PRAISE FOR THESE NATIONALLY BESTSELLING AUTHORS:

JAYNE ANN KRENTZ

"A master of the genre…"
—*Romantic Times*

"Who writes the best romance fiction today?
No doubt it's Jayne Ann Krentz."
—*Affaire de Coeur*

BARBARA DELINSKY

"When you care to read the very best, the name of
Barbara Delinsky should come immediately to mind."
—*Rave Reviews*

"One of this generation's most gifted writers of contemporary
women's fiction."
—*Affaire de Coeur*

ANNE STUART

"One of the most original authors in or out of the genre."
—*Romantic Times*

"Before I read an Anne Stuart book I make sure my day is free,
because once I start, she has me hooked!"
—bestselling author Debbie Macomber

ABOUT THE AUTHORS

JAYNE ANN KRENTZ

is one of today's top contemporary romance writers, with an astounding twelve million copies of her books in print. Her novels regularly appear on the *New York Times,* Waldenbooks and B. Dalton bestseller lists. First published in 1979, Jayne quickly established herself as a prolific and innovative writer. She has delved into psychic elements, intrigue, fantasy, historicals and even futuristic romances. Jayne lives in Seattle with her husband, Frank, an engineer.

BARBARA DELINSKY

was born and raised in suburban Boston. She worked as a researcher, photographer and reporter before turning to writing full-time in 1980. With more than fifty novels to her credit, she is truly one of the shining stars of contemporary romance fiction! This talented author has received numerous awards and honors, and her books have appeared on many bestseller lists. There are over twelve million copies of her books in print worldwide, so Barbara's appeal is definitely universal.

ANNE STUART

has become synonymous with sizzling romance. She published her first book in 1974, and in the over fifty novels and countless short stories she's written since then, has demonstrated an uncanny ability to touch readers with witty repartee and her trademark taut sexual tension. Anne Stuart has won every major writing award, including three prestigious RITA Awards from the Romance Writers of America, and, in 1996, a Lifetime Achievement Award. She lives in Vermont with her husband, daughter and son.

Dangerous DESIRES

JAYNE ANN KRENTZ

BARBARA DELINSKY

ANNE STUART

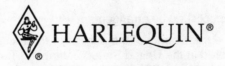

HARLEQUIN®

TORONTO • NEW YORK • LONDON
AMSTERDAM • PARIS • SYDNEY • HAMBURG
STOCKHOLM • ATHENS • TOKYO • MILAN • MADRID
PRAGUE • WARSAW • BUDAPEST • AUCKLAND

ISBN 0-373-83431-4

DANGEROUS DESIRES

Copyright © 1999 by Harlequin Books S.A.

The publisher acknowledges the copyright holders of the original works as follows:

TOO WILD TO WED?
Copyright © 1991 by Jayne Ann Krentz

MONTANA MAN
Copyright © 1989 by Barbara Delinsky

FALLING ANGEL
Copyright © 1993 by Anne Kristine Stuart Ohlrogge

Visit us at www.romance.net

Printed in U.S.A.

CONTENTS

Too Wild To Wed?

Jayne Ann Krentz

CHAPTER ONE

XAVIER AUGUSTINE WAS BACK in Tipton Cove.

Letty Conroy heard the arrogant purr of the hunter-green Jaguar and eagerly looked out her study window. It was nearly midnight and the storm that had been hovering offshore earlier that day had finally struck land an hour ago. Through a solid sheet of cold Oregon rain Letty watched the elegant car pull into her narrow drive. Her heart soared. Xavier was back a whole day early.

And he had come directly here to her, Letty realized, even though it was very late. Right here to her house. At midnight, no less. What would the neighbors think? she wondered with a soft, delighted chuckle.

She wanted to do more than chuckle. She wanted to laugh out loud. No, she wanted to sing. Xavier Augustine might look like a raffish, decidedly dangerous thug, but the truth was he had the manners of a saint.

Showing up here at her front door at this hour was completely out of character for him. Xavier, Letty had learned to her chagrin, was never the least bit improper. Since he had first started courting her three months ago, and *courting* was definitely the appropriate word, he had been the very soul of propriety. Indeed, he had been excruciatingly circumspect in every aspect of his wooing.

It could be rather depressing, not to say distinctly frustrating, to be romanced in such an old-fashioned manner. Letty had discovered to her astonishment during the past few months that she was apparently a woman of passion. She just wished she could find a way to set that passion free. She knew now that the only man who was capable of doing so was Xavier. But until now he had shown very little interest in the task.

The blunt truth was that Letty had never met a man so concerned with a woman's reputation, at least not in this century. Xavier's behavior had begun to seem uncomfortably close to that of some medieval lord bent on protecting his lady's honor at all costs.

It was true Tipton Cove was a very small academic town and

Letty's position as an assistant professor of medieval studies at Tipton College was vulnerable to gossip. A certain level of deportment was expected of the faculty of the college. And, as she had reminded herself over and over again, it was wonderful in this day and age to meet a man who cared about protecting a woman from wagging tongues.

Nevertheless, she feared Xavier took his concern for her reputation a bit too far. After all, the man had dated her for nearly three months before asking her to marry him a week ago but he had yet to take her to bed.

Letty admitted to having had a few qualms concerning her beloved's sexual orientation at first. But her own woman's instincts reassured her. The hint of fire in Xavier's kisses and the glimpses of raw, glittering sensuality she had seen in his catlike green eyes when she had surprised him covertly studying her were unmistakable proof of his all-male eagerness.

No, the flames were there, all right, but for some inexplicable reason Xavier kept them carefully banked.

Lately she had begun to wonder if he suffered from some physical difficulty that was too embarrassed to confess. She wanted to tell him she would understand and would love him regardless of his prowess in the bedroom, but she was too shy to bring up the subject for fear of insulting him.

It was all very complicated, Letty thought.

Out in the drive the door of the Jag closed with the soft, solid chunking sound made by very expensive, very classy car doors. Everything about Xavier Augustine was first-class and expensive— something else that had given Letty an occasional qualm in the midst of the magic of the past three months.

She was not used to going first-class on a college professor's salary.

Letty watched her fiancé stride quickly toward the old-fashioned porch that fronted her quaintly detailed Victorian-style house. Xavier seemed unconcerned with the rain pelting down on his thick dark hair. He had an expensive leather briefcase in one hand and a superbly tailored jacket slung over his arm. He wore European clothes—his shirt had been made in France, his shoes in Italy and his tie, which was unknotted and hung loose around his throat, came from England. The gold and steel chronometer on his muscled wrist had been precision engineered in Switzerland.

The man looked like a walking advertisement for the elegant, civilized life, but all the expensive accoutrements in the world could not conceal the very earthy, excitingly uncivilized, bluntly masculine aura he projected. At least not to Letty. She had been drawn to him from the first moment like a moth to the flame.

Xavier was a lean, tall, broad-shouldered man and he moved with the easy coordination of a hunting cat. He was thirty-eight years old, Letty knew, but there was no sign of softness about him. She doubted if there ever would be, regardless of his age or physical status. The hardness came from within and was a trait of the man himself. In the harsh yellow glare of the porch light she could see the rough planes and angles of his subtly fierce face. His eyes glittered in the shadows.

As Xavier approached, Letty felt a primeval thrill sweep through her—a very female sense of anticipation. She stood up quickly, leaving the last of the stack of exam papers she had been grading on the desk. She tightened the sash of her prim, high-necked, quilted robe as she hurried toward the door. Her thick fluffy slippers made no sound on the bare wood floor in the hall.

Xavier was here. At midnight, no less.

Letty caught a brief glimpse of herself in the hall mirror and winced. The problem with unexpected midnight callers was that you never had the chance to properly prepare for them. She thought about the dainty, frivolous lingerie she had bought for her trousseau this past week and sighed with regret. Everything was carefully packed in tissue and stashed in the bottom drawer of her dresser. There was no time to change into the beautiful peach-colored peignoir she had picked out with loving care last Saturday. Nor was there any time to apply some lipstick or take down her hair from the lopsided knot on top of her head.

The doorbell chimed impatiently. Letty pushed her glasses up higher on her nose and went through the clumsy, time-consuming ritual of unhooking the chain, unlocking the deadbolt and unlatching the new door lock, all of which Xavier had insisted she have installed two months ago. The man had a strong protective streak.

Letty at last got the door unsealed and opened it with a sense of exuberant excitement. She could always unpack the peach-colored peignoir, she told herself.

"Xavier."

Then she got a good look at the man she loved and knew that

he was not in any condition to sweep her off her feet and into bed tonight. Concern welled up, nudging aside the hopeful passion.

"Good heavens. I wasn't expecting you. You look absolutely exhausted. You must have had an awful drive in this storm." She touched the side of his face with her fingertips as she stood on tiptoe to brush her mouth a bit shyly against his.

His lips were hard and warm and she could smell the distinctly masculine scent—hints of his aftershave, leather from the car's upholstery and rain all in one.

"Sorry about the time, honey," he said. "I know I shouldn't have surprised you like this. I was going to wait until morning. But when I landed in Portland a couple of hours ago I just got into the car and kept driving toward the coast. I considered waking up somebody down at the motel, but I decided I'd come over here instead." His teeth gleamed briefly in his familiar, fleeting smile. He was very sure of his welcome. "Do you mind?"

"Oh, no, not in the least." Letty blushed happily, not caring that her feelings for him were blatantly obvious. She reached out hastily and took the briefcase from him. "Here, let me take that." She staggered backward a step under the unexpected weight of the leather case and realized she needed both hands to lift it.

He frowned. "Are you sure you can handle that?"

"Of course. My own weighs almost as much. Come on in, Xavier, and don't worry about the time. I mean, we are engaged, after all, aren't we? It's freezing out there. And you're soaking wet."

"Thanks. It's really coming down." He ran his fingers through his dark hair, shaking off water droplets onto the rug. Then he blocked a huge yawn with the back of his hand. "Just set that down anywhere. I'll go back out and get my suitcase in a few minutes. Hell, I'm really beat. I thought Waverly would never sign those papers. Took me all day to talk him into it."

"But your business went well?"

"No major problems." He yawned again and rubbed the back of his neck. "Unless you count jet lag."

"Why don't you go on into the parlor and sit down. I'll make you a nice cup of tea."

"I'd rather have a shot of brandy."

"Brandy. Oh, yes. Certainly. Brandy." Letty thought fast. "I've got some, I think. I'll get it right away. You can put your jacket in the hall closet."

"Right. Thanks."

Anxious to please him so that he would be more inclined to stay, Letty hauled the briefcase halfway down the hall, dropped it on the floor with a thud and rushed into the kitchen.

Please let there be some brandy left in the cupboard, she prayed silently. *And please let it be a decent label.*

"Did you get your portion of the invitation list made up?" Xavier called out casually from the parlor.

"Yes. The invitations will go out next week. Everyone on the faculty is included, just like you said. And the library staff. And the trustees."

"I brought my list with me. You can add the names to yours."

"Is it very long?" Letty asked, trying to keep the uneasiness out of her voice. She opened a cupboard and discovered to her relief that she did, indeed, have some brandy left. Unfortunately it was an unprepossessing label that she had purchased primarily to use in cooking. Xavier was bound to notice. He was very aware of such things. He would never buy cheap brandy, not even for cooking.

"No. Only about fifty people or so. Business acquaintances for the most part. I don't have any family to invite, as I told you."

Fifty? Letty rolled her eyes heavenward and stifled a groan as she reflected on the added effort of addressing fifty more wedding invitations. Xavier had taken three months to ask her to marry him but once he'd popped the question and gotten Letty's immediate answer, he'd moved forward with ruthless efficiency to set events in motion.

Before he'd left on this latest business trip, he'd given her a long list of tasks to do in preparation for the wedding, which he had decreed would be at the end of the month.

When she'd asked why the rush, he'd told her he liked the idea of a June wedding. It was traditional, he'd explained with an air of authority that had made her smile. She was given to understand Xavier Augustine wanted a formal affair with all the trappings. First class, all the way.

Letty had been working like a demon for the past couple of weeks what with having to grade end-of-term papers and exams while trying to plan the full-scale wedding production Xavier had insisted upon having. She would not have accomplished nearly as much as she had in the short span of time if not for the help of her friend, Molly Sweet.

"Guess what?" Letty called brightly, as she hurried out of the kitchen with the two glasses and the bottle of brandy. "I went shopping for the dress with Molly and we found the most gorgeous gown. I can't wait for you to see me in it."

"I'm looking forward to it," Xavier said. He sounded indulgent.

"It's really beautiful. Sort of old-fashioned looking with a square neckline and loads of white lace and little pearls around the hem and yards and yards of petticoats and skirts and—ouch." Letty broke off abruptly as her toe struck the massive briefcase in the hall. She sucked in her breath and squeezed her eyes shut for a few seconds. "Damn."

"You okay?" Xavier asked from the parlor.

"I'm fine. Just fine. No problem, really." Letty gritted her teeth and stood on one foot while she waited for the pain to subside in the other. At least she had not spilled the brandy, she noticed. A small miracle under the circumstances. "Be right there."

"I think I'll build a fire. All right with you?"

"Yes, please go ahead. Sounds lovely." Letty glowered at the briefcase as she went past. Then she forgot about her sore toe as it dawned on her that it was looking more and more as if Xavier meant to spend the entire night here.

Her rising sense of euphoria plummeted briefly when she reminded herself he would probably insist upon sleeping on the sofa. But just maybe, it she got enough brandy into him, he could be persuaded to head for the bedroom.

Oh, Lord. After all these months of anticipation and frustrated desire and the deepest sense of longing she had ever known, maybe *tonight* would be the night.

Letty rounded the corner into what had once been the front parlor of the old Victorian house and saw that Xavier was down on one knee setting a match to a pile of kindling on the hearth. He had removed his tie. His white shirt was open at the throat and the sleeves were rolled up on his sinewy forearms. He glanced up as she entered the room and she realized again how drawn and tired he looked.

"Just what I need," Xavier remarked, his eyes moving to the brandy. He finished lighting the fire and got to his feet.

He took the bottle of brandy and one of the glasses from her hand. Letty held her breath as he briefly examined the label. But he made no comment as he filled both glasses.

"What a hell of a day." He swallowed half the contents of the glass and smiled wearily at her, green eyes glinting in the light of the rising flames. He brushed his knuckles affectionately along her cheek. "You look good, honey. I missed you."

"I'm glad. I missed you, too." Letty wanted to catch hold of his hand and keep his knuckles pressed against her skin. She wondered why the bubble of happiness on which she was standing did not simply leave the ground entirely and carry her up to the ceiling.

All the hard work of the past week was suddenly totally unimportant. In another three and a half weeks she would be married to this man and it would all be worth it. She raised the brandy glass to her lips and firelight sparkled on the large emerald in her beautiful engagement ring.

"I got a couple of things accomplished beside closing the Waverly deal," Xavier said matter-of-factly, as he walked across the room and sat down on the chintz sofa. "Picked up the cruise tickets."

"Did you really? How exciting. Did you bring them with you?" The one thing Xavier had insisted on handling personally was booking the honeymoon cruise. Letty knew he planned to take her first-class and she was quite dazzled by the prospect. She had never been on a luxury cruise.

Xavier smiled slightly at her obvious enthusiasm. "The tickets are in my briefcase. Along with a brochure describing the ports of call." He sprawled on the sofa and unbuttoned another shirt button. Firelight revealed the shadows beneath his eyes and the hollows below his high cheekbones.

"I'll go and get your briefcase," Letty said readily. She set down her brandy glass and hurried toward the hallway. "I can't wait to see the brochure."

Out in the hall she found the massive leather briefcase, seized it with both hands and dragged it back into the parlor.

"You're such a little thing," Xavier observed. "Better let me handle that." He went to pick up the briefcase and opened it, pulling out a colorful brochure. "Here you go. What do you think? Does it look like the perfect honeymoon trip?"

Letty took the brochure and opened it eagerly. Brilliant photographs of tropical islands, a gleaming white ship and a seemingly endless array of exotic shipboard food was spread before her. "Xavier, it looks fabulous. I can see I'm going to have to do some more shopping, though. I don't have the right kind of clothes for a trip like this."

"Get whatever you need. And don't worry about the cost. I'll pick up the tab." Xavier downed the rest of his brandy and leaned into the corner of the sofa, resting his head on the high cushioned back. He massaged the bridge of his nose, gazed into the flames and stifled another yawn with the back of his hand.

"No, you will not pick up the tab, thank you very much." Letty turned another page in the brochure and scanned an array of scenes that showed happy couples drifting about on the ship's dance floor. "I have a perfectly good career, remember? Tipton College may not pay the best faculty salaries in the state, but I can certainly afford my own clothes."

"I want you to have the right things for the trip." Xavier frowned slightly and poured himself a little more brandy. "We'll be traveling first-class and I want you to feel—" he paused "—comfortable among the other passengers. Clothes have a lot to do with how others treat you—how much they respect you."

"I suppose so." Letty bit her lip and risked a quick glance at Xavier. He was still studying the dancing flames, his dark lashes half-closed as he lounged wearily on the sofa. He had one elegantly shod foot up on the coffee table and he looked as if he was about to fall asleep.

This was probably not the best time to tell him she was not particularly concerned with how expensively dressed she was on the cruise, Letty decided judiciously.

The issue of Xavier's insistence on always doing things first-class would have bothered her more if she had not sensed intuitively that he did not actually judge others by how well they dressed or how much money they made. He certainly had not judged her by her clothes or her income, which was nowhere near his.

Nor did Xavier treat others differently according to their financial status. Money or the lack of it was obviously not the issue for him when it came to dealing with people.

But Xavier liked having the best for himself; he insisted on doing things in what he called the right way, the proper way.

Letty was beginning to think there was something about the outward trappings of what he termed *class*, that were too important to Xavier Augustine. At times it was almost as if he had something to prove. And yet there was so much sheer arrogant strength in him, she reminded herself. It was one of the many aspects of the man that had initially attracted her. Surely he had nothing to prove to anyone.

Xavier Augustine was as solid as a rock in all the ways that counted. Once he made a commitment, you knew he would stand by it come hell or high water. That sense of reassuring strength was something Letty had never found in any other man, something she had been waiting all of her life to find.

Now, for the first time, she wondered if it was possible for a man to be *too* strong, too self-controlled, too intent on running his own private world. As she watched Xavier doze in front of the fire she finally acknowledged that part of her was definitely getting worried about the relationship in which she found herself.

She did not know all that much about Xavier Augustine. In fact, all she really knew was what everyone else in Tipton Cove knew. He was a quietly but brilliantly successful entrepreneur, an independent consultant and owner of his own firm, a company called Augustine Consulting. A few months ago he had been invited by the chairman of Tipton College's newly established School of Business Administration to give a series of guest lectures.

The lectures had been popular beyond the chairman's fondest dreams. They had been riveting. Several members of the faculty outside the School of Business Administration, such as Letty Conroy from the history department, had heard about them and dropped into the lecture hall on Wednesday afternoons to see what all the excitement was about. Letty had not been disappointed, although she was the first to admit the subject of business held little innate interest for her.

Tipton College had not been disappointed, either. In addition to a lively series of lectures, Xavier had endeared himself forever to the small private college by personally endowing a faculty chair in the School of Business Administration. It was, of course, to be called the Xavier Augustine Chair in Business Administration. Certain delighted trustees were privately calling it the Saint Augustine Chair.

Letty had been introduced to Xavier at a faculty tea. She had been shy initially, acutely conscious of Xavier's effect on her senses. It had taken her a while to realize that what she was experiencing for the first time at the age of twenty-nine was a compelling physical and emotional attraction to a man. The effect was almost lethal to her inexperienced senses. She'd had an occasional crush in the past but nothing like this.

She had struggled valiantly to deal with the unfamiliar overwhelming sensations and had tried to conceal her rioting reactions behind a ladylike facade. Then Xavier had smiled at her in such a way she'd instinctively sensed the attraction was mutual.

From that point on Letty knew she had not stood a chance. Xavier had pursued her with an archaic correctness and an attention to propriety that would have graced the most chivalrous knight of old, but he had definitely *pursued* her. There had been no doubt of that.

Looking back on the past three months, Letty decided it was just as well she had been attracted to her modern knight from the start because she was not at all certain she could have escaped him.

Now she was engaged to marry him. She gazed down at the beautifully designed gold and emerald ring she wore. It had, of course, been purchased from a jeweler who dealt only in the finest gems. Xavier had selected the ring himself. In the glow of the firelight the elegant stone reflected the same fire Letty occasionally saw in his eyes.

This marriage would work, she told herself fiercely. There were some unknowns in the equation, but surely she could trust her instincts. She loved this man, even if she did not know a great deal about him. Everyone approved of Xavier, from the college president right down to the secretaries in Admissions. She was not making a terrible mistake, Letty told herself. She was seizing the opportunity of a lifetime. Everyone said so.

"Xavier," Letty said tentatively, "I was just wondering if you planned to, well, you know, stay here tonight? I mean, it's perfectly all right with me. Goodness knows there's plenty of room and I wouldn't mind in the least. In fact, I..."

Letty's voice trailed off into thin air as she looked up from the colorful brochure and realized the love of her life had fallen asleep on her sofa. Disappointment gripped her for a moment. And then a rueful amusement made her smile to herself. There was no way she would ever be able to get him into her bed tonight. And she really did hate to wake him. He looked so exhausted.

She got to her feet and went to fetch a blanket from the hall closet. Her initial disappointment faded a little as she realized that even though he was not actually in her bed, Xavier was going to spend the night right here in her cozy little house. Definitely a step in the right direction. It was better than having him go back to the Seaside Motel the way he had all the other nights of their courtship.

Tenderly Letty removed the expensive Italian shoes and arranged Xavier's legs on the sofa. It was not easy. Everything about Xavier was strong, smoothly muscled and surprisingly heavy.

Eventually she managed to get him looking halfway comfortable. He mumbled something once as she bent over him to adjust the blanket.

"What did you say?" she whispered.

He opened one glittering green eye and regarded her with a sleepy, blatantly sexy expression. His mouth quirked. Then he lifted his hand and wrapped it around the nape of her neck. His fingers were warm and strong and very sure.

"I said, you're sweet," he muttered, dragging her down so that he could kiss her. His mouth moved lazily, lingeringly, on hers. His tongue slid briefly into her warmth. "You even taste sweet. Almost too good to be true. But you are, aren't you?"

"Well, I certainly hope I'm not *that* good." She laughed at him with her eyes. "It sounds dull."

He shook his head slowly and closed his eyes again. "Not dull. Suitable. Classy. Just what I wanted. You're exactly the way you're supposed to be—a real lady." He turned his head into the cushion and exhaled deeply. "I've got the proof," he concluded in a soft, indistinct mumble.

"Xavier?" Letty straightened and stared down at him uncertainly. "What proof? What do you mean by that?"

But Xavier was sound asleep. Letty did not have the heart to shake him awake and demand an explanation. Perhaps he'd been half caught up in a dream.

She took a step backward and the back of her leg collided with the heavy briefcase. The leather case toppled over, spilling some of its contents onto the rug.

Letty hurriedly bent down to collect the various papers and manila envelopes that had fallen out. She glanced automatically at the documents as she started to stuff them back into the briefcase.

The first envelope bore the name of a small Oregon bank. The second had Waverly written on it in Xavier's bold scrawl and the third, a legal-sized envelope, had her first name jotted on it in pencil in the upper right-hand corner. *Letty.*

Xavier's writing again. Something he'd meant to give her, Letty decided. Perhaps more information on the cruise trip he had planned.

Letty stared at the envelope and then turned it slowly in her hands to read the return address. Her insides went cold as she realized she was looking at the name of a Portland-based firm of private investigators. Hawkbridge Investigations.

You're exactly the way you're supposed to be. I've got the proof.

Letty could not believe her eyes. She held the envelope as if it were about to explode in her hands. Surely Xavier had not had her investigated. He was smart and savvy and as hard as nails in some ways, but surely he would not have chosen a bride based on the recommendation of a private detective agency. Perhaps it was all a mistake. Perhaps her name jotted on the outside of the envelope had nothing to do with the contents.

Letty moved to the chair in front of the fire and sat huddled there for a long while, the envelope in front of her. The longer she stared at it, the more certain she was that she had to find out what was inside. She was dealing with her future here.

She looked across at the sofa and saw that Xavier was deeply asleep. Then she lowered her eyes once more to the ominous envelope. Slowly she opened it and pulled out two sheets of paper. The first was a short, handwritten note scrawled boldly on Hawkbridge Investigations letterhead:

Here's the final report, Xav. I ran the check myself, as I said I would and it was done with complete discretion. There were no surprises, as you will see when you read it.

Ms. Conroy has obviously spent the past twenty-nine years just sitting around waiting for you to show up. Take some advice and marry her fast before someone else gets his hands on her. Your bride-to-be is exactly what you've been looking for, a real lady.

Don't forget to invite me to the wedding,

Hawk

With dawning horror Letty unfolded the second sheet of paper and read the report the investigation agency had compiled for Xavier.

When she was finished, she wept.

When the tears were dried she sat for a long while staring into the flames. And then she made her decision.

CHAPTER TWO

HE WAS DROWNING in a white sea.

Xavier came awake with a start and slashed at the billowing creamy white satin that was threatening to suffocate him. He sucked in his breath and got a mouthful of pearl-studded lace, which he promptly spit out.

"What the hell?" He was buried beneath waves of white petticoat netting, trapped by yards of heavy, gleaming white fabric that covered him from head to foot.

He jackknifed to a sitting position on the sofa and fought free of the frothy white fog, finally surfacing beneath the folds of a wedding veil to see Letty on the other side of the room.

She was wearing a pair of jeans that snugly fitted her sweetly shaped derriere. Xavier had an excellent view of that derriere, even through the veil, because Letty was bent over at the waist, thrusting something red and frilly into an open suitcase.

Slowly he lifted the delicate netting away from his face. His first thought was that he had fallen asleep like a damn fool instead of making love to Letty last night as he had intended.

He had spent the whole of the long night drive from Portland thinking about taking Letty to bed. The time had finally arrived, he had told himself with a great deal of satisfaction. He had all the reports, the engagement was official and Letty was waiting to fall into the palm of his hand like a sweet, ripe plum. He planned to catch her very gently.

But the long, frustrating business trip to conclude the Waverly deal followed by the drive to the coast had taken more out of him than he had realized. Apparently he'd collapsed on the sofa after only a couple of glasses of Letty's lamentable California brandy. Xavier made a mental note to buy her a bottle of the good French stuff.

He stared for a moment at the cold ashes on the hearth and then at the yards of white satin that surrounded him and wondered if he was still dreaming. Something was definitely wrong but he could not imagine what it could be. Everything was supposed to be under control.

"Do you like the wedding gown, Xavier?" Letty asked in a strangely brittle voice. She did not turn around. "I certainly hope so, because it goes straight back to the store today. This is the only opportunity you'll ever have to see it."

"Good morning to you, too." Xavier pushed aside another wave of white satin and wondered what had gone awry in his neatly constructed world.

"Don't you dare call this a good morning." Letty straightened and spun around to glare at him through her little tortoiseshell glasses. "This is the worst morning of my life. The only thing good about it is that I have at last discovered the truth about my knight in shining armor. He's a no-good, rotten, scheming, conniving untrusting sonofa—"

"That's enough." Xavier held up a hand to silence her. "Not first thing in the morning, if you don't mind. I need a cup of coffee before I can deal with this. And after the cup of coffee, I'd like an explanation. A rational, straightforward, logical explanation, not a lot of feminine screeching."

"If you don't like the sound of my *screeching*," Letty shrieked, "you can take your first-class cruise tickets and your first-class shoes, and my beautiful, first-class wedding gown and get into your first-class car and get out of my life. The sooner, the better, as far as I'm concerned."

Xavier experienced a twinge of genuine concern. He wondered if Letty was ill. He'd heard strange things about the effects of PMS. He also recalled hearing about something called bridal jitters. "Are you feeling all right, honey?"

"No, I am not feeling all right," she yelled furiously. Her small hands clenched into fists around a lacy little black bra. "I am feeling damned mad. And hurt. And I am totally disgusted with you, Xavier Augustine. I thought you were the love of my life but you're really an arrogant, cynical, self-centered clod. You don't love me. You never did love me."

"Letty," he said, wondering if she wore that little scrap of black lace regularly and if so what she looked like in it, "you're not making any sense."

"Who the hell do you think you are to have me investigated? What right did you have to check out my past to see if I was good enough to be your wife? How could you do that, Xavier Augustine? How could you do such a horrid, untrusting thing to me? I thought you *loved* me."

Xavier went very still as he finally began to realize what had happened. She must have found the letter from Hawkbridge Investigations. His gaze flicked to the briefcase. It yawned open revealing a myriad of envelopes, documents and papers. He did not see the incriminating envelope.

"I think you had better calm down and explain why you're so upset," Xavier said, opting for an air of calm authority.

"Why I'm upset? *Upset?*" She stared at him as if he'd lost his senses. "I'm not upset, I'm enraged. Outraged. Furious. Insulted to the core. Madder than hell. I'd like to stake you out over the nearest anthill and pour honey on you."

"Why?"

"Because I've just discovered you deliberately checked out my past before you did me the great honor of asking me to marry you. You had to make certain I was classy enough for you, didn't you? You had to see if I was good enough to go with your expensive car and your fancy wine and your hand-tailored suits."

He sighed. "So you did find that letter. I never meant for you to see it, Letty. I knew it might upset you."

"I told you, I'm a hell of a lot more than a trifle upset. What right did you have to that? I wasn't applying for the post of Queen of England, you know. If you wanted to find out about my sordid past, all you had to do was ask me. I would have told you everything. But, oh, no, you didn't trust me enough to just ask, did you? You had to run a full-scale investigation. How much did that fancy outfit charge you, anyway?"

Xavier smiled faintly and rubbed the back of his neck. "Your past is anything but sordid, honey," he pointed out gently. He ignored her question about the price of the investigation. Hawkbridge Investigations charged an arm and a leg for its services but it had been worth every penny as far as Xavier was concerned. Hawk ran a top-notch, utterly reliable outfit. "There was nothing in the report to be embarrassed about."

"Oh, God, I know only too well there was nothing exciting or sordid to report on me. You don't have to remind me of what a dull life I've led until now." Letty dropped the black lace bra and stalked over to the table where a familiar-looking envelope lay.

She shook out the report Xavier had commissioned on her. "Look at this. Just look at it."

Xavier glanced at the few brief lines on the page—evidence of a pristine past. He knew everything on that sheet by heart. His future wife was twenty-nine years old and well on her way to becoming an old maid.

She had grown up in a small town in eastern Washington, the unexpected and rather late-in-life child of a highly respected local judge and the daughter of one of the county's oldest, most established families.

Letty's parents, who had long since given up on the possibility of having children, had been thrilled with and quite overprotective of their little girl right from the start. They had also been unusually strict with her, at least by modern standards of child rearing. As staunch pillars of the local community, the judge and his wife had impressed upon their one and only child the supreme importance of not doing anything to disgrace them or herself.

In spite of her carefully supervised upbringing, or perhaps because of it, Letty had been a happy, well-loved child who had displayed her intellectual abilities early on and been encouraged to develop them. She had been a model student all the way through high school and college, never once getting into any kind of mischief. She had rarely even dated.

Her history studies had been her chief interest in life and she had concentrated on them to the exclusion of almost everything else. She had graduated with honors in history and gone on to complete a Ph.D in Medieval studies at a small, private, very distinguished college back east. She had returned to the Pacific Northwest to join the faculty of Tipton College the year she had completed her studies.

A copy of Letty's doctoral dissertation, a lengthy treatise entitled *An Examination of the Status of Women in the Medieval World*, had been included along with the preliminary report from the investigation. Xavier had read every word. He had also read several of the papers and articles she'd had published in obscure academic history journals since graduating.

Her parents had been killed in the crash of a small plane piloted by Letty's father four years ago. Since their death Letty had continued to lead a quiet, decorous existence that consisted of a busy round of study, teaching, research and faculty teas.

In addition, there were occasional trips to England during summer vacations where she toured castles and buried herself for days
on end in such places as the Bodleian Library and the British Mu-
seum.

Until Xavier had arrived on the scene, Letty's relationship with
men had been limited to the occasional quiet date with a fellow
member of the history department. During the past year a certain
Dr. Sheldon Peabody, an associate professor also specializing in
medieval history, had escorted Letty to a handful of chamber music
performances and a production of *Hamlet*. Letty had been home
shortly after midnight on each occasion and Peabody had hung
around just long enough for a cup of tea before taking his leave.

Xavier had made it a point to meet Dr. Sheldon Peabody and
had not been particularly worried by the competition.

All in all, Xavier had concluded early on, Letty Conroy was an
eminently suitable wife for him. There was an air of class about
her. *Real* class. The kind that could not be faked or bought or
learned—the kind *he* had worked so hard to cultivate.

Letty was not stunningly beautiful, but he had learned long ago
not to let himself be blinded by a woman's superficial attractions.
In any event, her lively features held a piquant charm and intelligence that appealed to him on a deep, fundamental level.

She had huge hazel eyes, a tip-tilted nose and a soft, vulnerable
mouth that responded beautifully to Xavier's kisses. She was slender and feminine with high, round, pert little breasts. Her hair,
which she almost always wore in a classic knot at the nape of her
neck, was a thick, lustrous chestnut color. Last night it had glowed
with the reflected light of the fire. As he had drifted off to sleep,
Xavier had imagined flames burning in that thick, sleek hair.

And she had the most delightful way of deferring to his wishes,
Xavier reminded himself a bit smugly. She was always terribly
anxious to please him.

She also had excellent manners, stimulating conversation, a
sweet temperament and she was head-over-heels in love with Xavier Augustine. Most important of all, she was an honorable, old-
fashioned sort of woman who would take such things as wedding
vows very seriously.

The perfect wife—an eminently suitable wife. Exactly the sort
of wife he wanted, Xavier thought with satisfaction and not for the
first time. All he had to do now was smooth her ruffled feathers.

Husbands had to do that sort of thing occasionally. He might as well get in some practice.

The truth was, he did not really mind this unexpected display of temper now that he was past the first shock of surprise. Temper indicated passion and he definitely wanted passion in his wife. He was a man of strong, sensual appetites himself and he could not imagine a worse fate than being married to a woman who did not respond to him physically.

"I was very pleased with that report," Xavier said carefully, searching for a way to defuse Letty's volatile mood. "It confirmed everything I already knew or suspected. You are exactly what you claimed to be."

"Well, you aren't what you claimed to be at all, Xavier Augustine. You're a fraud. Do you hear me? A complete fraud."

Xavier felt as if he'd been kicked in the stomach. For an instant, genuine panic set in. There was no way she could know the truth, he told himself desperately. No way at all. He had buried it long ago.

He found his breath with an effort and stood up abruptly to cover his startled response. "What are you talking about, Letty?"

"You let me think you were in love with me," Letty wailed. "I thought you trusted me. I thought you cared for me."

The sick feeling was washed away by a wave of relief. She did not know anything, after all. Xavier started toward the kitchen. "I do care for you. Very much. And I trust you, sweetheart." *I trust you completely now that I've seen that report,* he added silently. He smiled down at Letty and ducked his head to drop a quick kiss on her forehead as he went past.

She stepped back hurriedly but not in time to avoid the light, possessive touch of his mouth. Her eyes narrowed behind the lenses of her glasses as she glowered up at him. "If you trust me so much, why did you have that background check run on me?"

"Routine, honey. Just routine." He walked into the kitchen and started opening cupboard doors.

"Routine? You expect me to believe that?" She hurried down the hall after him and came to a halt in the kitchen doorway, her expression fierce. "I've got news for you, Xavier, it is definitely not routine to hire professional investigators to run checks on future spouses."

"It's not as rare as you think, Letty," he said quietly. "Not for a man in my position.'' He opened another door and found a package of coffee. "Ah, here we go. I'll be in better shape to defend myself after I've gotten some caffeine into my system. Are you always this feisty in the mornings?'' He went across the room to where the drip coffee machine sat perched on a tiled counter.

"Don't you dare try to make a joke out of this.'' She stalked into the kitchen and snatched the package of coffee out of his unresisting hand. "I have been badly hurt and humiliated and I will not have you making fun of me on top of everything else.''

"I'm not making fun of you, sweetheart.'' He leaned back against the counter and watched in amusement as she opened the package of coffee and measured some into the machine. This was his Letty, he thought with satisfaction, so very feminine in her ways that she was even making him coffee while she raged at him. It was touching. "And I assure you I never meant for you to be hurt or humiliated. That was the last thing on my mind.''

"Is that right?'' She shoved the glass pot under the faucet, filled it with water and dumped the water into the coffee machine. Then she stabbed the switch. "What was the first thing in your mind? Making certain I wasn't some floozy? Some gold digger who was going to try to take you to the cleaners? Give me a break, Xavier. I've got a perfectly good career of my own and I love it. I don't need your money and you ought to damn well know it.''

"I never thought you were after my money,'' he said honestly.

"Then why the investigation? Did you think I'd murdered my last three husbands and buried them in the backyard or something?''

"No.''

"What were you looking for, then?'' she demanded, her voice rising another notch.

This was going to be a little difficult to explain, especially in her present mood. Xavier chose his words thoughtfully. "I did not go looking for anything in particular, Letty. I told you, it was just a routine background check.''

She nodded with savage conviction. "Just a routine check to make certain I was worthy of being married to the great Saint Augustine. You wanted to make certain I was as first-class as everything else you own, didn't you? You had to make sure there were no embarrassing scandals in my past.''

"Now, Letty...''

"No awkward little brushes with the law. No ex-husbands or alcoholic fathers or brothers lurking in the woodwork who happen to be compulsive gamblers. No family history of insanity or criminal connections. That's what you wanted to check out, wasn't it? You wanted to see if I was really suitable wife material."

"Don't twist this all up into little knots you won't be able to unravel, Letty."

"Damn you, the least you owe me now is the truth. Admit you checked up on me because you had the unmitigated gall to want to be certain I was good enough to be your wife."

"You're overreacting." Xavier was beginning to grow irritated now. "In this day and age when people marry strangers instead of the girl next door, it pays to be a little cautious." He'd learned that lesson the hard way, he reflected bitterly.

"Then you must think I'm a real idiot, because I didn't hire anyone to do a background check on you," she shot back. "Why on earth would you want to marry an idiot? It's probably hereditary and you told me you want children."

"The coffee's finished."

She looked at the full pot in outraged horror. "Talk about idiocy. What on earth am I doing making coffee for you like a good little wife? I must be out of my mind." She yanked the pot out from under the filter basket and dumped the freshly brewed coffee down the sink.

Xavier winced. "That wasn't really necessary."

"Oh, yes it was," she stated, slamming the pot down onto the kitchen counter. "I am no longer going to cater to you, Xavier Augustine. Our engagement was ended the minute I found that letter from the investigators. I need to start somewhere and this is as good a point as any."

He eyed her expression with misgivings. "What, exactly are you going to start?"

"Living a more exciting life," she announced. "Do you know what the worst thing was about that damn report the investigators filed on me?"

"Honey, there was nothing bad in that report."

"That was the worst thing about it," she stormed. "I looked at that report last night and realized that my entire life had been summarized in less than a single page. There wasn't one single, thrilling, scandalous item to put down. No torrid relationships, no dan-

gerous adventures, no unsavory incidents. The long and the short of it is, my life has been a dead bore to date.''

"Damn it, there is nothing wrong in being a dead bore." Xavier closed his mouth abruptly but it was too late. The words had already been spoken and hung in the air like grenades waiting to explode.

"My God, that's the bottom line, isn't it?" Letty's eyes filled with horror. "You wanted to marry me precisely because I am a dead bore."

"I did not mean that the way it sounded and you know it," Xavier said through set teeth. "What I meant to say was that there is nothing wrong in having lived a blameless life. You should be proud of yourself."

"Well, I'm not. I'm furious when I think of what a little goody two-shoes I've been. And to be married for that reason is the final straw." Letty lifted her chin in proud defiance. "From now on, Xavier, I shall dedicate myself to only one goal and that goal will be to live a life-style that will absolutely, positively guarantee to make me totally unsuitable to be your wife."

She stomped back past him out of the kitchen, red flags of anger flying in her cheeks, her slender frame stiff with tension.

"I can't believe I'm hearing this." Xavier swung around and went after her. "Letty, you're behaving like a child. When you've had a chance to calm down, you'll realize you're completely overreacting."

"I'll overreact if that's what I feel like doing." She was back at the suitcase, tossing more frilly underwear inside. "From now on I will do whatever I feel like doing. No more Ms. Nice, Proper, Boring Dr. Conroy. Henceforth, I am a new woman and the last thing anyone will ever say about me in the future is that I'm untainted, unsullied or boring. I'm going to go for the gusto."

He scowled at the suitcase. "Are you planning to go somewhere in particular for this gusto?"

"Yes."

He drew a breath, telling himself to be patient. "Where?"

"None of your business, really. But since you ask and since I have no objection to telling you, I'll answer the question." Letty folded a tiny pair of red lace panties and placed them on top of what appeared to be a filmy peach-colored peignoir. "I am going to spend the next few days boning up on the pleasures of life in the fast lane.''

Xavier stared at her. ''What the hell are you talking about now?''

She straightened abruptly. ''I am going to accept a long-standing invitation to attend the quarterly convention of what I understand to be a lively, fun-loving group of amateur historians called The Order of Medieval Revelers.''

Xavier folded his arms across his chest and stood, legs braced, glaring at her. ''And just who the hell issued this long-standing invitation?''

''Dr. Sheldon Peabody.''

''*Peabody?* That pompous ass in the history department?''

''I believe you've met him at one or two of the faculty teas,'' Letty said in lofty tones. ''He figures in the investigator's report as one of my 'occasional, insignificant relationships with members of the opposite sex.' I think that was how it was phrased. Such a delicate way of saying I have a boring love life.''

''Stop calling your life boring,'' Xavier ordered.

''Any life that can be summed up in one page is boring. And while we're on the subject, I would like to take this opportunity to point out that my dull love life didn't get any more exciting after you came on the scene.''

It took him a few seconds to realize the nature of the accusation she was hurling in his face. Xavier's jaw dropped. Then his teeth snapped together. ''Now hold on one blasted minute here. Are you saying you're mad because I didn't take you to bed?''

''Not mad, just bored.''

He lost his temper at that point and reached for her. ''You know something, lady? You've got one hell of a lot of nerve.''

''Don't touch me.'' Letty stepped back quickly but not quickly enough. Xavier's fingers closed around her shoulders and he hauled her up against his chest. Her wide, startled eyes were only inches away from his own furious gaze.

''Bored, were you?'' he gritted. ''After all I went through to behave like a gentleman? After all those nights I went back to the motel room alone and stood under a cold shower? And you have the nerve to tell me you were bored?''

She bit her lip. ''Well, maybe bored isn't quite the right word.''

''No, it is definitely not the right word.''

She got a grip on herself and defiance blazed in her eyes once more. "Try frustrated. Or confused. Or worried."

"Worried about what, for crying out loud?"

She made a little sound to clear her throat and her eyes flickered uneasily. Her cheeks blushed a bright pink as she lowered her gaze to his chest. "I did wonder if perhaps you had some sort of, uh, masculine problem, if you know what I mean."

Xavier was so outraged he could barely think coherently. "A problem? Hell and damnation, woman. You better believe you won't have to worry much longer about any problem I might have in that department."

"Now, Xavier, there's no need to feel offended. Lots of men have problems of that sort," she said soothingly. "I've read all about them. I understand most of them can be quite easily remedied with modern medical technology. There are even little devices you can use to sort of pump yourself up, I hear—"

"Not another word out of you," he roared. "It will give me real pleasure to demonstrate that all the basic equipment I possess is in full working order. Trust me, by the time I've finished proving I don't have any problem in bed, you won't have any lingering questions left on the subject. You'll be lucky to be able to walk."

"Promises, promises," she taunted. "And stop yelling at me. You don't have any right to yell. Or to make threats. It was perfectly reasonable of me to question your sexual prowess under the circumstances. After all, I had no way of knowing you were simply biding your time until you had the final report on my background."

"Damn it, Letty."

"Why did you wait? Weren't you attracted enough to me to want to go to bed with me? Did it take that stupid report to make the thought of making love to me bearable?"

"That's enough, Letty. You're carrying this whole thing too far."

"It was your own future comfort you were really thinking about, wasn't it? You'll be living full-time in Tipton Cove now that you're moving your business headquarters here. You'll be giving more guest lectures at the college. You'll be socializing with all sorts of high-profile, conservative, respectable people. I can see where it would have been embarrassing to have had a brief fling with one of the junior members of the history department. What if she made things a trifle awkward after you finally found a really *suitable* wife?''

"Letty, I'm warning you..."

"Admit it, Xavier. Admit you couldn't be bothered to seduce me until you were sure I was good enough for you. You know something? I think that is the final insult.''

"That does it. You're beyond reason at the moment. I'm getting out of here while you cool down.'' Xavier released her before he lost any more of his normally ironclad self-control. He strode across the room and put on his shoes. Then he snatched the offending letter from the investigation firm off the end table, shoved it into the briefcase and latched the buckles.

Letty stood tensely, watching his every move. "Going to be a little embarrassing leaving my house bright and early in the morning like this, isn't it, Augustine? What will the neighbors say?''

"They'll say you spent the night with your fiancé. Happens all the time these days. Even in small towns like Tipton Cove. Perfectly acceptable. Don't worry. Your reputation won't suffer.'' He started for the door.

"Oh, gee, thanks. Well I'll tell you something, I don't give a damn about my reputation anymore. But what about yours, Xavier?'' She sprinted after him as he opened the front door and stepped out onto the porch. "What will they all say when they find out I ended my engagement after only one night with you? They're bound to think you must have been a heck of a disappointing lover if you couldn't even please a dull, boring, terribly naive little history professor.''

Xavier glanced across Letty's tiny, neatly groomed front yard and saw her neighbor, the elderly Dr. Knapthorpe, Professor Emeritus of English Literature. The good professor was engaged in the process of pruning his rosebushes, which bordered Letty's drive. Knapthorpe was close to eighty but there was nothing wrong with his hearing. Xavier knew the old man was taking in every word.

"I don't know what the neighbors will think about you standing out here shrieking like a fishwife at your fiancé, Letty.'' Xavier strode over to the Jaguar and opened the door. "Why don't you ask them?''

He had the satisfaction of seeing her blush furiously as she realized Dr. Knapthorpe was listening.

"Beast," she hissed.

"By the way," Xavier advised as he slid into the leather-upholstered seat, "don't bother returning that wedding gown. You're going to need it when you marry me at the end of the month. Unless, of course, you find the idea of being married in a formal gown a little too conventional and dull for your taste. You're welcome to show up naked at the church if you like, but one way or another, you will be there."

"Never," she yelled after him.

But Xavier was no longer listening. He was too busy wondering if she was really serious about taking that suitcase full of frilly lingerie to the quarterly convention of Sheldon Peabody's Order of Medieval Revelers.

CHAPTER THREE

"HONESTLY, MOLLY, it was the most humiliating moment of my entire life." Letty shuddered.

Molly Sweet grinned cheerfully around a mouthful of anchovy and onion pizza. "From the sound of it, that isn't saying much. Apparently your life has been so blessedly bland that you haven't had any real experience with supremely humiliating moments."

"Don't remind me." Letty eyed the remains of the pizza and wondered what had happened to her normally healthy appetite.

She was usually more than capable of downing her half of the giant pizza she and Molly always ordered at this particular off-campus pub. Maybe if she sprinkled some more hot peppers on her half she could work up some interest in the dripping pizza. She reached for the bottle of crushed dried peppers.

"So he actually had you investigated? By a real detective agency? Like one of those on TV?"

"Yes. An outfit called Hawkbridge Investigations. And they didn't find one single exciting thing in my past. Twenty-nine years old, Molly, and not one event worthy of mention. You should have seen that single-page report. I could have died. Dull, dull, dull."

"I'd love to see it." Molly's eyes widened behind her glasses. "Oh, not because I'm curious about you."

"Thanks," Letty muttered sarcastically. She had to pitch her words over the sound of recorded rock music, clinking beer mugs and the noise coming from the pool table in the corner of the pub. "Apparently everyone's curiosity about me is very easily satisfied. Nothing of interest to anyone except someone looking to marry a woman without a past."

"Now, don't take offense. I just meant I'd like to see what a real background check looks like, that's all."

"Believe me, there wasn't much to it." Letty glanced up from her contemplation of the pizza and smiled reluctantly as it dawned on her that her friend was genuinely fascinated. In the subdued pub lighting she could see the intent interest in Molly's eyes.

The two young women had met shortly after Letty had arrived
at Tipton College. They had discovered immediately that they had
a great deal in common in terms of personal temperament, intellect
and interests. They even shared a few physical similarities. Both
wore glasses and both were twenty-nine years old.

Beyond those salient features, the two were quite different in
appearance. Letty was a conservative dresser who favored button-
down shirts with her jeans and always wore a suit and pumps to
class; Molly Sweet opted for bright colors and off-the-wall styles.
Tonight she had on a pair of black jeans, boots and an oversized,
violently chartreuse-green knit top that glided over her slender
frame all the way to her thighs. The flashy, whimsically designed
earrings she wore were so long they brushed her shoulders.

Letty's dark chestnut mane was almost always anchored neatly
at the nape of her neck, but Molly's golden brown hair was cut in
a short sassy style that suited her vivid blue-green eyes and delicate
features.

Although the two had a lot in common, their intellectual interests
had taken them down different career paths. Letty's single-minded
obsession with medieval studies had led her to specialize in research and teaching in the field of history. But Molly's eclectic
interests together with a host of quirky enthusiasms had led her to
choose a more generalized field. She was a reference librarian at
Tipton College Library.

Letty picked up a slice of peppered pizza. "It gives me the
creeps just thinking about it."

"What? The investigation?"

Letty nodded, wrinkling her nose as she chewed. "The thought
of somebody sneaking around behind me, following me, watching
my every move, making notes. It just makes my skin crawl."

"Actually," Molly said, looking thoughtful, "I would imagine
there was very little, if any, of that sort of investigation. That's the
way it was done years ago. Times have changed. Sometimes you
spend so much of your life living in the medieval world, Letty,
that I think you forget about the modern one. These days I'll bet
investigations are done by computers."

"Computers?"

"Sure. The same way credit checks and reference checks are
run. You can find out almost anything you want to know about
someone if you know what you're doing with computers."

Letty stared at her. "You could?"

"I think so." Molly's brows rose. "Why are you looking at me like that? Is there an anchovy hanging out of my mouth?"

"No, no, I was just thinking. Molly, you know a lot about computers. You search sophisticated data bases all the time when you do research for grad students and faculty."

"Uh-huh. Academic-oriented data bases for the most part."

"But you could get into others?"

"Sure, although it's surprising what's available in the academic ones."

"Would it be illegal?"

"No. Some data bases are publicly accessible, some you pay a fee to search and, as a librarian, you'd be amazed at how many I could get into just by asking permission. What are you getting at?"

Letty put down her unfinished slice of pizza. "Could you, hypothetically speaking, run a discreet little investigation on Xavier Augustine?"

Molly's mouth fell open and she, too, put down her pizza. "Are you serious?"

"Shush. Keep your voice down." Letty leaned over the table. "Is it possible?"

Molly thought about it. "Theoretically and hypothetically speaking, yes, I imagine so. But do you think there's anything to find?"

"Probably not." Letty sat back in disgust. "The man is so noble and so terribly conscious of doing everything in the right and proper fashion that his background is probably not much juicier than my own."

Molly drummed her nails on the table. "I wouldn't be too sure of that. Xavier Augustine is a self-made man from all accounts. He didn't inherit money, he made it the hard way. Take it from me, Letty, no one gets as rich and successful as our Saint Augustine without leaving a few bodies buried somewhere along the way."

Letty turned that over in her mind. "Like some landless medieval knight who decides to make his fortune by becoming a professional mercenary."

"They did that back then?"

"Certainly. There were a lot of knights who had no fortune or land of their own. The only way up in the world was to sell their swords to some lord who needed manpower to defend his castle or raid his neighbors' property. When the mercenary had enough money and power of his own he got himself some land, selected a wife suitable to his fine new status as a respected man of property and went about siring as many sons as possible.''

"A lowly, landless knight who had been able to turn himself into a powerful lord would probably have had all sorts of unpleasant little secrets in his past—'' Molly observed ''—human nature being what it is and all.''

"You know, I'm beginning to think my knight in shining armor may be more like the original version than I initially thought. The real thing was a tough, arrogant warrior who would have done all sorts of horrid things himself, but insisted upon having a wife who had a spotless reputation.''

"A little unreasonable, to put it mildly.''

Letty shrugged. "Of course it was. Typically male, though, isn't it? The reasoning behind it was that a man's honor was tied up with that of his lady. If she brought dishonor on herself, he was dishonored. So he protected her honor as fiercely as if it were his own, which was very fiercely, indeed. Castration was a common punishment for a man who dared to seduce a lord's wife.''

"The lord, of course, got to run around to his heart's content, though, I'll bet.''

"Right. While he was watching over his wife like a hawk, he took a little time out to seduce all the pretty castle servants and the daughters of the peasants.''

Molly's mouth tilted wryly. "Well, that's one thing you don't have to worry about. Xavier hasn't seduced anyone around here as far as we can tell. And in a small community like this, believe me, we'd know if it happened.''

Letty groaned. "True. He hasn't even seduced me. Nevertheless, I have a hunch you're right. I doubt that Xavier Augustine is quite the saint he tries to make everyone think he is. Molly, I want you to do it. I want you to run an investigation on him.''

"Why bother? You already said you were canceling the wedding.''

Letty felt a wave of depression sweep over her at that thought. "I know. I guess I just want some vengeance.''

"Have you considered the fact that he may be right? That you are overreacting because you feel hurt? Letty, you told me, yourself, that you loved him. Are you sure you want to give him up?''

"No,'' Letty admitted candidly, aware of tears welling in her eyes. She blinked them back. "But it's done. I told him this morning I was calling off the wedding. Molly, I can't marry a man who doesn't trust me. What kind of marriage would we have?"

"You might be able to teach him to trust you."

"I will not prove myself to any man, damn it. I fell in love with him and trusted him completely. I deserved the same degree of love and trust in return."

"True. But men can be a bit weird, Letty. Let's face it. They don't always think the way we do. They get all muddled up when it comes to dealing with emotions."

"I realize that, but it's just not fair. Molly, I feel so terrible. I really thought Xavier was the right man for me. I was so sure of him."

"I know," Molly said gently. "Have some more wine and pizza. You'll feel better. Are you really going to go off to one of those meetings of that society Sheldon Peabody joined last year?"

"Yes, I am."

"I'm not so sure it's a good idea." Molly looked seriously doubtful. "From what little I've heard about the Order of the Medieval Revelers, it doesn't really sound like your kind of thing."

"You're talking about the old, dull Dr. Letitia Conroy. The new fast-forward Letty is going for wider and wilder experience."

"All the same, I'm not sure how Dr. Stirling would feel if he found out his precious little golden girl, whom everyone knows he is grooming for promotion and tenure, was out carousing with a group like the Revelers. You know Stirling thinks the world of you."

Dr. Elliott Stirling, patrician-featured, silver-haired and much respected in academic circles, was chairman of the history department. He had been extremely pleased when the new assistant professor of medieval studies had begun writing papers that had gotten Tipton College's department of history mentioned in several prestigious journals.

"Stirling may have taken some notice only because I've gotten a few things published in some of his favorite journals," Letty muttered. "You know the old saying, Molly. In the academic world, it's still publish or perish. Stirling would lose interest in promoting me tomorrow if he thought I was never going to get another paper in print."

Stirling had made no secret of his satisfaction with Letty and she would have been naive, indeed, not to realize she was slated for rapid advancement at Tipton College. Unless, of course, she blotted her copybook so badly that Stirling became annoyed.

Letty cringed inwardly at that thought. After all, until she had made the mistake of getting engaged to Xavier Augustine, her academic career had been the most important thing in her life. And there was no denying that in a small, inbred academic community such as Tipton College, the double standard in behavior still applied to a certain extent, just as it did in the modern corporate world.

The flat truth, although everyone denied it, of course, was that the social rules for men were still different than those for women, just as they had been during the Middle Ages. People might turn a blind eye to the peccadilloes of a male member of the faculty but they would frown severely on similar behavior on the part of a female faculty member.

Not that some progress had not been made in the past eight hundred years, Letty reminded herself wryly. Back in the Middle Ages women had not even been allowed to join an academic faculty, let alone given an opportunity to struggle for tenure.

"I realize Stirling is delighted with you because you've brought some prestige to the department," Molly said patiently. "You can't hold that against him. In a lot of ways he's no different than a manager in a large corporation who promotes the people under him because they made his department look good. That's the way the real world works and you know it. You can't do anything to jeopardize your career."

"I'll be discreet," Letty vowed.

"Even Sheldon has the sense to keep fairly quiet about his activities with the Revelers. No one around here really knows what goes on at those meetings he attends. All we've heard are a few rumors and I, for one, don't like the sound of them. From all accounts there's a lot of partying and general carousing."

"What's wrong with that?" Letty asked defiantly.

"It's not you, Letty."

"It is now."

Molly sighed. "I think you should reconsider the idea of rushing off to join this crowd. Find some other way to show Augustine you aren't suitable wife material."

Letty scowled. "I'm not doing this to prove anything to Xavier. I'm doing it for myself."

Molly grinned. "Don't give me that. You were perfectly content with your life until this morning. If you'd felt the need to experiment with walking on the wild side, you'd have tried it years ago. Even you must have had a few opportunities along the way. You weren't that sheltered."

Letty slapped the table with her palm, thoroughly outraged now because Molly was too close to the truth. She had been very content with her life until this morning. "It's the principle of the thing, damn it."

"Hey, hey, hey," said a jovial new voice. "Did I hear the word principle? Sounds like an academic sort of argument going on here. Nothing I like better. Mind if I join you, ladies? I need a beer, a lively discussion and some female companionship to bring me back to life. I think that last batch of exam papers I just finished grading had petrified my brain."

Letty and Molly looked up at Sheldon Peabody who was looming over the table with a hopeful, appealing expression on his handsome face.

Dr. Sheldon Peabody was thirty-six years old and rather good-looking in a soft, dissipated sort of way. His sandy hair, blue eyes and regular features gave him a boyish charm that he had used to advantage all his life.

Peabody had started to put on a little weight in recent years and had lost some of the athletic look that had been part of his attractiveness. But the slight paunch around his middle was well concealed tonight by a black pullover that he wore with his jeans.

Peabody had risen to the rank of associate professor in Tipton's history department. He had not yet gained tenure or a full professorship, however, and people were starting to notice that fact.

Gossip had started to the effect that Peabody's career advancement was stalled until he got something important into print. He had apparently fallen behind in his research and writing during the past couple of years and had not had any papers published for some time.

"You can sit down, Sheldon," Molly said politely but without much enthusiasm, "if you promise not to stick us for your beer tab the way you did last time."

"Thanks." Sheldon dropped carelessly into an empty chair and signaled the waitress for a mug of beer. "What have you got on that pizza?"

"Anchovies, onions and peppers on what's left of it," Molly told him. "I already ate my half. Help yourself. Letty doesn't seem very hungry tonight."

Sheldon eyed the remains of the pizza and grimaced. "No thanks. Even if I liked anchovies and onions, which I don't, it looks like there are enough hot peppers on it to set fire to the thing." He turned his winning smile on Letty. "Got your note in my box this afternoon. So you finally changed your mind about attending one of our little conventions at Greenslade Inn, hmm? That's great."

Letty was not sure she liked the intense satisfaction she saw in Sheldon's eyes. It made her uneasy. But she was committed now. The new Letty was trapped inside, waiting to spring free. "You've been telling me how much fun it is so I've decided to give it a try. If the invitation is still open, that is."

"Oh, it's definitely still open, my dear. I'll be glad to get you a guest membership for this quarter's convention. I'll even put your name in for full membership in the Order, if you like. About time you let your hair down a little and did some fast living. You'll have a great time. Trust me. I'll see to it personally."

"Uh, thanks." Letty hid a small shiver of apprehension. It occurred to her that this notion of attending a meeting of the Revelers might not be one of her better ideas after all. Then she thought of that single-page report that had summed up her whole life and she hardened her resolve.

"Where is this Greenslade Inn?" Molly asked coolly.

"Down the coast toward the California border." Sheldon smiled genially as his beer was set in front of him. "Great old place. It's all by itself, a couple of miles from the nearest town and it sits right on a cliff overlooking the sea. Lots of atmosphere, you know? Built by some rich timber baron back in the eighteen-hundreds. Even looks something like a castle, which makes it perfect for the Revelers. The management books the entire inn for our use while we're meeting there."

"It sounds interesting," Letty allowed.

"You'll love it," Sheldon assured her. "Say, why don't you and I drive down together tomorrow? No sense taking two cars."

Letty gnawed briefly on her lower lip as she caught Molly's

narrowed glance. "I think I'd rather have my own transportation available, Sheldon. Thank you, anyway."

"Suit yourself." He shrugged dismissively and took a swallow of beer. "I'm glad you're coming but I'll admit I was a little surprised to get your note. Didn't think that new fiancé of yours would let you off the leash for something like this."

"It's none of Xavier's business," Letty said in a tight voice.

Sheldon chuckled and gave her a conspiratorial glance. "So Augustine doesn't know, huh? What is this, Letty? Eat, drink and be merry because at the end of the month you're going to be shackled to a tyrant?"

Letty swallowed. She had not yet told anyone except Molly that the engagement to Xavier was off. She drew a deep breath. "Well, Sheldon, to be perfectly blunt, there isn't going to be a marriage."

His eyes narrowed in obvious speculation. "Oh-oh," he said softly. "So that's how it is, is it? Sorry to hear that." He did not sound sorry at all. He sounded pleased.

"Pretend you didn't hear it," Xavier Augustine advised in a cold voice from directly behind him. "Because the wedding is definitely going to take place on schedule."

Letty, Molly and Sheldon swung around in surprise. Letty flinched and felt her pulse rate quicken as she saw the implacable expression in Xavier's green eyes. She told herself that anger was the emotion she was feeling, not trepidation. The man was truly overbearing. He radiated all the innate arrogance and authority of a genuine medieval knight.

"What are you doing here, Xavier?" Letty asked, sounding peevish, even to herself.

"That should be obvious. I dropped in for a pizza. Hi, Molly."

"Hi, Xavier. Have a bite. Letty obviously isn't going to finish hers."

Xavier sat down next to Letty and reached for a slice. "What the hell have you got on this thing, anyway? It looks like it's covered with hot peppers."

"It is. Also anchovies and onions. I like my pizza, as well as a few other things I could mention, very, very hot." Letty smiled with taunting innocence.

Xavier's eyebrow climbed as he nonchalantly took a large bite of the over-peppered pizza. "I'll keep that in mind." His gaze did not so much as flicker as he calmly chewed and swallowed the spicy pizza.

Sheldon scowled at Letty. "What's going on here? You two getting married, or what?"

"Yes," Xavier said around a mouthful of pizza.

"No," Letty said simultaneously. She rounded on Xavier. "Stop contradicting me."

"You're still wearing my ring," he pointed out, taking another bite of peppered pizza.

She looked down in horror and instantly yanked the emerald off her finger. How on earth could she have forgotten to remove his ring? "Here, take it. You should be able to get your money back. I'm sure a really *first-class* jeweler will be happy to refund your money."

Xavier pocketed the ring and continued eating pizza. "I'll hold onto it until you've gotten over your little problem."

"What little problem has she got?" Molly demanded, clearly intrigued.

"Bridal jitters," Xavier diagnosed authoritatively. He signaled for a beer. "Letty's suffering from a bad case of cold feet. But she'll recover."

"Maybe my feet will get warmed up this weekend," Letty threatened furiously.

"Yeah," Sheldon murmured as he took a sip of beer. "Maybe."

Xavier finished the pizza and leaned back in his chair to contemplate Letty with a detached expression. "So you're still planning on going to that convention of Revelers you told me about?"

Letty, who had been suffering serious doubts on that subject, reminded herself once more she had to stand firm. Only a very boring person would lose heart now. "Yes, I am. And that's final, Xavier. There's no point trying to talk me out of it."

"Good for you," Sheldon said, hoisting his beer mug in a mocking salute to her courage.

"I'm not going to try to talk you out of it," Xavier said mildly. "I'm planning on attending, myself."

Sheldon choked on his beer. "You can't," he sputtered indignantly. "Attendance at a meeting of the Order is by invitation only."

"So you're going to invite me, aren't you, Peabody?" Xavier smiled a dangerous smile. His eyes were green glaciers.

"The hell I am. Why should I do that?"

"Because if you don't, I will seriously consider withdrawing my commitment to endow the new chair in business administration and I will see to it that the trustees of the college know that you were the reason I changed my mind."

Sheldon's handsome face paled and then tightened with fury. He knew as well as everyone else at the table what that threat would mean. Quite literally it spelled the end of his career at Tipton College. The trustees would never forgive him for depriving the school of a major endowment. They would see to it he was fired.

"You're a real bastard, aren't you, Augustine?" Sheldon's voice was hoarse with fury.

"I can be when I'm crossed. Otherwise, I'm really very easy to get along with. Just ask anyone."

Sheldon got to his feet with a jerky movement and regarded Xavier with a frustrated hostility that was obviously just barely under control. "You think you're so damned smart, don't you? Go ahead and show up at Greenslade. I'll tell the people in charge that you've got a personal invitation from me. We'll see how much you enjoy the quarterly meeting. You don't know what you're getting into, Augustine."

"I think I can handle anything you can come up with, Peabody."

"Don't bet on it." Sheldon turned away from the table and strode through the crowd to the door.

Letty sat frozen in shock. A glance at Molly revealed that her friend was just as stunned by the outrageous threat Xavier had so casually issued as she was. Xavier himself appeared oblivious of the scene he had just caused. He was reaching for another slice of Letty's pizza.

"How dare you?" Letty squeaked as she finally found her voice.

"It's not that bad," Xavier said, regarding the peppered pizza with a considering eye. "A bit heavy on the anchovies, but otherwise pretty tasty."

"I'm not talking about the pizza. I'm talking about what you just said to Sheldon. That was absolutely appalling, Xavier. How could you threaten him like that?"

Xavier gazed at her as he munched pizza. "I hate to tell you this, but it was amazingly easy."

"My God, you're impossible." Letty shot to her feet and tossed down her napkin as if it were a gauntlet. "I have never been so embarrassed."

"You're in for a lot more embarrassment if you continue to throw Peabody and me into a ring together," Xavier warned.

"I am not doing any such thing," Letty stormed. "Furthermore, I want to make it quite clear that I don't want you at Greenslade. Do you hear me?"

"Everyone in the place can hear you," Xavier said.

Letty gave up. She glanced desperately at Molly, who got to her feet like the good friend she was and prepared to follow her out of the pub. The two women turned their backs on Xavier and stalked out of the restaurant.

"Whew," said Molly as they stepped outside into the cool night air. "I think you're right. Whatever else he is, your Mr. Augustine is no saint."

"I want you to dig up anything you can on him, Molly."

"I'll get started on it right away," Molly promised. "Should prove interesting. A man like that is bound to have lots of skeletons in his closet. But even if I find them that still leaves you with the problem of what to do with them."

"I'll think of something. I'm going to teach Xavier Augustine that he can't treat me as if he were some lord from the Middle Ages."

"Uh-huh." Molly sounded doubtful.

"I will," Letty assured her fiercely.

"Just leave me a number where you can be reached."

"I will."

Molly nodded. "I don't know if it's any consolation, but you can take comfort in knowing that we all just stuck Xavier with the bill for the pizza and drinks."

"So we did," Letty said. The thought cheered her somewhat. "I guess there is some justice in the world, after all."

THE RED MESSAGE LIGHT on the telephone was flashing when Letty was shown to her room at the Greenslade Inn the following afternoon.

"Just pick up the phone and ask the front desk for the message," the bellman said as he dropped her suitcase and took the dollar she was holding out to him. "The costumes are in the closet over there." He nodded to a wardrobe across the room. "They're provided by the Order for all new guests. Regulars bring their own and some are pretty spiffy. Cocktail party starts at six. Banquet at seven-thirty and then we batten down the hatches.''

Letty blinked. "I beg your pardon?"

The bellman grinned. "This your first Revelers' meeting?"

"Yes, it is."

"Well, have fun. That's the main goal, as far as I can tell. I've worked half a dozen of these conventions and they're wild. I'll be running up and down these halls all night. You'd never think a bunch of folks who claim to be interested in ancient history would get so crazy. Some of them can be a real pain. But the tips are great. Enjoy yourself, Miss Conroy. And thanks.'' He closed the door behind himself.

Letty gazed around at the room with a sense of surprise and relief. She had not known quite what to expect but she was delighted with the old-fashioned canopied bed, the huge, carved wooden wardrobe and the lovely view of the windswept sea. When she walked to the window and looked down she could see the breakers crashing on the rocks of the cove below. Very picturesque. The perfect honeymoon spot, in fact. That thought made her sigh. She would not be going on any honeymoons now.

The inn was just as Sheldon had described it—a majestic old mansion built of stone and stout timber. It occupied a high bluff situated on a particularly isolated section of the coast. Two newer wings of rooms had been added on to the old section to provide additional space, but Letty was glad to discover she had been put into the original portion of the structure. Her room was on the third floor above the large rustic lobby.

Letty noticed there was a door in one wall, which meant there was a room adjoining hers. She made a note to be certain the door was locked from her side before she went to sleep later. Then she picked up the phone.

"You have a message from a Miss Molly Sweet," the desk clerk said cheerfully. "She wants you to call at once."

Frowning over the apparent urgency of the message, Letty hung up and dialed Molly's home number in Tipton Cove.

"Molly? It's Letty. Is everything okay?"

"Boy, am I glad you called." Molly's voice was laced with excitement. "Are you alone?"

"Of course."

"I mean, Augustine isn't there with you?"

"I told him he wasn't welcome, remember?" Letty said, irritated by Molly's assumption that Xavier could simply show up when and where he wished. She had seen no sign of him thus far and she was praying his statement that he would be attending the Revelers' meeting was an empty threat. "What's going on, Molly?"

"I started the search," Molly said quickly. "Just as we agreed. I've got to tell you, Letty, this is fun. I could really get into this investigation business."

"Molly, will you please just tell me what you found out?"

"Okay, okay. I plugged Augustine's social security number into every data base I could find. The first thing I can tell you is that he's healthy. Donates blood regularly."

"For heaven's sake, Molly, I already knew that." Letty was disgusted. "He was behind me in line at the last Tipton Cove Community Blood Drive, remember?"

"He's got a great credit rating," Molly offered helpfully.

"That's not exactly news. I didn't figure him to be on welfare."

"Well, if that doesn't impress you," Molly said with slow relish, "try this on for size. There is no record of Xavier Augustine existing until ten years ago."

"*What?*"

"You heard me. It looks like he invented the name and a whole new identity for himself thirteen years ago."

Letty felt as if she'd been pole-axed. "But people don't do things like that."

"They do if they've got a good reason for burying their old identity."

"Oh, my God."

At that moment, the door that connected Letty's room to the adjoining one opened and the man who called himself Xavier Augustine walked in.

CHAPTER FOUR

PANIC SEIZED LETTY. For one long, stricken moment she could only stare wide-eyed at the stranger lounging in the doorway. Xavier Augustine, the stranger she had very nearly married.

"Letty?" Molly's voice sounded very far away. "Is something wrong? Are you all right? I know this is something of a shock. But it's actually kind of exciting when you think about it. I mean, there's a real mystery here. Just think, you almost married the man and you don't even know who he really is. Letty?"

"Hello, Xavier," Letty said weakly. "What are you doing here?"

"I accepted Peabody's invitation, remember?" Xavier said with patient calm. He folded his arms across his chest and leaned one broad shoulder against the door frame. His cool, brooding gaze never left her face.

"Xavier's there?" Molly yelped in Letty's ear. "Right there in your room?"

"Yes. Yes, he is, as a matter of fact." Letty's fingers clutched the receiver. "He just walked in."

"Good grief. I'd better get off the phone. Listen, Letty, be careful, do you hear me?"

"I hear you."

"Don't confront him until we know more," Molly advised quickly. "We don't know what we're dealing with yet. He could be anything, anything at all."

Letty frowned, her gaze still on Xavier. "Like what, for heaven's sake?"

"Oh, I don't know. Maybe a gangster or a jewel thief or an undercover agent of some kind. Listen, if he's a criminal he might turn violent if he knows you're on to him."

"I'll keep that in mind," Letty snapped as irritation overcame her initial panic. Molly's thinking always had an imaginative bent.

"Goodbye, Molly," she said very clearly. "Thanks for checking up on me. As you can see, I arrived safe and sound and I'm looking forward to the next few days. Don't worry, I'll give you a full report when I get back.''

''Right,'' Molly said conspiratorially. ''That's the spirit. Play innocent. Don't let Augustine know we're checking up on him. I'll get back to you when I've got more info. 'Bye.''

Letty gently put down the phone and glowered at Xavier.

''That was Molly, I take it? Checking up on you?'' Xavier asked.

Letty cleared her throat with a small cough. ''Checking up on...me. Yes. Right. Me. She was checking up on me. She just wanted to make certain I'd arrived safely.''

''A good friend.''

''She certainly is.''

Xavier smiled grimly. ''So naturally she's on your side in this little war we find ourselves waging.''

''Well, of course she's on my side. What other side is there?'' Letty retorted.

''Mine?''

Her scowl deepened. ''Don't be ridiculous.'' She pushed her glasses up a bit higher on her nose. ''What war?''

''Haven't you noticed? You've retreated inside your castle walls and locked and barred the gate. I'm left with no option but to lay siege.''

Letty blinked. ''What a ridiculous analogy.''

He appeared thoughtful. ''Do you think so? I was rather proud of it. It seemed sort of appropriate under the circumstances.''

''How would you know?'' she demanded.

''Letty, my sweet, I don't claim to be an expert, but neither am I a total write-off when it comes to medieval studies.''

''What?''

''I've read almost everything you've ever written and published on the subject and I'm told it's some of the best stuff being done in the field today.''

That stunned her. She stared at Xavier, aware of an immediate sense of warmth at the realization that he had gone to all that bother. ''You have? Everything?''

''Everything I could find.''

''I hadn't realized you'd looked up all those papers.'' She blushed with embarrassed pleasure. ''You never mentioned them. Some of them were awfully dull.''

"I read every word," he assured her gently. "And I didn't find a single one of them boring."

"Oh." Then it struck her that it was undoubtedly his private investigation firm that had dug up the articles and papers she'd authored. Xavier had probably received neatly annotated summaries of each one presented to him as part of the firm's final report. Just a few more boring entries in her very boring file. The brief warmth faded. "Well, don't worry, there won't be a quiz."

"I could pass it."

"I'll just bet you could. Look, Xavier, I don't know why you felt you had to follow me here to the Revelers' convention. I assure you, it's not going to be your sort of thing at all and it's bound to be awkward for both of us."

"Not for me," he said.

"Don't be so sure," she retorted. "I understand things get a little wild around here. This is a real rowdy crowd. Party animals. Even the bellman said so."

"I think I can handle a little partying."

She eyed his unconcerned expression with a deep sense of wariness. "I hope you're not going to try to get in my way, Xavier, because I won't tolerate any interference from you. Our engagement is over and I consider myself free."

"You're not free." Xavier's voice was surprisingly gentle.

"Oh, yes I am."

He unfolded his arms and crossed the room in three long, stalking strides. He came to a halt in front of Letty and tipped up her defiant chin with one long finger. Then he looked down at her with a disturbing awareness.

"You're locked away inside your castle for the moment," he said, "but when you finally surrender and decide to open the gate and lower the drawbridge I'll be waiting to enter."

Letty went very still. She licked her suddenly dry lips. "Don't be so sure you'll want to carry out the siege. When you get to know the new me, you'll undoubtedly decide I'm not the sort of wife you want after all."

Xavier's smile was curiously enigmatic, as if he knew something she did not. "And maybe when you get to know me a little better you'll realize I'm not the sort of man who gives up something that belongs to him."

"But I don't belong to you," Letty sputtered.

"Yes, you do, Letty. You just haven't realized it yet. But you will." He brushed his lips lightly, possessively, over hers. "You will. If it's any consolation, I blame myself for the situation we're in now."

"You should blame yourself. It's definitely all your fault."

"I know. If I'd taken you to bed a month ago or two months ago instead of trying to play the gentleman, you wouldn't be so skittish now."

"Don't be too sure of that. I'd have turned very skittish the minute I saw that horrid report from the private investigators. Having me checked out as if you were thinking of employing me in a top security job was just too much, Xavier."

He nodded soberly. "My second mistake was not destroying that report after I'd read it. As I said, the present situation is all my fault. I take full responsibility."

"Stop saying that. I'm not asking you to take responsibility, I'm telling you that you should be ashamed of yourself for showing so little trust in the woman you claim you want to marry. Admit it, Xavier. What you were planning was nothing more than an old-fashioned arranged marriage to a suitable woman you had carefully chosen to meet your specifications. The way you went about the whole thing was positively medieval."

"I'd think you, of all people, would have appreciated that." There was a distinctly whimsical glint in his emerald eyes. "Given your intellectual interests, you ought to have found it romantic."

"Well, I didn't. Not in the least."

"I'll have to see what I can do to correct all the mistakes I've made lately."

Before Letty could find an appropriate response to that outrageous remark, Xavier walked back toward the connecting door. He stepped through it and closed it softly behind him.

Letty stared blankly after him for a stunned moment. Then she leapt to her feet and darted over to the door, intent on locking it securely. There was no bolt, just a simple old-fashioned doorknob lock. She pushed it firmly and heard the reassuring click.

Then she slumped in relief against the door and tried to take stock of the situation.

The thing she could not figure out was why Xavier Augustine, man of mystery, had followed her here to the Revelers' convention. Apparently he did not yet understand that she was very serious about her decision to turn around her dull, boring life. He needed to be convinced that she was soon going to be a totally unsuitable candidate for the position of wife to Saint Augustine.

Out in the hall a horn sounded and a loud voice called out, "Hear ye, hear ye. The festivities are about to begin. Sir Richard, Grand Master of the Order and Lord of Revelry for this convention, commands all guests to appear in the main hall in half an hour. Those summoned shall obey Sir Richard's command to eat, drink, be merry." Another blast on the horn followed the announcement.

Letty straightened away from the door and went purposefully toward the wardrobe to see what costumes had been provided. She was going to have fun, she vowed silently. She was going to kick up her heels and *live*. And Xavier Augustine, whoever he was, could have his fancy private investigators go find him another suitable wife.

Letty flung open the wardrobe doors and gazed at the apparel hanging inside. A small thrill of delight went through her as she reached out to touch the brilliant orange and red and blue garments. She took one gown off the hangers and examined it with a sense of wonder. Everything looked beautifully authentic, just like clothing out of a textbook on medieval costume design.

Letty made her choice for the evening and placed the garments on the bed while she took her shower. A few minutes later she stood in front of the mirror and carefully arranged her attire.

First came a *cotehardie*, a long gown with long tight sleeves and a flared skirt that moved delightfully around her ankles. It was a wonderful shade of sapphire blue and it neatly skimmed her figure, drawing attention to her slenderness. The neckline was wide and rather low. There was also a leather belt studded with bright glass jewels that rode low around her hips.

Over the long gown went a sideless jumper called a *cyclas* that was open from shoulder to hip to display the sapphire dress and the belt. The cyclas, done in panels of red and orange, had a deep neckline to show the low-cut neckline of the cotehardie.

When she had finished adjusting the gown Letty studied herself for a long moment and then decided to go for the whole effect. She brushed out her dark chestnut hair, parted it in the middle and arranged it into a heavy coil over each ear. Then she picked up a *crespinette*, an elaborate gold hair net, and put in on over the coils. She anchored the hairpiece with a gold fillet studded with blue glass gems. The fillet circled her forehead, fitting like a small crown.

Letty grinned as she surveyed herself in the mirror. She felt wonderfully medieval and altogether daring. She loved the long, graceful lines of the gown and the subtle sensuality of the cutaway cyclas. Through the opening at the sides of the garment one caught glimpses of the low, jeweled belt. It glittered and sparkled with each step she took.

The only anachronism was her glasses. Spectacles were not unknown in the Middle Ages, Letty knew, but they had been quite rare and had certainly not been worn by women of fashion. But Letty was not about to spend the evening wandering around in a fuzzy haze. She left the glasses on her nose.

Then she slipped her feet into the soft, absurdly pointed shoes that had been provided and decided she was ready for the world to meet the new Letty Conroy. Dropping her room key into a small, hidden pocket in her gown, she went out the door to try a taste of the exciting life.

LETTY STEPPED OUT of an elevator on the balcony overlooking the main lobby of the old Greenslade mansion and studied the remarkable scene below. She was instantly enchanted by the colorful medieval spectacle that awaited her.

The rustic hall was filled with laughing, chatting people in full period costume. The women were dressed in outfits similar to the one Letty wore. Some had elaborate wimples and veils held in place by small hats and fillets. The men were attired in tunics and surcoats anchored with low-slung belts. The main difference between their costumes and those of the women were that the tunics were cut much shorter, often just to the knee. Under them they wore brightly colored hose and soft pointed shoes.

Everywhere there was brilliant, gemlike color. The people of the medieval period had loved rich hues. Letty caught glimpses of fanciful heraldic devices picked out on several of the costumes and wondered if it signified some status within the Order of Medieval Revelers.

A fire blazed on the massive stone hearth that occupied one entire wall at the far end of the room. Everyone appeared to be drinking from metal or earthenware goblets. Letty decided that most of the members probably brought their own. She hoped some-one had stocked a few plastic glasses for newcomers.

There was a minstrels' gallery at the far end of the balcony where she stood and several musicians in period costume were warming up the lutes, harps, flutes and drums.

The laughter from the main hall drew Letty down the grand staircase. She moved slowly, wary of the unfamiliar feel of the pointed slippers and long skirts of her costume.

Sheldon Peabody hailed her as she reached the bottom step. He elbowed his way through the throng, his goblet raised high in greet-ing.

"Ah, the fair Lady Letitia. Welcome, my dear, welcome to your first meeting of the Order of Medieval Revelers. May I say that the style of the times becomes you. You are truly a vision, my dear. Allow me to fetch you some wine."

"Thanks." Letty smiled in relief at a familiar face. "That sounds wonderful."

"This way, my lady." Sheldon took her arm and steered her toward a bar that had been set up against the far wall.

Letty examined Sheldon surreptitiously, noting that the green tunic he wore over yellow leggings were emblazoned with an he-raldic device that appeared to be a griffin swigging a cup of ale.

"The ancient and honored coat of arms of the Sheldon family?" she asked with a grin as a costumed bartender took her order for red wine.

Sheldon chuckled. "Are you kidding? My family is from Kan-sas. Their symbol would probably be an ear of corn. No, my lady, this device I so proudly wear is one I designed myself. I felt it suited my particular skills."

"I should have guessed."

"To tell you the truth," Sheldon continued, "I'm hoping to replace it soon with the heraldic device of the Inner Circle of the Order of Medieval Revelers."

"What's the Inner Circle?"

Sheldon shrugged. "Basically it's the board of directors of the Order. The Grand Master this year is Richard Hodson. He's also serving as Lord of Revelry at this convention. The guy's an author. You may have heard of him."

Letty's brows rose behind the frames of her glasses. "The Richard Hodson who writes those clever mysteries set in medieval England?''

"The same." Sheldon grimaced. "The man doesn't even have a degree in history, but the editors and the public love those medieval settings he uses. Can you believe it? Makes you wonder if we're wasting our time trying to teach the real stuff to thick-headed undergraduates, doesn't it?''

"Well, I have to admit I enjoy teaching," Letty said cautiously. She had caught the underlying note of bitterness in Sheldon's voice and suspected it was directly related to his own inability to get published recently.

"You wouldn't if you'd been at it as long as I have and discovered that no one in our business appreciates good teaching. All the powers-that-be demand is a good track record in getting your papers into the right journals. It's all politics. Publish or perish, Letty.''

"I understand.''

"I doubt it." Sheldon's angry scowl cleared as if by magic and he gave Letty his genial, boyish grin. "But that's because you're still fresh in the game. You haven't come up against the publish or perish problem yet, have you? You're still the department's rising star.''

"I don't know about that." Letty felt suddenly awkward. In an effort to change the subject, she glanced around, hoping against hope to see a familiar face in the crowd. But it was useless. She was in a room full of exotic strangers.

One of the them—a young, pretty woman with a mass of burnished gold hair flowing out from under a fillet—spotted Sheldon and started toward him. The woman's gown was cut considerably lower than Letty's and revealed a great deal of healthy cleavage. She looked to be about college age. She was fit and tan and extremely energetic. There was something in the sway of her walk and in her open, fresh good looks that spoke loudly of Southern California beaches.

"Hey, Shelly babe," the young woman exclaimed in the bright breezy accents one associates with cheerleaders, "gee, I'm glad you made it. I've been looking forward to seeing you again." She gave him a quick, proprietorial kiss on the cheek and then turned speculative eyes toward Letty. "Oh, hi there. Who's your little friend, Shelly?''

An oddly flustered expression appeared in Sheldon's eyes for a few seconds. He got control of himself quickly. "Dr. Letty Conroy, meet Jennifer Thorne." Sheldon smiled warmly at the blonde. "Jennifer's father is one of the trustees of Rothwell College. You've heard of Rothwell, haven't you, Letty?"

"Rothwell," Letty repeated thoughtfully. "Isn't that the college down in Southern California that features pictures of students playing beach volleyball on the cover of its brochures?"

"Rothwell is what is familiarly known in the trade as a party school," Sheldon said. "Isn't that right, Jennifer?"

"Like absolutely for sure, Shelly. At Rothwell we believe in having fun while you get an education," Jennifer said. She giggled and her cleavage bounced exuberantly in response.

"You're attending Rothwell?" Letty asked politely.

"For sure. I'm a senior this year."

"Majoring in history?"

"Oh, no. I'm a drama major. What on earth would I do with a degree in history? I'm going to be an actress. But I just love fooling around with medieval history, don't I, Shelly babe?"

"Er, yes. Yes, you certainly do, Jennifer." Sheldon cleared his throat and gave her a serious, confidential look. "Would you mind if we got together a little later, babe? I have a few things to discuss with Dr. Conroy."

"For sure, Shelly babe. See you later." Jennifer smiled her blinding smile and waggled her long-nailed fingers. It was apparent she did not consider Letty much of a threat. "'Bye, Doc." She swayed off into the crowd.

Letty wrinkled her nose. "Doc?"

"Hey, babe, you've got a Ph.D.," Sheldon said, clapping her jovially on the back. "Might as well flaunt it. Most of the other folks here tonight are real amateurs—dentists, stockbrokers, secretaries, all kinds of people who just happen to get a charge out of the medieval thing, you know?"

"I think that's nice. It's good to see non-academic people taking an active interest in history."

"I'll let you in on a little secret. The Inner Circle would like to attract a few more members with some legitimate academic credits. They see it as a way of raising the academic credibility of the Order. Get my drift?"

"I didn't realize the Revelers were interested in raising their academic credibility."

"Well, it's true, they're all amateurs and hobbyists, but a lot of 'em think they should get more respect from mainstream historians." He winked broadly. "Play your cards right with Sir Richard and I have a hunch you're a shoo-in for membership."

"Sir Richard? That would be Richard Hodson? The Grand Master of the Order?"

"You got it. He'd love to get a few more genuine historians on board. It would make him look good. By the way, Letty," Sheldon continued amiably, "speaking of academic credits, I read your last paper. The one on medieval marriage contracts of the early thirteenth century. Very interesting." He nodded with a wise air. "Not a bad job, my girl."

"Thank you."

"I've been wanting to discuss it with you. I detected one or two weak points, but on the whole, I believe you're on the right track. Recently I've been doing some new research in the same period and it occurs to me we ought to consider doing a joint paper on the subject of the property rights of medieval widows."

Letty sipped uneasily at her wine. The last thing she wanted to do was get involved in a joint project with Sheldon Peabody. Xavier was right. Sheldon Peabody was something of a pompous ass. She felt a bit sorry for him, but she had no intention of writing a paper with him.

"Well, medieval widowhood is a fascinating subject, of course," Letty admitted carefully. "After all, the only time a woman had any real freedom or rights to speak of during the era was after she became a widow. Until then she was under the control of either her father or her husband. But I don't think our work is focused in the same direction, Sheldon. You've always emphasized the study of medieval patterns of warfare."

"Warfare is out of fashion. Social history is the in thing these days. Family life, the role of women, that kind of thing. I've decided to explore new directions. Just think about it, Letty," Sheldon urged, his smile more charming than ever. He draped a familiar arm around her shoulders and pulled her against his side, blithely ignoring her effort to resist.

"Sheldon, I don't know. I really do think..."

"My lady, I have a feeling the two of us could turn out something pretty spectacular together. And I'm not talking about just a single paper, either. Hell, we might even get a whole book out of it. Yeah, pretty spectacular."

"If you don't take your arm off my fiancée," Xavier said in a deceptively casual tone from directly behind Sheldon, "something spectacular is going to happen right here in front of the entire assembled multitude of the Medieval Revelers. And it won't be pretty."

"Xavier." Letty jumped at the sound of that all too familiar voice. She whirled around, recognizing the steel in it, even if Sheldon did not.

"Oh, it's you, Augustine." Sheldon's arm fell away from Letty's shoulders. "I was wondering when you'd show up. It was too much to hope you'd get lost en route, I suppose." With a bored air, he held his goblet out to the nearest bartender for a refill.

Letty fixed Xavier with a repressive frown. "Xavier, if you don't stop going around implying we're still engaged, I'm going to have to take serious measures. I really won't tolerate—oh, my goodness." She broke off in amazed wonder at the sight of Xavier Augustine in medieval garb.

He looked devastating. There was no other word for it, Letty decided. Xavier wore a stark black tunic emblazoned with a gold leopard. His leggings, boots and the shirt, which he wore under the tunic, were all black. An ornate belt rode low around his lean hips. The total effect, taken together with his riveting green eyes and midnight dark hair, was extremely unsettling.

Letty's nerve endings felt as if they'd had a close brush with electricity. She had no problem at all imagining Xavier donning a suit of armor, mounting a big destrier and riding off to do battle. She reminded herself firmly that history scholars were frequently accused of being overimaginative.

"Yes, Letty? What serious measures are you going to take?" Xavier accepted a glass of wine from one of the bartenders.

"Never mind," she muttered. "This isn't the time or place for this sort of discussion."

Xavier shrugged. "There's nothing to discuss as far as I'm concerned."

"An interesting perspective on the problem," Sheldon drawled.

"It's the only perspective. The trouble with you academic types is that you're inclined to view things from strange angles."

"So now you're an authority on the academic approach?" Sheldon's mouth tilted sarcastically and he slanted an amused glance at Letty. "No wonder you called off the wedding, my dear. Our Saint Augustine seems to think his business success is more impressive than your academic accomplishments."

"Letty knows I have nothing but respect for her academic accomplishments, don't you, Letty?" Xavier smiled at her.

Letty stared at him, horrified by the suddenly charged atmosphere between the two men. "Well, I thought you did, but I..."

"It's the accomplishments of one of the other members of the history faculty that leave me unimpressed," Xavier murmured.

"Why, you son of a—" Sheldon bit off the remainder of the epithet. "Damn you, Augustine, you think you can throw your weight around and get away with it, don't you? Let me tell you something. If you had the guts to fight fair instead of using your clout with the trustees to threaten me, I'd teach you a lesson you wouldn't forget."

"Hell, why not?" Xavier took a swallow of his wine. "Consider the threat lifted. I only needed it to make sure I got an invitation to this convention, anyway. I hereby swear not to use my clout to get you fired from Tipton. If you want to teach me a lesson, Peabody, you go right ahead and try."

"Gentlemen, how dare you," Letty yelped, frantic now. "This is getting out of hand. I feel as if I'm standing between a couple of genuine thirteenth-century hotheads trying to stage a quarrel in the castle hall. Xavier, how can you act like this? It isn't like you at all."

"How would you know?" he asked softly, green eyes glinting.

That brought Letty up short for an instant. The man had a point. According to Molly, she knew nothing about him. But Letty could hardly acknowledge that at the moment. "You're a civilized, well-mannered gentleman and I expect you to behave like one."

His smile was cool and dangerous. "Is that right? I got the impression you didn't appreciate my gentlemanly behavior."

Letty felt herself turning a brilliant shade of pink as she realized he was referring to her comments on his restrained method of courtship. "For heaven's sake, Xavier."

"Besides, you wanted to spice up your life a little, remember?" he continued smoothly, paying no attention to her admonishing scowl. "Nothing like having a couple of quarreling knights stage a small duel with you as the prize to add zest to your placid existence, right?''

Letty stared at him. ''Xavier, are you crazy?'' she hissed. ''This isn't like you. You're going to cause a scene.''

''Scenes are the very stuff of the exciting life,'' he informed her.

Sheldon narrowed his eyes and straightened his shoulders. ''Don't worry, Letty, I'll make sure Augustine here doesn't embarrass you.''

Xavier turned his cold smile back on Peabody. ''Now that should prove interesting.''

''I'm warning you, Augustine,'' Peabody began, only to be interrupted by a woman's voice.

''Oh, there you are, Sheldon. I've been looking for you.''

Letty and the two men turned to watch the newcomer approach. She was a plump woman with beige hair who appeared to be in her late forties. She was attractive in a hard-edged kind of way. Her gown was dark blue and fuchsia. She was wearing a transparent veil over the back of her hair that was anchored in place by a fillet. When she reached Sheldon, she slipped her arm through his and smiled at Letty and Xavier.

''Hello,'' she said with a bright salesperson's smile. ''You must be new. I don't recognize you and I know almost everyone at these conventions. I'm Alison Crane. From Seattle. I'm in real estate. High-end condos mostly. I do a fair amount of business among the Revelers. Here, let me give you a card.''

''Uh, Alison, this is Dr. Letitia Conroy from Tipton College,'' Sheldon said quickly as Letty automatically extended a hand to take the business card.

''I'm Xavier Augustine,'' Xavier said blandly when it became apparent Sheldon was not going to bother introducing him. ''No, thanks. I don't need a card. I'm not planning on buying any real estate in Seattle in the near future. But I'll keep your name in mind.''

''How do you do?'' Letty said, grateful for the opportunity to defuse the quarrel that had been building between Xavier and Sheldon. ''You've been attending these conventions for some time?''

''Ever since they started five years ago,'' Alison assured her. ''Made some great contacts here.''

Letty looked at her. ''That's why you come? To make business contacts?''

"One of the reasons. But history was my major when I was in college and after I graduated I turned it into a hobby. Just like most of the other people in this room. Something fascinating about medieval history, isn't there? I subscribe to a couple of major academic journals and I believe I've read one or two of your articles on women's roles in the Middle Ages, Dr. Conroy. Fascinating stuff. Absolutely fascinating."

"Thank you," Letty said, quite flattered. "Please call me Letty."

"Certainly. You know, you really ought to consider writing a book on the subject of medieval women aimed at the non-academic market. Your writing style is extremely readable. Not in the least dry or pedantic. I should think there would be a sizable market."

Sheldon looked sage and thoughtful. "What a coincidence. Alison, I was just telling Letty that she and I should get together to collaborate on a book, wasn't I, Letty?"

"Well," said Letty, feeling pressured again and wishing she could think of a polite way out of the situation. "I don't know, Sheldon. I mean, I've never tried anything for the popular market. I'd want to do a lot of thinking before I committed myself to anything like that."

Xavier stepped closer to Letty in a move that emphasized his claim on her. "Forget it, Peabody. If Letty wants to write a book, she'll do it on her own. She doesn't need a collaborator."

"Why don't you get lost, Augustine?" Sheldon threw him a scathing glance and took another gulp of his wine.

"Don't hold your breath, Peabody. I'm not going anywhere without Letty."

Letty was mortified.

Alison's smile went up another couple of watts as she serenely ignored the byplay between the two men. "Do think about it, Letty. I'm sure you would do a wonderful job. Now, if you'll excuse me, I've got to run. I see an old client of mine over in the corner. Oh, by the way, I'm having a little after-hours get-together in my suite after the official festivities are finished tonight. Drinks are on the house. Room 209. Come on up, if you get the chance. Both of you. And you, too, Sheldon. You always do."

Alison floated away through the crowd in search of her ex-client and Letty watched her go with a pang of regret. She did not like being left alone with Xavier and Sheldon.

But before she was forced to deal with the two quarreling knights, a horn sounded from the far end of the hall. A man dressed in the costume of a page held up a large scroll and cleared his throat.

"'Hear ye, hear ye, me lords and ladies. All members of the Order of Medieval Revelers are hereby summoned to the grand banquet. Sir Richard shall lead the way.'"

"Listen, Letty," Sheldon said earnestly as the crowd surged toward the banquet hall doorway, "I'll be eating at the head table. I'd like to ask you to join me up on the dais but there wasn't time to make arrangements for tonight's meal. Your decision to come to the convention caught me by surprise."

"That's quite all right, Sheldon," Letty said quickly. "Don't worry about it, I'll be fine."

"Right," said Xavier, taking her arm. "She'll be fine. She'll sit with me."

Sheldon smiled thickly at Xavier. Then he shifted his gaze quickly back to Letty. "Enjoy yourself, Letty. I've arranged a little surprise for you toward the end of the banquet when the jongleurs show up." He turned and got swept up in the throng.

"What are jongleurs?" Xavier asked.

"Traveling minstrels. It was fashionable for the knights to write poems to their ladies. They often had the jongleurs set them to music and sing them. Haven't you ever heard of troubadour poetry?"

"I think I read about it in one of your papers. A lot of nonsense about some idiot knight pining away for a lady who won't give the guy the time of day, right?"

"In a nutshell. You're such a romantic," Letty said.

"Don't I get any bonus points for trying? Let me tell you something, Letty, I wouldn't dress up in this funny outfit for just any woman."

CHAPTER FIVE

NO DOUBT ABOUT IT, Xavier thought midway through the lavish feast, he had definitely screwed up when he had inadvertently allowed that investigation report to fall into Letty's hands. He still did not completely understand why she had gotten so upset but she had. And he was paying for his carelessness now by having to sit through this crazy parody of a medieval banquet.

The scene that confronted him was downright bizarre as far as Xavier was concerned. The room had been draped in heavy tapestries depicting scenes of hunting, warfare and other events of medieval life. Everywhere there was color and outrageous pomp. Women in fancy headdresses and brilliant gowns were seated next to men dressed in tunics, tights and pointy shoes. Several of the men wore odd caps made out of felt. Gaudy jewels that anyone could see at a glance were fakes, gleamed in the belts and glittered from the head wear. The laughter and chatter was getting louder and more raucous as the wine glasses were refilled. It was a damn good thing nobody was driving home tonight, Xavier decided.

The diners were seated at two long rows of tables that extended out from the head table. Harried-looking waiters and waitresses garbed as pages and serving wenches scurried back and forth with huge platters of food.

Sheldon Peabody and several other high-ranking Revelers were all sitting under a yellow and white striped canopy on a raised platform at the far end of the room. Although he pretended to ignore them, Xavier was fully aware of the frequent glances Sheldon sent toward Letty who was clearly enjoying herself immensely.

Xavier had to admit that his lady did look lovely in her strange gown and the silly gold hair-net she was wearing. The little circlet of metal that went around her head like a delicate crown gave her a regal air. It only went to prove that true class showed regardless of what a woman wore, Xavier told himself proudly. Letty would look good in anything.

Tonight there was a captivating, otherwordly charm about her

that made him want to pull her close and protect her from Peabody's lecherous gaze. Xavier sipped his wine and idly wondered
how many medieval ladies went to banquets wearing glasses.

"What's wrong?" Letty demanded in a low voice. She shot him
a sidelong glance as he narrowed his eyes over the wine. "You
don't approve of the Burgundy, Sir Xavier?"

"It isn't a genuine Burgundy. It's a cheap California red."

"My, my, how depressing for you. But you seem to be holding
up manfully under the stress of having to drink cheap wine."

"Yeah." Xavier took a closer look at her strange hairstyle.

"What are you smiling at?" Letty asked irritably as she helped
herself to more vegetables.

"I was wondering what you'd done to your hair. It looks like
you're wearing ear muffs." Xavier continued to examine the rich,
dark chestnut coils that gleamed inside the gold net.

"I'll have you know this style was the *height* of fashion in the
late Middle Ages."

"Is that right? What was the *depth* of fashion?"

"The codpiece," she informed him with grim relish. "It came
into vogue at the end of the medieval period and truly flowered,
one might say, during the Renaissance. Be grateful your costume
is from the fourteenth century. If it had been from the fifteenth you
might have had to wear one and somehow I just can't see you in
a codpiece."

Xavier wondered if she was actually teasing him. If so, it was a
good sign. "You don't think I could have managed to fill one out
properly?" he asked politely.

"Nobody actually *filled out* a codpiece," Letty said sweetly. "At
least not by virtue of natural endowment. The men stuffed them
with cotton wadding or something."

Xavier grinned. "Sort of like putting tissue inside your bra, I
guess." He was rewarded with a hastily muffled giggle from Letty.
"Would you mind passing me the peas?" he continued. "Looks
like I'll have to eat them with my spoon. Have you noticed there
aren't any forks on the table?"

"Forks weren't around in medieval times," Letty explained.
"People used spoons and knives and fingers. At least we've got
real plates. In the old days they used trenchers made of large slabs
of stale bread to hold the food. And there would have been rushes

down on the floor to catch the stuff that got spilled. And lots of dogs running around under the table, of course.''

"The local health department probably put its foot down when the Revelers applied for a permit for rushes and dogs in a public restaurant. We should all be grateful. I assume most of this food is not particularly authentic, either.''

"Well, there isn't any larded boar's head or roasted peacock, but other than that a lot of it would have looked familiar to a medieval diner. The main difference between the food we eat now and what people ate back then is in the preservation and preparation techniques.''

"I suppose they were a little short on refrigerators and freezers.''

"Right. But they were very good at concocting thick, rich sauces and gravies to cover up food that was past its prime. And they had all sorts of exotic spices, some from the Far East. They routinely cooked with ginger and cloves and cinnamon. Some of the recipes were incredibly complex.'' Letty paused and then smiled in delight. "Oh, look, here comes the entertainment.''

Xavier glanced up and saw a team of jugglers dressed in green and orange costumes with whimsical pointed caps. They were taking up positions in the middle of the floor between the long tables. The crowd roared its approval as the entertainers began tossing soft colored balls into the air.

"Xavier, are you really intending to stay here the whole four days?'' Letty asked bluntly, her eyes on the jugglers.

He contemplated her profile, trying to figure out what she was thinking. "If that's what it takes.''

She turned her head, eyes flashing behind the lenses of her little glasses. "If that's what it takes to do what? Just what is it you expect to accomplish? I'm not going to change my mind, you know.''

He sighed and leaned back in his chair, hooking his thumbs in his low-slung belt. "Letty, two days ago you were in love with me,'' he reminded her gently. "I don't think anything has changed. You're just feeling a bit anxious. You'll get over it.''

"This is not a case of bridal jitters, Xavier Augustine. I am angry and hurt and I will not be changing my mind. Don't give yourself any false hopes.''

He smiled wistfully. "All I've got left is a little hope, sweetheart. Would you take that away from me along with everything else?''

She blinked and then her brows came together in a fierce expression. "Don't you dare try to make me feel sorry for you. I don't believe for one minute that you ever really cared deeply for me. Go find another suitable wife. I'm out of the running."

"Not yet," he drawled, wanting to laugh at her determination to move into the fast lane. "You haven't done anything to disqualify yourself yet."

"I will."

"I doubt it. You're too damned smart to do anything really stupid just to spite me."

She slammed her knife down on the table. "You're insufferable."

"Just desperate. I want you very badly, Letty."

He watched the blush rise in her cheeks as she glanced around hurriedly. She was obviously afraid that someone on either side of them might be eavesdropping. Xavier could have told her not to worry. Everyone else was either laughing at the jugglers' antics or talking loudly to his or her neighbor. For all intents and purposes, Xavier and Letty might have been alone in the crowded room.

"Stop talking like that," Letty muttered as she sank her small white teeth into a chunk of dark bread.

Xavier leaned closer to murmur in her ear. "I'm sorry you were upset by that investigator's report. I never meant to hurt you."

"Then why did you pay someone to spy on me?"

He frowned. "It wasn't exactly spying."

"Yes, it was."

"All I can say is that I had my reasons."

She turned to him with glittering eyes. "What reasons?"

Xavier contemplated her for a long moment, wondering how much to tell her. Damn, what a mess. But it was clear Letty was going to demand some answers from him. "It's a long story, love. And it has nothing to do with us."

"The hell it doesn't."

Xavier started to argue that point but was interrupted by another annoying blast from a horn followed by a monotonous drumming. He looked around to see that the jugglers had retired and had been replaced by a group of musicians dressed as minstrels.

"Now what?" he growled.

"The jongleurs," Letty said, looking expectant. "This should be fun."

One of the musicians stepped forward and held up his hands to call for silence and attention. When he had it he removed his belled cap and bowed deeply to the room full of people.

"My lords and ladies, I beg you to listen to the song I am about to sing for you. Pray remember that I am but a messenger, a humble servant of the bold knight who has commissioned me to convey his deep admiration for his fair lady. His only plea is that she listen to his heartfelt words of appreciation for her beauty, grace and form."

A round of applause greeted this announcement and the jongleur stepped forward to stand directly in front of Letty. Xavier saw her eyes widen in pleased surprise. She glanced toward the dais and Sheldon Peabody inclined his head with what was probably meant to be knightly grace.

"Damn," Xavier said beneath his breath. Out of the corner of his eye, he saw Peabody preen beneath the yellow and white canopy as everyone clapped again. It did not take much guesswork to figure out which bold knight had arranged for this performance. One of these days, Xavier decided, he was going to have to do something about Dr. Peabody.

The minstrel began to strum his lute and sing in a slow, mournful style. Xavier lounged in his chair and drummed his fingers impatiently on his belt.

Oh, I would tell you of my lady fair;
She with the dark flames burning in her chesnut hair
Ye shall hear of her radiant gaze, of eyes that glow like crystal
pools;
Of lips as sweet as fine spiced wine and of how she breaks
this heart of mine.
Each part of her is sheer perfection; each more beauteous
than the rest
Oh, how I shall languish until I am free to kiss her noble brow
and caress her fair, white breast.

Rage boiled in Xavier's veins as the last lines of the song sank home. When they did, he leapt to his feet.

"*Caress her fair, white breast,*" he roared. "Who the hell do you think you are, Peabody? Nobody, and I mean *nobody*, talks about my fiancée's fair, white breast except me."

"Xavier," Letty hissed, tugging frantically on his sleeve, "Xavier, please, sit down. It's troubadour poetry. They always sing about breasts and eyes and hair. Sit down, for heaven's sake."

Xavier ignored her, his whole attention on Peabody's mocking smile. "I want an apology, Peabody. And I want it now."

"You want me to apologize?" Sheldon looked amazed. "Why on earth should I apologize to anyone? What you have heard is nothing more than a humble tribute to a beautiful, intelligent, utterly charming woman."

"It's a damned insult, that's what it is, you bastard. And you will apologize, by God." Xavier planted one hand on the white cloth and vaulted lightly over the table.

He landed easily on the floor in the middle of the room and started striding toward the platform where Peabody sat. The musicians scrambled out of the way, a couple of them tripping over their long pointed shoes. The crowd hushed.

"Xavier, what do you think you're doing?" Letty called out anxiously. "Please come back here. You're causing a scene."

"I don't give a damn about embarrassing Peabody," Xavier declared, aware that the entire assembly of Revelers was watching in stunned silence. "He deserves it for embarrassing you."

"But I wasn't that embarrassed," Letty said in a small voice. "Honest. It was just a poem, Xavier."

Xavier paid no attention to her weak protests. He'd had enough of Sheldon Peabody. He came to a halt in front of the head table and reached out to sweep aside the dishes and trays of food behind which Peabody was barricaded. Platters, goblets, knives and trays cascaded across the white tablecloth.

"What the hell?" Peabody leapt to his feet as wine trickled into his lap. "What do you think you're doing, Augustine?"

The other diners seated under the canopy quickly edged out of the way, but made no effort to halt the scene. It was apparent the crowd was beginning to enjoy this new sport.

Sir Richard, a large, florid-faced man in his late forties, picked up his knife and rapped on his goblet for attention. "I see we have a little matter of chivalry and honor to settle here. It would seem these two bold knights both seek the attention of the same fair lady. What say you, my lords and ladies? How shall we deal with this?"

"Let them both compose poems and we'll all sit in judgment

tomorrow,'' yelled one man dressed in a red and gray tunic. ''The winner gets to entertain the lady tomorrow night.''

''Let the lady choose between them,'' a woman in a high, wide headdress and veil suggested.

''Aye, aye, let the lady choose,'' Alison Crane echoed. ''It's her right.''

''I say we let them compete for her,'' someone else suggested. ''Let them engage in an archery contest or a chess match.''

''No, a quest. Make it a quest.''

''Yes, a quest. Let's stage a quest.'' The cry was echoed around the room and accompanied by loud applause.

Sir Richard rapped his goblet once more. ''As Lord of Revelry, I must make the choice and I shall have to think on the matter.'' He turned toward Xavier and Sheldon. ''Do you prefer archery, chess or a quest, sir knights?''

Xavier looked at Peabody. ''What I prefer to do is wring Dr. Peabody's neck until he apologizes for insulting my future wife.''

Peabody turned a dull red. ''You think you can do it, Augustine? Go ahead and try.'' He leaned over the table, his expression viciously taunting. ''Just go ahead and try. But be warned, I've studied with a master in the martial arts.''

''I'll keep that in mind.'' Xavier put his hands on Peabody's shoulders and hauled him bodily across the table. Then he released him.

Peabody squawked loudly as he fell in a heap at Xavier's feet. ''How dare you treat me like that? I'm going to wipe the floor with your face, Augustine. You'll pay for this.''

Xavier stepped back out of reach as Peabody jumped up and lashed out with his foot. Xavier caught hold of the other man's ankle and yanked. Peabody went back down on the floor, rolled to one side and climbed back up to his feet. He looked murderous.

Xavier risked a quick glance at Letty and saw the horrified expression on her face just as Peabody lunged forward.

''You think you're so smart, Augustine? Try this on for size,'' Peabody bellowed. He swung wildly, a huge, roundhouse punch that was obviously a mile off.

Xavier considered Letty's expression and abruptly changed his mind about his tactics. He had been intending to pound Peabody into the floor but another strategy now beckoned. He gritted his teeth and waited for Peabody's fist to connect.

When it finally did with a dull, smacking sound, Xavier rolled with it so that the impact was not nearly as bad as it looked. But he made the most of it.

Amid startled shrieks from the audience, he crumpled magnificently to the floor and sprawled full-length at Peabody's feet.

For a moment no one in the room moved. Xavier looked up at Peabody through slitted lashes and realized the man was uncertain what to do next.

Peabody stood over his fallen victim, looking as surprised and confused as everyone else in the room at first. But that expression was soon replaced by a look of pompous satisfaction as it dawned on the professor that he had just vanquished the challenger in a single blow.

"I warned you, Augustine. Don't say I didn't warn you," Peabody crowed.

It was Letty who broke the stunned tableau. "*Xavier*. Oh, my God, Xavier, what has he done to you?"

Xavier lay still and listened contentedly to the sound of crashing dishes and silverware as Letty leapt out of her seat and scrambled over the table to get to him. He sighed in satisfaction as he heard her softly slippered little feet pattering madly across the floor and then she was crouching at his side, touching him with anxious, gentle hands.

"You've hurt him, Sheldon. How could you? Look at him, he's unconscious. You might have broken some bones or given him a concussion. Someone call a doctor. Hurry." She touched Xavier's bruised lip and cheek. "Speak to me, Xavier. Wake up, darling, and speak to me."

"Don't call a doctor," Xavier mumbled. "I'll be okay."

Relief flared in Letty's worried eyes. "Thank heavens, you're not unconscious. I was so frightened. Does it hurt very much?"

"A little," he admitted, opting for the stoic touch. "But I'll probably feel a lot better once I start the lawsuit proceedings."

"*Lawsuit.*" Peabody's voice was suddenly several notches higher. "Now see here, Augustine, you've got no right to sue me. You started this."

"Did I? My memory is a little foggy at the moment." Xavier rubbed his jaw. "Probably a result of the blow."

"I've got a hundred witnesses, damn it," Peabody retorted. "Tell him he hasn't got grounds for a suit, Letty."

"No one's going to sue anyone," Letty said soothingly as she put an arm under Xavier's shoulders and helped him sit up. "You were both at fault. But you shouldn't have hurt him like that, Sheldon. That sort of violence was uncalled for."

"He started it, damn it," Sheldon yelped.

"Well, I know, but all the same, physical violence is never the answer," Letty reminded him primly. "Are you sure you don't need a doctor, Xavier?" she added in concern. "You look a little odd."

"I'll be fine," he said bravely as he stifled a laugh. "But I'd like to go upstairs and get a cold compress on my jaw, if you don't mind. I've heard it's good for keeping the swelling down."

"Swelling. Good heavens, yes. You need to get a compress on that jaw immediately. I'll help you. Lean on me, Xavier." She staggered under his weight as she assisted him to his feet. When he swayed, she gripped his waist and tugged his arm around her shoulders. "Be careful, darling."

"Thanks, honey," he said weakly. "Sorry to disrupt the festivities. I'm sure no one will mind if we leave now." Over the top of Letty's head he smiled a victor's smile at Peabody whose eyes narrowed in sudden suspicion.

"He doesn't need any help, Letty," Peabody said.

"I'll be the judge of that," Letty informed him with fine hauteur. "You should be ashamed of yourself, Sheldon."

"But, Letty..."

"So long, Peabody," Xavier said. "See you around. Hey, no hard feelings, big guy. I had it coming." He raised the hand that was resting on Letty's shoulder and waved good-naturedly. "Win some, lose some."

Sheldon's face turned purple. "Letty, don't get suckered in by this jerk. He's not badly hurt."

She glared at him as she eased Xavier toward the door. "Don't try to tell me he's not hurt, Sheldon. I saw you hit him. You knocked him down. It was dreadful."

"He walked straight into it—deliberately, I'm beginning to think," Sheldon muttered as he hurried along beside her.

Xavier groaned in pain and leaned more heavily on Letty's shoulders. She responded by pulling him closer and giving Peabody another furious glance.

"I saw it all," Letty announced. "You knocked him down, Sheldon. Now please get out of my way. I have to get him upstairs so we can apply cold compresses.''

"Damn it, Letty, I'm telling you..."

"Telling me what?''

Peabody groaned and gave up. "Never mind." He gave Xavier another narrowed glance. "You think you're so damn smart, don't you, Augustine?''

"Who, me? I don't have a Ph.D. like you, Peabody. How could I possibly be smarter than you?''

Peabody started to reply to the taunt but at that moment a well-endowed young woman with acres of blond hair bounded forward out of the crowd.

"Hey, Shelly babe, are you all right?'' The young woman grasped Peabody's arm. "That was just super, the way you decked him. Like absolutely awesome. I've never seen anything like it. Wow. You really flattened him. Totally. Are you sure you're all right?''

"I'm fine, Jennifer.''

"That was a really super song you wrote. Some people just don't appreciate real talent.'' Jennifer shot a cool glance at Letty.

"Not now, Jennifer,'' Peabody muttered, his frustrated gaze still on Xavier.

The banquet hall door closed on Sheldon Peabody's twisted grimace of frustrated fury. Letty did not appear to notice. She was too busy guiding Xavier across the lobby.

"I can't believe what happened in there,'' she said as she steered her charge into the elevator and punched the button. "Two grown men brawling over the banquet table.''

"Welcome to the exciting life.''

She glowered. "Xavier, this is not a joke. You could have been seriously injured.''

He hung his head and tried to look chastened. "I know. I was a fool. I just couldn't handle it when I heard that verse about caressing your fair, white breast. I went a little crazy. Hell, Letty, even I haven't caressed your fair, white breast.''

"Neither has Sheldon Peabody, so don't get upset,'' she retorted. "Honestly, Xavier, I told you it was just a song in the tradition of the medieval style of chivalric love. The knights who wrote the poems sang a lot about longing to caress their ladies, but the fundamental principle of chivalric love was that it was platonic and unrequited. The ladies weren't supposed to actually respond.''

''Don't try to tell me Peabody was only thinking of worshipping you from afar when he wrote that damned song for you. And don't tell me you weren't responding. You were enjoying that stupid poem.''

She had the grace to blush. ''Well, it is the first time anyone ever wrote a poem to me, I must admit.''

''It was an insult, by God.''

''Listen, Xavier. You want to talk about insults? I'll tell you right off that I was a lot more insulted when I found out you'd had me investigated than I was hearing I had fire in my hair and fair, white breasts.''

Xavier recognized a bad strategy when he saw one. He retreated quickly, groaning loudly and rubbing his jaw. ''Ow. Sure hope Peabody didn't loosen any of my teeth.''

Letty immediately stopped berating him and started fussing nicely. ''I can't believe Sheldon hit you. How dare he? He always seemed like such a nice, civilized sort of person. This is so unlike him.''

''Uh-huh.''

Xavier considered going back down to the banquet hall and shoving Peabody's teeth down his throat. Common sense overrode male hormones, however. After all, Xavier told himself, he was the one alone up here with Letty. Peabody was downstairs, no doubt stuffing himself at the head table and wondering why the fair lady had left with the loser.

Xavier grinned faintly at that thought. Obviously Peabody was better at writing stupid love songs than he was at understanding how women like Letty thought.

''What's so funny?'' Letty eased Xavier off the elevator at the third floor and started down the hallway.

''Nothing. Just a grimace of pain.''

''Oh, dear.'' She looked up anxiously. ''Is the pain getting worse?''

''I'll survive. I think.'' He searched for the pocket in the strange clothes he was wearing. ''Here's my room key.''

She took it from him and opened his door. ''I have never been so shocked in my whole life as when you leapt over the table and went to confront Sheldon.'' She switched on the light and helped him sit down on the edge of the bed. "I've never seen two men fight before. It was sickening."

"It's even more sickening to lose."

"Who could have guessed Sheldon would have turned so violent? Just be grateful you weren't hurt any worse than you are." She went into the bathroom. "Stay where you are. I'll fix up a compress."

"Thanks." Xavier listened as she ran water into the sink. He caught sight of himself in the mirror and winced at his grim image. Dressed entirely in black with his dark hair rumpled and nursing a split lip he was probably not a maiden's delight.

"Here we go." Letty came out of the bathroom with a damp washcloth neatly folded into a compress. "Lie down and I'll adjust it."

Xavier did as she directed and leaned back against the pillows. The folds of her brightly colored gown wafted around him as she bent to apply the compress to his bruised jaw. Surreptitiously he inhaled the delightful scent of her as he gazed at the expanse of skin exposed by the low neckline of her costume. Her hands were wonderfully gentle as she dealt with his wounds.

"Thank you, Letty," he murmured. "That feels much better."

She frowned. "You're sure a cold compress is enough? You don't want me to drive you into town to the emergency room?"

He shook his head and smiled faintly. "No. I'll be fine. I'm sorry I embarrassed you."

"I suppose it's not your fault that you aren't very familiar with the traditions of medieval poetry and songs."

"I overreacted."

"Yes, you did, but it's understandable." She smiled suddenly as she adjusted the compress. "Actually, now that I think about it, your reaction could be seen in a somewhat noble light. I mean, you did think you were defending my honor in a way, didn't you?"

He watched her from beneath half-lowered lids. "I'm glad you understand."

Her smile widened and her eyes warmed. "I'll let you in on a little secret, Xavier. It could have been worse. A lot of medieval verse is a great deal bawdier than what you heard tonight. Lots of sexual allusions to battering down castle gates and plucking roses from well-guarded towers. The poems were full of tales of knights inventing ways to sneak into ladies' bedchambers. They were an earthy bunch back in those days.''

Xavier scowled. "I don't think I want to hear about it. If Peabody tries to sneak into your bedchamber, I really will throttle him. *Ouch.*" He touched his sore lip.

"Sorry. Did I hurt you?"

He gave her a sharp glance and saw only innocence radiating from her concerned gaze. "No. It's my fault. I should have moved a little quicker when Peabody threw that punch.''

Letty started to say something but broke off at the sound of high-spirited shouts out in the hall. They were followed by laughter, footsteps and a couple of distinctly feminine squeals. "Sounds like things are getting into high gear out there, doesn't it? Sheldon said this was a real party crowd.''

Xavier experienced a moment of panic wondering if Letty was planning to join the others as soon as she had finished tending to his wounds. "I don't think I'll be up to any more fun and games this evening. I'd better keep the cold compress on this face of mine.''

"Yes, I suppose so." She sounded uncertain. "Do you think you'll be all right up here by yourself?''

Xavier shook his head doubtfully and groaned. "You never know about the after-affects of a punch like the one Peabody landed. Takes a couple of hours to see if there's going to be any real problem.''

"It does?''

He nodded. "Right. I'll just sit up here and watch TV by myself. You go off and have fun. That's what you came for, isn't it?''

"Well, yes, but I feel bad about leaving you up here alone watching television while everyone else is having a great time.''

"I've spent worse evenings, believe me. Run along and enjoy yourself, Letty. Don't worry about me. It wasn't your fault I got beaten up.''

She stood up abruptly. "I will worry about you and that's all there is to it. And it is my fault you're hurt. At least, in a way it is. Sort of. Tell you what. I've got a deck of cards in my room. Why don't we play some gin or something?''

Xavier smiled slowly. "That's very kind of you, Letty.''

"I'll get the cards.''

Xavier waited until she had gone through the connecting door before he picked up the telephone and called room service.

"I want a bottle of your best champagne, no, not the California sparkling wine, the real thing. From France. What have you got?" He listened to the limited selection available in the inn's cellars as it was reeled off. Then he chose the best label on the list. "And two glasses. Oh, yeah, send up a tray of snacks. Something classy. Got any good pâté or caviar?"

"Yes, sir, we do," the room-service waiter responded. "Which would you prefer?"

"Send up both."

"Right. We're getting real busy down here, sir, but we'll take care of your order as soon as possible."

"Do that." Xavier put down the phone with a sense of satisfaction. He ignored the shrieks and shouts of laughter that were getting louder out in the hall. He was going to see to it that Letty enjoyed a very private party right here in this room tonight.

He intended to show her she did not need Sheldon Peabody and his Order of Medieval Revelers in order to spice up her life. And while he was at it, he also intended to show her in no uncertain terms that all his male equipment worked just fine.

CHAPTER SIX

A LONG TIME LATER Letty put down yet another winning hand of cards and smiled triumphantly at Xavier who was stretched out on the bed, shoulders braced against the pillows.

"Gin," she announced with glee. "Again."

"I'm obviously out of my league here." Xavier folded his cards. "My only excuse is that it's getting hard to concentrate with all that racket going on out in the corridor."

The din from the corridor had increased during the past two hours. There were parties going on in nearby rooms and people were bellowing down the hall at friends or laughing uproariously. The sound of footsteps and loud music filtered through the walls.

"The bellman who showed me to my room said they battened down the hatches around here after the official festivities were over for the evening. I think I'm beginning to see why." Letty shuddered and picked up her glass of champagne. "It sounds wild out there, doesn't it?"

Xavier, apparently unfazed by his sixth losing hand in a row, put down his own cards and picked up the bottle of champagne to refill his glass. "It sure does. Sorry you're missing out on it?"

She sighed. "To be perfectly honest, no. I'm beginning to wonder if I really fit in with this crowd, Xavier. It was fun dressing up in these costumes and I did enjoy the banquet, at least I did until you and Sheldon started brawling."

"Sorry about that."

"But," she continued, "I'm not sure I would enjoy those after-hours parties going on out there. I'm not certain I would know what to do at one, if you know what I mean."

"Maybe you tried to move into the fast lane a little too quickly," Xavier said with a slow, sensual smile. "You're not used to this kind of life-style."

That observation annoyed her. "What do you suggest I do? Go back to my humdrum, boring existence in Tipton Cove? No thanks."

"I wasn't going to suggest anything so dull." Xavier covered her hand with his own, his fingers strong and warm.

When she raised her eyes to meet his, Letty drew a sharp breath at the glittering sexuality in his hooded gaze. She had seen hints of that very masculine, very exciting expression before in his eyes when he had taken her into his arms. But Xavier had never followed through on the subtle promise that had always sent shock waves through her. In the past he had always carefully disengaged himself, said good-night and left her to her lonely bed.

"No," Letty said quite firmly as she snatched her hand out from under his. "No, absolutely not."

"No, what?" His gleaming gaze narrowed briefly as he dropped his hand to rest possessively on her thigh.

"No, you are not going to do it to me again, Xavier Augustine. I've had it with your passionate good-night kisses that never go anywhere. You're not going to get me all hot and bothered again tonight and then send me off to my own room. So don't even bother to try." She stood up quickly and stepped back from the bed.

Xavier did not move. "Who said I was going to send you off alone to your own room this time?"

"It's what you did all those other times you kissed me good-night. I'm not taking any chances. You've set me up once too often. I'm calling it quits before you even begin this time."

He got to his feet with lazy grace and caught her gently around the waist. "Tonight will be different, Letty."

"I doubt it. Let go of me." She batted ineffectually at his hands as he pulled her close against his hard, lean length.

"Letty, you still love me, don't you?" He brushed his mouth lightly over hers. "You can't possibly have fallen out of love with me in the space of only two days."

"Want to bet?"

"I want you, sweetheart. I've wanted you all along." He wrapped his arms tightly around her and simply held her close, making no effort to kiss her again. He tenderly pushed her head down onto his shoulder. "And I'm through trying to play the gentleman."

"I told you, it's too late to try to seduce me." Her voice was muffled against the fabric of the tunic. "The engagement is off, Xavier. Over. Finished. Terminated."

"All right," he said thoughtfully.

Letty went very still. She hadn't expected him to agree quite so easily. A niggling disappointment shot through her. "All right?" she repeated blankly. "You mean, you're going to stop running around telling everyone I'm just suffering a bad case of bridal jitters?"

"I'll run around telling everyone we're having an affair, instead. How does that sound?"

"An *affair?*" Letty planted her palms against his chest and shoved herself back a few inches to look up into his face. "What on earth are you talking about? We're not having an affair."

"Why not?" He smiled slightly as he cupped the twin coils of hair over her ears. He held her that way as he kissed her brow. "You want to do something exciting, don't you? Why not have an affair?"

"With you?" She felt dazed. Her mind whirled as she tried to take in what he was saying.

"Naturally. Who better to have an affair with than the man you once loved enough to marry? So much safer than picking up a stranger these days. After all, you already know a lot about me. And you like me. We're compatible in lots of ways. What better basis for an affair? Hell, it was good enough to get us engaged, wasn't it?"

Letty stared up at him, belatedly remembering the phone call from Molly Sweet. "But I don't know all that much about you."

"Sure you do. You knew enough to agree to marry me." Xavier's eyes glittered with sexy humor. "If you have any questions, you can always check my references."

"References?"

"Certainly. Starting with the trustees of Tipton College. If that's not enough for you, I'll be happy to provide you with a list of my business associates. Will that do?"

Molly's words came back. *There is no record of Xavier Augustine existing until ten years ago.* Letty wondered what Xavier would say if she asked for a list of people who had known him for longer than ten years. But she did not dare to bring up the subject or demand explanations until Molly had done more research.

Letty did not want to look like a fool if it should turn out that Molly had simply not done a proper search on her computers. Perhaps further inquiries would reveal that Xavier Augustine could easily be traced right back to his date of birth. No, better to keep quiet for now.

Besides, she had other problems at the moment.

"Well, Letty?" Xavier eased the gild fillet off her head and removed the crespinette. He dropped the golden hair-net on the bed. Then his fingers moved in the coils of hair over her ears, loosening them.

"Please, wait, Xavier. I have to think. I don't understand what you're doing." Letty tried to catch his hands and failed. Her hair tumbled free around her shoulders as she looked up at him with a disconcerting mixture of apprehension and desire. She felt the fierce, wild rush of longing she always experienced when Xavier took her in his arms but she told herself she had to stay clear-headed.

"I'm starting an affair with you." His hands moved beneath her hair and his fingers caressed the nape of her neck. "Doesn't that sound exciting?" He slanted his mouth across hers in a slow, erotic kiss. "Doesn't that sound like a real change of pace?" His tongue teased her lower lip. "Doesn't that sound like a way to completely alter your life? Turn it around? Add some spice?"

"I'm not sure," she said slowly.

"Please, darling. No more insults aimed at my virility. I don't think my ego can take it."

Letty was swamped with guilt. She hugged Xavier urgently. "I didn't mean to insult you. Really, I didn't. It's just that I'm trying to think my way through this whole thing."

"That's the old Letty talking. The new Letty doesn't think her way through to a decision. She surrenders to the moment."

"But I hadn't planned on having an affair. At least not with you," Letty explained baldly.

He winced. "I thought you promised there would be no more insults."

"I just meant I never expected you to be interested in having an affair with me," she amended hastily. "You certainly never showed much interest in having one in the past."

"I was a fool. Since you're bent on calling off the marriage, I no longer have much choice, do I? I've decided that an affair is exactly what I want. Can't you see that it's the perfect solution for you, too?"

"I don't know." She was still doubtful although her pulse was beating strongly now and her stomach was doing tiny flip-flops.

"Let me convince you." Xavier eased the jumperlike cyclas off over her head and dropped it down onto the bed. Then he searched out the fastenings of the sapphire-blue gown.

Letty stirred uneasily. She circled his strong wrists with her fingers and looked up at him anxiously. "Xavier, are you sure you want to do this?"

His mouth curved in an unreadable smile as he framed her face with his hands. "Trust me. I know what I'm doing."

"Oh, Xavier. I'm going to do it. I'm going to surrender to the moment." Letty flung her arms around his neck as the last of her qualms fell away. She did love Xavier. "I can see your point perfectly. Who better to have an affair with than the man I once loved enough to marry?" She lifted her face eagerly for his kiss. "You're right. I can see that now. An affair is the perfect answer."

"I thought you'd see the light. I think we'll use your bed. It's larger. And I like the canopy, don't you? Very romantic."

"Oh, yes. Very."

He laughed, a low, husky sound that sent ripples of excitement down her spine. Then the room spun around Letty as Xavier picked her up in his arms and carried her through the open connecting door into her room.

He stood her on her feet beside the canopied bed and removed her glasses. He set them down on a bedside stand and slowly eased her out of the blue gown. Letty held herself very still, mesmerized by the compelling eroticism of his touch. His hands were strong and sure and gentle. When the archaic dress pooled at her feet, she stepped out of it, suddenly aware of the scraps of lace covering her breasts and the bit of silk that shielded her secrets.

"The trousseau lingerie?" Xavier smiled as he unclipped the bra.

"Yes. I bought it for our honeymoon," she admitted, wondering why her eyes were suddenly filled with tears.

"Don't cry, darling." He kissed away the drop of moisture that squeezed out of her closed eyes. "Think of this as our wedding night."

She sniffed back the tears as raucous laughter echoed out in the hall. "No, I'll think of it as the first night of our affair. Which is exactly what it is."

"Whatever you want, sweetheart. We'll talk it out in the morning."

"There's nothing more to discuss, is there?" Letty looked up at him, feeling an odd sense of regret.

"Yes, there is. But now isn't the time. Hush, love."

"But, Xavier..."

Xavier was no longer paying any attention to her words, however. His mouth was moving over her cheek, seeking out the tender skin behind one ear. His teeth closed briefly around her earlobe and Letty gasped.

"You're trembling," he whispered.

"I can't seem to stop."

"I'm a little shaky, myself," he admitted with a small smile as he freed her breasts. "I've waited a long time for this night, Letty."

"No one said you had to wait," she reminded him a bit irritably, even as her nipples tautened beneath his thumbs.

"I know, I know. It's my own damn fault. I make mistakes once in a while, but I always take care of them."

There was an unexpectedly hard edge in that statement. Letty raised her head to search his face but all she could see in the shadows were his gemstone eyes. They glittered with a powerful desire that took away her breath.

"Fair, white breasts," Xavier murmured wonderingly. "You are very lovely, sweetheart. You set my blood on fire. Do you know that? I was afraid to touch you like this before because I knew you'd have this effect on me. I knew that once I'd started making love to you, I wouldn't be able to stop."

"Oh, Xavier, I wanted you so." She swayed against him, clinging to his waist and resting her head on his broad shoulder.

"I'm glad. I'm very, very glad you wanted me like this." Xavier's hands slid down her bare back to the base of her spine and then closed around her rounded buttocks. He squeezed gently and groaned deep in his chest when Letty shivered. "I'm burning up, love. I'm going to bury myself in you until you put out the fire. There is no other way this time. No cold shower in the world would work tonight."

"Good." She kissed his throat. "I'm glad."

Xavier released her. He leaned down to pull back the covers on the canopied bed and then he swept Letty back up into his arms.

When he deposited her in the center of the bed she instinctively reached for the sheet and pulled it up to cover her breasts.

Xavier watched the movement with hungry eyes as he undressed beside the bed. "Shy?" he whispered.

"A little."

"You'll get over it. I'm going to touch every inch of you and then I'm going to kiss every place I've touched. By morning you won't know the meaning of the word shy."

She watched him toss aside the black tunic and shirt. The sight of his smoothly muscled chest made her ache deep inside. She held her breath as he shed boots and leggings. Then Letty's eyes widened as she caught sight of his gloriously aroused body.

Xavier chuckled softly as he came down beside her. "Why are you looking at me like that, sweetheart? Measuring me for a codpiece?"

She licked her lower lip as his heavy thigh settled over her bare legs under the sheet. "No, of course not. But I must say you, uh, certainly wouldn't need any additional padding in order to fill one out," she managed, trying for a light, sophisticated tone.

His eyes softened knowingly. "Don't worry, Letty." He bent his head to kiss her shoulder. "I'm going to fit perfectly inside you."

"I'm not so sure about that."

"I am."

Xavier tugged the sheet free of her clutching fingers and pulled it slowly down to her waist. His mouth followed the receding line of the sheet, moving with slow heat across her sensitized skin. When his teeth settled tenderly around one nipple, Letty stopped worrying about whether she and Xavier would fit together properly. She just knew he was going to be perfect for her.

She arched herself against his mouth, her fingers tightening in his night-dark hair. Hot, liquid excitement poured through her and she realized she and Xavier were made for each other. She had known that since the day she had met him.

His hands moved lower, sliding over curves and hollows; seeking out her feminine secrets. When his fingers found the inside of her thigh, she moaned and sank her teeth into the skin of his shoulder.

"I knew you were going to be a passionate lover," Xavier said with deep satisfaction. His hand closed over the damp, flowering place between her legs. "So hot and sexy and wet. Sweetheart, I want you. How I want you."

"Yes. Oh, yes, *please.*"

"Touch me." Xavier's voice was thick now. He caught hold of one of her hands and dragged it down the length of his body.

She felt her fingers glide through crisp, curly hair and then she was touching his sleek, powerful shaft. It throbbed beneath her fingertips as she gently circled it.

"Ah, no. Wait, honey. Bad idea." Xavier sucked in his breath and eased her hand away from himself. "Too much, love. Another couple of seconds of that and I'll explode and I want to be inside you when I do that."

She smiled mistily up at him as it finally dawned on her that she had as much power in this encounter as he did. Her hands trailed lovingly over his hip and flattened on his back. "You're so strong and so sleek," Letty whispered in soft wonder.

"And I'm about to go out of my mind. Tell me that you want me, sweetheart." His fingers slid gently inside her and then withdrew very slowly.

Letty gasped, shivering in response. "I want you. More than anything else in this world."

"Take all you want, love."

And then he was moving, pulling her gently beneath him and settling himself between her legs. The sounds out in the hall faded into the distance. Letty was aware of nothing except the need to have Xavier inside her, to be joined with the man she loved. She clutched at his shoulders, her nails biting into his skin and her whole body started to tighten.

"Easy, honey." Xavier's fingers slid into her warmth again, testing her readiness. "You're so small. I don't want to hurt you."

"You couldn't hurt me. You'd never hurt me." Somehow she was utterly confident of that.

"No, never."

He parted her gently and fitted himself to her. His mouth closed over hers and with a slow, steady, inevitable stroke he filled her completely.

Letty moaned in reaction to the tight, full feeling. But the small sound was lost in Xavier's mouth. She held herself very still as her body adjusted to the delicious invasion and then Xavier began to move.

The rhythm of his lovemaking was slow and deep and unbeliev-ably sensual. The reality of making love with Xavier was far more thrilling than the fantasies she had entertained during the past few months. She had not realized how exciting the sheer weight of him would be as he lay on top of her. She could not have imagined the effect his curly chest hair would have on her tight nipples. She had not understood how the sexy, masculine scent of his body would tantalize her.

But most of all she had never been able to conjure up in her dreams the blazing heat that now sent her senses soaring. She had not even guessed at the sheer intensity of the experience.

Xavier's lovemaking was just like Xavier, himself—hard, strong and fiercely tender. She felt incredibly safe and protected even as her senses were being pushed to the limit.

The passion consumed her. Something inside Letty twisted tighter and tighter with each long, filling stroke. Then Xavier was reaching down between their bodies, finding her, touching her, tor-menting her until she could stand it no longer. She was lost.

"Xavier."

"Yes. *Yes.* All of it. All of it, sweetheart. Give it to me."

The tension was released all at once in a gentle explosion that sent ripples all the way down to Letty's toes. Somewhere in the middle of the haze, she heard Xavier's hoarse shout of satisfaction and he wrapped her so tightly to him she could barely breathe.

Eventually Letty was aware of Xavier collapsing heavily on top of her, his body slick with sweat. He muttered something low and deep in her ear but she could not make out the words. It was too much effort to ask him to repeat himself. Besides, she did not really want to talk right now. Her emotions were confused and disjointed. Nothing was clear. Things were not quite what they were supposed to be tonight.

This should have been our wedding night, Letty thought. Instead she was starting an affair with the man she had once planned to marry.

"Letty?" Xavier's voice was a dark, velvet whisper.

"Yes?"

"Everything's okay now, isn't it?"

She did not understand what he meant. Instead of answering, Letty put her arms around Xavier's sleek back and held him close.

For a long while she lay quietly listening to the noisy revelry going on outside her room and then she fell asleep.

THE SOUND OF THE PHONE ringing beside her bed brought Letty awake the next morning. She was aware of the unfamiliar sensation of a hard, muscled, masculine leg lying alongside her thigh. Then she opened her eyes and found herself staring up at the equally unfamiliar sight of a canopy over her bed.

Memory came back in a blinding flash.

The phone rang again and the heavy leg shifted. There was a loud clatter and a muffled curse as Xavier reached out for the receiver.

"Who the hell is this?" he demanded irritably as he finally got the phone to his ear. "If it's you, Peabody, you can take a flying...What? Oh, hi, Molly. No, you haven't got the wrong room. What do you mean—*who is this?* It's me, Augustine. Who did you think it was?"

Letty sat up clutching the sheet to her breasts and reached for the phone. "Here, let me have that, Xavier. It's for me."

Xavier gave her a slow smile filled with lazy sensuality and smugness. "She's right here, Molly. I'll put her on." He handed the receiver to Letty who scowled briefly at him.

"Molly?"

"Letty, is that you?" Molly sounded alarmed. "What's going on there? It's seven o'clock in the morning. What's Augustine doing in your room? Did he spend the night with you?"

Letty propped up a pillow and leaned back against it, aware of Xavier idly listening to every word of her side of the conversation. "Well, yes, as a matter of fact, he did."

"Good Lord, the engagement's not back on or anything, is it?"

"No." Letty avoided Xavier's possessive gaze. It was harder to ignore the big hand stroking her thigh. "No, nothing has changed."

"But you're sleeping with him? Letty, I'm not so sure that's a good idea. Things are getting curiouser and curiouser."

Letty drew up her knees and wrapped her arms around them. She slid Xavier a speculative glance which he ignored. "What's happening, Molly?"

"Remember I told you there's no record of any Xavier Augustine matching the description or social security number of your Xavier before ten years ago?"

"I remember." A small shiver went down Letty's spine.

"Well, I assumed he changed his name legally so I went looking for some record of that and you'll never believe what I got back."

"What?"

"A query," Molly said, sounding really excited now. "Somebody wants to know why I'm asking for information on Xavier Augustine."

"I don't understand. You mean someone knows you're...uh..." Letty broke off uneasily, sliding another quick glance at Xavier who finally began to take some interest in the conversation. "Someone knows you're doing some research?"

"Right. Which means that someone set up a few traps in the system to catch anyone who might come looking. A very clever someone. Letty, this could mean anything. I don't know what to tell you to do. We could be opening up a real can of worms here. I can try ignoring the query and try coming at the problem from some other direction. But I don't know what will happen. Do you want me to continue the investigation?"

"Yes," Letty said stoutly, "go ahead."

"This could be serious stuff, Letty. We may be dealing with anything from the mob to the government."

"Oh, my God."

"I know. Very mysterious." Molly echoed Letty's grim tone but underneath it, the thrill of the hunt was clearly bubbling. Molly was enjoying herself.

"Molly, this isn't dangerous or anything is it?" Letty whispered into the phone, turning her head away from Xavier's increasingly watchful gaze.

"I don't think so. Not at this stage. I don't think anyone could figure out where the search is originating and even if someone did, he'd only know it was somewhere in Tipton College. It could be anyone who happened to sit down at one of the dozens of computers here on campus."

"Just be careful, all right?"

"Listen to who's talking. You're the one who's sleeping with the mystery man, for heaven's sake. Try following your own advice."

"Yes, I will. Goodbye, Molly." Letty handed the receiver back to Xavier who replaced it without taking his eyes off of her.

"Anything going on here I should be aware of?" Xavier folded his arms behind his head, leaned back against the pillows and studied Letty intently.

"No. No, nothing at all." Letty reached for her glasses and slid them on. She peered at Xavier, thinking that he had never looked quite so raffish and dangerous as he did this morning. "Molly was just chatting about some project she's working on. She's very excited."

Letty knew her voice was much too high and thin. To conceal her agitation, she made a production of getting out of bed, trying to take the sheet with her.

"Hold it, Letty. Come back here." Xavier halted her efforts to escape by gently taking hold of Letty's arm and pulling her back down onto the bed.

She gave up the useless struggle and tried a bright, unconcerned smile. "Something wrong, Xavier?"

He glazed thoughtfully down at her. "This is the second time Molly's called since you arrived yesterday afternoon. I know you two are close friends, but this is a little ridiculous. Is she that worried about you being here?"

Letty seized on the excuse. "Yes, I'm afraid so. She wasn't at all sure I should accept Sheldon's invitation, you see."

Xavier considered that explanation and then shook his head. "No, there's something else going on here. You sounded as concerned about Molly as she was about you. Come to think of it, you've acted strangely both times you've talked to her since we arrived. What's up, Letty?"

Letty decided hauteur was her best line of defense. She sat up again and lifted her chin. "Honestly, Xavier. I don't see that it's any of your business. Molly and I were having a private conversation. It has nothing to do with you."

"Interesting."

She narrowed her eyes. "What's interesting?"

"I've never seen you try to tell a lie before. You don't do it very well, Letty. Probably haven't had enough experience," he concluded complacently.

Letty was stung. "Is that right?" she retorted rashly. "I suppose you've had plenty, haven't you?"

Something cold entered his gaze. But his voice was dangerously soft. "I've had plenty of what? Experience telling lies? Is that what you're saying?"

Too late Letty realized she had stepped into very deep water. She made another leap for freedom, dragging the sheet with her, and finally managed to stand up beside the bed. "Forget it. I was just annoyed. I hate it when you tell me how naive and prim and proper I am. I've told you, I'm changing my image."

"Letty..."

"Now, if you'll excuse me, I'd like to take a shower and get dressed." She fumbled with the sheet, trying to wrap it around herself so that Xavier would not have an unrestricted view of her derriere as she headed for the bathroom. "There are a couple of seminars I'd like to attend this morning and I want to have breakfast first."

"Letty, you're dithering."

"I am not dithering." She was suddenly enraged at the unfair accusation.

"I'm not going anywhere and neither are you until you tell me the real reason Molly called yesterday and again this morning."

Letty stared at him, furious with his implacable attitude. "I don't owe you any explanation, Xavier Augustine."

"The hell you don't. We're engaged."

"We are not engaged," Letty howled.

His eyes grew as cold as the bottom of a green sea. "You're still saying that after what happened between us last night?"

"We started an affair last night. We did not reinstate our engagement," Letty shouted as she edged backward toward the bathroom. The sheet trailed along the floor. "I thought you understood that. It was your idea, damn it. Remember? 'Why not have an affair with the man you love, Letty?' 'What better way to move into the fast lane?' Nice and safe, you said."

"Do you?" Xavier asked softly.

"Do I what?" She was feeling totally confused and agitated now.

"Do you still love me?"

"What do you care?" She was almost at the bathroom door. Another couple of steps and she would be safe.

"I care a lot, as it happens." Xavier got up off the bed, utterly heedless of his own nudity, and started to stalk toward her. "And I want some answers, Letty. What was that phone call all about?"

"Why should I tell you?"

"Because you're not leaving this room until you do tell me," he stated calmly.

"All right," Letty snapped as she reached the safety of the bathroom doorway. She lifted her chin proudly, the sheet still clutched to her bosom. "I'll tell you what it was all about. I'm checking up on you, Xavier Augustine. I'm finding out just who you really are. After all, if I'm going to have an affair with you, I ought to know a little something about you, don't you think? A woman in my position can't be too careful."

"Checking up on me? What the hell do you mean? What's Molly got to do with this?"

"She's running an investigation on you through her library computer system," Letty informed him coldly. "The same sort of investigation you ran on me. Fair's fair, Xavier."

"An investigation? On me?" Xavier's eyes were colder than ever and there was no trace of warmth or gentleness left in the lines of his fierce face.

"That's right." Letty was genuinely scared now. She had never seen Xavier in this mood. She grabbed the trailing edge of the sheet and yanked it through the doorway. Then she slammed the bathroom door in his face and locked it. "And I'll tell you something else," she yelled through the wood. "Molly has already found out some very interesting facts about you, *Saint* Augustine."

"Like what?" Xavier roared back.

"Like the fact that you didn't even exist until ten years ago." Letty experienced a brief satisfaction at the realization that she had finally managed to gain the upper hand over Xavier Augustine.

And then Xavier's fist slammed against the door, rattling it on its hinges.

Startled, Letty leapt back and stumbled over the commode. She found her balance and stared wide-eyed at the locked door.

"Xavier?"

But there was no answer, only an ominous silence from the outer room.

CHAPTER SEVEN

XAVIER PACED his room, fighting to keep his emotions under control. He had closed the connecting door to Letty's room because he was very much afraid if he saw her when she at last ventured out of the bathroom, he would lose his temper completely. He had not been this angry in a long, long time.

And he had never before in his life been this scared.

Letty was having Molly Sweet run an investigation on him. He could not believe it. Of all the nerve. Of all the sheer, unadulterated female gall. Who the hell did she think she was?

She was a lady bent on vengeance, that's what she was. She was doing to him exactly what he had done to her.

Xavier came to a halt at the window and stood looking down at the sea. Letty was getting even. And in the process she might get more revenge than she even dreamed. She might destroy the new life he had built for himself.

He had obviously made a very big mistake when he'd hired Hawk to run a check on his future bride, Xavier decided grimly. Everything he had worked for, everything he had planned so carefully was coming apart before his very eyes because of that investigation.

And last night he had been so certain that he'd repaired the damage he'd done, so sure he had her back in the palm of his hand again. Letty had given herself to him completely, surrendering so sweetly, so beautifully that he had felt dazed. Making love to her had been more satisfying than he had ever imagined and he was certain he had satisfied her, too. She had burst into flames in his arms.

But now she claimed she not only had no intention of conducting anything more serious than an affair with him, she was checking out his past, just as he had hers.

Unlike hers, however, Xavier knew his past could not withstand close scrutiny.

The real question here was just how good was Molly Sweet with a computer? How clever could one little librarian be, anyway?

Taking advantage of the fact that Letty was in the shower, Xavier came to a decision. He turned away from the window, dropped into a chair and picked up the phone. When he got an outside line he dialed a number from memory.

His call was answered on the second ring.

"Yeah?" The familiar voice was dark, male and thick with sleep.

"Hawk? You awake?" Xavier's fingers tightened on the receiver.

"No. I'm sound asleep. Damn. Is that you, Augustine? I've been trying to get hold of you. Where the hell are you?"

"At a little inn on the Oregon coast," Xavier explained impatiently. "Hawk, is something going on with my old files?"

"Someone's asking questions, pal." There was no more sleep in Hawk's voice now. "Don't know how he got this far, but he did. Must have gotten lucky. I tried to call you last night and got no answer. What's going on? Anything serious? This doesn't look like a routine credit check."

Xavier sighed. "You'll never believe it. My fiancée has got a friend of hers searching a computer for information on my background. This friend has already managed to find out I didn't exist until ten years ago."

"No kidding?" Hawk was clearly impressed. "That's fast work. Who is this friend? He's good. I'll give him that much."

"Her name is Molly Sweet."

"Yeah? A woman?"

"She's a librarian at Tipton College and I don't care how good she is. I want her stopped."

"I sent back a query asking for identification but she backed off immediately. Then she apparently went off-line for the night. I didn't get any more responses when I tried to coax her back."

"I don't think she's going to give up. Not as long as Letty is giving the orders. You can handle it?"

"I'll try. But it might be simpler to just tell your sweetheart the truth."

"No," said Xavier. "Not yet. I've got enough trouble at the moment as it is."

"What kind of trouble?"

Xavier rubbed the back of his neck. "She's trying to call off the wedding. Claims she just wants to have an affair."

"Our sweet, prim and proper little Dr. Conroy has called off the wedding and opted for an affair instead?" Hawk gave a crack of laughter. "I don't believe it. What brought this on?"

"She found the investigation report you worked up for me and she hit the roof," Xavier admitted, feeling like an idiot because it was all his own fault. "At first I think she was merely insulted. But then she decided she didn't like the fact that her whole life could be summed up on one page of paper so she's decided to change her image."

"Your little scholar has cut the strings and decided to run wild, is that it?"

"I'm glad you're finding this so damn funny, Hawk. I don't."

"No, I can see that." Hawk made an effort to get his laughter under control. "So where are you now? Chasing after her?"

"Yes." Xavier's voice was clipped. "We're having a wild four-day weekend at a convention of medieval history enthusiasts."

"A convention of history buffs? That's your lady's idea of running wild? In that case, I wouldn't worry too much, if I were you, Augustine. How much damage can she do fooling around with a bunch of history enthusiasts?"

"You don't know this crowd," Xavier told him with great depth of feeling. "I've already been in one fight since I got here. Some jerk from the Tipton College history department wrote Letty a love poem and had it sung in front of the whole crowd. I took exception."

Hawk chuckled. "I'd like to have seen that. So what did you do? Stomp him into the roast beef platter?"

"Hell, no. I let him take one good swing and then I went crashing to the floor like a felled ox. Letty's the kind of woman who always empathizes with the underdog."

"That figures. So you played wounded warrior and let her tend your bruises, huh? Good move."

"It's not over yet. She's still talking about having an affair instead of getting married and she's still got Molly Sweet hunting up information on me. Listen, Hawk, I don't need any more complications right now, understand? I need time to soothe Letty's ruffled feathers. I'll tell her whatever she wants to know after I've got a ring on her finger."

"What difference would that make? She can walk out on you just as easily after she's married to you as she can now."

"Not Letty," Xavier said with great certainty. "Marriage vows still mean something to women like her. Once we're married there will be a time and place to tell her everything. But I don't want to try to explain it all now. I don't trust the mood she's in. Her father was a judge, for crying out loud."

"She knows there's a mystery now," Hawk pointed out thoughtfully. "There's no stopping a woman once she senses a mystery. She'll want answers."

"I'll figure out something."

"This," said Hawk, "should be amusing. You know something Augustine? When I ran the investigation on her, I decided your Dr. Letitia Conroy sounded like a very nice lady. Now she's beginning to sound like a very intriguing lady. I always did like a little spirit in a woman."

"You can say that because you're not the one having to deal with the problems caused by a woman with a 'little spirit'," Xavier growled. "I liked Letty just fine the way she was."

"How about the way she's turning out to be now?" Hawk asked gently. "Still like her?"

Xavier blinked as it struck him quite forcefully that the word *like* did not begin to cover the way he felt about Letty today. None of his emotions toward her now could be labeled with bland words such as *like*. She was driving him crazy this morning even as his body was still basking in the afterglow of last night. He wanted to yell at her for having the nerve to investigate him but he also wanted to take her into his arms and kiss her senseless.

"As a matter of fact, I don't like her much at all right at the moment," Xavier muttered. "I'm mad as hell at her. But the woman belongs to me now, whether she knows it or not, and I'll deal with her. I'll take care of things on this end. You just do something about Molly Sweet."

"I'll see what I can do to satisfy Ms. Sweet's curiosity without giving away your dark secrets," Hawk promised. "Good luck with your courtship. You still planning the wedding for the end of June?"

"You better believe it." Xavier hung up the phone and told himself to start thinking carefully and clearly. He had a problem on his hands.

LETTY DID HER BEST to keep her attention on the young man giving
the lecture on medieval methods of training falcons for the hunt.
The speaker was a young veterinarian who had made falconry a
hobby and he certainly knew his material. Normally Letty would
have been extremely interested in what he had to say.

But Letty's thoughts kept going back to Xavier's lovemaking
during the night. When she did manage to get them momentarily
off that subject they leapt instantly to the scene that had taken place
in her room that morning following Molly's phone call.

"A good falconer was expected to be part veterinarian, part
trainer and full-time nursemaid to his valuable birds," the lecturer
informed his audience.

Everything had felt so right last night, Letty recalled sadly. She
and Xavier had come together so beautifully—she just knew they
had been meant for each other.

"The first stages of training were carried out in a darkened
room," the speaker was saying. "Nervous birds are more easily
handled in darkness. The falcons were first taught to perch on a
human wrist and then gradually introduced to the hunt."

Letty gave a start as someone sat down in the empty chair beside
her. She did not know whether to be relieved or alarmed when she
realized it was Sheldon Peabody. Sheldon was dressed in a short,
dark green surcoat over light green hose. He wore a jaunty little
felt cap that matched the surcoat and a pair of shoes with points
that extended a good six inches beyond his toes.

"Hi, Letty," Sheldon whispered, "I've been looking all over for
you."

"Good morning, Sheldon." Letty glanced at him warily. Sheldon had a distinctly pained expression on his handsome face. She
frowned. "Are you all right?"

"Yeah, sure. A little too much partying last night. But I'll live.
Things got a little crazy there toward the end. Jennifer Thorne
insisted on demonstrating her idea of what a medieval cheerleader's
routine would have been like."

"I can just imagine Jennifer leading the cheering squad at a
fourteenth-century tournament."

"It does boggle the mind, doesn't it?" Sheldon agreed thoughtfully.

Up on the stage the lecturer continued his talk. "The falcons
were highly valued and their training carefully supervised. A lord's

favorite bird often slept on a perch in the same chamber as its master. Hunting was more than just a sport for the medieval lord, it was a way of life that perfectly complimented his half civilized, half warrior lifestyle. Society saw itself mirrored in the hunt.''

Sheldon leaned closer. "Come on, Letty, let's get out of here. This is basic stuff. You're not going to learn anything new about falcon training from this guy. Let me buy you a cup of coffee. Lord knows I need one.''

"I don't know, Sheldon. I really did want to hear some of the lectures.''

"Forget the lectures. They're just an excuse for the partying that comes later. Everyone knows that. Besides, I want to talk to you.'' He took her arm and urged her to her feet.

Letty reluctantly allowed herself to be led out of the room. She and Sheldon slipped through the doors at the back and started toward the downstairs café. Letty kept an eye out for Xavier but there was no sign of him.

A few minutes later she found herself sitting opposite Sheldon near a huge window that overlooked the sea. The morning fog was just beginning to lift, revealing craggy cliffs and the vast expanse of the Pacific.

"Better," Sheldon breathed in relief as he took a long swallow of coffee. "Much better. What a night. One down and three more to go. How's the wounded victim?''

Letty studied her coffee. "Xavier's all right.''

"Glad to hear it," Sheldon said dryly. "Quite a performance he put on last night.''

"He really was hurt, Sheldon. You cut his lip and there was a bruise on his jaw," Letty flared, feeling obliged to defend Xavier for some obscure reason.

"He set me up, knowing that you'd fly to his side the minute he took the fall." Sheldon shook his head. "The guy's a lot sharper than I gave him credit for in the beginning, I'll admit that. I guess it's the business shark in him. But I'm still surprised at you, Letty. I thought you were smart enough to see through him.''

"I'd rather not discuss this, if you don't mind." Letty made a move to get to her feet.

"Hey, sit down. Take it easy. I'm sorry." Sheldon reached out and caught her arm, urging her back down into the chair. "I apologize. For everything." He gave her a crooked, endearing little smile. "You can't blame me for feeling a trifle annoyed with the whole situation. After all, I've been doing my best to get your attention for the past year and I've hardly made any headway. Augustine walks into Tipton Cove and you fall at his feet without a murmur."

"It wasn't like that," Letty insisted, knowing perfectly well that it had been exactly like that.

"Maybe not, but it sure seemed that way. I thought maybe you'd come to your senses when you told me that the engagement was over. But after the way you left with him last night, I guess nothing's changed."

"The engagement *is* over," Letty declared, feeling pressured.

Sheldon gave her a skeptical look. "Really?"

"Really."

He nodded thoughtfully. "Well, then, there's hope for me, hmm?"

"Sheldon, please, I'm not ready to discuss another relationship," Letty said in a choked voice. She turned to gaze out to sea, wondering frantically how to put a halt to Sheldon's overtures.

"I understand. Ending the engagement must have been traumatic."

"It was."

"He didn't understand you, Letty. How could he? His background is very different from yours. You two had nothing in common."

Letty's head snapped around. "What do you know about Xavier's background?"

Sheldon's shoulders rose and fell in a negligent shrug. "Just what everyone else knows. He comes out of the business world. I know he drives an expensive car and wears smart clothes but you're not the type to be impressed by that kind of superficial glitter. You need someone from the academic world. Someone who's intellectually oriented the way you are."

She sighed and turned her attention back to the sea. "I don't know what I need at the moment."

Sheldon smiled his charming smile and touched her hand as it lay on the table. "You need someone like me, Letty. And I need someone like you. I've been increasingly aware of that for the past few months. The feeling has been growing slowly but surely. We could be a great team, honey. We have so much in common."

"Sheldon, I said I don't want to talk about another relationship right now." Letty grabbed the most convenient excuse at hand. "It's too soon. I hope you understand."

"Of course." His expression was one of sincere concern and deep understanding. "You're a very sensitive creature. You need time to recover. But you're going to have to watch out for Augustine. He's as crafty as the devil, Letty. Don't let him manipulate you the way he did last night."

"I can handle Xavier," Letty declared stoutly.

"Okay, okay. I get the point. You're a big girl." Sheldon smiled again. "I know you can take care of yourself. I admire your independence, really I do. But you can't blame me for feeling protective."

Letty groped for a way out of the uncomfortable conversation. "Thank you, Sheldon, but I'm quite capable of managing my own life. Now, I'd better be on my way or I'll miss the lecture on the construction of medieval kitchens."

"It's all elementary stuff, Letty, just like the lecture on falconry," Sheldon said impatiently. "I told you, strictly amateurs giving the talks to show off their hobbies. You won't learn anything you don't already know. Why don't you and I start talking seriously about doing a book together? Alison Crane was right when she said we could turn out something interesting. What do you say we have lunch later and discuss the idea?"

"I'll have to check my schedule." Letty rose quickly and flashed Sheldon a bright smile as she fled the café.

It occurred to her that for a woman who had until recently enjoyed an extremely dull love life, she was certainly picking up steam in that department. Last night she'd begun—and possibly concluded—an affair with one man and this morning she had another male breathing down her neck telling her he thought he was falling for her.

All things considered, Letty decided, she was definitely living a more exciting existence these days. She had actually begun to accomplish her goal of leaving her boring life behind.

She wondered why the whole thing was making her so uneasy. Apparently this sort of life-style took some getting used to.

XAVIER HAD STILL NOT sought her out by the time Letty joined the rest of the Revelers and a small crowd from the nearby town on the inn's front lawn. A medieval fair had been set up on the grass. Dressed in another of the costumes she had discovered in her room, a yellow gown and a crimson surcoat with a white hart embroidered on it, Letty strolled leisurely around the stalls.

Now that the fog had vanished, the day had turned out warm and summery. Brightly hued pennants and banners snapped in the light breeze off the ocean. Striped awnings and tents sheltered the many craftspeople who had come from as far away as California and Washington to sell their wares. A wide variety of leather goods and jewelry as well as reproductions of medieval weapons and costumes were for sale. Vendors of meat pies and ale were making small fortunes as the Revelers spent money with a lavish hand.

It was easy to distinguish the townsfolk from the conventioneers. The locals were the ones dressed in faded jeans, boots, tractor caps and Stetsons. They had arrived in pickup trucks and four-wheel drives for the most part. From the murmured comments, chuckles and jokes Letty overheard, it was apparent that most of the local people had come primarily to gawk and grin at the strangers running around in outlandish costumes. The two groups did not mingle, but kept a certain distance from each other.

Letty paused for a few minutes to watch a wrestling match and decided it was not her style of entertainment. She did not care if wrestling had been very popular in the Middle Ages. The sight of the sweating, straining men reminded her too much of the fight that Xavier and Sheldon had engaged in the previous evening. The memory brought back others of what had followed. She moved quickly on to a puppet show that was taking place beneath a blue and white awning.

"Good morning, Letty." Alison Crane, her hand tucked under Richard Hodson's arm, smiled a cheery greeting. "Sir Richard, here, has asked to meet you. Richard, this is Letty Conroy, Sheldon Peabody's friend. Letty, meet the Lord of Revels and current Grand Master of the Order, Richard Hodson. The author. You've heard of him, I'm sure."

"I certainly have. In fact, I've read all your books." Letty extended her hand. She was mildly disconcerted when Hodson bent over her fingers and kissed them. "Oh." She hastily retrieved her hand.

"I am delighted to make your acquaintance, my dear." Hodson smiled with oily charm, his eyelids drooping in what he probably thought was a worldly, seductive gaze. "The Revelers are always eager to recruit members of your caliber. I am pleased you are attending our quarterly gathering as a guest."

"Thank you. I'm having a lovely time." Letty switched her smile to Alison. "I love that hat, Alison."

"Thank you, dear." Alison touched the brim of the open-crowned toque she was wearing over a veil. "I had it specially made from an old pattern I discovered in a book of medieval costume design. Turned out rather well, didn't it? Please excuse us. Richard, I believe we ought to be moving on. I see Judy Coswell over by the stage. I think I can talk her into giving me the listing on her condo."

"Yes, of course." Hodson gave Letty a lingering glance, eyelids drooping another quarter inch, mouth lifting at the corners with just the right touch of knowing intimacy. "We'll meet again, I'm sure, Lady Letitia."

Letty nodded and watched the pair as they drifted into the crowd. They she went toward a jewelry stall.

"Enjoying yourself, Letty?"

Letty spun around at the sound of Xavier's sardonic voice. He was not wearing a costume like the other Revelers, she noticed. Instead he had on a quietly expensive button-down shirt and a pair of dark, close-fitting trousers that had obviously been made to order. His hair gleamed in the sunlight and his eyes were very green. He looked a little dangerous, she thought. But, then, he always looked that way. He could not seem to help it. If Molly's suspicions were correct, he might very well be dreadfully dangerous.

But he had been so tender last night....

"Hello, Xavier," she managed to say coolly. "I wondered where you were. I thought perhaps you'd gotten bored with all this fun and games business and decided to drive back to Tipton Cove."

"Not without you," he said. "I think it's time we had a talk, Letty."

"Honestly, you sound just like Sheldon. Why do so many people want to have serious talks with me lately?" She turned away to examine a gaudy necklace that sparkled on the table of the jeweler's stall. It was a cheaply made item, but it looked quite pretty in the sunlight.

"Peabody's been trying to talk to you, too? Figures. He's bent on finding a way to use you."

That annoyed Letty. "Has it occurred to you he might actually find me interesting and attractive?"

"He thinks he can get you to write a paper or a book with him and help him salvage his sagging career," Xavier said impatiently. "Don't be a fool, Letty. Steer clear of him."

"I'll tell you the same thing I told him. I can take care of myself."

"Uh-huh." Xavier leaned over her shoulder and picked up the necklace she had been studying. He examined it with a critical eye.

"You don't have to sound so skeptical. I'm an intelligent woman and I can take care of myself."

"Whatever you say."

"Xavier, let's get to the point. Are you going to explain why Molly can't turn up anything on you prior to ten years ago?"

He shrugged, still studying the necklace. "I changed my name. No big deal. It was a business decision. Nothing more."

"There's more to it than that, I can tell."

He slanted her an unreadable glance. "Can you?"

"Yes, but you're not going to tell me anything else, are you?"

"There's nothing else that you need to know. Besides, why should I make Molly's job any easier?" Xavier turned the necklace over and looked at the catch. "Are you thinking of buying this?"

"Yes, I was," Letty said.

"Don't bother. It's a piece of junk."

"It is not a piece of junk," she retorted, thoroughly incensed. "It's beautiful. I like it and if I decide to buy it, I will."

Xavier dropped the necklace back onto the velvet. "It's cheap and tacky and you know it. If you decide to buy it, it will only be because you're trying to prove to yourself that you don't need my advice."

He was right, damn him. "You know something, Xavier? I think Sheldon was right when he said you don't fight fair."

His eyes slid to hers. "I fight any way I have to in order to win. Remember that, Letty."

She stared mutely up at him and suddenly the day did not seem as warm and sunny as it had a few minutes earlier. There was a cold fire burning in Xavier's green eyes and Letty felt the now-familiar shiver flash down her spine. But it was not fear she felt. It was excitement.

Dangerous, she thought. *I know that. So why aren't I as frightened as I should be?*

"I don't like being threatened, Xavier," she said boldly.

"Neither do I."

"I haven't threatened you."

"Yes, you have," he countered. "You've threatened to end the
engagement."

"That wasn't a threat, it was a promise," she shot back. "A
vow. A fact. A fait accompli."

His eyes narrowed faintly as he studied her. "You're certain you
want to call off the marriage?"

"Yes, I am," she insisted, knowing she was lying through her
teeth. She was not at all certain what she wanted right now.

"Then why go to all the trouble of having Molly research my
background?" Xavier asked softly.

"Revenge. Pure and simple. Besides, I've started an affair with
you, remember?"

"How could I forget?"

For some reason his ready agreement on that point made her feel
much better. He was not going to walk out of her life, after all,
even if he was angry.

"In addition to sweet revenge," she told him, "I'm having you
investigated because a woman in my position can't be too careful.
If you turn out to be a mob boss or something, I want to know
before the FBI knocks on my door."

"I see." Xavier took her arm and led her toward a stall where
shortbread was being sold. "I've got a hypothetical question, Letty.
If we were still planning on getting married, what would Molly
have to turn up in her investigation to make you change your
mind?"

Letty scowled up at him as he bought her a piece of shortbread.
"What are you talking about?" She took a bite of the buttery
cookie.

"I'm just asking you what sort of things in a man's background
would make him unsuitable as a husband." Xavier munched his
own shortbread, apparently not overly concerned with her response.

"Speaking hypothetically?"

"Of course. Our marriage has already been canceled according
to you, so I'm just asking out of sheer masculine curiosity. What

would a woman like you find unacceptable in a man's background?''

Letty considered that closely for the first time. When she had told Molly to carry out the search, she had not really stopped to think about what she might find.

''I don't know. I guess it would depend,'' she finally said honestly.

Xavier shot her a quick glance. ''What the heck does that mean?''

''It means I don't know. It's hard to make judgments out of context, if you see what I mean. Of course, there are a few things that would certainly make me think twice.''

''Such as?'' he pressed.

''Well, if it turned out you had a half-dozen ex-wives running around, I'd be seriously concerned about your inability to make a meaningful commitment.'' She gave him a saucy smile, trying to lighten the atmosphere. ''Or if you really are an ex-hit man or something along those lines, I'd be a little wary.''

''So you don't approve of ex-wives or criminal records. Anything else?''

''Xavier, this is a ridiculous conversation.''

''You started it when you told me you were having me checked out.''

''I started it? What nonsense. *You* started this, Xavier.'' Letty came to a halt and swung around to confront him. ''What about you? What sort of things in my past would have made you decide not to marry me?''

He gazed out over the throng of people milling around the brightly colored stalls. ''It doesn't matter now, does it? The engagement is off, according to you.''

''Damn it, Xavier, I want to know.'' Letty stepped closer and grasped a handful of his shirt in each hand. She stood on tiptoe and beetled her brow ferociously.

He was silent for a long moment as he looked down into her angry eyes. ''A few months ago I could have given you an answer,'' he finally said quietly.

''I'm asking you right now. What would it have taken for you to decide I was unsuitable to be your wife?''

He shook his head slowly, his eyes steady and thoughtful. ''I told you, I don't know. I can't think of anything you could have done in the past that would make me change my mind now about marrying you. Not now that I've gotten to know you.''

Letty stood perfectly still, balancing herself on her tiptoes as she crushed the expensive fabric of Xavier's shirt. She stared into his unfathomable eyes. His answer unnerved her but she refused to admit it.

With a soft exclamation of dismay, she released him and stepped back. "Honestly, Xavier, I don't know what to make of you. I just don't understand you at times," she muttered.

"I'm not so difficult to comprehend." He reached out and caught her hand in his, lacing her fingers through his own. "I'm just a man and I want you for my own. What's so hard to understand about that?"

Letty struggled to stifle the warmth his words caused to well up inside her. "The trouble with men is that they're never as simple and straightforward as they make themselves out to be."

"The trouble with women is that they can't resist making things a lot more complicated than they really are."

THE OFFICIAL INVITATION from the Lord of Revels to attend him in his suite arrived at Letty's door shortly before dinner. She scanned the brief note with a considering frown. It was elegantly short.

> My Dear Lady Letitia,
> As Grand Master of the Order of Medieval Revelers and Lord of Revels, I hereby request that you do me the honor of attending a small gathering in my suite at five this evening. Sherry will be served and full membership in the Revelers will be discussed.
>
> Yours,
> Richard

After a brief hesitation, Letty decided to attend the small party before dinner. After all, she was here to broaden her social horizons. In any event, she looked forward to having an opportunity to talk to Richard Hodson about his medieval mysteries.

She selected another colorful costume from the wardrobe and began to dress, aware of Xavier moving about in his room. She considered letting him know where she was going but told herself she should be more independent. She was sleeping with the man, but she was not married to him.

Letty just knew that if she gave Xavier an inch, he would take a mile. He was perfectly capable of commandeering the rights of a husband even if he was merely a lover. Something told her Xavier was the possessive type. She really should not get into the habit of always letting him know where she was going.

At five minutes after five, Letty arrived at Richard Hodson's suite. She listened for the sound of people within the room but there was no noise. Tentatively she raised her hand and knocked.

The door was opened immediately by Hodson. He looked very elegant in his gold and white surcoat and matching tasseled cap of soft white felt. The belt around his hips was a massive affair studded with imitation gems and ornate fittings.

"My dear Lady Letitia. How charming you look this evening. I'm delighted you could stop by for a glass of sherry." He smiled suavely down at her, his eyelids drooping with what was obviously intended to be rakish charm.

"Am I early?" Letty looked doubtfully past him into the suite and realized it was empty except for Hodson.

"Not at all, my dear, not at all. Right on time. Do come in." Sir Richard stood back from the door and beckoned her inside with a gracious gesture of his beringed hand.

"Thank you." Letty took a quick glance at one of the rings on his fingers and decided it looked like a real diamond. Apparently the medieval mysteries were paying well. Perhaps Sheldon was right in prodding her toward the non-academic market.

"A glass of sherry, my dear?" Richard went over to a tray containing a bottle and two small glasses.

"Yes, please." Letty glanced absently at the label on the sherry bottle and hid a small smile. She had been with Xavier when he shopped for sherry and she knew that particular label was one he disdained as cheap and bland. "Where is everyone else, Sir Richard?"

"I thought we would make this a private occasion, my dear." Hodson poured the sherry and handed her the glass with a small bow. "I wanted to meet you and talk to you alone, you see. I have a particular interest in encouraging you to join the Revelers. I have long admired your work in the field."

Letty relaxed. So this was going to be shoptalk—it was reassuring. "Thank you, Sir Richard." She wrinkled her nose thoughtfully as she tasted the sherry. It did taste rather bland.

He chuckled. "Just call me Richard. No need to stand on formalities. We are only playing games here at Greenslade, are we not?"

"Yes. But the games are rather fun." Letty smiled back at him as he drew her over to a sofa that faced the window. "Actually, I'm delighted to have an opportunity to talk to you. I don't want to sound like a gushy fan, but the plain truth is that I've thoroughly enjoyed all of your books."

"Have you? I'm honored." He sat down close beside her, his thigh brushing hers.

"I think you do a wonderful job with the research. Medieval history is obviously a passion of yours." Letty tried to edge her knee away from Hodson's but did not succeed.

"Passion is the perfect word for my interest in the medieval world," Richard said, sitting a little closer. "I find myself attracted to the period precisely because it was a time of high passion. Life was so much more vivid in those days. It was a world of extremes. The pageantry, the color, the warfare, the chivalric code and, yes, the great sexual liaisons. They were all taken to the limits of human emotions, enjoyed to the fullest by the people who lived then. Don't you agree?"

"Uh, yes." Letty took a quick sip of her sherry and tried to put some distance between her thigh and Richard's. "It was certainly a very colorful period. But quite brutal in many ways. And primitive. I mean, the sanitation standards were very low. Privies, chamber pots, garbage in the streets..."

"But for people like us, Letty, it was the ideal moment in history, I think." Richard struck an attitude of deep reflection. "It was a time that would have suited us admirably."

Letty coughed slightly and set down her unfinished sherry. "People like us?"

"People of intense passions," he explained. "I look at you, my dear, and I see a woman with a potential for truly great passion."

"You do?"

"Oh, yes, definitely." Richard edged closer. "Endless wellsprings of passion are buried in you, my dear. Oceans of passion. You were born out of time, just as I was, Letty. We belong to the age of Great Loves and High Passions."

"Excuse me, Richard," Letty cut in swiftly. "About my membership in the Revelers?"

"It is the duty of the Grand Master of the Order to personally interview and approve of all candidates. It is certainly my pleasure to carry out my duty in this instance. I think we have a great deal in common, my dear. And I know you will make a great contribution to the Order of Medieval Revelers."

"You do?" Letty asked doubtfully.

"Yes, I do." Hodson's arm slithered around her shoulders. "What's more, I believe you can make your contribution at the highest levels. You can serve as my personal assistant, Letty. How does that sound? Together you and I can transform the Revelers from a group of amateur medievalists to a dynamic organization of respected historians. Together we can lead the group into the future—help it achieve its full potential—gain academic acceptance of its accomplishments. Will you meet the challenge with me, my dear?"

"Uh—well, I've been giving the matter some thought and to tell you the truth, I haven't yet decided whether or not to become a full member. I'm certainly enjoying myself, you understand, but...oh, heavens. Just look at the time." Letty smiled brightly and leapt to her feet. "I've promised to meet someone. If you'll excuse me?"

"But, my dear, we have several things to discuss concerning your membership. We very much want to encourage people such as yourself who have academic credentials." Richard got to his feet and took her hand in his.

At that moment a sharp knock sounded on the door of the suite.

"Damn." Richard frowned. "Excuse me, Letty, while I take care of this. I left orders I was not to be disturbed."

He crossed the room and opened the door. "I thought I told everyone that I didn't want to be bothered before dinner. Oh, it's you, Augustine. What do you want?"

"Letty," Xavier said easily as he shouldered his way into the room. "I came to tell her we're going to be late for dinner. Ready to go, Letty?"

"Yes." She summoned up a smile that contained more relief than anything else. "I was just noticing the time. You will excuse us, Richard? Thank you so much for the sherry. I hope you'll autograph one of your books for me sometime."

"I'd be delighted." Richard gave Xavier a stiff smile, but his eyes were cold. "I don't believe anyone said anything about putting your name in for full membership, Augustine."

"Don't worry, I'm not applying. One of these conventions is enough for me. Let's go, Letty." Xavier dragged Letty out into the hall.

The door of the suite slammed shut behind them.

"I do believe," Letty said, "that I have just been entertained by what my mother would have called an aging roué."

"I found his note in your room. What the hell did you think you were doing going to his suite alone?"

"I thought there would be a crowd. It was supposed to be a pre-dinner cocktail party."

"Some party."

Letty started to giggle.

"What's so damned funny?" Xavier muttered.

"There was nothing to worry about," Letty said with a grin. "I wasn't in any danger. It was very cheap sherry. My standards have been considerably elevated since I met you, Xavier. Nowadays I would never allow myself to be seduced with a second-rate sherry."

MUCH LATER THAT EVENING Xavier opened the connecting door to Letty's room and walked in as if he owned the place. Letty, dressed in her prim, quilted robe, was standing in front of the closet, hovering over her selection of new nightgowns. She whirled around when she heard the door open and close behind her.

Xavier was wearing only a pair of black trousers. His broad shoulders gleamed in the bedside light. For a moment she simply stood there drinking in the sight of him.

"What's the matter, Letty?" He moved forward and lifted one of the wispy gowns out of her hands. "Can't make up your mind which one to wear for me?"

"I wasn't absolutely positive you'd show up here tonight," she admitted shyly.

"We're having an affair. Where else would I be at this hour?" He pulled her into his arms and covered her mouth with his own.

Letty sighed softly and wrapped her arms around his waist. His back felt sleek and strong and beautifully contoured. His masculine scent, tinged with soap and a recent shower, made her senses swim.

Xavier lifted his head and smiled as she melted against him. "Forget choosing a nightgown. You won't need one tonight."

He gently stripped off her robe and turned her so that she faced the full-length mirror that hung on the closet door. Letty gasped softly at the sight of herself standing naked in Xavier's arms. He slid his hands slowly down her sides to her hips and tugged her back against his thighs. He was hard with his arousal.

Xavier bent his head and kissed the curve of her shoulder. Letty leaned back against him, her knees suddenly weak. A fine trembling went through her. She knew Xavier felt it when she saw his slow, sexy smile in the mirror.

"Xavier?"

He cupped her breasts in his hands and nibbled gently on her earlobe. She felt his tongue on the inside of her ear and another shock of pleasure sizzled through her.

Then his hands were sliding down across the small curve of her stomach to the triangle of her hair below. Letty closed her eyes, her fingers clutching his forearms as she felt him part her softness. One long finger slid slowly into her and she cried out.

"You flow like warm honey." Xavier's voice was thick with desire.

"Please," she whispered.

"Yes." He wrapped one arm around her waist to hold her upright when she threatened to slide to the floor at his feet. With his other hand he probed her slowly and deliberately, finding the small, hidden bud and coaxing it into throbbing fullness. All the while he watched her in the mirror.

"Xavier." Letty caught her breath. Her fingers tightened around his arm. The tight, twisting sensation built. Letty grew frantic, wondering why he did not carry her over to the bed. "Xavier, the bed," she managed.

"Soon," he promised, his fingers still stroking, teasing and coaxing.

And then it was too late. Letty felt the great release and the pleasure that followed and cried out again. She lost what little remained of her strength and sagged against him with a soft moan.

"Oh, *Xavier.*"

"Now we'll try the bed," Xavier whispered as he picked her up in his arms and carried her across the room.

CHAPTER EIGHT

THE FOLLOWING EVENING the huge lobby of the Greenslade Inn was crowded as the night's festivities got underway. The musicians were getting warmed up and the Revelers made a colorful sight as they milled about in their spectacular costumes.

Letty noticed the spot of wine on her gown a moment after Alison Crane, who had paused to chat, swept off in search of a potential real estate client. Letty touched Xavier's arm.

"I'll just be a minute. I'm going down the hall to the ladies' room to sponge this wine out before it stains the gown. Be right back."

Xavier nodded and Letty headed for the door and stepped out into the hall.

The long skirt of her golden yellow gown swished lightly around her soft, pointed shoes as she walked quickly through the empty corridor. Behind her the muffled music from the ballroom filtered out into the hall.

She had left Xavier talking to a young amateur enthusiast who happened to be an expert on medieval warfare techniques. They had been deeply engrossed in a conversation about trebuchets and mobile assault towers, the terrifying engines of medieval warfare.

Letty pushed open the door of the women's room and thought about what was going to happen after the ball. A small rush of anticipation went through her as she admitted she was looking forward to Xavier's lovemaking.

And he was most definitely going to make love to her. She had no doubt at all about that. He had made his intentions very clear all evening long. Every time his glittering green gaze had caught hers, he had made his desire plain. He wanted her.

To think she had once questioned his virility. Letty grinned briefly to herself as she finished her business in the restroom and stepped back out into the hall.

"Oh, Letty, I've been looking for you." Alison Crane, dressed in a green gown and white cyclas and wearing a silver crespinette,

came swiftly down the corridor. There were two more women behind her whom Letty did not know. They were both giggling.
"There's something you simply must see."

"What is it, Alison?" But Letty was already being swept down
the hall by the three costumed women. "Xavier will be expecting
me back in the ballroom."

"This will only take a minute." Alison pushed open a door at
the end of the hall and urged Letty out into the chilled night.

"Please, Alison, I really don't think—" Letty broke off as she
saw the two knights waiting outside near a car. "What in the world
is going on here?"

"Don't worry, Letty," Alison said reassuringly as the two
knights swept deep bows and took hold of Letty's arms. "It's just
a game. Part of the fun at the Revelers' conventions is initiating
new members. Tonight your Xavier is going to prove his knightly
valor by rescuing you. And just to make things interesting, he's
going to have a little competition."

"No, wait, I don't want any part of this." Letty started struggling in earnest but she was vastly outnumbered.

Laughing, the knights and ladies bundled her into the backseat
of the car and slid in beside her, locking the doors. One of the men
got behind the wheel.

"Don't worry, Lady Letitia," one of the knights said cheerfully.
"You're the prize in a quest. It's all part of the fun and games."

Letty turned her head to gaze helplessly back at the inn as the
car drove off into the night. "Xavier is not going to like this," she
warned.

"'HEAR YE, hear ye,'" the man holding the scroll intoned following a dramatic drumroll and a couple of blasts on a horn. "'Sir
Richard, the noble Grand Master of the Order of Medieval Revelers
interrupts the revelry to announce a quest. All members of the
Order will pay attention.'"

Shouts and applause broke out around the lobby and then an
expectant silence descended as Sir Richard and his entourage made
their way toward the dais.

"Sounds like something's up," the young man next to Xavier
said.

Xavier gave up trying to learn more about the firepower of medieval catapults and reluctantly turned to face the front of the room.

He watched cynically as Richard Hodson, dressed in a heavily embroidered white surcoat, ascended the elevated platform and sat down in a heavily carved thronelike chair.

Xavier, wearing the black tunic with the gold leopard embroidered on it, decided he was getting bored with the endless games played by the Revelers. He wondered if he could talk Letty into leaving early. They could find their own private place on the coast, he thought as he glanced impatiently at his watch.

Where was Letty, anyway? Maybe there had been a long line in the ladies' room. Or perhaps she had run upstairs to her own room for something.

"My lords and ladies of the Order," Sir Richard said, speaking very solemnly into a microphone, "I fear we have a damsel in distress who must be rescued."

A cheer went up. Xavier frowned and glanced toward the door of the ballroom. There was still no sign of Letty.

"I wonder what this is all about," murmured the young authority on medieval war engines.

Sir Richard leaned toward the microphone as the cheers died down. "I have taken counsel with the members of the Inner Circle and we have reached a decision to send two bold knights on a quest to rescue the fair Lady Letitia from the clutches of the villains who hold her captive."

The crowd gave a roar of approval to this notion.

"Letty." Xavier was suddenly paying full attention to what was taking place on the dais. "What the hell is going on here?"

"Sounds like you're about to find out," the young engineer observed.

Sir Richard held up a hand for silence. "We summon Sir Sheldon and Sir Xavier before us."

The engineer leaned closer to Xavier. "You'd better go up there if you want to find out what's happened to Letty. Sometimes the Order's idea of a game gets a little out of hand."

Xavier shot him a quick speculative glance and then turned and strode toward the front of the room. The crowd parted to allow him to pass.

"Go for it, Sir Xavier," a man called out. "My money's on you."

"He's too new at this kind of thing," someone else yelled. "No experience in quests. I'll bet on Sir Sheldon."

"I'll take Augustine," a woman declared. "Always stand on the side of the saints, I say."

Xavier ignored them all as he approached the dais. He saw that Sheldon Peabody was there ahead of him, resplendent in a short brocaded green satin tunic and a dapper little cap. He wore a flowing orange cape trimmed with elaborately scalloped edges. Xavier decided Peabody looked like some sort of comic book hero.

"What's this all about?" Xavier asked, making an effort to control his irritation. He came to a halt in front of Richard Hodson. "Where's Letty?"

"Ah," said Sir Richard with a knowing wink, "that is for one of you two stout knights to determine. A list of clues to her present whereabouts has been drawn up by the Inner Circle. The knight with the purest heart, the strongest sword and the most untarnished honor shall no doubt find her first. When he has rescued her from her captors, he will deliver her safely back here."

Sheldon gave Richard his most charming smile. "And is there any reward for the winner of this quest? Aside from the gratitude of the lady, that is?"

"Most definitely," Hodson said. "Whichever one of you returns with the fair damsel shall be rewarded not only with the lady's company for the evening, but with an honorary place among the valiant members of the Inner Circle for the duration of the year."

Another round of applause went up.

"Sounds good to me," Sheldon murmured, giving Xavier a sidelong glance.

Xavier ignored him. "This is stupid. Is Letty safe?"

"Quite safe. She is attended by three fair ladies and two of our most noble knights," Richard assured him. "And now the clues." He held out his hand with a regal gesture. Someone handed him two rolled-up scrolls. "Before you leave, you will kneel and make your solemn vow to strive to be successful in your quest."

Sheldon dropped dramatically to one knee, his cape swept back over his shoulders. "I vow to rescue the fair Lady Letitia and return her safely to this castle," he said in ringing tones.

Xavier gave him a disgusted look. Then he stepped forward and snatched one of the scrolls from Richard's hands. "Let me see that." He unrolled the paper swiftly and scanned the long list of obscure clues. "'A door of green,' 'a sea view,' 'an arrow's flight from the hamlet'? This is garbage."

"May the best man win," Sheldon drawled as he stood up and took the other scroll.

The last of Xavier's limited supply of patience finally evaporated. He looked at the Lord of Revelry. "I don't feel like playing your silly games, Hodson. I want Letty back here right now."

"Sorry, Sir Xavier. But the game is afoot and the only way to end it is to play it out and rescue your fair lady." Sir Richard chuckled jovially as he rose and started down the steps of the dais. "See you later."

Xavier watched Hodson make his way through the crowd for a moment, aware that Peabody was wearing a very satisfied smirk on his soft face.

"Well, well, well," Sheldon said. "Looks like you're going on a quest whether you like it or not. That is, of course, unless you'd rather let me go out alone to find the fair maiden. I imagine Letty would be a bit disappointed if you didn't show any interest in rescuing her but perhaps I can console her."

Xavier's gaze followed Richard Hodson's white tunic as it moved through the brightly garbed throng. "I don't play games, Peabody."

"You're playing this one." Sheldon chortled. "And you're going to lose. Now, if you'll excuse me, I'm going to start working on these clues."

Xavier did not bother to respond. Without a backward glance he headed into the crowd, making his way toward the doors at the far end of the room. Hodson had just disappeared through one.

Progress was slow because everyone wanted to give him an encouraging word or warn him that Sheldon Peabody was already getting the jump on him.

"Better get started, Sir Xavier. I'm afraid Sir Sheldon has the advantage. He's been on quests before," one man said as he clapped Xavier on the back.

"Thanks for the advice," Xavier muttered as he neared the doors.

"Good luck, Sir Xavier," a woman called out. "Remember, your lady's counting on you."

Xavier paid no attention to the well-wishers. He opened the ballroom door and stepped out into the wide corridor. When he glanced to the left he saw a white tunic disappearing around the corner at the end of the hall. Xavier followed. Sir Richard was headed for the castle privy.

The door of the men's room opened just as Xavier reached it. A balding, middle-aged knight came out. He was busy adjusting his tunic.

"Is it crowded in there?" Xavier asked easily.

"Nope. Just Sir Richard," the man said with a cheerful grin. "Plenty of room."

"Thanks."

Xavier walked into the white-tiled room. Hodson was standing at the sink, straightening the elaborate white and gold striped cap he was wearing. He glanced toward the entrance as Xavier entered.

"Hello, there, Augustine. Trust you're going to be a good sport about this," Hodson said smoothly. "Don't worry, it's all in fun."

"Sorry, I'm not going to be a good sport about it at all." Xavier grabbed the startled Hodson by the shoulder and slammed the man up against the tiled wall. He pinned him there. "Where's Letty?"

Alarm replaced the amusement in Hodson's astonished gaze. "Hey, what do you think you're doing, Augustine?"

"I asked you a question." Xavier drew back his fist.

"Hey, hold on a second, will you? It's just a damn game."

"What have you done with her?"

"Let me go. She's safe, I tell you."

"I'm not going to play your stupid game, Hodson. Nobody gets away with dragging Letty off into the night. Tell me where she is or I'll take you apart. Starting right now."

Hodson stared at him for a few seconds. What he saw in Xavier's eyes obviously made him decide that the game was over. "Look, it's no big deal, okay? Peabody wanted a quest that would pit the two of you against each other. The members of the Inner Circle thought it would be entertaining for the others so they agreed. We do it all the time. You two are both interested in Letty Conroy, so we made her the object of the quest. Simple."

"Did Letty agree to this?"

"Well, no, not exactly. She didn't know anything about it until Alison Crane and the others tricked her and got her into a car. Look, she's all right, I tell you. It's early. Nobody's started drinking. No one's in any danger."

"Where is she, Hodson?"

"You're supposed to follow the clues to find her," Hodson said, sounding desperate. "No, wait, don't get excited, I'll tell you," he added quickly as Xavier shifted his weight in preparation for the blow. "Damn it, man, you're serious, aren't you?"

"Yeah, Hodson. I'm serious. I don't like your games."

"Okay, okay. They've taken her to a little cottage on the other side of town. Take the main road along the ocean until you see a sign for Seaview Point. The house is on the right. It belongs to one of the Revelers."

"If you're lying to me, Hodson, I'll be back. And I'll be mad. Understand?"

"Yeah, yeah, I understand. What's the matter? Haven't you got any sense of humor?"

"Not much." Xavier released his victim and stepped back. "Remember, Hodson, if you've lied, I'll feed you your teeth."

Hodson straightened himself warily, shaking out his rumpled costume. "Hey, I believe you. What the hell am I supposed to tell Peabody?"

"I don't give a damn what you tell him as long as you don't tell him where she is. He likes quests. Let him follow those stupid clues."

Xavier was already at the door. A plump-looking knight dressed in green and pink entered just as Xavier went out.

"Say, there, Sir Xavier," the knight called out. "You'd better get going on your quest. Sir Sheldon just headed for the parking lot with a few of his buddies."

"I'm on my way."

"Good. My money's on you," the man yelled after him.

Xavier did not respond. He was striding down the hall, fishing for his car keys beneath the black tunic.

The Jaguar was right where he had left it in the parking lot, but it had been imprisoned. It was now barricaded behind a ring of other vehicles that had been strategically parked around it.

Obviously Peabody had taken his own approach to giving himself an edge in the quest. Several Revelers sat on the hoods of their cars, laughing and grinning as they waited to see what Xavier would do to rescue his besieged warhorse.

Xavier did not pause. It would take time to force several Revelers to move their cars. He ignored the hoots and shouts from the people sitting and leaning on the cars and walked toward an aging black Camaro that was parked on the outskirts of the steel ring. A man in a dark tunic and a woman with an elaborate headdress were lounging against the fender. They grinned at him as he approached.

"This your car?" Xavier asked casually.

"Yeah, it's mine," the man said. The woman beside him giggled. "What about it?"

"I think I'll borrow it."

The man straightened, alarmed. "Are you kidding?"

"You want to give me the keys or would you rather I hot-wired it?" Xavier was already reaching for the door handle.

"Now just a damned second here. You can't take my car."

"Watch me." Xavier slid into the front seat and bent down, seeking under the dash with knowing fingers. It had been a few years since he'd tried this. He'd have to trust that the old feel was still in the fingers.

The owner of the car leapt forward with a strangled yelp, obviously recognizing expertise when he saw it. "Wait, don't start ripping up my wiring, for crying out loud. Here, take the damn keys."

"Thanks. I appreciate it." Xavier caught the keys as they were hurled at him. He slammed them into the ignition and put the Camaro in gear.

"Well, hell," the Camaro's owner breathed as Xavier spun the wheel and sent the vehicle racing out of the parking lot. "This is going to be interesting." He rounded on a friend who was watching curiously. "Hey, Sam, let's follow Augustine."

Xavier heard a few enthusiastic shouts behind him as he drove out onto the main road, but he did not bother to glance back. He was in a hurry.

LETTY SAT in the corner of the old sofa, her knees drawn up under the skirts of her gown and stared glumly at the checkerboard. "I wish you would listen to me, Alison. Trust me, this is not a good idea. Xavier is going to be very annoyed."

"Relax, it's a game. Everyone has a good time and we all party afterward." Alison sat back from the checkerboard. "Your move."

Letty reluctantly pushed a piece on the board. The rest of the group who had spirited her away into the night were munching potato chips while they watched television and made bets on how long it would take for Peabody to show up.

"Afraid Sheldon will probably be the winner," one of the men had confided as he dumped more chips into a bowl. "He's been on quests before and he knows how to follow clues. It's sort of like a scavenger hunt. Augustine ever been on one?"

"I doubt it," Letty had said. She could not imagine Xavier Augustine going on a scavenger hunt. "He's not the type."

She was not exactly a prisoner in the beachside cottage, Letty knew. She had already made one trip to the bathroom to scout out the situation and had discovered there was nothing to prevent her climbing through the window.

The problem was what to do after she was out of the cottage. The night was cold, rain was on the way and she did not have a coat with her. Letty was quite sure none of the others would give her the keys to the car so her only option was walking all the way into town, a distance of perhaps three or four miles. The road back to town would be a long and lonely one.

In a true emergency she would have risked the hike, of course. But given the fact that she was in danger of Xavier's uncertain temper, she had decided not to try to escape. She would just have to wait for her *verray, parfit gentil* knight to show up.

"Nice little cottage, isn't it?" Alison said in a chatty tone as she made another move on the checkerboard. "One of my clients owns it. It was a steal. Estate sale, you know."

"It's very pleasant." Letty hesitated, wondering how much of an advantage Sheldon's previous experience on quests would give him. "Alison, I wish you'd listen to me. Xavier is not into this kind of thing. He's going to be worried about me and he will definitely not be in a good mood when he gets here."

One of the men sitting in front of the TV glanced over his shoulder. "Don't worry, we'll explain it all to him. Just a game. All the new members have to go through a quest or something. Revelers have a reputation to uphold. If you want to be a member in good standing, you've got to know how to have fun."

Letty shook her head. "I don't think Xavier wants to be a member in good standing."

"Then he can get lost," the other man, whose name was Carl, said lazily.

"Don't be a spoilsport, Letty." Alison jumped two of Letty's men and crowned a king for herself. "Let's talk about something else."

"Like what?"

"How about that book I was telling you to write?"

"I'll think about it." Letty shifted a bit on the couch and strained to hear the noise of an approaching car. She thought she could hear a distant roar but knew it was probably the sound of the ocean. "It's kind of isolated around here, isn't it?"

"That's the beauty of the place," Alison assured her. She picked up a checker, started to put it down and then paused, tilting her head attentively to one side. "Hey, everyone, I think I hear a car."

Letty leapt to her feet. The distant roar she had heard was a vehicle after all. But it did not sound like the sophisticated purr of Xavier's Jaguar, she realized, disappointed. She hurried to the window. "Someone's coming. More than one car."

"Maybe Augustine and Peabody are neck and neck," Carl said as he joined her at the window. "Get ready to be rescued, Letty."

"What the heck?" The other knight peered out the window into the darkness. "There's a whole bunch of cars coming this way. What's going on?"

"Do you suppose a few of the Revelers decided to follow the two knights on their quest?" Alison asked.

"I don't know." Carl frowned. "I'm not sure I like the looks of this. They're arriving too soon. There hasn't been time for the two knights to figure out the clues. And there are some pickup trucks in that group of cars following the Camaro."

"Pickup trucks?" One of the other women who had accompanied them leaned closer to the window and frowned. "I don't think I remember any pickups being parked in the lot at the Greenslade Inn. Where did those come from? What in the world is happening out there?"

"I'm not sure, but they're definitely coming this way." Carl edged back from the window, digging out his keys. "You know, it might not be a bad idea if we got in the car. This is making me a little nervous."

"Wait a second, I recognize that black Camaro in the lead. That's Bob Frazer's car, isn't it?"

"Maybe. Maybe not. This is turning weird."

"Why would Frazer be leading the rest of them? He's not a member of the Inner Circle and he's not on the quest. How would he know where we went with Letty?"

Everyone turned to stare accusingly at Letty, who shrugged her shoulders. "Don't look at me. Xavier doesn't play by other people's rules."

"Hell, let's get moving." Carl was already leading the way outside.

The others, including Letty, followed quickly into the cold night.

The black car in the lead was pulling into the drive, its headlights sweeping across the small group of people hurrying toward Carl's car.

The Camaro came to a shuddering halt and the driver's door was thrown open. Xavier, looking exactly like what he was supposed to be in his black attire—a medieval knight bent on rescue and retribution—leapt out.

"Letty, over here. Hurry." He ran toward her.

Letty turned at the sound of his voice. *"Xavier."* She picked up her skirts and dashed toward him.

He caught her up in a grip of steel and bundled her into the front seat of the Camaro.

Carl yelled at him over the top of his own car. "Augustine? Is that you? What's going on?"

"I picked up a few camp followers. Some of them are friendly but I don't know about a few of the others. They're from town. You know how it is, everyone loves a parade." Xavier was already behind the wheel of the Camaro, shoving it into gear. "If you want my advice you'll get the hell out of here."

"Damn." Carl jumped into his car and his friends piled in after him.

Xavier gunned the Camaro's engine and roared out of the drive. Carl was close behind.

Letty turned in the seat and stared out the window at the line of cars angling off the main road into the cottage drive. Horns were sounding, tires were screeching, music blared from car speakers and people were yelling. It was quite a sight.

"You always do things first-class, don't you, Augustine?" she murmured as she leaned back and fastened her seat belt. "I have never been rescued before, so I can't speak from personal experience. But something tells me this little scene is going to pass into legend in the chronicles of the Order of Medieval Revelers."

"Unfortunately, it isn't over yet." Xavier pressed his booted foot down harder on the accelerator. "We still have to go back through town. Bound to pick up a few more followers. This time the cops are likely to notice.''

"Oh, my.'' Letty fell silent as she envisioned the size of the thundering horde that would be arriving back at the Greenslade Inn. "Xavier, this is getting a little out of hand. What are we going to do when we get back to the inn?''

"You are going to follow orders.'' Xavier checked his rearview mirror. "We've got a few minutes' lead. They're all still milling around back at the cottage, trying to figure out where the action is. Except for the idiots who kidnapped you. They're right behind us.''

"It wasn't exactly kidnapping and they're not idiots, Xavier. Just an overzealous group of fun-loving history enthusiasts.''

"They're idiots. And it was kidnapping as far as I was concerned. You didn't go with them willingly, did you?''

"Well, no. I didn't want to go, but it was a little hard to refuse, if you know what I mean. They were very insistent.'' Letty sighed. "I told them you weren't going to like it.''

"You were right. I hope you've had a good time during the past three days, Letty, because it's all over now.''

She shot him an uneasy glance. "What do you mean?''

"I have a hunch the quarterly meeting of the Order of Medieval Revelers is about to come to an unexpected conclusion. With any luck at all, we'll miss the fireworks. Now, listen up, Lady Letitia. When we get back to the inn, I'm going to park at the rear entrance. You and I are heading straight upstairs to our rooms. We're going to pack all our things in five minutes flat and then we're going to get in our cars and drive straight home to Tipton Cove.''

Letty's eyes widened. "All the way back to Tipton Cove? Tonight? Xavier, it's after midnight. I don't feel like a two-hour drive.''

"You'd better get in the mood, because that's what you're going to do.''

"But why?''

"Because I have a hunch the Revelers are going to make a few headlines tomorrow morning and I don't want you showing up in the news photos.''

"News photos.'' Letty was aghast. "Xavier, what do you think is going to happen?''

Xavier glanced into the rearview mirror again, his mouth grim. "When that crowd behind us roars back through town a second time and picks up a police escort, there will be hell to pay. There's already some tension between the locals and the Revelers. Didn't you notice it yesterday at the fair? We're going to be safely back in Tipton Cove when the big raid gets plastered across the front pages.''

"Oh." Letty digested that. Then she sat back in the seat and smiled to herself.

Xavier shot her a sidelong glance. "What are you thinking about now, Letty?"

"I was just thinking that it's all been quite exciting. In the past three days I've broken off an engagement, I've had two men do battle over me, I've started an affair, I've been the intended victim of a seduction by an aging roué, I've been the object of a quest, I've been rescued by a knight riding a black destrier and now I'm in danger of figuring in a scandalous newspaper story."

"Yeah, I see what you mean," Xavier said coolly. "I guess it doesn't get any better than this, does it?"

"Go ahead and be sarcastic if you want," Letty said, folding her arms under her breasts. "But I'm telling you this is the most excitement I've had in my entire life."

He threw her a burning look. "Tell me something. Out of all the exciting things you've done this weekend, which was your favorite?"

"Oh, that's easy. Starting the affair."

Xavier was silent for a long moment and then he grinned slowly, a very wicked, male grin that spoke volumes. "What a coincidence. That was the thing I liked best, myself."

Letty smiled in the darkness. "You know something, Xavier?"

"What?"

"I knew you'd rescue me. I never doubted it for a moment."

"Is that right?"

"Uh-huh. I don't know what you did before you materialized as Xavier Augustine ten years ago, but whatever it was, you must have been good at it. I can't wait until Molly finds out just who and what you were before you became a saint."

"Letty?"

"Hmm?"

"This is not a good time to bring up the subject of the investigation you and Molly are trying to conduct into my past. I am not feeling indulgent."

"Right. Whatever you say, Xavier." Letty started to laugh and then she spotted a familiar car passing them, going the opposite direction. "Oh, look. There goes Sheldon."

"He must have finally figured out the clues Lord Richard gave him."

Letty's brows came together in a thoughtful expression. "Everyone kept saying Sheldon had the advantage because he'd been on quests before and knew how to decipher the clues. How did you manage to get to the cottage ahead of him? And why are you driving this car instead of the Jag?"

"I don't always play by the rules."

Letty smiled with satisfaction. "That's just what I told Alison."

CHAPTER NINE

"LETTY? Letty, honey, wake up."

"Not time to get up," Letty mumbled into the pillow. "We just got into bed."

"It's five-thirty. Up and at 'em." Xavier leaned over the bed, pulled back the covers and gave Letty an affectionate slap on her rear.

"Five-thirty?" She forced open her eyes and turned to peer resentfully up at Xavier. Even without her glasses she could tell he looked far too vigorous considering the circumstances. He was dressed in sweats and a pair of very expensive, very high tech running shoes. "We didn't get in until late last night. Why do we have to get up now?"

Letty had been drooping with weariness when she finally pulled into the drive of her little Victorian house in Tipton Cove last night. Even as she had opened the car door, the lights of Xavier's Jaguar had swung into the narrow lane behind her. He had followed her closely all the way from the Greenslade Inn.

They had barely made it out of the inn's parking lot as the first of the parade of cars had begun returning. The vehicles that had chased after Xavier on the outward bound trip had been supplemented by several more pickup trucks and a smattering of four-wheel drives on the return trip.

Letty, driving away from the inn at a discreet speed, had heard the first of the police sirens in the distance. Xavier had been right, she had reflected as she reached out to turn on the radio. Things were about to get even more lively at the quarterly convention of the Order of Medieval Revelers.

She had experienced a brief moment of regret at being obliged to miss the excitement that was bound to ensue, but staying around to participate was out of the question. A glance in her rearview mirror had revealed Xavier's Jaguar already hard on her tail, herding her forward on the long drive home.

When they reached Letty's house, both she and Xavier had literally fallen into bed and gone straight to sleep.

"Letty," Xavier said again, disturbing her memories of how she came to be in her own bed this morning, "you have to get up now. I'm not joking."

"Give me one good reason."

"All right, I will. You have to get up so you can go for an early morning run in the park."

"Running? You want to go running? After all that dashing around last night? You're out of your mind." Letty shoved her face back into the pillow.

Xavier swore softly under his breath. "Letty, pay attention. You have to go for an early morning run so that by noon everyone in Tipton Cove will know that you were right where you should have been when the big raid at the Greenslade Inn took place."

That comment finally succeeded in riveting Letty's attention. She sat straight up in bed, clutching the sheet. "What raid?"

"The one that netted our esteemed Lord of Revelry and a certain member of the local Tipton College academic community." Xavier handed her the *Tipton Cove Herald*, the town's slender morning paper. Then he held out her glasses.

Letty put on the glasses and looked down at the front page of the newspaper. The *Herald* generally featured extensive coverage of such titillating topics as the fate of the latest sewer bond issue or Tipton College's recent academic appointments. But this morning it had a much juicier story to report. "Celebrity Author and Tipton College Prof Key Figures in Fracas."

"'Fracas'?" Letty looked up. "Is that what they call it?"

"I believe fracas is a professional journalistic term meaning something along the lines of a barroom brawl."

"Oh." Letty stared down at the headline for a long while. Beneath it was a photo of Richard Hodson and Sheldon Peabody being assisted into the back of a police cruiser. They were still wearing their medieval attire. The expression on his florid face made it clear Hodson was trying to explain just how famous he was. The policeman did not look impressed. Perhaps he did not read medieval mysteries.

Sheldon, on the other hand, was trying desperately to conceal his face with the hem of his tunic. He hadn't succeeded.

The lights of the Greenslade Inn blazed in the distance, revealing the entire, sordid scene. A throng of knights and ladies could be seen standing on the lawn behind the police car. They were apparently engaged in exchanging insults with a crowd of local farmers and cowboys. Beneath the photo was a caption.

Well-known author Richard Hodson and Tipton history prof taken into custody during an altercation between townsfolk and convention goers at Greenslade Inn. No charges were filed and the pair was later released.

"Oh, my goodness." Letty dropped the paper on the bed and raised her eyes back to Xavier's cooly amused gaze.

"My point, precisely," Xavier said. "Our goal this morning is to show everyone that you were nowhere near the Greenslade Inn when the 'altercation' occurred." He tossed her a red long-sleeved sweatshirt and matching pants. "Move, honey."

"What if I don't mind everyone knowing I might have been involved in something like that?"

"I mind." Xavier bent down and yanked her flannel nightie off over her head. He stood gazing down at her breasts for a moment, looking regretful. "And while there are other things I would rather do this morning than go for run in the park—" he touched one nipple and watched with appreciation as it went taut "—I must be strong for your sake."

"But we're not going to get married, so my reputation or lack of it, doesn't matter any more." Vividly aware of her nipples puckering in response to his touch and the look in his eyes, Letty grabbed the sweatshirt and put it on. Then she reached for the pants.

Xavier threw her a thoroughly disgusted look as he went to the closet to find her running shoes. "What about your career, Letty? You want Stirling to think you were mixed up in that raid?"

"I don't care what he thinks," she said defiantly as she put on the scuffed and worn shoes.

"Easy to say now. You'll feel differently when you've had a chance to think about it."

"Oh, yeah? Says who?"

Xavier handed her a brush. "Says me."

"Why are you still trying to protect my reputation? We're merely involved in an affair now. It's okay to have affairs with fast women, you know.'' She got up, went into the bathroom and yanked the brush through her hair.

Xavier's mouth kicked up at the corner as he watched her. ''I don't have affairs with fast women,'' he said gently.

''What kind do you have them with? Slow women?''

''Don't get sassy.''

She closed the door on his wicked grin. ''What is this, Xavier?'' she called out as she ran water in the sink. ''You're so upright and proper that even your mistresses have to be above reproach?''

''You're really looking for an argument this morning, aren't you? Yesterday morning wasn't much better, as I recall. I think I'm beginning to see a pattern here. Are you always this hostile when you wake up?''

''Sometimes I'm worse,'' she assured him as she walked back out into the bedroom.

''I'll keep that in mind. Come on, I don't have time to spar with you now.'' He grabbed her hand and hauled Letty firmly toward the front door.

''Do we have to go through this?''

''Stop whining. It's for your own good.''

''You mean it's for your own good,'' she sniped, feeling distinctly peevish as she stepped out into the crisp morning air. ''I don't think I'm up to running. How about a nice, leisurely morning walk?''

''You have to look fit and robust. Can't have anyone thinking you might be hungover or otherwise suffering from your three days of orgies and debauchery.''

''Such a lovely word, debauchery. You know, Xavier, I don't feel that I really had a chance to experience much debauchery at Greenslade. I was just starting to get the hang of it when you made me leave.'' Letty allowed herself to be urged down the front steps and along the path to the garden gate.

''You've had plenty of excitement lately. What about the brawl? What about beginning an affair? What about getting kidnapped? Wild times in the fast lane, if you ask me.'' Xavier unlocked the front gate.

''I'm not saying that what there was of it wasn't exciting.''

''I suppose I should be grateful for that much,'' Xavier muttered as he closed the gate.

Letty frowned thoughtfully. "You know, Xavier, it occurs to me that you caused most of the excitement I did get to experience."

"Me?" He gave her a reproachful glance as they started past Dr. Knapthorpe's rosebushes.

"Yes, you." Letty warmed to her topic. "You were the one who actually started that brawl. You were the one I had the affair with. You were the one who caused that fracas at Greenslade by refusing to play the quest game by the rules."

"I'm hurt."

"Hah. You know something else? I'm beginning to suspect you're something of a fraud, Xavier. You're not the saint you pretend to be, are you?"

"I never pretended to be a saint. Just a man who prefers a nice, peaceful existence. I don't think that's too much to ask out of life. Morning, Knapthorpe." Xavier raised a hand in greeting as Professor Knapthorpe, dressed in a bathrobe, came out onto his porch and waved.

"Good morning, Augustine. Letty." Knapthorpe nodded genially. "Thought I heard you two come in last night. Missed all the excitement down the coast, I see." He indicated the headlines on the *Tipton Cove Herald* he was holding.

"We left the convention early," Xavier explained, leaning casually against the white picket fence. "It wasn't quite what we had expected. Letty and I realized shortly after we got there that it really wasn't our kind of thing."

"I should say not." Knapthorpe shook his head and tut-tutted. "Peabody certainly seems to have made a fool of himself. Can't think what Stirling will have to say about this."

"A very unfortunate incident," Xavier said, looking grave.

"Yes, isn't it? You two certainly showed good sense leaving the convention early. But, then, that's only what I would expect of you both. Neither one of you is the type to involve yourself in a messy situation like this nonsense down the coast."

"No, sir," Xavier agreed. "Letty and I much prefer the quiet life, don't we, Letty?"

Letty gave him a saccharine-sweet smile. "Our muscles are going to tighten up in this cold air if we don't get moving."

"Right you are," Xavier said cheerfully. "Can't have tight muscles. Off we go. See you later, Professor."

"Certainly." Knapthorpe nodded in a friendly fashion and

turned toward his front door. He paused briefly and glanced over his shoulder. "How are the wedding plans coming?"

"Invitations are going out this week," Xavier said before Letty could open her mouth.

"Excellent. I'm looking forward to it."

"That reminds me," Xavier said. "Letty has no one to give her away. We were wondering if you'd do the honors?"

"*Xavier.*" Letty's voice was a high-pitched squeak of dismay.

Knapthorpe looked vastly pleased. He beamed at Letty. "Why, I would be happy to do so. Very kind of you to ask. Never done that sort of thing before. Never had any daughters of my own. It will be a delightful experience. I shall look forward to it."

"It's settled then. See you, Professor." Xavier took Letty by the arm and urged her off at a slow trot.

Letty was still recovering from the shock. She had never been so incensed. "Xavier, how many times do I have to tell you, the wedding is off? How dare you go and ask Knapthorpe to give me away? What am I supposed to say when he finds out the truth?"

"We'll worry about that later. Right now the important thing is to make everyone think things are perfectly normal. Run, lady."

"Please, Xavier, I can barely move, let alone run."

"I told you, this is for your own good."

Letty sighed deeply and managed to move from a slow trot to a jogging run as they headed around the block to the park.

As with many college towns, Tipton Cove was filled with fitness enthusiasts and on any given morning one could count on the park to be filled with runners, joggers and people walking briskly along its shaded paths. This morning was no exception. Letty and Xavier passed at least ten people by the time they reached the pond at the far end. Each person they saw seemed surprised and somewhat relieved to see them.

"Morning, Letty. Morning Augustine. Glad to see you didn't get mixed up in that mess down the coast."

"Hi, you two. I see you're back early. Good thing. Hear it got a little hairy at that convention of medievalists."

"Hey, I didn't realize you two were here in Tipton Cove. Thought you'd gone off down the coast. Just as well. Word has it Peabody got himself arrested at that convention. Can you believe it?"

"Letty. Augustine. Glad you're back in town. Heard there was a big riot at Greenslade. Good thing you weren't involved."

Letty groaned as Xavier prodded her along the second lap of the park course. "Talk about being the focus of all eyes. I get the feeling everyone in town knows we went to that convention and they all seem to know what happened last night."

"Told you so."

"Please, Xavier. Not at this hour of the morning. I'm barely surviving this marathon as it is. I don't need you telling me you told me so."

"Sorry."

"You don't sound sorry in the least." She shot him a glowering look, aware that he was moving easily without any apparent effort beside her, deliberately slowing his pace to match hers. He was not even breathing hard. "How can you run around like this after a night like the one we just had?"

"Fear is a great motivator."

"Fear of what people will say about me if they don't see us out here?"

"Exactly. Tell you what, I'll buy you a nice fresh cinnamon roll at the Park Street Café," Xavier said. "How does that sound?"

"Assuming I make it as far as the Park Street Café, it sounds all right," she allowed grudgingly.

"Bound to be a crowd in the café by this time," Xavier noted, glancing at his watch.

"I get it. More witnesses to the fact that we're here in Tipton Cove instead of languishing in jail."

"You're catching on fast."

The first person Letty spotted when Xavier opened the door of the Park Street Café a short time later was Dr. Elliott Stirling, chairman of the Tipton College history department. The professor was paying the cashier for the cup of coffee he had just finished consuming.

Stirling glanced up expectantly when Letty and Xavier walked into the cozy restaurant. He frowned slightly into the morning sunlight behind them and then his noble brow cleared as he recognized his bright, young medieval studies scholar and her fiancé. He nodded his patrician head in regal acknowledgment of their presence.

"Dr. Conroy. What a surprise. Heard you'd gone down the coast to attend that convention of amateur medieval history buffs."

Xavier smiled blandly at Stirling as he escorted Letty to a nearby table. "Letty and I gave it a whirl but decided to come back early when we realized it wasn't a genuine, academically oriented convention."

"Quite." Stirling gave Letty an approving look. "I wouldn't have said it was your sort of thing, Dr. Conroy. Glad to see you had the sense to leave early. Too bad certain other members of the department didn't demonstrate the same degree of intelligence." Stirling nodded once more and then went out the door.

"Poor Sheldon." Letty sighed and picked up her menu.

"As far as I'm concerned, he got what he deserved," Xavier said.

"How can you say that?"

"He was trying to use you, Letty. I told you that."

"I wish you'd stop saying that," she muttered.

"I'm saying it because it's the truth. You want one cinnamon roll or two?"

"One."

"I'll order two for you. That way I can eat the extra one." Xavier closed the menu and smiled at the waitress. "Two cinnamon rolls for the lady and I'll have two, also. And two cups of coffee."

"Right. You two see the morning paper?" the young waitress inquired with a bright-eyed expression.

"I glanced at the headlines on the way out the door this morning," Xavier admitted.

"Really weird about Professor Peabody, wasn't it? I had him in History 205 last quarter. It seems strange to have a professor do something stupid like that. Be right back with your orders."

Letty glared across the table at Xavier. "I hadn't realized just how little privacy there is around this town."

"Told you so."

"Say that one more time, Augustine, and I'm going to cram my napkin down your throat. I didn't ask you to rescue me, you know."

"It was my pleasure."

Letty sighed. "I guess, now that I think about it, it's a good thing I'm here this morning and not in the headlines along with poor Sheldon."

Xavier grinned, looking pleased with himself. "You know,

Letty, this would be a very good time for you to start wearing your engagement ring again.''

She eyed him suspiciously. ''Why?''

''Because it will help stifle speculation and gossip. You don't want them talking about you the way they're going to be talking about Peabody. Don't worry, you can always take it off again in a few days after all the fuss has died down.''

''I don't know, Xavier, it seems sort of dishonest.''

''Think of it as protective camouflage.'' Xavier had already reached into his pocket and pulled out the ring. He took her hand gently in his and slid the emerald back into place. ''There, that should help quell some of the comments.''

Letty gazed sadly down at the emerald. It winked back at her in the sunlight. ''Well, all right. If you're really that worried about what people will say, Xavier.''

''Thank you, Letty. I appreciate it.''

There was more than humble gratitude in his tone, Letty thought. There was also one heck of a lot of cool, masculine satisfaction.

THE RED LIGHT was glowing on Letty's telephone answering machine when she and Xavier walked back into the house an hour later.

''You go ahead and take a shower,'' Letty said to Xavier. ''I'll listen to my messages.''

''Fine.''

There had apparently been several calls. Letty pushed the playback button and heard Molly Sweet's anxious voice.

''Letty? Where are you? I tried the inn but they said you'd checked out in the middle of the night. What's going on? I have to talk to you.''

The second message was in a similar vein but there was no doubt but that the anxiety level had escalated in Molly's voice.

''Letty? Call me as soon as you hear this. I have to talk to you. Things are getting sticky.''

The third call sounded even more urgent. ''Letty, I'm not kidding. This is serious. I must talk to you ASAP. It concerns you-know-who. Call me. Oh, damn. Where are you?''

Letty frowned in growing concern as the last of the anxious messages concluded. She sat pondering the situation for a moment, listening to the sound of the shower going in the bathroom. Then she picked up the phone and dialed Molly's home number. Her call was answered midway through the first ring.

"Letty? Is that you?"

"It's me, Molly. What's happening?"

"I don't know." Molly sounded extremely agitated. "But I'm afraid I may have gotten all of us into some very deep water. I have to talk to you. Someplace private. Don't bring Xavier, whatever you do."

"Why can't I bring Xavier? Does this have something to do with your computer search?"

"Yes. I've been getting more of those strange inquiries from some source that won't identify itself. They're getting spooky, Letty."

"Threatening inquiries?" Letty's fingers tightened around the phone.

"Veiled threats, if you know what I mean," Molly said in an ominous tone. "Letty, this could be dangerous."

"Dangerous? To whom? Xavier?"

"Maybe. Or maybe to us. I just don't know. Look, I'm afraid to say anything more over the phone."

"Oh, my God. You think whoever's sending those threatening inquiries over the computer might have tapped your phone, too?"

"I just don't know. We can't take any chances. Meet me at the pond in the park. That's out in the open so it should be reasonably safe. Ten minutes."

"I'll be there." Letty replaced the phone, wondering what sort of excuse she could give to Xavier for dashing back out of the house. She suddenly realized the shower had gone off while she had been talking to Molly.

"Any important messages?" Xavier asked casually from the hallway.

"Oh, no." Letty jumped and swung around to see him fastening his trousers and stuffing his shirttail into his waistband. She wondered if he had overheard anything. He did not sound curious or suspicious. She cleared her throat. "That is, no important messages. Just Molly trying to get in touch with me. Xavier, I've just realized I'm out of milk. I'm going to run down to the convenience store on the corner and get some. Be right back."

His brows rose. "I thought you were exhausted from our early morning run."

"Yes, well, I've recovered. Women recover from exercise much faster than men, you know. Scientific fact. And I won't actually be running to the store. Just sort of sauntering along." Letty pinned a bright smile on her face and edged toward the door. "Be right back." She let herself out the door and closed it firmly behind her.

Xavier crossed the parlor and looked out the window. Letty was running, not sauntering back toward the park. He wondered when she would realize she had not taken her purse.

Xavier went over to the phone and dialed Hawk's number.

"What's going on, Hawk?" Xavier drawled when the phone was picked up on the other end. "Threatening inquiries? Phone taps?"

"Maybe a few of the former but definitely none of the latter, although it might prove interesting." Hawk was totally unperturbed. "I'd like to hear Molly Sweet's voice. The lady is sounding more and more interesting by the hour. How's it going on your end?"

"You've got Molly and Letty agitated as hell. What have you been doing?"

"I've been blocking all of Ms. Sweet's data base queries. I'm letting her think she's getting into forbidden territory. Implied she was asking for top secret information and asked to see her clearances. She keeps backing out and trying from new directions. Very clever, our Ms. Sweet. I'm having fun. Want me to keep up the good work?"

Xavier leaned back in the chair, propped his feet on the ottoman and stared thoughtfully out the window. "Yeah, I think so. Stall for a while longer."

"Still having problems with your lady, huh?"

"My lady thinks she's into excitement these days. And she's decided having an affair with me is a lot more exciting than getting married to me."

"She's calling off the wedding?"

"The wedding is still on," Xavier informed him roughly. "She just doesn't know it."

"Still not ready to tell her about your past?"

Xavier's mouth tightened. "No."

"Sounds like you've made up your mind and once you do that, you're like a rock. I won't even try to change it for you." Hawk chuckled. "I'll just go back to playing games with Ms. Molly Sweet. What's she look like?"

"Who? Letty?"

"No, not Letty. Molly."

"Oh." Xavier frowned, trying to think. "Wears glasses. Got kind of a bizarre taste in clothing. She's about Letty's age." He floundered, unable to think of any other salient characteristics. "Smart. Sort of attractive, I guess."

"Married?"

"No." Xavier suddenly realized where this was leading. "You sound like you're interested."

"I like her persistence," Hawk said. "She's gutsy."

"Just keep her out of my past," Xavier muttered. "At least until I figure out how to salvage my future."

"I'll do my best. Good luck." Hawk hung up the phone.

LETTY SAT on the park bench beside Molly and stared at the ducks on the pond. "This is beginning to make me very nervous."

"Tell me about it." Molly, dressed in a fuchsia and electric blue striped top over tight black leotards, scowled behind her glasses. "But I've saved the worst until last. I think he knows where I am, Letty. I think he even knows my name."

"What?" Letty was horrified. "Are you certain?"

Molly nodded grimly. "He started making little jokes on the computer. Wordplays on my last name. The inquiries all start with some dippy salutation like, 'Hi, sweetcakes' or 'You again, sweetheart?' This morning it was 'What do you want this time sweets?' He knows my last name is Sweet, Letty. And if he knows that much, he knows too much."

"I see what you mean. That does sound suspicious."

"I think I'd better stop the search, Letty. I don't know what I've opened up here."

"I think you're right." Letty stood up abruptly. "I'm going to have a talk with Xavier. This has gone far enough. I am going to demand some answers."

"Be careful, Letty." Molly got to her feet, looking worried. "The more I think about this, the more I'm afraid we may be in big trouble."

"I'll call you as soon as I talk to Xavier. I'm going to tell him what's happened and tell him I need to know if you're in any danger."

"I'm going straight home," Molly said. "I'll wait for your call."

Letty nodded and broke into a run. She was certainly getting her exercise this morning, she reflected bleakly.

She arrived back at her house a few minutes later, pushed open the garden gate, dashed up the porch steps and threw open the front door. The aroma of hot coffee drifted down the hall from the kitchen.

"Xavier?"

"In here," he called from the kitchen. "Get the milk?"

"Forget the milk. We have to talk." Letty hurried down the hall and came to a halt in the kitchen doorway. Xavier was fiddling with the coffee machine. "Xavier, I have something to tell you. Something serious. And I need some answers."

He hesitated and then turned around slowly to face her. He looked a little dangerous and a little wary. "What is it you have to tell me?"

Letty drew a deep breath. "I told you I asked Molly to make some inquiries about you."

"So you did." He folded his arms across his chest, his eyes never leaving her face.

Letty chewed her lip. "The thing is, someone seems to have discovered that she's asking questions."

"And?"

"And Molly is afraid we may have opened up a very big can of worms," Letty concluded in a rush. "She thinks whoever discovered she was prowling around in the computer data bases now knows who she is and maybe even where she lives. Xavier, you have to tell me the truth. Is Molly in any danger because of the way she's been probing your background?"

Xavier blinked, as if that was not quite the question he had been expecting. "No," he said slowly. "There's no reason for Molly to be in any danger."

"Are you absolutely certain?" Letty pleaded.

"Absolutely certain. Molly's in no danger."

A rush of relief went through Letty, emboldening her. "Then I think it's time you leveled with me, Xavier."

His eyes glittered. "What do you want to know?" he asked a little too softly.

"Isn't it obvious? I want to know if you're the one who's in danger."

He looked blank for a moment. "Depends on how you define danger, I guess."

"Xavier," she yelped, "don't pussyfoot around the issue. Does this have something to do with a...a legal problem in your past?"

"That's a tactful way of putting it. Look, Letty, I think I..."

"It's all right. You don't have to explain everything now. Just tell me this much—would it be awkward for you if people found out about your past?"

"Yes," Xavier said.

"I knew it. Oh, God, you are in danger." She hurled herself across the kitchen and into his arms, burying her face against his very expensive shirt. "And it's all my fault."

His arms closed fiercely around her. "Honey, it's all right."

"No, it isn't all right. If I hadn't told Molly to conduct that search none of this would have happened. Oh, Xavier, I'm so sorry. I never meant to put you in danger. I was just trying to get a little revenge because you had me investigated. Please forgive me."

He kissed the top of her head. "I forgive you."

She raised frightened eyes to search his face. "Do you swear it?"

"I swear it." He smiled slightly. "Word of honor."

"And Molly's safe?"

"Perfectly safe."

Letty stepped back. "Then we have to get out of here. Now. Before he comes looking for you."

"Before who comes looking?" Xavier asked curiously.

"The person who's tracking Molly in the computer. Don't you see? Whoever he is, he already knows too much. He's figured out that Xavier Augustine is you. By searching for your past, Molly's accidentally tipped him off that you're still around. What's more, she's afraid he now knows where she lives. Which means he can figure out where you are."

"This is getting confusing, Letty."

She grasped his shoulders and tried to shake him. It was like trying to shake Mount Everest. "Don't you see? Xavier, whoever it is you've been hiding from for the past ten years now knows where you are. We have to get out of here right now. We can't afford to waste another minute."

"Where are we going?"

"Into hiding, of course. We're going to lie low until the heat dies down."

CHAPTER TEN

"I CAN'T TALK long. Letty went out to pick up dinner. She'll be back soon." Xavier paced back and forth in front of the motel room window, his eye on the parking lot. It was filled with eighteen-wheel trucks, pickups, and a variety of aging Chevvies and Fords. There wasn't a BMW, Mercedes or Jaguar in sight. Across the street a garish neon sign signaled a fast-food restaurant.

"What the hell is going on?" Hawk demanded.

"I told you, we're on the lam. Hiding out. Living on the run. Heading for the border."

"The Mexican border?"

"No, not yet. Right now we're heading for the California border. But at the rate things are going, we may be on the way to Mexico next. Or Canada. I'm not sure. This is Letty's operation. She's saving me, you see. At the moment we're holed up for the night in a cheap motel off the Interstate."

"A *cheap* motel?" Hawk laughed. "That doesn't sound like you, Augustine. You always go first-class."

Xavier spotted Letty hurrying across the parking lot with a white paper bag in her hand. She had the collar of her windbreaker pulled up high around her ears and she was casting suspicious glances over her shoulder. He grinned. "I told you, Letty is managing this escape and she thinks we'll be more inconspicuous in a budget motel."

"Isn't having a Jaguar parked outside the room going to look a little strange?"

"We left the Jag hidden in Molly's garage. We're driving Letty's little compact. Look, she's coming back to the room now so I've got to hang up. Just wanted to let you know what was happening."

"A thrill a minute," Hawk said dryly. "You want me to keep up the pressure on Molly Sweet?"

"Yeah. For a while longer. Letty says we have to stay out of sight until Molly gives the all clear. Molly says she'll do that when she's convinced that whoever's backtracking me through her computer has given up.''

"Right. I get it. I'm the bad guy. Guess I'll go play the role of unseen computer menace," Hawk said. "Hey, Augustine?"

"Yeah?"

"You know something, old buddy? You sound like you're actually having fun."

"I am."

"Looks like you've got all the proof you need now that the lady isn't about to ditch you because of your sordid past."

"Funny how things turn out. I never planned it this way, but that's what happened. It feels good, Hawk."

"Well, good luck on your run for the border."

"They'll never take me alive," Xavier vowed. "Talk to you later, Hawk." He put down the phone as Letty inserted her room key into the lock. Then he went to open the door.

"Everything okay?" Letty asked as she shot one more glance back over her shoulder and quickly slipped into the room. She turned to throw the bolt.

"No problem." Xavier smiled at her as he took the paper bag from her hands. She was breathless and disheveled and there was a scattering of raindrops on her jacket. Her hair had long since slipped its moorings and chestnut tendrils floated around her shoulders. "Nobody around out there except a few truckers pulling in for the night. What did you bring us?"

"Fish and chips from the fast-food place across the street. Oh, and I got a bottle of wine from the convenience store next door and some plastic glasses." Letty looked at him uncertainly. "It's just a jug wine, I'm afraid. Nothing special. They didn't have much of a selection."

Xavier pulled the screw-cap bottle of generic red out of the bag and did not even wince at the sight of the cheap label. "I need a glass of this. You serve dinner, honey, and I'll pour the wine."

"Okay." Looking relieved, Letty set about unwrapping the contents of the paper bag. The aroma of fried fish and chips filled the small room. "I know this isn't quite what you're accustomed to, Xavier, but I figure no one will look for you in a place like this."

"You're probably right." Xavier hid a rueful smile as he glanced around the tacky little motel room, noting its faded drapes, sagging bed and worn shag carpeting. The television was chained to the wall. "It's a great place to hide out."

"I just wish we knew how long we'll have to lie low." Letty's brows snapped together over the frames of her glasses as she sat down at the small table.

"I don't think we'll be on the run for long," Xavier said, thinking of the wedding invitations waiting to be addressed and mailed. "Not for more than a few days at the most."

"You think whoever Molly alerted will give up that quickly?"

"Probably. I don't think he's the persistent type. Just doing a routine check." Xavier poured the wine into two disposable cups.

"I'm not so sure about that. He seems to be taunting Molly. She was very nervous."

Serves her right, Xavier thought wryly. "Trust me. Molly is safe." Xavier took a swallow of the red. "You know, this stuff isn't all that bad."

"What? The wine? Oh, good." Letty tried hers. "Tastes like the kind they serve at the pizza parlor in Tipton Cove."

"The perfect accompaniment for fast food," Xavier declared, taking another taste. "Did you bring any catsup?"

"It's in the bag." Letty gave him a narrow glance. "You know, something, Xavier?"

"What's that?"

"You don't seem quite as worried about what's happening as you should be."

"You have to be philosophical about this kind of thing, Letty. A survivor learns to roll with the punches."

"When are you going to tell me what it was you survived ten years ago?" she asked softly.

Xavier plunged a French fry into the catsup. "It's a little hard to talk about after all these years."

She reached across the table to touch his hand. "Don't you think I ought to know what we're facing?"

"Maybe. But I haven't talked about this with anyone for ten years, Letty."

"I understand. Don't worry, I'm not going to push you." Letty withdrew her hand and picked up a plastic fork. "I can see you don't feel comfortable in confiding in me yet. But I hope you will one of these days."

He exhaled heavily. "Soon, Letty. Soon. I promise."

The fish and chips and cheap red wine served up on a rickety table in a budget highway motel room proved to be one of the finest meals Xavier had ever enjoyed. He knew he would treasure the memory for the rest of his life and he knew why. He was beginning to believe that Letty could love him in spite of his past.

When he had asked her to marry him, Xavier had been confident that Letty had fallen genuinely in love with the man he was today. She had fallen for the very successful and eminently respectable Xavier Augustine, a man who endowed college faculty chairs; a man who knew the difference between real French champagne and California sparkling wine; a man who always traveled first-class.

But now Xavier allowed himself to wonder if maybe, just maybe, Letty could love the man he had once been.

"I'll take the remains outside and dump them in the garbage bin," Xavier said when the last of the fish and chips had disappeared. "Otherwise this room will smell of fried fish all night."

"Be careful," Letty said, looking anxious again.

He kissed the tip of her nose. "Relax. No one's going to see me."

He bundled up the wrappers and let himself out into the damp night. The smell of rain was in the air, making everything seem fresh and new. Xavier found himself whistling as he walked over to the garbage bin. On the way back to the room, he glanced up and saw the moon winking down at him through scuttling clouds.

Life, Xavier decided as he let himself back into the cheap little motel room, looked very good tonight.

Letty was just emerging from the bathroom, wrapped in her prim, quilted robe and wearing a pair of fluffy slippers. Her hair was loosely pinned on top of her head and her face was freshly scrubbed. She pushed her little round glasses higher on her nose and smiled tentatively at him.

It occurred to Xavier that she was feeling somewhat shy. He smiled back at her as he closed and locked the door. "The thing about affairs," he said gently, "is that one is usually obliged to conduct them in hotel and motels rooms. Which is what we've done so far, isn't it?"

"You're an authority?" she asked tartly.

He shook his head as he started unbuttoning his shirt. His eyes never left hers. "No. But I've heard tales."

Letty sat down on the edge of the bed, clutching the lapels of her robe. "Well, I don't imagine it would be much different if we were married," she said briskly. "We'd still be on the run and still forced to stay in places like this."

"Somehow," he said as he sat down beside her and unlaced his shoes, "I think things would be a lot different if we were married."

"Why?"

"Just a feeling." He let his shoes drop to the floor and sat beside her, his shirt hanging open. He gazed thoughtfully at the darkened TV set across the room. "Letty?"

"Yes?"

"There's something I'd like to know."

She stirred slightly. "What's that?"

"Well, I was just wondering if an affair is all you're ever going to want from me."

"Xavier..."

"I mean, now that you've turned over a new leaf and you're into excitement and adventure, maybe you're going to get bored with me as soon as the heat is off and we're no longer on the run."

Her eyes widened. "Xavier, how can you say that? I can't imagine ever getting bored with you. Even when you were playing the part of the perfect gentleman, I was never, ever bored. Frustrated at times, but definitely not bored."

"Yes, but you're a new woman now. You might not feel that way when our lives return to normal. If I went back to my old life, you might decide to go out and find someone more exciting."

"Stop saying things like that."

"I don't know, Letty." He got up slowly, went across the room and switched off the overhead light. The neon light from the fast-food restaurant sign made the curtains glow a dull orange. "I've been thinking it over and I'm not sure I want to go on like this."

In the dim orange glare filtering through the drapes he could see the sudden alarm on her face.

"Like what? You don't want to go on having an affair?"

He shook his head as he sat back down beside her. Then he leaned forward and rested his elbows on his thighs, his hands clasped loosely between his knees. "It's the uncertainty, you see. I don't think I can handle it. I've already got too much uncertainty in my life as it is."

"You do?"

"I'm afraid so. There's the basic uncertainty of my business, of course. People in my line of work are always at financial risk. And then there's the uncertainty of not knowing when or how my past might catch up with me. That's a constant concern, especially at the moment. It all adds up to a lot of pressure. I'm not sure I can handle the added uncertainty of having an affair with you."

"I hadn't thought about it quite like that. Was that why you had me investigated, Xavier? Because you were trying to eliminate some of the uncertainty in a relationship?"

"In a way. Do you think you can ever forgive me for that, Letty?"

Her fingers tightened on the lapels of her robe. "I suppose I'll have to after what I've done."

"Don't blame yourself for what happened when you started digging around in my past. You couldn't have known."

"True," she agreed. "To tell you the truth, I expected your past to be as dull as my own."

"I never considered your past dull. Not for a minute."

"That's because you wanted a woman without a past," she reminded him grimly.

"I just wanted to know what I was getting into." He turned his head to look at her. "But it wouldn't have mattered what I found. I'd still have wanted to marry you."

Her eyes searched his. "You say that now when you know there's nothing in my background to cause you any problems. But what would you have said when you first got the report if the investigation had shown some major scandal in my past?"

"There's nothing I can say or do now to prove that I would have married you anyway. But doesn't it mean anything to you to know that I still want to marry you, even though you're into the fast life these days?"

"Well..."

"Letty, do you still love me a little?"

She threw her arms around him. "Xavier, I still love you a lot," she whispered against his chest. "I've never stopped loving you."

"You're not just saying that because I've gotten more exciting lately?"

"No, I swear it. I do love you, Xavier. I love the old you and the new you."

"I wish I could be sure of that," he said, stroking her slender back with gentle hands. "Things have gotten so mixed up lately."

"Xavier, I promise you there is nothing uncertain about my feelings for you."

"You're sure?"

"Absolutely sure. What do I have to do to prove it, for heaven's sake?"

"Say you'll marry me. Even though we're on the run."

"Yes, damn it," she said, sounding thoroughly exasperated, "I'll marry you. Now, please stop trying to talk about it. I'm the one who's getting confused."

She pushed him abruptly down onto the bed and kissed him with a fierceness that took away Xavier's breath. He felt an overwhelming urge to laugh in soft, loving triumph but there was no opportunity. Letty was all over him, raining kisses across his mouth and his throat. Xavier's rush of satisfaction turned into flaring desire.

"*Letty.* Ah, sweetheart, that feels so good."

Her small, delicate fingers trailed across his chest, sliding under his shirt to find the flat nipples hidden in the crisp, curly hair. Her tongue touched his skin and Xavier groaned.

He felt as if he were being attacked by a horde of butterflies. It was a wonderful sensation. Within seconds he was hard with need. He started to unknot the sash of Letty's robe.

"Xavier, I do love you so. Please believe me."

"I believe you." He had her robe open now. Underneath it she wore a transparent peach-colored nightgown. Xavier knew he was looking at another one of the new gowns she had purchased for her trousseau.

Even as he started to ease the robe off her shoulders, Letty was busily at work on his belt. He obligingly lifted his hips when she started awkwardly pushing his trousers and briefs down over his thighs. At last he was wearing only the unbuttoned white shirt. He felt himself throb when her fingertips touched him intimately. Xavier breathed deeply, fighting to control the raging need. His blood ran hot.

"Damn, Letty. You don't know what you do to me."

"I'm glad you want me," she whispered. "For a while I wasn't sure that you did."

"You know better now, don't you?" he growled. He managed to get her robe off at last. Then he shifted position so that he was lying full-length on the bed. He pulled her down on top of him. The skirts of the peach-colored gown swirled around his hard body.

"Show me how much you love me, sweetheart." He caught her face between his hands, dragged her mouth down to his and kissed her deeply. "Show me how much you want me."

"Yes. Yes, my love."

She kissed him back with frantic eagerness, her hands touching him everywhere. There was an endearing, sweet wildness in her lovemaking as she struggled to please him.

Xavier gloried in the waterfall of feminine sensuality that was pouring over him. He felt the weightless nightgown glide along the inside of his leg, teasing and tantalizing him. Letty's hips ground against his. Her bare foot slid along his calf. Her tongue plunged daringly into his mouth.

Xavier was vaguely aware of the harsh glare of the orange neon sign illuminating the bed. From time to time a whiff of frying hamburgers found its way into the room. There was a dull, distant roar of engine noise from the traffic passing by out on the Interstate. Somewhere a trucker leaned on his horn. A television blared next door.

None of it mattered. The only thing that mattered was the scent and taste and feel of the woman in Xavier's arms. She loved him.

He reached down and pulled the hem of the peach gown up over Letty's sweetly shaped buttocks, all the way to her waist. Then he caught hold of her silken thighs and parted them until she was sitting astride him.

Bracing herself with her palms flattened against his chest, Letty gasped and looked down at him.

"Xavier?"

He smiled, reached up and plucked off her glasses and set them down on the dresser beside the bed. Then he slid his hands slowly up along the insides of her legs to where the womanly wet heat awaited him. When he found her slowly with his fingers she closed her eyes and shuddered. Her reaction electrified all his senses.

"Letty, you make me feel like the most powerful man on the face of the earth." He lifted her slightly away from him and then eased her down onto his heavily engorged manhood. The gossamer fabric of the nightgown foamed around his thighs and drifted across his flat stomach.

Xavier urged her gently downward, filling her slowly and surely with himself.

Letty sucked in her breath as she adjusted to him. Xavier luxu-

riated in the sensations ripping through him. He had to set his teeth
to keep from rushing the climax.

"You feel so good," he muttered, his voice hoarse and rasping
with sexual tension. "So good." He lifted his hips experimentally.
He could feel her clinging all along the length of his shaft. His
head whirled.

"Oh, Xavier, *please.*"

"Yes," he said through his teeth. *"Yes."*

He guided her into the rhythm and she responded with everything that was in her. Xavier closed his eyes as he surged into her
again and again.

She cried out softly and trembled in his grasp. He opened his
eyes to watch the play of emotion across her expressive face as
she found her release. Xavier thought he had never seen anything
so glorious in his life. She loved him even though she thought he
was on the run from a past he could not tell her about.

She loved all of him, past and present.

He felt the last of her gentle, rippling climax begin to fade and
then he let himself go, driving himself deeply into her one last
time. His guttural, half-stifled shout blended with the sounds from
outside.

Xavier tightened his arms around Letty and held her close
against his sweat-dampened chest as she collapsed against him.
When he opened his eyes a while later he found himself staring up
at the patterns created by the orange neon glow on the ceiling.

He thought he could see his future and his past in those patterns.
And for the first time, they were joined together in a way that at
last felt right.

LETTY STIRRED beneath the covers, instinctively exploring with one
big toe for Xavier's muscled leg. She frowned into the pillow when
she did not discover it.

That was when she realized she could hear him talking somewhere. She turned amid the sheets and yawned.

"Xavier?"

"Over here, honey. Just a second."

She opened her eyes and saw that he was sitting at the small
table, talking into the phone. He was dressed only in his trousers,
his chest bare. His hair was still rumpled from sleep. He gave her
a quick, intimate smile and then went back to his conversation.

"That's right, it's all over, Hawk. Leave poor Molly in peace. And don't forget, we'll be expecting you at the wedding." Xavier paused, listening. "Damn right, it's going to be formal. And since you're going to be best man, you'd better start shopping for a tux. What?... You better believe it. First-class, all the way. So long. I'll talk to you later." He hung up the phone.

Letty struggled to assimilate the meaning of the mysterious conversation. "Hawk? As in Hawkbridge Investigations? Xavier, what's going on here?"

Xavier leaned back in the chair, legs wide apart and ate her up with his eyes. "Don't move. I'm coming right back to bed in a minute but first I just want to look at you."

She held up a hand. "Hold it right there, Augustine. What was that call all about? Hawkbridge Investigations is the firm you hired to run that background check on me. Any connections to the person on the phone?"

"Yes."

"Well? Why are you talking to that outfit again? Why did you tell whoever it was that we're going to have a formal wedding?"

"Because we are. Just as I planned all along. The man I was talking to is a friend of mine. The best one I've got. His name is Hawkbridge but everyone calls him Hawk."

"You said something about leaving Molly alone. He's the one who's been terrorizing her on the computer?"

"He was just trying to stall her while I sorted things out on this end." Xavier smiled with satisfaction. "But we've got everything sorted out now, don't we?"

Letty scowled as a vague suspicion rose in her mind. "Xavier, are you playing some kind of game with me?"

"Not exactly. Well, maybe. In a way. It's a little difficult to explain, Letty. But I'm going to try over breakfast."

She reached for her glasses and put them on. Her intuition told her something was very wrong here. "You will explain now, please."

He grinned lazily. "I'd rather wait. I've got more interesting things to do at the moment." He stood up and started to unsnap the fastening of his trousers.

Letty tensed. "Sit down, please. I want the explanation now,

Xavier. I don't like this feeling that something's been going on behind my back."

He studied her briefly, amusement still edging his hard mouth. "What the hell. Why not? Might as well get it over and done." He sat down again, one arm resting casually on the table. He rubbed his jaw thoughtfully. "This is a little complicated."

"Don't worry about the complexity," she retorted. "I'm quite bright."

He grinned. "That's right, you are, aren't you? Ph.D. and everything."

"Is it so difficult to remember?" she asked very sweetly. "Perhaps you keep forgetting because I have this nasty habit of making a fool out of myself around you?"

"Whoa. Take it easy, honey. I never said that."

"Tell me why you were on the phone first thing this morning to that man named Hawk."

"I told you why. I'm calling him off the case. I no longer need him to stall Molly." Xavier leaned forward, his eyes growing serious. "It's a long story, Letty, but I'll try to keep it short because it's not a very interesting story."

"Suppose you start with who you really are."

"I really am Xavier Augustine."

"Legally?"

"Very legally. I told you, I changed my name ten years ago. Perfectly legal."

She stared at him. "Why?"

He sighed. "Because my life was a mess, my career was in ruins and my fiancée, who had played me for a chump, had just run off with the man I had been working for. On top of that, I had come very close to taking the rap in a case of fraud. I damn near went to jail, Letty. My reputation was in shreds. There was no way I could salvage it. So I walked away from my past and started fresh under a new name."

"My God."

"Yeah." His smile turned wry. "Hawk was a friend. The only one I had left when it was all over. He runs a firm that handles investigations and security matters for business. He knows how to pull apart someone's past. That means he also knows how to construct a new one."

"And he did that for you?"

"He helped me build up a new identity after I changed my name. He also set up some computer traps and triggers in certain major data banks used for credit checks so that he'd get a warning if anyone ever started prying to closely into my background. Having someone discover the truth about my past could have seriously jeopardized my new business relationships. Once you've been tainted in a fraud case, it's impossible to convince clients you're clean."

"So he was alerted when Molly started checking on you?"

Xavier nodded. "Right away. He called me while we were at the Revelers' convention and asked me what I wanted to do. When I realized you were behind the check, I told him to stall. I didn't want you finding out about my background at that stage."

"You were afraid I wouldn't approve? Is that it? Xavier, how could you think that?"

"You have to look at this from my point of view," he said patiently. "You're a classy lady."

"Oh, for pity's sake..."

"It's true. You've got it, honey. The real thing. Not flash and glitz, the kind of class anyone can buy, but *real* class. You're a lady in the old-fashioned sense of the word. You come from a whole different world than the one I hail from. You've got a fine education, a clean, respectable past, a good reputation. You've got the respect and admiration of others in your field. And on top of everything, you're very nice."

"Nice?" Letty was appalled. "That's all you can find to say about me? I'm *nice?*"

Xavier paused, obviously searching for the right words. "You're kind to people. A good friend. People trust you. You're honorable. You've got integrity."

"I sound like a Boy Scout," Letty said in disgust. "I keep telling you I'm not that virtuous," she snapped. "Never mind. Keep talking."

Irritation flashed in his glance. "You know what your problem is? You take it for granted."

"Take what for granted?"

"Your good name. The respect people have for you. The whole bit. You've always had it, so you assume it's the norm. But it wasn't. Not for me, at any rate." He ran a hand through his hair.

"Damn. There were times when I wanted respect so badly I could taste it. I would have paid any price for it."

"What are you trying to say?" Letty asked quietly.

"I was born on what they used to call the wrong side of the tracks. My parents split up when I was three years old. I never saw my old man again after he left. My mother waited tables to support me. I started getting into trouble the day I realized people judged her by her clothes and her background and the kind of car we drove. It was my way of fighting back. I wouldn't let anyone get away with treating her like dirt."

"Oh, Xavier..."

"I was into one scrape after another at school and had a couple of brushes with the law. Then my mother died in my senior year of high school and I dropped out. I never even finished high school, Letty."

"You're self-educated. So what?"

"That's only the beginning," he told her. "The worst is yet to come. I finally landed a job in the mail room of a small investment firm in Southern California. I worked my tail off to get noticed and within six months I was out of the mail room and working as an assistant in one of the offices. After that there was no stopping me. Once on board, I didn't waste time. I had a flair for that kind of thing. I learned fast and I was willing to work twenty-four hours a day. The boss was a red-hot entrepreneurial type. He didn't care about anything except the bottom line and I always delivered."

"So you moved up fast?"

"Very fast. The money started rolling in. I'd never seen so much money in my whole life. And along with the money came respect and that was even better. People knew I was successful and they admired me for it. It was a heady thing, Letty. For the first time in my life, I was making it."

"What went wrong?"

"Along with the money and the respect came a very beautiful, very sophisticated woman named Constance Malton. I'd ever seen anything like her. She was the perfect Southern California dream made flesh. She knew more about life in the fast lane than you could ever hope to learn, Letty, even if you devoted your whole life to the project. Hell, I think she was born in the fast lane, although I sure didn't realize it at the time."

Letty bristled. "I see."

Xavier smiled indulgently. "Believe me, honey, you aren't the type. Hell, your idea of fast living is to run off to a convention of history buffs and get yourself kidnapped by a bunch of folks wearing medieval costumes."

Letty felt suddenly extremely naive. "You must have found it awfully amusing when I told you I intended to become a more exciting sort of woman."

"No, Letty, I was not amused. I was angry with myself for having made you think you had to change, though."

"What happened to your Southern California dream girl?"

"We were going to get married. Had it all planned. Just as soon as my boss concluded a monster land deal he was working on. In the meantime I had to handle the office." Xavier's eyes hardened. "He pulled it off, all right. And as soon as my boss had stashed the money in a Swiss bank, he and my fiancée left for foreign climes. The government walked into my office before I'd even realized I'd been set up to take the fall."

"It was an illegal deal?"

"It was a very complicated piece of fraud. A scam. I was set up by my fiancée and my boss to look guilty. Some wealthy, powerful people got taken and when the smoke cleared, I was the only one left around to prosecute. I was innocent. I'd had no idea of what was going on with the land deal. But before it was all over I spent everything I had on lawyers trying to clear myself. I managed to do it. Then I found it didn't really matter. Everyone still thought I was guilty."

"You couldn't shake the stigma of having been connected to the fraud, is that it?"

Xavier nodded. "That's it. The fact that I was found innocent of all charges didn't seem to mean anything. My business reputation had been shot to hell."

"So you started over."

"With Hawk's help," Xavier agreed. "He also helped me finish things."

"What does that mean?"

Xavier paused a beat and then said deliberately, "I finally figured out a way to bait a trap for Constance and my ex-boss. I needed Hawk's expertise. He helped me put the plan together, helped me pull it off. We lured them back to the States with a deal that was too good to be true. They fell for the setup and the Feds were waiting.''

Letty shivered at the ice in his voice. "So you got your revenge on them."

"Did you think I'd let them get away with what they had done?" Xavier asked softly.

"No," Letty said. Xavier would have been implacable in his vengeance. Just like any medieval knight in shining armor. She turned that over in her mind for a minute. "Why did you feel you had to run an investigation on me?"

Xavier exhaled slowly. "If I'd had the sense to check Constance Malton out earlier on, I would have discovered that she was a professional conartist. She'd lured more than one male to his financial doom. I was very young and desperate to prove I could succeed. That made me easy pickings for her. After Constance, I swore I would never let another woman set me up for a fall."

Letty pondered the tale. "So what it basically comes down to is you had to be certain I wasn't another Constance Malton before you asked me to marry you."

"Can you blame me?" Xavier asked softly.

That did it. Letty leapt off the bed and grabbed her robe. "Yes, damn you, Xavier Augustine, or whatever your name is. I do blame you." She raced around the small room, stuffing her things into her suitcase. "You've made a fool of me right from the start. You don't love me, you love my pristine reputation and my naiveté. You've manipulated me for the past few days. You even tricked me into thinking you were in danger from something that had happened in your past."

"Letty, honey..." he began soothingly.

"When I think of how you must have laughed to yourself yesterday after I told you I was going to go into hiding with you, I could scream." She yanked on her jeans and grabbed a shirt. Then she stepped into her loafers.

"Letty, are we going to go through this scene again?" Xavier asked coldly. "Because if so, you might as well know I'm tired of it. This has gone far enough."

"I agree completely." She headed for the door, suitcase in hand.

"Letty, come back here." He realized belatedly that she was actually going to leave. He got up and went to the door as she opened it and went out. "I said, come back here."

"Forget it."

"What do you think you're doing?" he yelled after her. "You told me you loved me, by God."

"I do." She opened the car door and threw her suitcase inside. Then she slid into the front seat. "The old Letty would have forgiven you instantly, taken pity on your traumatized past and thrown herself into your arms. But this is the new Letty and I've had it with being sweet and understanding."

"Come back here."

"Pay attention, Xavier Augustine. Until you decide you love me, *me,* not my virtuous past or my stalwart integrity or my respectable academic reputation, you can forget any idea of marrying me or of having an affair with me." She turned the key in the ignition.

"Listen to me, honey."

"I don't feel like listening to you. You're not saying anything I want to hear. Do you know you've never once told me you loved me? Not once." She shoved the gear lever into reverse and stamped her foot down on the pedal.

The car roared out of the parking lot.

Xavier stood in the doorway for a long time after the little car had disappeared. Then he turned back into the room and packed up his belongings.

When he was ready he walked out to the road that led to the northbound on-ramp and stuck out his thumb. Fifteen minutes passed before a big rig slowed to a halt. Xavier recognized it as one that had spent the night in the motel parking lot alongside Letty's car.

The trucker watched as Xavier opened the door and climbed up into the cab. "That your little gal I saw leaving like a bat out of hell a few minutes ago?"

"Yeah. Thanks for stopping."

"Sure." The trucker shook his head as he cranked the eighteen-wheeler onto the Interstate and headed north toward Portland. "Got yourself a little domestic crisis, I take it?"

"Uh-huh."

"Sorry to hear that. She important to you?"

"More important than she knows," Xavier said. "But it looks like I haven't done a very good job of telling her."

The trucker nodded sympathetically. "The thing about women is that they like to hear the words, you know?"

"I gave her plenty of words but they weren't the right ones."

The trucker shot him a curious glance. "You got 'em straight now?"

"Yeah. I've got 'em straight now."

CHAPTER ELEVEN

LETTY GAZED MOROSELY down at the anchovy and onion pizza that occupied the center of the table. "I shouldn't have done it, Molly. I was an idiot to do it. It was too big a risk. He'll never come after me now. He has too much pride. I shouldn't have pushed him that far."

"Why did you?" Molly helped herself to a slice of pizza.

Letty sighed. "Finding out he'd let me make a fool of myself by thinking I was saving him from his past was, well, it was the last straw. He doesn't love me, Molly. Not really."

"I wouldn't be too sure of that."

"No, it's the truth. I have to face facts. He was making me prove myself again, just as he did when he had me investigated. He enjoyed watching me try to rescue him. I tell you, Molly, I'm sick and tired of proving my love for Xavier Augustine. He can damn well prove his love for me this time around."

"How's he going to do that?"

"By apologizing and telling me he loves me. Do you realize he's never actually said it?" Letty shook crushed hot peppers on the pizza. "Not once, damn it."

"You'd believe him if he did say it?" Molly asked curiously.

Letty was astounded at the question. "Of course. Xavier would never make a commitment like that unless he meant it."

"I see. Well, he's been awfully persistent for a man who's not in love," Molly said thoughtfully.

"It's not love, it's a constitutional dislike of having his carefully laid plans thrown into disarray," Letty explained. "I imagine it's the businessman in him. He's accustomed to getting what he wants. And he doesn't always play by the rules."

"You're overlooking something here," Molly said. "If he still wants you after everything he's been through, he must see you as more than just a business acquisition. Seems to me you've done plenty of things in the past few days to make him think twice about your suitability as a wife."

"This time I've gone too far. After the way I abandoned him at that motel this morning, he's not going to want me any longer. He'll wash his hands of me and look elsewhere for a suitable wife. I just know it. I blew my last chance to make the relationship work." Letty sprinkled a few more peppers on her half of the pizza.

"Wait and see."

"No, it's over. Finished. I should have stayed there and talked instead of running off like that. But the truth is, I've had it with being made to look like a fool."

Molly made a face as she chewed pizza. "If it's any consolation, I'm not feeling like the sharpest brain on campus at the moment, either. Not after I realized how my own investigation had been monitored and sabotaged right from the start by that mysterious Hawk person."

Letty looked up. "Did he finally identify himself to you?"

"Uh-huh. I turned on the computer this morning and there was a message from him. The first one he's signed."

"What did it say?"

"It said 'see you at the wedding.' That was my first inkling that I'd been had." Molly finished the bite of pizza and reached for her wine. "I tell you, Letty, if I ever meet that jerk in person I'm going to have a few well-chosen words to say to him."

"Don't worry," Letty said. "You won't be seeing him at the wedding. There isn't going to be one." A shadow fell over the table and she glanced up quickly, hoping against hope. She stifled her disappointment when she saw Sheldon Peabody smiling genially.

He was wearing a pair of artfully faded jeans, a flower-print shirt unbuttoned halfway down his chest and several gold chains around his neck.

"Well, well, well. I believe this is where I came in." The gold chains glinted in the dim light as Sheldon sat down without waiting to be asked. "You two still have lousy taste in pizza, I see." He signaled for a beer.

"You don't have to eat any of it," Molly told him.

"Don't worry, I won't." Sheldon beamed at them as the beer was set down in front of him. "But to show you what a great sport I am, I'll pay for it."

Letty and Molly stared at him in shock.

Letty recovered first. "You'll pay for it? You're going to buy us dinner?"

"Are you feeling all right, Sheldon?" Molly asked.

"I have never felt better in my life," Sheldon declared. "I'm celebrating." He hoisted his glass of beer. "Join me in a salute to the dazzling new future that awaits yours truly."

"What dazzling new future?" Letty demanded.

"Does this have anything to do with the missing buttons on your shirt and all those gold chains?" Molly inquired.

"It does, indeed. I am going off to find my destiny in Lala Land, ladies. I am blowing this two-bit burg," Sheldon announced grandly. "I'm shaking the dust of Tipton Cove from my feet and heading for life in the fast-forward lane where I belong. You may congratulate me, my dears. I have been invited to accept a position on the history faculty of Rothwell College. Full professor with tenure."

Letty stared at him. "Do I detect the fine hand of Jennifer Thorne?"

"Ah, yes. Dear little Jennifer." Sheldon inclined his head in acknowledgment. "The lovely Ms. Thorne has decided I would make a great scholarly contribution to Rothwell and she prevailed upon her father to so inform the trustees of the college. Once Mr. Thorne let it be known that there would be no more Thorne endowments for the college unless they made the appointment, they fell all over themselves making me an offer I couldn't refuse."

Molly grinned slowly. "Congratulations, Sheldon. Something tells me you'll do very well down in Southern California."

"Listen," Sheldon leaned forward to announce with exuberant confidence, "I was born for Southern California."

Letty smiled. "Good luck, Sheldon," she said sincerely.

"Thank you, my dear. I want you to know you are at least partially responsible for my good fortune. Jennifer Thorne was quite taken with the way I decked Augustine at the banquet that first night. She says she's been looking for a man with real machismo."

"And since you're looking for a woman with connections, the match should be a perfect one," Molly murmured.

Sheldon chose to ignore that. "Speaking of our dear Saint Augustine, where is he?"

"Right here," Xavier said from directly behind him. "And I

want everyone to know upfront that I am not feeling in a really saintly mood.''

Letty jumped at the sound of his deep, rough voice. *"Xavier!"* She looked up at him with undisguised longing and was startled by what she saw.

Xavier needed a shave. He had always reminded her of a well-groomed gangster but tonight the dark shadow of a beard gave him an even more dangerous look. He was wearing the expensive trousers he'd had on this morning and one of his beautifully tailored white shirts. But both garments had dust and grease stains on them and they were distinctly rumpled. There were scuff marks on his handmade shoes. He looked like what Letty had briefly assumed him to be, a man with an unsavory past.

"How did you get back?" Molly asked with open curiosity.

"I hitched a ride with a trucker as far as Portland and then rented a car to drive over here to the coast. It's been a long trip, to put it mildly. I have suffered. Nothing but lousy truckstop coffee and greasy truckstop hamburgers for the entire trip."

"Oh, dear." Letty turned red. "I'm sorry, Xavier."

"You should be." He sat down.

"No offense, but you look like hell, Augustine." Sheldon smiled cheerfully.

"Peabody, if you have any sense at all, you will keep your mouth shut," Xavier told him.

Sheldon shrugged good-naturedly and leaned back in his chair to sip his beer.

Xavier turned to Letty who was toying with a slice of pizza. "Now that I've finally caught up with you at last, we are going to have a short talk."

He was going to say goodbye, once and for all. Letty just knew it. "Xavier, please, I know I shouldn't have run off like that this morning. I really am sorry. I realize you probably don't understand and it's hard to explain, but I—"

"Open your mouth, Letty," Xavier ordered calmly. He picked up a slice of pizza.

Letty's mouth dropped open more in surprise rather than in response to the command. "Huh?"

Xavier inserted the tip of the pizza wedge between her teeth. "Close your mouth."

Letty obeyed, bemused.

"Now, let's get one thing clear before we go through any more chase scenes," Xavier said. He folded his arms on the table and narrowed his eyes. "I love you."

Letty's eyes widened and she struggled to speak around the pizza. "Youff douff?" She chewed and swallowed hurriedly.

"Yes." Xavier inserted more pizza before she could finish the first bite, effectively silencing her again. "Nod your head if you still love me."

Letty nodded frantically.

"In spite of my past?"

Letty nodded again, wishing she had not put quite so many hot peppers on the pizza.

"What past is that?" Sheldon asked.

Xavier paid no heed to the question. His eyes were fixed on Letty's face. "I am sorry I didn't tell you everything right from the start. My only excuse is that I was afraid of losing you. You have my word there won't be any more secrets between us, ever. Good enough?"

"Yeff." Letty swallowed another bite of pizza. When Xavier made a commitment, you knew he'd stand by it. "Oh, yes, Xavier."

"Good. That's settled, then. On to other things. I want your solemn vow that you will never again abandon me in a cheap motel on the Interstate. That was an extremely tacky thing to do, Letty."

Still struggling with a mouthful of pizza, Letty started to nod and then shook her head quickly.

Xavier smiled a little dangerously. "Is that a yes or a no?"

Letty swallowed the pizza. "It's a yes. I mean a no. I mean I won't abandon you in any more cheap motels on the Interstate."

"This is beginning to sound more interesting by the minute," Molly observed. "Does that vow include not abandoning him in luxury resort hotels, too?"

Xavier again ignored the interruption, his entire attention on Letty who just stared back at him, knowing her heart was probably mirrored in her eyes.

"I think," Xavier said coolly, "that we have been through enough fun and games. I am now officially declaring this case of bridal jitters at an end."

"Oh, Xavier, are you sure?"

"I've been sure since the beginning." Xavier got to his feet. His mouth edged upward at the corner. "Come on, honey, we have things to do."

"Like what?" Letty got to her feet.

"Like addressing wedding invitations. But first things first." Xavier caught her around her hips and tossed her lightly over his shoulder.

"Xavier, for heaven's sake. Everyone's watching," Letty gasped, torn between giggles and outrage.

Xavier glanced at a grinning Molly. "By the way, Molly, Hawk says to send his regards and to tell you he intends to go hunting soon."

Molly's grin turned instantly into a thunderous scowl. "I do not approve of hunting wild animals."

"I don't think wild animals are the quarry Hawk has in mind," Xavier said. "Good night, Molly. So long, Peabody. I hear you're going to Southern California. Something tells me you'll like it down there."

"Bound to be a lot more exciting than Tipton Cove," Sheldon agreed.

"I wouldn't be too sure about that," Xavier said. He swung around and strode through the crowded restaurant with Letty over his shoulder. A cheer went up as the diners realized what was happening.

"Hey, look," a young woman sitting at a nearby table remarked to her companion as Letty was carried past. "Isn't that Professor Conroy?"

"Yeah," her friend said in obvious amazement. "It is. Who would have thought she was the type to get herself carried off over a man's shoulder? Saint Augustine's shoulder, no less."

"He doesn't look too saintly right now," the young woman observed. "In fact, he looks kind of exciting."

"You know," Letty said to Xavier as she craned her head to wave farewell to Molly, "things like this never used to happen to the old Letty Conroy."

Xavier laughed as he carried her outside to the waiting Jaguar. The sound echoed through the night, deep and rich and full of male happiness.

A LONG TIME LATER, Letty stirred amid the tangled sheets of her bed and stroked her fingertips along Xavier's smoothly muscled shoulder.

"When did you know for certain that you loved me?" she asked.

"I knew you were just biding your time until you asked that question. Couldn't resist, could you?" Xavier propped himself up on one elbow and looked down at her. His green eyes gleamed in the shadows.

"Well, you didn't love me at first," she insisted.

"What makes you so sure of that?" He put his hand on her hip.

"The fact that you had me investigated. The fact that you didn't try to make love to me for a long while." Letty started counting on her fingers. "The fact that you originally selected me for the great honor of being your bride based on my dull past and equally uneventful present. Shall I go on?"

"No." He snagged her fingers and trapped them on the bed. Then he studied her thoughtfully for a long moment. "You're wrong, you know."

She smiled gently. "It's all right, Xavier. You don't have to pretend it was love at first sight the way it was on my part. As long as you're sure you love me now, I don't care."

"I think it was love at first sight." He smiled at her skeptical expression. "It's true, Letty. I'll admit I didn't label it love in the beginning. To be bluntly honest about it, I wasn't thinking in those terms. I was just keeping an eye out for the woman who met all my specifications. The minute I was introduced to you, I knew you were the one."

Letty gave a choked laugh. "So I met your specifications and you noticed right off? That's not what I'd call falling in love at first sight. You chose your bride the same way you would have if you'd been living in medieval times and you know it. You wanted a suitable wife."

"I found her. And then she made me woo and win her. Which she had every right to do." Xavier drew her fingers to his lips and kissed them warmly. "I found myself chasing after her, doing battle with rivals for her hand and rescuing her. Then it began to dawn on me that what I was feeling might be what people call love. I knew it for certain when you decided to save me from my past."

"Really?" Letty glowed.

"Really." Xavier's eyes were very intent now. "No one's ever tried to rescue me before, Letty."

"I felt like such a fool when I realized it was all a game," she confided.

"It wasn't a game. Not the way you mean. I was indulging myself in the luxury of knowing you cared that much." He kissed her fingers again. "It was very reassuring. Men like a little assurance, too, you know. Forgive me?"

"Yes." She was feeling wonderfully magnanimous at the moment. "Especially since I've decided that the investigation you had your friend Hawk carry out was a good thing in the end. After all, if it hadn't been for that, I might still be leading the same uneventful life I've been leading for the past twenty-nine years. As it is, I'm a whole new person. I owe it all to you."

Xavier groaned. "At the risk of repeating myself, I would just like to point out one more time that I was perfectly content with the old you."

"Don't be silly. I'm sure I'm a lot more interesting these days." Letty kissed him lingeringly on the mouth.

"That's not what I was thinking when I found myself hitchhiking a ride out on the Interstate." Xavier cupped her breast in his hand.

"No? What were you thinking?" She kissed his throat.

"I was thinking that I should have fulfilled your craving for a taste of the wild side a lot earlier in our relationship by taking you to bed. I think if I'd done that, I could have saved myself a lot of exhausting effort."

"But you're so good at chasing around after me," she murmured.

"Making love to you is a lot more interesting." Xavier eased her onto her back and came down on top of her. "Something tells me I am never going to get tired of it."

"What about the rest of those wedding invitations we're supposed to be addressing?"

"First thing in the morning," he vowed. Then he clasped her wrists in his hands and moved them up above her head, stretching her out beneath him. His mouth closed over hers, hot, possessive and loving.

Letty felt her whole body quicken once more beneath his touch. "I love you, Xavier," she whispered.

"I love you, too. And the next time you want proof, just ask, okay?"

"I'll do that," she said with a soft smile.

But there was no need for proof. Their love glowed between them, clear and bright and strong enough to last a lifetime.

Montana Man
Barbara Delinsky

CHAPTER ONE

He was a cowboy. Lily Danziger wasn't blinded enough by the falling snow to miss the faint bow of his long legs or the telltale Stetson on his head. Nor was she troubled enough by the worsening weather to ignore his sheer size. He was a mountain of a man, wrapped in a sheepskin jacket with its heavy collar up against the wind, and he was flagging her down.

She'd never picked up a hitchhiker before. It was lunacy. Just the week before she'd read that a huge percentage of hitchhikers were wanted by the law for one reason or another.

She didn't want to consider whether this one was wanted, or, if so, for what, because her predicament was precarious, to say the least. She was miles and miles from nowhere; hers was the only car on the road; the driving was getting more difficult with the thickening snow; and she was growing more worried by the minute.

What it boiled down to, she decided in the brief time that elapsed from when she first spotted the cowboy's waving hands to when she gingerly applied the brake, was that she was willing to overlook the danger of taking a stranger into her car in exchange for the small comfort it might bring. She'd been alone for the past eight months, but that aloneness was totally different from what she felt now. If her car slid off the road, there would be no one to see, no one to hear, no one to help.

Except perhaps this cowboy.

Her sporty Audi came to such a slow and muted halt that she half wondered if it was final. The thought didn't help her peace of mind much. Nor did the fact that the cowboy had begun to lope toward her even before she'd stopped.

He tugged at the door handle, then bent over to peer into the car, gave an impatient knock and pointed to the door lock.

For the space of a shaky breath, Lily hesitated. Up close and half-covered with snow, the man looked even more formidable than he had before. She thought of the risk. Then she pushed it from mind, because she couldn't *not* open the door, she realized. Not in

as remote and hilly a spot in a storm like this. For humanitarian
reasons alone, she had to let him in. He hadn't had his thumb in
the air. He'd been waving her down as though something were
wrong. Something *had* to be wrong for him to be out there at all.

Reaching across the passenger's seat, she released the lock, then
returned to her side and watched him open the door, toss a duffel
bag onto the floor in back, brush the worst of the snow from his
jacket with hands that looked half-frozen, then fold his large frame
into the seat beside hers. With the slamming of the door behind
him, she felt the chill he'd brought in. Casting a worried glance
toward the back seat, she pulled her own thick parka closer against
her neck.

"Thought you were going to change your mind," he muttered
in a voice that came from deep in his chest. He alternately rubbed
his hands together and held them out toward the nearby heating
vent.

"I almost did," she said, hoping that it would serve as a warning
that she was on her guard. She couldn't see much beyond the collar
of his coat, couldn't see whether his features boded well or ill.
"What were you doing out there?"

"Trying to beat the storm, same as you." He tossed his head
toward a point beyond the hood of her car. "I might've made it if
I hadn't gone off the road."

She had guessed he'd been dropped there by someone else, since
she didn't see his car. "You were driving?"

"Is there any other way of passing through this godforsaken
place?"

She thought of horseback, then thought again. "Did you skid?"

He snorted. "Fell asleep at the wheel. My car's nose-down
against a tree. There's no hope of getting it back up in weather
like this."

Peering harder through the swing of her windshield wipers, Lily
finally made out the tail end of a car sticking up in the snow. Its
presence vouched for the cowboy's story, and while that relieved
her, she couldn't help but stare at the car. It was headed down what
looked to be a steep ravine.

"You were lucky there was a tree to stop you."

He grunted. Taking the Stetson from his head, he opened the
door again, whacked the snow off the hat, stuffed the hat back on
his head and slammed the door. Then he tucked his hands in his

pockets and slid a little lower in the seat, looking for all intents and purposes as though he planned to resume the sleep his mishap had disturbed.

To Lily's knowledge, he hadn't looked at her once, which was just fine with her. She didn't need charm and conversation as much as a bodyguard. As out of place as a cowboy was in northern Maine, this one would serve the purpose if she got stuck and needed a push.

Aware that the storm was getting no better, she shifted into gear, carefully pulled back into the center of the road and, gripping the steering wheel with both hands, drove on.

"How long were you out there?" she asked.

He shifted his legs, which were too long for the space allotted them. His voice sounded just as pressed. "Better than an hour."

"And no other cars went by?"

He made a sound that was halfway between a grunt and a dry laugh. She thought he was going to leave it at that when he muttered, "Gotta be mad to drive in weather like this."

Or desperate, Lily thought. She wondered which of the two he was. "Where are you headed?"

"North."

That much was obvious, she thought, and hadn't realized she'd said it aloud until he muttered, "So why did you ask?"

She shot him a short, sharp look and decided that he had a chip on his shoulder, which no doubt accounted for his breadth. And while she wasn't one to tackle chips single-handedly, she'd vowed when she left Hartford that she was going to be strong, and being strong meant sticking up for herself. Though she hadn't had much practice at it, now was as good a time as any to start.

"Because," she said, taking a breath, "I was hoping you'd say you were on your way to Quebec to do something innocent, like visit your mother. From my point of view, that would be preferable to your heading for the Canadian border to escape the State Police or the FBI or the DEA or someone like that."

"I'm not running from the law." He passed off the statement with such utter indifference that Lily believed him.

"*Are* you on your way to see your mother?"

"No."

"A friend?"

"No."

"Then you must be here on business." She wanted to believe it. A business trip was respectable.

"You could say that," he answered, sounding more weary. Tugging his hat low over his eyes, he set his head against the headrest in a silent declaration that he was done talking.

For the time being Lily settled for the little she'd learned. She had her bodyguard if she needed him, though what she needed most just then was to concentrate fully on the road.

She drove on. Ten minutes seemed like twenty, twenty like an hour. The snow continued its steady fall, mounting on the car, the road, the surrounding landscape until things began to blur together. She drove at a slow pace, which was as fast as she safely could, and even then her rear wheels spun out every so often before regaining traction. Her fingers grew tighter on the wheel, then tighter still when a gust of wind rocked the car. Her eyes strained to see the road. She held her breath for long stretches, as though that would enhance her control.

Intermittently she glanced at the man beside her. He seemed to sleep for a while, then waken with a small jolt, then stare out the front window for a bit before falling asleep again. Though she couldn't see much more than his eyes in the narrow strip between his hat and his collar, the way his brows hugged them was ominous.

She wasn't surprised when after the car fishtailed wildly enough to shake him from his sleep, he swore. "Damn car's too light for this kind of travel."

"I'm sorry," she said quietly. "If I'd realized it was going to snow, I'd have taken the dogsled."

Ignoring her sarcasm, he grumbled, "Didn't you hear the forecast?"

"Obviously not."

"So you set out into the woods in the middle of January without a thought to the weather."

"I gave a thought to it. I just didn't know what it was going to be." Not that it would have mattered, she knew. She'd had to get away fast. The weather had been the least of her worries.

"Real smart," he remarked.

Lily was thinking it was a case of the pot calling the kettle black, but she didn't bother to say it. There seemed no point, particularly when driving demanded so much of her attention. If anything, the snow was gusting harder. Her windshield wipers were working double-time, yet the glass never seemed to quite clear.

When the road took a sudden turn, she managed to negotiate it with only a small skid—through which, a nervous glance told her, the cowboy slept. Within minutes she handled another turn, and, to her relief, the car began to descend. She figured the lower altitudes would bring an easing of the snow, and, if not that, certainly a return to some form of civilization. She wasn't asking for a thriving metropolis, just a place to take shelter until the storm passed. She wasn't desperate enough to risk life and limb, yet she seemed to be coming closer to that by the minute.

A small motel would be ideal. In the absence of a motel, she'd happily pay for the use of a compassionate Mainer's spare room. Hell, she'd settle for a gas station, if that was all she'd be able to find. She needed gas, anyway.

Almost incidentally her gaze flicked to the gas gauge. Her eyes widened, then returned to the road with greater intensity. Finding a gas station was suddenly her first priority.

To her dismay there was no sign of a gas station, or any other relic of civilization along the road, and where she would have preferred to coast downhill, she had to keep her foot on the gas to propel the car through the drifts. Worse, with each passing minute, the road seemed to narrow. If she didn't know better, she'd have said she was on a logging road in the middle of a forest.

That was impossible, of course, she told herself. Just to prove it, she fished her road map from a pocket on the door. But she couldn't take her eyes from the road long enough to study it. One false move and she'd find her own car hopelessly ground against a tree.

As though goaded by her thoughts, the Audi suddenly slid sideways on the road. She twisted the wheel in an attempt to stop the slide, but the shoulder of the road had angled. After a glide that was brief and utterly silent in contrast to the uproar inside her, the car came to a jarring halt against a cluster of dense, low-growing pines.

The cowboy awoke with a start.

"No problem," Lily said. Determined to ward off panic, she shifted into reverse and stepped on the gas, shifted back into drive and did the same, then repeated the procedure several times.

"We're not moving," he stated.

"Give me a minute. One of the tires is bound to catch on something."

"Or get buried deeper." He swore, then growled, "Leave it to a woman," and opened his door. "Put it in reverse," he ordered as he climbed out. "I'll push."

Lily was grateful she hadn't had to ask, grateful that he seemed willing to take charge. She readily obeyed him, all the while fighting off the terrifying thoughts that seemed to be rushing headlong her way.

Bracing his hands on the front of her car, the cowboy pushed when she gunned the gas. The car moved a bit, but slid right back to where it had been the instant he let up the pressure. He gestured for her to try again. She did. The car moved a bit more, then a bit more. It was only a matter of time before they were back on the road, she told herself, grasping at fragile threads of hope.

The next time she stepped on the gas, though, the engine sputtered, sputtered some more, then went dead, and those fragile threads snapped. Nervous perspiration beaded on her nose as she repeatedly pumped the gas pedal. She shifted from one gear to the next, praying that anything else was wrong with the car but what she feared.

The passenger's door flew open. "What in the hell's wrong?"

"Nothing's happening!"

He slid into the seat, bringing the snow and cold right along with him, and promptly leaned sideways to study the dashboard.

Lily shrank into the far corner of her seat and waited for his explosion. It didn't take long.

"God*damn*it!" Straightening, he pushed back his hat, turned to glare at her and said in a voice that was low and threatening, "You're out of gas."

His voice wasn't all that was threatening. For the first time, she saw his face, and a darker one she'd never met. Tension radiated from his features—from the lean line of his mouth, his straight nose, the low shelf of his brow. His skin was bronzed, and there were crow's-feet at the corners of his eyes much as she'd have expected of a man who spent a good deal of his life squinting against the sun. But where she'd always assumed cowboys to be mild-mannered sorts, this one wasn't. His eyes were coal black, even darker than the hair that had escaped from his hat to fall in scattered spikes onto his brow. Those coal-black eyes bore into hers.

"I've been looking for a gas station," she argued in her own defense, "but there wasn't one."

"Surprise, surprise."

"I've been looking for a long time."

"Not long enough. Don't you know to gas up before you hit the back roads?"

"I did. I started with a full tank."

"When?"

"This morning."

"Where? New York?"

"Hartford. And I didn't think I was *on* the back roads. The line on the map was thick and black."

His mouth tightened. "Thick and black. So what did you think you were seeing out here? Superhighway? Didn't you begin to wonder when there weren't any other cars on the road?"

"I assumed that's just how Maine roads are."

He nodded. "You assumed that's how Maine roads are." His voice hardened. "Baby, no main road is like this." He shot a scowl through the windshield. "Where the hell are we, anyway?"

Grateful to have something to do, Lily quickly lifted the map from her lap and studied it. "Here, I think," she said, pointing to a thick black line that undulated through northwest Maine.

"You think wrong," the cowboy informed her, "unless you've managed to cover a hundred miles since you picked me up." They both knew she'd come nowhere near that. "I went off the road right about here." He fixed a lean, blunt-tipped finger on a spot some distance from her thick black line.

"But I wasn't supposed to be there at all," Lily protested. Her voice shrank. "I must have missed a turn."

"You must have missed more than one. That's quite a feat."

"I followed the road. Where it turned, I turned."

"You were supposed to stay on the main drag."

"I thought the turns *were* the main drag. In case you haven't noticed, the visibility's awful!"

"That's because we're surrounded by trees."

He seemed to have an answer for everything. She tried a few of her own. "It's because the storm's worsening. And what were you doing when I made those wrong turns? Maybe if you hadn't been sleeping—''

''Goddamned thing doesn't look like much of a road at all,'' he decided, ignoring her accusation. He studied what he could of the landscape.

Lily was beginning to tremble. ''It has to be. I was following *something*.''

''Damned if I know what it was,'' he growled and speared her with a condemning look. ''Damned if I know where we are. Damned if I know how we're gonna be found. You didn't listen to the weather, you didn't get gas, and you didn't bother to stay on the main road. Baby, when you blow it, you really blow it.'' He sat back in his seat, returning his glare to the window. ''Just my luck to be picked up by a spoiled little rich girl.''

Lily had never been that in her life. The irony of his thinking it would have made her laugh, if he hadn't followed up with ''Fancy car, fancy clothes, fancy face—'' he turned his head slowly her way ''—and...no...brains.''

The tension inside her burst into anger. ''I had enough brains to pick you up.''

''No brains there. It was a stupid thing to do. You don't know a thing about me. For all you know, I'm a killer.''

''If that were true, I'd have been dead by now, and I'm not. So where would you be if I hadn't stopped?''

''In someone else's car, safe and warm and on my way north.''

''Or frozen to death by the side of the road.''

''It's not that cold.''

''Good,'' she said, raising her head a notch. ''Then you can get out of my car and walk. If you're in such a rush to get to wherever it is you're going, be my guest. *Hoof* it. You're not much use to me anyway. You couldn't even push my car out of a rut.''

His dark face came closer. ''Rut? You call what we're in a rut?''

She refused to back off. ''Go on. Get out and walk.''

His dark eyes flashed. ''You're the one without the brains, lady. Me, I'm a survivor. I don't go out walking lost in the woods in the middle of a blizzard with night closing in.''

Her bravado faltered. ''Night's not closing in.''

''It's dusk.''

''No. It's only dark because of the trees.''

''It's dusk. Look at the time.''

Lily did. "It's not even four-thirty in the afternoon!"

"Dusk *falls* at four-thirty in the afternoon this time of year."

She swallowed. "It can't!"

"You gonna stop it?"

Her mind raced on. "After dusk comes darkness, and once it's dark, we'll be stuck."

"We *are* stuck. When's that gonna sink in?"

She fought it, though her insides were shaking harder. "Stuck in the snow, but—"

"Stuck out here. Lost. Marooned. Isolated. Cut off from the rest of—"

"Maybe you could try pushing again?" she interrupted, begging and not caring that she did.

"But you've got no gas!" he shouted as though he'd decided she was deaf as well as stupid. In frustration, he slammed a fist against the roof. "I don't believe this. I should've stayed with my own car. Better marooned on the road with myself than on some cow path with a woman—" A sound from the back seat cut him off, and he went utterly still. When the sound came again, he glanced sharply around, and when it continued, he managed a low "What in the hell's that?"

Snapped from oncoming panic, Lily was already dropping the back of her seat. When it was as flat as it would go, she climbed over it to the carrier that was safely strapped behind the cowboy. "It's my baby," she said softly and not at all apologetically. If there was one thing she'd done right in her life, it was giving birth to the small bundle that she now lifted into her arms. "It's okay, Nicki," she murmured softly, gently, more calm than she'd been moments before. Settling in directly behind the driver's seat, she eased the baby's snowsuit back from its face and put a slender fingertip to first one side of the infant's tiny mouth, then the other. "Shhh. Mommy's here." The baby quieted like a charm.

Twisted in his seat, the cowboy stared back at her in disbelief. "A baby?"

"Yes."

"You've got a *baby* in this car?"

She shot him a dry look.

His voice rose a notch, horrified, now, as well as disbelieving. "We're stuck in the middle of nowhere, for the night—maybe longer—and you've got a *baby* in this car?"

Ignoring his prediction, she smiled at Nicki. "I do believe that's what I'm holding."

"How can you say it so *calmly?*"

"How can I not?"

"Aren't you worried?"

Her smile was gone when she looked up at him. "I'm terrified. But it won't do any good to let the baby know it—unless you'd like to listen to her scream for a while."

The cowboy dropped a frown to the bundle in pink. "She'll probably do that anyway."

"Not for long. She's a good baby."

"All babies scream."

"She's a good baby," Lily repeated, but no sooner had she said it when the baby began to whimper. "Oh, honey, what's wrong?" she cooed softly. She clicked her tongue several times and began a gentle rocking motion, but the baby's whimpers were soon full-fledged cries.

"She's hungry," he informed her.

Lily turned her back on him. "I know that."

The baby's cries were small, but so was the car. Lily was used to it. Clearly the cowboy wasn't.

"Well, aren't you going to do something about it?" he demanded. His dark eyes looked a little wild. "Don't you have a bottle or something? Christ, you don't even have any way of warming milk! Didn't you think *any* of this out before you left New York?"

"Hartford. I left Hartford."

"Same difference. So what are you going to do about that baby?"

"Feed her," Lily said. Sitting sideways on the seat facing away from him, she pushed aside the layers she'd been unbuttoning, unhooked her bra and put the baby to her breast.

The silence inside the car was sudden and sweet, as was the gentle tugging created by the baby's suckling. Settling the infant more comfortably in her arms, Lily rested her cheek against the velour upholstery. Outside, the snow whipped the world into a wild frenzy, but she closed herself in a small cocoon with her child.

For the longest time the cowboy said nothing. Lily refused to look up, refused to let him intrude on her private time with Nicki. Nor did she want to be made to feel self-conscious. She wasn't in the habit of nursing the baby in front of people, much less strange men. She kept herself safely angled for privacy, and what the position didn't do, the layers of clothes surrounding her did.

Though she wasn't watching, she clearly felt it when the cowboy finally faced forward. He remained silent for a time. She was beginning to wonder what scathing comment he'd come out with next, when he asked, "How old is she?"

His voice was lower, more civil. Responding to that, Lily said, "Five weeks."

After a short pause came a scathing, "How can you subject a five-week-old child to this?"

She knew he was facing front, looking out at the storm. She didn't have to look to feel the wind. "I think," she said quietly, "that we've been through this before. I had no idea the weather was going to get so bad."

"Why didn't you stop somewhere when the snow began to pile up?"

"There was nowhere to stop. I kept thinking that it might be worse if I turned back. For all I knew, the center of the storm was where I'd come from. Besides, I hadn't passed anything alive for miles, so there was nothing to go back to. I figured there had to be something ahead."

"Might've been if you'd stayed on the main road."

Lily didn't respond. She worked her way through the fold-over mitten of the baby's snowsuit and watched the infant's tiny fingers curl around hers. They were so perfect, those fingers, so small, but perfect. So was the little chin, and the button nose, and the soft gray eyes that held hers.

Lily wondered what those eyes saw. The books she'd read said that during the second month of life those eyes would be unfocused when the baby sucked, that the child couldn't actively look and suck at the same time. Lily wasn't sure she believed it. Her baby's eyes were clear, and she could swear they were focused. Of course, it was possible she was simply seeing her own very focused reflection in them.

Her head shot up when the cowboy suddenly opened the door and started to get out. "Where are you going?" she asked quickly.

"I'm taking a look around while there's still some light left." He slammed the door loudly behind him.

"Go ahead," she said lightly, then whispered to the baby,

"That's fine. We don't need him in here. Now, if he scouts around and happens upon a bustling logging camp, we'll be forever indebted to him." She gently waved the tiny hand that held hers. "What do you think of that idea, Nicki? Hmm? Sound like an adventure?"

Nicki continued to suck at a steady pace. After a bit Lily looked up and around, searching for sign of the cowboy. But the snow was covering increasingly larger portions of the windows, and, to her horror, the light beyond was indeed growing dim.

For a split second, she imagined the cowboy not returning. She imagined being left alone, totally alone in the woods in the storm with Nicki, and she felt chilled to the bone. A disgruntled bear of a man was better than nothing, she realized.

Swallowing away her fear, she said to Nicki, "Whaddaya think? Think he'll find a logging camp out there?"

Nicki broke the suction of her tiny mouth.

"*Are* there logging camps nowadays?" Lily asked in a deliberate singsong as she raised the baby to her shoulder and gently rubbed her back. "It's the middle of January. Would loggers be working through the dead of the winter? I can't imagine it, but you never can tell." She gave several pats. "He'd better find *something* out there, or we could be in big trouble—"

The baby burped.

"That's my girl," Lily said with a grin and transferred the infant to the cradle of her other arm. Normally she'd have taken a minute or two to play at that point, but she wanted to finish nursing before the cowboy returned.

Nicki began to take her time, though. As her stomach filled, she grew increasingly content—which wasn't to say that she was done. Lily knew from experience that if she forced an end to the feeding, there'd be fussing. That—and a weakening sense of relief—was why she didn't so much as move a muscle when the door opened and the cowboy slid back into the car.

It was a minute before he brushed himself off, another before he fit himself satisfactorily into the seat. Still he didn't speak.

Unable to bear the suspense, Lily finally blurted out, "Did you find anything?"

"Woods," he said without turning.

"No camp?"

Apparently he hadn't shared her fantasy. "Camp?" he asked blankly.

"Settlement. Houses. House, singular."

"No."

Her hopes sank. She looked down at the baby and, for her own comfort as much as the child's began a slow rocking back and forth. "I guess we stay here, then?"

"You guess right." Though his trek through the storm had taken the edge off his anger, his voice remained hard. "Some shelter is better than none. Come morning, when we're guaranteed light, I can go farther looking for help."

"Maybe the snow will have let up by then."

"Maybe."

"Do you think—is there a chance that someone will pass by here?"

His snort was eloquent.

But Lily wasn't quitting. "What if you tried hiking back the way we came? You'd hit the main road and—"

"I'd be lost in the storm long before that."

"Maybe in the morning?" she asked more timidly. She needed something to cling to.

He turned to her quickly, about to speak, then faced front again just as quickly and growled, "How long does that take?"

She knew what he was talking about. She'd felt the same jolt he had when he'd looked back. As irrelevant as it seemed, there was still something about his being a man and her being a woman. "Usually about forty minutes. She's almost done."

"How often does it happen?"

"Every four hours. She goes for a longer period during the night."

Pulling his hat off, he drove a handful of fingers through his hair. "Knowing my luck, she won't this time."

"She will. She has to. And if she doesn't, I'll just feed her more often."

"Great," he muttered under his breath.

Lily studied him. Though the light in the car was growing dimmer by the minute, she could see that his hair was dark and thick and that though it needed a cutting, the last one had been good. He didn't look unkempt. His jacket and jeans, which was all of his clothing that she could see, looked comfortably worn but clean, and he didn't smell of horse.

Okay, so he was embarrassed when she nursed the baby. There were worse things he could be.

Then again, there weren't many worse situations she could imagine herself in. His earlier words came back to taunt her. In a small, discouraged voice, she repeated them. "I really did blow it, didn't I."

He pushed out a breath. "Yup. Too bad you can't fill up this tank the way you do that kid."

Ignoring his crudeness, she turned her attention to Nicki, who was by now clinging to her nipple for the sake of comfort alone, rather than the nourishment. "All done?" she asked softly. Disengaging the baby's mouth, she put the child to her shoulder, alternately rubbing and patting her back until she'd bubbled. Then, righting her own clothes, Lily tucked her close to her warmth.

"Would you turn the car on for a minute, please?" she asked.

The cowboy looked back and, seeing that she'd finished nursing, held her gaze this time. "What for?"

"Heat. I know it'll drain the battery but—"

He looked like he wanted to laugh but wasn't sure how. "You won't get any heat out of this car. Not without gas."

"Sure, I will. Try it. Turn the key."

"If I turn the key," he said in a slow and tempered voice, "The fan will go on. Just the fan. By now the engine will have cooled off. You won't get a thing but cold air, probably colder than what's in here now."

Refusing to believe that, Lily held his dark-eyed gaze. "Try."

"It'll be counterproductive."

"Try anyway."

He did. Within seconds, cold air was blowing from the vents. She had enough time to extend the fingers of her free hand to discover just how cold that air was before he turned off the fan.

"You were right," she said in a small voice.

"Naturally." He faced front.

"Are you always right?"

"Usually."

"No modesty there," she softly told Nicki. "Too bad he fell asleep while I was driving. If he'd been paying attention to where I was going, we wouldn't be in this mess."

"I thought you admitted you were the one who blew it," came the grim voice from the front.

"I think I'd rather share the blame." She felt the weight of responsibility on her shoulders, and if he was going to be arrogant about it, he could just take a little of that weight.

The only problem was that aside from getting nervous about the baby, he struck her as a competent man. There was a firmness to his voice and a directness to his eyes. While she started to shake each time she thought about what lay ahead, he was calmer. Annoyed, yes, and disdainful of her, but calmer. She guessed he was a practical man, and, just then, with the snow blowing and night falling, a little practicality was in order.

"What do we do now?" she asked.

"Nothing."

"We just sit here?"

"And try to keep warm." He turned to scan the back seat. When he had trouble seeing what he wanted, he went front toward the glove compartment. "Have you got a flashlight in here?"

"I...no."

He slammed the cover and sat still in his seat. She didn't doubt for a minute what he was thinking. But she'd never in her life had use for a flashlight in her car, and there'd been no way she could have known she'd need one now.

Feeling more inadequate than ever, she asked, "Do you want to turn on the overhead light?"

"Not until we're desperate. The battery will only last so long." He turned to her. "Our major worry is warmth. Since we won't get any from the engine, we'd better start thinking about substitutes. I don't know what you've got stashed back there, or in the trunk, but if you've got anything we can use, we'd better get it now. It's gonna be pitch-black before long."

The thought of things being pitch-black sent a shiver through Lily. She tried to concentrate on all she'd packed into the trunk of the car. "The diaper bag is back here. There are lots of clothes in the trunk—mine, and the baby's."

"Baby clothes won't keep us warm."

"There's an afghan." It was the last thing her mother had made her. She hadn't been about to leave it behind. "And two heavy coats. One of them is a fur." On principle alone, she hadn't been about to leave that behind.

"Ah, the advantages of wealth," the cowboy murmured as he reached for the keys, but Lily stopped him.

"You can only do it from in here." Holding Nicki tightly to her, she came forward, barely managing to wedge open the door on the driver's side enough to flip the trunk release on the side panel. She slammed the door as fast as she could, but not before snow fell into the car. "Hell," she whispered, brushing snowflakes from the baby's face.

The cowboy was already out, wading through the snow toward the trunk. Covering Nicki as snugly as she dared, Lily returned the infant to her carrier and scrambled over the seats after him.

Cold nuggets of snow hit her the instant she got outside, and she sank knee-deep. Without a thought to the fine leather of her boots, she pulled up her hood and, head-down, worked her way to the back.

The cowboy was standing by the open trunk trying to figure out what was where. Within seconds Lily had her hands on the two coats and the afghan, all of which had been tucked around her suitcases. He took them from her and quickly deposited them in the car. Under the faint illumination of the trunk light, they soon had their arms filled with the heaviest and warmest of the clothes Lily had brought.

"Any food back here?" he yelled above the wind.

She shook her head and headed around the car. By the time she'd tossed in what she carried and climbed in herself, Nicki was whimpering again, and Lily knew why. Wet diapers had a way of upsetting even the most peaceful of babies. Pushing aside the clothes she'd been carrying, she set about remedying the problem.

It broke her heart to have to expose the baby's skin to the chill, to see the tiny legs shake and touch the baby's new, paper-thin skin with her cold hands. The darkness didn't help. Nor did the setup in the car, which was a far cry from the convenience of the white wicker dressing table she'd had for the baby in Hartford. Fumbling around when necessary, she worked as quickly as possible, all the while crooning sweet nothings to Nicki and trying not to think that this could be the best it would be for a while.

The cowboy, meanwhile, made several more trips to the trunk. By the time he climbed into the front and closed the door behind him, there was a mountain of clothing on the driver's seat. Lily

didn't realize how much he'd carted in until she had Nicki put
back together and snugly zipped into her snowsuit.

"What have you *got* there?" she cried.

"Insulation," was his succinct response. He lowered the back
of his seat and reached for the baby carrier. "How does this thing
come undone?"

"Why?"

He paused in his groping to look at her. Though his face was
shadowed, his tone left little to the imagination where his opinion
of her intelligence was concerned. "If I can move it, I can get back
there and stuff clothes under the window. In case you haven't realized it yet, the longer we sit here, the colder it's going to get.
This car may be state-of-the-art chic, but it ain't gonna keep us
warm for long without heat. So we need insulation. Understand?"

Lily did and was annoyed at herself for not anticipating what he
had in mind. To compensate, she reached down and released the
seat belt that held the carrier in place. Once the bulky piece was
wedged between the two front seats, she set Nicki in it and began
helping line the back window, then the seams of the doors and the
front windows with shirts, skirts, slacks and sweaters. She was
grateful for the activity. Not only did it warm her up, but it kept
her mind off the reality of what was to come.

Too soon, the cowboy muttered, "That'll have to do." Curving
his spine to the back seat, he extended his long legs over the lowered front.

Nightfall had further darkened the interior of the car, but Lily's
eyesight adjusted to some extent. Sitting back on her heels, she
looked around. The afghan, the coats, several sweaters and the baby
things were dark blurs on the driver's seat and in the hollows before
the two front seats. She dragged the afghan back to where she was,
then reached for Nicki. With the child in her arms, she pulled the
afghan up chest-high and made herself as comfortable as possible
in her own corner of the back seat.

Outside, the snow swirled relentlessly. Lily listened for a bit,
rocked Nicki for a bit, tried to imagine the future when she might
look back on this experience and laugh. Laughter of any sort was
hard to imagine now. Her sense of optimism seemed to be hovering, not sure which way to go.

She glanced at the cowboy. "What do you think?"

He didn't answer at first, and when he did, his voice was low and tight. "About what?" He had his head back and his eyes closed.

"Can we make it?"

"We have to."

"I know that, but can we?"

"If we're lucky."

"Lucky how?"

"If the snow stops before too long. If it doesn't get too cold after that. If someone sees my car and starts wondering—"

"Were you expected somewhere?" Lily asked hopefully. "Will someone be looking for you when you don't show?"

He killed her hope with a short, deep "Nope," turned his head against the seat back and opened his eyes. "How about you?"

She shook her head.

"No one?" he asked.

Again she shook her head.

"What about the kid's father?"

"He's not in the picture."

The cowboy's gaze pierced her through the darkness. "You just got knocked up for kicks?"

"No, I—"

"—had the hots for a married man and didn't stop to think of birth control."

"No, I—"

"—wanted a baby. Didn't want a husband."

"*No. I was* married. I'm just not anymore."

"But you have a five-week-old child. Surely the father knows about it and is going to worry when you don't show up somewhere."

"He knows about the baby. But he won't worry. He doesn't know where we are, where we're going or what we're doing. He doesn't want us any more than we want him."

The cowboy stared at her. Lily refused to look away, but she felt as though she were being skewered. Clearly he was wondering what was wrong with her that her husband would divorce her when she was pregnant. It was a typically male way of thinking. Lord, she was tired of it.

"We wanted different things," she finally said when she could take no more of his silent scrutiny.

"So you took the car, the fur and the kid."

"And my clothes. And the afghan my mother made me. And what little was left of my pride." There were other things she'd taken, but she saw no need to enlighten the cowboy further.

"Then this is the big escape?" he asked with dawning awareness. "You're not just off to see someone or take a vacation?"

"It'll be a long time before I take a vacation, and there's no one I want to see," she said and for an instant regretted her forthrightness. But she pushed her regrets aside. Nothing about the cowboy had suggested that he'd hurt her. She had no reason to believe him to be evil.

Of course, he was a man, and she wasn't thinking too highly of men as a group just then. Then again, she didn't have to like him. All she had to do was weather his company until they found a way out of the mess they were in.

The cowboy straightened his head and closed his eyes.

"Are you going to sleep?"

"Might as well."

"Whenever you go to sleep, something happens. First your car went off the road and then—"

"I'm tired."

"You must be, to have fallen asleep at the wheel in the middle of the day."

"I've been up for nearly thirty-six hours straight getting this far."

"Where did you start?"

"Montana."

"Where are you headed?"

He was quiet. Lily wondered if he'd fallen asleep when his voice came to her, deep and slow. "New York, I thought, but when I got to New York, they said Boston, and when I got to Boston, they said Quebec." He yawned. "If I don't find what I'm looking for in Quebec, I'm goin' home."

She was surprised that he'd said as much. He'd been more laconic until then, keeping personal things personal. Perhaps, she decided, he realized the impossibility of privacy in their situation. Or perhaps her opening up had inspired a little in him. Or perhaps it was simply fatigue, doing in his defenses.

Whichever the case, she wanted to take advantage of it. "What are you looking for?" she asked.

But he didn't answer.

"Are you asleep?" she whispered loudly.

"Almost."

"You won't tell me what you're looking for?"

"Not now," he murmured sleepily.

"What if you fall asleep and freeze to death?"

"You'll wake me before that."

"What if *I* fall asleep and freeze to death?"

"The kid will wake you before that."

"What if she freezes first?"

"Wrap her inside your coat and she won't. You've got body heat. Use it."

His suggestion was a good one, particularly since Lily had a canvas carrier tucked into the diaper bag. By strapping Nicole to her chest, zippering her own coat around them both and covering them with the afghan and a coat, she stood a fair chance of keeping the baby warm.

Not that she was moving just yet. The baby was happily clutching her finger, and the air inside the car was far from frigid. But it was a good thought for the future.

On its heels came another thought. "Is there any chance of our asphyxiating closed in here like this?"

The cowboy didn't answer.

"Uh...excuse me...are you still awake?"

"Barely," came the deep, distant voice.

"Did you hear what I asked?"

"Mmm." He paused, then mumbled, "No gas, no fumes."

She breathed a sigh of relief. "That's good."

"I'm goin' to sleep now. Can you keep still?"

Lily wasn't sure she wanted to keep still. Talking, hearing the sound of her voice, hearing the sound of his was a comfort in the dark. But he was exhausted. Thirty-six hours was a long time to go without sleep. She had to respect his needs if she wanted him to respect hers.

"I'll be quiet," she agreed softly. After no more than a minute, though, she said, "What's your name?"

"I thought you were going to be still?"

"I will. Tell me your name first. That way I can wake you before you freeze."

He was quiet for a very long time. Watching him, Lily could have sworn that his eyes were open for part of that time. At the end, though, they were closed and his breathing was low and even. She was about to give up on him when he said, "Quist."

"Excuse me?"

"The name's Quist."

"Quist?"

"Mmm."

She'd never heard anything like it, didn't even know whether it was a first name or a last name, but when she would have asked, he suddenly shifted, turning away from her.

She let him be. It was only fair, she reasoned. Besides, if luck was on their side, morning would come and with it rescue, and she would never need to know anything more than that the man she'd been stranded with for a night in the snow was Quist from Montana.

CHAPTER TWO

Quist came awake to a strange sound. At least, it was strange until he got his bearings. There had never been a baby in his life, not of the human variety. He'd had his share of experience with newborn calves, colts and fillies, dogs, cats and the occasional bear, but he'd been spared the joy of human squalling until now.

Opening his eyes to the darkness, he looked around, remembered where he was and why, and slowly turned his head. Though the woman had her back to him, the car wasn't large enough to separate them by much, particularly since they were both stretched out from the back seat forward. If he moved his arm, it would brush her shoulder.

He didn't move his arm.

She was shushing the baby, but the baby had a mind of its own and kept crying while she started fiddling under the afghan. Then came the silence, as abrupt as it had been earlier, and Quist knew she was nursing the child.

He wasn't sure why that made him uncomfortable, and he wasn't about to brood on it, but it did.

He hadn't thought she'd be the type to nurse. Nursing babies was for women who were willing to be tied to home and hearth for months, and he wouldn't have pegged her that way. She looked rich. He guessed that her sporty red car was no more than a year old, that her hip-length turquoise-and-white parka had a designer label inside, that her boots were imported, that her pencil-slim jeans cost three times as much as one pair of his functional Levi's.

Besides that, she didn't look hardy enough to nurse a child, let alone give birth to one. Thanks to the bulky parka, he hadn't been able to see much, but what he'd seen looked small. Her face was slender, her features delicate. Her legs were slim. And standing, as she'd done for a brief time by his side when they were digging things from her trunk, the top of her head hadn't reached his shoulders.

There was a fragility to her. He kept thinking about how she'd gone through childbirth only five weeks before. Her body had to still be recovering. And beyond the physical was the emotional. She might be calm with the baby, but she meant it when she said she was terrified. He'd seen it in her eyes, even when she tried to keep her voice calm.

She had every right to be frightened. They were lost in the woods in an area that very possibly hadn't seen traffic in years. If the situation were different, just him and her, they could stay with the car until the snow ended, then bundle themselves up and hike back toward the main road, even if it meant several days' exposure to the cold.

But he wasn't sure how far she'd make it in the snow, and then there was a baby involved. A five-week-old infant couldn't survive exposure like that. So the options were limited and the responsibility greater, none of which pleased him.

He wanted to be in Montana, not Maine. He wanted to be back home on the ranch, which he knew and loved. He worked hard there, but the work made sense. There was an order to it. Emergencies cropped up all the time, but he could deal with them. He could deal with most anything on his own turf.

This was something else entirely. But then, women had always been the bane of his existence. He doubted that was ever going to change.

"Quist?" came a whisper from the edge of the afghan.

He grunted.

"We woke you, didn't we?" She paused. "I'm sorry. I settled her as soon as I could, but everything's so dark that I had to fumble around." She paused again. "It's still snowing."

That figured. He didn't expect things to get easy all of a sudden. They were bound to get worse before they got better, and worse, at that moment, meant colder. His feet were feeling the drop in temperature in the car.

Sitting forward, he thought of the advantages of being car-bound with someone rich as he reached for the fur coat and wrapped it around his lower half.

"My boots got wet when I went outside," Lily said quietly. "They're still damp. I wasn't sure whether I'd have been warmer if I'd taken them off. You left yours on, so I figured I'd do the same."

"Are you cold?"

"I'm okay."

"What does that mean?"

"It means that I'd be a lot more comfortable if we could build a fire in here, but that I don't think I'm on the verge of frostbite yet."

"How's the baby?"

"She's all bundled up. It's a miracle I can find her under the hat and hood and snowsuit. I've kept her inside my coat, like you told me to. She's still pretty warm."

Quist looked at his wristwatch, then burrowed more deeply into his coat.

"What time is it?" Lily asked.

"Almost ten."

She moaned. "I feel like I've been sitting here forever. I was sure it had to be at least one or two in the morning."

"Time flies when you're having fun."

His sarcasm went right by her. "I want morning to come. I don't like the dark."

"Did you sleep?"

"Uh-uh. I'm too nervous." She'd spent the time since he'd fallen asleep imagining any number of possible scenarios for the next twenty-four hours. Most of them were depressing.

"Are you hungry?"

"Starved. I was waiting for you to wake up to eat."

That brought Quist slowly around. "You have food?"

"Leftovers from lunch. There's a bag on the floor on my side. Can you reach it?" She would have done it herself if Nicki hadn't been so comfortable, attached to her breast.

When he leaned over to feel around on the floor, the side of his head touched her thigh. Though she was covered not only by jeans, but by the afghan and her coat, she still felt a moment's awkwardness, which was probably why she began to talk more quickly.

"There was a Burger King on the highway. I stopped there to use the rest room and change Nicki, and I figured that I had to get something, even though I wasn't very hungry." When he straightened with the bag in his hand, she felt a little less crowded. "I don't think there's more than half a hamburger, a few fries and some cookies, and they're probably rock hard by now, but they're better than the rest of the food this airline's serving."

Quist snickered.

"If you don't mind my germs" she added.

Germs were the least of his worries. Removing the contents of the bag, he laid them out on the empty baby carrier.

Lily eyed the dim shapes. "I suppose it's lucky we can't see. We might think twice about eating."

"Not much chance of that," he said, but he made no move to take any of the food.

"I'm sorry there isn't more. I should have ordered a whole lot, but I never dreamed dinner would be a problem."

Neither had Quist, and as he stared at the meager spread, he couldn't help but wonder how many dinners in the future would be a problem. Reaching to the floor on his own side this time, he tugged out his duffel, opened it and rummaged around inside. He set down several foil cubes beside the Burger King remains, rummaged again and came up with several more.

Lily couldn't make out details in the dark. "What are they?"

"Chunky bars."

"Chunky bars?" Her voice rose. "I haven't had a Chunky in years!"

"Don't get excited. We'll have to ration them, too. It may be a while before we get our hands on anything more."

"Ration. Right."

"It's a sensible thing to do, isn't it?"

"Sure. Ooops—okay, Nicki," she said softly as she lifted the infant to her shoulder. She put her mouth to the baby's cheek and began to pat her back, breathing, "That's my girl. What an angel you are. Got a bubble in there for me?" Stopping her patting for a minute, she groped in the diaper bag, which was jammed between her leg and the side of the car. Coming up with a cloth diaper, she slid it between the baby and her shoulder. "Just in case," she murmured under her breath and started patting again.

"In case what?" Quist asked.

"In case she cheeses on my shoulder. It smells vile."

"Oh. Great. By all means, then, take the precaution. The last thing we need in here is something that smells vile."

Lily bit her lower lip, wondering what he was going to do when she changed certain diapers. In that respect she was grateful Nicki was so young. Even the worst smells weren't all that bad. Of course, that was easy for Lily to say. Nicki was flesh of her flesh.

Nuzzling the infant's cheek, she found pleasure in the sweet baby scent that lingered even now from her morning bath. How long ago that seemed, a world away. That sweet scent would disappear, she knew, if they didn't somehow get help. Thought of Nicki going without a warm bath, without lotion and powder and clean clothes disturbed her. Oh, she had the lotion and powder and clean clothes with her, but there was no way she was going to undress the infant for other than the quickest diaper change. It was too cold.

Quist interrupted her grim musings. "The only thing here with protein is the hamburg. I think you should have half now and save the rest for tomorrow."

"Me? What about you? Don't you want some?"

"I can do with the other stuff."

"But you said it yourself—this is the only thing with protein. There's none in the other stuff."

"You need it more. You're the one who's eating for two."

"That was when I was pregnant. Nicki eats for herself now."

"What—hamburg? French fries?"

"Uh, not quite."

"Exactly," he said, annoyed that she was making him spell it out. "She drinks milk. Does she eat anything solid yet?"

"No."

"So milk is it, and you're the only milkman around here, which means you need that protein more than I do."

"But you're the one who's going out in the snow tomorrow looking for help."

"I'll be fine."

"You may be walking for miles."

"I'm in shape."

"To go through a blizzard?"

"I'm not going through a blizzard. I'm not budging unless the snow stops."

"What if it doesn't" Lily asked. She tried to keep her voice steady, though it was higher than before. "What if it keeps on for two or three days—or more? What if four or five feet pile up out there? I've read of that happening in the North, and we're pretty far north. What if—"

Nicki burped. Lily held the breath she'd been about to expel, then released it slowly.

"It won't do either of us any good to worry about *what ifs*,"

Quist said, using an assured voice in the hope of calming her. "The fact is that for now, we're okay. We have shelter and a little food. We'll make that last as long as possible and then worry. One thing at a time. Okay?"

Lily wished she could see his face, but it was too dark, so she had to put her faith in the low command of his voice. "Okay," she whispered, then added, "I'm sorry. I try to be strong, but it doesn't work sometimes."

Her whisper, and the words she said, did strange things to Quist. Something stirred inside him, something like compassion. It was totally uncharacteristic and entirely unwanted, but he felt a definite softening. He guessed it was her honesty. At least he thought it was honesty. It had been so long since he'd connected honesty with a woman that he wasn't quite sure whether to buy it or not.

"Take the hamburg," he insisted crossly and thrust it in her direction.

"Let me finish with Nicki first."

"I thought you were starved."

"I am, but another fifteen minutes won't hurt."

"Can't you eat and nurse at the same time?"

"Yes, but then I'd be diluting each of the pleasures."

He put the hamburg down again and drawled, "And you're a lady who likes her pleasures."

Vaguely stung by his sarcasm, Lily said, "Certain ones more than others. Nursing Nicki is the best. It's the most rewarding experience I've ever had in my life, and the most innocent pleasure in the world. It's a time when there's just the two of us, and we're both doing what we were made to do. While I'm nursing, I like to give her my undivided attention. So why should I eat? It's not like I have a whole list of things to do when she's done."

That said, she transferred Nicki to her other arm, tucked her inside her coat and began the second half of the feeding.

Quist took several of the fries, slouched back into his side of the car and began to eat them slowly, one by one.

"And anyway," Lily's voice came through the darkness after several minutes, "there haven't been as many pleasures in my life as you think. I've earned everything I have."

"You work?"

"Every woman works."

He grunted. "In some form or another." He was thinking of

Belinda McClean and the horizontality of her occupation. Not that
he was a hypocrite. He'd enjoyed Belinda plenty and had paid her
well. Then she'd gotten greedy and had blown the arrangement to
bits. But that had been years ago. Ancient history.

Lily coupled his muttered comment with something else he'd
said. "You don't like women, do you?"

"I don't trust women. They're only out for themselves."

"I could say the same about men."

"Then you've just met the wrong ones."

"Maybe. And maybe the same is true with you and women."

"I doubt it. In forty years, I've seen lots of women come and
go, and not one of them's been able to change my mind."

Given the iron beneath his words, Lily had no doubt that he fully
believed what he said. "That's very sad."

"No, it's very smart. I know what to expect and what not to. I
go through life with my eyes wide open. Wide open." Having
issued what he felt to be an adequate warning, he fell silent. But
something was nagging at him. After several minutes, he gave in
to that nagging. "So what *do* you do to get paid so well?"

"I never said I was paid well. I said I've earned everything I
have."

"Did you earn the car? The clothes?" He'd seen quite a few of
those clothes when they'd been taking things from the trunk, and
everything he'd touched had been top-notch.

"Every last piece," she said with conviction.

"How?"

"By making a warm, welcoming home for a man who took
every possible opportunity to put me down. By cooking for him,
only to be told that the meat was tough—and cleaning for him,
only to be told that the professional service did it better—and dressing up for him, only to be told that the particular color I'd worn
made me look sick. By being there when he needed me, then having to stand by and watch when he decided he needed someone
else." She caught a quick breath. "He was never particularly generous. Maybe he was just distrustful, like you. Maybe he felt that
I was out to take him for whatever I could get, so that made him
cautious. But what he gave me, I earned. So help me, I did."

Her voice hung in the silence of the car for a minute, then
dropped, leaving nothing but the sounds of the storm to fill the

void. Listening to the elements' anger, she was drained of her own. After several minutes she breathed out a small, rueful laugh.

"So much for giving Nicki my undivided attention." She pressed a gentle kiss on the infant's forehead, and said in a soft breath, "Forgive me, Nicki? I think it's the darkness that brings out the demons. Either that, or I just need to hear the sound of someone's voice, even if it's my own. I'll be better from now on. I promise I will."

True to her word, she spent the rest of the feeding doing all the little things, some vocal, some not, that told Nicki how much she was loved. And through it all, Quist sat and listened. There was more he wanted to ask, but he couldn't get himself to interrupt. Strangely, though he'd felt uncomfortable earlier, he suddenly wanted to turn on the overhead light for a minute. He wanted to see the lady beside him. She was taking on a personality, shaped by voice and words, but there was an unreality to it in the darkness.

He waited until she'd put the baby to her shoulder again. Then he asked, "How old are you?"

The question surprised her. She hadn't thought he'd care one way or another how old she was. But she had no big secrets on that score. "Twenty-nine."

In turn, that surprised him. He'd have guessed she was younger. "How long were you married?"

"Four years."

"And he just walked off with someone else and left you with a newborn child?"

"Oh, no. He left me the day I told him I was pregnant. He said I'd plotted it just to keep him." She pressed her cheek to the baby's and whispered, "As though I hadn't wanted you all along. I'd been trying all that time to get pregnant and he knew it." She spoke up again for Quist. "He thought I knew he'd been fooling around, the jackass. I wouldn't have put up with that." Her voice fell, though this time not for the baby's sake. She'd thought long and hard about what might have been, and each time she had doubts. "Then again, maybe I would have. If he'd said that his thing with Hillary was a mistake and that it was over, I might have stayed. I'm not sure I would have been able to believe him, but I did want the marriage to work."

"Why?"

That was harder to answer, because it went beyond self-doubt.

Lily knew what her weaknesses were, and she wasn't proud of them. Not even cover of darkness—or the fact that Quist was a stranger—made it easy to confess. "Oh, lots of reasons," she murmured, but said no more.

He let it go, mainly because he didn't feel he had a right to pry further. The reasons why she'd wanted her marriage to work had no bearing on their present predicament. As to that predicament, all he needed from her was a little cooperation, and he felt sure he'd get that. What they *both* needed was a little luck.

Finishing off the last of the few fries he'd allotted himself, he listened to the wind and wondered about his luck. Actually he'd had his share. He had the ranch, which he'd won in a card game twenty-one years before. He'd been nineteen and brash as all get-out then, and though he hadn't known what in the hell to do with two hundred acres of land, three ramshackle buildings, a small herd of cattle and two aging cowhands, he'd known enough to take advantage of the windfall. Working his tail off and learning as he worked, he turned the ranch around, eventually adding to the acreage, the buildings, the herd and the crew. Sure, hard work had been most of it, but he'd had certain breaks, too. He'd lucked out more than once when it came to contacts and timing and deals, health and weather.

He sure as hell hadn't lucked out with women, though.

"I take it you're not married," Lily said. Much as she tried, she couldn't put the discussion to rest.

"You take right."

"Have you ever thought about being married?"

"Nope. Never even came close."

"I mean, have you ever imagined yourself being married and thought about what it would be like?"

"No."

"Never thought about how you'd handle it, how you'd react to some things as a husband?"

"Never."

Since she wasn't getting the answers she wanted, she turned her attention to Nicki. "Where's that bubble?" she whispered gently. She brushed her lips across the infant's forehead, then ran a thumb over her cheek and would have repeated the gesture if her hands hadn't been so cold. Tugging the sleeves of her jacket over them, she began rubbing firm, flat-handed circles over the baby's back.

Several rounds of that brought a soft burp from the small bundle. Lavishing whispered praise, she righted her clothes and returned the baby to the crook of her elbow.

Quist propped a foot on the gear shift. "Why do you ask?"

"Ask what?"

"About marriage." There had been three questions, one right after the next, all about the same thing. He wanted to know why.

"Oh, I was just wondering about something, but if you've never imagined what married life would be like, there's no point in my asking."

"Ask."

"No. I think not."

"Why?"

"Because you don't like women, so I know just what you'll say."

"That's one of the things I like *least* about women. They think they know it all." He raised his voice. "You don't know me. How can you know what I'll say?"

Annoyed that he was making something out of nothing, she burst back, "All I wanted to know was whether you thought Jarrod was right. If you got married, if you took vows and promised to be faithful, would you turn around and cheat on your wife? Do all men do it? Is there some justification for it that I'm missing? I mean, I took those vows seriously. Am I the one marching to a different drummer? Is that my problem? Am I misinterpreting the rules of the game?"

Quist didn't know what to say. She was clearly hurt, but he was no healer.

"And it wasn't only Jarrod," she went on, as though once started she couldn't hold it in. "It was loads of guys we knew. I always heard women talk about this one or that one who was fooling around. No one ever named Jarrod in front of me, and I was never sure whether to believe them about the others until Jarrod told me, and even *then* I might have thought he was exaggerating, trying to okay what he'd done by claiming all the guys were doing it, until Michael came on to me. *Michael*. Jarrod's own *brother*—"

Only after she'd said it did she realize what she'd done. Breathing hard, she buried her face by Nicki's until she'd regained a bit of control. Then she raised her head enough to be able to speak clearly—softly, but clearly.

"I'm sorry. I got carried away. It's history—water over the dam. There isn't a lot I can do about what happened. But it still hurts. I guess I'm still pretty angry."

Quist could believe that. But he wasn't about to pass judgment, to say whether or not she had a right to that anger, because he'd only heard one side of the story. For all he knew, the innocent-sounding little mother huddled close by had been a shrew of a wife. For all he knew, she was a lousy lover, or, conversely, a pathological liar who hadn't taken her marriage vows half as seriously as she'd like him to believe. For all he knew, she'd been feeding him a line of bull.

He didn't think so, but what the hell, he didn't even know her name. It was, he realized, time to change that.

"Who are you?"

"Excuse me?"

"Your name—you never told me what it was."

She was silent for a minute. He was starting to think that she did indeed have something to hide, when she laughed. It was a soft, self-conscious sound. "I don't believe it. I just dumped all the sordid little details of my marriage in your lap, and you don't even know my name."

"Well?"

"Lily. Lily Danziger."

"Is Danziger your—"

"Maiden name. Nicki's birth certificate reads Danziger, too." Her voice hardened. "Jarrod didn't want any part of us, and the feeling's mutual."

"What about child support?"

"What about it?"

"Don't you want any money?"

"No."

"Don't you *need* any money? I hear raising a kid is expensive these days."

"It's always been expensive, but people manage."

"How will you? Do you have money of your own?"

"I'm not independently wealthy, no."

"Then you must've got a great divorce settlement."

"Why do you say that?"

"Because it makes sense," he said, and because he was naturally cynical when it came to women. "The guy you married has money—he leaves you for another woman the day you tell him you're pregnant—you go through the pregnancy all by yourself and give birth to the child alone. I mean, it's a tear-jerker."

"I don't hear you crying."

He snorted. "I'm not."

"You're just a hard-as-nails kind of guy."

His voice took on the hard-as-nails sound she'd heard so much of at the start. "I'm a survivor. I do what I have to do, say what I have to say, feel what I have to feel."

"And you're out for number one, just like Jarrod."

"Lady, if I was out for number one, I wouldn't have offered to share my Chunky bars with you."

"It's Lily, not lady," she huffed, "and you can keep your damned Chunky bars. I wouldn't eat them, anyway."

"Why not?" he asked, vaguely affronted.

"Because if I eat chocolate while I'm nursing, the baby is apt to get diarrhea."

"Oh."

"Yes, oh." With that, she turned her back on him, making herself as comfortable as possible with Nicki safely tucked inside her coat. She didn't want to talk to Quist anymore. He annoyed her. So she half sat, half lay on her side of the car with her hooded head pressed to the wool slacks she'd used to line the window.

The wind blew. She tried not to hear it, tried not to hear the hard nuggets of snow that swirled with it, hitting small bared patches of the car. She tried not to think about the cold that had settled in her hands and feet and threatened to spread, and she tried not to think about the future. Mostly she tried not to cry, which was what she really wanted to do. She'd been wanting to do it a lot lately, and it had nothing to do with a snowstorm. It had to do with facing a future that was unknown and daunting. It had to do with feeling very alone and very frightened.

Quist, too, listened to the storm, but his eyes were on her huddled form, trying to make sense of it in the darkness. He didn't know why he bothered, didn't know why he didn't just turn over and go back to sleep. He was still exhausted, but he wasn't as cold as he figured she was, and that made him feel bad.

She seemed so damned fragile. He wanted to think her irresponsible when it came to driving, lousy when it came to keeping a husband and greedy when it came to getting rid of one—still, she seemed fragile. And if there was one thing he had to hand her, she seemed like a devoted mother.

Which was a hell of a lot more than his own had been, he mused, then broke into his musings when he heard a strange sound. It wasn't the baby, at least he didn't think it was.

He held his breath for a minute and listened, then cautiously said, "Lily?"

There was a pause, then a muted, "Mmm?"

He waited, trying to hear the sound again, but it didn't come. "Are you all right?"

After another pause, she said, "I'm fine."

Sitting up, he reached forward and switched on the overhead light.

Lily's head came around fast. She didn't have to squint; the light was too small for that. But it wasn't small enough to hide the tears that pooled on her lower lids—or the defiance behind those tears.

"Don't you dare say a word," she warned, eyes glittering. "Don't you dare tell me that I'm weak or that there's something wrong with me—because I'm tired of hearing it."

He hadn't been about to say either of those things. He'd been about to swear, because tears usually meant that a woman wanted something, and he didn't have a damn thing to give just then. But he decided that swearing wasn't such a good idea, either. It would only upset her, and he didn't want her upset. It wouldn't help the situation.

"I just wanted to make sure you eat," he said. He picked up the half hamburger and held it out. "Like I said, you're the only one who can feed the kid."

The sight of the cold sandwich reminded Lily of how hungry she was. "Can you tear it in half?" she asked. When he'd done it, she took one of the two pieces. "Are you sure you won't have the other?"

"I'm sure."

"If you want it later, you can have it."

But he shook his head. He felt guilty enough about eating the few fries he had, since she wouldn't share his candy. So what was hers was hers. He'd still give her a Chunky if she changed her mind—and it might come to that if the choice were between some milk and no milk—but he wasn't taking any more of her food. She needed it.

Setting the uneaten quarter hamburger on the carrier with the rest of the food, he turned off the light again and sat back. He could feel Lily beside him, eating slowly. He couldn't hear whether her breathing was even—the wind made that hard—but at least he didn't hear another gasp or swallow or whatever the hell it had been. He didn't want her crying. He didn't like women at all, but women who cried were the worst.

On that thought he closed his eyes, slid lower on the seat and went to sleep.

When he awoke, it was six-thirty in the morning, dawn was just beginning to break and Lily was feeding the baby. He wasn't at all where he wanted to be, which put him instantly on his guard and made him cross. He would have complained that the infant's cries had woken him if it were true. But he couldn't remember hearing the baby. He'd been exhausted. Though he'd gone with little sleep many a time back home, the sheer frustration of this trip had taken the toll that physical strain rarely did.

Now there was physical strain, too. Gingerly he stretched muscles that were stiff from the unnatural position he'd slept in and from the cold.

Feeling his movement, Lily peered around the hood of her parka. She was relieved that he'd awakened to face the day with her, but Jarrod's dark early-morning moods had conditioned her to caution.

Quist had never awoken to a woman's stare before. "Something wrong?" he demanded in an edgy voice.

"No."

"Why are you looking at me that way?"

Quickly she looked away, toward where Nicki was nursing under the afghan. "No reason." She took a fast breath. "The wind is down, but I can't tell if the snow has stopped. Everything's quiet. That has to be a good sign, doesn't it?"

Quist flexed his shoulder. "Snow doesn't make much noise when it falls on itself." He studied her downcast face. Even in profile, even in the dim light of dawn, he saw signs of strain. "Did you sleep?"

"I dozed. I kept thinking...lousy things."

He didn't want to hear what those lousy things were.

But she couldn't help herself. The night had been so long, hour

after hour with only the briefest of catnaps, and during those waking times her imagination had been in full swing. Now that there
was someone to talk to, she needed reassurance. "I kept thinking
that maybe there'd be so much snow piled up around the car that
we wouldn't be able to open the door."

"We'll be able to open the door."

"I kept thinking that maybe it would freeze shut, and that we
wouldn't have any way of melting the ice, so we'd be stuck in
here, *really* stuck in here." She swallowed and whispered, "That
won't happen, will it?"

"No." The question, he knew, was whether there was anything
outside that could offer them better shelter than the car. Sitting
forward to stretch the cramped muscles of his back, he glanced
around toward the general vicinity where the baby would be under
the afghan. "Is she all right?"

Lily nodded. "She slept, thank goodness, and she's drinking
well. I don't look forward to changing her. She's so small, and it's
so cold. Her legs tremble pathetically. But if I don't change her,
she'll be uncomfortable that way, and if she gets diaper rash, it'll
be worse." She fell silent for a minute, then raised her eyes to
Quist and said in a small voice, "When I'm not thinking about
being frozen solid in this car, I'm thinking of being rescued. Do
you think it will happen?"

"Nope," was Quist's blunt reply. "No one's going to find us
here. It's up to us to find someone or something out there." He
reached for one of the Chunky bars, peeled back the foil covering,
snapped the bar in half and popped one of the halves into his
mouth. Rewrapping the other half, he put it back with the rest of
their meager store of food. Then he crawled into the front seat,
jammed the Stetson onto his head and forced the door open. He
was out, with the door slammed shut behind him, before Lily could
tell whether the swirling snow was simply snow dislodged from
the car or a continuation of the storm.

The minutes crept by, and with each, Lily grew more apprehensive. She had no idea whether Quist was gone for the day, gone
for good, or simply looking around outside. As had happened the
evening before when he'd left the car, she felt an overwhelming
aloneness. At least it was getting lighter out, but that was small
solace if, in fact, he'd set off on his own.

When the door opened, she felt an inordinate sense of relief. Her gaze clung to his snowy figure as he slid back into the car. Nervously she awaited his verdict.

Hauling his duffel from under the seat, he began rummaging inside. "It's stopped snowing for now, but there's more to come. The sky's still filled with it. I'm going to see how far I can get before that happens." Shrugging out of his heavy sheepskin jacket, he pulled a sweater on over the one he was already wearing.

Lily's eyes clung to his shoulders. Their breadth represented the strength she'd soon be losing. "Which direction are you going in?"

"Ahead." He pulled on the jacket. "Behind is a waste. You didn't see anything there yesterday. There won't be anything there today." Reaching into the bag, he pulled out several pairs of socks. "Besides, it's all uphill, and I don't have snowshoes. Better to hike down. I'll go for three or four hours or until the road comes to an end. With luck I'll hit something before then." He stuffed a pair of socks in each of his pockets, took a third pair in his hand and looked her in the eye. "It may be a while before I get back."

"How much of a while?" she asked, unable to hide her fear.

"That depends on what I find. But I don't want you to leave the car. Do you understand that? If you start wandering around, you'll get lost."

"What about you? What if you get lost?"

"I won't. I'm a tracker." His eyes sharpened. "But it won't do me any good to go out searching for help and come back and find you gone. Stay right here with the baby. I don't care how impatient you get, do not wander away from this car. If you start stumbling around in the snow, you'll be in trouble. Do you understand what I'm saying?"

He was speaking in such a slow, clear, elementary kind of way that she couldn't help but understand. "I'm not dumb."

"But you're scared, and scared women do crazy things. So I'm telling you—stay here, stay as warm as you can and remember to eat. Sooner or later, I'll be back."

"Sooner or later?" she echoed in a small voice.

"I can't tell when it will be."

"Will it be today?"

"With luck."

"And if it's not?"

"If it's not, you'll spend another night like the one you've just spent, and I'll be back tomorrow."

"Will you?"

"Yes."

"Do you promise?"

Quist wasn't used to having his word questioned. He wouldn't have put up with it, if Lily hadn't looked so damned frightened. And vulnerable. Damn, he didn't need vulnerable. "I just said it, didn't I?"

She nodded. "But can I believe you?"

He studied her closely. "You're not a very trusting sort."

"I've trusted and been hurt."

That much was clear from the factual way she said it and the sober look in her eye. It also jibed with things she'd told him about herself. Feeling an empathy he didn't want, Quist drew himself up as straight as he could within the confines of the car. "Then you've trusted the wrong men. Me, I'm a man of my word. If I say I'll be back, I'll be back."

Looking into the coal-black eyes that told her nothing in the dim light of dawn, Lily wavered for a minute. Then she thought back on the past fourteen hours and realized that though Quist had his moods, he'd behaved responsibly. She also realized that she had no choice; if she was to make it through his absence with her peace of mind intact, she had to believe that he'd be back.

"Okay?" he asked in a low, cautious tone.

She nodded, then watched him tuck the half of the Chunky bar he hadn't eaten into his pocket.

"In case I get hungry," he explained, then snorted and added, "as if I couldn't eat ten of them now." His dark eyes met hers. "So you've got the rest of the food. I'll have to come back to get it, won't I?"

Before she had time to respond, he let himself out and slammed the door.

CHAPTER THREE

For Quist, the trudge through the snow was cold and frustrating. He followed the narrow break in the trees on the assumption that it was a road, though eighteen inches of snow had obliterated any sure signs. Save for that lean swath, the landscape was reduced to an endless expanse of snow-laden woods. A winter wonderland? More like the twilight zone, he knew. Oh, he was hardy enough. He could survive cold and lack of food; he'd done it before and he'd do it again.

The problem was Lily. He figured she'd be able to make it through another couple of nights in the car, but after that there'd be trouble. She was cold, and unless he got something to eat, her milk would dry up, and if that happened, the baby would starve, and if *that* happened—he didn't want to even think about it. God only knew why he cared; Lily Danziger and her baby were nothing to him but a pain in the butt. Still, he couldn't just let them freeze.

The more he thought about it—and he had little else to think about as he trudged on through the snow—it was incredible. From the cradle on, he'd had no need for a woman, yet he'd been involved with his share, and each one had been trouble. Hell, he would never have been in the goddamned Maine woods in the first place if it hadn't been for a woman, and now another's plight had him stomping his way for help.

Sure, he'd be stomping his way for help even if he'd been the only one stuck. He wasn't about to freeze to death, either. But the fact was that if he'd been alone, he'd never have left the main road in the first place. And if he were alone, he wouldn't feel the responsibility he did now.

He knew what he wanted. He wanted to hit a bona fide thoroughfare, flag down a car, find a can of gas and some chains to get Lily's fancy red Audi out of the snow. He wasn't even sure if chains would do the trick, especially if it started to snow again. Playing it safe, he'd probably snag a tow truck to go in after her.

If all went well, he'd be in his own motel room for the night, then back on his way to Quebec in the morning.

If all went well.

Somehow he didn't think it would. After plodding through the snow for nearly two hours, he saw no sign of civilization. There wasn't the faintest smell of a wood fire. There wasn't the slightest sound of a snow plow. Maine was nowhere near as big as Montana, and the terrain wasn't nearly as rugged, still he felt well and truly isolated from humanity. In Montana that was good. In Maine, he wasn't so sure.

For Lily, the wait was interminable. With the full dawning of day, she stepped out of the car into knee-deep snow, which did nothing to reassure her. Even if she had gas, she doubted the Audi would be able to make it back to the main road. True, it had stopped snowing, but the sky was still that pregnant, pale gray shade it had been the day before. Quist was right. The snow wasn't done.

Back in the car, she piled every imaginable layer over her for warmth, then played with Nicki, who was right with her under all the covers. She sang; she cooed and babbled and hummed. She took advantage of daylight to do all the things she wouldn't be able to do once night fell again, though she prayed something would happen before then. She wasn't a camper. A city person born and bred, she'd never spent time in the country. As hard as it was to believe that she'd already spent one cold night in the car, it was that much harder to believe that there might be more nights like it.

She wondered how long she'd be able to survive that way, then decided not to think about it. But minutes later she was wondering what would happen if Quist was lost or hurt in the snow and never made it to civilization. Her car, she realized, could be sitting just where it was, unseen by human eyes until spring came, if then.

She wouldn't let that happen. If Quist didn't return in a day or two, she knew that despite what he'd told her, she'd set out on her own. She wasn't about to let Nicki die. She wasn't about to die, herself. She had something to prove, something to do with basic human worth, and she was damned if she'd let a snowstorm and a few wrong turns stand in her way.

Still, her empty stomach knotted. She listened for the sound of a rescuing tow truck, but none came. She waited for Quist to return with the news that he'd found a settlement several hills over, in which case they could laugh at the night they'd spent thinking themselves marooned. But he didn't come.

One hour passed, then two, then three. Nicki slept for a bit and awoke hungry. After Lily fed her, she finished off the last of the cold hamburger. An hour later she had a cookie, but by then she realized the importance of saving whatever she had. Quist had been gone for four hours. Clearly he hadn't found something nearby. Things didn't look good.

Noontime came and went. She rocked Nicki, sang playful songs to her, though playfulness was the last thing she felt. At one point tears came to her eyes and, holding Nicki tight, she cried quietly. She felt she had that right. With the exception of Nicki's arrival, the past year had been a nightmare, and the nightmare went on, more vivid, if anything, in the week now past. From Michael's attack, to her precipitous departure from Hartford, to the long drive, the snowstorm and now this—she feared to think of where it would end.

If her parents were alive, she'd have had a haven, humble as it was. But her mother had been dead for ten years, her father for four, and she had no siblings to ask for help. All she wanted, she realized, was to feel a little less alone.

Sitting in her car, snowbound and lost in the middle of God's country, did nothing to ease that feeling of aloneness. Nor did Quist's continuing absence. By the time one o'clock came, he'd been gone for nearly six hours. She told herself that he'd reached help, but that it would take time for that help to get back to her. Still she felt abandoned—and colder and more frightened by the minute.

At one-forty, just when she was beginning to despair, there was a sudden wrench on the door. It opened with a yawn and a snow-covered figure fell inside.

Had it not been for the Stetson, Lily wasn't sure she'd have recognized him, but the Stetson came quickly off, as did the socks that had been tied end-to-end to cover his ears and the large sheep-skin jacket, and before she knew what was happening, he was in the back seat with her, crawling into the nest that her body heat had managed to keep warmer than the air.

"Damn, it's cold out there," he said hoarsely. He pulled her close, baby and all.

"You're freezing!" she cried. She was shocked not only by the chill of his body but by the sudden intimacy he'd forced on her. Much as she told herself that the circumstances were extenuating, it had been a long time since she'd been so close to a man.

"I know. Warm me a little before we go back out?"

Her shock yielded to a glimmer of hope. "You found something?"

"A cabin. It's a one-room job, but it's been lived in as recently as last summer." He took a shivering breath against her forehead. "There's a woodstove, plenty of wood and some food—canned goods and staples. I would've lit the stove if I hadn't been afraid to leave it untended. Didn't want to get you and the kid there and find the place burned down." He paused. "It's a three-hour walk. Can you make it?"

"I can make it."

"You just had a baby. Are you sure?"

"It's been five weeks."

"Still, you must be—your body can't be right yet."

"It's okay. I can make it."

He figured he had to take her word for it. "Fine, then. Strap the kid close to your body and wear as many layers of clothes as possible. We'll carry whatever else we can. God knows how long we'll be there."

Lily started to get up, but he snagged her back with an arm around her waist.

"In a minute," he murmured, his voice a deep rumble against her temple while his legs tangled with hers. "Just a minute. You're the only thing warm worth a damn for miles, and I'm cold. Give me another minute. You owe me that much."

He was right, she knew. He'd found a place that would keep them alive, and he could easily have stayed there to warm up, eat and relax for a while, but he'd turned right around and come back to her. That had to say something for his character.

Not that his body was all that bad, either. With the passing of her initial shock, she realized that the closeness felt good. She guessed it had something to do with the hours she'd just spent alone and fearing the worst. She half suspected she'd have welcomed the closeness of a baboon. But Quist was no baboon. He smelled of the cold outdoors, of snow and of man in a pleasant sort of way. Though he burrowed close, she didn't feel stifled, and beneath the surface chill of his body was a certain strength.

She could have done worse, far worse than this cowboy, she knew, and yes, she owed him.

Maintaining a safe grip on Nicki, she slipped her free arm around his head to cover his ears, which, in spite of the thick hair that brushed them and the makeshift earmuffs he'd worn, were red from the cold.

Quist wasn't about to reject the gesture. He welcomed anything of a warming nature after the trek he'd made, and the trek wasn't over. They had to make it back to the cabin by nightfall, which wouldn't be a problem if he was alone, but he doubted Lily could match his pace. The snow on the ground was deep, and new snow had begun falling a short time before. The additional inches wouldn't make things any easier.

He supposed that the sooner they set out, the better. But he didn't move. It felt too good to lie there absorbing the warmth of a woman, even if she was a scrawny thing—with a bawling kid.

"What's wrong with her?"

"I think she's being squished," Lily said and loosened the arm she'd wrapped around Quist's head. It was a minute before she extricated herself enough to push up against the seat, another minute before she'd worked through the layers to reach the baby's face. "What is it, pumpkin?" she whispered. "Shh. It's all right. Shh."

Nicki kept crying, her tiny features pinched and pink.

"Is she hungry?" Quist asked, sitting up beside them.

"She shouldn't be. Not for another hour."

"Can you put her down while we get ready to go?"

"She'll cry, but that's okay." She paused. "If you can take it." Expectantly she looked up into his face. It was closer than she'd thought, and though he wore a day's worth of stubble and a frown, she wasn't frightened.

Intrigued was more like it. Tanned from the sun and ruddy from the cold, he was the image of health. With his shadowed jaw, the squint marks by his eyes and the general set of his features, he was also the image of ruggedness. Not bad looking, she had to admit. Something like the Marlboro man.

She'd never met a Marlboro man before. Ruggedness wasn't

something a man developed at Harvard Law, or Columbia Law, or Yale Law, and since she'd worked in posh law offices for years, most of the men she'd known had gone to one of the three. That meant they'd graduated with credentials to match their egos—largely overrated, in her modest opinion.

Ruggedness, on the other hand, was hard earned. In that sense, Quist was refreshing. He was also looking into her eyes in a way that was every bit as cock-sure as any one of the high-powered lawyers she'd known.

"I can take it," he said. "We'll stuff my duffel and one of your bags. And that diaper thing over there. And anything else that can be strung over a shoulder. Right before we leave, feed her, change her, do whatever else you have to to keep her happy while we hike. You won't be feeding her again until we reach the cabin."

Lily agreed that the plan made sense. "Is the cabin on the main road?"

"Main road?" he asked in a mocking tone that brought back yesterday's folly.

Lily figured she owed him that, too. "This road," she conceded without a fight. "Will we have any trouble finding it?"

"I'm a tracker. I told you that. I don't get lost." He didn't tell her that he'd had to try several different forks in the road before he'd found one that led to a cabin, because it didn't matter. He had found the cabin. And he could find it again. Enough said.

Lily studied his face for a minute longer, then took a deep, resigned, if faintly unsteady breath. "You came back for me when you didn't have to. I suppose I can trust you not to lead me out into the snow for nothing."

The element of resignation struck Quist the wrong way. He bristled. "It's my life, too, lady. Just remember that."

"Lily. It's Lily, not lady."

He put his face even closer. "Warm me up, and it's Lily. Talk snotty, and it's lady."

"I didn't talk—"

"You sounded all stuck-up and put out."

"I didn't—"

"You're the one who got us into this mess, remember?"

"I thought—"

"You thought wrong. Fancy city girl screws up again, only this time the stakes are higher than usual. Face it, sweetheart, you need me.''

''I am not your sweetheart.''

His eyes flashed hotly. ''And ain't it a shame. You'll never know that particular pleasure, will you?'' Leaving Lily tongue-tied, he bolted forward, tugged on his coat, hat and makeshift earmuffs, then stomped out of the car to get a bag from the trunk.

Lily spent a minute getting over her astonishment, then another trying to figure out what had happened. Snotty...stuck-up...put out...she hadn't felt any of those things. She thought she'd been telling him she trusted him. It should have been a compliment. Obviously he hadn't taken it that way. He certainly did expect the worst where women were concerned.

But he expected other things, too. That last look in his eyes told her so. It had been different. Hot and flashing. Challenging in a sexual kind of way. No doubt he'd been thinking of one of the women he loved to hate.

A dull thud from the trunk brought her around. Reluctant to give Quist cause for further complaint, she gave the still-crying Nicki a quick hug. ''Hush, Nicki. I have to put you down for a couple of minutes. Please don't cry. Please.'' When the crying momentarily lessened, she set the infant in the car seat and quickly went out after Quist.

It didn't take them long to select the most malleable of Lily's canvas bags and empty it of all but practical items. Returning to the car, they repacked it with the heavier clothing that they'd brought in the evening before. When that was done, they stuffed Quist's duffel and the baby's bag with more of the same, sliding diapers into every imaginable crevice.

They worked in silence. As though to compensate, Nicki kept up a stream of sound that varied from faint whimpering to all-out rage. Finally Lily picked her up and changed her, then put her to her breast. Only then was she still. And only then, with that brief idle time to pass until they left, did Quist pull a can from his pocket. Using one of the arms of his pocket knife, he opened the can, and using a flat blade, scooped out a helping of its contents.

''Here.'' He held out the knife with its offering. His tone brooked no argument, and Lily gave him none. She was desperately hungry, feeling weak from it. ''Carefully,'' he warned as she closed her mouth around the food. Gingerly she drew it into her mouth without cutting herself on the blade.

"Hash?" she asked with a curious smile. It was hard to tell with everything so cold and Quist's large hand obliterating the label on the can.

He helped himself to a mouthful, talking around the food. "Sure ain't caviar."

"It could be. It tastes heavenly. Thank you for bringing it."

"I figured it'd help before the walk."

"You figured right. My legs are a little wobbly."

He gave her another helping of the hash. "Are you sure you can make it? Better think about it before we set out."

She swallowed. "What's my alternative?"

"Staying here. Waiting for me to bring help back in."

"That's no alternative. I'm going."

"It's a long walk. If you get tired, I can't carry you."

"You won't have to," she informed him with her chin set firm. "I may have just had a baby, but I've probably had more exercise since she's been born than in the year before. I can hold my own. And Nicki. All you have to do is lead the way."

Between the look in her eye and the determination in her voice, Quist saw that she meant it. "Done," he said and knifed more hash into his mouth. He continued alternately feeding Lily, then himself, while she fed the baby beneath cover of her clothes. When she'd finished, she strapped Nicki onto her chest, pulled on several additional sweaters, her long woolen coat, then her parka, secured the fastenings as best she could, grabbed hold of the diaper bag and followed Quist out of the car.

As promised, he led the way. Carrying both his duffel and her large bag, with her fur draped over his head, he looked even more mountainous than he had when Lily had first picked him up. She had a better idea of what was inside now, though, and he wasn't the enemy.

Nature was. Snow was falling in large, moist clumps that accumulated with frightening speed on top of all that already lay on the ground. With each footstep, she sank up to her knees in the stuff, and though she walked in Quist's tracks, her boots were quickly coated.

Mercifully there was little wind, which meant that the cold wasn't exaggerated. But it was bad enough. Stealthily it crept through seams, folds and the tiniest openings that she'd thought secured. She feared to think what would have been if she were less voluminously covered. Though the layers of bulky clothing she wore made walking more difficult, they were a protection. Keeping Nicki from the chill was critical. She felt she was doing that.

The first hour passed. Quist, who had been regularly turning to check on Lily, waited for her to catch up. "Are you okay?"

She managed a stiff-jawed, "I think so."

"Need to rest?"

"No!" she insisted. "Keep going!"

With a single nod he turned and headed off again. He'd have stopped if she'd had to, but he, too, wanted to keep on. The large, moist flakes of snow had given way to smaller, colder chips that were coming down in even greater intensity. If he were to guess, he'd say that those chips were the start of an entirely new storm, which meant that the sooner he and Lily reached the cabin, the better.

By the end of the second hour, Lily was tiring badly, but again, when Quist asked if she wanted to stop for a rest, she refused. She set her sights on resting at the cabin, with a roof for shelter and a woodstove for warmth. She didn't protest, though, when he pressed one of the leftover cookies into her mouth. She needed quick energy. She needed energy, period.

On and on they plodded. Lily kept her head tucked low against the sharp nuggets that were being driven now by a rising wind. There were times when she closed her eyes and concentrated on nothing more complex than the heavy rhythm of the trek. Once when she was doing that, she plowed right into Quist, who had stopped for a minute. She nearly fell. He steadied her with a hand on either arm.

His eyes sought hers. "What's wrong?"

She wanted to tell him that she felt lousy, that her back hurt, her shoulder pinched, her insides ached, her feet were half-frozen and *where was his goddamned cabin already*. Instead, she said, "Nothing."

"How's the kid?" he asked. Thinking to lighten the mood, he quipped, "Is she still alive and kicking in there?"

It was the wrong thing to say. Lily's eyes filled up. "Of course, she's alive! I can feel her squirming. But you don't hear her screaming, do you? She's being good. So good."

Quist wasn't sure he'd be able to hear a thing through the layers Lily wore, and what small peeps might have escaped would be swallowed up by the wind. But he wasn't about to make the same mistake twice. "You're right. She's being very good. We're lucky." He paused. "Think you can make it a little longer?"

She nodded.

Some of her discouragement must have shown in her eyes because he said, "You're doin' real well, Lily. Keep it up, we're almost there," before he turned and went on.

The third hour was the tough one, as Quist knew it would be. For one thing, dusk was approaching, and though there was still enough light to see the way, night became a deadline, fast closing in. For another the terrain grew trickier closer to the cabin, and Lily's fatigue didn't help. She had trouble on the inclines, even more on the declines. He could feel the strain of those downhill stretches in his own thighs and had to believe that it would be even worse for her. At one point he turned to find that she'd stumbled and fallen in the snow, and the look on her face was so pathetic when he helped her up that he stayed by her side, rearranging the bags on his shoulders so that he could link an arm through hers to help her along.

Once she recovered from the fall, she protested his help. "I'm okay."

"You're not."

"I can manage."

"Another fall like that and you might really hurt yourself."

She'd already hurt herself, if the new discomfort in her wrist was any indication. "But I'm slowing you down."

"You'd slow me down whether I was holding your arm or not. Now keep still and walk. We're almost there."

He'd been saying that for hours, Lily thought, but she didn't have the energy to point it out. And the fact was that she did appreciate his help. Her legs seemed a great distance away, barely belonging to her, they were so cold and numb. Her gloved hands were nearly as bad, and the rest of her felt a rising chill.

Aside from the occasional stirring she'd mentioned, Nicki slept on, for which Lily was overwhelmingly grateful. She wasn't sure whether it was the steady movement that kept the infant sated or the crying she'd done that had exhausted her, but Lily couldn't begin to think of what she'd do if the baby woke and began to fuss. She couldn't very well change a diaper in the snow. Or nurse. If her milk wasn't frozen solid. Lord, what would she do if something happened to her milk?

The storm intensified as dusk deepened, and every one of Lily's fears paraded in turn through her panicked mind. While not panicked, Quist grew increasingly concerned. The cabin was ahead; he knew he hadn't taken a wrong turn, but he feared he might if they didn't reach it soon. Between the wind-whipped snow and the dark, visibility was decreasing by the minute.

"Where is it?" Lily wailed at the moment her knees buckled.

Quist caught her up. "Whoa," he said, hugging her to him for a minute, "take it easy. We're almost there. Almost there."

"I don't feel well," she cried softly.

"Just a little longer. Hang in there just a little longer."

"How much?"

"Ten, fifteen minutes, maybe."

"I don't...know if I can."

"Sure you can. You've come this far. A little longer's a piece of cake."

"No, it's hell."

"Then it's hell," he agreed in a harder voice, "but you've got to do it. If you can't do it for yourself, do it for Nicki. Or do it for me. I've been puttin' out for you all day. It's right time you put out for me, babe."

She was silent for a minute, and he was beginning to fear he had a *real* problem on his hands when she muttered stiffly, "It's Lily. Not babe. Lily."

"Fink out on me, and it's babe. Give me that extra go and it's anything your sweet little heart desires. So. Are we on?"

In answer, she straightened, pulled herself away and set off— unfortunately in the wrong direction, but Quist was quick to correct that, and they were soon once again huddled together, plowing through the storm.

Ten or fifteen minutes, he'd said, but Lily's concept of time was as distorted as the landscape, an endless expanse of snow and trees of a deepening indigo hue. She was sure they'd been walking for another hour before they stumbled over a rise and he tightened his grip on her arm.

"There. There it is. See it?"

She wanted to so badly, but things were blurring. "No," she cried feebly. Her lungs hurt. "It's too dark."

"Come on. When we're closer you'll see."

And she did, though at first she thought she was hallucinating. Quist tugged her up to the door and pushed it open, then pulled her inside and shouldered the door shut against the havoc of the snow. Leaving her balanced against the rough-hewn wood, he dropped the fur coat and made his way in the dark across the small room to the table where he'd deliberately left a hurricane lamp and a box of matches. It took a bit of fumbling—his fingers weren't much warmer than Lily's and he was trying to hurry—but he soon lit the wick. The lamp cast a low glow to the room.

Lily didn't think to look around. Sliding down the door to the floor when her legs refused to support her any longer, she kept her eyes on Quist, who went on to light the woodstove. Dry and ready, the kindling caught, then the logs, and the glow cast by the lamp was heightened by a warmer one. He knelt for a minute with his hands held out to that warmth before tossing aside his hat and earmuffs. Sitting back on the floor directly in front of the flames, he tugged off his boots, then stood and went at his coat. When it was off, he looked back at Lily. She hadn't moved.

Swearing softly, he crossed to the door and knelt before her. Small baby sounds were coming from under the layers of her clothes. Lily heard them, but for the first time since the baby's birth, she simply lacked the strength to move.

"I'll just...rest for a minute," she whispered.

"Nuh-uh. Not yet." He tugged her feet out from under her, ignoring the muffled moans the movement caused. When he'd pulled off her boots, he unfastened both her parka and the wool coat she'd worn beneath it.

"Nooo," she cried softly when he slid a hand inside and pushed the two coats away. "I'm too cold."

"The fire will warm you now." As quickly as he could, he stripped off the two oversized sweaters she'd worn. With the baby still strapped to her chest, he scooped her up, carried her the short distance to the woodstove and sat her down on the floor. "Don't move."

Why she'd have wanted to, she didn't know. He was right; the fire was warming. She couldn't quite feel it in her hands and feet, and those parts of her face that had been exposed still felt as though they belonged to someone else, but elsewhere she was beginning to feel the blessed relief of the newborn fire. If anything, though, that small thawing made her more aware of her exhaustion, which raised another point. She couldn't have moved if she'd *tried*, other than to keel over, and she didn't want to do that. The baby was crying. She had to take care of the baby.

Quist returned, dragging a mattress across the floor. With an ease that belied his own fatigue, he lifted her onto it, repositioning her directly before the flames. In the next minute he was draping an old blanket around her shoulders, and in the next, he was beside her, trying to figure out how to lift the whimpering baby from her chest.

He'd never held a baby before, and even if he knew what to grab, this one was bundled up in a snowsuit that made it difficult to see what was where. He pushed a hand between the back of the snowsuit and the canvas carrier, but there was no hold there. He reached for either arm of the snowsuit, but the baby's own arms felt so fragile through the bulky material that he was sure he'd break something if he pulled. Carefully he closed his fists on the snowsuit material alone, hoping to haul the child up that way, but the entire carrier rose with his tugs. Frustrated, he began to fiddle with the carrier itself, but the only thing contact with the side straps taught him was that though Lily's body was slender, her breasts were firm and full.

Snatching his hands away, he growled. "How in the hell does this come off?"

Lily's numbness was beginning to fade, but she'd started to shiver. It was the cold's way of exiting her body, she supposed, and in that it was good, but it did nothing to help the cause of her hands. Futilely she picked at the fastening that held the carrier close, but it was Quist who completed the job, while she cupped an arm around Nicki.

Bending forward, she deposited the baby onto the mattress, and, by a miracle of will, managed to unzip the snowsuit on the first try. She got as far as freeing the baby's tiny arms and legs from their covering when she stopped, eyes filling with tears.

She wasn't sure if it was the sight of Nicki, so relieved to be out of her snowsuit for the first time in a day and a half that she'd stopped crying and was propelling her little arms and legs in wild circles. Or if it was the simple realization that they'd made it alive through the storm. Or an accumulation of everything that had happened. But the tears trickled down her cheeks while more welled up, and she could do nothing but yield to the quiet sobs that shook her.

Staring at her, Quist felt more helpless than he ever had in his life. Oh, yeah, she was a crier, and he hated women who cried, but this one was different. Her tears were spontaneous. She wasn't turning them on for his sake, because he doubted she was aware of his existence just then. She was crying because she'd gone through a hell of a lot in the last day and she needed the outlet.

He wasn't sure he could complain. She'd been strong when strength was called for. She'd made her way through the snow—albeit with a little goading now and then—and when it came right down it it, she hadn't slowed him down much more than the storm would have done, anyway. He supposed she deserved a bit of respect for that.

So he granted her the respect, but he was feeling something else. He was feeling compassion again, and the strangest need to take her into his arms. She really was a small thing. Sitting there in a sweater and jeans, with her hair—light brown, he saw now, and matted from spending so long under her hood, but still pretty—brushing her shoulders, her head bowed and her arms drawn into herself, she was the embodiment of loneliness. At least, it seemed that way to him. Looking at her, he relived every lonely moment he'd had in his own life, and though he hadn't needed the solace then, he did now.

Gently he pulled up the blanket, which had slipped to the floor. Then he wrapped an arm around her shoulder and drew her against his chest. She didn't melt; her body remained stiff, and her sobs continued to come, but she didn't push him away, and he was glad for that. Holding her made him feel better. And that was all he did, just held her. He didn't stroke her or whisper soft words that he didn't mean. He just held her, just let her feel the solidity of his body and hear the beat of his heart.

After several minutes her sobs subsided, and he could have sworn he felt the slightest relaxation of her body against his. Before he was quite sure, though, she took a deep, shaky breath and made a small movement in search of her freedom. He dropped his arms and sat back on his heels to watch while she gingerly eased herself down on the mattress and drew the baby close.

Her movements were unsteady, not quite coordinated. She was physically hurting, and he could understand that, since he was feeling the same way. Everything that had been close to frozen not long before was beginning to ache—that, in spite of the fact that the warmth from the woodstove felt wonderful.

Lying on her side with an arm draped lightly over the baby, Lily closed her eyes. Quist guessed that she was asleep in less than two minutes, and though he had plenty to do—not the least important of which was to fix something to eat—he sat for a while watching her.

She'd pushed herself to the limit that day, he knew, and though neither of them had had a choice in the matter, he wondered once again whether she'd been up to it. Lying there curled up, with the blanket half-on and half-off, with her hair fallen into her face and smudges visible beneath her eyes, she seemed a far cry from the woman he'd first seen the day before. The sporty car was left behind, her makeup worn off, her fancy clothes, pared down to the basics. She could almost have passed for a ranch girl.

Almost. But not quite.

The baby made a sudden squeak. Quist's eyes flew to her. She was batting the air with all four limbs. He moved closer, wondering what was wrong with her. He fully expected her to start crying any minute, and while he thought that would be a shame, when Lily was finally getting a rest, he wasn't about to save the day by picking her up.

Strangely she didn't start crying, but made another sound, this one the tiniest coo that he almost suspected came out by accident, if the look of surprise on her face was for real. As he watched her, Quist found other things even more surprising.

For one thing, she was even smaller than he'd thought. No longer hidden by the snowsuit, she was wearing a one-piece terry-cloth thing that moved with her. The only point of padding was her diaper, which crinkled softly as she kicked. Though her feet were covered, her hands were free, and smaller, more delicate fingers he'd never seen in his life.

For another, though she didn't have much hair to speak of, she looked like a girl. No doubt, he decided, it was because she was wearing pink and because he *knew* she was a girl. Still, she had the same delicacy to her features, albeit small-scale, as her mother.

He couldn't imagine a baby boy looking like that, or if one did, he pitied it.

For a third, she was looking at him as though she possessed some sort of advanced intelligence. She didn't blink. She just stared right at him with eyes that were large and gray. He moved a little to the left; she followed him there. He moved back to the right; so did she. He felt as though he ought to be carrying on some sort of intent conversation with her, but for the life of him, he didn't know what to say—and he could have sworn she knew it, the minx!

Then she sneezed. Her tiny body recoiled along with the small, sweet sound, face puckering, arms and legs flinching. Quist was entranced—until her face stayed puckered and she started to cry.

Lily moved at the sound. She opened her eyes, groggily lifted her head and reached out for the baby's hand, which instinctively curled around her thumb. "Shh," she whispered and closed her eyes again. "Let Mommy rest a little more. Just a little more."

But Nicki wasn't about to do that. She was hungry, and she had no better way to communicate it than to intensify the force of her cries. She proceeded to do just that.

Lily gave a soft moan. She ached all over, and what didn't ache, tingled. Beyond that, she felt totally drained, not at all up to shouldering responsibility. She wanted to *have* a mother right then, not *be* a mother. But the clock couldn't be turned back. And this particular responsibility couldn't be handled by anyone else.

Without rising, she drew Nicki close, unbuttoned her sweater and bared a breast for the child's taking. At the first hint of the nipple's presence, Nicki turned her little head and latched on. In turn, Lily closed her eyes and focused on this small pleasure to counter her larger aches.

Quist hadn't moved. He sat on his heels not far from Lily, his hands splayed on his thighs, his eyes glued to the tableau before him. It was the first time he'd watched her nurse, and though a small amount of the discomfort he'd felt on other occasions remained, something stronger held him in its thrall. He wasn't quite sure what it was—whether it had to do with the bend of Lily's slim legs under the blanket, the graceful line of her back and the curve of the arm that held the baby close, or the peaceful look that had crept over her face. He wondered whether it had to do with the exposure of her breast, which looked full and creamy, or the disappearance of her nipple into the baby's mouth, or the small, sucking motion of that mouth, or the tiny hand that looked so pink on Lily's ivory flesh.

He guessed that it wasn't any one of those things, but several or all of them that contributed to his fascination. The picture before him was very beautiful. It stirred him.

Realization of that stirring was enough to break the spell. Closing his eyes tightly, he hung his head, and, without conscious intent, swayed on his heels against the pain he felt deep inside. It was the pain of sadness, the pain of wanting something and knowing that it was never to be.

The pain lasted for just a minute. In its wake came the refortifying of Quist's defenses—and an anger that those defenses had been breached at all—and the determination that it wouldn't happen again.

CHAPTER FOUR

What the cabin lacked by way of running water and a bathroom, it made up for in food. The kitchen, which consisted of a full wall of shelves and a large sink, contained canned goods ranging from soups and stew to fish, vegetables and fruit. Airtight containers held staples such as sugar, flour and salt. There was a large jar of peanut butter, several smaller jars of wax-sealed jelly that looked to have been home done, and a tin of thick crackers. And there were envelopes of powdered milk and cocoa.

Not bad, Quist decided. If need be, they could stay holed up there, well-fed for a month. Not that he had any intention of doing that. He wanted out, and the sooner the better. He still had Quebec to hit—though whether Lily's little folly would screw that up, too, he didn't know. If he was so late getting to Quebec that Jennifer had run somewhere else, he'd be pissed off. He wasn't sure he'd follow her. Enough was enough. He wanted to be back home, where things were normal.

Taking a handful of crackers from the tin, he sampled one. It was bland and stale, still he chased it down with a second. Intense hunger had a way of humbling even the most discriminating of men, and he'd never been that. Maybe in some things, but not food.

He shot a glance at Lily, thinking to start her eating, too, but her eyes were closed. She was in another world. He had no wish to intrude.

Setting the rest of the crackers within munching distance, he took a large can of stew from the shelf, opened it with the can opener that lay nearby and dumped the contents into a saucepan. When he was satisfied with the way the stew was starting to heat on top of the woodstove, he put on his boots, took a large pot and headed outside to fill it with snow.

He hadn't even reached the door when the cold hit him. It hadn't been as noticeable before, since he'd been so cold himself, but now that he'd warmed up, the contrast was marked. The cabin might have been lovingly used in spring, summer and fall, but he doubted that its owners used it much in winter. If so, they'd have insulated the walls better against storms like this one. Frigid air, even bursts of fine snowflakes were driven by the wind through cracks that the human eye could barely see. That made the temperature by the front walls, where the two cots flanked the door, a good twenty degrees cooler than the air by the woodstove, which stood deeper into the cabin. It was a sure bet that he and Lily would be centering their existence by the latter, and a small space it was, indeed.

On that discouraging note, he slammed out the door.

Lily roused at the noise and looked around just as Nicki was taking a break. Struggling to a sitting position, she laid the baby across her lap and gently burped her, then put her to the other breast.

Moments later Quist returned. He brought with him a fierce gust of wind and a large pot of snow. After brushing himself off, he set the pot on the floor by the woodstove. Once melted, its contents would provide water for drinking, washing and whatever else they wanted. What *he* wanted was a double shot of whiskey. Naturally, it was the only thing the kitchen didn't have.

Ignoring Lily as best he could, he stirred the stew, then put several scoops of snow into a smaller saucepan and set it on to heat for cocoa.

"We lucked out, huh?" Lily said softly.

He shot her a glance, then looked away when he found she was still nursing. Her breast was very much covered to the point where the baby's mouth was attached. Still, the image was there, etched deeply in his mind along with memory of the stirring he'd felt. That stirring meant trouble.

"Lucked out?" He wasn't so sure. There was nothing lucky about being a sap, and if he allowed Lily to get to him, that was just what he'd be. She was a woman, with an agenda of her own. It was totally different from his.

"Warmth. Food. It could have been worse."

"Wait till you see the plumbing."

She looked around, searching the shadows at the perimeter of the room.

"Don't bother," he said. "It's nonexistent. There's an outhouse. The door's half-off, but it serves the purpose." He paused, waiting for her reaction to that bit of news.

If there was dismay on her face, it was lost amid the fatigue.

"That's okay," she said quietly—so quietly that he didn't feel any of the satisfaction he'd hoped for. Against his will, he was vaguely concerned.

"How do you feel?"

"Okay."

"Tired?"

"Very."

"Sore."

"A little." It was more than that, but she didn't want to complain. A good night's rest and the soreness would pass, even that in her wrist, which was throbbing. Fortunately it was her left wrist. She could work around it.

"Are you warm enough now?"

"I think so." She glanced at the lower half of her jeans. "These are wet. I'll change when I'm done with Nicki." She kept her head low. "Quist?"

He was wondering what he was supposed to do while she changed. The cabin was a single, open room with neither a divider nor facility for one. His first thought was to watch her, and that angered him. So he snapped, "What?"

At his tone she hesitated, but only for a minute. "I'm sorry—about before. I don't usually fall apart that way, but it's been hard—" Her voice cracked. She took a deep breath. "I've always been one to cry. I cry at everything—books, movies, graduations, weddings, funerals, you name it—but lately it's been worse. It must be post-partum depression, or something."

"Yeah, well..."

"Crying is a sign of weakness."

"Who told you that?"

"Jarrod. Over and over and over again."

"He sounds like an asshole."

She raised tentative eyes to his. "I'd have thought you'd agree with him."

"I do in one sense. I hate crying."

She waited for him to go on, brows lifting slightly. He'd have been happy to leave the subject there and then, and might have if it hadn't been for that silent invitation. In its innocence, it was powerful, a challenge to his own sense of truth.

"Crying can be manipulative," he said. "It can be melodramatic and phony as hell. And messy."

Still she waited with that same air of expectancy, and it occurred to him that he was being manipulated without a tear in sight. The thought wasn't terribly reassuring. Still, he was driven to finish his thought.

"But it can also have a positive purpose. Certain of life's circumstances are pretty hefty. At those times, crying can be the expression of honest, gut-wrenching emotion, and in that sense, it's a strength." He paused, his frown deepening at the slight change in her expression. "What's the matter now?"

She shook her head. "Nothing."

"Why are you staring at me like that?" He felt as though she were judging him, and he didn't like it one bit.

She looked away, then back. "I'm surprised, that's all. I didn't expect an answer like that. I mean, it's almost like you've spent time thinking the whole thing through—"

"You didn't expect me to think?"

"It's not that. I didn't expect that you'd—"

"Feel? What do you take me for, an ignorant clod?"

"Of course, not."

"Ah, but I'm a cowboy. I'm not supposed to be a hell of a lot brighter'n my horse."

"You're a *man*," she cried in frustration. "Men aren't usually insightful, or sensitive when it comes to feelings. They don't say things like you just did. They have an image to uphold, and crying doesn't fit the image."

"I didn't say that I cried," he warned.

"See? You say it can be a strength, but still you want to make it clear that you don't do it. That is very male of you."

He shook his head. "Practical. It's practical. I don't cry, because as an outlet it doesn't work for me. I'm not saying it never did, just that I don't do it now."

"You used to cry?"

He shrugged.

"When?"

"I don't know."

"When you were little?"

"Every kid cries. You did. I did." He tossed a hand toward Nicki. "She does."

"But when you were five. Or six or seven. I can't picture you crying then. You're too tough."

"I cried," he argued. He wasn't ashamed of feeling what he had at that point in his life. It showed that he was human, and that he had depth. Suddenly telling her became a matter of pride. "My mother walked out on my dad and me soon after I was born. I didn't miss her at all except for certain times, like birthdays and Christmas and special days at school when all the other kids had mothers visiting. I hated those times. I felt angry and hurt and alone, and I didn't understand any of it. So I used to race home, run down to the basement of the triple-decker we rented, hide behind the furnace where no one would hear me and cry."

Lily's eyes had widened as he spoke. They envisioned a little boy, a confused little boy who wanted something without quite knowing what it was. "That's so sad," she whispered.

But he didn't want her pity. "That's not the point. The point is that I cried because at that time it was the only way I could express what I was feeling. When I got older, I found other ways."

"Like?"

"Like pounding fence posts into the ground, or hacking old cedar stumps to bits, or riding hell-bent for leather to the outer pastures to check on my stock." He took a fast breath. "So don't think I don't think or feel just because I don't cry like you do. I handle my feelings differently, that's all." He stirred the stew with more force than was necessary, and announced sharply, "This is almost ready. When are you going to be done?"

"Soon," Lily said distractedly. She was still thinking of Quist as a little boy, and looking down at Nicki, she felt an awful fear that without a father the child might experience similar pain. "Not if I can help it," she whispered fiercely as she bent low over her. By the time she'd relaxed her grip, Nicki had had enough milk. Lifting her to her shoulder, Lily looked around.

The cabin was a utilitarian affair. A small trestle table flanked by broad benches stood not far from the woodstove. Closer to the front of the cabin were a pair of Adirondack chairs with cushions of a nondescript brown plaid. The front wall held the cots, which doubled as sofas, she guessed, and just around the corner from those were two crudely-fashioned dressers.

With an effort and a small, involuntary groan, she managed to get to her feet. Her legs still felt foreign—stiff and shaky at the same time, and weak—but they did respond to commands of her brain, enough to get her to one of the dressers. The drawers held towels and more blankets, but she wasn't interested in their contents. Finding an empty one, she used her right hand to haul it completely out and lug it toward the woodstove, while she kept her left arm curved protectively around Nicki.

Dropping the drawer on the mattress, she lined it with the blanket Quist had put around her, then double-lined it with the softer receiving blanket that she took from the baby's bag. Nicki had burped by then, and Lily gently lowered her to the makeshift crib. The fit was fine. Eyes on her mother, the baby gently waved her arms and made such sweet gurgling sounds that Lily couldn't help but lean forward and laugh. Nor could she help but congratulate herself on her inventiveness. To date, Quist had been the one in charge. It was time she took over some, at least where she and her child were concerned.

Bearing that in mind, she forced herself back to her feet and once again left the circle of the woodstove's warmth. The floor by the door was littered with all they'd discarded when they'd first come in. Most of it was wet, now that the snow had melted, and she knew that anything that wasn't spread out or hung to dry would stay wet. So she picked up first her boots, then Quist's and stood them against the side of the chair facing the fire. Then she went back for more.

"What's wrong with your hand?" Quist asked. He was leaning against the trestle table, watching her.

"Nothing."

"You're favoring it like it hurts."

She shrugged off the problem. "I landed on it when I fell, but it's just a sprain. It'll be fine."

"Let me see." He started toward her, but she held up a fast hand to stop him.

"It's *fine. Really.*"

At the insistence in her tone, he backed off, but he continued to watch. His mouth twisted when he saw her pick up the fur coat. He should have known she'd worry about it, and he supposed he couldn't blame her. It was worth a mint. Still, she had quite a time spreading it out on the bare metal springs of the cot whose mattress he'd moved. She made a show of using her left hand, but her right was the one that did all the work. Likewise when it came to draping her parka over the back of a chair. When she bent to pick up her wool coat, he'd seen enough. "Leave it," he barked, turning away.

Lily, who had been concentrating on the mechanics of the chore, whirled around. "What?"

"I said, leave it. You can pick up later. Supper's ready."

Supper. The word alone made her mouth water, but she'd been in the outer parts of the cabin long enough to be acutely aware of her legs. "Give me a minute. I have to change."

Dragging her bag onto the cot, she fished inside until she found the warmest wool slacks she'd brought. Then she paused, wondering where she was supposed to change. She was in the darker part of the cabin, still Quist could see plenty.

"Do it there," he told her, as though he'd read her mind. But his voice was more impatient than smug. "I won't look."

When she glanced over her shoulder, he was turning away. Determined to seize the moment, she quickly reached for the top button of her jeans. But what was simply done with two hands wasn't quite as simple with one. She pushed, pulled and tugged, but the metal button wouldn't slide through its hole. When she tried to use the fingers of her left hand to anchor the denim, the only thing to come from the effort was a low moan of pain.

Clamping down on her lower lip, she worked feverishly at the fabric until, at last, the button was freed. But there were still four more. With a whispered cry of frustration, she went to work on the second.

"Let me see your hand," Quist demanded.

Lily jumped. He was right behind her, then beside her. "You weren't supposed to be looking," she protested.

"You were taking forever. The stew's done, and I'm hungry. Let me see your hand." He reached for it before she could pull away, and then the only thing she could do to minimize the pain was to move right along with the hand. That brought her flush against Quist. Leaning over her, he began to examine her wrist.

Despite his gentleness, she sucked in her breath.

"Hurt?" he asked.

"Yes," she whispered.

He moved his fingers, prodding as lightly as he could while still assessing the damage. "Here?"

She gasped.

"A lot?" he asked.

"Enough."

He probed one more spot, using his thumbs to explore. This time, she would have jumped sky-high at the pain if he hadn't had her anchored to him with his elbows. "I think you've broken the wrist," he announced.

She shook her head against his chest and said in a shaky voice, "Oh, no. It's not broken."

"How do you know?"

"I know. It's not broken."

"I felt it, Lily. That last time, I felt the bone moving. And see how swollen it is." Putting his palms under hers, he held her hands side by side. The difference between them was marked.

"It's sprained. That's all. If I pamper it a little, it'll heal just fine."

"It'll take more than pampering. It should be immobilized and elevated. I'll have to splint it."

"But it's not broken," she insisted, tipping her head back this time to look into his face.

He'd never seen such pleading or such fear, and he was touched so quickly that he didn't have time to tell himself that he didn't want to be touched. "I'm not going to cut it off. Just splint it."

"But if it's broken, I can't use it," she said in a small, high voice. "And I have to use it. I have to be able to take care of Nicki. She has no one else, just me."

"She's a little thing. You'll be able to handle her fine."

"Not if you do something to my hand."

"You're the one who did something. I'm only going to try to fix it."

She looked down at the hand and repeated firmly, "It's just a sprain. No big deal. Leave it alone, and it'll be better in the morning. You'll see."

"Leave it alone, and it'll be worse," he argued, then deliberately gentled his voice. She felt so small and vulnerable, leaning against him like she was. "I'm telling you, Lily, I know about these things. Bones break lots in my line of work. Ignore them, and you're in big trouble. If the bone you've broken knits wrong, you'll have a choice between surgery to rebreak and reset it, in which case you'll be in a cast even longer, or a permanently bum wrist." He paused and tipped his head, coaxing, "All I'm suggesting is that you let me immobilize it until we reach civilization. You can have it X-rayed then, and you'll find out for sure whether or not it's broken. If it's not, good. You'll have taken a precaution, that's all."

Lily was torn. His deep voice was so reassuring, his body so large and warm and supportive, that she wanted to say, "Yes, yes, do whatever you want, take the responsibility, I'm so tired." Still, she didn't want to believe that anything was seriously wrong with her wrist. When and if they were rescued, she had so much to do. She had to finish the drive north, find a place to stay, a job, a bank, a supermarket, a pediatrician, day-care—the list went on. A broken wrist would complicate things horribly.

"It isn't broken," she stated in a last-ditch attempt to believe it.

Removing his hands from hers, Quist held them up and took a step back. "Okay. It's not broken. I guess you know best." She was a big girl, he decided. He couldn't force her to do something she didn't want to do. It was her wrist, her future. If she wanted to mess it up, so be it.

Without another word on the subject, he returned to the stove and began to dish out the stew. After a minute, Lily followed him. He sent her a scowl.

"I thought you were changing your pants."

"I'll do it later," she mumbled.

He stared at her averted face for a minute, then swore and dropped the spoon back into the pan of stew. "You'll do it later, hah. You won't do it later, any more than you'll do it now, because you can't manage those stupid buttons with only one hand." Taking her firmly by her good arm, he ushered her back to her bag. "What in the hell possessed you to buy button-fly jeans, anyway? They went out when zippers came in, for one good reason. When a man wants his pants open, he wants them open fast."

Lily would have gasped at what he said if he hadn't said it so factually. "Button-fly jeans are in fashion," she offered meekly. He made a sound that told her what he thought of fashion. When he began pulling things from her bag, she cried, "What are you doing?"

"I thought I saw you pack a pair of sweatpants in here. Where are they?"

She had her hand on them quickly. They were pink, rather than gray, which was probably why he hadn't spotted them. "What do you want with my sweatpants?"

"I don't want them," he growled, squatting before her. "*You* do." Before the words were out, he was working on her pants.

She tried to stop him. "What are you *doing*?"

He pushed her hand away. "Undoing these. You can't manage it yourself, and there's no other way to get the damned pants off." With half of the buttons undone, he paused and looked up at her. "You're going to have to take them off sooner or later, whether it's here or in that outhouse. Better here—take my word for it." He returned to his work. "And better now. You need dry and warm, not wet and cold." He tugged at one stubborn button. "Besides, these jeans are skin-tight, and you haven't eaten all day. Once you've had a little of that stew, there'll be even less room to maneuver the buttons."

Lily turned beet red. "I know. My stomach isn't as flat as it used to be." All the buttons were undone. He began to work the denim down her legs. She clutched his shoulder for balance, speaking quickly to cover her nervousness. "I've been doing sit-ups. That helps. It's much better than it was at first. I only gained twenty-three pounds during the pregnancy," she balanced on one foot, while he freed the other, "and all but the last five are gone, but those five pounds don't want to move." She shifted her balance. "Some women are lucky and have no problem. I guess I'm not one of them."

Quist tossed the jeans aside. He wanted to say something about Lily's propensity for problems, but the words didn't come. His attention was focused on the five pounds she'd been talking about. Only he couldn't seem to see them. He saw a slim waist and hips, and a stomach that was ever-so-gently rounded as to be utterly feminine. She wore a pair of white bikini panties, nylon with lace that dipped in a V beneath her navel and was a perfect foil for that soft, gentle rounding.

She was lovely. Soft, gentle, feminine. Unable to help himself, he let his eyes run down her legs. They were slender but shapely and sheathed in the same ivory hue as her stomach and her breasts. He curved a hand around her heel and skimmed it lightly up over her calf, past the back of her knee and her thigh to come to a whisper-soft halt just under her bottom.

That was when he realized what he was doing. It was when he noticed the fine tremor in his hand, and when he saw the movement at Lily's middle that reflected her own quickened breathing.

His eyes met hers, which were wide with something that wasn't quite fear, wasn't quite surprise, wasn't quite desire but had elements of all three. Awareness. That was what he saw. In the instant when he'd touched her, she'd become aware of him as a man.

Her hand, which had never left his shoulder, was gripping it more tightly. At the same time, he caught an almost imperceptible shake of her head.

So she didn't want it, either, he realized and felt a glimmer of relief. If there had to be an attraction between them, at least it was mutually unwanted. It wasn't that he didn't trust himself—though he supposed he didn't. When he was attracted to a woman, he usually followed the attraction to its limits. Sometimes he did so against his better judgment, but if the woman was willing, his brain didn't have much of a chance against the demands of his body. He was glad Lily wasn't willing.

Tearing his eyes from hers, he reached for the pink sweatpants. He knew he should get up and walk away, but he was determined to finish what he'd started. In the process of doing that, the first thing he touched was her damp socks. Reaching again, this time into his own duffel, he replaced those damp socks with a pair of his own clean, dry, wool socks. He figured it was some compensation for thinking lascivious thoughts. Besides, there was nothing at all sexy about a lady wearing wool socks that were way too big, or about a lady wearing pink sweatpants over those socks.

"There," he said when he'd finished, but he had to clear his throat before he spoke again. "The elastic waist is easier."

Rising to his full height, he had to stifle a moan. He was stiff in more ways than one. Peeved at that, he crossed the room and finished spooning stew into the bowls.

It was a minute before Lily followed. She spent that minute trying to understand the warm curling she'd felt inside when Quist had seen her undressed. And when he'd touched her. That had been incredible. The feeling had been so unexpected, but good. She couldn't deny that. Of course, good was all there was to it—a moment's pleasure from physical contact with another person, flesh on flesh, a deeper warmth. It wouldn't go any further than that. It was the circumstances, that was all.

Feeling a slight chill, she took a pair of sneakers from her bag and, perching on the edge of one of the Adirondack chairs, tried to put them on. The bulk of Quist's wool socks would have made the task next to impossible even if she'd had both hands to work with, but without both hands, she couldn't even come close. About all she could do with her left hand was to pick at the laces, and ineffectually, at that. Rather than make an issue of her wrist again, she gave up the struggle.

Shoving the sneakers out of sight, she took several small, bright, rubber toys from the baby's bag, put them on the trestle table and went to get Nicki. She managed it by sliding her right hand under the baby and using her left elbow to help. Grateful that she could do that much, she put Nicki on her stomach on a receiving blanket on the table.

Quist set down the bowls of stew, deposited the tin of crackers nearby and sat opposite Lily. If there was a lingering awkwardness from what had happened before, it quickly passed. Hunger and its assuagement was foremost in their minds. They ate in a silence broken only by Lily's occasional soft chatter to the baby. Quist refilled each of their bowls, and they efficiently went through seconds.

Lily was still savoring the very last of the stew, thinking that nothing canned had ever tasted so good, particularly when she'd been growing up and canned food was frequent fare, when Quist set a mug before her.

"Milk," he said. "Powdered. Probably tastes lousy, but I think you need it."

She did. Since midway through her pregnancy, she'd been drinking several glasses a day. Now, nursing Nicki, it was more important than ever, yet she hadn't had a drop in a day and a half. She didn't care how the powdered version tasted. For Nicki's sake, she'd drink it.

It wasn't half-bad, she found. She was thirsty anyway, and it quenched that thirst. Quist was drinking cocoa. She'd have loved to have had some of that, but she didn't dare.

Stacking the bowls, she gave a vague look toward the sink. "I'm not sure how to do this."

"Never roughed it?"

"Why are there spigots if there isn't any running water?"

"There is in the summer. Whoever owns this place drained the pipes before winter so they wouldn't freeze and burst. Makes sense."

She supposed it did, but that didn't solve the immediate problem. Of course, the immediate problem was exacerbated by the pain she felt each time she moved her left hand, but she was going to have to learn to work around that, too.

Quist watched her face. He could practically read the thoughts going through her mind, particularly since she was gingerly holding that left hand at her waist. It needed to be splinted, and badly. But she was going to have to reach that conclusion herself. He wondered how long it would take her.

Though his first instinct was to do the cleanup himself and let her concentrate on the baby, he sat back leisurely drinking his cocoa. "There's a basin by the sink," he said. "Fill it with the water that's left on the stove. Add enough cold water from what's on the floor so you don't burn yourself. Soap and stuff is by the basin."

It sounded nearly as simple as it was. Lily managed to clean everything they'd used for dinner, and conveniently there was a draining rack by the sink, so she didn't have to worry about drying, which she guessed would be more difficult.

When she was done, she felt buoyed. Returning to the table, she sat down, put her face on eye level with the baby and said, "How's it going, Nicki?"

Nicki, who'd been nudging a soft plastic ring in the general vicinity of her mouth, lifted her head and looked at Lily with round eyes that expressed excitement at having her mother's attention again.

"What a bright little girl," Lily whispered in praise. Smiling, she ran her hand over the baby's soft brown hair.

"What does she do?" Quist asked.

Lily looked up. "What do you mean?"

"Is this it? She sleeps, eats and cries, lies around kicking her arms and legs and making faces?"

Lily wasn't offended. Quist just didn't know. Two months before, she'd probably have asked the same question. So it was easy to be patient. "She looks around. She absorbs what she sees and tries to make sense out of it. She responds to the people she's with." Lowering her head again, Lily said in a soft, mommy voice, "Isn't that so, Nicki? There's so much to see in the world, even in this dark, old cabin. There's the sound of the wind and snow outside, and the buzz of the fire and the light from the lamp. There's my face and his face and the table and your toys—" She broke off, because Nicki grinned, and it was such a delightful thing to see that Lily laughed. When she reached for the baby to hug her, though, the laugh ended with a sharp cry. Without thinking, she'd tried to use her left hand. It was a mistake.

Coming to her feet, she did manage to get Nicki into her arms, but the hug she gave her was selfish, more to comfort herself than anything else.

"Your face went white just then," Quist informed her.

"Thanks."

"It's going to get worse."

"No. I just forgot for a minute. When Nicki smiles, I forget about everything else."

Quist hadn't seen the smile, because he'd been studying Lily's face at the time. He'd been trying to understand how a woman who looked tired and bedraggled could suddenly start to beam. He supposed it was what she said, that Nicki made her forget about other things, but having never had an experience like it, he couldn't quite understand. He'd never been so caught up with another human being that he'd forgotten who he was, what he was doing and why.

"Does she smile often?" he asked.

Cradling Nicki between her body and her left arm, with the injured hand angled away, she used her right to tease the baby's chin. "More and more now. Her first smiles came and went so fast that I wasn't really sure what I'd seen, or whether it was a real smile or a gas pain. Lately the smiles come at appropriate times." Lily grinned and her voice went up. "Like now."

He saw it that time, toothless and wide, and there was something about it that made him smile inside. She looked so happy, Nicki did, so happy in such a wholehearted, innocent way that it would have been impossible for him to do anything else. When her smile disappeared, he was sorry and found himself watching closely to see if it would come again.

It did. So did several others, all in response to Lily's coaxing and cajoling. In time, though, as was inevitable, Nicki tired. Her little face remained serious. Then she began to squirm and grimace. Lily did her best to restore her good mood, hoping, among other things, to prolong her wakeful period as much as possible so that she'd sleep longer through the night. But the whimpers came next, and when they persisted, Lily knew she had to do something.

Changing a diaper, particularly those of the disposable, painless variety, was a relatively easy chore. Lily had changed dozens in the past five weeks. She felt she'd become an expert.

Always before, though, she'd had two hands, and never before had she had an audience. If she'd thought ahead, she'd probably have changed the baby in her drawer on the floor, where her one-handed awkwardness would have been hidden. But she didn't think beyond the ease of changing the baby on the table, and once she'd managed to scoop up the diaper bag from the shadows, juggle both the bag and Nicki, then deposit Nicki on the receiving blanket, she wasn't about to lift her again so fast.

So with Quist watching, she went about the task. Unsnapping the lower part of the terry jumpsuit was easy enough to do with one hand, as was freeing the baby's tiny feet. Lifting the jumpsuit out of the way without lifting the baby was a little tougher. Lily pushed and tugged. She tried to act natural doing it, though she was sure that she looked incompetent, which was very much how she felt. But the diaper had to be changed, and there was no one to do it but her.

She kept at it. Talking soft gibberish to Nicki, which was what she always did when she changed her, she ever so carefully held one part of the diaper down with the very tops of the fingers of her left hand, while she tore first one tape, then the other. Thanking her lucky stars that the baby was only wet, she lifted the two little feet in her right hand and pushed the diaper out of the way with the side of her left.

That brought a closed-mouth moan.

"Lily," Quist warned.

"It's okay," she said quickly.

"Each time you do something like that, it makes it worse."

"It's sore. That's all."

"You're risking greater damage."

"Oh, hush. You're just trying to make your point."

"Damn right, I am. That wrist is broken—"

"Sprained. It'll be fine," she said with determination. Drawing the new diaper close, she lifted Nicki's feet again and nudged the diaper under her. Though she didn't moan that time, tiny dots of perspiration broke out on her nose. Weak-kneed, she lowered herself to the bench.

"What's wrong?" Quist asked, concerned by her pallor.

Lily took a premoistened towelette from its pack. "I wish I could bathe her. It's been so long."

He was relieved that was all. "She looks pretty clean to me."

"She is, I suppose." Using her one good hand, she managed to wipe the baby's bottom.

Quist watched everything she did. He wasn't feeling as smug as he had before. She wasn't giving in to the pain like he thought she would, and he was beginning to really worry about her wrist. But aside from that worry, he watched out of pure curiosity. Without her sleeper, Nicki was smaller than ever. He couldn't say that she was scrawny, because she looked healthy and well fed, still she was small. He doubted her foot was as big as his thumb. Looking at her, he found it hard to believe she would grow up one day to have the kind of gentle, womanly curves her mother did.

Annoyed that he'd even thought that, he scowled. Seconds later, when Lily liberally coated the baby's bottom with Vaseline, he said on a note of distaste, "That looks like the most uncomfortable thing in the world. Who wants to go around with a greasy butt?"

"A baby who doesn't want a rash. The Vaseline protects her." Lily arched a brow his way. "She's not riding a horse, Quist."

That shut him up, but it was a short-lived victory for Lily. Securing the new diaper on Nicki was a trial, as was getting her dressed again. By the time she was done, Lily was frazzled and her wrist was worse.

"What now?" Quist asked. He hadn't moved an inch, still sat at the table with his forearms flat and his mouth set.

"I'm going to bed," Lily answered. She didn't know what else to do. She was feeling lots of things—annoyed that he'd watched her struggle without offering to help, afraid that he was right about her wrist, fearful that the storm had worsened and that they'd be stuck in the cabin for days. Mostly, though, she was feeling exhausted. She hadn't done more than doze the night before, and now, with a full stomach after a day that had been endless and tense, she wanted the blissful escape of sleep.

First, though, she had to put Nicki into her blanket sleeper. She did it with the baby in the drawer this time, still it was an ordeal. Between the frustration and the pain, Lily was near tears by the time she finished. Sheer force of will kept her from breaking down again—that, and Nicki's precious face looking up at her from amid the blankets.

"You're such a love," she whispered, leaned low and kissed the baby's soft cheek. The contact felt so good that she stayed there for a minute. For another minute she actually debated having Nicki sleep with her on the mattress. She wanted to hold—or be held— anything to ward off the fear she felt.

Given the tender state of her wrist, it was a bad idea, she decided. So she took a deep breath and stood. With her back to Quist and her head down, she said, "I have to use the outhouse. Where is it?"

Quist closed his eyes briefly, only then admitting to the suffering he'd felt watching Lily try to manage Nicki with one hand. Now she had to use the bathroom, which meant putting on boots and a coat, then taking them off again. He'd wanted to make a point before, but he just wasn't enough of a bastard to carry it to the extreme.

"Come on," he said and went for his boots.

Lily grew alarmed. "Uh, you don't have to go out. Just tell me where—is it to the right or the left—how far away—"

"It's wild out there."

She could hear it. The wind had been howling around the corners of the cabin since they'd arrived and showed no sign of letting up. Still, she didn't want Quist taking her to the bathroom. It was embarrassing.

"I'm taking you."

"That's not necessary."

"I think it is," he said firmly. He knelt and held her boot.

Lily stared at the boot for a minute, but that was all it took for her to realize that, as had been the case with changing her pants, embarrassment was impractical. Gripping his shoulder, she pushed her foot in. After he'd held the second boot in the same manner, he held her coat for her. He was duly patient when it came to the left hand, which she took more time easing in.

When he tossed on his own coat, she made a final plea. "I'd feel better knowing you were here with Nicki."

He shot a fast glance at the baby, but she was little more than a silent bundle of blankets in her drawer. "You think she might get up and run off?"

"Of course not, but—"

"Someone may come and abduct her while we're gone? A kid-napper? In this blizzard?"

"What if something happens, like a spark coming out of the woodstove—"

"I've been watching that woodstove since I lit it, and it doesn't send out sparks. It's perfectly safe."

"Still—"

"Look at it this way," he said with a tired sigh. "The chances of something happening to Nicki alone in here are far less than something happening to you alone out there. So I'll come—unless you're planning to spend two hours in the outhouse, in which case, thanks, but I will stay here."

"I'll only be a minute."

"That's what I thought. Let's go." Pushing the Stetson onto his head, he took the hurricane lamp and her arm and drew her out the door.

The storm was as wild as he'd said. Snow was heavy underfoot and overhead, a fury of bright white dots whipping around in the light of the lamp at the mercy of the wind. She ducked her head against the cold, stinging flakes and let Quist forge the way. She heard him swear, or thought she heard him, though with her hood over her ears and the thunder of the wind she couldn't be sure. But she was glad he'd come. Even if she'd known where she was going, she wouldn't have liked being out there alone. It was dark and cold and wet and scary.

The outhouse stood a dozen yards behind the cabin in what seemed a never-never land of snow. By the time they reached it, Lily wouldn't have cared if Quist had come inside. But he shoved her in with the lantern, yelled, "Hurry," and pulled the door closed.

She was as quick as she could be, given her hand, the cold, and the utter foreignness of the place. She didn't stop to look around; she was afraid of what she'd see. So she simply relieved herself, thanked God that Quist had had the foresight to put her in sweatpants, straightened her clothing and left.

Not about to waste the trip, Quist took his turn while Lily stood outside, huddling against the snow-encrusted wood with her arms wrapped around herself and her face buried in her coat. As soon as he came out, they trudged back to the cabin. The return should have been easier, since they'd already made tracks, but the sheer volume of snow worked against them.

Once inside, Lily went straight to Nicki, who was sound asleep, none the worse for the few minutes she'd spent alone. Quist made no comment, but helped her take her things off, then took off his own and dropped into one of the Adirondack chairs.

Taking a pillow and blanket from another of the dresser drawers, Lily lay down on the mattress in front of the stove, shivered under the blanket until the cold from outside had left her, then closed her eyes. She felt bone tired, more so than she could ever remember feeling. But sleep didn't come. Her wrist hurt. She shifted from one side to the other, from her back to her stomach, but there wasn't any escape from the pain. It was relentless, stretching each minute to an agonizing extreme. She tried to will it away, but Quist's words kept echoing in her mind.

"It's broken...I felt it...I felt the bone moving...see how swollen it is...it should be immobilized and elevated."

Shifting her head to one side of the pillow, she propped her wrist on the other. He'd said to elevate it, and that was the one thing she could do without much effort. It was also, she realized after what seemed another eternity of trying to sleep, not doing as much as she'd hoped. The throbbing went on.

"That wrist is broken...you're only risking greater damage...if the bone knits wrong."

Sitting up, she eyed the wrist as though it were an old friend that had turned traitor. It looked guilty—fat and ugly. And broken. There. She admitted it. But admitting it didn't make the pain go away.

She looked over her shoulder at Quist. He was slouched in the low chair with his legs outstretched, his fingers loosely laced over his middle and his head back against the slats. At first she thought he was asleep. Then she caught the tiny flicker of light reflected in his eyes, and she knew he was looking at her.

"Can you do something?" she asked defeatedly.

"About what?"

"My wrist."

"Not much to do for a sprain," he said, but she heard the challenge in his voice.

She lowered her head. "I can't sleep. It really hurts. I think you're right. It may be broken. I don't want it to be, but what I want isn't always what I get." She raised her eyes to his. "Please."

Quist was out of his chair in a minute, silently cursing himself for making her spell out what she wanted. He didn't like hearing her beg. Somehow it didn't seem right. From what she'd told him, well apart from her wrist, things hadn't gone her way much. If she'd been stubborn before, it had been out of fear. From what he'd seen of her, she wasn't naturally mulish.

"Go sit at the table," he said. He went to the far corner of the room where the dry logs were stored.

Lily wondered what he was doing, but she did her wondering from the table. She watched him take several somethings from the corner, then go back to their bags and get a pair of socks from hers and a shirt from his. She was looking nervous by the time he joined her, which prompted him to explain exactly what he was going to do.

"These are pieces of shingle. I saw them when I took wood for the stove. Someone must have done some repair work on the roof last summer and left the remnants there." He took one of her socks, which were long and cotton, stretched the neck enough to get the piece of shingle going, then shimmied it inside. "They're fiberglass, so they'll be rigid enough to work as a splint without being heavy." He repeated the process with the second piece, then began to tear strips from his shirt.

Lily couldn't believe he was ruining a perfectly good shirt. "Wait, there must be something of mine—"

But he ignored her. "These will hold the whole thing together. You won't be able to move your wrist, which is how we want it." Swinging a leg over the bench, he came down behind Lily. With an arm on either side of her, he was positioned to work on her hand as though it were his own. "I'll have to touch it again to make sure it's okay," he warned. His voice was low but gentle, his breath fanning her temple.

Lily steeled herself for the pain. When it came, she bit her lip and leaned back into him. It was as though one part of her had to escape his prodding, though she didn't move her hand. It was also a move toward a haven that promised warmth and strength.

As gently as he could, Quist continued to probe his way through the swelling to feel the bone that was broken and make sure it was straight. He knew the discomfort he was causing, and again wished for that double shot of whiskey, though not for himself this time. Lily did her best not to make a sound, and except for sharp little gasps when the pain was at its worst, she succeeded. But he could feel the way she pressed back against him, leaning away from the pain, and the way she clutched the table with her good hand and the way she was beginning to tremble. At one point, when she seemed particularly tense, she pressed her face to his arm. He wet his lips and probed on.

"I think that's it," he murmured when he was satisfied that he had the bone aligned. Carefully he slid one of the sock-covered shingles under her hand. He put the second shingle on top, then bound and secured the cotton strips. "I've left your fingers hanging out. You'll be able to use them a little once the swelling goes down."

"When will that be?" she asked. Her face was no longer buried against his sleeve, but her voice was thin. It would have told him she hurt even if he didn't already know.

He rested his hands beside hers, making no move to get up. "As soon as tomorrow, if you keep it raised. The point is to elevate it above your heart so the blood runs away."

"When will it feel better?"

"Tomorrow or the next day, if I've done it right. As long as the bone is aligned and you can't move it, there should be steady improvement. I may have to tighten these strips once the swelling goes down, but that's no big deal."

"Fine for you to say. You're not the one in agony."

He almost wished he were, he felt so badly for her just then. "Got any aspirin?"

"No."

"There's a first-aid kit on one of the shelves." It was a small pack that didn't look capable of containing much more than Band-Aids and disinfectant. But it was worth a try. "Maybe it has aspirin, or something stronger."

"No," she said quickly. "I don't want anything."

"It would help with the pain."

"I can bear the pain as long as I know it's not permanent."

"It's not permanent," he assured her and continued to hold her gently. The tension he'd felt in her body while he'd been working was beginning to drain away, leaving her limp and pliant. She conformed nicely to his frame. While he wasn't sure it was wise of him to appreciate something like that, he knew he'd stay exactly where he was until she showed signs of wanting to move.

After sitting for another minute with her head lolled back against his chest, she slowly drew herself forward. "I should let you sleep."

"I'll sleep later."

"Then I should let me sleep."

It was what she needed most, he knew. He also knew that he wouldn't sleep until she did. Leaving the bench, he went back to the dressers and took out another pillow and three more blankets. He returned to the woodstove just as Lily was checking on Nicki.

"Sleeping?"

She nodded. "I don't know for how long. It could be another hour, or five."

"Then you'd better try to get whatever rest you can now."

She nodded again, but she stayed where she was, sitting on the edge of the mattress with her splinted hand carefully placed on her thigh. Her eyes were soft with fatigue when she looked up at him. "Where will you be?"

He shrugged. "I'll sit here a little, then bring over the other mattress."

She studied her hand for a minute, then looked up again. "Thank you for doing this."

"How does it feel?"

"It still hurts."

He imagined that would go on for a while yet, and since she wouldn't take aspirin, the only other thing he could do was to elevate her hand and try to give her a little relief that way. Without thinking of the absurdity of it, he dragged one of the Adirondack chairs forward, propped a pillow against it and sat down on the floor. Then he took Lily's pillow, put it against his stomach and gestured for her to lie down.

Lily wasn't thinking of the absurdity of it, either. She was remembering how nice it was to be close to Quist's body. She wanted more of that comfort. It would be better than aspirin, she knew.

Crossing to where he sat, she put her head on the pillow and her splint on the blanket he folded on his knee. She felt him cover her with the third blanket, but she'd already closed her eyes, and she had no intention of spoiling the moment by uttering so much as another thank-you. Just before she fell asleep, she imagined she felt a hand smooth her hair back from her cheek. She held the gesture to her until exhaustion took it and all else.

CHAPTER FIVE

By the time Nicki stirred, Lily and Quist had shifted to the mattress. They were tucked against each other with Lily in front, nearest the woodstove. Her wrist was still elevated. Quist had woken periodically to make sure of that, and though the wrist still ached, the throbbing had eased. She'd actually been sleeping quite soundly when she'd heard the first of Nicki's tiny cries.

Maternal instinct had awoken her then, a second sense that registered certain sounds while overlooking others. Not being a mother, Quist was without benefit of that instinct. The first he knew of anything amiss was when the softness that had been pressed against him stirred, then inched away. He was slow to realize what was happening, but once he did, he came quickly awake.

"Don't lift her," he said suddenly and loudly.

About to do just that, Lily jumped. She was sure she'd left him asleep. "I have to take her out to feed her," she explained. She returned her attention to Nicki, who wasn't pleased with the delay, but she'd no sooner freed the fussing infant from her blanket than Quist materialized on the opposite side of the drawer.

He was hunkered down, hands poised, voice all business, if a bit groggy. "Tell me what to do."

He was so earnest about it that Lily couldn't help but stare. "You can't feed her, Quist."

"I know that, Lily," he mocked, "but I can get her up and put her in your arms. There's a reason why I made the effort of splinting your wrist, and I didn't have fun doing it, no matter what you think. So let's give the damn thing a chance to heal, huh?" He looked at Nicki again. "Now what do I do? What do I grab?"

Lily felt suddenly light-headed. She figured it had something to do with sleeping so soundly and waking abruptly. She wondered if it had to do with sleeping with Quist. As a compromise she decided it had to do with simple relief that he'd offered to help. Between that light-headedness and the absolutely precious look of intensity on his face, she wanted to laugh. She knew better.

"Slide one hand behind her head and neck, and the other under her bottom. Head and neck. That's right. There, she's fine."

"Why's she screaming?"

"Because she's hungry." She held out her arms.

But Quist kept staring at the bundle in his hands. "She doesn't like the way I'm holding her."

"She likes it just fine." Just as she'd known not to laugh, Lily knew what to say. She was no fool. Quist's offer of help was a godsend. She wasn't about to offend him by telling him he was holding the baby like she was a sacrifice to a pagan god, though the image was apt. He did look half-heathen, dark and mussed and badly in need of a shave, and his arms were tense. "You can relax your hands a little. They're big and she's small—they'll support her without much effort. That's right."

"She's still crying."

Again Lily reached for her. "She wants milk." When he still made no move to hand Nicki over, she lowered her arm and said, "Try bringing her in a little closer to your body. She likes to feel sheltered. There's a comfort in that." As Lily knew from personal experience. "Ah, see? She's quieting down."

"Not all the way. I'm still doing something wrong."

"No, you're not."

"She's uncomfortable with me."

Lily wanted to say that Nicki was wet and hungry and would be uncomfortable with *anyone* who held her just then, but in fact she was crying less loudly than she'd been a minute before. "Hold her like she's a football."

He was horrified by that idea. "Are you kidding?"

"No. You know how they do it when they've got the ball and they're running down the field? Well, shift her around a little so her head's kind of tucked into your elbow."

"How do I do that without dropping her?"

"Slide the hand that's under her head down her back so that your arm keeps supporting her head."

"It'll wobble if I don't, won't it?" he said, but he was following her direction and there wasn't a bit of a wobble.

"That's it. Now ease her up into the crook of your elbow. There." Inordinately pleased, she sat back on her heels. "Perfect. You can even take away the other hand. She's very comfortable there."

Indeed, she was. She'd stopped crying altogether, and although her little mouth was set in a way that threatened she might start in again at any time, she simply looked up at Quist.

He made a small, weighing motion with his arm. "She's very light."

"She's very little."

"Littler than most babies?"

"Littler than some, but none are real big at this age."

He made the small, lifting motion again. "This isn't so bad."

"What did you expect?"

"I don't know. I thought maybe she'd squirm right out of my hands. Know what I'd feel like if that happened and she fell on the floor?"

Lily had asked herself the same question dozens of times in the past five weeks. "She won't."

Nicki continued to study Quist with eyes that looked large and round in her face. Only her hands moved. They were linked in a random way that kept shifting, one tiny index finger on a knuckle, then a pinky around a wrist, then a thumb in a palm. Intrigued, Quist followed the changes.

"Does she know she's doing that?"

"She knows she's touching something that's reassuring and warm. Does she know it's her own hand? Probably not."

"She looks like she does. She looks like she knows a whole lot more than we think she does."

Lily felt a swell of pride, but said nothing. She thought Nicki was brilliant. That didn't mean she was going to boast about it to strangers.

Then again, Quist wasn't really a stranger. Not anymore. She didn't know the details of his life, didn't know what kind of ranch he had or how many men he employed or why he'd been heading for Quebec, but she had a feeling that she knew things about him that other people didn't. She knew that there was a gentle side beneath the gruffness, a caring side beneath the indifference. She knew that though he claimed to dislike women, he didn't like see-ing one hurt, and that his aversion to babies wasn't so much aver-sion as fear, and that though one part of him didn't want to, he liked physical closeness a lot. What else could explain the way he'd chosen to sit when he'd tended her wrist, or the way he'd held her while she'd fallen asleep, or the way he'd kept her curled against him after that, or even the way he was holding the baby now. He still wasn't entirely comfortable with it, but he didn't rush to hand her back.

He was, Lily decided, an interesting man. She'd taken one look at him in the snowstorm and labeled him a cowboy, but there was much more to him than a Stetson. He had a depth that few of the men she'd known possessed. Thirty-six hours—not even that— she'd spent with him, and together they'd run through a gamut of emotions. Still she had a feeling that she'd only seen a few of his layers.

Strange, she mused as she continued to study him, but that top layer had changed since they'd met. She hadn't thought him particularly attractive at first. He'd been too large, too dark, too forbidding. She saw him differently now. Beneath the bulk of his outer clothing, he was well built. Though his shoulders were broad, they tapered to a lean waist and hips and long, strong legs. And while his face was shadowed by a two-day stubble, he didn't look darker, so much as rugged. He had high cheekbones and eyes that weren't coal black, as she'd originally thought, but softer, rich like sable, warm when the defensive walls inside him began to melt. They were doing that now, and he wasn't looking at the baby. He was looking at her, in a way that said they shared something special.

She'd never seen that kind of look in a man's eyes before. God knew Jarrod had never looked at her that way. It made her heart beat faster and her blood heat and her breath trip over itself before rushing on.

In that rush, with her eyes still on Quist's, she whispered, "Maybe I'd better feed her. It's still the middle of the night. I've been trying to teach her that I won't play with her when it's dark. That's the only way she'll learn to sleep through." She took a fast breath. "Besides, I'm feeling full. It's time."

Quist's gaze fell to her breasts. He didn't say a word, just looked, but Lily felt an intense tingling warring with that sense of fullness. This tingling went deeper, curling down through her body until it settled in her womb. The sensation was nothing like the contractions she used to feel when the baby nursed. This sensation was sexual and unexpected. It had been a long time since Lily had thought of herself as a sexual being.

He raised his eyes to hers for a final, hot second before turning his attention to Nicki. Very slowly and more than a little awkwardly, reversing the motions that had brought her in to his elbow, he handed her over. Lily was able to take her in her left arm without hurting the splinted wrist, while she used her right hand to unbutton her Henley-style sweater. She was about to push the wool aside, when she paused. Her bra was already undone, since she hadn't been able to do it up with one hand after the last feeding, and pushing aside the wool meant baring her breast. Quist had seen it before, but that had been when she'd been cold and exhausted and hurting. She hadn't been thinking about him then.

She was now. She was thinking about the heat in his eyes and the heat inside her. She was thinking that it was both inappropriate and frightening, and that the smartest thing would be to turn away while she nursed. But when she started to do that, he said, "Don't. Let me watch."

His voice was low and smoky, a caress and a plea, and she couldn't say no. After all he'd done, she couldn't deny him this. Or so she told herself as she gently eased back the wool, tucked it outside her breast and brought Nicki to her nipple. But there was more. Though she kept her eyes on the baby, she could feel Quist's eyes on her. She could feel the heat. Yes, it was inappropriate and frightening. But it felt good.

Quist wasn't so sure. He was aroused—the pressure behind the placket of his fly was fierce—and he didn't know where it had come from. One minute he'd been holding the baby, thinking totally innocent thoughts, and the next he'd looked up to find Lily looking at him in a way that had turned him on.

He didn't know what was so arousing about her. He liked his women tall and shapely, with long, thick, wavy hair that could toy with a breast before he'd even put his fingers there. Lily wasn't like that at all. She was small and slender. Her hair just grazed her shoulders. Granted, her breasts were large, but that was because they were filled with milk, and because of that, he reasoned, they shouldn't turn him on.

So what was it? He supposed it was lots of things, and he supposed it had been building for a while. Nursing or not, a breast was a breast, and he was definitely a breast man. He guessed he had felt something the first time he'd seen Lily's. He knew he'd felt something when he'd helped her out of her jeans, when he'd seen the shapeliness of her legs, the softness of her skin, the curvature of her stomach. She'd been embarrassed by that, but he'd thought it sexy as hell.

And then she'd looked at him as if she found him attractive, when he'd counted on her not wanting him. He'd counted on her nixing anything before it started. He'd counted on her being the ice water to cool his fire.

Maybe it was an aberration. Maybe she was thinking of someone else, like her ex-husband or that brother-in-law she'd mentioned. No, not one of those two, he decided, but maybe someone else. He knew she was headed for Quebec to start a new life, and he knew she was alone. Still, maybe there was an old love in Quebec, someone she was planning to see, someone she'd been thinking about when she'd looked at him that way.

The thought angered him, but then, he was easy to anger when he was aroused without hope of relief. He was still aroused. *Why didn't the damn thing go down?*

It didn't go down, he told himself, because he'd asked her to let him watch her nurse, and a strangely erotic sight it was. His gaze drifted from her bare breast to her bent head to the slender fingers that, over and over, smoothed the baby's fine hair. Yes, it kept him aroused, but there was also a peace to the scene that held him there. Lily was nurturing her child as women had nurtured children since the start of time. She was loving that child in unspoken ways, and the feeling that emerged was one of serene beauty.

Quist watched with growing envy. The one thing he'd missed in life had been the kind of relationship that was so close as to be beautiful. Lily had it. Nicki would grow, and perhaps mother and daughter would have their differences, but at the moment they had something precious.

Aware that his body had finally begun to relax, he got up and added wood to the stove, then sank into the chair to watch it burn while he thought about relationships and what made them the way they were. When he saw Lily take Nicki from her breast, he found himself sitting forward and quietly asking, "Need help?"

But she easily shifted the baby to her shoulder. "I'm okay."

"Does the wrist hurt?"

"It aches, but it's better than it was. The splint helps."

Quist sat back again, this time propping his jaw on a fist. He thought back to the start of the time they'd spent together, when he'd been able to chalk Lily off as just another troublesome female and ignore her. That time had passed. He didn't think he'd ever be indifferent to her again. Even now, when his body was finally under control, he'd leaned forward and asked for more. Either he was a masochist, or Lily sparked something in him that no other woman ever had. He wasn't sure he wanted to know which it was, but in either case, he knew he couldn't sit by and watch her struggle. Time enough for struggling once they were back in civilization and went their separate ways.

Prompted by the thought, he went to the window, pulled back a shutter and peered outside. It was too dark to see much, but the low light leaking from inside the cabin revealed snow sweeping past the pane. He couldn't detect the slightest letup of the howling wind. It made him nervous to think about how much more snow had accumulated since he'd been out last.

"What time is it?" Lily called softly.

"Four-fifteen."

"No improvement?"

"Nope." He returned to his chair and sat there until Nicki was done. When Lily laid her on the mattress, he came forward. "What can I do?"

She reached for the zipper of the sleeper and began working it down, jerk by jerk, with one hand. "Uh, I don't think you want to do this."

Pushing her hand aside, he had the zipper down in a minute. Then he sat back on his heels. "What next?"

"Her legs. You have to take them out of the sleeper."

He managed that a little more slowly, gingerly holding her legs with his thumb and forefinger. Remembering what Lily had done the last time, he unsnapped the bottom of the jumpsuit, then pulled the terry cloth until first one, then the other of Nicki's feet popped free. Lily lifted both feet in one hand.

"Push the stretchsuit out of the way."

He did that. Again remembering, he carefully tore each of the diaper tapes. Then he sat on his heels and tucked his hands into the back of his jeans. He couldn't have said, "This part's yours," any louder.

Lily didn't complain. She was impressed that he'd done so much. As quickly as possible, given the handicap of her wrist, she did her part. When she reached for a clean diaper, he came forward again to help, and though he did things more slowly than she might have if she'd had two hands, he worked faster than she could with one.

When Nicki was back in her drawer with the blankets pulled up around her, he went for the second mattress and put it foot-to-foot with the first.

Lily was vaguely disappointed. She'd enjoyed the warmth of Quist's body. But separate beds were the wisest thing, she knew. Vividly she remembered the heat that had simmered between them, and though it had cooled to a comfortable level, she knew it could rise again. Separate beds were definitely the wisest thing.

Quist turned down the hurricane lamp this time, leaving the cabin lit only by the golden glow from the stove. With the pain in her wrist nowhere near as sharp as it had been, Lily fell quickly to sleep.

As though sensing her mother's need to rest, Nicki slept for a full five hours. It was after nine-thirty in the morning when her small cries woke Lily from a deep sleep.

She yawned, then stretched, and the first thing she thought of was not her daughter, but a delightful warmth by her feet. It was a minute before she realized that those feet were entwined with Quist's. For a minute they remained that way. She could hear the storm raging outside, and the warmth inside felt so good that she didn't want to lose it.

But Nicki wanted attention. Reluctantly Lily sat up, only to have Quist wave her back down. "I'll get her," he murmured in a groggy way that was offset by the speed with which he was on his feet. He lifted the baby a little less awkwardly this time, and when she immediately stopped crying, he scowled at her. "I thought you were hungry."

"She just wanted to get up," Lily explained, rubbing sleep from her eyes. "She's probably hungry, too, but the first priority is recognition."

Quist went on scowling at Nicki. "They learn fast."

Lily considered that as she came fully awake. "We teach them. First children, especially. From the start, we come to them when they cry, so they start crying when they want us to come. Some mothers have the demands of other children or a husband or a job, so they don't do it as much. Me, I only have Lily. I've spoiled her, I guess."

"She doesn't have any grandparents?"

"My parents are dead, and if Jarrod's know she exists, they don't care. It's just as well, I suppose. If they wanted to see her, I'd have to take her back to Hartford to visit, and I don't want to do that."

The hardening of her voice was subtle, but Quist caught it. He knew that her marriage had ended badly. As odd as the time seemed now, he wanted to know more. "Was it bad all the way through?"

Disentangling herself from the blanket, Lily pushed it back and got up. "Not really." She went to her bag, took out a brush and worked it through her hair.

"What does that mean?"

She sighed. The last thing she wanted to discuss, especially two minutes after she'd woken up, was her marriage. But she couldn't be angry with Quist. He was being so helpful, and he was only curious. "It means that while I was living through it, I thought it was okay. It's only afterward that I look back and know differently." Returning the hairbrush to her bag, she looked longingly at the clothes she'd brought. She wanted to bathe in a bad way and, even more, to put on fresh things. But that would have to wait.

Coming back to Quist, she saw that Nicki was perfectly happy. Lily wasn't quite sure why, since he was holding her as if she was a sack of potatoes, albeit a valuable one, but she guessed that the novelty of his features intrigued her. Funny, his darkness hadn't made her cry. But then, she was too young to put a symbolic meaning to dark and light. Or maybe she was too smart.

"You have a way with her, Quist."

He grunted. "She'd be staring at me even if I was a side of beef."

"No. She doesn't like sides of beef. I tried that in the supermarket once. She screamed. Actually, it wasn't a side of beef. It was a steak that I put into the carrier with her. Something about it frightened her. You're much bigger, but she's not frightened." She paused to look up at him. "Will you hold her a minute longer? Since she's quiet, I can try to get some breakfast going. She may not be starved, but I am."

So was Quist. "There aren't any eggs."

"I didn't expect there would be."

"Or bacon or sausage."

So he was an egg and bacon man, she mused, crossing to study the kitchen shelves. Actually, she was an egg and bacon woman, but she hadn't expected to find either of those, and she wasn't complaining. Yesterday's fear of starvation was too fresh in her mind.

She lifted a few lids and peered inside, then bent down to scan the contents of a lower shelf. "Quist?"

"Yes?"

He was directly behind her. She shot up straight, then went red. "Sorry."

He noticed the color on her cheeks and realized that she looked better. The shadows under her eyes had faded. She didn't look as frightened or as helpless, though there was still a question in her eye. For a split second, he entertained the notion that the question had to do with sex. Then he forced himself to think sanely. "You started to ask something."

It was a split second before she remembered what it was. "The weather. We're not going anywhere today, are we?"

"Not unless the wind suddenly dies and the snow stops within the next half hour."

"Why in the next half hour?"

"Because when I go out, it's got to be first thing in the morning. It may take me a while to reach help, then a while to get it back here, and I want to be back by nightfall."

She wanted to ask why, but that seemed like pushing a good thing too far. Still she was touched. He was an incredibly kind man. For that, she decided, he deserved the best breakfast she could invent.

Actually, she didn't have to invent a thing, since pancakes had been breakfast fare for generations. She supposed lacing them with peanut butter was a novelty, and she doubted she'd want to enter the recipe in the bake-off, but the end result was edible and nourishing.

Quist loved it. He was great at opening cans and cooking up frozen dinners and reheating leftovers, and he could fry a mean egg and grill a rasher of bacon just right, but he wasn't one to put together a meal from scratch. He was surprised that Lily had done it. He hadn't expected she'd be much of a cook, but she'd managed well, even with a bum hand. Nicki had started to cry just as the first batch of pancakes were done, so he'd taken over with the spatula, but that was okay. It wasn't like Lily had left the kitchen in the middle of things to polish her toenails. He could wield a spatula. And the pancakes were great.

With Nicki fed and changed, Lily laid her on the table and sat down for her own breakfast. Nursing a second cup of cocoa, Quist watched her eat. Though she talked softly to Nicki from time to time, she seemed otherwise content with the silence. He wondered whether she'd become as used to solitude as he had, or whether she'd always been that way. He didn't ask, though. The silence was too comfortable just then.

When she'd finished, Lily looked at him and smiled. Seconds later, she shifted her gaze to the window and the smile faded. "This is unreal," she murmured.

He'd liked her smile. It had done things to him, and he was sorry it was gone. But he knew what she meant. Unreal was one word for their situation; bizarre was another. "Uh-huh." He saw her looking down at her splinted wrist. "How does it feel?"

She hesitated before answering, "Okay."

"Does that mean better?"

She nodded. It still ached, but the ache was more dull than acute. One part of her wanted to think that it wasn't broken, after all. The other part recalled the pain she'd felt when Quist had manipulated it the night before. No sprain felt like that.

"I should have known it was broken."

"You didn't want it to be."

"No, but I should have known. I always manage to do things like that."

"You didn't do it on purpose."

She sighed, still looking down. "I didn't purposely come down with chicken pox the night before I was to play Dorothy in my seventh grade class's production of 'The Wizard of Oz,' either. Or break out with poison ivy the day before my high school prom. Or have my rental car stolen with all my things inside when I was driving to college to start my sophomore year." She frowned, feeling the pain inside her head rather than at her wrist. "This couldn't have happened at a worse time." Her voice dropped to a whisper. "I have so many things to do."

"So you'll just do them slower."

She shrugged and got up from the table with the dishes. She didn't want to think about it. It was too discouraging. So many things to do, simple but important things that were going to be twice as difficult for her now. It wasn't fair.

Quist carried a pot of hot water to the sink. "I'll do them this time."

"*I'll* do them," she insisted. Swishing the dishes around in soapy water was one of the few things she could do single-handedly, and while she regretted her snappish tone, she had to be assertive. Quist was doing far too much.

Preoccupied wondering how she was going to do all those other things, she finished the dishes without another thought to Quist. When she was done and turned, though, she went very still.

He was shaving. Sitting at the table with his back to her, he was stripped to the waist. A small mirror was propped against the worn leather shaving kit. A small pan of hot water stood before that. He was stroking the blade up his neck, making neat, consecutive furrows in the shaving cream.

But it wasn't his neck to which her eyes were drawn, so much as his back. It was a broad expanse of skin stretched over tight muscles that moved with each stroke. She'd already guessed him to be fit. She'd already guessed at his tapering shape. She hadn't guessed at the raw power of his body, or at the powerful effect seeing it bare would have on her.

Her heart began to pound as she stood there, unable to take her eyes away. She noted the way spikes of dark hair fell over his nape when he tipped up his chin, the way the muscles of his shoulder bunched when he reached the apex of each stroke, the way tufts of dark hair shadowed his armpits. She saw a pale scar, jagged but old, lying somewhere in the vicinity of his waist, but it was hard to tell just where that waist was, since his jeans rode low on his hips. She traced his spine up to his shoulders, then dropped her gaze again until it hit his jeans. But her mind didn't stop at denim. It went on to the small of his back, then stole around to his front to see what was there.

Covering her eyes with her arm, she tried to get hold of herself. The baby would help, she decided, so she went to the table, leaned over Nicki, cooed to her for a minute and lifted her. Then, with the baby held tightly in her arms, her eyes went to Quist.

His chest was breathtaking, his muscles well-defined without being overdeveloped. He wasn't heavily haired, but what there was created a soft pelt that was broad and tapering, a visual echo of the shape of his body. His nipples were small and dark brown. He had a beauty mark just below the right one and a scar several inches below that.

"Lily."

She raised her eyes to find that he'd stopped shaving.

"What are you doing?" he asked in a low voice.

She tried to moisten her lips, but the inside of her mouth was dry. Her throat must have been, too, because her voice came out sounding parched. "Holding Nicki."

"That's not what I mean."

She swallowed. "I'm thinking that maybe I could bathe her when you're done."

His eyes glittered, daring her to tell him the truth.

"Well, you were just sitting there," she burst out. "I mean, I was doing the dishes and suddenly turned around and there you were with your shirt off. What did you expect me to do?"

"I didn't expect you'd stare that way," he said very quietly. "You've seen a man with his shirt off before."

"I know."

"You've seen a man shave before."

"Yes, but—"

"Is it just that it's been a long time, that you're hungry?"

"I'm not!" she cried. "I just had a baby. The *last* thing on my mind is sex."

He paused before saying, still in that same very quiet voice that was more pointed than a shout and every bit as dangerous, "It was there just now."

"And it's your fault!" She dropped her voice to mutter, "Sitting there like that, with a chest like yours," then raised her voice again, "What do you expect?" Turning on her heel, she stomped off to the front of the cabin and glared at her open bag.

"I expect," Quist said from directly behind her, "that you'll use a little self-control. I'm a man. You can't count on me for it."

"You don't need it. I'm not the one who's sexy."

"Who told you that?"

"I know it. I'm not gorgeous to begin with, and now that I've got a baby, I'm about as attractive to a man as a piece of mush."

His voice was closer. "I wouldn't say that."

"You would if you weren't shut up in this tiny place with me."

"But I am shut up in here with you, and it doesn't help things when you look at me the way you just did."

She knew that he was directly behind her. The heat of his body reached out to her, joining with the images of his bareness in her mind to play havoc with her insides. To blot out those images, she buried her face against Nicki's head, but the name she whispered was Quist's.

The heat came even closer then, a line of fire touching her from her shoulders to the backs of her knees. "I want you, Lily."

She shook her head, but couldn't utter a word.

Lowering his head over hers, he put his lips to her temple. The rest of his body did a similar kind of nuzzling. "You're not my type, still I want you. Can you feel it?"

A little frantic, she nodded.

"Then I would suggest," he said slowly and with deliberation, "that you make a point not to encourage me. If you let on that the feeling is mutual, I can't promise I won't take you." The last was said against her neck and was punctuated by a slow, suckling kiss that made Lily feel faint. But just when she needed him most, he stepped back. Furious in her frustration, she put a hand to the spot he'd kissed and whirled on him. "You gave me a hickey."

"Not this time," he said. More softly, he promised, "Next time," and before she could think of an appropriate comeback, he was sauntering back to the table.

Senses in an uproar, she collapsed onto the bare springs of the cot, held Nicki close and rocked back and forth. The squeaking of the springs joined with the sounds of the storm to emphasize the absurdity of the situation, as did a certain scent that was coming to her. It wasn't exactly the musky, male scent that had already etched itself on her brain, but a more immediate scent.

Touching her temple, she brought her hand down with traces of shaving cream. She found them on her neck, too, and would have screamed if it would have done any good. But self-control was what she needed, certainly not another confrontation with Quist. She was attracted to him. Okay, she was. But she'd get past it. It was nothing more than another hurdle to be cleared.

Taking several deep breaths, she sat up straight and turned her attention to Nicki.

Quist finished shaving and bathed himself as best he could with the water that remained and one of the towels he'd taken from the drawer. When he was done, he went for a clean shirt. That meant passing close by Lily, but she seemed determined not to look. He looked at her, though, as he buttoned the clean shirt, and when he was done, he said, "Do you want to bathe the kid?"

"Yes."

Pulling his boots on, he went outside to refill the largest pot with snow. He set the whole thing on top of the stove to melt. The process gave Lily plenty of time to undress Nicki, which she did on a blanket directly in front of the woodstove, where it was comfortably warm. By the time the water was hot, she was ready to go.

Quist watched. He told himself that he wanted to make sure Lily didn't injure her hand, but there was a definite curiosity factor involved. He wanted to see what she was going to do and how. He also wanted to see her doing it, because he liked watching her care for Nicki. It brought out the serenity factor, and though it reminded him of everything he missed, and in that sense was painful, he was helplessly drawn to it.

That serenity factor wasn't as strong, now, though, as it had been at other times, and Quist could see why. Splinted and awkward, Lily's wrist kept interfering with what she was trying to do. She shifted, lifting Nicki different ways, doing the best with what she had, but it clearly wasn't enough to satisfy her. Though she continued to talk softly and gently to the baby, her features grew tense, reflecting her frustration.

By the time she'd wrapped a wet and naked Nicki in a towel, she was near tears. That was when he came forward. "Damn it, won't you ever ask for help?"

She sat back on her heels, put her hands on her hips and, looking at the baby, said stonily, "I don't want help."

"Maybe not, but it'd be a hell of a lot easier on both of us if you admitted you could use it."

"I have to do this myself."

"Why?"

"Nicki's my responsibility."

"Yeah, but I'm sitting here doing nothing. Why not make use of me?"

She looked him in the eye. "Because that puts us close. Better we shouldn't be close."

He ran a hand through his hair, which had already dried from the dunking he'd given it and fell right back over his brow. "Better you should get this done. It's worse watching you."

Lily wasn't sure exactly what that meant, but she didn't have time to ask before he was leaning over to pat the baby dry. While Lily took care of the delicate parts, he helped with the others, and Nicki was happy enough with the dual attention to kick and coo and smile. By the time he handed her over, she was dressed in a pretty pink stretchsuit, her hair was brushed and her cheeks had the polish of early apples. Closing her eyes, Lily breathed deeply of that sweet baby smell she adored, and smiled. When Nicki yawned, she kissed her tiny, button nose and held her for several more minutes, then neatened the drawer and put her in for a nap.

Quist's voice came from the world behind her. "Are you next?" He had a clean towel in his hand. Rising, she took it. He lowered his voice. "Want me to help?"

"Of course not," she whispered, eyes wide and glued to his.

"Can you manage by yourself?" The intimacy of his tone was matched by his look.

"Yes," she said in the wisp of breath he left her. She was able to breathe more deeply only when he turned away.

Disposing of the water she'd used for the baby, he refilled the smaller pot with hot water and set it on the table. When he looked at her again, his eyes were dark and sensual. "If I were a martyr, I'd offer to go out and wander around in the storm for fifteen minutes, but I'm no martyr." He turned one of the Adirondack chairs so that it faced the front of the cabin, dropped into it and said, "I won't watch."

Lily swallowed and stood stock-still. The air was pregnant with a silence that not even the storm could fill.

"Well?" he prompted without turning. "You'd better get to it. Like I said, I'm no martyr. I won't sit here forever."

That brought her to life. Taking clean clothes and a small bottle of lotion from her bag, she went to the table. For another minute she looked at Quist; only his dark hair and navy sweater were visible through the slats of the chair. Realizing that she had no choice but to trust him, she turned around, eased the sweater over her head, then over the wrist with the splint, and began to wash.

Quist didn't look once. He wanted to, and several times he came close—mainly because he hoped that the real thing would be less impressive than his imagination—but he stayed true to his word.

His mind was so preoccupied thinking about what she'd be like naked, though, that he was unprepared when she materialized by his side fully clothed, looking fresh and combed and even more sweet-smelling than the baby. She wasn't on a pleasure mission, though.

"I think this needs tightening," she said quietly, cradling the splinted wrist in the good one. She looked a little pale.

"It hurts?"

She nodded.

Urging her down in front of him, he took the wrist onto his thigh and, one by one, released and retied the strips of cloth that held it tight. When he'd finished, he took the fingers extending from the splint and very gently moved them.

"Hurt?"

"A little."

"But not as much as yesterday?"

"No."

"That's good." With the splint braced on his thigh, he held her fingers in his palm, traced their slenderness with his thumb. "You don't wear a ring."

She looked at her hand, saw what his thumb was doing, found it soothing. "I'm divorced."

"Did you get the divorce, or did he?"

"He did. He wanted it fast."

"What was the rush?"

"His girlfriend was pregnant."

"So were you."

She raised her eyes. "So?"

"So his loyalties were misplaced. You were his wife. He should have stayed with you until you'd had the baby."

"I didn't want that any more than he did," she said, and he saw the pride that lifted her chin.

"But it must have been hard, being alone through all that."

"It would have been worse if we'd been together. Everything would have been right there—the anger, the resentment, the distrust. I'd have been a nervous wreck, and Nicki would have suffered." She shook her head. "Better being alone than living with that."

He could understand the rationale. It was one he'd adhered to most of his life. "Did you ever see him after that?"

"Not if I could help it."

"What about your brother-in-law?"

Her features tightened. "What about him?"

"Did he offer to help?"

She looked back at her hand in time to see her fingers curving around his. "Did he offer to help? I guess you could call it that." She took a shaky breath. "He offered to take credit for Nicki in exchange for my...servicing him."

At thought of the service, Quist swore softly. At thought of Nicki, he said, "Take credit for her? But she already had a father."

"That's right. Michael threatened to say that he'd had an affair with me, that Jarrod wasn't her father at all. The only way I could keep him from doing that, he said, was to sleep with him."

"Did he want you that much?"

"Me?" She gave a brittle laugh. "He didn't want me. He wanted to sock one to Jarrod. They'd been rivals all their lives. He thought he could take advantage of the way I was feeling to get back at his brother. It would have given him great pleasure to let Jarrod think he'd been making it with his wife."

Quist made a face. "What kind of sickness is that?"

"Sickness?" She raised sad eyes to his. "You don't know the half. When I refused him, he got ugly."

"Ugly? Like how?"

"Yelling. Name-calling. Violent, I guess."

"You guess?"

"He started throwing things. If it hadn't been for my next door neighbor knocking on the door, I'm not sure what I'd have done."

Quist was quiet, staring into her eyes for a long time. At last, very quietly, he asked, "When was all this?"

Taking her hand back into her lap, she stood. "Three days ago." She went to the window, wrapped her arms around herself and stared out at the gusting snow.

It was easy enough to figure out. "So you ran."

Hurt in her eyes, she whirled around. "I had to. I couldn't stay there, not living under that kind of threat, *especially* not with Nicki's welfare to consider." Her eyes followed him, barely aware that he'd come out of his seat. "You don't know these people, Quist. They have power and money, and they have no qualms about using either or both when it suits their purposes." Her eyes rose as he approached. "Michael would have kept after me, maybe

threatened something else, and Jarrod might have lashed back, but
I'd be the one hurt. Me, and Nicki. So why should I stay in Hartford? I stayed there during my pregnancy because my doctor was
there and a few friends, but all along I knew that I'd be leaving.
There was no future for me there. Thanks to Michael, I made the
move sooner, that's all.''

Feeling the need to comfort, Quist lightly stroked her arms.
''What's in Quebec?''

''I'll find out soon.''

''Do you know anyone there?''

She shook her head. ''It's supposed to be a nice place, and if I
don't like it, I'll move on. I'm a legal secretary, and a good one.
I can work anywhere there are lawyers.''

''What about Nicki?''

She swallowed hard. ''I'll find someone to look after her while
I work.''

''Is that what you want?''

''It's not what I want at all,'' she cried, ''but what choice do I
have? I'm not like Jarrod or his family. I don't have contacts in
scads of cities. My parents were quiet, private people who struggled
to pay the bills until the day they died.'' She caught in a breath
and added, ''I thought I'd escaped that.''

''Is that why you married him?'' Quist asked, but even before
the words were out she was shaking her head.

''I thought I loved him. I thought he loved me. I thought we
were a solid couple, because I was a foil for his flamboyance. I
calmed him down, so he said. I thought it was true. I thought that
I was sensitive enough to understand his mood swings and smart
enough to anticipate his needs. I thought that the differences in our
backgrounds didn't matter and that his parents would come around
in time. I thought we'd have a house and a car and kids and a dog.
I thought—I thought we could have it all.'' She sucked in a breath
and held it for a shaky second before releasing it in a ragged
whoosh. ''I thought wrong.''

Tears shimmered on her lower lids, underlining the anguish in
her eyes. Quist felt the pain of that anguish, but before he could
act on it, she said in a soulful whisper, ''All I wanted...all I wanted
was to be a good wife. I didn't want personal recognition. I didn't
want a career. I didn't even want to be named to the board of one

of the corporate subsidiaries. All I wanted was to keep house, to be a good wife and a good mother. Was that so awful?''

He drew her close and wrapped her in his arms. She didn't cry. But her body trembled as it sank into his, and her arm stole around his waist and clung.

She drank in his strength without thought as to why she shouldn't. She needed him just then, needed him to hold her, to tell her she was worth holding. She'd been alone for too long with her fears and her worries. She needed to feel that she had a friend.

She'd never had one quite like this, though—one whose body could protect and comfort and at the same time excite. She'd never had one who made her feel delicate, while he held her so tight, or one who felt so vibrant or smelled so good in such an unadorned way.

So many sensations, so many emotions. She felt dazed when he drew back and looked down into her face. His own was as dark as always, but his eyes were alive, relaying the message of his body. Her lips softened. Her pulse raced. She wasn't so dazed that she didn't know what was happening when he lowered his head—nor was she so dazed that she didn't know that, right then, she wanted his kiss more than anything else in the world.

CHAPTER SIX

His mouth touched hers. It was a tentative touch, a brief sampling that quickly called for another. The second, then the third were the same, gentle enough to be nonthreatening, firm enough to offer the comfort for which they had been originally intended.

At least Quist told himself he was offering comfort, but the question was to whom, and the issue was drawing the line between comfort and desire. He knew he was doing something to Lily, because her lips softened beneath his and her body went pliant, losing the tension he'd felt when she'd been telling her story and he'd first touched her. And he knew that he felt better with her in his arms, tasting her mouth, breathing in her sweet woman's scent. But his body wasn't pliant; it was growing harder by the minute. So, was desire a comfort? That depended on where it led, he supposed.

But supposition had its place, and it wasn't there, at that moment in time. Sensation was taking over, driving him to deepen the kiss. His tongue outlined her lips, first outside, then inside. When it met resistance at her teeth, he returned to a more innocent caress, and soon, with a tiny sigh of surrender, she asked him in.

He didn't wait to be asked twice. With gentle force, his tongue swept the hidden depths of her mouth. He breathed her breath and gave his own in return, and in so doing, possessed her in ways that went far beyond a kiss.

She was lost, unaware of anything but Quist. The storm might well not have been, nor the cabin, nor Nicki. Quist filled her senses to overflowing—the strength of his body as he held her, the gentleness of his touch, the fire he sparked. He made her forget everything else, and she needed that. He made her feel feminine, and she needed that, too. But he gave her a sense of hope, and that was what she needed most of all.

It was also, in the end, what made her draw back. Her body was heated and trembling, arching into his with a primal ache, yet she made a small sound and tore her mouth away. She didn't release her hold of his waist; she couldn't quite let go of everything at once, and besides, she didn't trust her legs to support her. But she laid her head on his chest and closed her eyes in an attempt to corral her senses into some kind of order.

Quist kept one arm around her back. He cupped her head with his free hand and held it close while he raised his own high and dragged in labored breaths in an attempt to regain firm footing on the ground. Only when he felt he'd done that did he lower his head.

"Lily?"

Her voice was muffled against his sweater. "I'm okay."

"I won't apologize for that."

"I don't want you to." She paused, then asked very cautiously, "Was it me?"

He didn't know what she meant. "You?"

"Me. As opposed to someone else."

"There's no one else here."

"In your life."

"What are you talking about?"

She let out a small, muffled sigh. "Has it been a long time since you've been with a woman?"

"It's been a while."

"Oh."

She sounded disappointed, which surprised him. He'd have thought she'd be pleased. Bemused, he cupped her head with both hands and turned her face up. Her cheeks were flushed, her eyes large and gray. He would have kissed them closed if he hadn't been distracted by her reaction. "What in the devil's going through your mind?"

"You're horny."

That much was obvious, since his erection was pressing against his jeans, which were in turn pressing against hers. "A man can't hide things like a woman can."

"But you're horny because you haven't had a woman in a long time. So it wasn't me. It was my being a woman. That's all."

He was beginning to get her drift. She was feeling insecure, and based on what she'd said about her marriage, he could understand why. She was also distrustful of men, but she'd told him that at the start. He hadn't imagined then that it would bother him so much.

Tightening his hold of her head, he said with some force, "I see women. I see them all the time. I may be a goddamned cowboy, but it's not like I'm out on the range for six months at a time. I'm in town two or three times a week, and I travel farther at least once a month. So there are women. If I haven't had one for a long time, it's by choice, which means that it's also by choice if I want one now."

His eyes fell to her lips and lingered there. "You taste so damned good," he muttered under his breath. As though chagrined by the admission, he looked her in the eye and went on more sternly. "So don't ever suggest that I'd take just any woman. I'm picky. I don't make love to one while I'm thinking of another, and I don't make love *at all* unless it's to the woman I want." He stared hard at her for another minute before softening. "I've already said you turn me on. You'd better believe it."

Lily wanted to. Then again, she didn't. In fact, the more she thought about it, the more she realized that she didn't want to believe it at all. She didn't want it to be so. She didn't want to be involved that way with Quist, not when her life was in such a state of confusion.

"I need a friend," she whispered, "not a lover."

Arching a dark brow, he drawled, "That wasn't no friendly kiss you just gave me, baby."

"I didn't give you anything. I just...*let* you—" she gritted her teeth "—and it's Lily, not baby. I hate being called something I'm not." Pulling free of him, she moved a step back. That was all it took to put her up against the wall. To compensate, she tipped up her chin.

Quist took in the staunchness of her expression and remembered other times she'd taken similar exception to what he'd said. Suddenly he realized why. "He did that, didn't he? Your husband did that."

"Ex-husband, and yes. When I worked in the office, I was his girl. When I dated him, I was his honey. When I married him, I was his sugar. But the worst, the *worst*, was baby. That started sometime during the second year of our marriage, when the glow had worn off and the monotony set in. I told myself it was nothing more than another little term of endearment, but it always bothered me. It was short and crude and condescending. More than that, it's a cop-out. A man can call any number of women baby, or sugar or honey. It's easy. He doesn't have to remember a name, and he doesn't risk using the wrong name on the wrong woman.'' She took in a fast breath and her tone grew pleading. ''So, please, call me Lily. Not lady, or sweetheart, or baby. Lily. Or nothing at all.''

As abruptly as she finished talking, she dropped her chin and looked at the floor. Quist allowed that for just a second before he took her chin in his fingers and lifted it.

''Let's get a few things straight,'' he said.

''A few *more* things,'' she corrected.

''Okay. A few *more* things. First off,'' he began, dark eyes flashing, ''I am not like your ex-husband. I don't use women—or if I do, they know it right from the start and agree to the terms. Second, when I use words like lady or sweetheart, I do it to express something I'm feeling at that moment, whether it's anger or affection. I don't do it to avoid calling one woman by another's name. I don't have to. Because—point number three—I believe in monogamy. I have never been involved with more than one woman at a time. One woman is about all I can handle, and if she isn't, then she's all wrong for me. And fourth,'' his fingers tightened on her chin, ''I want *you*, not just any woman, and not just because we're marooned out here in the middle of a goddamned blizzard. There's nothing sexy about being stuck here when I'm supposed to be somewhere else, and there's nothing sexy about that bare-bones mattress on the floor over there. I'm forty years old. I've roughed it plenty. I've earned the right to creature comforts, and making love on a skinny, lumpy bed isn't one. Nor is doing it on a hardwood floor or against a drafty wall.''

He paused, mesmerized by the wide-eyed look on her face. She was so innocent. It was hard to believe. ''Besides,'' he said more quietly, even distractedly as his attention drifted to her mouth, ''There's no way I could confuse you with any other woman I've known. You're different from the rest in every possible way.''

Lily wanted to think that was a compliment, but she wasn't sure. ''What are the others like?'' she heard herself whisper.

With a sniff, he shot a glance toward the eaves. ''Tall. Buxom. Curvy. Blond.'' He brushed the pad of his thumb on her chin. ''And none of them have kids.''

''Why didn't you marry one of them?''

''I'm not interested in marriage. You should have guessed that.''

''Because you don't like women?'' He'd been blunt about that from the first. "For a man who doesn't like women, it sounds like you've been involved with an awful lot. I'm surprised one of them didn't con you into it."

He straightened. "No one cons me into anything. And that's a vow." As though to second it, the muscle in his jaw jumped.

Lily knew what he was thinking. "It's not a vow, it's a warning, but it's unnecessary. I couldn't con you if I wanted to. I don't know how. Besides, I don't *want* to con you into anything. The only thing I want is to get my car out of that snowdrift and get back on my way to Quebec."

Curling his fingers around her neck, he said, "It'll be at least two or three days before that happens, and in the meantime…"

"In the meantime, what?" she asked, but she could tell from the look in his eyes what he was thinking.

"In the meantime, anything can happen."

"It won't."

"It almost did, right here, a minute ago."

"That was just a kiss, for God's sake."

"It was more than that, and you know it. It was a preview." He leaned closed. "You felt it deep inside, just like I did."

She shook her head.

"Yes, you did, Lily." His voice lowered. "You feel it even now." His hand came from the back of her neck. He rubbed the backs of his fingers over her throat. "And don't say you've just had a baby so you're not interested in sex, because I'm not convinced one follows the other. You may not have kissed me back, but you enjoyed what I did."

"I didn't ask for it."

"But you enjoyed it." His voice grew more intimate. "And you'd enjoy it if I touched you more." He ran the backs of his fingers down between her breasts to her middle, ignoring her gasp of surprise. "Come to think of it, having a baby is a pretty sexy thing. There's only one way to get pregnant."

Lily's heart was beating faster. "Not today. There are lots of ways today."

He was drawing light circles just above her navel. "But sperm has to meet egg and do its thing. There's something inherently sexual about that, regardless of where it takes place."

"You're playing with words," she said a bit breathlessly.

"And you're picking at straws." His hand came slowly up, fingers dragging along her sweater, creating friction and an incredible heat. "Admit it. You're feeling sexy."

"I'm not."

He caressed the side of her breast. "How about now?"

She shook her head.

He brushed her nipple. "And now?"

A tiny sound came from the back of her throat, still she shook her head.

"You're a liar," Quist whispered, but with an odd affection, as he settled his hips against hers. "Why deny it? It's no crime." Back and forth went the backs of his fingers over that tightly budded crest. His cheek was against her forehead, his voice not much more than a breath against her eyes. "I can feel it. It's hard and aching."

Lily could feel it, too, but from the inside. His touch was pulling all kinds of strings linking her breast to the center of her being. "I don't feel sexy," she managed in a husky voice. "I feel aroused. There's a difference."

He was willing to settle for aroused. God only knew he was that, himself. Breathing more roughly than he had moments before, he opened his palm and cupped her breast fully.

"Don't."

"Shh. It's okay. I won't hurt you."

Hurting her wasn't the problem, at least, not in the traditional sense. She was beginning to ache inside, wanting something she couldn't have. And his hand wasn't helping with its sweet stroking, the kneading that gave definition to her flesh. Each time he buzzed her nipple she felt a surge of heat.

"Please," she gasped.

"Please, what?"

"Stop. Please, stop."

But he didn't. He kept touching her, and she didn't so much as grab his hand, because what he was doing felt so good. She felt as though she was awakening after a long sleep, as though she was stretching and purring and coming alive in ways she'd never been before. Her breathing was shallow and fast, her forehead pressed to his cheek. She felt female all over.

Quist thought so, too. While one of his hands stroked her breast, the other was exploring things like her waist and her hips, even her thighs, and nothing he found was a disappointment. But he was, after all, a breast man. Wrapping that other arm fully around her waist to anchor her close, he slipped a hand under her sweater and, before she could protest, cupped her swollen flesh.

She gasped, then followed it with a tiny moan of helpless pleasure and mindless need. She hadn't expected the sensual onslaught. She wasn't prepared for it at all.

"Quist," she whispered, and there was a frantic edge to the sound.

He heard it. Not for a minute did he think it anything but what it was. She wasn't asking for more, though one part of her wanted it. She was asking him, one last time, to stop. She was saying that she wouldn't be able to ask him again, but that she didn't want to make love. She was frightened.

So was he, in his way. He'd had his fire stoked many a time, but never to quite the combustible level he was at now. His muscles were tight, his blood heated. He was on the verge of losing control. He had to think, had to decide whether that was what he wanted to do.

Breathing hard, memorizing the feel of her for a final greedy moment, he dragged his hand over her flesh and out from under her sweater. "This is absurd," he grumbled. "This whole thing is absurd. There shouldn't be any attraction between us."

"I know," she cried in a wobbly voice.

"We're as different as night from day."

"Yes."

"We want different things. Once we leave this cabin, we'll go our separate ways and never see each other again."

She nodded against his chest.

"So what are we doing?"

"I'm not doing anything. You're the one who's doing—and don't say that I didn't fight you, because I know I didn't, so I'm as bad as you are."

"Worse," he said. Unfulfilled desire always made him cranky. "I told you not to count on me for control, but you did it. So where does that leave us now? I'm hard and you're scared."

"Maybe you'd better let me go."

"But I like the feel of you against me."

"It's useless. It can't go anywhere."

He moved then, not far, but enough to allow for breathing space. "Can't?" It was a possibility he hadn't considered, but he eyed her in concern and considered it now. "Was there some problem when you had Nicki? Are you not completely healed or something?" She'd done pretty well going through the snow, right up until the end. It was hard to remember she'd been through childbirth such a short time before.

"I meant can't, as in won't."

But he wasn't convinced about the other. "Are you okay, Lily? If things were different, if we knew each other in normal circumstances, if you wanted to do it, could you make love?"

She was a long time answering, and then it was in a defeated voice directed at the far wall. "I should say no. That would be best for both of us. You'd know that you couldn't do it, and I'd know that I lied, so I wouldn't deserve to do it." She looked meekly up. "I haven't been to the doctor yet. I was supposed to see him next week." She hesitated for another minute, finally admitting very quietly. "But I'm fine. I know my body. It's healed."

Quist was glad for her, not so glad for him. Temptation was staring him in the face, and he didn't like it.

Crossing her arms over her waist, Lily balanced her splinted wrist in the crook of her elbow. Her face was averted. "I was only with one man before my husband, and that was long before my marriage. I'm not good at things like this."

"Neither am I," Quist said. "The other women I've been with have known the score."

Her head went lower. "I'm sorry. I wish I was more sophisticated—"

"Oh, please," he snarled, turning away with a hand at the back of his neck. "If you were more sophisticated, I probably wouldn't want you so much. Besides, wishes are pointless. They don't do us any good."

She pulled in her arms. "What will?"

"Determination." He faced her again, and his expression was as firm as his voice. "We're not making love. That's that. The attraction is skin-deep. You don't want a cowboy any more than I want a new mother. We'll be here together for another one, two, maybe three days, but after that it's over. So we're just gonna have to use a little self-control."

"You said I couldn't count on you for it."

"I'm not sure you can. I'll try. You just be sure to try double hard."

Lily put her head back against the wood and closed her eyes for a minute. She could try double hard. She was good at doing that. It seemed she'd been doing it all her life. Ah, but she was tired of the struggle.

Her eyes flew open when Quist suddenly grasped her arms and hauled her away from the wall. She was thinking that his resolve hadn't lasted long at all, when he said, "You'll freeze standing there." He dropped one hand, kept the other at her arm as he led her to the chair nearest the woodstove. When she'd settled into it, he turned the other around to face the same way and sank down. He stretched out his legs, propped his elbows on the broad wooden arms, pressing his fists together against his mouth. Seconds later he mumbled something.

Lily looked up. "Hmm?"

He dropped his fists to his lap. "You didn't feel the cold, did you?" It was more a statement than a question. No, she hadn't felt the cold, and they both knew why. "And your wrist wasn't hurting." He didn't even attempt to make that one a question. She'd been aroused. Everything in the periphery had fallen away. "It was powerful," he said a bit wistfully, keeping his eyes on the slow-burning logs.

There wasn't much Lily could add. He'd captured the feeling in two short statements and three words. Dwelling on it, though, wasn't going to help with self-control. They needed a diversion.

"Why are you headed for Quebec?" she asked. It seemed as good a diversion as any, and besides, she wanted to know.

He shot her a fast glance before looking back at the woodstove, and he was silent for a while. Finally he rubbed a finger across the bridge of his nose. "I'm looking for someone. Last I heard, she was there."

"She?" Lily felt stung.

"My half sister."

The sting eased. "Your mother's daughter?"

His nod was slow and tight. "She's in some kind of trouble. Called me two weeks ago from New York and asked if I'd come, but when I got there she'd gone to Boston, and when I got there, she'd gone to Quebec. I'm giving it this one last shot, and if she isn't in Quebec, I'm on my way." He half sang the last, the message being that he'd be on his way without regret.

"What kind of trouble is she in?"

"Man trouble. She got involved with someone who wasn't very nice. The question is whether he takes the fall alone, or whether he drags her down with him."

"What can you do?"

"Get her a good lawyer."

"She can't do that herself?"

"She's only nineteen."

"Nineteen! That's...surprising."

His mouth grew hard. "My mother was seventeen when she had me. She was thirty-eight when she had her. For all I know, there were others in between, but I only heard of Jennifer. I got a call from a lawyer one day saying that my mother had died and there was a daughter I was supposed to be told about. So I was told."

There was more that he wasn't saying. "You've never seen her, have you?"

"Nope."

"Were you in touch with her at all before this?"

He pursed his lips and shook his head.

She offered him a tentative smile of admiration. "Still you've come all the way across the country to help her. I think that's nice."

"Not really. I'm just satisfying my curiosity."

"It has to be more than that," she chided, still wearing that tentative smile. "If it was only curiosity, you'd have come to take a look at her long ago."

"I didn't know about her long ago. It's only been five years since my mother died."

Lily's smile faded. "Did you ever see your mother again, I mean, after she left?"

"No."

She rubbed her arm against the chill in his voice. "You never tried to find her?"

"Why would I have done that? She was the one who left. She didn't give a damn about me. Was I supposed to care what happened to her?"

"Weren't you ever curious?"

"I had enough to keep me busy so I didn't have to think of it."

"But she was your mother."

"An accident of birth."

Lily glanced toward the drawer in which Nicki was napping, and it occurred to her that one day her daughter would say the same thing about Jarrod. And Lily would do nothing to discourage it. Lord knew, *she* didn't want contact with Jarrod. "But Nicki may be curious," she told herself. Realizing that she'd spoken aloud, she sent Quist a self-conscious look. "I was thinking about Nicki and her father."

"Obviously."

"I'm not sure how I'll handle it."

"When she asks about her father?"

Lily nodded. "It's not an immediate problem. While she's little, she'll accept the answers I give her. But if she decides she wants to see him when she's older, I don't know."

"You can't forbid it."

"I don't want her hurt. What if she pops up on his doorstep and he slams the door in her face? Can you imagine what she'd feel?"

"I can imagine," he said, and Lily realized that he, more than most, could imagine, indeed.

"God, I hope that never happens," she whispered, nervously fiddling with the ragged ends of the cloth strips binding her splint.

"What if he comes looking for her one day?"

Her eyes flew up. "He has no right."

"He has every right. He's her father."

But Lily was shaking her head. "As far as I'm concerned, he surrendered his rights where Nicki's concerned the day he walked out on us."

"A court would say differently."

"Whose side are you on?" she cried.

"I'm not taking sides. I'm just being realistic."

Calming herself a little, she realized that he was right. Only he didn't know the facts. "I have papers. Jarrod signed them. He agreed to leave us alone."

Quist considered that. "In exchange for what?"

She had to hand it to him; he was quick. And it seemed silly, since she'd already told him so much, not to tell the rest. "A lump-sum settlement that was below what I might have gotten if I'd wanted to fight him. Jarrod's family is powerful. They never accepted me as one of them, and I could imagine all kinds of nasty things happening if they decided they wanted part of Nicki. I won't have her used that way. I was willing to give up the money for a certain peace of mind."

"So now you have to work."

"I don't have to. The settlement was still a good one. But I want to put it away for Nicki—for education, maybe travel or a home when she's grown." She rubbed her arm. "I don't want that money for myself. I'd rather work."

Quist had to admire her for that, but his thoughts were straying. He was remembering what it was like growing up with one parent and no siblings. "She'll be lonely."

"Maybe not. I'll be there most of the time. And if I meet the right man, I'll remarry and have more kids."

He eyed her warily. "Is that what you want?"

She had no qualms about saying, "Yes," and looking him in the eye. "I meant it when I said I didn't want a career. I can work, and I'll happily do it as long as I have to, but I'm not ambitious that way. I want a home and a family. I want to bake bread and drive car pools and barbecue hotdogs on Sunday afternoons. That's all I've ever really wanted."

When she'd said it before, it had been in the context of her marriage to Jarrod. He hadn't given it much thought then. Now he did. "You're a throwback. Women aren't wanting to do things like that nowadays. They want to be out having fun, making money, putting men in their places, or trying to."

"Not me," she said simply. Resting her head against the back of the chair, she closed her eyes.

Quist stared at her, waiting for her to look at him and tell him how cynical he was, or that he knew the wrong women. The fact that she didn't move, didn't speak, didn't even open her eyes somehow gave greater credence to her claim. If she was a throwback to women of an earlier age, she was making no apologies for it.

He almost envied the man she married, and she would marry, he knew. She wasn't meant to be a loner. She'd make some man a good wife. She was nice to be with, eager to please, willing to do her share of the work. She was bright and attractive. And sexy. He looked at the way her sweater fell loosely over her breasts and remembered how that flesh had felt in his hands. Too quickly he felt a stirring in his loins.

Fortunately Nicki woke up just then, and he was almost relieved. He needed something to take his mind off Lily's body. Picking the baby up, carrying her to Lily, helping change her diapers were the kinds of things that—novice that he was—demanded his full attention. He had to confess that he liked it when Nicki looked at him and smiled, which he found he could make her do by tickling her under her chin, which he could do without a lot of fuss while Lily's back was turned. He liked doing it then. He didn't feel foolish. And with Lily off across the room, he knew Nicki's smile was for him. That gave him an odd kind of satisfaction.

Odd or not, he needed *some* satisfaction, because with Lily so often close, the breaks were few and far between. He spent the time she was nursing Nicki at the window, looking out at the storm, wishing it would end, wondering when it would, planning the action he'd take when it happened, but no sooner did he return to the center of the room than he felt that same unbidden excitement deep inside. Increasingly that excitement led to a sense of deprivation, which made him testy.

Lily's version of testy was edgy. No matter what other things she thought of, when Quist came near, she was acutely and physically aware of him, and when that happened, she got nervous. She fumbled around his large hands for the diaper tapes, bobbled the can of soup he opened for her to heat, twice lost the stirring spoon in the pot. Though she could blame the clumsiness on her splinted wrist, she knew its true cause.

Quist was exceedingly virile. Everything about him smacked of man, from his height, to his physique, to the gentle bob of his Adam's apple when he drank, the fine hairs on the backs of his hands and the veins on his forearms. His walk, especially, intrigued her. It was tight-hipped and spare of movement, but it got him where he was going just when he wanted to be there. Of course, he wasn't going far within the cabin, but that meant that wherever he did go, she could watch.

It was a trying pastime. Too often, when their eyes met, that special heat flared, and their eyes met often. Sheer boredom led to that. There wasn't much to keep either occupied in a way that was separate from the other. The cabin was too small, their activities too enmeshed.

Lily was taking her turn at the window, looking helplessly out at the storm, when, from out of the blue, she said, "Are you really a cowboy?"

Quist was feeding the stove, whose heat was slightly depleted after having provided them with a lunch of hot soup. Her question made him pause. Twisting on his heels to look back at her, he said, "I thought that was a given."

She came away from the draft. "Are you one?"

He shrugged and turned back to the woodstove, pushing the log where he wanted it. "Depends how you define the term. If you mean, do I live on a ranch with cattle and horses and branding irons and dust, the answer is yes. If you mean, do I swing into the saddle every morning wearing chaps and spurs to do all kinds of fancy tricks with my rope, the answer is no." He closed the grate and stood, brushing his hands against each other. "My ranch is a business. When I'm not in my office, I'm in town contracting for supplies, and when I ride the range, it's usually in a Jeep."

Nothing he said diminished the slightly romantic notion she had of a cowboy and his life. She could see him doing those things. Dark head, bronzed skin, tight hips and long, denim-covered legs—he made a handsome cowboy. "Do you like the work?" she asked and watched him sink into the chair she'd come to think of as his.

"Yes."

"Do you miss it now?"

He stretched out his long legs and nodded.

"Is it nice, Montana?"

He shot her a glance. She was standing by the chair he'd come to think of as hers. "Never been there?"

She shook her head.

"It's real pretty. Green and blue. Lots of wide-open spaces. I like wide-open spaces."

She could imagine he would, given his size. She could picture him standing on his front porch, taking a long, deep breath of the fresh air, then striding easily off toward the corral. He was the commanding type, with the more to command, the better, she guessed.

That raised another issue. "Who's taking care of things while you're gone?"

"I have a foreman."

"Is he good?"

"He's been with me for fourteen years. I trust him." He looked at her again. "Why all the questions?"

She shrugged. "I don't know. I was just wondering. That kind of life is totally foreign to anything I've ever known."

"A city girl born and bred?" he asked with a dry twist to his lips.

"Something wrong with that?" she asked right back. Picking a fight with him was better than panting after him.

"Wrong? That depends on what you want in life. City living's great if you want headaches, stomach aches, traffic jams, lines everywhere you turn and either cockroach-infested apartments or ticky-tacky houses on quarter-acre lots. Me," he took a breath, "I'd die living like that."

She brushed her fingertips on the arm of the chair. "But you did it once."

"Did I tell you that?"

"You said you lived in a triple-decker. I've never heard of a ranch with a triple-decker. You know the pitfalls of city living very well. And then there's the way you talk. You don't talk like a cowboy."

He was amused. "How is a cowboy supposed to talk?"

"With a drawl. With *ain't*s and *dunno*s and *mama*s. And *darlin'*s. You've never called me darlin'." She slipped into the chair and settled back. "If you were a native cowboy, you'd have done that."

He snorted. "You've been watching the wrong programs."

"Cowboys don't use words like that?"

"Some do, some don't. But you're right," he hurried on, because she'd already picked up on too much, "I was born in the city." And once started, it seemed a shame not to tell it all. "We lived in Seattle, my father and me. Then we moved to Denver, then Detroit."

"Why so many moves? Did it have to do with his work?"

"Maybe. He was a restless kind of guy."

"Do you think he was looking for your mother?"

The muscle in his jaw jumped. "If he was, he never told me, and he sure as hell never found her."

Lily was amazed at the anger that the mere mention of his mother stirred in Quist. Not wanting to make things worse, she redirected her questions. "What happened after Detroit?"

"*In* Detroit. He died."

She turned her head against the wood slats to find him staring at the woodstove, not quite angry, but sober. "And?"

"I raised hell for the next four years. Then I won the ranch."

"Won?"

"In a game of five-card stud."

"You're kidding."

Slowly he shook his head.

"You *won* it?"

He nodded.

"Men actually do that—put something as valuable as a ranch up as a stake?"

"Damn right they do," he said, but he remembered how stunned he'd been, himself—no, what had stunned him was the lousy hand the guy had. Poker players were usually more careful when something as vital was at stake. "Not that the ranch was worth a hell of a lot back then, but it was more than I'd ever had." He looked at her. "So I took it."

"That's incredible," she said with a smile of amazement. "And you made it work."

He basked in her smile, letting its warmth seep through him. She was so pretty when she smiled, he thought. No, she was pretty all the time, but when she smiled, she lit up, and that lit him up inside.

Her smile, he realized, was totally innocent, seductive in the broadest sense of the word, and dangerous.

That thought was sobering. In a darker voice, he said, "I made it work, all right. I fought and sweated and bled to get it in shape, and once I'd done that, I fought and sweated and bled some more to get it growing. That place is me."

"Mmm. Big and dark and rough," she teased, but he didn't smile.

"Not dark, but big and rough. It's a man's place."

"Without a woman's touch?"

"Don't need a woman's touch."

"Do the women who see it agree?"

"Women don't see it."

Lily frowned. "Where do you see *them*?"

"Anywhere but the ranch. The ranch is mine. Besides, a ranch is no place for a woman."

Lily stared at him, then made a face. "That's the dumbest thing I've ever heard. Women have lived on ranches since the beginning of time. Who do you think did all the cooking and cleaning and sewing while the cowboys were out getting dirty?"

"Correction," he said, looking back at the fire. "A ranch is no place for the women *I* know. I love it—they'd hate it. I don't need that kind of grief."

Whether it was something in his voice or the grim set of his face that did it, Lily wasn't sure. But she suddenly wondered whether he was afraid of rejection. After all, he'd been rejected early on by his mother.

"Why would they hate it?" she asked more gently.

"It's not fancy. It's not society. It doesn't have four-star restaurants or exciting nightlife. It doesn't have nightlife, period, because the days begin at dawn. It relies heavily on routine. It's quiet and isolated. And peaceful," he tacked on, because that was the way the ranch made him feel.

Lily thought it sounded nice. "What about creature comforts?" she asked, teasing again.

This time, his mouth relaxed into a sheepish half smile. He remembered what he'd told her. "It has those."

"Then maybe it isn't so bad. Maybe you underestimate your women."

His smile went the way of the warmth in his eyes. "No. Never that." He was out of his chair in a minute, stalking to a corner of the kitchen. There, he turned to glare at Lily, who was sitting demurely in her chair. "Don't look at me that way." She didn't blink. "What are you staring at?"

"You. You really do know the wrong women. You're typically male."

"What do you mean by that?"

"Men want women who are fast and free and glitzy. What was it you said—your women are tall, buxom, curvy and blond? It's an ego thing. You think you're hot stuff if you attract hot-shot women." She pictured Jarrod, pictured his new wife, whom she'd known quite well and who was the embodiment of glitz. Then she deliberately blinked them away. "Well, of *course* those women won't fit on a ranch. That's not to say that other women wouldn't do just fine."

"They would not."

"They would, too."

"Ranch life is hard."

"Uh-huh, with your office and your Jeep and your creature comforts."

"Ranch life is *hard*."

"And a woman's too soft?" She heard just about enough. Coming out of her chair, she advanced on him. "You want to believe that. You want to believe it so bad that you keep your eyes closed to the alternative." Her own eyes were angry. "For your information, women can be every bit as hard as men, if not harder. We have to be, if only to survive the mess you guys make of things!"

She whirled away, but he caught her arm and whirled her back. "I've never made a mess of anyone's life—"

"—but your own. You're missing out on a whole lot, Quist, and some day you'll die a lonely old man!" As soon as the words were out, she regretted them, and it had to do only in part with the rigidity of his features. She'd confused the issues, let her own anger jade her judgment. "I'm sorry," she whispered. "I shouldn't have said that. It's not my place to tell you what's right or wrong. I haven't done such a super job with my own life."

Quist wanted to say, "Damned right, you haven't," but the words wouldn't come. He stood there staring at her, wondering how she could be hard and soft at the same time, knowing she was. She was so different. Whether she was being quiet and vulnerable or vocal and insistent, he wanted her.

He could see that she wanted him, too. It was there in her eyes as she stood before him. It was there in the faint tremor that gave her body a gossamer feel, and in the quickening of her breath.

Taking a deep one of his own, with his hand still on her arm, he led her across the room. "We're going out," he muttered.

"Out?" she said shakily. "We were out before, and it's still snowing."

"I need fresh air."

"Then you can go out."

"You need it, too," he said and looked at her in such a way that she didn't say another word. She submitted to being helped on with her boots and her coat. She waited while he put on his own things. Then, holding the back of his coat, she let him lead her out into the storm.

Heads bowed against the wind, they waded through the thigh-high snow to circle the cabin twice before making a stop at the outhouse. Quist, who had that much more strength than Lily and commensurate sexual energy to expel, made two more circles before joining her inside. She'd managed to shrug out of her coat and work her boots off with her feet, but when she turned to him, he caught his breath.

Her hair was still matted by the hood of her coat, and the moss-green sweater she wore didn't exactly go with her pink sweatpants. But her eyes were clear, her cheeks red, her lips moist. She looked good enough to eat.

In the space of a breath he was before her, taking her face in his hands, covering her mouth with his. He kissed her with the hunger he thought he'd just walked off. Then he murmured against her mouth, "This isn't going to work. I want you too much."

Lily moved her hand over his jaw, trying to warm it with a hand that was none too warm, itself. Then, trying to warm her hand, she buried her fingers under the crew neck of his sweater. The skin there was warm and firm, and just that little bit fuzzy.

"Lily," he warned.

"I know," she said quickly and withdrew her hand. "It's okay." She turned from him. "Nicki's due up any minute." Sitting on the mattress beside the drawer, she held her hands in her lap and watched the baby until she awoke.

But Quist was right. It wasn't going to work. No matter how hard she tried to concentrate on the baby, she was aware of him. If it hadn't been for her wrist, she decided, she'd have been able to do everything on her own. But her wrist was broken. So she needed help. And he was more than willing—no, he insisted on giving it.

Afternoon wore into evening. The snow let up a little, which was the only hopeful thing that happened. They continued to struggle with thoughts and looks and accidental touches. Tension ran high between them, and though it was sexually-induced, it took different outlets. Quist snapped at Lily for using up the hot water without telling him; she snapped back at him when he diapered Nicki too loosely; he told her that the bread she'd made to eat with the stew wasn't real bread at all, and she said that it couldn't be since she didn't have yeast, so it was quick bread—and between them they ate every crumb.

By the time Nicki went to sleep at eight o'clock, Lily felt the night had already been endless. She sat by the stove for a bit, then lay down on the mattress and pulled the blanket to her chin. But though she was tired, she couldn't sleep. Her insides were astir with feelings and thoughts that she shouldn't have been feeling or thinking. So she tossed and turned on her mattress.

In time, Quist lowered the lamp and turned in, too, but his rest wasn't any more peaceful than hers. At one point, without considering for a minute that she might be asleep, he growled, "Is it your wrist?"

"Is what my wrist?"

"Whatever it is that's making you squirm."

"No, it's not my wrist."

"Do you have to go to the bathroom?"

"No! I'm restless. That's all."

"You're keeping me up," he alleged.

"You're keeping yourself up," she told him and flopped over again.

Quist was in fact up in the most sexual of senses and had no way to relieve it. He ached to take Lily, but he wouldn't. His body was punishing him for his chivalry.

After long periods of thinking about the ranch, plotting strategies for diversifying his herd and counting the heads of cattle in the pen he drew in his mind, he fell asleep. When he awoke, it was four in the morning, Nicki was whimpering, and he was hard as a rock.

Ignoring the last, though it caused him a moan when he pushed himself up, he went to the drawer, lifted the baby and deposited her into Lily's waiting arms. On impulse, he sat down at the base of the chair and pulled Lily back against him. "Do it here," he said with a huskiness that could have been due to a number of things. "Indulge me."

"Quist..."

He fitted her more snugly into the notch of his thighs. "Nothing can happen. You've got Nicki."

On the one hand, he was right. Lily drew up her sweater and put Nicki to her breast, and all was fine. She switched breasts midway through, and all was still fine.

The trouble came when she was done.

CHAPTER SEVEN

Quist carefully put Nicki back in her drawer and watched Lily tuck her in. But when she turned toward her own mattress, he caught her hand and in a single fluid movement had her in his arms.

She barely had time to cry his name when his mouth came down over hers, and what she'd so diligently tried to suppress for so long sprang to life. There was nothing tentative or exploratory about this kiss, nor was it gentle. It was hard and hungry, like Quist's body, and it wasn't about to be denied.

His mouth plundered hers. It slanted and sucked, drawing her deeper into his desire. She was stunned by the force of that desire, stunned even more by the understanding that the desire was her own. She'd never thought of herself as a woman who craved. In times past when she'd been with a man, his needs had directed and dominated the dance. Jarrod had barely cared whether she achieved satisfaction, and, in truth, she hadn't cared much, either. The pleasure was in the giving.

Something was different now. She opened her mouth to Quist, took his tongue and gave her own in return, but the giving was greedy. She'd never felt such hot and intense a need, and though a small voice in her brain warned her to caution, the rest of her didn't listen. She was caught up in sensation and in an irrational but irrevocable feeling that what she was doing was right.

Quist wasn't thinking any more clearly than she was. Holding her head still, he devoured her mouth. He tasted her, drank her, breathed her until even that wasn't enough. Sliding his arms around her body, he crushed her to him with a force that made Lily cry out.

Immediately he loosened his hold. "Are you okay?"

"I think so," she said with a breathless little laugh. When he backed into the chair he'd just left and brought her down on his lap, she whispered a hurried, "Maybe we shouldn't, Quist." Her arms, even the one with the splinted wrist, were draped over his shoulders, and though she was having trouble catching her breath, her eyes held his.

"We have to," he answered. Voice, gaze, touch—all smoldered with barely banked heat. "We have to. I can't explain the need," it was as much emotional as physical, as much a need to stake a claim as to slake a desire, "but it's too strong." He took her head in his hands. "I need you, Lily. I'm making you mine."

Like the fierceness of his kiss, the boldness of his words excited her. He didn't ask. He didn't beg. He told her what was going to happen and why, and since Lily was feeling everything he was, she couldn't argue with his conclusion. Instead, her body began to tremble in anticipation.

He kissed her again until she was gasping for breath. Then he brought the hem of her sweater up and took it over her head and off, leaving her naked above the waist. He held her back to look at her, first her eyes, then for a long time her breasts.

Her breath came more shallowly. She was acutely aware of her nakedness, of the rapid rise and fall of her breasts, of their heaviness, of the paleness ribboned by veins that had come with motherhood, and she might have tried to cover herself if it hadn't been for the look in his eyes. That look was incredible. It made her feel warm and beautiful. And sexy. No man had ever made her feel sexy like that. Not a word, just that look, and she soared.

But the soaring had just begun. When he put his hands on her breasts, she sucked in a breath. She let it out in a soft sigh of pleasure when he began to knead her flesh, and when he lowered his head and took a distended nipple into his mouth, she cried out.

He paused, fearful again that he'd hurt her, but she pushed her fingers in his hair and urged him back to her breast. He lingered there just long enough to drive her wild before relinquishing the wet nub to his fingers and moving on to the next. Small sounds of pleasure came from deep in her throat. She urged him closer, then closer still as the crux of the heat moved downward. Pressing her legs together didn't help. Neither did shifting her hips.

Clutching fistfuls of his hair, she whispered his name and tugged. He lifted his head and looked at her, still with the desire and appreciation that made her feel so wanted. The wanting made her desperate.

"I'm on fire," she cried brokenly. "Help me."

He didn't need further urging. His hands went to her sweatpants and pushed them down. He shifted her until the heavy material was free of her hips, then her legs, leaving her in the V-shaped scrap of silk and lace that he found so sexy. With the flat of his hand he touched her stomach, her hips, the small of her back, her bottom, and by the time he returned to her front, he'd breached the barrier of her panties to find the dampness that gave proof to her arousal.

Lily hadn't been so indifferent to satisfaction in the past that she'd never had an orgasm. She knew the feeling, knew when it was imminent, and at that moment she was on the edge. If Quist touched her more deeply, if he slid a finger inside she'd come, and she didn't want to. Not without feeling the iron of him, not without knowing that they were fully coupled.

"Your sweater," she cried against his mouth as she grabbed a handful of it and pulled. More than ever before, she wished for two good hands. Fortunately, Quist had them.

Setting her on her feet, he rose and tore off his sweater. She barely had time to reacquaint herself with the marvel of his chest when he had his zipper down, then his jeans. When he came back to her, he was buck naked and magnificent. Kneeling, he slid her panties down, leaned forward and put his mouth to the hair that was still too short to curl.

Her knees buckled. She slid down until her breasts grazed his chest, and he lowered her to the mattress. His breathing was rough; his arms shook with the force of his desire as he held himself above her, poised between her widely parted thighs.

"Hurry," she whispered and lifted toward him. She was frantic to have him where it seemed he belonged. That sense of rightness had survived the fire of foreplay and was as strong, if not stronger than ever.

But he held back. He looked into her eyes, looked deeper, into her soul and felt touched to the core of his being. She was his. She was bare before him, inside and out. He felt responsible for her, and while he'd always before shunned responsibility where women were concerned, this time he welcomed it. It made him feel possessive, protective and strong. It was also humbling, so much so that instead of thrusting hard into her as his body was telling him to do, he moved forward more gently.

Lily would never know how he'd known to do that, but it was another thing to marvel at. She was tight. She hadn't realized how much so. Involuntarily her body tensed at his initial incursion and she gasped.

"I'm hurting you," he whispered against her temple.

"No. It's...from the baby...I'm very..."

Sealing her mouth with his lips, he began to caress her, first her breasts, then her belly, then the small bud that had hardened between her legs. Little by little, he pressed inside as he built her arousal to an ever higher pitch. He moved his hips in slow, gentle circles, stretching her, allowing her to get used to his size. Only when he was fully buried inside her, when he felt her tightness hugging him to the hilt, did he allow himself a moment's selfishness. Closing his eyes, he arched his long torso, threw his head back and shuddered with pleasure, then, unable to help himself, gave a low cry of triumph.

The triumph was Lily's, too. She'd never felt so much a part of a man, and it wasn't just that Quist was more man than she'd ever met. There was something else. They shared a special feeling. She couldn't comprehend the extent of it just then, because all that was happening inside was near to overwhelming, but she was more satisfied by what they were doing than she'd ever been by any orgasm.

Sensing and sharing that satisfaction, Quist held himself still. After a time, he breathed in a long, shaky breath, opened his eyes and looked down at her. What he saw made his heart pound harder against his ribs.

Lily's gray eyes were warm and velvet and there was a soft smile on her lips. Her cheeks were pink, her skin dewy. Her breasts rose and fell with the short breaths she took, while her knees hugged his sides. She looked as though she'd be perfectly content to stay right where she was for an eternity, and he wasn't sure he'd have minded. She was without a doubt the most beautiful, the most serene, the most honest woman he'd ever made love to.

He gave a small smile. "Ahh, Lily." When her brows rose in question, he whispered, "I could almost be tempted to look at you like this all day." Bowing his head, he opened his mouth on her neck and gave her the hickey he'd promised.

"You rat," she whispered back, but her smile grew wider. "Haven't you got better things to do with your mouth?" Coming up off the mattress, she used her own on his nipple. When he let out a guttural cry, she wound her arms around his neck and gave him the kind of kiss that made him think of all those better things he could do.

He did a good many of them in the next few minutes, and if there were some that he missed, neither of them noticed. Laying her down, he made love to her fully—withdrawing and gently reentering, withdrawing and coming back harder, withdrawing and thrusting home with the force of his ardor.

Lily egged him on. Once past her initial tenderness, she was a creature she'd never known. She writhed in response to the fire he lit and demanded he tend it. It never occurred to her to lie still, as a vessel for his pleasure; that simply wasn't part of their relationship. With Quist, she was a free agent, a woman letting herself blossom without set rules or preconceptions. He was a rough-edged man prone to wild passion, and wild passion was what he inspired. She gave and she took with rapturous fury.

Their bodies grew sweaty as they worked toward a near-violent crest. At its height, she felt a moment's fear, the sensation was so intense. His name was a frantic cry on her lips, but he was fast to soothe her.

"That's it, Lily," he panted, pumping more quickly. "Let it come. Let go for me. That's it."

Catching in a breath, she arched up off the mattress, closed her eyes and went very still for an instant before erupting into a series of shuddering spasms. She was still in their grip when Quist thrust deeper than ever. With a low, agonized sound, he gained his release—but not before he'd found the wherewithal to pull out of her.

Lily missed him instantly. Though their damp bodies remained entwined, she felt a sudden and stark emptiness inside. It brought tears to her eyes. "Quist?" she whispered, still breathless from the power of what she'd experienced.

It was a minute before the harshness of his breathing eased, another before he raised his head from her shoulder. One look at the tears in her eyes and he said, "Oh, no, don't do that." He brushed the moisture from her lids with his mouth. "Don't cry. Not now."

"Why did you do that? It was so perfect until that."

He'd been afraid she regretted having made love and was deeply relieved it wasn't so. Shifting to cradle her gently against him, he lifted her splinted wrist to his chest. Then he ran his thumb under her eyes to catch the tears that remained. "You've just had a baby," he said and felt protective. "You don't want another so soon."

Lily was surprised; thought of birth control hadn't entered her mind. In self-defense, she said, "I wouldn't have gotten pregnant. It was just one time."

His smile was indulgent, the rolling of his eyes more eloquent than that. So she tried again.

"A woman can't get pregnant while she's nursing."

"Is that a fact? Has it never happened? Not once?"

"Well, maybe once or twice," she conceded, "but those are the exceptions."

He studied her face, stroked her damp cheek. "Look at you," he said, feeling concern this time. "You have a new baby and no home. Can you even begin to imagine what it would be like to be pregnant on top of that?"

It would be terrifying, she knew, still she felt the same emptiness she'd felt when he'd first withdrawn. "I liked being pregnant," she said almost as an afterthought and lowered her face to his chest. He had a nice chest. It was firm and well shaped and had just enough hair to lightly cushion her cheek. Besides, his chest held his heart, and its steady beat was a comfort by her ear.

Looking over the crown of her head to the ivory skin that extended below it, Quist felt a swell of affection. She was so incredibly sweet, sweet to taste, to smell, to hold. And she said sweet things. No other woman had ever complained when he'd put on a rubber. He hadn't had a rubber here, but he'd deliberately waited until she'd climaxed to reach his own peak and withdraw. Still, she was sorry he'd left. That made him feel special.

In fact, he was feeling special in lots of ways. And relaxed. And content. Which was really odd, given the cabin and the storm and the fact that he still had to find his way out of it. Still, at that particular moment, he felt special.

"Quist?"

When she used that tentative tone, he knew something was up. "Mmm?"

"Do you really think I'm sexy?" she asked, keeping her eyes on the lean plane of his middle.

"How can you ask that, after what we just did?"

"For all I know, you go wild with every woman you bed."

He rolled on top of her, partly to feel her again that way and partly to set her straight. "I like sex, and I like it hard and fast. But I've never done what we just did."

All eyes, she looked up at him. "What do you mean?"

He couldn't answer at first, because he wasn't sure *what* he'd meant. Then again, he was. What he'd done with Lily had been more than sex. It had been lovemaking. He couldn't tell her that, though, because she might get the wrong idea. She might think he loved her, and it wasn't that at all. He liked her, liked her in some ways that weren't at all physical, so that when he'd taken her physically, he'd felt more than usual. But like wasn't love. And she was waiting for an answer.

Wrapping himself in the velvet of her gaze, he said in a voice vibrant with attraction, "I've never entered a woman slowly, the way I entered you. I've never really cared if she was uncomfortable at first." He stopped for an instant. "I've never taken a virgin before."

"I'm no virgin," she whispered, cheeks going pink.

"But I imagine it was like that. You were new. You haven't been touched since the baby." He thought about that and slid halfway to her side so that she wouldn't bear the brunt of his weight. Then he asked in a quiet voice, "You were cut there, weren't you?"

She nodded. They'd just made love, which was as intimate as two people could get, still his question seemed even more so. His interest made her warm all over.

"Did it hurt?"

"There was local anesthesia. I didn't feel it."

"Afterward?"

"I felt it then, but it didn't bother me. It was part of having Nicki. I'd do it again in a minute."

"In a minute?"

She smiled. "Well, maybe not so fast, but I wouldn't hesitate to have more children."

"You really enjoyed being pregnant?"

She nodded, and Quist believed her. It was in keeping with everything else she'd said. Besides, she didn't lie. He'd already learned that, though at times like this he wished it weren't so. She was looking up at him with such guileless warmth that he felt his blood stir. Slowly, inevitably, his gaze fell from her face. He moved to see her body better, and when the visual wasn't enough, he touched her.

His hands were large, his fingers calloused but gentle. The heady combination sparked a renewed tingling deep in Lily's belly. Grabbing his hand, she dragged it to her throat and held it there.

"What's wrong?" he asked.

She took in a shaky breath. "You touch me and I start to burn. I don't know what it is about you, Quist. I was never like this before."

He seized her mouth to still her words, which were as much a turn-on as anything else. But a taste of her mouth led to a taste of her neck, then one breast, then her stomach. She'd released his hand by then and was touching him wherever she could, and by the time he straightened beside her, he was feeling hot and bothered. Taking her hand, he lowered it on his body. "Touch me," he whispered hoarsely. "I've dreamed of having your hands on me here—" He groaned the last as he curled her fingers around his arousal. Oh, yes, he'd dreamed of that; it was why he'd been so hard when Nicki's cries had woken him. But the dream paled in comparison to reality. He hadn't dared to dream that Lily's fingers would take him higher, and with such untutored skill.

The skill was a product of instinct, in turn a product of curiosity and desire. Lily was intrigued by the length and strength of him. She explored his thickness, the velvety tip and the heaviness beneath, and felt pride when he grew even harder.

His low moan brought her gaze to his face. In the dim light filtering from the woodstove, she saw that it was covered by a sheen of sweat. His eyes were closed, his mouth drawn into a thin line as he struggled to retain a measure of control.

She wanted him to lose it. To that end, she grew even bolder with her hand and her mouth. Tasting his body, brushing her nose through the hair on his chest, dragging her lips along the line that tapered to his navel while she continued to caress his hardness— he was soon breathing roughly, and she wasn't doing much better. Everything about him turned her on. She felt a flame inside that was every bit as hot as it had been not so many minutes before.

Wanting to see how far she'd go, Quist drew her on top of him. Knowing she couldn't put weight on her left wrist, he supported her under each arm. Her legs straddled his hips, and for a prolonged minute of torture, she held herself just inches above him while, taking short, shimmering breaths, she looked down into his eyes. Then, closing her own, she let her hips settle, taking him fully in one smooth glide.

Quist felt possessed. It was a turnaround, but he wasn't displeased. He filled Lily, yet he was the one who felt filled, and the filling was with an almost unbelievable pleasure. It smacked of oneness, which was something he didn't know much about. But like Lily, he acted on instinct, and that instinct was to help her, to make her movements his own, make her rapture high.

At first, he did nothing more than lightly run his hands over her body. When she began to undulate with him inside, he drew her forward so that he could love her breasts with his mouth, and when she dropped her weight to her elbows, he grasped her hips. Guidance or caress—the line blurred, and it didn't matter, because neither of them was analyzing what happened. Instinct and sensation dominated the thrusting sweep of their bodies, and if instinct and sensation were in turn dominated by a deeper underlying emotion, neither of them was analyzing that, either.

They burned, then exploded. In the end, Quist rolled over Lily and afforded her the same protection he'd given the first time. Though she knew what he was doing this time, she still felt the loss, but the heat of her climax carried her through until he held her tightly to his side again.

There were no words when it was over, nothing to describe what had happened. Their bodies continued to communicate for a time, lying limply, then more peacefully entwined. When Quist drew up the blanket, they fell asleep. Neither one of them moved again until Nicki's small cries broke through the morning silence.

Lily stirred first, trying to burrow more snugly against the warmth of Quist's large body. When she realized what the sound was that had awoken her, she started to turn, but he held her still.

"I'll get her." His voice was groggy, and, contrary to his words, he drew her in closer and buried his face in her hair.

Nicki cried again.

"I'd better go," Lily whispered.

But with a kiss to the top of her head, he disengaged himself from her body. "Stay here. I'll bring her over."

Settling her head on the pillow, Lily watched him climb out from under the blanket. His body was beautiful, not only in the throes of passion but now in the morning's light. What she'd only felt earlier she could finally see, most notably the masculine make of his legs and the way his sex lay amid a dark nest of hair. He was impressive in any state of arousal, a pleasure to look at.

But he was reaching for his pants, threatening to deny her that pleasure.

"What are you doing?" she asked, vying with Nicki to make herself heard.

He balanced precariously on one foot as he tried to get the other into his jeans. "I can't very well go to her like this." He glanced down at himself.

Lily was torn between admiration of his body and amusement. "Why not?"

"She's a girl. She could be traumatized."

"She's just a baby. She won't see a thing."

"She sees," he said earnestly, as though he had great insight into the matter. "She understands more than you think."

Pressing her lips together to stifle a grin, Lily gave a slow but confident shake of her head.

He paused. "No?"

She repeated the slow headshake.

"But I'm a strange man. She doesn't know me. I'm not even her father."

"She knows you better than she does her father," Lily said, "but that's neither here nor there. The fact is that she won't know whether you're naked or not, and I don't want you dressed."

That brought a softer look to Quist's face. Nicki kept on crying, but he stayed still where he was with his jeans on one leg and no more. "You don't?"

She shook her head.

"Are you sure?"

She nodded.

Nicki's cries grew more strident. Shucking the jeans, Quist strode to where she lay and picked her up. She quieted right away, which made him grin. "Like that, do ya?" he asked the child in a voice that was light, a little playful, very masculine. "Are you a sexy little thing like your mama?" He placed her carefully in Lily's arms.

"I'm not sexy," Lily chided in a half whisper. Turning onto her side, she put Nicki to her breast.

After fueling the stove, Quist pulled the blanket up to cover

Lily's back and stretched out, propping himself on an elbow, to watch her nurse. "What do you mean, you're not sexy?"

"I'm not."

"Sure could've fooled me. Sure could've fooled my body."

Lily felt a heat rise in her cheeks, but she kept her eyes on Nicki. Quist watched them both. He thought of the first time he'd seen her nursing and remembered how uncomfortable he'd felt. He was jealous then. He saw a closeness that he'd never had, and irrationally, he was jealous. That jealousy had eased, mostly because he'd become involved with Lily. Now when she nursed Nicki, it was a specific, rather than a generic activity. But there were still times when he felt pangs of something else, when he looked at the two of them and the warmth they shared and ached to be part of it.

This was one of those times. To get his mind off the aching, he asked, "What does that feel like?"

"It's peaceful," Lily said, smiling into Nicki's eyes. "And very satisfying."

"I mean physically. When she sucks. Is it like when I do it?"

The color in her cheeks deepened. After a minute, she raised her eyes to his. Her voice was feminine without being seductive. "It's the same, but it's different."

"Explain that." When she sent him a pleading look, he said in a voice that was masculine without being seductive, "I want to know."

"But it's hard to explain, and it's embarrassing. Here I am, at the same time nursing my baby and thinking about a man doing... putting..."

"Sucking." His mouth twitched. "Spit it out, Lily. No need to play prim. After all, you're the woman who insisted I stay naked."

"You keep me warm when you're naked." She looked at his chest. "Besides, I liked what we were doing."

"We were sleeping."

"Before that," she said and took a breath. He was right. There was no reason to be prim, after what they'd done with and to each other. Meeting his eyes again, she said, "The difference between what you do and what Nicki does is in intent and outcome. When Nicki nurses, the sucking sensation brings out maternal things like love and pride and protectiveness. The satisfaction is in the doing. When you, uh, do the same thing, it makes me want more."

He grinned. "Does it now?"

She nodded, and for several minutes, they simply looked at each other, neither one of them saying a word. Finally, with a bit of the devil in it, his grin broadened. "There. You did a real good job with that explanation."

Lily was entranced by his grin. It made him look younger, less stern, almost happy, and the bit of the devil in it was highly endearing. Without thinking, she raised her splinted wrist and touched the tips of her fingers to his chin. He took her hand and gently held it to his neck.

"How does it feel?" he asked.

"Rough. A little stubbly. Very manly."

"Not my chin. Your wrist."

"Oh. Okay."

He sighed. "What does 'okay' mean?"

"Better than yesterday."

"Still ache?"

"A little. It's more an annoyance than anything."

He lightly rubbed her arm just above the splint. "First priority when we hit civilization is a hospital. A cast will be neater and easier to manage than this."

When we hit civilization. The words echoed in Lily's mind, but they didn't have the element of relief they'd had twenty-four hours before. She was feeling safe just where she was, she realized. Safe and happy. Holding Nicki, looking at Quist, it suddenly occurred to her that she wouldn't mind it a bit if they were snowbound for months.

But that made her stop and listen, and what she heard was silence. Eyes widening, she glanced toward the window, then looked back at Quist. "It's over?"

"Sounds it," he said calmly. Rather than getting up to check, he waited to see what she was going to say next.

She didn't say anything at first. She looked down at Nicki, lowered her head and rubbed her cheek against the baby's hair in an attempt to recapture the sense of solidarity she shared with Nicki. They were a twosome, mother and daughter. They'd gone through nine months and five weeks together. They'd left Hartford to make a new life for themselves, and that was just what they'd do.

Now, though, there was Quist. She wasn't sure where he fit into the life they were making, but it had to be somewhere. He was too special; what she'd done with him was too intimate. Even if their

relationship proved to be nothing more than an aberration, a product of being caught together in an isolated cabin in the midst of a
blizzard, she'd remember him. She wasn't sure she was ready to
say good-bye.

When she raised her eyes to his, they were filled with tears. "We
were just starting to have fun," she whispered.

Quist didn't know whether to laugh or cry. He'd been thinking
the same thing, but hadn't wanted to say it. "Don't you dare go
weepy on me now."

"If the snow's stopped, you'll be leaving."

"I don't know for sure that it's stopped."

"Aren't you going to look?"

"Me? And freeze my butt off? I'm not dressed." He took a lazy
breath. "Maybe later."

"But you said you'd have to set off first thing in the morning,"
she argued. Even as she did it, though, something in his expression
registered. He was looking a little too content, almost to the point
of smugness. Slowly the meaning of the look set in. He was giving
them an extra day. "Thank you," she whispered, and this time the
tears that welled were ones of happiness.

Quist wanted to scold her, but couldn't. Her tears, he was learning, were as expressive of what she was feeling as a laugh or a
sigh or a moan. They came and went quickly, and were eminently
honest. He couldn't fault her for that, particularly since in this case
she was crying because she was pleased to be spending another
day with him.

He wondered what was going to happen when the time came
for them to part. It wouldn't be the lightest of moments, he knew,
and determined to push it out of his mind.

Actually that was easily done. Once Nicki was fed, they did
dress to make a trip to the outhouse. The snow had stopped, and
the forest was beautiful, which added to the idyllic feeling they
brought back into the cabin with them. While Lily played with
Nicki, Quist put together a breakfast that, while it wasn't quite as
imaginative as Lily's had been, filled their stomachs. When they
were done, he helped her bathe the baby, and when they were done
with that and Nicki had been rocked and sung to and put in for a
nap, they bathed themselves. All three baths were a joint effort.
The last two led to something far hotter than the water.

"I've never been like this in my life," Lily murmured when,

once again, they lay sweaty and spent in each other's arms. "You've corrupted me."

Quist gave a weak laugh, which was all he could muster after the physical exertion he'd just made. "I think you got that backward. You're the corrupter. I'm just an innocent cowboy."

"For an innocent cowboy, you sure know how to do some naughty things."

He opened an eye and looked down at her. "And you loved them. Admit it. You loved them."

"I admit it," she said simply. Pressing a kiss on his chest, she put her head down. "This is all so unreal," she breathed.

"Mmm."

"Hard to believe how we met."

"Hard to believe what we've done since we met."

She laughed softly, almost to herself, but the laugh quickly died. She was thinking that it would be a story for the books, one to tell the grandchildren, only she didn't know whose grandchildren she'd tell. She and Quist wouldn't have any together.

"Quist?"

"Mmm?"

"When do you think you'll leave?"

He was quiet for a time. Finally he said, "Tomorrow. You ought to have your wrist casted right, Nicki's running out of diapers and I'm getting sick of hash."

He was right on all counts, she knew. She also knew that she'd give just about anything to stay another day, then another day after that. But it couldn't be. He had to leave. Thought of that brought new worries.

"The snow's deeper now than when we hiked in here. The going will be tough."

"I've got long legs."

"But you may get lost."

"I'll follow the break in the trees, same way I did to get us here, and I won't have the wind and the snow."

"What about animals? They'll be out foraging for food. I think I read somewhere that there are bears in northern Maine."

"They're in hibernation." Taking her chin, he tipped her face to his. "I'll be okay, Lily."

"I'll worry."

"But I'll be okay. And you will be, too."

Lily wasn't so sure. The thought of Quist leaving, of his being gone for a long time gave her a desolate feeling. She was going to have to learn to live with it, she supposed, but that didn't mean it wasn't real.

"Kiss me," she whispered, wanting a little forgetfulness.

He gave her that and more, then repeated the good deed while Nicki was napping that afternoon. He might have been sick of hash, but his appetite for Lily was endless, so much so that he was almost willing to consider staying put for another day when the decision was taken out of his hands. The sound of an engine broke through the silence of the forest, waking him from a doze. Slipping out of Lily's arms, he went to the window in time to see the arrival of a pair of snowmobiles.

In an instant he was back shaking Lily's shoulder. "Up you go, sweetheart. We've got company." He was into his pants in a flash, then helped Lily into hers. She had just managed to pull on a sweater when the door burst open.

Their guests, it seemed, weren't guests at all, but the son of the owner of the cabin and his girlfriend. It was a toss-up as to who was the most uncomfortable—Lily and Quist for having been caught in the love nest they had created, or the two younger lovers who had come to create their own.

Civilization, it seemed, was an hour away by snowmobile. With a little arm twisting, Quist managed to convince his male counterpart to return with him for help. Leaving the young girl with Lily, and feeling better that she wasn't alone, he set off.

Shortly before dark he returned with a snowplow and its driver, the boy and his snowmobiles, plus two gallons of gas.

CHAPTER EIGHT

The next few hours passed in something of a blur for Lily. With Quist's help—and that of the young girl, who was anxious to see them gone and be alone with her boyfriend—she neatened the cabin and repacked the things they'd carried through the snow. Strapping Nicki to her chest, she climbed into the cab of the truck to sit between the driver and Quist.

The distance to the car was no more than four miles. What had taken Lily and Quist more than three hours to trek through on foot in the storm took the snowplow thirty minutes. Between the two men, the Audi was shoveled off, towed onto the newly plowed path, gassed up and warmed in another thirty minutes. By the time darkness was complete, Lily and Quist were following the truck back to town.

Quist drove. With his Stetson on his head and the collar of his sheepskin jacket up, he looked so much like the distant cowboy she'd picked up in the storm that Lily felt lonely again. Occasionally he glanced at her, but the night masked his expression. Only once, when he reached out to touch her, did she feel a breath of the warmth they'd shared.

He stopped in town to settle up with the driver of the snowplow and make arrangements to have his abandoned rental car retrieved and returned to an agency outlet. Then, as promised, he set off for the nearest hospital. It turned out to be an hour north of where they'd emerged from the woods. Nicki, who had awoken hungry halfway through the drive, was already fed by the time they arrived, and again, Quist took charge. Holding the baby like a pro, he ushered Lily inside, had an X ray taken and an orthopedist examining her arm before she'd had time to do more than fill out a cursory form, and while Nicki slept in his arms, he watched the doctor put a lightweight, waterproof cast on Lily's wrist.

Back in the Audi, parked under the bright lights of the emergency entrance, Quist turned to her. His voice was deep, quiet. "Quebec is four hours north of here. It's ten now. We could be there by two. Or we can find a place to spend the night and make the drive in the morning.'' He watched her closely, trying to look through the frail mask of her defenses. Cautiously he said, ''I say we find a place. I want a hot shower and a big bed. How about it?''

He'd read her well, she mused with a smile and a nod. She was feeling tired, though she didn't know why she should, since she and Quist had dozed on and off for a good part of the day. Perhaps more than tired, she was drained. Leaving the security of the cabin had thrown her once more into the limbo of her life. Finding a room somewhere, with four walls and Quist, sounded just right.

What they found, actually, was a ski lodge that had plenty of midweek vacancies. They took one room; there was never any question of taking a second. Quist registered in his name, and if the clerk chose to assume that they were a family, that was fine. All they asked of him was the room key and a portable crib, both of which he produced without pause.

The room wasn't fancy, but it was warm, carpeted and blessed with a king-size bed. Nicki was quickly changed and put into the portable crib, and while Lily rubbed her back to help her fall asleep, Quist took the shower he'd been dying to have. When he'd finished, he came back for her.

Reluctant to wet her cast until it had fully hardened, Lily opted for a bath, and nothing, she swore, nothing had ever felt so good— at least, that was what she told Quist, who was helping her at every turn. The fact that he made her feel better than the bath was something she kept to herself. She wasn't sure whether he'd take it as calculated flattery, and she didn't want that.

What she wanted was to go to Montana with him. She wasn't sure when she'd gotten the idea, but it had come to her and stuck like glue. But she knew what he thought of women, in general, and women on a ranch, in particular. Granted, he had to know by now that she wasn't a piece of fluff, still she had to be careful. She couldn't do anything to suggest she was trying to manipulate him. If she was to go to Montana, the idea had to come from him.

So she simply smiled her pleasure as she floated in the hot bath water. He helped her soap up, even washed her hair, and by the time he'd finished drying her off, the towel he'd wrapped around his hips was too small.

They made love on the clean sheets of the king-size bed, and even apart from the cleanliness of the bed and their bodies, the experience was new and different, special in ways that Lily couldn't begin to name. Hunger, greed, joy, desperation—so many things entered into their mating that it was hard to sort one from the other. The past was a dream, the future an enigma, yet they were affected by both. And in the aftermath, when Lily lay with her head and an arm on his chest and a slender leg between his longer, more ropey ones, she knew that she loved him.

Morning came all too soon. Though they lingered in the waking, taking time with Nicki and each other, and then lingered over breakfast in a nearby coffee shop, inevitably they had to drive on.

It was midafternoon when they reached Quebec. Again Quist took a room, this time at the Hilton, which, he told Lily, had a shopping arcade so that she'd have something to do while he was out taking care of business. Lily wanted to tell him that she didn't like shopping, and that she'd be glad to go with him to confront the half sister he'd never seen, and that if anything she ought to be looking for an apartment for Nicki and herself.

She didn't tell him any of those things, not because they weren't true, but because he was gone before she'd had a chance.

So she stayed in the room to feed and change Nicki, and by the time she was done, it was too late to start apartment hunting. Besides, she wanted to be there when Quist returned, if only she knew when that would be. He had an address, she knew, but whether he'd find his half sister there, or whether he'd have to go elsewhere, and if he did find her how long they'd spend talking, Lily didn't know.

The complicating factor, of course, was that Lily didn't know quite where she stood with Quist, and that was the one thing that made her most uneasy as the minutes piled up. Playing with Nicki was a distraction and a comfort, but when Nicki began to doze off, the distraction was gone. So she bathed. With the comfort and compactness of the cast on her wrist, she had greater use of her fingers than she'd had before. She brushed her hair until it shone, put on the smallest bit of makeup, dressed in a sweater and skirt. Frustrated with the waiting, she put a sleeping Nicki into the carrier, slid the straps over her shoulders, anchoring the baby to her front, and went down to sit in the lobby and wait for Quist there.

He returned ninety minutes after he'd left. Lily saw him instantly as he strode from the revolving door. Even without the Stetson, which he held in his hand, he stood head and shoulders above the rest, but he didn't look pleased.

Hurrying to join him, she weathered a tense glance as they stepped into the elevator. He didn't say a word, simply punched their floor then stood with his jaw set and his eyes on the digital readout. With other people in the car she knew he wouldn't talk, but once they reached the privacy of their own room, she waited apprehensively.

He stalked to the window, pulled back the sheer and stared at the night lights of the city.

"Quist?" she prodded.

Slowly he turned and in an equally slow but very angry voice said, "She wasn't there. At the first place they sent me to a second, and at the second they sent me to a third. At the third place they told me she'd left town." His nostrils flared with the carefully controlled breath he took. "She left town. I came all this god-damned way, lost three days in a damned blizzard, not to mention the two days I spent checking out New York and Boston, and she left town."

Lily gave a small moan of disappointment. "When?"

"Day before yesterday."

"In the storm?"

"They said it wasn't so bad here. She probably figured she'd use it to her benefit by getting a jump on anyone who might be on her tail." He thrust a hand through his hair, then hooked both hands on his hips and scowled. "If I'd have gotten here when I was supposed to, I'd have caught her, and if I'd have done that, I'd be back home right now."

"And if I hadn't taken the wrong turns," Lily put in, because she knew he was thinking it, "you'd have gotten here when you were supposed to." She paused. "I'm sorry, Quist. I messed you up."

"Women always mess me up," he grumbled without acknowledging her apology. "I'm the man, but they're the ones doing the screwing. I haven't met a woman yet who was good for her word. Jennifer calls me and asks if I'll come—I come and she's gone. She's just like her mother. Runs away and keeps running. I don't know why I thought it would be any different."

Lily didn't like being lumped with his women, particularly since she'd been honest from the first. But the argument was better saved for later. When it came to anything to do with his mother, and Jennifer had to do with his mother, he was raw. "Did they say where she'd gone?"

"Chicago."

"Chicago!"

"That's what I said."

"What's she going to do in Chicago?"

"Same thing she was going to do here, I guess—hide out until things quiet down."

"But if you were able to find out where she's headed, so will whoever it is who's following her."

He shook his head. "She had protective friends. I had to show an ID to get the information. At least she had enough brains to give them my name and say I'd be coming. But what in the hell does she expect me to do, follow her all over the goddamned northern hemisphere?" Swearing again, he turned back to the window.

Lily took in the rigid set of his shoulders and his tight stance, and although the circumstances were completely different, she couldn't help but remember when they'd first met. He'd been angry then, too—at himself for falling asleep at the wheel, at her for being a woman picking him up in a sporty red car, at the world for stranding him on a mountain road, at whatever it was that had made it snow.

She'd been able to shrug off his anger then, because she hadn't known him at all. She knew him now, though, and it bothered her to see him upset. Slipping her arms out of the carrier, and laying Nicki in the center of the bed, she went to him.

"What will you do?" she asked in a softer voice. When he didn't answer, she put a tentative hand on his back, and when he didn't move away, she slid it up and began to lightly massage his shoulder. "She's young. Probably frightened and confused."

"She should have stayed put," he growled. "I told her I'd come."

"But she doesn't know you. Maybe she's as wary of men as you are of women."

"Then she shouldn't have called me in the first place."

"But you're her half brother. You may be the only living relative she has."

"Does that give her the right to use me?"

"It gives her the right to ask for your help. You could have refused her at the start."

"I should have."

"Why didn't you?"

"Because she's my half sister," he snapped. "She may be the only living relative *I* have."

Which said a lot, Lily mused. It said that though Quist didn't have family, he wanted it, and that made her love him all the more. Unable to help herself, she slid an arm around his waist and fitted herself to his side. "You're a softy, do you know that?"

"I've never been a softy," he muttered.

"Maybe not on the outside, but inside—" she flattened a hand on his chest "—you've got heart."

"I won't be taken advantage of."

"Who's trying to?"

He hesitated for a minute before shooting her a look. "You. I know what you're thinking. You're thinking that if I've come this far, I owe it to myself to go to Chicago. It's on the way home, if I was driving. But I'm not, and you know it."

"I wasn't thinking that at all, but since you mention it, it's not such a bad idea."

"She could be gone when I get there. This has been a wild-goose chase so far. Who's to say Chicago isn't just the next bogus stop?"

"Can you call her first? I assume you have an address. Do you have a phone number?"

"No, and I can't get one. She's staying with a friend. I have the address but no name, and the lady I spoke with didn't know it."

"Chicago is on the way."

"Not as the crow flies."

"But as American or Delta or TWA flies. You could easily stop there on the way home."

He grimaced. "Damn it, I shouldn't have to do that."

"What's your alternative? After you've gone through all this, can you really go home and forget about her? Won't you always wonder what happened? Won't you wonder whether she got into trouble? Won't you feel guilty that maybe you weren't there when she needed you?"

"I *was* there, but she *moved*," he argued, feeling more frustrated than anything else.

Quietly, Lily said, "You'll always wonder, Quist."

He stared at her hard. "You're laying a guilt trip on me."

"No. I'm trying to put into words what you won't. You make yourself out to be a callous kind of guy, but you're not that at all. And I think that if you don't follow this thing through, you'll always wonder if you should've."

He continued to stare at her, but the hardness was easing. "You're being manipulative."

"Me? Manipulative?" She'd tried so hard not to be. "How am I being manipulative?"

"Your words. Your tone. They're so damned reasonable. And the way you've got yourself plastered to my side—how can I think straight when you do that?"

She started to move away, but he tugged her right back, and then it was his long arm that sandwiched her in. "If you're such a tough guy," she said, tipping up a defensive chin, "you should be able to withstand anything I do. And while we're on the subject," she grabbed at a breath, "I want to make a couple of things clear. I am not a manipulative woman, nor have I ever tried to take advantage of you—" her voice dropped "—well, maybe I did when we first met, because I thought you could help me if I got stuck in the snow, but after that plan fell through, I wasn't thinking at all in terms of what I could get out of you." She paused to recoup, and her voice rose again. "And the fact that I'm telling you this should make my next point. I've never lied to you. I've never gone back on my word. So don't group me with women you've known in the past. It's not my fault you're a lousy picker of women."

Finished, she closed her mouth, but in the next blink it was open again. "If it hadn't been for the storm, we'd never have met. If you'd seen me on the street, you wouldn't have looked twice. You've said it yourself, I'm not your type. Well, I say 'hallelujah' because it doesn't sound to me like your type is so hot."

Held captive by the vibrancy of her features, Quist felt a swelling in the area of his heart. Lily was unreal, that was all there was to it. She was a vision he'd conjured up to fill the void in his life—which was truly remarkable, since before this trip he hadn't given great thought to that void. She was sweet and agreeable, industrious, domesticated, feisty when she felt he was being unjust, and dynamite in bed.

She gave him a dark look. "What are you grinning at?"

"You're dynamite in bed. Do you know that?"

She made a face. "Is that relevant to this discussion?"

"I think so." His gaze fell to her lips and stayed there.

"How?"

"It has to do with our relationship," he said, but his voice was lower, almost distracted as his eyes traced the shape of her mouth. "You turn me on even when you're telling me off. How can that happen?"

A slow warmth was starting to seep through her. "Maybe because what I say is the truth, and because an honest woman turns you on."

"I doubt it. I think it's because you're such a little thing, and when you get up on your soapbox your cheeks turn pink and your eyes flash, your lips caress the words and your breasts go up and down with each breath. I'm a breast man."

"Do tell."

"I'd rather show." But it was her chin that he took in his fingers, and her mouth that he seized. His kiss was long and thorough. When he let her up for air, he said against her mouth, "So you really think I should go to Chicago?"

Her voice was a wisp of air. "Think? How can I think anything when you kiss me that way?"

"You said I should go to Chicago. I want you to come."

Her head cleared a little. "To Chicago?"

"To Chicago." He gave her another long, drugging kiss. "Or else I might change my mind halfway there. You're my conscience."

"I thought," she whispered, "I was dynamite in bed." Her eyes were heavy-lidded, her head back, her lips moist and parted.

Unable to resist their lure, he kissed her again, and this time he couldn't stop. His hands got into the act; his whole body got into the act. In no time, it seemed, clothes were strewn around the room, and they were making love on the plush dove-grey carpet. At one point Lily thought she heard him murmur, "I need you with me," but, if so, the words were overshadowed by deeds, and she lost all but the moment.

There was, of course, no question but that she'd go to Chicago with him. She loved him. As improbable as it seemed, when a week before she hadn't known he existed, she'd fallen hard. While her feelings for Jarrod had been conscious and rational, what she felt for Quist was more passionate on every count. It wasn't necessarily wise; she had no idea where it would lead, but it was strong enough to keep her from turning away. She was happy. Traveling with Quist, spending days and nights with him gave her pleasure. She had a right to that, she reasoned.

Quist was strong, perhaps headstrong at times, but gentle and caring as well. As angry as he might be at the fates, he couldn't sustain anger against her. Looking back on it, she realized he'd never been able to do it. Even at the beginning, he'd been more bark than bite. He made her feel protected; more than that, he made her feel worthy of his protection.

And he was good with Nicki. Lily loved the way he held the baby, careful but now steady and competently. Despite all his grumbling at the start, he seemed genuinely attached to Nicki. He didn't shy from carrying her, bathing her, even changing her diapers, and Lily suspected that if there was food to be spooned in, he'd do that, too. She wanted to believe that having Nicki and her in his life meant something special to him, and though he hadn't said as much in words, nothing of his actions suggested differently. After all, he could have been free of them in Quebec, but he was insisting they continue on with him to Chicago.

So she was going. Quebec held nothing special for her. She'd chosen it because it was new, because she'd heard good things about it, and because it was a safe distance from Hartford and the long arm of Jarrod's family. The irony that she'd met Quist because his half sister had chosen to run there, too, didn't escape her. But she didn't dwell on it. Nor did she dwell on—or Quist raise the issue of—if, when and how she'd return to Quebec. She was taking one day at a time.

That seemed to be what Quist was doing, too. Though he kept a steady pace, he didn't break any speed records on the way to Chicago. He was keeping in daily touch with the ranch, though, enough to know that snow had fallen there, too. If there was more, he told Lily, and if the temperatures fell much, he was going to have to airlift hay to large numbers of his herd. He had to get back soon, he knew. Still, he wasn't racing.

Chicago was their crossroads. Though neither of them said as much, both knew that there were decisions to be made there. It was one thing to leave Quebec and head for another way station, but once they left Chicago—and Quist swore he wouldn't, couldn't go any farther in search of Jennifer—the next stop would be Montana. Lily's going there was a step that would take some discussion.

The discussion, though, once they reached Chicago, revolved around Jennifer. Reaching the city in the middle of the afternoon, they drove directly to the address Quist had been given. It was a small house on the outskirts of the city, modest verging on shabby. Lily was surprised. With the jumping from large city to large city that Jennifer had done, she'd expected something more cosmopolitan.

"They've all been places like this," Quist told her as he studied the house. "Very plain." He looked at Lily. "I'll go see if she's here. If she is, I'll be back for you." To the objective observer, he looked perfectly calm, but Lily had spent long enough studying his face to recognize the subtle tightness around his nose and mouth.

"Won't you want to see her yourself?" she asked. "Nicki and I can wait here."

"In the cold, no way. If I go in, you go in." He paused. "Aren't you a little bit curious?"

She gave him a crooked smile. "I suppose." She offered her mouth when he leaned over in search of it, then she watched him unfold his tall frame from the car and approach the house.

Two minutes later he came back for her. The tension remained around his nose and mouth, and Lily could have sworn she saw something approaching fear in his eyes. But it was gone before she could be sure, and after he helped her out, he took Nicki in his arms.

It occurred to Lily then that she and Nicki were Quist's security. They were his family as he confronted someone who was also his family but in whom he had no faith at all. Lily knew that she was a calming force for him; she'd seen it different times when he'd been tense or angry, when looking at her or touching her had relaxed him. The situation with Jennifer clearly put him on edge. It also opened up feelings of vulnerability. If Lily gave him confidence, that was good. She found deep satisfaction in being there for him.

Jennifer Simmons had no one to give her confidence. Her vulnerability was right there on the surface, along with features that were young and lovely and eyes that were years too old. She was dressed simply, in jeans and a shirt, and she looked up at Quist as though she didn't know whether to hug him or run away.

Awkwardly she introduced them to the older woman with whom she was staying, and showed them into the house. When they were seated in the living room, she swallowed hard. She looked down at her hands, which were pale and tightly clenched. She looked up at Quist.

"Thank you for coming," she said in an unsteady voice. "I wasn't sure you'd follow me here."

Quist wanted to be angry with her. She was his mother's daughter, and he'd been angry at his mother all his life. But at first glance Jennifer looked more unwitting than evil. So rather than be angry, he was cautious. "You gave my name to your friends. I assumed you expected me."

She shook her head. Her hair was dark like Quist's but shorter and fine. It hugged her head and would have made her look waiflike if she hadn't been so tall. Lily guessed her to be five nine. She also guessed that she could have been a model if she'd wanted to.

"I didn't know what to expect," Jennifer said, still unsteadily, "but I had nowhere else to turn."

Where else but to blood kin, Lily thought as dozens of questions flooded into her mind. If she'd been Quist, she'd have been wondering whether Jennifer looked like her mother, whether they'd been close, what her mother had been like, whether Jennifer had any other siblings, whether her mother had remarried and finally settled down, whether she'd ever mentioned Quist.

Quist wasn't unaware of those questions. But he was guarded, not yet ready to open up that part of the relationship. "You told me there was a man, that he was involved in embezzlement and that he planned to implicate you in it."

Jennifer held herself straight, but there was a fine trembling in her arms that made her shirt shimmer as though there was a wind whispering through the weave. She hesitated for just a minute, seeming as reluctant to trust Quist as he was to trust her. Then a tiny flicker of resignation crossed her features, suggesting that she had no choice.

"His name is Walker Keane. I've known him most of my life, but it's just been the last two years that we've been together."

"You're having an affair with him?" Quist asked bluntly.

She looked down. "Yes. We—I thought he was a good person. He had a nice place to live, and he was always buying me things.

All he asked was that I look good for him. He liked to show me off. I made him feel younger.''

That sounded ominous. "How old is he?''

"Forty-three.''

Quist was silent, trying to reconcile the twenty-four-year difference in ages. He thought of Lily's being eleven years younger than him, but eleven years wasn't twenty-four.

Jennifer made no attempt to rationalize the difference. If anything, she seemed eager to get away from it. "We were living in Albany. He was a free-lance business manager. He would hire himself out to different companies for a limited period of time. That meant he could work as much or as little as he wanted to, and it meant that we could go away a lot. He liked doing that, going off on trips.''

"Did you?''

She hesitated, then nodded. "Walker's the only man I've ever really known. I trusted him. From the first I can remember, he was always around, and even though he used to get into some awful battles with Mom—''

"He's been around that long?''

"Since I was seven or eight.''

The guy sounded perverse to Quist. "He was attracted to you back then?''

"Not to me," Jennifer said. "To Mom.''

Nicki started crying. Only after Quist handed her over to Lily did he realize how tightly he'd been holding her. With a determined effort, he relaxed his muscles.

But Jennifer was leaning forward, smiling at Nicki in a way that made the girl look fifteen. "She's adorable. How old is she?''

"Almost six weeks now," Lily said.

Jennifer's gaze skipped back and forth from Nicki's face to Lily's, then Quist's. "She looks like you," she told Lily, and Lily didn't say a word as to why that should be so.

Neither did Quist, but only in part because he didn't mind being mistaken for Nicki's father. The other part was still trying to comprehend what Jennifer had said about her mother and Walker Keane. It disgusted him to think that mother and daughter had been involved with the same man, even if it had been at different times.

"How did Keane get into trouble?" he asked a bit sharply.

Jennifer looked up from Nicki, and her smile quickly faded.

"I'm not sure how or when it started. All I know is that he's been accused of stealing hundreds of thousands of dollars from different ones of the companies he worked for."

"Where do you come in?"

"He doesn't have much of a defense, I guess, so he's going to say that I put him up to it."

"A nineteen-year-old girl?" Quist asked skeptically.

"And before me, my mother. He'll say that the original scheme was hers, and that I just carried on after she died."

"Does he have proof?"

"How can he have proof if it's not true?" she cried. It was the first time she'd betrayed any of the frustration she was feeling, but she quickly regained control of herself. "He has proof that we helped him spend the money, and we did that, only we thought he'd come by it honestly."

"Your mother cared about things like honesty?" Quist blurted out. He couldn't control the asking any more than he could the bitterness behind it.

Jennifer remained quiet, thinking, choosing her words. "I know you have no reason to feel anything for her. She wasn't much of a mother to you."

"Much?" he echoed tartly.

"Okay, she wasn't a mother at all," Jennifer said, and both her tone and her look said that her guard was down. "But she was to me. She never got divorced from your father, so she never married mine, and he didn't stick around long enough for it to matter. So I grew up with one parent, too, except that after a little bit we had Walker. But the whole time, Mom tried. She worked as a book-keeper until Walker said she didn't have to work anymore, and I was glad he said it. She worked too hard. She worked too hard trying to be good with Walker, too. Sometimes she was his mother and sometimes his lover, and sometimes she was something in between. That was when there was trouble. But all she wanted was to have us be together, Walker and me and her. Maybe she felt she'd blown it once—I don't know, because she never mentioned you to me, but I do know that she liked the idea of family."

She stopped and was studying Quist. "You're older than I thought you'd be."

"She was seventeen when I was born."

"Maybe she was too young to handle having a baby. Did she love your father?"

"I doubt it."

"Do you remember her at all?"

"No. I was an infant when she left."

Jennifer frowned and looked away. "I wonder what she did all those years in between." She looked back up at Quist. "What do you think? She never talked about the past. It was like her life began when I was born. When I used to ask her questions about where she was born or what it was like when she was little, she'd give me general answers that said nothing at all."

Quist wanted to offer some kind of dark speculation as to what the woman had done after she'd abandoned his father and him, and though he had plenty of words at the ready, he couldn't get himself to utter a one. He was coming to wonder whether Jennifer Simmons wasn't, in her way, a victim of her mother, too. Jennifer had loved the woman. He couldn't see deliberately hurting her for the sake of his own vengeance. Far safer to stick to Jennifer's present predicament.

So he cleared his throat. "Where is Keane now?"

"In Albany."

"Has he been indicted?"

She nodded. "He's out on bail."

"And he actually told you what he planned?"

"He was drunk, but he didn't deny it when I pinned him down the next day."

"So you ran?"

"As fast as I could. I went to stay with someone in Albany, but he came for me there. I thought I could lose him in Manhattan, but I got a call saying he was on his way."

"Who are the people you've been staying with?"

"Friends of my mother. We used to visit them a lot when I was little but not so much after we moved in with Walker. I was counting on their loyalty lying with me."

Quist was grateful she'd had that much sense. She'd been pretty dumb carrying on with a hand-me-down from her mother, but then, she was young, seventeen at the time she'd started in with Keane. Seventeen was the same age his mother had been when she had him and left. And at seventeen, he'd been no cherub, himself. Maybe bad judgment at that age ran in the family.

But that was as far as he wanted to go with family analyses. "What do you want from me?" he asked. It didn't matter that he felt an unbidden affinity for the girl; he wasn't about to be used without knowing the score.

"Advice." She looked at him straight on and would have conveyed utter confidence if it hadn't been for that same fine trembling in her arms. "I think I need a lawyer, but I don't know the first thing about how to go about getting one who would be good for something like this. I tried to reach Henry Melnick—he was the lawyer who called me after my mother died and told me about you—but he's dead, and I don't know where else to turn. My mother's friends—the people I've stayed with—don't know. Walker was in control of just about my whole life." Looking off to the side, she said more quietly, "I don't have much money, and I can't get a loan from the bank." She looked back at him with as determined a gaze as he'd received from her. "But I'll pay you back. I'll work for you, or work somewhere else and make payments to you every week from my salary. I can type, or file, or do whatever somebody trains me to do. But I don't want to go to jail."

The silence that followed her words was abrupt and final, indeed like the steel doors of a prison clanging shut.

Quist continued to study her, but Lily's words were the ones echoing in his mind. *Can you really go home and forget about her? Won't you feel guilty? You'll always wonder.*

"You won't go to jail," he said at last.

"If Walker implicates me, I will."

"He's only using you to take a little of the weight off him. No prosecutor will charge you without solid evidence." He truly believed that, but he had no intention of leaving it to chance. Rising from the sofa, he reached down to take Nicki from Lily. "There's a lawyer I trust in Billings. He won't handle the case himself, but he'll give us the name of someone in New York who can."

With Lily at his side, he went to the door. There, he turned back to Jennifer, who was standing in the hall looking nearly as unsure as she had at the first.

"I'll make the calls from the hotel. We'll be staying at the Hyatt. If you want to join us there for dinner, I may have something to tell you. Say, eight?"

Jennifer nodded.

Only after they were back in the car and stuck in the rush-hour traffic did Lily turn to Quist. "What do you think?" she asked cautiously. He'd been looking dark since they'd left the house.

He shrugged.

"Is that a 'she's nice'?"

"It's a 'she's young and lost and I don't know what the hell else, because I barely spent twenty minutes with the girl.'"

"You liked her."

"I didn't spend *long* enough with her to like her."

"But you'll help her."

"A few calls. I'm making a few calls, and I'll pick up the tab, but only because I have the money and I got nothing better to do with it. And, anyway, she'll pay me back."

Lily doubted he'd make her do that, but she said nothing. Well, almost nothing. "You and Jennifer have the same nose."

There was dead silence for a minute, then a rather annoyed, "So?"

"Just making an observation."

Quist made the same observation that night at dinner. Shortly afterward, he gave Jennifer the name, address and phone number of a top-notch lawyer in New York who was expecting to hear from her the next day. He also gave her an airline ticket, plus a check made out to the lawyer. "This will more than cover his retainer. He's to put the excess in an account for your use. I want you to stay in New York until he tells you you can leave. Keep in close touch with him, and whatever you do, don't go running off. This lawyer is your ticket to freedom from Keane."

Jennifer's gratitude was written all over her face. She looked as if she would have thrown her arms around him if he'd shown the slightest receptiveness to that. But he didn't. And though Lily, who knew how warm and physical Quist could be, could have kicked him for keeping his distance, she understood that he needed time.

For Lily, though, time was running out. She had to know where she was going, whether it would be back to Quebec or on to Quist's ranch. The issue weighed heavily on her mind when they returned to their room, and once Nicki had been put to bed, she couldn't put it off any longer.

"Quist?"

He'd just put down the phone from talking with his foreman, but his eyes had been on her the whole time. "Mmm?"

There was a different intonation to his hum. She had a strong suspicion he was thinking the same thing she was. So without preamble, she asked, "What now?"

His eyes dropped to her shoulders, then her breasts, and he invited her over with a toss of his head. Always pleased to be close to him, she rounded the bed and slipped under the arm he offered. He didn't speak, though, but put his lips against her hair.

"Quist?"

"I'm thinking."

"You have to go home."

"I know."

"Maybe I should be heading back to Quebec."

"You can't drive."

"Why not?"

"Alone in the car for that distance with Nicki, it's too much. Maybe if your wrist wasn't broken."

"My wrist is okay. It just aches once in a while. I can do most everything with the cast on."

"You shouldn't do much."

"I have to. I have to get on with my life, Quist."

He didn't say anything, but she could feel the acceleration of his pulse. Taking her face in the V of his hand, he tipped it up. "Kiss me," he ordered and took her lips hard.

She kissed him, loving the hardness for the passion it contained. He was a hard-driving man with a good heart. She wanted to be the one who gave that heart a workout. But his kiss went on, filling her senses, increasingly, to the exclusion of all else.

"Quist, wait," she whispered once, but he didn't allow her any other words. He kept her mouth busy with his own, and by the time he moved on to other parts of her body, she wasn't thinking of talk. Before long they were naked and in bed, writhing against each other in a timeless drive toward release, and when it came, it was better than it had ever been before.

Which was precisely what she'd thought the last time they'd made love, and the time before that, and the time before that.

I love you, she wanted to say, but she didn't dare. What she did say, when they'd regained their senses, pulled up the blanket and relaxed comfortably against each other was, "We have to talk, Quist."

"No need," he murmured sleepily. "You're coming to Montana. This is too good to give up."

"This...what?" she asked.

"What we have.

"What's that?"

"Something good."

"Something good in bed?"

"That, too."

She watched him closely, looked at the way his eyelids lay perfectly at rest and the way the muscles of his face were calm and the way his chest expanded with each slow, sleepy breath he took. And while she wished he was wide awake, looking her in the eye and telling her that he loved her, she had a suspicion that just then, warm and spent and unguarded as he was, he had come as close to that admission as he could.

Forty years of resistance wasn't about to topple in a few short days. Loving Quist, knowing that she wanted to be with him, Lily figured that she could give it a little longer.

CHAPTER NINE

After four months of living with Quist, Lily didn't regret her decision. She loved the ranch. That wasn't to say that she'd loved it from the start. It had looked big, barren and cold when she'd first seen it in January. Very much the city girl Quist had accused her of being, she was overwhelmed by the expanse of snow-covered prairie and the harshness of the hills, by the distance the ranch was from others, by the pervasive darkness of the night. More than once she pined for the noise and lights of the city.

She didn't tell Quist that. She didn't want him to think she couldn't hack it, when she knew she could. Okay, so the land was large and foreign. So she felt more comfortable inside the house and most comfortable when Quist was with her. Everything was new. She was flexible. She could adapt.

She did. As the days passed, she got used to the largeness of things. She realized that she wouldn't be swallowed up by the land if she went out for a walk with Nicki. Nor would she meet a bear. Nor would a catastrophe happen with no one around to help. If anything, *because* there were fewer people around, those people were more attentive.

The ranch house itself was a pleasure. A single-story, sprawling structure, it blended into the prairie with far more charm that she'd expected to find in Montana. Quist had been right about creature comforts. While she wouldn't have called the house plush, it had all the modern amenities she could want. And once she'd softened the rooms with things like plants, decorative baskets and wall hangings, she felt very much at home.

Yes, she loved the ranch, but mostly she loved what she did there. Her days were filled with taking care of Nicki, polishing the handsome oak furniture, baking things like cinnamon-raisin bread, fresh carrot muffins and Swedish apple pie—and her nights were filled with Quist, which was the icing on the cake.

Her wrist had healed well and was long since forgotten. With the gradual onset of spring, she thrived. Nicki thrived, too. Quist had found a pediatrician they both liked, and one glowing report after another came each month. Still a baby but looking more like a little girl each day, Nicki had the kind of sunny temperament that brought smiles to the faces of those around her, and that included the ranch hands, whom she charmed to a man.

Quist was the most charmed. He never made a big thing of it in front of Lily, but time and again she would find him in a quiet corner playing with Nicki. He always checked on her before he went to bed, and looked in on her again when he awoke at dawn. In turn, Nicki came alive when he entered the room, and when he came close, she raised her arms to him in a bid to be held.

There were times when Lily grew teary-eyed watching the two of them together. She loved Quist for adoring Nicki and loved Nicki for adoring Quist. Each blossomed under the other's attention. Their relationship was innocent and sweet.

But there were times—granted not often, because Lily did everything she could not to think about it—when she grew teary-eyed wishing the relationship were more. Though he fit the role well, Quist wasn't her husband. Nor was he Nicki's father. Lily didn't know what Nicki would call Quist when she started to talk, or how she'd explain his position in her life to little friends when she went off to school. Something had to happen before then, Lily knew, but she couldn't push the issue.

She was too happy to risk that. It sometimes frightened her to think that if she'd stayed in Hartford a day longer, or taken early shelter from the storm in a motel, or taken a different road or even the same road at a different time, she'd have missed Quist. As unlikely as any relationship between them had seemed back then, she couldn't imagine life without him. He filled every one of her needs. Even after four months together, her pulses raced when he came near. After that length of time, any critic who would have attributed their relationship to the experience of being snowbound together had to be silenced.

To Lily's knowledge, though, there weren't any critics. Quist had friends and acquaintances at neighboring ranches and in town, and they welcomed her warmly. Several of his ranch hands went so far as to say that Quist's disposition had taken an upswing since she'd come, and though one part of her wondered whether they weren't just buttering her up for the sake of the mocha-nut cake she made, which they loved, the other part of her accepted their compliment with pride.

There was one critic, though. Like a bad dream, she'd thought of him from time to time since she'd come to live with Quist. But Quist made her feel safe and protected, and Montana was a long way from Connecticut. It wasn't Jarrod; he had remarried and would do, she knew, everything he could to forget that Lily existed. It was Michael. She hadn't dreamed that he would follow her.

He did just that. Late one Monday morning in the beginning of June, he showed up at the door. Unsuspecting, she went to answer his knock. She was wearing jeans and a shirt, and was wiping her hands of remnants of the bread dough she'd just put in the oven. She came to an abrupt halt several steps from the screen when she saw who was there.

Her first thought was to look around for help, but she controlled the urge. "Michael," she said with cool civility.

He dipped his head in greeting. His blond hair was as perfectly groomed as always, his skin as perfectly tanned, his slacks and cotton sweater as perfectly chic. With all that perfection, he looked distinctly out of place. "Aren't you going to let me in?"

"That depends." She resumed wiping her hands on the dish towel. "What do you want?"

"To talk."

"About what?"

"What you've done with yourself in the past few months."

"I don't see why that should be of any interest to you," she said, and though she'd tried to say it evenly, something of her inner feeling must have come through. The battle lines were drawn.

Without invitation, Michael opened the screen and stepped inside. Lily countered by quickly sidestepping him, hooking the towel on the coatrack and escaping to the porch he'd just left.

"D.J.!" she bellowed at the top of her lungs. "D.J.!"

"What in the hell are you doing?" Michael cried, holding the screen door open. "I just want to talk."

She drilled him with a look. "Last time you said that, you ended up throwing things at me." She looked back at the barn in time to see a young man striding purposefully toward her. "I've learned not to make the same mistake twice," she added, then called to D.J., "Can I have your help for a minute? This man wants to talk with me, but I don't care to be alone with him."

"Sure thing, ma'am," D. J. said with a drawl and a smile. He took the two front steps in one stride, then posted himself against the porch rail.

Michael should have been humiliated, but he wasn't. Not Michael. He stared at the young man for a long minute before turning to Lily. "You're a coward."

"Uh-huh." She felt better now that D.J. was there, but that didn't mean she was calm. Her insides shook. She wished she were five ten and robust. She wished she wore armor. She wished Quist were around, but he was out in the Jeep. "So, what do you want?"

Again Michael looked at D.J., but the younger man showed no sign either of looking away or leaving. Finally he decided to ignore him, and, in a pleasant voice, asked Lily, "How have you been?"

"Just fine."

"You're seeing something of the country, I take it." When she didn't respond to that, he smiled and asked, "Do you miss the east yet?"

"Not really."

"This is...different."

"Uh-huh."

He looked off toward the barn, then the open range, then back toward the inside of the house. "A rancher's mistress. Funny, I hadn't pegged you for the mistress type."

Lily felt a momentary chill, but she shook it off. "Wasn't that what you had in mind for me back in Hartford?"

"Of course not. I wanted to marry you."

She'd never heard anything as absurd, but it didn't seem worth her breath to tell him so. "What are you here for, Michael?"

"You," he said. When she gave him a you-must-be-crazy look, he insisted, "I want you to come back with me."

"Why would I want to do that?" she asked in disbelief.

"Because you and I could be good together."

"I don't believe this," she murmured. She turned her head toward D.J. "I don't *believe* this." She glared back at Michael. "Last time you were threatening me with all kinds of ugly things, and that was before you got violent."

"I was upset. I said things I shouldn't have."

"You certainly did, but that's not even the issue. The issue is that there's nothing between us. There's never *been* anything between us, despite what you threatened to say. Why on earth would I want to go back east with you?''

''Because this is no way to live.'' He shot a disparaging glance around. ''Animals live on places like this. People choose more cultured surroundings.''

Even aside from the fact that he'd just insulted D.J., who was within earshot, and Quist and all the others, who weren't, Lily felt personally offended. After all, she'd chosen to live on the ranch. She could have left at any time. ''I think you'd better go.''

''After I've come all this way to see you?''

That raised another issue, one she wanted answered out of sheer curiosity. ''How did you find me?''

But Michael was looking at the approaching ribbon of dust. ''Is that your rancher?''

Lily was relieved that it was. She was also relieved that D.J. didn't move. ''How did you find me?''

''You wired the bank to have your account transferred here. Where's Nicole?''

The chill she felt this time wasn't so easily shaken off, and at the back of her eyes, she felt the prick of tears. ''Nicole is none of your affair,'' she said on a note of warning.

''She's my niece.''

Lily held herself still. ''I have a paper that waives any claim you or your family may have on her.''

''I'm saying that I care. How is she?'' When Lily remained stone-faced, he said, ''She was very little when I saw her last. I'll bet she's grown.''

Lily refused to even acknowledge Nicki's presence, though she was, at that moment, close by, in a wind-up swing in the kitchen.

''Come on, Lily. I'm her uncle. I'm curious.''

''Nicki and I are doing just fine. Now that you know that, and now that you know I won't go back east with you, you can leave.''

''You really intend to raise her here?''

Lily didn't blink. ''You can leave, Michael.'' She didn't want him there. His presence was contaminating something that was good and pure and healthy.

''For God's sake, what kind of a life is this for a child? I mean, if you want to play the rancher's maid, that's one thing. But think of Nicole. She shouldn't have to live this way.''

"Live what way?" Lily demanded, trembling now with anger and doing little to hide it.

"A bare-bones existence. This isn't life. It's just survival. Where do you go to shop around here? Where do you go to eat out? No theater? No symphony? The two of you could be spending your days at the club. Nicole could be seeing other children like her, instead of groveling with cows and dust and people who probably haven't graduated from high school."

Lily was livid. "Are you saying that a diploma is a sign of intelligence? That, Michael, is probably one of the most ignorant comments I've ever heard."

"You know what I mean."

"No, I don't. The people I've met here are open and intelligent, and when it comes to common sense, or perceptiveness, or sensitivity, they're head and shoulders above you and Jarrod—*combined.* 'I should be at the club,'" she mimicked. "I *hated* the club. When I think back to the people I met through you two, I thank God Nicki's not there. I'd rather have my daughter growing up knowing people like D.J. any day."

Michael's mouth twisted as he shot a derisive glance at the young cowhand. "Are you putting out for him, too?"

Tears gathered on her lower lids. She was rigid with fury. "Leave, Michael."

But instead of leaving, he narrowed his eyes. "Think, Lily. Think back to when you conceived Nicole and all the things you wanted for her then. This isn't for you, and it's not for her." He darted a glance at the Jeep, which had reached the driveway to the house. "And what kind of relationship do you have with that guy, anyway?" He grabbed her hand, ignoring D.J., who had remained immobile in the face of personal insults but now immediately straightened. "No wedding band. He hasn't married you. You've been living here servicing him all this time, and he hasn't married you? That's dumb, Lily. Really dumb. Oh, not on his part. I have to give him credit for that. He knows a good thing when he sees one. He's got a cook, a laundress, a housekeeper and a lover all for free. What kind of woman is going to put up with that bull?"

Lily yanked her hand back. "No bull, and I know what it looks like, because you and Jarrod gave me plenty. Everything I have here is good. I've never been happier." She heard the Jeep pull to a halt not far from the steps.

"And you think it'll last?" Michael asked, but his words were lower and coming quickly, as though he knew that he was running out of time. "You think he'll still want you in a year, or two or three? He'll tire of you. Or Nicole. Wait till she gets bigger and starts making demands. You think he's going to want you then? You'll be out in the cold, Lily. Out...in...the...cold."

"What's going on here?" Quist asked. His voice was deep and steel-edged, and his eyes were on Michael as he put a possessive arm around Lily's shoulder.

"This," Lily said shakily, "is Michael, my former brother-in-law. I told you about him. Do you remember?"

Quist certainly did. He remembered everything Lily had said and the way she'd said it. "What's he doing here?"

"He came to see how I was. But he's just leaving. Weren't you, Michael?"

The expression on Michael's perfectly tanned face suggested he was feeling thwarted, but he didn't let on to it in words. And Lily could understand why. Michael was tall, but Quist was taller. Quist was also broader and more heavily muscled, a fact that was made abundantly clear by the snug fit of his chambray shirt across his chest and the sinewy forearms that extended beyond the roll of his sleeves.

Michael recognized a formidable opponent when he saw one. Without saying a thing, he sent a final hard look at Lily. Then, exhibiting perfect posture to match his perfect attire, he walked past her, down the steps and to his car.

Quist went after him.

"Wait, Quist," Lily cautioned.

He held up a hand to reassure her, but he didn't look back. Lily watched apprehensively while he leaned low at the driver's window. She couldn't hear what he said. The distance was a little too far, his voice a little too low, the breeze a little too active in the grasses beyond the barn. The instant he straightened, Michael's car shot forward.

"I'll be goin' back to work now, ma'am," D.J. said.

Lily had momentarily forgotten his presence. At the sound of his voice, she swung a surprised look his way. "Uh, oh, sure, D.J. And thanks. Thanks for being here." Softly, just a hair above a whisper, she added, "Please forget what you heard. I don't want to upset Quist."

"Sure thing, ma'am," he said, and with a tip of his hat, he was gone.

Seconds later Quist came up the steps, but Lily was already on her way inside. Heart thudding, she made straight for the kitchen. Nicki was in the swing, just where she'd been left. Its wind-up had long since wound down, but she was perfectly content gnawing on one of the rubber teethers Lily had tied with a ribbon to the chain of the swing.

At sight of her mother, she began to gurgle and grin. Lifting her, Lily held her tightly, closed her eyes and swayed gently from side to side.

"Lily?" Quist came forward from the open archway.

"I'm okay," she breathed.

"You're shaking like a leaf. Did he threaten you again?"

"No. Seeing him was bad enough."

Babbling, Nicki began to kick against Lily's waist.

"He won't be back."

She opened her eyes. "What did you say to him?"

Quist wasn't going to tell her, because it was too crude. "Let's just say I made a little threat of my own. I think he understands that I'll carry it out if he comes near you again."

Again. Did that mean *ever* again, as in during the course of her lifetime? She couldn't ask, couldn't push.

"Hi, pumpkin," Quist said softly to Nicki. When she held out an arm, he took her gently in his. "How long was he here?" he asked Lily.

"Not long. Just a few minutes."

"Did he ask to see Nicki?"

"No. He asked how she was. That's all."

Quist wanted to know what they'd talked about, but he didn't ask. Sounding insecure, which perhaps he was, wasn't part of his image. Sounding distrustful, which perhaps had been true at one point, was no longer. He did trust Lily. He knew that her feelings for him were strong. He couldn't see her picking up and leaving him.

He figured that in her own good time, she'd tell him what Michael had said.

Unfortunately she didn't, and it would have been all right, if they'd settled back into their lives without any sign of the slightest disturbance. But Lily seemed to be quieter at times, not quite preoccupied, not quite as carefree in her silence as she'd been. It didn't happen often, but Quist was so keenly attuned to her that he noticed whenever it did. When he asked if something was bothering her, she put on her brightest smile and assured him nothing was, and then she'd be her usual self for a while, as though she was making a concerted effort not to let him see. He began to wonder how much time she spent when he was gone, thinking about whatever it was.

A few minutes; that was all the time she'd spent with Michael, but he'd said something that lingered. Quist knew it, and the longer he wondered what it was, the more unsure he grew. The wondering was like a chisel, chipping away at the fragile base of his trust.

In his mind, the issue was a simple one. He wanted Lily to stay with him. He feared that Michael had made her a counteroffer, and while he didn't believe that she'd seriously consider accepting, knowing how she felt about Michael, he couldn't help but wonder if she was rethinking her position in his life.

He wanted to ask her, but he couldn't seem to find the words. Actually he couldn't seem to find the courage. He didn't know what he'd do if she told him that yes, she was rethinking things.

In the end the words he found surprised even him, though the time and place didn't. They'd just made love on the charcoal-gray sheets on his king-size bed. It had been a hard, fiery coupling that had carried them long and far. Their bodies were slick with sweat and exhausted. As always at times like those, Quist's guard was down.

"Marry me, Lily," he said.

Lily didn't move for a minute. Her heart, which had just settled into a relatively even beat, began to pound again. She wondered if she'd heard wrong, or if she'd imagined the words because she'd wanted to hear them so badly. Levering herself up, she looked into his face. It was damp and slumberous, but his eyes were open and though he seemed a little unbalanced, he was looking straight at her.

"Well?" he prodded.

"Uh, what—will you say that again?"

"I want you to marry me."

She was ecstatic—and frightened. Tears came to her eyes, but she willed them back. "Why?"

"Because I like the life we have together. I think it should be formalized."

That wasn't what she wanted to hear. "Why formalized?"

"I don't know. It just seems right. We're living as husband and wife. Why not make it official?"

"Is that what you really want?" she asked warily.

Quist had been hoping for a warmer reception. He wondered if his fears were founded, after all. The thought of that made him more uneasy than ever. "I want to know you won't leave."

"I won't leave."

"Then marry me."

Lily studied his face for a minute, studied the firm set of his jaw, the straight line of his mouth, the dark eyes that were more enigmatic than they'd been in a while, and though she wanted to melt into him, say yes and make him happy, her own happiness rested on knowing more. She couldn't go through life wondering whether Michael's visit had prompted the proposal. "Why now?"

"Because it's time, don't you think?" He scowled for a minute, wishing he had more patience, but when it came to matters of the heart he was too much a novice to feint and parry. Taking her face a little roughly in his hands, he said, "I'd make you a good husband. I'd make Nicki a good father. I want to have more kids, and you do, too, but I won't do that unless we're married."

Lily loved everything he was saying, still he hadn't told her what she needed to know. So she argued, "Not so long ago, you didn't like women. You weren't interested in marriage."

"I've changed."

"Just like that?"

"No, not 'just like that.'" His hands gentled around her face, thumbs picking up the long teardrops that seemed suspended at the corners of her eyes. "It's been six months, and I fought it at first. One part of me still fights—old habits die hard—but I don't want to go back to the other way of living." When she still looked skeptical, he said, "I've been good with Jennifer, haven't I?"

Lily was the first to admit that he had. He'd kept in close touch with the lawyer from New York, and Jennifer had even been west for a visit, with another one planned for the fall. While there wasn't the kind of brother-sister closeness that came from siblings sharing a past, they had a start.

"You've been very good with her," Lily said. "But that's different. She's someone you can see or not, be close to or not. You don't pick your relatives, but you do pick your wife, and if you pick her for the wrong reasons—'' She sat up, effectively removing her face from his hands. Perching sideways, she drew her knees to her chest for the warmth she missed.

Quist grew cautious. "What is it, Lily?" His voice was low and slow as he studied her profile. "You're thinking something— you've been thinking something for a while now, and I've been trying to figure out what it is, but I keep coming up with zip. Tell me. I need to know."

Lily stared at the needlepoint wall hanging she'd made for the room; it was burgundy and gray to match the sheets and spread, but the gray was pale and soft, far more feminine than charcoal. It was her personal stamp on this room that was masculine in so many other respects, and it was symbolic of all she'd tried to do in his life. *It's time, don't you think?* he'd asked her. She figured he was right. If he didn't love her now, he never would. It was time to be completely forthright.

"I've been thinking about lots of things," she began. "I suppose that Michael—"

"Michael," Quist cut in. The name brought him sharply to a sitting position. "I knew it had to do with him."

"But it doesn't," she argued, eyeing him over the edge of her shoulder. "Not really. But he voiced things I'd been thinking about for a while. It's one thing when they're in your own mind, another when someone who doesn't even think the way you do says them."

Quist accepted that. Bending a knee, he propped an elbow on it and tried to look casual. "So what did he say?"

"He talked about me as your mistress. He said you had a good thing going, with someone to cook and clean and do everything else around the house. He said you'd get tired of me—"

"No *way*—" Quist began, but Lily cut him off with a hand on his arm as she twisted to face him.

"I know," she said softly. Her throat felt tight, but she pushed the words past it. "I think I knew it a long time ago, because you seemed legitimately pleased to have me here. But there was always that little question in my mind about *why* you were pleased. There was always that little question about whether it was me you liked having around, or a live-in maid, cook, lover. I didn't think about it all the time. I really didn't think about it much. I tried *never* to think about it, but that didn't work, because I've been used—and abused—once, and the hurt is still fresh. Then Michael came, and suddenly it was like he took all my little fears and put them in lights.''

''But I want to marry you,'' Quist insisted. ''*You*. Not anyone else I've known in my life. *You*. I could have hired a live-in maid, if that was what I wanted. Or a cook. Or a lover. I've got the money. But I never wanted to have anyone around. Then I met you, and things changed.''

''Things.''

''What I wanted.''

''Why?''

''What do you mean, why?''

''Why did things change? You'd been happy before. From what you said, you were perfectly content with your life.''

Quist looked off to the side. ''Yeah. That's what I said.''

''Weren't you?''

He looked down, thoughtful as his eyes focused unseeingly on the rumpled sheets. ''I suppose I was. I had a safe life. I wasn't taking any chances on women. I used them on my terms. I protected myself.'' He stopped. His gaze rose to the spot where the pale flesh of Lily's hip met the wrinkled sheet. ''Then I met you. You were so damned honest, it was hard not to trust you. But there was something else. For the first time in my life, I was taking care of a woman.''

He raised his eyes to find that hers had flooded. When he winced, she said quickly, ''It's okay. I'm okay. Go on.''

He stared at her long enough to make sure that the tears were staying put. Then he shrugged. ''What's to say? I enjoyed taking care of you.''

''You didn't feel you were being used?''

''How could I feel that, when you resisted my help, and then you were giving me back even more than I was giving.'' He scowled. ''Damn it, Lily, what do you want me to say? I want you here. I want to go on taking care of you. I want to go on taking care of Nicki. I want us to spend the rest of our lives together.''

''You could say that you love me,'' she blurted out, then quickly bit her lip. She hadn't wanted to say that. It was supposed to have come from him. She was about to say something to cover the gaffe when the look of incredulity on his face stopped her.

"Of course I love you," he cried in astonishment. "Isn't that what I've been saying? Isn't it what I've been *doing* for months?"

Tears shimmered in her eyes. "You never said it. I didn't know. You never said it. I need to hear the words."

Unable to hold himself apart from her any longer, he hooked an elbow around her neck and one around her waist and pulled her to him. He ducked his head, sliding his face against her hair. "I love you, Lily." He paused. "And I need to hear them, too."

"I love you," she said, letting the tears go at last.

He was holding her so tightly that it was a miracle she could move to breathe, much less cry, but she did the latter, with the smallest, softest sobs. "I hope it's happiness," he remarked against her cheek.

"And relief." She sniffled, cried a little more, then put her hand over the wet spot she'd made on his chest. The hair was matted; she rubbed it with her fingers, feeling the strength underneath. "I was so afraid. I tried not to be. I kept telling myself that you had to feel something for me, because you were so good to me, and you seemed so happy, but there was always this niggling little doubt."

She hurried on, ignoring the hiccoughing that broke the rush of her thoughts. "Then Michael started talking about the future and what kind of life I'd have here, and it made me realize even more how good it is. It's just the kind of life I want—I love it here, it suits who I am and who I want to be, *you* suit who I am and who I want to be." She took in a trembling breath. "But then I started thinking about what would happen if I ever lost you or lost what I have here." She looked up at him with eyes that were large, still damp but true windows to her soul. "I don't want that to happen, Quist."

For a minute Quist couldn't say a word. He was wondering what he'd ever done to deserve the woman he held in his arms. She was warm and giving, honest, strong enough to support him, vulnerable enough to need his support. And she did love him. It was there in her eyes, spilling from her soul. He'd seen it before, though he'd never had the courage to call it what it was for fear of losing it, but never before had he seen it in quite such a raw state. If he'd doubted before, he no longer did. Lily's love was a part of her being. She could no more free herself from it than she could do without a heart.

That was pretty much the way he felt, he realized. A future without Lily was no future at all. She gave his life dimension, depth and color. His love for her was boundless.

"So," he said a little hoarsely, "will you marry me?"

"Oh, yes," she whispered and offered her lips for a kiss to seal the vow.

EPILOGUE

Lily could look at him for hours, which was very much what she did during the first day of his life. She put him to her breast, but her milk hadn't come in yet, and still she found pleasure from his sucking.

Though he was sleeping quietly now, he had a strong pair of lungs. He was also long and had a shock of dark hair so like his father's that Lily grinned through her tears each time she combed it with her fingers.

He was a beautiful baby. Nicole had been beautiful, too, and still was. Inside and out. Lily was blessed.

"Anybody sleeping?" came a deep-murmured call from the door.

She looked up to see two faces peering around the door's edge. Quist was clearly making a game of it, with Nicki not quite sure she wanted to play. It was the first time she'd seen her mother since Lily had gone into labor. It was also the first time she'd been in a hospital since her own birth, and she looked apprehensive.

At the sight of them, Lily's throat went tight. But she smiled broadly, held out her free arm and wiggled her fingers in invitation. Quist brought Nicki into the room. She was clinging to his neck, pressing her cheek to his shoulder, peering at Lily as though she didn't want to, but couldn't resist.

"Hi, sweetheart," Lily finally said. "You look so pretty. Daddy put on your favorite dress?" It was lime-green gingham with gros-grain ribbon at the bodice and hem, and beneath it were white tights and tiny white strap shoes. "And he put a ribbon in your hair." Which was shoulder length, light brown and shiny. "You're my gorgeous little girl." Lily held out her arm. "Can I have a hug, gorgeous little girl?"

But Nicki tightened her arms around Quist's neck and turned her face into his shoulder.

"No hug for Mommy?" Quist asked softly. When she shook her head, he said, "Well, I want to give her one. She's my favorite big girl.'' He bent over and gave Lily an eloquent kiss, then sat down on the edge of the bed.

"You said *I* was your favorite big girl,'' came the tiny voice from his shoulder. For a three-year-old, Nicki was unusually verbal. But then, Lily mused, she was unusual in lots of ways.

Quist's eyes smiled at Lily over Nicki's head. "You're right. You are my favorite big girl. Mommy's my favorite *big* big girl.'' He tucked in his chin to whisper, "Want to see your brother? He's sleeping, but you can take a peek.''

She shook her head and didn't look. Quist did, though. He couldn't help it, any more than he could help looking at Lily again when he was done. She was beautiful, and she was the mother of his son. On top of all the other things he loved her for, he loved her for that.

In response to the exquisite look in his eyes, Lily touched his cheek. Then she gently rubbed Nicki's arm. "I've missed you so much, Nicki. I told the doctors that I had to go home tomorrow so that I could be with my daughter.''

"How are you feeling?'' Quist whispered.

She grinned and nodded, looked at Nicki, looked at the baby. "Incredible. I'm feeling incredible.''

"How's he doing?''

She continued to grin. "Incredible.'' She slipped her thumb into Nicki's loose fist. The small fingers tightened around it. "But the food here is lousy. I miss our special superburgers with bacon.''

"I had one yesterday,'' came the high little-girl voice.

"Did you?'' Lily feigned hurt. "And you didn't bring one here for me?''

"I wanted to,'' Nicki said, "but Daddy said we should wait and make one when you get home.'' She turned her head just enough so that she could peek at Lily.

"I think I can live with that,'' Lily decided. "What else did Daddy make for you?''

"Fluff and popcorn and Chunky bars.''

"Shhhh,'' Quist said. "You weren't supposed to tell her that.'' Nicki giggled.

Lily loved it, but she didn't let on. "Quist, that's *terrible*. Fluff and popcorn and Chunky bars?''

"Not together,'' he argued, as though that would excuse it.

"You're corrupting this child.''

"I like fluff," Nicki said. "And popcorn. And Chunky bars. Maybe baby wants a Chunky bar." She dared a glance at the infant.

"Mm, not for a little while, sweetheart. Babies only drink milk at the beginning."

"Did I?"

"Sure, you did." Lily had had the same conversation close to a dozen times with her daughter, but she didn't mind the repetition. Babies were something totally new for Nicki.

"His eyes are closed," the little girl said.

"He's sleeping. He'll do that a whole lot."

"When can I play with him?"

"When he's awake. Would you like that?"

She looked a little dubious, still she nodded.

"Come here," Lily said, and this time when she held out her arm, Nicki went right to her. When she was snuggled close to Lily's side, she reached out and timidly touched her brother's hand.

Lily smiled at Quist, who was smiling right back at her, and there were a myriad of messages going back and forth with those smiles.

Jonathan. I like the name Jonathan. After you. I like that, too.

They say he's perfect. Thank you for giving me a perfect son.

I'm glad it was a boy. Every man should have a son.

I'm glad we waited this long. We needed the time together, and Nicki needed the time with us.

Lord, do I love you, Quist.

Ah, Lily, you're the light of my life.

And the smiles went on.

Falling Angel

Anne Stuart

PROLOGUE

"This isn't working out, Mr. MacVey."

Emerson Wyatt MacVey III looked up and blinked. The light was blinding up there, endless bright white light set against a clear crystal blue. It gave him a headache. "Could you be more specific?" He managed to make his voice coolly polite.

The woman standing in front of him was an impressive figure, and he didn't like to be impressed. She was ageless, of course, with smooth, unlined skin, pure white hair, a long, slender body and large hands. She was possessed of the most frightening eyes he'd ever seen. Large, dark, powerful, they looked right through you, seeing everything you wanted to keep hidden.

Not that he needed to keep anything hidden, he reminded himself. He'd lived his life as he'd seen fit, and he didn't need to make excuses to anyone.

"How long have you been here?" the woman asked in a voice even colder than his. Augusta, that was her name. It suited her.

Emerson shook his head. "I don't remember. Time moves differently..."

"Then I'll jog your memory. You've been here for seventeen months, Mr. MacVey. And you've shown very little improvement."

"Seventeen months?" he echoed, shocked out of his determined cool. "It was only three months yesterday."

"As you've said, time passes a little differently up here," Augusta said sternly. "You've been dead for seventeen months, Mr. MacVey. And you're still the same arrogant, argumentative person you were when you arrived."

He tipped back in his chair, staring up at her. "Yeah? Well, maybe I wasn't ready to die. You ever consider that? Maybe thirty-two years old was a little young to have a massive heart attack. Maybe someone made a mistake, pulled me out a little too early."

"You've seen too many movies. We don't make mistakes."

"Then why am I here?" Frustration was building, ready to spill over. "Why aren't I floating around with the angels, playing the harp and all that crap?"

"You are an angel, Mr. MacVey."

That stopped him for a moment. He glanced down at himself. Same body, thin, patrician. Same English wool three-piece suit that he died in. It had been ripped off him when the medics had labored over him, trying to bring him back. Fortunately he'd been able to repair the damage. "Really? Then why don't I have pearly wings and a halo?"

Augusta smiled sourly, and suddenly she reminded him of his maternal grandmother, a cold-blooded old tartar who'd managed to terrorize three presidents, a prime minister and her only grandson quite effectively. "Your status is in no way assured, Mr. MacVey. There are two choices. Heaven, or the other place. We're not certain where you fit."

When he'd had his heart attack it had been a huge explosion of red-hot pain. This was cold, icy cold, and even more frightening. "What do you mean by that?" His voice stumbled slightly, and he cursed himself for showing weakness. Augusta wouldn't respect weakness, any more than his grandmother would.

"I mean that you need to earn your place up here. On earth you were petty, grasping, cold and heartless. All you cared about was making money and amassing possessions. Where are your possessions now, Mr. MacVey?"

"It's a little too late to do anything about that, isn't it?" He managed to muster a trace of defiance.

"On the contrary. It's not too late at all. You're going to be given a second chance. One month, to be exact. You're going back to earth and try to right some of the wrongs you've done. If you prove yourself worthy of redemption then you'll be allowed to move on. If you fail..." She made a desultory gesture.

"The other place?" Emerson supplied.

"Exactly." Her voice was sepulchral.

Emerson controlled his instinctive start of panic. He didn't want to go to hell. It was just that simple. But not simple enough that he wasn't ready to put up an argument. "Won't people find it a little surprising to see me running around again? I imagine they had a full-blown funeral, people weeping and all that."

"No one wept."

Again that stinging cold sharpness where his damaged heart should be. "Don't be ridiculous. People always cry at funerals."

"No one cried at yours. But then, not very many people showed up for it, either. Only one person cried for you, Mr. MacVey. And it was one of the people whose lives your selfishness destroyed.''

He racked his brain for people he might have injured, people he might have destroyed, but he came up with a comforting blank. ''I didn't destroy anyone.''

''Oh, you didn't set out to do so, I grant you that. In a way, that almost makes it worse. Does the name Caroline Alexander mean anything to you?''

''Not a thing.''

''She was your secretary for three months.''

He shrugged. ''I went through a lot of secretaries.''

''You certainly went through Carrie. You fired her on a whim, Mr. MacVey, on Christmas Eve, and that started a chain of events that totally devastated her life. She's one of your projects. You have to fix what you so callously destroyed.''

''And how am I supposed to do that? I don't imagine she'd want me anywhere near her.''

''You aren't going back as Emerson Wyatt MacVey III. Things aren't going to be quite so easy this time around. You'll have your work cut out for you. You have three lives to save, MacVey. And you'll have one month to do it. You go back on Thanksgiving. And you return on Christmas Eve. We'll decide then whether you've earned your right to move on.''

''But...''

''Don't fret, Mr. MacVey,'' Augusta said. ''You won't be going alone. You'll have a little help. An observer, so to speak. Someone to keep an eye on you, make sure you're not making things even worse. I don't have a great deal of faith in this particular experiment. I think you're a lost cause, but I've been overruled in this matter.''

Thank heaven for small favors, Emerson thought.

''Not a small favor at all,'' Augusta replied, reading his thoughts with an ease he could never get accustomed to. ''You will go back to earth and repair some of the damage you have caused, or you will be doomed to the other place. And you won't like it, MacVey. You won't like it at all.''

He had no doubt of that. ''What exactly am I supposed to do?''

Augusta smiled, exposing very large, very yellow teeth. ''You will fix Carrie Alexander's life, which, I warn you, is no small task. And you must find two other people you've harmed, and somehow make amends.''

"How am I supposed to find two people I've harmed?" he demanded indignantly.

"The problem, MacVey, won't be in finding people you've harmed. The problem will be in finding people you haven't hurt during your tenure on earth. Good luck," she said sourly. "You'll need it."

"But what about my observer? You said I was going to have some help," he said, no longer bothering to disguise the panic in his voice.

"We don't want to make it too easy on you, MacVey," Augusta said with saccharine sweetness. "You'll find out who your observer is in good time. As a matter of fact, no one's offered to take on the task. They all think you're a lost cause."

Emerson sat up a little straighter. He was a man who was used to challenges, would do just about anything to triumph over impossible odds. "Want to bet?"

"We don't gamble up here, Mr. MacVey."

"You just pass judgment."

"Exactly."

"Great," he muttered under his breath, despising the old woman almost as much as he'd despised his grandmother. "So you're going to dump me back on earth and the rest is up to me?"

"That about sums it up. Oh, and you'll be given a slight edge. Miracles, Mr. MacVey. You'll be given the opportunity to perform three miracles. How and when you choose to use that particular gift will be up to you. But you cannot use more than one per person."

"Great," he said again. "Any other rules?"

"You're not to tell anyone who you are. But you needn't worry about that—you won't be able to."

"What do you mean by that?"

"You'll find out. Are you ready?"

"Ready? Last time I looked it was August."

"It's late November. Thanksgiving, to be exact. Time to go."

"But..."

"No more questions, Mr. MacVey. You're on your own."

The light grew sharper, clearer, brighter still, until it felt as if his head were about to explode. The cold stinging in his chest was like a stiletto-sharp knife, a column of ice that speared through his body until it began to dissolve into a thousand tiny crystals. And then he was gone, cast out, drifting through the black night like the flakes of snow surrounding him, no two ever the same. And all was black.

CHAPTER ONE

He squinted at the swirling white light in front of him, trying to orient himself. He was cold, his feet, his hands, even the tip of his nose was cold. It took him a moment to realize the bright, fuzzy light in front of him was the headlights from the vehicle he was driving. It was snowing, heavily, and the light barely penetrated the thick darkness.

"Damn," he said out loud, he wasn't quite sure why. Maybe he wanted to hear the sound of his own voice, to prove he was alive.

Except that he wasn't alive. He'd been dead of a massive heart attack for almost two years now. And it wasn't the sound of his own voice coming from his throat.

He dropped his gaze, from the storm beyond his windshield, to his hands clutching the steering wheel. They weren't his hands. His hands were on the small side, neat, perfectly manicured, slightly soft. The hands in front of him were big hands, with long, slender fingers, short nails, calluses and scars marring the skin. They were the hands of a working man. Not the hands of a man who'd never done anything more strenuous than use the carefully padded equipment at his upscale health club.

"Damn," he said again, testing the sound. Lower than his voice. With a slight huskiness in it. No discernible accent. That was something at least. What the hell had Augusta done to him?

He glanced up in the rearview mirror, but all he could see was the swirling darkness behind him. He shifted it, angling his head to get a look at his face. And promptly drove off the snow-slick road into a ditch, banging his head against the windshield.

The engine stalled, the headlight spearing into the darkness. He hadn't been wearing a seat belt. How strange. He always wore a seat belt. Of course, in New York, where he'd lived, it had been the law, and he'd been a very law-abiding citizen. But he'd been wearing seat belts since he'd first ridden in a car. And what use had they done him? he thought bitterly. Seat belts weren't much good against a heart attack.

He jerked the mirror down, almost ripping it from its mooring in the tattered roof of the pickup truck he'd been driving, and stared down. It was no wonder he'd driven off the road. A total stranger stared back at him.

Emerson Wyatt MacVey III had been a compact, good-looking yuppie, with perfectly styled sandy blond hair, even features, clear-framed glasses and carefully orthodontured teeth. He'd had icy blue eyes, and a faintly supercilious expression on his naturally pale face.

The man who stared back at him was his exact opposite in every way. Dark brown, almost black, eyes, long, curling black hair that obviously hadn't been cut in months, a high forehead, high cheek-bones, a large, sensual-looking mouth, and a strong Roman nose all composed a face that didn't belong in his world.

He glanced down at the long, jeans-clad legs, the faded flannel shirt beneath the down vest, the big, strong hands that had first startled him. Whatever he had become, it was as different from Emerson MacVey as night and day.

Enough of his ingrained nature remained that he carefully turned off the truck lights, pulled the key from the ignition and locked the truck when he climbed out into the mini-blizzard. A stray thought hit him—who would steal an old truck from a ditch in the middle of a blinding snowstorm?—but he ignored that. Emerson was a man who locked his car. Even if he was currently possessed of an old pickup that looked as if it belonged in a junkyard, it was still his car, his possession, and he wasn't going to let anyone else make off with it. Who knew what else this stranger possessed?

He could see lights in the distance, through the swirl of snow. He shivered as a mantle of snow covered him, and he stared down at his feet. Way down, and the feet were big, like his hands. And wearing only sneakers to wade through the drifts.

He shivered again, grimaced, and then struck out toward the lights. He felt a little dizzy, and he realized there was a throbbing where he'd smashed his head against the windshield. He touched it gingerly, and beneath the melting snow he could feel a respect-able lump. Maybe that could explain away some of his confusion when he asked for help from whoever lived nearby. Because he sure as hell felt confused.

As he drew nearer, he saw it was an old farmhouse, in about as good condition as the truck he'd been driving. The front porch sagged, the windows had sheets of plastic stapled around them, rather than decent triple-track storm windows, and ripped tar paper had been tacked around the bottom of the house. He imagined that the roof was in equally shoddy condition beneath the thick blanket of snow. He could smell the rich, aromatic scent of wood smoke, and he stopped still. In his endless, timeless sojourn at the Waystation he'd been able to see and hear and even feel things. But there hadn't been anything to smell.

He took another deep sniff. Turkey. Roast turkey, and the faint trace of cinnamon and apples. And he remembered with a start what Augusta had told him. He was coming back on Thanksgiving, leaving on Christmas Eve. It was Thanksgiving, and someone was just sitting down to dinner.

And he was standing outside in a blowing snowstorm, freezing to death. He shook himself, running a hand through his long, thick hair in a gesture that was both foreign and automatic. And he stepped up to the ancient, scarred door and rapped.

In a moment the door was flung open, letting out a flood of warmth and light and noise. Someone was standing there, silhouetted against the brightness, and he could make out the slender shape of a woman. Beyond her were others, various shapes and sizes, friendly, nosy, he thought, swaying slightly.

"My truck's gone off the road," he said, then fell silent, shocked once more at the unfamiliar sound of his new voice. Deeper than his old one. Slower. "Can I use your phone?"

She moved toward him, reaching for him, hands touching his snow-covered sleeve, and he realized he hadn't been touched. Not since all those technicians had labored over him. And even then he hadn't felt it. He'd been a few steps back, watching them as they tried to save him.

"You must be frozen," she said in a voice that was light, musical, oddly charming. "Come in out of the storm and we'll warm you up. It won't do you any good to call anyone at this hour. Steve runs the only garage in town, and he's gone to his mother's for Thanksgiving. But there are a bunch of us here, we'll get you out."

He let her pull him into the kitchen, into the noise and warmth and hubbub, even as he wanted to pull back. It hurt in there. The bright light hurt his eyes, accustomed to the darkness. The friendly conversation hurt his ears, accustomed to silence. The heat hurt his skin, which had grown so cold, so very cold. It was life, he realized. For the first time in months, no, years, he was no longer dead, no longer in a cool, sullen cocoon, and the shock of it was intensely painful.

He turned to look at his hostess, the woman who'd pulled him into the kitchen, and got his second shock of the night. This time it wasn't a stranger's eyes he stared into. It was the warm blue-eyed gaze of a woman who'd once spent three thankless months as his incompetent secretary. It was Carrie Alexander, one of the people he'd come to save.

She looked the same, and yet different, somehow. She'd always been thin, a dancer, he thought he remembered. But now she was even leaner, almost skinny, and there were faint shadows behind her smiling eyes. And then she was no longer smiling, as a frown washed over her face, and he wondered for a moment whether she'd recognized him.

"You've been hurt," she said, reaching up, way up, to push his hair away from his face. He tried to jerk back, but she wouldn't let him, and her fingers on his chilled skin were warm and incredibly gentle. "You must have hit your head when you went off the road. Let me do something about that while Maggie gets you a cup of coffee to warm you up."

"Please..." he said, and wondered where that word came from. He'd never considered it an essential part of his vocabulary. "I just need to get my truck out of the ditch."

"Jeffie and I will help you."

A man stepped forward, a huge, lumbering bear of a man, except that for some reason his eyes weren't quite on a level with Emerson's. Once again he felt that dizzy, disoriented feeling, trapped in a strange body that was so unlike his own.

"I'm Lars Swensen, and this is my wife, Maggie." A plain, careworn-looking woman flashed him a friendly smile as she handed him a mug of coffee.

Emerson hated coffee. He drank Earl Grey tea exclusively. It must be the cold that made the coffee smell so good. He took a tentative sip, and his entire body vibrated with pleasure.

"That's it," Carrie said in a soothing voice. "Just come into the bathroom and sit down and I'll clean up that cut on your forehead. As soon as you have a nice hot meal inside you, you can deal with your truck."

For some reason he wasn't in the mood to argue. If it wasn't for the fact that he'd somehow managed to stumble onto one of the very people he was supposed to save, he'd be out of there before anyone realized what was happening. He didn't like accepting the kindness of strangers, and it was only when he convinced himself that he had something important to gain that he gave in and followed Carrie Alexander's slender, graceful figure out of the warm, crowded kitchen.

He had another startled glimpse of himself in the bathroom mirror before she gently pushed him down onto the edge of the old claw-footed bathtub. He had plenty of opportunity to watch her as she rummaged through the medicine cabinet, pulling out hydrogen peroxide, gauze bandages, swabs and pills. She'd gotten thinner, he was sure of it. He was a firm believer in the fact that no woman could ever be too thin or too rich. Carrie certainly had a problem with the latter. Anywhere he looked carefully, he could see signs of decay. The house was falling down around her ears, a fact she seemed cheerfully oblivious to.

And she was no thinner than Margot, the dancer from the Joffrey Ballet he'd been involved with for a few months. Carrie had been a dancer, too, hadn't she? He recalled something of that sort. She certainly moved with the same sort of innate grace Margot had had. And something more. The elegance of her movements in no way conveyed the sense of self-absorption Margot's gestures had. Carrie simply seemed to be someone at ease with her slender, fluid body.

She turned back to him, and once again there was that startled expression in her blue eyes. She began dabbing peroxide on his forehead, pushing his ridiculously long hair out of the way, and she bit her lip as she concentrated.

"What's wrong?" he found himself asking, wondering again whether she knew him.

She was eye level with him, and she managed a rueful smile. "It's just that you're so beautiful."

She'd managed to startle him. "I beg your pardon?"

"Like a Renaissance sculpture. A Botticelli angel, maybe." She shook her head, laughing at herself. "You must have heard that before."

"Not recently," he said, his voice dry.

Her fingers were cool now against his flushed skin. "Well, it can't be a novel experience. You must have spent…what is it, thirty years…with that face. Surely you must be used to people's reactions by now."

"Not exactly."

She glanced at him, startled, then obviously decided to drop it. She stood up, surveying her handiwork with satisfaction. "I think you'll live," she pronounced, and it was all he could do not to snort in derision.

"I'm Carrie Alexander, by the way. And you're…"

Inspiration failed him. He reached for the first name he could think of, then shuddered when it came about. "Gabriel," he said. He thought about that strange reflection in the mirror. "Gabriel Falconi," he said, wondering why it sounded right.

Obviously she thought so, too. "It suits you. Come and meet the rest of my Thanksgiving guests. If we wait much longer my turkey will dry out." She was out of the tiny bathroom, her long skirts swirling around her ankles, and he had no choice but to follow her, protesting.

"But my truck..."

"Your truck can wait. I'm not serving cold, dried-out turkey and congealed gravy to all these people. And you look like you're in need of a good hot meal yourself. Come along. Someone will have set an extra place for you by now."

"But..."

"Come along," she repeated firmly, sounding like a cross between Augusta and Mary Poppins. She was six inches shorter than his new self, and if his age was still relevant, about four years younger, and she was acting like his mother. He didn't like it.

He was, however, interested in having his first real meal in seventeen months. If he could smell things he could probably taste them, too. And the thought of turkey and gravy, and what was almost definitely apple pie for dessert, was too much for him to resist. He didn't even have to worry about cholesterol anymore.

He was amazed that there were only eleven people at dinner. Twelve, if you counted the small scrap of humanity that slept peacefully in an old wicker basket in the corner. He'd met Lars and his wife, briefly, at least, and he was introduced to their other three children, Kirsten, with thick blond braids and an adolescent shyness, Nils, a sturdy boy in his teens, and Harald, who was just a little younger.

There were the Milsoms, a middle-aged couple who seemed clearly devoted to each other, Jeffie Baker, a sullen-looking teenager, and Gertrude Hansen, a bent-over, white-haired old lady with thick, impenetrable glasses and a sweet, gentle manner. They all welcomed him like the prodigal son, and he found himself ensconced in the middle of the huge old table, surrounded by Hansens, Swensens and their ilk. And too far away from Carrie Alexander.

Without his asking, a plate arrived in front of him, piled high with turkey, rice, gravy and biscuits. His mug of coffee had appeared by his plate, refilled, and a glass of jug wine accompanied

it. He reached for his stainless steel fork, when a sudden silence
fell over the chattering party.

"Would you ask the blessing, Lars?" Carrie asked, and Lars
nodded.

Oh, God, he thought, writhing in embarrassment. He was going
to have to sit there and listen while they prayed, for heaven's sake.
He'd fallen into a bunch of religious fanatics.

Lars, however, was simple and to the point. "Bless this food
which you have given to us so abundantly. Bless our friends and
family, and welcome the stranger to our midst. Amen."

"Amen," the others muttered, heads bowed, and Gabriel cast a
worried glance around at them. But then, the uncomfortable moment passed. People began digging into their food, and conversation was once again at fever pitch, interspersed with the occasional
moment of silence as people paused to chew their food.

He kept his head down, concentrating on the meal with an almost
religious fervor, hoping no one would decide to cross-examine him.
Particularly when he wasn't certain what his story would be. He'd
come up with a name, thank God, though it was an absurd name.
He was just lucky he hadn't hit upon something worse, like Angelo.
Gabriel was bad enough. A fallen angel, all right. He only wondered how much further he was going to fall before all this was
through. Whether he'd be able to accomplish the overwhelming
task Augusta had set before him. Or whether he'd end up in the
other place.

He didn't want to go there. Bottom line, he wanted heaven, eternal happiness, wings and all that crap. At least he had a head start.
Carrie Alexander was only a few feet away. He wouldn't have to
hunt her down to solve whatever crisis his life had precipitated.

Though right now she didn't look very troubled. If only Augusta
had been more specific. The woman sitting at the head of the table
didn't look as if her life had been a series of disasters. She looked
calm, happy, at peace with the world. What in the world could she
want that he could possibly give her?

Three people, Augusta had said. Three people whose lives he'd
destroyed. Carrie didn't look destroyed, but looks could be deceiv-
ing. And where the hell was he going to find the other two? They
couldn't all be in this tiny little backwater...

He realized then that he didn't even know where he was. It might
be Upstate New York or Alaska or Siberia, for all he knew. Somewhere cold and snowy. The happy din had quieted somewhat, and

he drained his cup of coffee with automatic appreciation and caught Lars's eye.

"What's the name of this town?" he asked, hoping he sounded natural. He didn't dare ask what state he was in, besides the obvious state of confusion.

"Town?" Lars laughed. "I don't know if I'd call Angel Falls a town, exactly. More a dot on the map."

Gabriel's empty mug slipped out of his hand. "Angel Falls?" he echoed, getting used to the faint harshness in his new voice. This time, at least, it was justified.

"High-flown kind of name for such an unpretentious little town, isn't it?" murmured Milsom, the man next to him. "Named after the falls, of course, and they were named after the lake, and I think it was probably missionaries who named the lake some two, three hundred years ago. So we're stuck with the name, and it's gotten so most of us sort of like it."

"Especially during the Christmas season," Carrie said. She wasn't eating much, Gabriel noticed. She hadn't put much on her plate to begin with, and most of it was still there, just slightly rearranged.

"So what are you doing driving through this part of Minnesota during a snowstorm?" Lars asked. "Shouldn't you be with your family on Thanksgiving?"

"Minnesota?" he echoed, momentarily shocked.

"Where'd you think you were? Hawaii?" Jeffie Baker spoke up, breaking the sullen silence he'd maintained through most of the meal. Gabriel wished he'd continued to shut up.

"Guess I must have crossed the border without realizing it," Gabriel said.

"The border's about two hours in any direction," Lars pointed out, not unkindly. At least he let the question of family go. "What do you do for a living, Gabriel?"

"A living?" Instinctively he looked at his hands. Big hands, work worn. He hadn't the faintest idea what they were used to doing.

"Don't tell me," Lars said, and Gabriel breathed a sigh of relief. "I can tell just by looking at your hands. You're a carpenter, like me."

"Am I?" he muttered. "I mean, of course." He'd never touched a woodworking tool in his life, but at least he wouldn't be forced to prove it.

Lars held up his own hands. They were squarer, broader, but

they had the same look to them. "Takes one to know one. Were you looking for work around here? Because I have to tell you, there's not much. We're a poor community since the factory closed down, and it doesn't look like things are about to improve."

"I'm not planning to take any work away from you..." Gabriel said automatically, not even wondering why he'd say such an uncharacteristic thing. Emerson would take anything he could get in his quest for success.

"You'd be welcome to it if there were any," Lars said flatly. "We've just been scraping by. There's some logging work that might be opening up before long, but I don't know if they need more than one."

"I'm not looking for work."

As if on cue, everyone looked at him, at his threadbare flannel shirt, his obvious air of less than notable prosperity. "I've got work after Christmas," he explained. "Due on the job Christmas Day, as a matter of fact. I'm just passing through, looking for a way to kill some time until the job comes up."

They seemed to swallow that. After all, it was nothing more than the truth. "Well, you're welcome to spend your time in Angel Falls. Unless you've got family...?"

There was that question again. He didn't know about Gabriel Falconi, but Emerson MacVey didn't have a relative to call his own. "No family," he said.

"We have something in common then," Carrie said, her face smooth and unlined, her voice casual. And yet he felt her pain, as sharply as he'd ever felt his own. "Orphans of the storm. Stay and spend Christmas with us, Gabriel. We're a friendly town. We share what we have, no matter how little it is."

He wished he could tell her no. He wanted to get out of this warm, friendly community, away from the concern of strangers, the gentle prying. But Carrie Alexander was one-third of his ticket to heaven.

Gertrude Hansen was seated on his other side. She put a gnarled hand on his, and her eyes behind the thick bottle-lens glasses blinked sincerely. "Stay with us, Gabriel," she said, and he was suddenly, forcibly, reminded of Augusta.

Ridiculous, of course. This stooped-over, gentle creature had nothing to do with the harridan of heaven. He tried to move his hand, but her grip was surprisingly strong. "Stay," she said again, and her sweet, soft voice was joined by a chorus of others.

"Stay," Carrie said. "You've never experienced anything until you've experienced a real Scandinavian Christmas. We're all of Norse descent around here—Swedes and Danes and Norwegians. We know how to celebrate Christmas.''

''And you wouldn't believe the food,'' Mrs. Milsom leaned across the table to inform him.

He'd cleared the mound of food on his plate, he, who seldom ate anything more filling than nouvelle cuisine. ''You've convinced me,'' he said, glancing toward Carrie.

It hit him, harder than the windshield of his truck, harder than the blows of the paramedics as they'd labored over his chest, harder than anything he'd felt in his short self-absorbed life. She smiled at him, her blue eyes filled with warmth and pleasure, and he was lost. The emotional pull was immediate and shocking, so intense that he felt mesmerized. It no longer mattered what his task was, what Augusta's orders were, what his observer, whoever he was, would tell him to do. It no longer mattered about the two other people he was going to save.

He had no intention of leaving Carrie Alexander's side until he was forced to do so. Come hell or high water. And he doubted high water would have anything to do with it.

CHAPTER TWO

Carrie stood in front of the old iron sink, staring out into the wind-swept night as the four men trudged off into the darkness. Three men and a boy, she amended to herself, glancing at Jeffie's slight, childish frame. She was worried about him. His parents had taken off again, some joint business trip, and as far as she knew they hadn't even called to check in on him. They knew she'd have him over for Thanksgiving, and they figured their responsibility ended there.

Carrie wasn't quite sure when responsibility to your children ended, but Jeffie was only seventeen. And a very troubled seventeen-year-old at that. He needed parents, he needed people to care about him, to concern themselves with his well-being. Instead he had two workaholics who'd washed their hands of him when he'd failed to live up to their exacting standards. They still loved him, all right. They just didn't have much use for him. And Jeffie knew it.

"Let me take over," Maggie said, nudging Carrie out of the way with her comfortable bulk. "You've been on your feet all day and you look worn out. Kirsten and I can finish up these dishes."

Carrie didn't even consider making a token protest. She was exhausted, so tired she wasn't certain if she could cover it up. And she wanted to sit in a quiet place and think about the stranger who'd shown up on her doorstep.

The baby lay sleeping soundly in the old bassinet, not stirring as Carrie added more wood to the cast enamel stove. Sinking down in the shabby armchair that had once been her grandfather's favorite place in the world, she put her feet up, leaned her head back and closed her eyes.

Why did he seem so familiar? She'd never seen him before in her life, of that she was absolutely certain. If she had, she wouldn't have forgotten him. He looked like a Renaissance angel, with such classic, astonishing beauty that part of her wanted to just sit and stare at him. It had taken all her wavering concentration to keep up a normal front. She'd been working too hard, not taking proper care of herself. She knew it, and yet she couldn't change. Guilt was a powerful force in her life, one she didn't even try to combat.

Would he still be around tomorrow? He hadn't been very talkative. He said he was just passing through, and it was more than possible that once they got him out of his ditch, he'd move on, touching their lives only briefly.

But she didn't think so. She'd never been one for relying on her instincts—they'd failed her too many times. But she somehow knew that Gabriel Falconi had stumbled onto their Thanksgiving dinner for a reason. And he wasn't going to simply disappear without accomplishing whatever he'd come to do.

She shook her head, marveling at her own sudden fancifulness. She was overtired, overfed, though she'd barely eaten a thing, worn out by the stress and excitement of the day.

By the time tomorrow dawned and Gabriel Falconi drove away from Angel Falls, Minnesota, she'd see things more clearly.

A tiny snuffling sound alerted her, and she was out of the chair, lifting the sturdy bundle that was Anna Caroline Swensen into her arms. Her goddaughter, little Carrie, smiled up at her, sleepy, not yet ready to demand a feeding, and Carrie sank back down into the chair, cradling the four-month-old in her arms. "No turkey for you, little one," she murmured in a low voice. "Next Thanksgiving, maybe. If any one of us is still here."

"Is she all right?" Maggie, with the instinct of all mothers, stood in the door, her weary face momentarily lightening at the sight of her new daughter.

"She'll be demanding food before too long. I'll take your place in the kitchen..."

"I'll bring a bottle, if you wouldn't mind. She needs to get used to bottles, and to other people feeding her."

"Why?" Carrie asked flatly. "Are you having trouble nursing?"

Maggie shook her head. "I'm going to have to find work, you know that. I've waited too long already." She looked at her daughter, and her eyes filled with tears. "I'll bring the bottle."

"You aren't going to like this," Carrie whispered to the baby as her customary silent remorse swamped her. "I don't like it, either. Life isn't fair sometimes, little one. It's not fair at all."

Anna Caroline, however, wasn't so choosy. She accepted the formula with the placid good grace that she usually exhibited, and Carrie leaned back, thinking there were few experiences more peaceful than feeding a sleepy baby. So peaceful, in fact, that she didn't leap up when she heard the men return, stamping their feet on the front porch, their voices deep, jovial, that new voice, deeper, slower, joining in.

"He's not going anywhere tonight," Lars said when he poked his head in the door, his square face red and beaming, his graying blond hair wet with melted snow. "The tire's flat, the rim's bent, and I'm not too sure about the axle. Come daylight it might be better than it looks. Can you bed him down here tonight? We'd be more than happy to take him in, but we don't have space in the car…"

"Of course I will. It'll be company for Jeffie. He's not sure he likes having to stay here while his parents are out of town. Having another man around might make it more palatable."

Lars nodded. "I told him you'd insist, but he's a man who doesn't like to accept favors."

"He's not used to small towns," Carrie said, rising from the chair with silent grace, never disturbing the sleeping infant. "Let me set him straight."

Lars took his daughter in his burly arms, looking down at her with complete devotion. "You do that, Carrie," he murmured absently. "I've never known a man who didn't toe the line when you told him to."

"Flatterer," Carrie said dryly, walking into the kitchen.

Gabriel was standing by the sink, drying the dishes. He glanced at her when she walked in, then immediately began polishing the old Meissen that had been passed down from her greatgrandmother. Once again she was struck by the palpable intensity his presence brought into the room. And the odd, impossible feeling that she knew him from somewhere.

"You're stuck with Jeffie and me for the night," she announced cheerfully. "Don't bother arguing. You can't sleep in your truck, you'll freeze to death."

"A motel…" he suggested, not looking at her.

She wanted to see his eyes again. "Not for forty miles. No hotel, no boardinghouse, and the bed-and-breakfast places up by the lake are closed for the winter. You're stuck here, Gabriel."

"I don't like to be beholden to anyone." It was odd, the way the words seemed to surprise him when they came from his mouth.

"Don't worry, you won't be. I have a nice big wood box that needs filling, more firewood outside that could use some stacking. I've got things that need doing if you've got the desire to do them."

"I've got the desire," he said, and she got her wish. He looked at her, his eyes dark, almost black, in his face, and she felt herself slipping, falling, lost in a place that was foreign and yet familiar.

She stepped back, reaching behind her for the doorway, and she smiled briskly, remembering Lars's words. She could make any man toe the line, could she? She might run into a little trouble with this one if she didn't make certain things clear right away. Like the fact that she was no-nonsense, maternal, and a friend to all. Not a potential bedmate.

"Terrific," she said briskly. "We'll put you on the sofa, and first thing in the morning we'll get Steve and his tow truck out here. Assuming Steve's back from his mother's. We'll get you up and running again, and then you can decide whether you want to stay around here until your next job comes up."

He was still watching her, and she wished she'd never noticed his eyes in the first place. Now she couldn't look away. She couldn't rid herself of the notion that she'd looked into those eyes before. Except that they'd been a different color, held a different expression.

"Absurd," she muttered beneath her breath. Was she going to have to add delusions to her list of future symptoms?

He set the dish down on the pile, folding the faded linen dish towel in his big, strong hands. "I thought I'd stay," he said. "That is, if I can find a place closer than forty miles away."

Carrie glanced at Lars and Maggie, remembering their huge old house, made for a family of twelve, and their dwindling cash supply. "I have an idea or two," she murmured. "In the meantime, who wants to play charades?"

Gabriel blinked, just a momentary reaction, and she noticed his eyelashes were absurdly long. Typical, she thought, searching for her sense of humor. Just as she had decided to ignore her own selfish wants and embark on a mission to right the wrongs she'd inadvertently done, someone had sent her the most potent package of temptation she'd seen in her entire life.

Lars went over and slung an arm around Gabriel's shoulders. "Come along, Gabe," he boomed. "We'll show them a thing or two."

"Yeah," Jeffie piped up, for the first time not sullen. "Men against the women. We'll beat the stuffing out of them." And he looked up at Gabriel with shy, burgeoning adoration.

Lord, I hope I don't look the same, Carrie thought. "Wanna bet? Loser does the dishes tomorrow morning."

"Aw, Carrie..."

"Aw, Carrie, nothing," she said. "Don't you have any faith in your ability to stomp on us poor defenseless women?"

Jeffie cast another glance at Gabriel's unpromising expression. "We've got an unknown quantity on our side," he pointed out.

"Maybe I shouldn't play," Gabriel said in his slow, deep voice.

"Nonsense. What better way can we get to know someone? Especially since he's going to be around till Christmas. It's a trial by fire," Lars boomed.

"Trial by fire," Gabriel echoed. "That sounds about right." But the fire was in the depth of his dark, dangerous eyes. And despite the warmth of the old kitchen, Carrie shivered.

HE WAS ABOUT A FOOT too long for the sofa. Tucking his arms under his head, Gabriel stared up at the ceiling, watching the faint shimmers of light that filtered from the minuscule cracks in the wood stove. Emerson would have fit on the sofa, he thought. But not Gabriel. His feet hung over the end, his size-thirteen feet, he'd discovered when he'd taken off his snow-wet sneakers. His backbone was curved against the lumpy cushions, and his head was throbbing. He was probably going to be a mass of stiffened muscles when he woke up the next morning. But at least he'd be warm enough. The wood stove was kicking out the heat, and the quilt that covered him was thick, beautiful and smothering. If he could just manage to clear his mind of all the distractions he would manage to sleep.

Problem was, he didn't want to. Never had life seemed so precious to him, now, in the quiet of the fire-lit living room of the old farmhouse. He could hear the wind howling outside, the dry crackle of the firewood, the solid chunk as a piece broke apart in the flames. He could hear Jeffie snoring faintly, in a bedroom miles away at the rear of the house. He could hear Carrie breathing in the room above him, hear the faint, steady beat of her heart. He could even hear the flakes of snow as they dropped to the ground.

He felt odd, disoriented, thrust into a life that was as foreign to him as if he'd landed on Mars. Even the things that should have been familiar seemed somehow different. The taste of turkey, for instance. A hundred times better than he'd ever remembered. And coffee. Strong, biting, absolutely delicious.

Lars's hearty friendship, Bill Milsom's shyer warmth, were things that were foreign, as well. As was Jeffie Baker, for some obscure reason staring up at him as if he were God walking the earth instead of an itinerant carpenter who'd managed to land himself in a ditch on a snowy night.

This would be a dangerous place to live, he thought. You might start believing in people, in things. And then where would you be?

He closed his eyes, shifting uncomfortably on the couch, and he knew it wasn't the lumpy cushion that was making him restless. It was that damned game of charades.

He hadn't played charades since he was ten years old and at summer camp. Even then he'd thought it was an impossibly stupid game, juvenile and idiotic. He never would have thought adults would play it, and enjoy it. He never thought he'd be shouting out answers, completely involved. Until it had been Carrie Alexander's turn.

He'd vaguely known she was a dancer, but it hadn't meant anything to him. Until she'd risen and walked to the center of the room, elegant, simple grace radiating from her reed-slim body. He didn't even know what she'd been trying to act out. He hadn't heard the shouts from the women as they tried to guess, hadn't been aware of anything but the twist and flow of her, slow and sensuous and supple.

Hunger hadn't been his only physical appetite to return, he realized with a shock. Staring at Carrie Alexander, he knew a longing that was both intensely sexual and far beyond that. He wanted her with a need he'd never felt before. A need that shook him to the very marrow of his bones. A need he had no intention of giving in to. If he did, it would be an express ticket to hell.

But lying alone in that living room, he could give in to the fantasy. He could look through the darkness and imagine she was there again, moving, twisting, dancing, just for him. And then he shut his eyes tight, closing off the half-remembered vision, and let out a quiet, agonized groan. If he didn't make it through this sojourn, hell might end up being a picnic.

Another noise suddenly overwhelmed the intense peacefulness of the old house. A faint scrabbling sound that at first he identified as the never-before-heard sound of mice in the woodwork. And then he heard another sound, or lack thereof. Jeffie had stopped snoring.

He kept his breathing steady, not moving, as he listened to the sound of a door creak open. Someone was moving in the kitchen, someone so still and silent that Gabriel felt his heart stop. For a crazed, longing moment he thought it might be Carrie, coming to him. A moment later he dismissed the thought as patently absurd.

Then he saw Jeffie's shadow on the wall in the kitchen as he reached across the table. For the half-empty bottle of wine.

None of his business, Gabriel told himself. The boy was close enough to drinking age, and it wasn't his problem. He wasn't here to save Jeffie Baker.

"You think you ought to be doing that?" He could hardly believe the quiet voice was coming from the stranger's body he was currently inhabiting. "After all, she's a good lady, welcoming you into her home, feeding you, making you welcome. Is that any way to repay her?" He pitched his voice so low it would carry no farther than the kitchen. He kept the reproach out of it—simply giving Jeffie the choice.

The shadow was absolutely motionless. And then the bottle was replaced, untouched, on the table, and the phantom figure moved away. A moment later he heard the sound of the door closing once more.

"Damn," he muttered beneath his breath. He should have kept his mouth shut. Who was he to give advice, opinions, admonishments? Who was he to involve himself in other people's problems, when his own were beyond overwhelming, beyond life threatening? They were eternal.

He had no idea whether he'd made Jeffie's situation better or worse. He told himself he didn't care, but the odd thing was, he did. For no reason at all, it mattered to him. He didn't want to see an already troubled boy get mired even deeper into the kind of mess life could be.

It wasn't until he heard the faint, measured sound of Jeffie's snoring that he let some of the tension drain out of his body. He hadn't even realized he'd been wired, until he let go of it. At least he hadn't traumatized the boy. Maybe he just needed someone to point out a few things to him. It wasn't his job, it was his parents'. Clearly they hadn't been meeting their responsibilities.

And then his body froze again as he heard the almost imperceptible sounds of someone moving through the old house. Not Jeffie this time—he was still snoring lightly. That left only one person, moving down the narrow, steep stairs, coming toward him, dressed in a filmy negligee, reaching out for him...

She wasn't wearing a filmy negligee, she was wearing an enveloping flannel nightgown that reached almost down to her narrow toes. Her straight blond hair was tousled with sleep, her face open and vulnerable as she moved into the living room, silent as a wraith. And he knew she hadn't come for a romp on the narrow sofa with a horny stranger.

She sat down on the rocking chair opposite him. She was wearing a shawl over the white nightgown, and as she pulled it closer around her chilled body he considered asking her if she wanted to share the quilt. He didn't. He just sat up on the sofa, waiting.

"Thank you," she said, her musical voice pitched so low he could just hear it.

"For what?"

"For Jeffie. It was so stupid of me, to leave the wine out. I was too tired to think straight."

"You knew there was a problem?"

"I know Jeffie has a lot of problems. I can't lock everything away and keep him from himself. But I don't have to waft temptation under his nose."

He looked at her, and knew a lot about temptation wafting under his nose. "He's not my responsibility."

"Of course not. Any more than he's mine. But that doesn't keep me from doing whatever good I can along the way."

"What will it get you in the end?" he countered, playing the devil's advocate. He'd spent his entire life looking out for himself, and himself alone.

She shrugged her narrow shoulders beneath the thick shawl, a self-deprecating smile on her face. "A place in heaven?" she suggested.

He shut his eyes for a moment, wishing he even had the faith to say, why me, Lord? But he didn't. He'd had too much of coincidences, of not-so-subtle reminders, of Angel Falls, Minnesota, and the vulnerable-looking woman opposite him whom he couldn't remember wanting when he could have had her. Now that she was out of reach he seemed to have developed an instantaneous obsession.

"I'm not going to worry about that," he said finally. "I expect I'm a lost cause."

"No one's a lost cause. You helped Jeffie tonight, even if your brain told you not to bother. I think you've got good instincts."

"I don't believe in instincts. I believe in facts." That was Emerson talking, Gabriel realized. His old pragmatic self.

"If you say so," Carrie said, rising from the rocking chair and opening the wood stove. She reached into the wood box for a thick log, and he was up off the sofa before he realized what he was doing, taking the wood out of her hand.

For a moment she didn't move, didn't release her grip on the heavy log. She was shorter than he remembered, coming up to his chin. But no, he was taller than he remembered, that was it. He wasn't wearing a shirt, and his jeans were zipped but unsnapped, and if she made the mistake of looking downward she'd find he was far from immune to her presence, to the enveloping flannel nightgown, to the faint, flowery scent of her.

She didn't look down. She looked up into his eyes, but the startled awareness was there all the same. Identical to the sudden, sure knowledge that rippled through his body, and he wanted to toss the log across the room and take her slender body into his arms.

He didn't, of course. Enough of the old Emerson remained to keep him reasonably well behaved. She released the piece of wood and stepped back, letting him load the stove with more force than dexterity. When he'd closed the door he found she was out of reach, standing by the kitchen.

"Thanks again," she said, her voice smooth and warm, devoid of any kind of sexual awareness.

Maybe he'd imagined that heated moment. But he didn't think so. She was aware of him, as he was of her. But she'd pulled her defenses around her as tightly as that shawl, presenting a friendly, sisterly front.

He wanted to cross the room in two quick strides, pull the shawl away from her and explain to her in definite physical terms that he had no need of a sister. He didn't move.

"Anytime," he murmured.

She disappeared then as silently as a ghost, and he heard her light footsteps as they moved quickly up the stairs again. The wood stove was radiating heat, but he barely noticed it. He was so damned hot already.

First thing tomorrow morning he needed to get his truck out of the ditch, get the tire repaired and get the hell away from temptation. There was no way he could save her if he slept with her. She didn't need a lover who was going to disappear on Christmas Eve. She needed commitment, a man to cherish her, till death do them part. He'd already passed that point.

He was half tempted to get away from Angel Falls altogether. He had no more faith than the imperial Augusta had in his ability to accomplish his mission. Maybe he ought to give up before he started, enjoy his month and take his punishment like a man.

He didn't even know what Carrie needed from him. Where her life needed fixing, what damage he'd caused her. She looked happy enough. She had friends, a charming if slightly tumbledown house. What was missing? What was broken?

But eternity was too high a stake to wager. And he couldn't remember anything in life that would be worth giving up a chance at heaven. He was going to tough it out, he was going to win, damn it. He wasn't a man who admitted defeat. He had a month, he had three miracles, and he'd already found one of the people he had to save. If he could just keep his raging hormones under control he'd do fine.

He sank back down onto the uncomfortable sofa, thinking about the woman sleeping overhead. Except she wasn't sleeping. She was lying upstairs, her eyes open, staring at the ceiling, just as he was. And sleep was going to be impossible tonight.

For both of them.

CHAPTER THREE

Carrie lay alone in the big bed, the bed she'd never shared, and waited for sleep to come. The snow had finally stopped—moonlight was streaming through the frosted-up window, sending shadow patterns across the old, faded rug.

Odd, Carrie thought, shifting around, looking for a comfortable spot on the wide mattress. She'd never thought about the bed being lonely before. But she was thinking about it tonight. And thinking about the man downstairs. Hovering over her, so damned big and yet not the slightest bit threatening.

At least, not in the usual sense. Gabriel Falconi was a threat. To her peace of mind. To her carefully acquired plan of celibacy and self-sacrifice. To the safe little cocoon she'd spun around her.

It would be easier if he wasn't so extraordinarily beautiful. It would be easier if he wasn't so troubled, so obviously torn by conflict. She wanted to soothe him, comfort him, help him. She already owed so much to so many people. She could just add him to her list. She could do her best to help Jeffie, the Swensens, Gertrude and the Milsoms, she could save Gabriel, and she could deny herself and her own selfish wants.

An odd thought. Why should Gabriel need saving? He was clearly better off than Lars Swensen—at least he had a job to go to in another month. He didn't have six hungry mouths to feed, a mortgage to meet, a crushing sense of failure that was in no way his due.

But Gabriel had something eating at him. Darkness lurked behind his eyes, a darkness of the soul. And Carrie had the uneasy suspicion that his demons might prove too much even for her.

Her room was cold. She usually left the doors open to let the heat circulate, but tonight she wanted to be closed in, with barriers of wood between her and the man stretched out on her grandmother's old couch. She couldn't save everyone, fix everything. It was her foolish need to do so that had gotten Angel Falls into the disaster it was in. And Carrie had every intention of paying her debts. Not amassing new ones.

WHEN SHE AWOKE sunlight was streaming in the old multipaned windows, spreading across the quilt that covered her, reaching to her fingertips. She lay without moving, absorbing the heat, slowly coming to wakefulness. She had a reason to wake up today, something exciting had happened, but in the first mists of sleep she couldn't remember what.

She glanced over at the old windup alarm clock. It must have stopped last night, and she'd never noticed. It said ten-thirty, and she never slept past six in the morning nowadays.

But she could hear the steady ticking, a loud, comforting noise. She could hear another, rhythmic thud, coming from outside. And she remembered why she was happy. Too late to keep from feeling that pleasure. Gabriel was here.

Snow was melting from the trees outside her bedroom window as she quickly threw on some clothes. The storm last night was leaving as quickly as it had come, the thick wet snow disappearing. She frowned for a moment, leaning her head against the pane of glass. She'd been ready for snow. Once Thanksgiving came, it was part of the whole Christmas season, a welcome enough part as long as it didn't choose to storm on a day she planned to go shopping.

She wouldn't be doing much shopping this year, nor would most of Angel Falls, with the factory shut down. It was going to be a homemade Christmas, and probably better for it.

She could smell coffee, and she hoped it was Gabriel, not Jeffie, who'd made it. Jeffie had brewed it a couple of days before, and it had taken all her limited acting ability to choke down two cups of the stuff, which was closer to toxic waste than French roast.

There was no sign of either visitor when she reached the kitchen. She poured herself a cup of coffee, noticing with relief that the color was a normal dark brown, not black sludge. There were clean dishes in the drainer, and the heat in the room came from a freshly stoked wood stove, as well as the bright sunlight. She moved toward the row of windows, mug of coffee in her hand, and looked out.

They'd been busy, the two of them. There was a pile of freshly split wood in the melting snow. Jeffie was nowhere in sight. But Gabriel was there, in the warm winter sun. Stripped to the waist, he was splitting the oversize firewood.

She couldn't move. She was mesmerized by the ripple and play of the muscles in his strong back. By the faint sheen of sweat on his golden skin. He'd tied his hair back with a discarded strip of quilting material, out of the way, and his long, muscled arms moved in a steady, hypnotic rhythm.

She'd deliberately kept herself from thinking about his body when she'd gone back up to bed last night. His face was troublesome enough, his almost angelic beauty that still managed to be completely masculine. When he'd come so close to her the night before, she'd been mesmerized. By the smooth golden texture of his skin. The corded sinew of muscle and bone beneath that skin. The faint tracery of dark hair, not too much, not too little. The long, long legs, the narrow hips. Everything about him entranced her, brought back feelings she thought she'd managed to squash down permanently. They were back in full force as she stood in the window of her old kitchen and watched a stranger work on her woodpile.

He must have felt her eyes on him. He turned suddenly, looking back at the house, and through the old window his eyes met hers. And she realized with sudden faintness that his beautiful face, his strong, sexy body, were nothing, nothing at all, compared to the siren lure of his dark, troubled eyes.

And then the spell was broken as Steve's tow truck lumbered up her winding driveway, dragging a rusty old pickup truck. Jeffie was riding in the front seat, next to Steve, and he looked like a normal, excited seventeen-year-old. If only he always looked like that.

"She's all messed up," Jeffie called out jovially as he bounced out of the truck.

Gabriel turned to look at his vehicle, and his expression was pardonably dismayed. Dropping the maul, he reached for his abandoned flannel shirt and started toward the tow truck. The conversation was too low-pitched for Carrie to hear, and she stilled her curiosity. She could see well enough that his truck wasn't going to take him away from Angel Falls for the next few days at least. That was enough for now.

Draining her now-lukewarm coffee, she headed for the telephone. It didn't take her long to accomplish her objectives, so that by the time Jeffie and Gabriel walked into the kitchen, accompanied, of course, by Steve, she had everything neatly arranged.

"His truck's real messed up, Carrie," Steve, a balding, cheerful bachelor in his late forties, announced as he took her automatically proffered cup of coffee. "I'm gonna have to order a new wheel, and that axle'll be a bitch to straighten. I told Gabe here that he's gonna have to get used to spending a few days at the back of beyond.''

Carrie glanced over at Gabriel, who shrugged. "That's easy enough to say in a place that doesn't have a motel."

"I've taken care of that," Carrie announced cheerfully.

"Have you, now?" There was no reprimand in his low, even tone, but nevertheless Carrie felt some of her buoyancy vanish. She was used to taking care of people—in a small town like Angel Falls everyone looked out for one another, and she made it her business to make sure everyone was taken care of. She'd forgotten what it was like out in the real world. Where everyone had his or her own space and didn't like other people invading it. Where no one wanted to accept favors or let other people do for them. Out in the real world people wanted to control their own destinies, and most of them spent fruitless years trying to do just that.

"I've done it again, haven't I?" she asked, her voice rueful. "I was just trying to be helpful, and I got carried away. I'm sorry. I haven't committed you to anything. I just checked with Lars and Maggie to make sure they had room for you, if you wanted to board with them. You need a place, they could do with a little extra cash."

He didn't say a word, letting her babble. Once again she got the strange sense of dichotomy, almost a schizophrenia. On the one hand, he clearly wanted to tell her to stuff her concern. On the other hand, he seemed to be leaning toward accepting her help.

"Anyway," she continued, "it's a place you can stay if you need to. And if you don't have any money I know they'd be more than happy to put you up anyway. I just thought it would be a way to solve both your problems."

"Is that what you do, Carrie? Solve people's problems?" There was no edge to the question he asked. It was simply put, curious. And yet she felt oddly guilty.

"Course, it is," Steve said jovially, oblivious to the undercurrents in the room. "We count on Carrie around here. Course, she can't work miracles. She can't stop the factory from closing, she can't raise the dead. But she comes darn close."

There was an odd expression in Gabriel's dark eyes. "Darn close," he echoed softly. "As a matter of fact, I've got some money. Not a lot, but I have to live somewhere until my next job, and Angel Falls seems as good a place as any. If the Swensens will take me I'll be glad to stay there."

She felt slightly encouraged. "I might be able to come up with a little work for you. There's not much in town right now, what with the factory shutting down, but this house could do with a little shoring up before winter really hits.''

To her relief he didn't get that cold, distant expression again. ''Before winter hits? What was last night?''

Steve laughed. ''Last night was just a lick and a promise. When the snows really come you'll know it. Matter of fact, if you're staying, either here or anywhere north of Kansas, you're gonna be needing some snow tires on that truck of yours.''

''I don't know if my finances will go that far.''

''Maybe we can work something out. You could give me a hand at the garage to pay off your bill. Even in a depression people still need to keep their cars running.''

''I don't know anything about cars.''

Steve looked startled. ''That's funny. You seemed to have a pretty good sense of what you were doing when I opened the hood out there.''

''If Gabriel says he doesn't know anything about cars then he doesn't,'' Jeffie piped up, instantly defensive. ''Do you think he's lying to you?''

''Calm down, kid,'' Steve said. ''I wasn't meaning no offense. I just thought it was odd, is all.''

''Well, you can...''

''Never mind,'' Gabriel overrode Jeffie's protest. ''I've got good instincts, but not much knowledge. Let's see how the current bill goes and we'll take it from there.''

''Sure thing,'' Steve said. ''I'll just tow her into town now. Want a ride? I'll be going right past the Swensens.''

''Carrie can drive him,'' Jeffie announced.

''Who says she wants to?'' Steve was getting a little testy at this point, and Carrie decided it was time to intervene. She was beginning to feel a little like a juicy bone, being fought over by two hungry dogs. She knew perfectly well that Steve harbored certain fruitless romantic feelings toward her. What was new was Jeffie's possessiveness. She didn't have any illusions that he might have suddenly developed an adolescent crush on her. He wanted her for Gabriel.

As for the stranger, he hadn't said a word. If he knew what was going on, he gave no sign of it. His eyes met hers, and she felt that icy-warm shiver reach down to her toes. ''If you're willing to wait, I'll drive you in a couple of hours,'' she said. ''Jeffie needs to get some fresh clothes, and I wanted to get a start on my Christmas shopping.''

She startled him into breaking the mesmerizing eye contact. ''Christmas shopping?'' he echoed, obviously aghast. ''Today?''

''It's tradition,'' Steve explained. ''People always go Christmas shopping the day after Thanksgiving.''

''That's why it's the most crowded day of the year,'' Gabriel protested.

''That's what's so much fun about it,'' Carrie said. ''I usually don't even buy anything. I just like the crowds and excitement.''

''You're crazy,'' he said flatly.

''A little.''

Jeffie was looking worried. For some reason he seemed to have decided that Gabriel was the best thing since sliced bread, despite or perhaps because of their little run-in last night. While his new-found hero worship was extreme, Jeffie was still fairly protective of her. He clearly didn't like the idea of sparks between the two of them. But he wasn't sure which side to be on.

''As long as you don't drag me shopping,'' Gabriel said.

''I don't think anybody could drag you anywhere you didn't want to go.''

''I hope you're right,'' he said obscurely. ''Jeffie and I will fill the wood boxes. After that, you can show me what you want done around here.''

That easily he'd turned things around, taking control. Suddenly she was on the receiving end, and she wasn't sure she liked it. She accepted it, however, with good grace. She nodded, turning to Steve, who'd been watching all this with a preoccupied expression on his face. ''Would you like any more coffee?''

He roused himself with an effort. ''Nah, I've got to get going. I want to finish in time to do a little shopping myself. I have to get something for my best girl.'' He gave her a meaningful leer, one she responded to with a faint smile, and then Steve followed Jeffie out into the cool morning air.

Gabriel was still standing there, an odd expression on his face. ''Best girl?'' he echoed.

She wanted to tell him it wasn't any of his business, as it certainly wasn't. She wanted to go into lengthy explanations, all of which would have told too much and not enough. She countered with a question of her own. ''What's it to you?''

''Nothing. Nothing at all.'' He started toward the door, his back rigid, and she made the major mistake of not dropping it there.

"He's a friend," she said. "I have lots of friends."

He stopped at the door, not turning around. "He wants more," he said.

"I know. I don't give more. To anyone." She said it, out loud, clear and simple.

He turned to look at her then, a disturbed expression in his dark eyes, and she wondered if he was simply surprised by her statement. Or disbelieving. He'd felt the pull between the two of them as strongly as she had. She knew it.

But he didn't argue. He simply nodded, accepting. Agreeing. And then followed Jeffie out into the bright winter sunlight.

HE'D NEVER SPLIT firewood before in his life. He'd been grateful that Carrie had slept late, no witness to his miserable early attempts at turning a solid chunk of log into firewood.

Jeffie had tried to show him, but he was at that gangly, post-adolescent age, all arms and legs and gawky gracelessness. Besides, he'd been so eager to please that his clumsiness had increased, so that even Gabriel's feeble attempts had shown better results.

He hadn't said anything about the late-night visit to the kitchen. Indeed, Jeffie had studiously avoided mentioning it, being careful to fill any possible conversational openings with lively, slightly nervous chatter that precluded anything more meaningful. Gabriel was glad to leave it at that. He still didn't quite understand why he'd interfered the night before, and he wasn't eager to get even more involved. For some reason Jeffie, instead of resenting his interference, seemed almost pathetically grateful.

Gabriel took the wood-splitting instruction with good grace, discovering, if he just forgot to think about it, his body took over, falling into the rhythm with a naturalness that made his previous claims of knowing nothing about wood seem a blatant lie.

The same had happened with the pickup. When Steve had finally managed to drag the poor old wreck up the road, Gabriel had opened the hood with unerring instinct, poked around at parts he couldn't name, his hands knowing what his brain didn't.

He'd have to watch himself. At this rate, Jeffie would start thinking he was an alien. *Invasion of the Body Snatchers* wasn't far-off.

He couldn't help but wonder if there really was a Gabriel Falconi somewhere. A tall, muscular Italian carpenter with the face of a Botticelli angel. If so, what happened to him? Had he died, too? Or was he simply a figment of Augusta's sourly twisted imagination?

It didn't really matter. What mattered was getting through the next month in one piece. He was supposed to save three people. One of whom he'd already discovered. She was obviously his first priority—he'd have to assume someone would lead him in the direction of the other two once he'd taken care of Carrie.

He didn't want to be led away from her. He didn't want to save her. When he let his imagination drift, he found he really wanted to debauch her in some pleasant, mutually agreeable manner. She'd warned him off with words, with body language. But her eyes said something completely different.

What the hell was wrong with her? How was he going to save her, when he'd made such a mess of his own life? And how was he going to be around her for however long it took without touching her? Kissing her? Pushing her down onto that lumpy sofa that had been more torture rack than bed and making love to her on that beautiful quilt?

"You got any kids, Gabriel?" Jeffie asked as he arranged the firewood in an artistic configuration.

"No. But I'm only thirty-two years old."

"I've got a brother who's thirty-two."

Gabriel stopped what he was doing, looking over at the boy with the deliberately casual stance and the wary expression in his eyes.

"Do you? Does he live around here?"

Jeffie shrugged. "No one really knows where he is. He dropped out of college, joined some commune years ago. Every now and then he sends my parents some book about enlightenment."

"What does he send you?"

Jeffie's smile was twisted. "I think he's forgotten about me. I was only five when he left. I think he's up in Alaska now. Becoming one with the seals, or something like that."

"Sounds pretty flaky."

"That's what my parents say. They're pretty disappointed in him. Guess that's what parenting's all about. Disappointment."

Gabriel had a tendency to agree, but different words came out. "I don't know about that. I think being a parent's probably the most important thing anyone can do."

"Not if you ask my parents." Jeffie dropped another log onto the pile, and the neat stack collapsed in a welter of firewood. He swore at them, something quite astonishingly obscene, and Gabriel, who used such words frequently, had to bite back an uncharacteristic reproof. Jeffie would have to learn by himself not to use those words indiscriminately. Gabriel wasn't going to lecture him.

Besides, Jeffie wasn't his particular problem. Carrie was. "What do you think about her?" he asked casually.

Jeffie looked confused for a moment. "You mean Carrie? She's pretty neat, considering. I mean, she's like all grown-ups. Wants to take care of you, when you're old enough to take care of yourself."

"I noticed," Gabriel said dryly, thinking of her heavy-handed attempts to get him safely settled in Angel Falls.

"But she's still pretty cool. She'll do anything for anybody, no matter what it costs her, she's always willing to help out, and besides, she's the best cook I know. She never lectures, and she'll give me a ride anytime I call her, no questions asked. Like I said, she's neat."

It was a lot of information crammed into one artless speech. Gabriel picked it apart carefully, going for the most important aspect. "What do you mean, she'll do anything for anybody, no matter what it costs her?"

A variety of expressions crossed Jeffie's face. Remorse, furtiveness, guilt. "I'm not supposed to talk about it."

"Too late, you already did," Gabriel snapped, not caring if he sounded cold. He was going to get it out of Jeffie if he had to beat it out of him.

"Listen, I promised..."

Gabriel set the maul down and advanced on Jeffie. "You're about to break your promise. What did you mean?"

He heard the door open behind him as Carrie left the house. She was still out of earshot, but he only had a moment.

"Tell me," he said, "or I'll ask her."

"Don't do that, man," Jeffie said wildly.

"Tell me."

Jeffie glanced behind him at Carrie's approaching figure. "She doesn't take care of herself," he finally admitted. "She got pneumonia and almost died last year, she's accident-prone, and no one can get her to slow down. Maggie says she just doesn't care about herself anymore. She's punishing herself, and no one knows why. Maggie says something happened to her in New York, something that changed her, and sooner or later she's going to walk in front of a truck or something again, and there's not a damned thing anyone can do about it." He stopped, breathless, defiant, glaring at his newfound hero. "She's going to die, damn it. Unless some-one can find a way to save her. And I don't believe in miracles."

Gabriel looked across the snow-covered ground as she ap-proached. "Neither do I," he said in a low voice. "But we both might be surprised."

CHAPTER FOUR

Carrie Alexander drove an aging Japanese station wagon that had seen better days, but not, in Emerson Wyatt MacVey III's opinion, much better. Its muffler was making a loud, throaty rumble, the bumper was held on by a wire, the once-maroon paint was liberally splattered with rust, and the windshield was cracked. He climbed into the front seat, trying to stretch his too-long legs out in front of him, and stared at the pitted vinyl dashboard, the mileage counter that read well above one hundred thousand miles. It did, however, start on the first try.

"Good baby," Carrie crooned, reaching out a slender hand and stroking the aging dashboard as a mother strokes a child.

"You talk to your cars?" he asked, mesmerized by her hand, the long, delicate fingers, the unconscious sensuality of her caress. And the waste of it, on an inanimate old car that belonged in a junkyard.

She glanced over at him, and there was a glint of humor in her bright blue eyes. "Everything on this earth needs a little encouragement now and then. I've learned not to take anything for granted, including having a car start when it's supposed to."

"I don't wonder, with this car," he said wryly.

"It's not in that much worse shape than your truck."

"My truck's been in an accident."

"You know what I mean. Besides, it's a waste of time bemoaning the fact that you don't have a Mercedes when you'll never afford one. It's better to be happy with what you have."

He had owned a Mercedes, a car he'd taken for granted. He'd certainly never stroked the dashboard and crooned lovingly to the motor. "This is a very nice car," he said.

"It's going to get you into town, which is a lot better than walking," she replied cheerfully, putting the car into reverse and backing out the long, curving driveway without looking.

He didn't look, either, too busy watching her face and thinking about Jeffie's disclosures. It had to have been typical teenage dramatics, but Carrie had come up on them too quickly for Gabriel to cross-examine him. He'd have to wait till he had a few moments alone with Jeffie to beat it out of him, if need be.

What had happened to her in New York that had changed her? It wasn't MacVey—he refused to accept responsibility. But then, if he wasn't responsible, why was he here now? He had miracles, Augusta had told him. Perhaps he could simply mutter a few hookie-pookie words and Carrie would start taking better care of herself. First task accomplished, and then he could be on his way.

He didn't think it was going to be that simple. Even if he'd been given some miraculous healing touch, where all he had to do was reach out to the woman by his side and solve her problems, it wouldn't solve his. He wasn't ready to move on. Away from here. He wasn't ready to go anywhere. Even to heaven and some kind of eternal bliss.

"Do you want me to drop you off at your house, Jeffie, or do you want to come with us to Swensens'?" she asked, navigating the slush-covered roads with a singular lack of attention. The four-wheel drive vehicle held the road surprisingly well despite its decrepit appearance, and Gabriel forced himself to relax in the front seat. He'd never enjoyed being driven—he was a man who liked to be in control of his own destiny at all times. He'd had to accept the fact that never again would he control anything in his life.

"I'll come with you," Jeffie said promptly from the back seat. "Maybe Lars will let me work in the shop for a while."

"Are you making something for your parents?" Gabriel asked.

Jeffie snorted. "Not likely. I just like messing around with wood."

"So do I," Gabriel said without thinking, then stopped, surprised. He glanced down at his hands again, those large work-worn hands, and wondered what talents lay beneath the skin and bone and sinew.

"I have to stop by the drugstore on the way," Carrie said as they pulled into a small town. "Henry's closing early to go Christmas shopping. Do either of you need anything?"

"Are you sick?" Gabriel asked abruptly, remembering the pneumonia that had nearly killed her.

"Oh, man," Jeffie muttered in the back seat.

Carrie's cheerful expression didn't waver. "Nothing that a little aspirin won't cure," she said, parking outside a small storefront with the gilt-lettered Olsen's Pharmacy peeling off the windows. There was a Christmas tree in the window, a fake silver one, and the lights were flashing off and on with dizzying regularity.

"I'm coming with you," Jeffie said, reaching for the door.

Gabriel put his hand out and stopped him. "No, you're not," he said pleasantly. "Keep me company and tell me about this town."

Telling about a town the size of Angel Falls would take exactly thirty seconds, but Jeffie settled back, a mutinous expression on his face as he muttered again, "Oh, man."

Gabriel waited until Carrie disappeared inside the store. "So?"

"So what?" Jeffie responded.

"She's not going to be in there that long, and if you don't tell me now I'll ask you when she gets back out here. What did you mean, she's changed? That she's going to walk in front of another truck or something. Are you telling me she's suicidal?"

"Not exactly. She just doesn't look after herself, and around here life is tough enough that you need to. She's so busy taking care of everyone else that she forgets to eat, doesn't watch where she's going. Maggie says if she doesn't pull herself together it's only a matter of time before something terrible happens."

Gabriel digested all that unwillingly. "How has she changed since she was in New York?"

Jeffie shrugged. "I don't know, man. Neither does anyone else. Maybe she's just still run-down from the accident."

"What accident?"

"Man," said Jeffie, shaking his head, "that's where it all started. She walked in front of a taxi in New York City and nearly got killed. Apparently it was Christmas Eve, she'd just been fired from her job, and she was so upset she didn't watch where she was going." Jeffie stared out at the busy sidewalk. "I'd like to get my hands on the bastard who fired her."

"Who says it was his fault?" Gabriel said, trying not to squirm. "He didn't push her in front of the cab, did he?"

"Carrie still defends the pig. All I know is she nearly died. When she got back here, she was different. Quieter, sadder than anyone remembered. Whatever money she has goes to everyone else, and I know for a fact she barely has enough to get by on."

"Maybe she ought to put that energy into herself," Gabriel argued. "She needs to get a job, feed herself..."

"There aren't any jobs around here. She can't make enough quilts to support the entire town, and Maggie says that's what she's trying to do."

"Is that what she does? Makes quilts?"

"Man, don't you notice anything?" Jeffie's hero worship was

fading fast, something that ought to have relieved Gabriel. Instead, he felt curiously bereft.

He tried to stretch his legs out in front of him. "Sometimes I'm extremely unobservant," he said with a weary sigh.

"Hey, I'm sorry, I forgot you hit your head," Jeffie said, suddenly contrite. "You must be feeling like garbage, and here I'm bothering you with Carrie's problems."

"You're not bothering me," Gabriel said flatly. "I want to know how I can help her."

"You and everybody else. There's nothing we can do. Unless you happen to have a miracle available. Fat chance," Jeffie said with all the true cynicism of a seventeen-year-old.

"You'd be surprised," Gabriel said mildly, watching as Carrie left the store and moved toward the car with her usual grace.

She didn't look as if she were an accident waiting to happen. She was too thin and pale, but her eyes were bright, her soft mouth was smiling, and he wondered what had happened to her to make her feel that life wasn't worth living. He couldn't remember anything about the three months she'd been one of his secretaries— most of his past was a frustrating blank. But he hadn't been a monster; surely he couldn't have destroyed her life.

He wanted to take her narrow shoulders and shake some sense into her. Right now life seemed very precious indeed to him, and he couldn't stand the thought of her throwing hers away.

She dropped her package onto his lap. "What's this?" he asked.

"Aspirin. You have to have a prize of a headache, after that crack your skull got last night. You haven't complained, but you have to be hurting."

"Do I?" Actually he hadn't been hurting at all, not from the crack on his skull, not from using unexpected muscles when he split Carrie's firewood. Maybe coming back had its own strange blessings.

Before he knew what she'd planned, she reached out and touched his forehead, brushing back the too-long hair, and her hand was as gentle, and even more sensual, than when she'd stroked her car. "It's healing nicely," she said. "In a couple of days you won't even know you've hurt yourself." Her fingers still lingered, warm against his cool flesh. "Unless you cut your hair, of course."

"I was thinking of that."

"Don't you dare." She started to pull her hand away, but he caught her wrist, stopping her with gentle force.

Her eyes met his with startled wonder. "Why shouldn't I cut my hair, Carrie?"

"Maybe you should," she said breezily, not tugging at her hand. "You're a little too beautiful as it is."

His mouth curved in a wry smile. "It won't work."

"What won't work?" She yanked her hand away, and he let her go.

"You keep talking to me as if you're my maiden aunt."

"For one thing, I feel like your maiden aunt," she said with asperity. "For another..."

"For another?" he prompted.

Jeffie chose that moment to interfere. "Yeah, Carrie? For another what?"

"For another thing, I'm saving myself for you, Jeffie," she said cheerfully, starting the car. This time she didn't stroke the dashboard and croon to it. A good thing, too. He would have caught her hand in his again.

The town of Angel Falls was no more than a block long, with a diner, two gas stations, a bar, and a general store beside the pharmacy. Beneath the rapidly melting snow things looked very clean, very shabby, very depressed. It was a town on its way out but putting up a brave front nonetheless. The tatty, sparkling Christmas decorations were going up all around them.

"Isn't it a little early for Christmas decorations?" he asked.

He could sense Carrie's shoulders relaxing as he changed the subject. "It's a hard life up here," she said. "We have to celebrate anything we can. At least we wait till Thanksgiving. I know some places that start the Christmas season in mid-October."

"Like New York City."

She looked at him in surprise. "Did you used to live in New York? You don't seem the type."

"I don't know if there is a type." He avoided answering her question, turning to stare at the scenery. Half the vehicles they passed were pickup trucks, few of them newer than his. "This is a pretty poor town."

"Do tell. Ever since the mill closed down things have been pretty lean. A lot of people have moved out."

"But you moved back."

She didn't ask him how he knew. "I had no place else to go. The same with most of the people left around here. If they had a choice, they'd be gone."

He glanced around at the shabby, yet neat Victorian houses beneath their soggy blanket of snow. "I can see why. It's depressing."

"Not really. This town, and the people in it, grow on you. It's really very beautiful. But people have to make a living, and the summer people don't provide enough of an income for the whole town."

"It sounds like the whole town is in need of a miracle," he said.

"You don't have to sound so gloomy. No one's expecting you to provide it," Carrie said.

He looked at the old houses and narrow streets, and wondered whether that was true. Or whether he really was supposed to save the whole damned town.

The Swensen house was as big, or bigger, than the other old Victorian houses. The paint was peeling, but the woodwork was in perfect shape. Lars was standing on the broad front porch, wearing a flannel shirt and wool vest, hanging a Christmas wreath entwined with dried flowers and pinecones.

He pumped Gabriel's hand enthusiastically when he reached the porch, and there was no doubting the sincerity of his welcome, even to a man like Gabriel, who was used to doubting everything. "Good to see you, Gabriel," he boomed. "Maggie's already made up your room, and there's fresh coffee and bread in the kitchen." He leaned past him and gave Carrie a loud kiss on the cheek. "Some for you, too, little pigeon. We need to fatten you up."

"Bah, humbug," said Carrie with unimpaired good humor. "Jeffie will take you up on your offer. Teenage boys never stop eating."

"Aw, Carrie…" Jeffie protested, heading straight past everyone, presumably in the direction of the kitchen and food.

"Nice wreath," Gabriel murmured. Indeed, it was a piece of rare beauty, fashioned of blue spruce, the muted colors of the dried flowers complementing the greeny blue of the pine needles.

"He's been disapproving of all the decorations," Carrie piped up. "He thinks it's too early in the season."

"Don't you be putting words in his mouth," Lars said. "We put our wreaths up at Thanksgiving, and we leave 'em up until the needles drop off and they're brown, usually sometime in April."

"Why?" Gabriel couldn't keep from asking.

"To remind us that we should all have a bit of the Christmas spirit the year round," Lars said simply. "It's a lesson we all need to learn."

"Amen," Carrie said.

Gabriel tensed, waiting in fearful anticipation for one of them to burst into prayer, but that seemed to be enough for a moment. "Come along in," Lars said, stamping the loose snow off his feet. "And I'll see if I can roust Maggie."

The inside of the house matched the exterior. It was spotless and for a moment Gabriel paused. He'd always kept his own apartment pin-neat, with the help of an overpriced cleaning service, but it had never felt like this. Somehow cozy, homey, despite the neatness. The wallpaper was faded, but the woodwork on the curving stair was smooth and polished. The runner was unraveling on top of the shining oak floorboards, and the place smelled of lemon wax and coffee and cinnamon.

"This is what heaven should smell like," he surprised himself by saying.

"I imagine it does," Lars replied, pushing open the swinging door into the huge kitchen that was the heart of the house, the heart of the family. Maggie was sitting in an old rocker near the wood cookstove, nursing the baby, a cracked mug of coffee on the table close at hand.

She raised her head and smiled, and her careworn face looked as smooth and beautiful as a Madonna's. Gabriel could feel the instinctive flush rise to his face, his desperate need to escape watching her nurse.

But there was no way he could do so gracefully. He had no choice but to let Lars show him to a seat at the wide table and plunk a mug of coffee and a couple of fresh cinnamon rolls in front of him. He stared, with rapt concentration on the rich brown of his coffee, while Lars and Carrie made appreciative noises about tiny Anna Caroline Swensen.

"She's an absolute beauty, isn't she?" Lars boomed when his guest hadn't joined in with the appropriate praise.

"Gorgeous," Gabriel said, staring at his half-eaten cinnamon roll as if it held the answers to the universe. As indeed it might. It was good enough to cure cancer.

Carrie rose abruptly, and he realized in his acute embarrassment he hadn't even been aware that she was sitting close beside him. "Do you mind if I show Gabriel his room?"

Lars waved one burly arm. "Be my guest. It's the back bedroom under the eaves. We thought it would give him the most privacy. Want to go out to the shop, Jeffie?"

Jeffie rose from the table, his mouth still full of cinnamon bun. "You bet."

"Meet us out there," Lars said. "Carrie will show you the way."

Gabriel followed Carrie in complete silence, up the narrow, winding back stairway from the kitchen. Her blond hair hung half-way down her back this morning—she hadn't bothered to do anything more than tie it with a strip of material. A piece that matched the quilt he'd slept under, he realized suddenly.

She opened a burled walnut door and stepped into the room, surveying it with satisfaction. "This is where you'll be," she said. "There's a bathroom down the hall that you'll share with Lars and Harald, and around here you need to conserve hot water, cold water, electricity and heat." She moved forward, into the room, touching the old bird's-eye maple dresser. "They moved this in for you. Lars must approve of you."

It was a beautiful piece of furniture, the only beauty the bare room had to show. The bed was a narrow metal one with a sagging mattress, utilitarian white sheets and an old gray blanket. The one window looked out over the chilly gray landscape, and the chair and table looked extremely uncomfortable.

"It's very nice," he murmured, closing the door behind them, closing them in the room.

It was a small room. She was not a tiny woman, but he was a very tall man, and the room felt crowded, by the two of them, by the sensual awareness he couldn't escape as he looked down at her.

He knew if he lifted his hands they'd be trembling with the need to touch her. In his short, misspent life he'd never felt so quintessentially alive as he did now, standing so close to her he could feel the heat from her body, could breathe in the flowery scent from her skin. He wanted her with a desperation that was an ache in his bones, and he knew he couldn't have her.

She smiled up at him, and for a moment he thought she was serene and untouched by his burning need. Until he looked into her eyes at the troubled shadow that burned beneath the bright blue. He could see the rapid flutter of pulse at the base of her throat, the faint color in her skin. He could see the hardness of her nipples through the soft cotton top, and the room was toasty warm.

She took a step back, one that seemed perfectly natural, but he wasn't fooled. She was even more wary of him than he was of her.

"You should be comfortable here. As soon as you get used to Maggie."

The change of subject, even though the other was unspoken, startled him. "What?"

"How could you have reached the age of thirty-something and not seen a woman nurse a baby?" she asked, her voice a gentle tease.

"I've done my best to avoid it," he said gruffly.

"It's only natural."

"So is death. That doesn't mean I have to like it."

"You'll get used to it," she said serenely. "Won't you want your wife to breast-feed your children?"

"I don't have a wife."

"But you will someday."

"No."

He'd shocked her. "Why not?"

He was letting too much out. He shrugged. "I just can't imagine it. What about you?"

"I don't intend to have a wife," she said with an impish smile.

"What about babies and breast-feeding?"

He'd pushed enough to get a reaction, and he saw the pain and denial darkening her eyes. "That's none of your business."

"But my reproductive plans are yours?" he countered.

"You're right, I've been too nosy. It's a failing of mine."

She obviously wasn't going to have babies any more than he was. Not unless he could make a miracle. He looked at her and wondered what kind of miracle she needed. Whether he could put his hands on her and somehow cure her.

For the moment he was afraid to try. If he touched her he wouldn't be content with comfort, with healing. If he touched her he'd try to draw her down onto that narrow, sagging bed. And despite, or perhaps because of, her wariness, he knew there was a good chance she'd go with him.

He took a step back away from her, noting without comment the relief in her eyes. "That's all right," he said. "When I make my plans about babies you'll be the first to know."

And suddenly the relief vanished, leaving only the beginnings of an impossible longing. Impossible for both of them. And he started thinking that even the other place might be easier than this one. And a woman he couldn't touch.

CHAPTER FIVE

"You don't talk much, do you?" Lars Swensen was leaning over a piece of cherry-colored wood, running a strip of sandpaper down the edge with the tenderness of a mother smoothing her child's hair.

"No," Gabriel said, picking up a block of wood that someone, probably Lars, had begun carving and then abandoned.

"Well, I'm used to that. In case you hadn't guessed, I'm from Scandinavian stock myself, and most Swedes aren't much in the talking department. Course, Maggie says I make up for my family. I like a little conversation now and then."

"You won't get idle chatter from me." Gabriel leaned one hip on the high stool and picked up a tiny chisel.

"I don't need idle chatter. The shop gets lonely here. I'd appreciate the company, even if you don't want to talk. Though you strike me as a man who'd have a lot to say, given the right circumstances."

The wood felt rich, alive beneath Gabriel's rough fingertips. "I don't know what those circumstances would be," he said absently, digging a little bit into the wood with the razor-sharp chisel.

"You done much work with carving? That piece was part of the nativity scene I was doing for the church. I've done most of it, and then I get stuck. You know they talk about writer's block? Well, carpenters get it, too, sometimes. I've wasted more wood, trying to carve the rest of the figures."

Gabriel snicked off another chip of wood. "What have you got left to do?"

"I've done the holy family with no problem at all. I've got the shepherds and the wise men just about finished. But no matter how hard I try I can't carve the angels."

The chisel slipped, slicing into Gabriel's hand, and he dropped the block of wood back onto the workbench. "Really?" he said mildly enough, staring at the bright red blood welling from the shallow gash on his knuckle.

"Maybe you could give it a try," Lars continued, still concentrating on his block of cherry.

"Angels aren't my thing," Gabriel said.

Lars looked up then, obviously struck by something in his voice. "All right," he said finally. "But feel free to play around with it. I'm certainly not getting anywhere."

For a moment Gabriel's hands stilled as he stared at the wood. He knew nothing about carving, nothing about tools. And yet the plain block of wood had begun to take on a form. Not much of one, and yet he could see it clearly beneath the rough texture of the block of fine-grained cherry. The wings were delicately etched, widespread in silent flight. The face was calm, with an almost unearthly beauty. It was the face of the stranger he'd seen in the mirror.

He put the block down on the bench. "Maybe later," he said, and he could hear the strain in his deep voice.

She was standing behind him. He knew it without looking, without hearing, knew it with an instinct as certain as it was frightening. He didn't understand the effect she had on him, the feeling of destiny. And why couldn't he have felt it before, in another lifetime for both of them? Or had he?

He turned slowly, filling his eyes with her. She was standing silhouetted in the doorway, the baby in her arms, and he stared for a moment, wishing he could see a happy ending for her. Wishing he could see babies and health and a future, just as he'd seen the angel in the block of wood. But all he could see was a woman with a sorrow so deep and so eternal that no miracle of his could change it.

"Believe it or not, I'm going to the mall," she announced, her cheerful voice both startling and yet completely believable. "Maggie and I can't believe the Christmas season is really starting unless we partake of that madness, at least vicariously, so you've got the baby for the afternoon."

"I wanted to get some work done," Lars protested, reaching out for the child with welcoming arms despite his grumbling.

"It's the day after Thanksgiving. No one needs to work then."

"They do if they want to get the crèche ready by the first Sunday in Advent."

"You've got all of Saturday," she said. "Besides, you need Mary, Joseph and a donkey to start out with, right? You've already finished those."

"And an angel," he said morosely. "Don't forget the angel."

"Gabriel can do it. He's got the right name for it."

She wasn't looking at him, and he knew it was deliberate. He wasn't even surprised by her suggestion. If he questioned her she'd doubtless simply make a joke of it. But despite common sense, he knew there was a connection between the two of them, one she felt just as strongly as he did. The difference was, she didn't know what was behind it.

"You've got your choice, Gabriel," Lars said cheerfully, beaming down at his baby daughter. "You can hold the baby, or you can see what you can do for an angel. Carrie's right—we need one for Sunday morning. Mary, Joseph and the donkey start in the rear window of the church, heading toward Bethlehem. We need an angel waiting at the stable over on top of the organ."

For a moment Gabriel didn't move, once again certain he'd stumbled into a group of religious fanatics at the very least, or perhaps one of those extremely weird cults. Neither Lars nor Carrie seemed the slightest bit fanatical about it, however, merely matter-of-fact and almost alarmingly cheerful about the whole thing.

"What will happen if you don't have the angel? Does God strike you dead, or something?" he drawled, his hand drifting toward the piece of wood that held the angel imprisoned inside.

"Nope," Carrie said. "We'll use our imagination. Or maybe dredge up the battered papier-mâché angel from the Sunday school crèche." Her eyes narrowed as she looked at his hands, and she took a sudden step toward him. "You've cut yourself," she said, putting her small, delicate hands over his.

He looked down at them, at her hands on top of his large, strong ones, and for a moment he said nothing, feeling the life flowing through her into him. "Just a scratch," he said, and indeed, the blood had stopped.

"Let me get you a bandage...."

Gently he removed his hands from her grasp, and she released him, stepping back. "It's fine," he said. "Go shopping, and I'll see what I can do about an angel."

It was the wrong thing to say. Her eyes lit up, and she looked like a child who'd been given a new pony for Christmas. He didn't want to bring her that much joy. He wanted to save her life, right whatever wrongs he'd done her, and then leave her to some other man to live happily ever after with. Didn't he? His eyes met hers, and something danced between them, a current of feeling with a life all its own. He wanted to pull back, needed to pull back, and yet he couldn't. All he could do was stand there, watching her.

Carrie hadn't moved, staring at him, entranced. "Get a move on, girlie," Lars boomed, and the baby in his arms jumped at the sudden sound of his voice. "If you and Maggie intend to buy anything more than sore feet and a headache, you'd better get started. Let's leave the man in peace and see what he can come up with. This little girl needs changing, I need some coffee and doughnuts."

The moment passed almost as if that thread of silent communication had never happened. "We won't be too long," Carrie said, backing away, her eyes still lingering.

"Promises, promises," Lars grumbled cheerfully. "We'll probably see you a few hours before Saint Lucia's Day."

"That's part of why we're going. You know who the oldest girl is this year," Carrie said, her attention finally off Gabriel.

He could feel some of the tension ease from him. As long as she watched him, concentrated on him, he felt intensely, painfully alive. He preferred the dull cocoon of life he'd been existing in. Except it hadn't been life, had it?

"What's Saint Lucia's Day?" he asked anyway, knowing it would bring her eyes, her attention back to him, unable to resist.

"You don't know Saint Lucia? Then again, I don't suppose she's much of a Catholic saint. The Scandinavians have pretty much taken her over," Carrie said.

For a moment he was about to deny his implied Catholic heritage, then wisely closed his mouth. He was Gabriel Falconi from the North End of Boston. He couldn't be anything but Catholic.

"We've got a lot of saints," he muttered. "I always liked Saint Jude."

"Patron of lost causes? The people in Angel Falls know a lot about that," Lars said. "You'll like Saint Lucia's Day, Gabriel. The oldest girl gets to wear a crown of candles and a white dress and serve cake to everyone."

"It doesn't sound like much of a holiday to me," he drawled.

"Wait till you taste the cakes." Lars patted his own estimable stomach beneath the comfortable burden of the baby. "You're going to have the best Christmas season of your life."

Gabriel glanced over at Carrie. "I have no doubt of that whatsoever," he said evenly.

And Carrie blushed.

MAGGIE SLID back in the passenger seat of Carrie's old car, closing her eyes for a moment. "I shouldn't be doing this," she said. "I'm behind on the laundry, Nils needs help with his algebra, Lars needs to work on the crèche, not watch the baby.''

"You can't take care of all the people all the time,'' Carrie said in her most reasonable tone of voice.

Maggie turned her head and looked at her, a faint ghost of amusement in her weary eyes. "You might listen to your own advice. You're running yourself ragged.''

"Oh, a perfect saint I am,'' she mocked, uncomfortable. "You know perfectly well I don't have half the demands on my life that you have.''

"You only wish you did.''

The image of baby Carrie hit her hard, sneaking up on her as it did so often. "Well, I don't. And won't, for that matter. I told you, I'm not cut out for a family and kids. Look on the bright side, Maggie. I can come and get my baby-longing taken care of by a good solid dose of your kids, and it gives you a break at the same time. It works out very well for both of us.''

"Not that well for you. I just wish...''

"I just wish we didn't have to talk about it,'' Carrie said firmly. "It's the beginning of the Christmas season. Let's think about what we can afford to buy.''

"Not much,'' Maggie said in her gloomiest voice.

"What is this, *The Grinch Who Stole Christmas?* We can always come up with enough for a sack of peppermints, and what could be more Christmassy? I think our finances can spread to some new hair ribbons for Kirsten, maybe even some gold stars for her Saint Lucia crown. You were going to get some yarn for a new work sweater for Lars, one he can wear in the woods.''

Wrong subject, Carrie thought, as Maggie's face crumpled in sudden grief. "I'm frightened, Carrie. So very frightened. The woods are dangerous, and you know as well as I do that Hunsicker runs a sloppy operation. If two of his men hadn't been injured there'd be no work for Lars.''

It was an old worry, one that Carrie had tried to calm innumerable times. It was hard work, soothing Maggie's fears, when Carrie knew how reasonable they were.

"We just have to trust, Maggie. Too many bad things have happened in the past few years, since the mill closed down. It's only natural to expect more disasters to follow, but they're not going to. Lars is a careful worker, and he keeps his tools in top shape. He's not going to get hurt....''

"You're right,'' Maggie said abruptly. "Let's not talk about gloomy things. We can't do anything but get depressed, and Christmas isn't the time for depression. Let's talk about something more cheerful.''

"Like what?" Carrie asked warily.

"Like Gabriel Falconi. Pretty cute, isn't he?"

"I wouldn't call him cute."

"What would you call him? Don't try to pretend you haven't noticed what a hunk he is. He's the best-looking thing I've seen since Lars."

"Maggie!" Carrie said in mock horror. "And here I thought you and Lars were the perfect couple."

"Don't try to mislead me. You've got your eye on him. I see a romance in your future."

"I don't have my eye on anyone. I'm not interested in romance, and well you know it." She could hear the strain in her voice, and her hopeless longing hung heavy in the air—there was no disguising it with her oldest friend.

"Whoever he was, Carrie, he's not worth spending the rest of your life as a nun," Maggie said sternly. "Gabriel is here, he's gorgeous, unattached, obviously heterosexual...."

"What makes you assume that?" Carrie gave in to her curiosity.

"I've seen the way he looks at you when he thinks no one is looking."

It shouldn't hurt, Carrie thought distantly. It shouldn't feel like a spear in her belly, the ache spreading outward through her body in a white-hot heat. She'd shut off her feelings, her vulnerability, content to be a wise mother superior, spreading asexual kindness around her like alms for the poor. She'd told herself her heart was buried with the cold son of a bitch she'd fallen in love with in New York, and it worked best for her to believe it. But now, in the space of less than twenty-four hours, her life had been turned upside down again, and all by the dark-eyed gaze of a man who looked like a fallen angel.

"You're imagining it," she said flatly.

"I am not. Every time you walk into the room the intensity level rises ten degrees. He—"

"We're going to end up either furious with each other or in tears by the time we reach the mall," Carrie interrupted. "Wanna talk about recipes?" She got in line behind a motorcade of shoppers heading into the newly built mall on the outskirts of Saint Luke, the closest thing to a city their area of Minnesota boasted.

For a moment Maggie didn't say a word. Then she reached out

and put her work-worn hand on Carrie's. "I like to use a trace of cardamom in my sugar cookie recipe."

Carrie flashed her a grateful smile. "Cardamom's fine, if you don't use too heavy a hand."

"Then again, coriander adds a nice touch."

"I can never tell the difference. My heavens, a parking place!" Carrie gasped. "Do you suppose this is a sign from God?"

"To get a parking spot right near the entrance? Absolutely. We're going to have the best Christmas ever."

GABRIEL SET the half-finished angel down on the battered workbench and stared at it in wonder. It was late afternoon, and he'd been alone in Lars's shop for uncounted hours, stopping only when Lars would appear carrying apple pie and strong Scandinavian coffee. The first hour he'd sat alone, staring at the block of wood as he tried to figure out how to use the tiny chisels. The more he'd concentrated the more he'd fouled up. When Lars made his first appearance after putting the baby down for a nap, he hadn't said a word about the carving. He'd simply left the food, turned on the tiny radio and left.

Gabriel had drunk the coffee, devoured the pie with more appetite than he'd ever remembered, and listened to the music. Christmas music already, he told himself in disgust. And yet, as he listened to the music and thought about all the reasons he shouldn't be enjoying some new-age rendition of "Good King Wenceslas," his hands picked up the piece of cherry and began to work.

Each time he stopped to think about it his hands would become clumsy. He'd never been a slow learner, and obviously the part of him that was Gabriel Falconi was equally adept. If he thought about it he wouldn't know what he was doing. So he concentrated on the music, on the soothing, flowing sounds, and let his hands do the thinking for him.

"Fine work."

He hadn't heard Lars come in. The older man stood beside him, looking down at the angel. "You've got a real gift," Lars continued. "And I'm the man to recognize it, if I may say so without false modesty. She's a real beauty, she is. You've got the touch."

Gabriel looked down at his hands. They were nicked, scratched, big and clumsy looking to his unaccustomed eyes. "I guess I do," he murmured.

"She reminds me of someone," Lars said, lifting the figurine.

"Something about her face that I can't quite place. She's a regular tartar, isn't she?"

Gabriel looked down into Augusta's stern, judgmental face. "She is that."

"You wouldn't think of an angel being quite such an old grump, would you? She'd scare the bejesus out of me if I had to face her on judgment day. And yet she looks just right." He clapped a hand on Gabriel's shoulder and squeezed it. "Just right," he said again.

Gabriel looked at him. In his previous incarnation he might have thought that was mild praise. But the man he'd become was more sensitive than his old self. And Lars Swensen had given him high praise, indeed.

"Thanks," he said. "I'll finish her up tomorrow and do the other one. If you want me to, that is. It took me a while to get started."

Lars nodded. "It does, sometimes. It was worth the wait. What do you see for the other one? Another judge?"

Gabriel stared down at Augusta's dry-humored face. "I'm not sure," he said slowly. "I'll have to see what my hands come up with."

An energetic wail emerged from the house. "Someone's calling. The women haven't returned from shopping yet, so I suppose we'd better see what we can rustle up. How are you in the cooking department?"

He thought of the cooking courses de rigueur for an upscale bachelor. Somehow he didn't think Lars would appreciate slivers of raw octopus ringed with duck pâté ravioli. "I can cook," he said. "Steak and spaghetti."

"Sounds my speed. Except this is the day after Thanksgiving. It's un-American to eat anything but turkey hash."

"Turkey hash?"

"Good Lord, are they that uncivilized in Boston? You haven't lived until you've eaten real turkey hash. Prepare yourself for a culinary feast."

"What culinary feast, Pop?" Nils demanded when they stepped into the blast furnace of a kitchen. Gabriel hadn't realized how chilly the shop was, so intent on his work that he hadn't allowed any conscious thought to enter.

"Turkey hash."

"Gross," Nils replied emphatically.

"Yuck," said Kirsten as she rhythmically pounded the baby's back.

"What a thing to do to a perfectly decent turkey," Nils added. "Couldn't we just have turkey sandwiches?"

"You had them for lunch. Besides, Carrie bought a turkey the size of Minneapolis. Food is too precious to waste."

"How about tacos, Pop? We've got some ground beef in the freezer."

"Turkey enchiladas." For a moment Gabriel didn't realize the words had come from his own mouth.

"Say what?" Nils demanded suspiciously.

"I make turkey enchiladas." He might as well carry through with it. If he could carve something that looked fiendishly like his nemesis, Augusta, then he could probably make turkey enchiladas, as well. He'd never been fond of Mexican food. And yet suddenly he had a craving as fierce as that of any woman eight months pregnant. He wanted something rife with chili powder and tortillas, and if he had to use turkey and cook it himself to get it, then he would.

"Sounds great to me. What do you need?"

For a moment Gabriel drew a blank. Shutting his eyes, he went into that blank deliberately. "Tortillas, chili powder, tomato sauce, jack cheese and onions."

"I'll go to the store," Nils shouted.

"Not by yourself, you won't. You only have a learner's permit. I'll drive, and we'll stop and pick up Jeffie. He's alone too much as it is." Lars turned to Gabriel. "You don't mind holding down the fort, do you? Kirsten can handle the little ones."

It wasn't panic, Gabriel told himself. It was his sheer dislike of children. He'd always found them noisy, messy creatures, and he didn't want to be trapped with three of them, alone. Except that Lars's children were the exception. Kirsten was bright, pretty, sweet tempered. The younger boy, whatever his name was, had a mischievous smile that somehow reached past Gabriel's natural reserve. And even the baby had something about her that was far too appealing.

He'd survive. "Take your time," he said grandly, pouring himself another cup of that wickedly strong coffee. And he didn't regret his words for another twenty-three minutes.

CHAPTER SIX

It was snowing by the time Carrie and Maggie pulled into the steep driveway outside the Swensen home. The roads had gotten slick enough to make any normal amount of speed unwise, and for once Carrie had listened to her better judgment. She didn't like the fact that she wanted to get back to the Swensens', wanted to with something close to desperation. Because she knew perfectly well what it was she was trying to get back to. Something she didn't deserve and wasn't going to have.

"Do you suppose they were worried about us?" Maggie asked as she climbed out of the front seat, her arms laden with packages.

"Probably. Do you care?"

"Not enough to come back any sooner," she admitted. "I bet they're sitting around, grumpy, expecting me to cook them dinner."

"I thought Lars was above that sort of thing."

"Honey, no man is above that sort of thing. They all expect you to wait on them hand and foot, even the best of them."

"Lars being one of the best of them?"

"Absolutely," Maggie panted, struggling up the icy driveway. "I haven't decided how Gabriel stacks up in the hierarchy of perfect men."

"Lars being a ten?" Carrie took several of the bulky packages from Maggie's icy hands.

"I imagine Gabriel might be somewhere near a four," Maggie said thoughtfully.

Carrie's protest was immediate, instinctive and unvoiced. "You can't get me to rise to the bait, Maggie. For all we know he could be a minus three."

"Not when he looks like that. I'll give him four points just for looks alone. It's a good thing Angel Falls is singularly devoid of unattached women. You won't have any competition."

"Maggie," she warned, stamping her snowy feet on the sturdy front porch.

"Not that you should worry about competition anyway. Any

man worth his salt would choose you over an entire herd of Miss America contestants.'' She pushed open the door, and heat and light flooded out onto the porch.

''What's this about Miss America contestants?'' Lars's voice boomed out as his sturdy frame filled the kitchen doorway.

''No such luck, sweetheart. You've got me,'' Maggie said.

''And you've brought half the stores in Saint Luke back with you.'' There was no missing the worry in his voice. ''I thought we'd decided we couldn't afford much of a Christmas.''

''Don't give your wife grief,'' Carrie said, shutting the door behind her. ''She spent a pittance. Just be glad we came home to feed you....'' Her voice trailed off as she sniffed the air. ''What's cooking?''

''That doesn't smell like turkey hash,'' Maggie said in an accusing voice.

''It's not. It's turkey enchiladas, and it's only by the magnanimous goodness of my soul and the Christmas spirit that I managed to save enough for you two.''

''You've never made enchiladas.''

''I still haven't. Gabriel's the chef.'' He reached out for the packages. ''I'll hide these. You two go in and get something to eat before you waste away to skin and bones.''

''Impossible for me,'' Maggie said with a sigh, hanging her coat on a hook, ''and too late for Carrie.''

''It's never too late for Carrie,'' Lars said firmly, giving the women a little shove.

The kitchen was empty. Maggie looked around her in dismay. ''I'm not sure it's worth it,'' she said as she surveyed the pile of dishes in the sink, the pots and pans littering every spare surface of the kitchen she'd left spotless.

''Lars said he was a chef, not a scullery maid,'' Carrie pointed out, heading for the sink. ''I'll just get a start on these...''

''Oh, no, you won't.'' Lars was back in record time. ''You sit down and I'll serve you.'' He scooped a pile of dishes off the table, dumped them into the sink and turned with a fatuous smile. ''You won't believe what you're tasting. I didn't know leftover turkey had such possibilities.''

''I don't believe what I'm seeing,'' Maggie said tartly.

''Neither do I,'' Carrie echoed softly, sinking down in surprise onto the chair Lars held for her.

Gabriel was standing in the doorway. The mess from creating his culinary masterpiece hadn't left him untouched. Chili sauce adorned his eyebrow, spattered his chambray shirt and stained his jeans. But that wasn't the most surprising thing about him. In his arms rested little Carrie Swensen, cooing cheerfully, equally bedaubed in that evening's dinner.

"Baby!" Maggie cried, reaching out for her younger daughter. "Little Anna Caroline."

For a moment the baby was torn. "I'm not sure she'll go to you, sweetheart," Lars said, placing two overfilled plates in front of them. "I think she's in love."

Gabriel's face was a study in contradictions. On the one hand, he seemed supremely embarrassed at the baby's obvious adoration. On the other, there was a surprising competence in the way he held her, as if those arms were used to babies, despite his earlier insistence that he had never even seen a woman nurse.

"She got upset when Lars and Nils went to the store," Gabriel said in his deep, slow voice. "I just managed to calm her."

Carrie could imagine it. She'd seen the baby when she was in one of her tears, and it was not a pretty sight. Usually nothing outside of her mother's arms could calm her, but Gabriel seemed possessed of a magic touch. Maybe lying in his arms, listening to that deep voice rumble through his chest...

She dropped her fork with a noisy clatter.

"What's the matter?" Gabriel asked. "Don't you like my cooking?"

She looked up, meeting his dark, enigmatic eyes over the baby's curly head. It was flirtation, a mild, clumsy form of it that seemed to surprise him as much as it surprised her. "It's wonderful," she said truthfully. "I just never got in the habit of eating much."

"I keep telling her she's too thin," Maggie said, her fork scraping against her now-empty plate. "Tell her she's too thin, Gabriel."

"She's too thin," he said in that slow, deep voice of his.

It took all of Carrie's concentration, but she managed to shake off the slumberous effect of it. "Well," she said briskly, "I'll just have to be a disappointment to you all. Even if I ate twice as much, I wouldn't put on weight. My metabolism isn't geared toward comfortable curves."

"You'd think she'd be proud of it," Maggie mourned. "Are there any more enchiladas?"

"Nope," Lars said.

"Are you going to finish yours?" She cast a covetous eye at Carrie's barely touched plate.

"Yes, she is," Gabriel said, handing Maggie the baby and moving to loom over Carrie.

He'd flirted with her, maybe, just maybe, she could flirt back a little. What harm would it do? "What'll you give me if I do?"

He was too close to her. Maggie had risen, resigned to her empty plate, and Gabriel took her vacated seat, next to Carrie. "Dessert," he said.

Carrie just stared at him, visions of all sorts of things, none of them sugarplums, dancing in her head. She opened her mouth to say something, then shut it again, pushing the still-full plate away from her, pushing her empty heart away from her. "Not for me. I'd better get back home. The roads are slick and my stove's probably out by now."

"Spend the night," Lars suggested. "It's too nasty a night to drive all that way by yourself."

"My pipes will freeze, and I can't afford a plumber. Besides, that's what I got the car for. Don't worry about me, Lars. I'll be fine."

"I do worry about you, Carrie. We all do," Lars said earnestly, leaning over the table between them.

"Don't." The word was short, raw, the pain obvious to anyone attuned to it. She didn't deserve their concern.

"At least let me follow you back and make sure you get home safely...."

"No."

"Gabriel can follow you," Maggie piped up, keeping her attention on her daughter so that she couldn't meet Carrie's glare. "He can make sure your stove is going before he leaves."

"No," she said again. "I can take care of myself, and well you know it." She rose, not meeting Gabriel's dark, steady gaze. "But if you'd like to come out tomorrow and look over the work I have for you..."

"Tonight would be better for me," he said.

She thought he'd missed the byplay. "Why?" she asked flatly.

"Because tomorrow I have to finish one carving and do another, I promised Lars I'd take the stuff down to the church, and I wanted to check on my truck. It's tonight or next week."

"Next week would be just fine...."

"Give it up, Carrie," Maggie said. "The man wants to come tonight, let him come tonight. Let somebody do something for you for a change."

There was nothing she could do, short of causing a scene. Lars and Maggie were the best people in the world, but they might have invented the phrase "stubborn Swedes." And if truth be told, she wasn't sure that she wanted to drive on the slick surface of the long twisting road. Four-wheel drive was all well and good, but not when it came to glare ice.

"All right, I'm not going to keep fighting," she said wearily. "All I want to do is go home and go to bed. If you insist that Gabriel follow me to make sure I get there safely then I'm sure I can't stop you, even though there's absolutely no need. But I'm tired, I don't want to drag Gabriel all over the house in an ice storm showing him what needs fixing. He can follow me home, watch me get safely inside the house, and then go home. Satisfied?"

"Satisfied," Lars said. "Take my pickup, Gabe. She's old and rusty but she runs like a top, and you're going to need the four-wheel drive on a night like this." He turned to Carrie. "Sit yourself back down, have some dessert and a cup of coffee before you go out into the night."

Part of her would have killed for coffee, but the longer she delayed getting home the more she'd be playing into the Swensens' heavy-handed matchmaking. Besides, she was exhausted. She needed to collapse in her own bed as soon as possible, and accepting Gabriel's help was the path that would lead her home the quickest.

"No coffee, no dessert."

"No coffee?" Lars echoed, horrified. "Some sherry, then? Something to warm your bones."

"A kiss good-night," she said, leaning over and kissing his burly cheek. "I'll get you both for this," she whispered in his ear.

Lars didn't look the slightest bit chastened. "Don't do anything I wouldn't do."

Gabriel followed her out into the hall, Lars's keys in his hand, an unreadable expression on his face. She braced herself, waiting for him to make some comment, but he was silent, looming over her. He didn't help her on with her coat, a wise move on his part. She was already in a bad mood, having to accept help when she was the one who wanted to offer it, and if he'd been fool enough to be oversolicitous she would have lashed out at him, she who seldom said a harsh word to a living soul other than herself.

But he didn't say a word, didn't try to touch her, simply waited as she struggled into her coat, and she reminded herself she was being paranoid. He didn't know a thing about her and her myriad problems. No one knew all her problems, or the depths of the harm she'd done. No one needed to know. Her own conscience was punishment enough.

"You don't need to do this, you know," she said. "Lars and Maggie are overprotective. I've been driving these roads since I was sixteen, usually without the benefit of four-wheel drive or even snow tires."

"They care about you."

"A little too much, if you ask me."

"I didn't know that was possible," Gabriel said.

It was useless to argue. "It's fairly direct to my house—you shouldn't have any trouble retracing the path, unless you have no sense of direction."

An odd expression flashed into his eyes. "I don't know," he said simply.

She didn't stop to consider the ramifications of that statement. "Well, I guess you'll find out tonight, won't you? Have you done much winter driving?"

"Last night," he said, the faint trace of a smile curving his mouth.

God, she loved his mouth. Immediately she slapped down that thought. "That's not much of a testimonial."

"It was a fluke. I'll be fine."

"I don't want to be pulling you out of a ditch. Maybe you ought to stay home."

He took her arm. Major mistake, she thought. She liked the feel of his hand on her arm, strong, forceful without being bullying, protective. She didn't let people protect her, she was too busy protecting them. But, Lord, it felt good, if only for a brief, self-indulgent moment.

"I think," he said, "that we ought to stop arguing and get on the roads before they become impassable. Assuming you haven't changed your mind and decided to spend the night here?"

"I haven't changed my mind." He still hadn't released her arm, and not for a moment was she tempted to yank it free. "I hope I made myself clear—I want you to stay in the truck until I'm safely in the house and then drive straight back home."

He didn't answer. Instead, he opened the door, letting a blast of damp, icy air into the house. "Let's go," he said.

And since his warm, strong hand was still clasped around her upper arm, she had no choice but to follow.

GABRIEL DROVE SLOWLY, following behind her on the icy roads as
he considered his course of action. He was glad to see some sign
of temper in her. He'd begun to think of her as the saint of Angel
Falls. A hell of a combination, he thought with a sour smile. A
saint, and a broken-down angel. He was the one who was supposed
to be the good one, wasn't he?

He wasn't sure of anything anymore. There were times when he
felt like Gabriel Falconi, comfortable and familiar inside a strange
body, a strange head. Emerson Wyatt MacVey III was a dream,
someone he'd read about in a book. Not a very good book, at that.
One of those depressing anti-yuppie novels he'd struggled through
in a previous life.

He concentrated on the red taillights ahead of him. Lars was
right, the truck held the icy road fairly well. He found he was adept
at driving through bad conditions. He automatically steered into a
skid, using just the right amount of pressure on the gas pedal, and
took a moment to admire his expertise. The moment he did, he
began to skid again, and this time he overcorrected, sliding first
one way and then another on the slippery road.

He managed to pull it out of the spin, setting it back on the
straight and narrow, his palms sweating, curses filling the air. Why
couldn't he remember? He had all sorts of talents he never knew
existed, if he just remembered to use his instincts and not his brain.
If Emerson thought about driving on nightmarish roads he'd end
up in a ditch. If Gabriel concentrated on the woman ahead of him
and let his hands and feet, not his mind, do the driving, he'd be
just fine.

He followed her up the long, twisting driveway to the dark
house, watched as she turned off her car, waved goodbye in the
glare of his headlights and moved toward the door with deceptive
energy. He knew how tired she was, he could see the purple stains
beneath her blue eyes, the paleness of her complexion, even the
faint tremor in her hands. He could also see that there was no
smoke coming from the chimney overhead.

He waited until the kitchen lights came on, then switched off the
truck and bounded after her.

She was standing in the kitchen door, glaring at him. "I thought
I told you to go home."

"Then why are you standing in the door?"

"I knew I couldn't trust you."

"Sure you can, Carrie," he said. "I'm here to see you home
safely, and that's what I'm going to do. Now why don't you let

me in so I can see about your wood stove instead of standing there letting more cold air inside?''

It was reasonable, but he could see by the expression on her face that she wasn't in the mood to be reasonable. He decided to take it out of her hands, pushing past her very gently and closing the door behind him.

The kitchen was icy. "Why don't you make me some coffee while I get the stove started?'' he said.

"I can't.''

"Why not?''

"I already checked. The water's frozen.''

She was a strong woman, but her voice cracked slightly. He wanted to draw her into his arms, to warm her slender, weary body with his. He shoved his hands into his pockets to keep from touching her.

"I'll get the stove going first,'' he said. "Come into the living room and wrap yourself up in something while I work on it, and then I'll see what I can do about the water.''

"You're a plumber?'' she asked, her voice incredulous.

"Anyone can unfreeze water if the pipes haven't burst yet, and I don't think it's been that cold for that long.''

"You're a man of hidden talents,'' she said wryly, following him meekly enough.

"I know,'' he said wryly.

He almost asked her to turn on the radio. Something to distract him from that intermittent clumsiness that assailed him when he least needed it. There were a few coals glowing at the bottom of the blue enamel stove, and he hummed beneath his breath as he stirred the ashes, opened the draft just the right amount and dropped only a minimal amount of kindling on it. In a moment it blazed forth, eating into the logs he placed on top of it.

"You've very good at that,'' Carrie said. She was curled up on the sofa where he'd slept the night before, wrapped in the quilt that had kept him warm. It was that potent, dangerous distraction that had enabled him to be so efficient with the fire. "Most people don't understand the idiosyncracies of wood stoves.''

"I have a fair amount of common sense,'' he said. No, I don't, his mind protested. If I did, I wouldn't be anywhere near her. Or at least I wouldn't be thinking the kind of things I'm thinking. "You got a hair dryer?''

Carrie grimaced. "Where it belongs. Under the kitchen sink, bought for the express purpose of thawing frozen pipes. Listen, don't bother. I can handle it, once I warm up. You'd better go home before the roads get any worse.''

"It just kills you to accept help, doesn't it?"

"I didn't ask for help. I can manage on my own." She shivered, despite the rapidly warming temperature of the room, despite the brightly colored quilt bundled around her.

"I'm sure you can. But you helped me out yesterday. I like to repay my debts." It was the best possible thing he could have said. She couldn't accept someone's help. But she could accept someone else's need to even things up.

"All right," she said with a sigh. "If it will make you feel better."

It took him longer than he expected to get the water flowing again. As the heat from the living room stove began to filter through into the kitchen his hands began to lose their numbness, and he was finally rewarded with a sputtering, then steady, stream of water from the open faucet.

The adjoining bathroom was in worse shape. By the time he had water moving through all the fixtures he was tired, dirty and hungry. He washed one level of grime from his hands and face and headed out to the living room.

She was asleep on the sofa, her long blond hair fanned out around her pale face, her hands still clutching the quilt around her. He loaded the stove as quietly as possible, banking it down, and then squatted down beside her, watching her.

She didn't open her eyes. "Don't," she said, her lips barely moving, the sound so soft he thought he might have imagined it.

But he hadn't. "Don't what?"

"Don't look at me like that." This time she did open her eyes, staring up at him with a fearlessness he knew was completely fake. She was frightened of him, and he couldn't imagine why.

"Like what?"

"I'm not available. I'm not someone to help you while away some time spent in a high prairie town. I'm not a convenient bed partner, or even a one-night stand. I've made my life, and it's a solitary one. Don't jump to any conclusions."

"Who says I'm asking?" he demanded in a slow, deep voice, not moving.

Her pale face flooded with color. "I'm sorry," she said, her voice muffled. "I guess I was the one jumping to conclusions."

He should rise, say something friendly and walk away. And he knew he wasn't going to do that. There was a reason she was warning him away, and it wasn't just him she was afraid of. It was herself.

"No," he said. "You're not." And he leaned over and brushed her lips with his.

CHAPTER SEVEN

Sunday morning dawned still and clear, with a warm front coming through and melting the layer of snow and ice that had clung to the stubborn Minnesota earth since Thanksgiving. Gabriel arrived at the Messiah Lutheran Church with the Swensen family, all of them scrubbed and combed and spruced up. He'd had to make do with the contents of the duffel bag. There were no Italian suits, no tailored wool blazers, not even a reasonable pair of khakis. Clearly Gabriel Falconi's idea of formal dress was a pair of unpatched jeans and a fresh cotton shirt.

He'd pushed it a bit, trying to iron the wrinkles out of one of them, but apparently that bit of domestic art was beyond even the estimable Gabriel. He tried whistling, tried concentrating on the inane but funny plot of the sitcom the Swensen family had watched the night before, to no avail. His hands were clumsy, impossible as he tried to iron, and even succumbing to the ultimate distraction only led to disaster.

Carrie's lips had tasted better than anything he'd ever kissed. They'd been soft, unresisting, surprised, and it had taken a self-control he'd never known he possessed to simply brush her mouth with his, not deepen it as he'd longed to, not push her back on the couch and warm his cold body and hers with a heat that had been burning inside him since he first saw her.

But he hadn't. He'd moved away without a word, leaving her staring up at him in numb surprise, and he'd left her before she could gather her wits together.

He'd driven back home over the slick roads, remembering the feel of her mouth, and that memory hadn't been far from his mind for the past thirty-six hours, culminating with a huge triangle-shaped scorch mark on his best shirt.

He'd given up then, settling for wrinkles, but been fool enough to ask Lars for a tie. Lars had looked at him as if he were crazy, but handed him a subdued narrow tie that should have felt at home around Emerson's neck. It strangled Gabriel.

"No one wears a tie to church anymore, Gabe," Lars said kindly when he brought it back. "You won't be offending anyone. It's not going to make any difference in the eyes of God, and no one in heaven's going to care."

Gabriel thought of Augusta's flinty eyes. "You'd be surprised," he'd said glumly.

Now he stood just inside the church, surveying the congregation while the younger Swensens whispered and fought, and he thanked God he'd at least had a look at the place the day before when he'd helped Lars with the pieces of the crèche.

It was unlike any church he could remember. When he'd bothered to go to church, he'd frequented Saint Barts on Fifth Avenue and 50th Street, an old, elegant church attended by all the right people. He sensed the eyes he was looking through were more accustomed to pomp and circumstance and stained glass. The Messiah Lutheran Church was plain, sturdy, with maple pews, oak trim, and a huge unadorned silver cross hanging from the front of the church. The organ was in front, and on top was a deliberately crude-looking stable filled with straw, one of Lars's beautifully carved cows, and the first angel.

Augusta perched on top of the miniature roof, arms outspread, face stern and judgmental. He'd had qualms about putting her right up there. The second angel had been much more user-friendly, an adolescent male with blond curls and a vulnerable face. He had no idea where that vision had come from. On the surface, he was much closer to the traditional idea of angels—sexless, pretty boys with outspread wings. It was only when you looked closer that you could see the fear in the wide, blank eyes.

Lars's carvings of Mary and Joseph were in a back window, along with a donkey, starting their journey toward Bethlehem, Lars had told him. Gabriel had wanted to sneer at the notion. Instead, he found himself strangely moved.

There'd been no way he could get out of going to church that day, not unless he'd asked directions to the nearest Catholic church. And while the overt religiousness of the Swensens, and indeed, everyone he'd met in Angel Falls, made him acutely uncomfortable, at least they didn't try to foist it upon him, and didn't spend hours ranting. Their faith simply seemed to be a part of their lives, just as shopping and driving cars and eating were.

Besides, he'd kept away from Carrie Alexander quite deliberately yesterday. He wanted to give her time to think about that kiss, to see what she was going to do about it. And he wanted to give himself time to get his unaccustomed libido under control.

He'd spent the day in Lars's workshop, finishing up Augusta, carving the young man. At least Lars saw no arcane resemblance in the young man's perfect face.

The word on Gabriel's truck wasn't encouraging. Steve had hemmed and hawed and muttered about differentials and main cylinders, phrases that meant nothing to Gabriel, but the bottom line was there'd be no moving on for him, even if he'd wanted to, for at least another week.

It was still an option, he thought. Gabriel didn't have much money, but he was possessed of a gold credit card, a miracle in itself. He hadn't had a chance to check the credit limit, but he suspected he could probably manage to fly to New York and live out his month on earth in the manner to which he'd become accustomed.

For some reason that notion didn't particularly appeal to him. Not that he thought there was a chance in hell, pardon the expression, to redeem himself, right the mysterious wrongs Augusta had insisted he'd committed, and make it past the Waystation. No, he was going to be roasting in the other place, there was no doubt about it, and he ought to be enjoying his brief sojourn on earth.

And he was. The room under the eaves at the Swensens was cold and barren, the bed narrow and saggy, the food plain and riddled with cholesterol. And yet he'd slept better in that narrow bed, beneath Carrie Alexander's quilt, than he ever had in his life. The food tasted better, and he no longer had to worry about cholesterol, did he? Besides, butter and cream tasted so damned good.

But not as good as Carrie Alexander's mouth. He saw her sitting in the choir, dressed in a blue robe, her face serene and untroubled. Looking like a saint again, he thought gloomily. He shouldn't want to tarnish that sainthood. It wouldn't sit well with the powers that were overseeing him. It would send him to hell for sure, and they might not wait until Christmas Eve.

He should have asked more questions at the Waystation, he thought as he followed the train of Swensens down the center aisle to a spot near the front of the church. Near the choir. Would he be sentenced to the other place without hope of parole? Or did he get time off for good behavior? Credit for at least trying? Maybe it would behoove him to forget the potent effect Carrie had on him.

Damn it, he hadn't been that rotten in his previous life! It wasn't fair that he was sent back to make up for all the wrongs he'd committed. As far as he could remember he'd been no better or worse than the next man.

It wasn't going to be up to him. He sank into the pew next to little Harald, and a moment later Gertrude Hansen sat down beside him, her eyes unreadable behind the thick-lensed glasses.

"Good morning," he whispered, having ascertained that a certain amount of preservice talking was allowed in this church.

Obviously not by Gertrude. Her mouth thinned disapprovingly, and he wished he'd worn a tie. "Good morning," she replied. "What were you thinking about?"

Lustful thoughts of a choir member, he wanted to tell her. "I was admiring the simplicity of the church," he whispered back.

"Were you?" Gertrude's gaze must be sharp behind those thick glasses. She reached out and patted his hand with her own aged one. "We're glad you're here with us, Gabriel."

Not if you knew what I'd really been thinking, he thought, smiling faintly at her and turning his gaze back to the front of the church. And found himself gazing directly into Carrie's eyes.

If she remembered the circumstances when she'd last seen him, she'd appeared to put it out of her mind. Scratch that, of course she remembered. There was no doubt in his mind that she hadn't been kissed nearly enough. Even so, she'd obviously managed to wipe the memory from her mind, her gaze serene and impersonal, almost maternal.

Gertrude, sitting next to him, could be maternal. He wasn't about to accept that from the woman in the choir. He also wasn't about to send her lascivious messages from his seat in the congregation, not with Gertrude on one side and an impressionable Harald on the other. He simply stared at her for a moment, and his eyes said, "later."

She blinked, startled out of her serene state. Before she could react, the organ started, the congregation surged to its feet, and they were in the midst of "Wachet auf."

If he'd worried that she'd try to escape once the service was over he needn't have. The Scandinavian population of Angel Falls wasn't about to let an occasion go by without eating, and immediately after church he was plied with coffee and a thin, wonderful pastry called kringle as he was introduced to Larsens, Swensens, Hansens, Johannsens, Rasmussens, and all the "sens" that flesh is heir to.

He knew she was standing behind him before he saw her. Even as he made strained conversation with the gentle, slightly befuddled Pastor Krieger, he could feel her presence, feel it through his clothes and skin like a soft spring breeze. He'd never feel a spring

breeze again, he thought before turning, and a sudden wave of
sorrow hit him. He would have liked to have felt the spring breeze
against his skin. With Carrie beside him.

"You're very gifted," she said when he turned to look at her.

She'd divested herself of her blue choir robe, and she was wearing some sort of shapeless dress. He found himself wondering exactly what kind of shape she had under there, and then stopped
himself. He was still in church, even if the service was over. He
could at least make an effort at behaving himself. "I am?" he said,
resisting the urge to touch her mouth with his fingers.

"The angels. I love them both. It's hard to believe that someone
as talented as Lars would show up. I've decided you must be a gift
from heaven."

He was getting used to it by this time, the odd, random statements that meant nothing to anyone but him. He didn't even choke
on the piece of pastry he'd just swallowed. "How's your water
doing?"

"Just fine. I didn't get a chance to thank you for your help on
Friday night." She said it calmly, not avoiding his gaze.

Two could play at that game. "Anytime," he said.

He was rewarded with a faint color in her pale cheeks. "Who
did you have in mind when you carved the second angel?" She
quickly changed the subject. "He looks so familiar, and yet I can't
quite place him."

A sudden uneasiness trickled down his spine. Both angels had
looked familiar to him, and he'd had no idea where the vision had
come from. Wherever it had sprung from, it had bypassed his conscious mind entirely. "I have no idea. I don't really think about
what I do, I just do it." Truer than she realized, he thought.

"Of course I recognize Gertrude, and I think it's very clever of
you to have seen through that myopic sweetness of hers. She loves
to act charming and befuddled, but beneath those thick glasses
she's really quite a formidable woman."

"What?" The sound of his shocked voice was enough to make
several heads turn, and he immediately lowered his pitch. "What?"
he demanded again.

"Gertrude. Your first angel is the spitting image of her, without
her glasses, of course. Don't tell me you didn't realize it?"

"Where is she?" he demanded hoarsely.

"I think she got a ride back with the Milsoms. She left something behind for you with Lars."

"I imagine she did," he said, feeling oddly shaken.

"Were you still interested in doing some work for me?"

It took him a moment to regain his concentration. "What?"

"I asked if you were still interested in doing some carpentry work for me?" she repeated patiently, with still that faint trace of color in her cheeks.

He knew what she was doing. She was trying to prove to him, and to herself, that she was immune to his presence. That she could treat him with the same friendly distance she used for everyone.

"Do you think that's a wise idea?" he asked, more for her reaction than real hesitation. Wise or not, nothing was going to stop him from working on her ramshackle old house. Or on her.

"Why wouldn't it be?" She raised her chin defiantly.

"You tell me." He glanced over at the door. Lars was standing there, his brood surrounding him. "It looks like my ride's leaving. When do you want me out there?"

"Whenever's convenient for you. Tomorrow morning?"

"Assuming the Swensens will lend me a vehicle. Steve says my truck's going to be out of commission for a while."

Carrie made a face. "I don't think that will be a problem. If it is, I'll come and get you. I need to show you what needs work, and we can discuss how much I can afford to have done. And we need to make a few things clear."

He couldn't help it. He grinned, a slow, lazy grin that made the pale pink of her cheeks darken. "You mean like Friday night?" he murmured.

"Aren't you looking pretty?" One of the Hansens or Larsens came up and gave the flustered Carrie a big hug. "And aren't we lucky to have someone new in town? The way all the young people have been leaving, we've been afraid we'll turn into a ghost town."

"Why have all the young people been leaving?" Gabriel asked.

"When the mill closed down there was no work, outside the tourist trade," the elderly lady said. "I hear it's been happening all over the country, big corporations buy up little companies, and then they sell them off for a profit. It doesn't matter to some wheeler-dealer in New York that our lives are depending on them. It doesn't matter that's it's people they're dealing with. They just see it as numbers on a paper."

He wasn't enjoying this morning at all, he decided. There were only so many revelations he could handle at one time. Finding Augusta lurking behind a thick pair of glasses was bad enough. The fate of Angel Falls's mill was worse.

"What was the name of the factory?" he asked, not bothering to hide the strain in his voice.

For some reason Carrie was looking acutely miserable. "Precision Industries. Not a very distinctive name, was it? They made furniture, not very distinctive furniture, either, but good solid work."

He remembered Precision Industries, but just vaguely. There were so many companies along the way, bought up on a whim, disposed of just as lightly. He had made money on Precision's dissolution, but then, he always had made money. How much had it been—half a million dollars? Less? And where was it now? Beyond his reach.

"It happens," he said. "That's the way the system works."

"We don't think it works too well around here," the old lady said tartly, and he was reminded of Gertrude. And Augusta. "And considering the rest of the country, I wouldn't be too optimistic about how the system works."

There was nothing he could say to that. Fortunately he was spared trying to defend a system that had effectively destroyed the entire town of Angel Falls by the timely arrival of Lars.

"We're ready to go. Maggie's got some julekage rising and she needs to get back before it goes over the top. Why don't you get a ride back with Carrie?"

"No!" Carrie said with what he might have considered unflattering haste. Except that her nervousness around him was one of the deepest compliments he'd ever received. "I mean, I've got a million things to do," she floundered, looking miserable. Saint Carrie, who spent so much time trying to take care of others, was making a botch of it as for once she tried to protect herself.

"I'll come now," Gabriel said easily. "What time do you want me tomorrow?"

It was an innocent question, blandly stated. It shouldn't have caused that darkening in her eyes, the awareness she was fighting so hard. "Anytime in the later morning. Can he borrow a vehicle from you, Lars, or should I come get him?"

"Take the truck," Lars said with something dangerously close to a wink. "Take all the time you want."

Time was the one thing he didn't have. "Tomorrow morning," he said. A threat and a promise.

The aging American sedan that had held all six Swensens and his own lanky body was waiting out front. From a distance he could hear baby Carrie crying, Nils and Kirsten fighting, Harald whining, and Maggie's voice rising in the age-old sound of a mother driven to temporary distraction. He opened the front passenger door and took the baby from Maggie's arms without even considering what he was doing. In a moment the deafening howls had ceased to damp, shuddery sighs, and then she managed a small beatific smile up at him.

He stared down at the baby in his arms in utter astonishment. It had amazed him last night, when he'd had no choice but to take her, it amazed him this morning, when he'd willingly gone to her.

"You've got the touch, Gabe, my boy," Lars said cheerfully.

Gabriel met his gaze over the hood of the car. "You mean with children?" he asked, still dazed.

"Possibly. Definitely with women. Maybe just women named Carrie." He was grinning, obviously pleased with himself, and Gabriel wished he could respond. With a joke. With a moment of male camaraderie. But the fact remained that whatever had been born, was growing, between him and Carrie Alexander was doomed from the start. He needed to right the wrongs, save the souls he'd wounded. He couldn't leave Carrie in a worse place than the one where he'd found her three short days ago. Not if he wanted to end up in heaven.

So he said nothing, handing the now-cheerful baby back to her mother to strap into the car seat before cramming himself into the back seat with the three other Swensens.

"Gertrude left this for you," Harald said, handing him a heavy hardcover book.

"Thanks," Gabriel said absently, turning the book over with a sense of foreboding.

At least it wasn't Dante's *Inferno*. Not a religious tract, or a description of after-death experiences. It was something much more subtle, a message from Augusta, loud and clear. A novel, with the unsubtle title, *Fools Rush In*. And he remembered the rest of the quote. "Where angels fear to tread."

Was she calling him a coward or a fool? He really didn't give a damn. All he could think about was Carrie. At least for the time being. For now, the town of Angel Falls and the other lost souls could wait their turn.

CARRIE DROVE TOO FAST on the slush-covered roads, cursing herself all the way. Why in heaven's name had she been so foolish? She'd survive the winter if the house wasn't banked. She simply wouldn't leave on the very cold days, staying close to the fires to

make sure they were putting out enough heat to keep the pipes
from freezing. If they did freeze, she was capable enough to thaw
them with the hair dryer.

She could take care of herself. She ought to eat more. Think
about herself every now and then. When she'd come down with
pneumonia last year, she'd ignored it until only Lars and Maggie's
round-the-clock nursing kept her out of the hospital she couldn't
afford. She mustn't let that happen again.

When it came right down to it, what was more important? Her
uneasy awareness of Gabriel Falconi? Or the debt she owed the
town of Angel Falls?

Never in her life had she been at the mercy of her libido. No,
scratch that. Once, just once in her life had she made a complete
fool of herself over a man. And it hadn't been as simple a matter
as unexpected desire. She had loved Emerson MacVey. It had made
no sense, but beneath those chilly blue eyes, that cool, heartless
elegance she had glimpsed a lost soul.

She'd paid for her foolishness, paid in spades. She wouldn't
make that mistake again. She could resist Gabriel, resist that faint
trace of desire that flared up at unexpected moments.

"Liar," she said out loud, turning into her driveway. It wasn't
a faint trace of desire. It wasn't an uneasy awareness. It was more
powerful every time she saw him, fast becoming an obsession. That
brief, tantalizing kiss had left her shaken, confused and longing for
things she thought she'd given up and wouldn't even miss.

But she could fight it. She knew perfectly well he had the same
sort of awareness of her, that kiss had been more than a hint. But
they were in far different positions. He was self-reliant, a loner, on
his way to a new life. She had the weight of the world on her
shoulders. And there was no room in her life, even temporarily,
for Gabriel Falconi.

She could do it. She was strong, determined. She could make
things clear, in a calm, matter-of-fact way, that there could be nothing between them. And he'd accept it, turn his beautiful gaze toward someone else.

It was the least she could do. She needed help to make it through
the winter, she had to face it. And she could either do what was
painful, almost impossibly difficult, and have Gabriel Falconi
around her house, working, and keep him at a distance. Or she
could ask the Swensens, or someone else in Angel Falls, for help.

And she'd die before she'd do that. For one simple reason. The
town was dying, turning into a ghost town because of the loss of

the mill. Families were splitting apart, people moving away from a place where their grandparents had lived, and Lars Swensen was going to have to go into the woods and risk his life on a dangerous logging site.

No one would accept money from her if she offered them work. They foolishly thought she sacrificed too much for the people of the town as it was. Little did they know she had hardly begun. And that she owed so much more than she could ever repay.

There was one person to blame for all the catastrophes that had hit Angel Falls, and that was Caroline Alexander. If Gabriel Falconi was part of her penance, it was a small enough price to pay.

CHAPTER EIGHT

The tiny house was warm when Carrie walked in. She'd loaded the fires, tossed a few sticks of cinnamon into the bowl of water she kept on top of the stove, and the house smelled of Christmas. She hung her coat on the hook in the hallway and sank down at the kitchen table, folding her hands in front of her.

Something was nagging at the back of her mind, driving her crazy, and she couldn't figure out what it was. It was there, just out of reach of her conscious mind, and she wouldn't be able to concentrate on a thing until she remembered.

At least it had nothing to do with Gabriel Falconi, she knew that instinctively. It had been his presence that had sent the thought skittering away from her, and it would take her sternest self-discipline to call it back. Not to think about strong, work-worn hands, a tall, rangy body and the face of a fallen angel.

Angel, that was it! The angels that Gabriel had carved were beautiful and, oddly, eerily familiar. Lars had recognized Gertrude's expression in that stern old lady angel, as well, but none of them knew the golden-haired boy. No one in Angel Falls had ever seen the man who bore an uncanny resemblance to that innocent angel.

Only Carrie, who'd looked at that youthful face and seen the man she'd once been crazy enough to love.

Indeed, it should have come as no surprise to her that she'd made a fool of herself over Emerson Wyatt MacVey III. In truth, she'd been an accident waiting to happen, an emotional bundle of female ready to fall in love with the first unlikely prospect.

She couldn't dance. What had been astonishingly gifted in Angel Falls, Minnesota, was stunningly mediocre in New York. Her gift was a dime a dozen, her love of the dance worth nothing. She'd left the small dance company where she'd finally managed to land a job, left before they fired her. Accepting failure, accepting the loss of her lifelong dream with what she'd foolishly assumed was a Scandinavian stoicism. Instead, she found she was simply numb.

The pursuit of that dream had taken most of her life. She'd never had time for more than friendships in her adolescent years, too caught up in pursuing her dream of becoming a great dancer, somewhere along the lines of Martha Graham crossed with Twyla Tharp. If it hadn't been for a particularly determined young man in college she would have reached the advanced age of twenty-three still a virgin. As it was, her sexual experience was minimal and not all that exciting when she went to work for Emerson Wyatt MacVey and found herself falling, illogically, head over heels in love with him.

It wasn't as if there were much to recommend him, apart from his rather conventional blond good looks. The women she worked with despised him, he seemed to have no friends, and his prevailing attitude was one of icy condescension toward all and sundry. He was utterly, completely alone.

It was that very aloneness that called to her. She thought she saw vulnerability beneath his remoteness, she thought she saw a wounded child who needed love and compassion. She thought she saw someone she could heal, and in doing so she would heal herself.

She'd been a fool, she knew that now. But back then, three seemingly endless years ago, he'd seemed to be everything she wanted. And the cooler, more foul tempered he was, the more she managed to convince herself that he needed her.

At first it had been subtle enough, her attraction to him. It might have stayed an unfocused maternal feeling if she hadn't seen him with his current girlfriend, seen the remoteness vanish into uncompromising sensuality, in the way he touched the striking young woman, in the way he looked at her. There was no warmth, but there was heat, and Carrie absorbed it, unobserved, shocked to find she wanted that heat directed at her.

She wanted him to notice her. She wanted to please him. In addition to that, she wanted to do something for her friends in Angel Falls, where the only viable industry, the mill, was running into deep trouble.

Emerson MacVey knew how to bring fresh life to failing businesses. He bought and sold them, invested in them, made them profitable. She'd thought if he directed even a fraction of his steel-trap mind toward Precision Industries of Angel Falls, Minnesota, then there would be no more layoffs, no more hard times.

She'd been subtle, knowing he wasn't a man who responded to pressure tactics, simply mentioning it in passing. The morning, early in December, when he'd stopped by her desk and asked her to get him all the information about Precision Industries had been a triumphant one. It was the beginning of the Christmas season, and she was going to secure for her hometown the greatest Christmas gift of all.

He wasn't a man who had affairs with his underlings. He wasn't a man who was prey to any weakness whatsoever. But the night of December twenty-third Carrie had come back to the office late, to pick up a present she'd left behind. MacVey was due at a fundraiser with his polished girlfriend, and the place would be deserted.

It wasn't. She used her key, letting herself into the tastefully decorated suite of offices, and began rummaging through her desk for the present she'd bought earlier that day, when she heard a sound from the inner office.

Music. Christmas music, but not the cheery kind. Something classical and Gregorian, more like a dirge than a carol. And she heard the clink of ice in a glass.

She stood motionless, feeling absurdly guilty. Wondering if he was alone behind that partially closed door. Wondering what he was doing.

Emerson Wyatt MacVey wouldn't be doing anything undignified, inappropriate or impulsive. She pushed the door open just slightly, thinking she'd ask if he needed anything.

He was sitting behind his glass-and-chrome desk, a bleak, cold expression on his handsome face. His blue eyes were distant, his Armani suit jacket had been discarded, his Egyptian-cotton shirt unbuttoned. She'd never seen him without a tie. With his blond hair ruffled. She'd never seen him with any emotion other than faint contempt.

"What the hell are you doing here?"

He never swore, either. His voice was rough, and she knew he'd been drinking. His eyes were red, but she didn't think that came from the amber-colored liquid in the glass beside his elegant hand.

"I left something."

"Go away."

She knew she should. MacVey was a private man—he wouldn't want her seeing him vulnerable. And vulnerable he was right now. Her heart cried out for him, and she stepped inside the room, closing the heavy door behind her. "Let me get you some coffee," she said gently.

He glared at her. "I don't need coffee. I've gone to a great deal of trouble to get drunk tonight, and I'm certainly not going to ruin the effect by drinking coffee. I'm not nearly drunk enough. You can go out and buy me more Scotch."

She shook her head, crossing the room to stand in front of the desk. "What happened?"

"'What happened?'" he mimicked, his voice savage. "Do you want to soothe my fevered brow, Carrie? Nothing happened, nothing whatsoever. It's Christmas, and I hate Christmas. The only suitable response was to get drunk."

"Where's Ms. Barrow?"

"Left me for another man."

"I see."

"No, you don't," he shot back. "You think I'm here drowning my sorrows because she left me. She was good in bed. Period. She was elegant to look at, and she didn't ask me stupid questions. But she wanted 'commitment.'" His voice was mocking. "She wanted 'intimacy.' She wanted me to bleed all over her, and I bleed for no woman."

"So why are you getting drunk?"

"A tribute to the season. Goodwill toward men, and all that crap."

She reached out for his half-filled glass of whisky, but his hand shot out and caught her wrist, stopping her. He hurt her, but she knew he didn't mean to. He just didn't realize how strong he was. They stayed that way for a moment, unmoving, as he sat there watching her, her wrist imprisoned in his hand.

And then his eyes narrowed, and a faint, mocking smile began to form on his thin mouth. And his thumb caressed her wrist. "You have a crush on me, don't you?"

Color flooded her face, and she tried to pull away. "Don't be ridiculous."

"I know the signs. It happens often enough, God knows why. It's usually the younger ones, who think I just need a good woman to make me happy. I don't need a good woman, Carrie."

"I'm sure you don't," she said stiffly. He released her finally, and she could still feel the warmth of his skin where he'd held her. "I'll be going now."

He rose, circling his desk, coming after her. Stalking her, though that notion was absurd in such a civilized man. "I just need a woman," he said, his voice low and cool and undeniably beguiling. "Do you want to be that woman, Carrie? Do you want to see whether you can save me?"

She'd reached the door, pulled it open, but his arm shot out and slammed it. She spun around, leaning up against it, staring at him. He wasn't much taller than she was, and in his cool, determined face she could still see the look of a lost child. One she wanted to comfort.

He stood there, his arms imprisoning her, his body not touching her. "It's up to you, Carrie," he said in a low voice. "Do you want me to let you go?"

He was warm. No, he was hot. He was staring at her out of pale, sensual eyes, and for the first time in her life she felt intense sexual attraction.

She would have denied it. She would have fought it, but her brain had melted, and somehow she thought that if she didn't take it, seize it, seize the moment, then the chance would never come again.

"No," she said, staring at him.

"No, what?"

"No, I don't want you to let me go."

He smiled then, a slow, cool smile that should have warned her. And then he set his mouth against hers, and no force in heaven or on earth could have stopped her.

He tasted of whisky. He tasted of coffee. He tasted of anger and despair. And all she wanted to taste was love.

She didn't want to remember that night, but there were times when it still haunted her, sleepless nights when she could feel his hands on her body.

He'd pulled her down onto the thick shag carpet and taken her fully dressed, only her serviceable cotton underwear flung away. He'd taken her on the leather sofa, naked, slippery, with the city lights all around them. He'd taken her leaning against the sink of his private washroom, he'd taken her in the marble shower stall. He'd taken her, had sex with her, shown her things she hadn't even imagined about her body that she thought she knew so well. The only thing he hadn't done was make love to her.

She had no illusions when she left just before dawn, left him sprawled and sleeping on the wide leather sofa, a cashmere blanket thrown over him. He hadn't allowed her to say a word of love, of affection, he hadn't allowed a caress from her. She was the recipient of his angry passion.

She was late to work the next morning. By the time she reached the office the other secretaries were bustling around importantly, and Megan greeted her with a grimace. "You had to pick today of all days to be late?" she questioned caustically.

Carrie wasn't about to give her the real reason. "It's Christmas Eve. No one does much business on Christmas Eve."

"You forget we're working for the Grinch. He was already at work when I arrived here this morning, and he's in the midst of dismantling one of his recent acquisitions. Nice job for the Christmas season."

Carrie had known. The sense of disaster had hung about her like a dark angel from the moment she'd left his arms that morning, and she'd tried to fight it off. "What do you mean?"

"You know as well as I do what he does," Megan snapped. "He buys up companies and guts them for parts, makes a huge profit, and leaves disaster in his wake. Lord knows why he picked on a small factory in Minnesota for destruction. There must be a profit in it somewhere."

"Where in Minnesota?" She barely recognized her voice.

"That's right, you come from around there, don't you?" Megan popped a chocolate into her mouth, staring at her coolly. "It's a place called Precision Industries in Angel Falls. He's sold the equipment to a company in Utah, he's closing the plant, and right now he's deciding between an offer from someone to dismantle the building for scrap or to just leave it a rusting hulk as a tax loss. Nice Christmas gift for that town."

"I have to see him."

"As a matter of fact—" Megan sounded a little more human "—I'm afraid he's got a little Christmas gift for you." She handed Carrie a long envelope.

Carrie just stared at it for a moment. She didn't want to take it, but the other two women in the office were watching her, as well, and the only thing she could salvage was her pride.

She took it with a brief, unconcerned smile. "I need to talk to him."

Megan shook her head. "He said no. I've already cleared your desk for you. You'll find your severance package more than generous. You can continue with your medical coverage, and you've got severance pay…"

Carrie opened the envelope. The check was there, insultingly large. Along with a scrawled note. One word, written in his bold, slashing handwriting. "Sorry."

Carrie ripped the envelope in half and dropped it onto the floor. "I don't need any benefits," she said. "I just want to see him."

"He's authorized me to call security if you prove difficult."

Carrie just looked at her. Without a word, she turned and walked from the building, leaving the pathetic box of her belongings behind her, leaving her heart and her innocence behind her.

She hated him. She wanted to kill him, she who was the gentlest of creatures. He'd destroyed her, he'd destroyed her town, for nothing more than a whim and a profit. She had no illusions about why he'd fired her. She'd seen him at his most vulnerable last night. He wouldn't want a reminder of that.

And he wasn't even man enough to face her, to tell her himself. He let his secretary do the dirty work, and if she had any sense at all she'd hate him. And she would, as soon as she got over the shock, as soon as her mind settled, as soon as she realized...

She'd never seen the taxi. One moment she was struggling for her sanity, the next she was struggling for her life. By the time she was well enough to think about Emerson Wyatt MacVey, he was already dead of a heart attack. And all she could do was cry.

She hadn't wanted to think about him, Carrie thought, staring out into the snowy Minnesota countryside. She thought she'd been able to put him out of her mind, concentrating instead on somehow making things better for the poor beleaguered town she'd brought to destruction. Atonement, penance, all those nice, stern biblical phrases that had little to do with the innocent joy of Christmas.

But ever since Gabriel Falconi had shown up at her doorstep she'd been thinking about Emerson. Remembering.

She had no difficulty understanding why, whether she wanted to accept the truth or not. Gabriel and Emerson had absolutely nothing in common, apart from an odd kindred expression in the back of the eyes, one she couldn't even begin to define.

The only thing they shared was Carrie Alexander.

For the first time since Emerson MacVey she was attracted to someone. She didn't like it, didn't want to accept it, but denying it seemed impossible. She was attracted to Gabriel, with his deep, slow voice, his strong hands, his angelic beauty and his tall, graceful body. And it was only logical that her attraction would bring back memories of the last man she'd been fool enough to want.

She couldn't deny her attraction, but that didn't mean she had to give in to it. She'd done her best to make it clear to Gabriel that she wasn't in the market for a brief affair with an itinerant carpenter. She wasn't in the market for a long-term commitment with Prince Charming, for that matter. She wasn't going to think about her wants, her needs, her weaknesses. She had her penance, and nothing was going to get in the way of it.

She should eat something, she knew it. A lifetime of watching her weight had left her with little interest in food, but she knew she had to keep her strength up. She should open a can of soup, then start work on the Christmas quilt she was making for Mrs. Robbins.

It needed to be special. Mrs. Robbins had commissioned it as a Christmas present for her only granddaughter, the granddaughter she hadn't been able to buy a wedding present for. The amount Carrie was charging her wouldn't even cover the materials, but Mrs. Robbins didn't know that. It was just one small thing Carrie could do to try to make amends.

Mrs. Robbins was only one of the people whose lives had been torn apart by the closing of the mill. Her two sons had lost their jobs, and they'd already taken their families and relocated to Saint Cloud. The only family the elderly lady had living nearby was her newly married granddaughter, and she was there on borrowed time. If there were no jobs, they wouldn't be able to afford to stay, and Mrs. Robbins would be alone.

Fresh snow was falling, and a brisk north wind was whipping the flakes against the house. Carrie hoped it wouldn't be a windy winter. The old house was snug enough as long as the wind didn't blow. Once it did, not even the wood stove could make a dent in the chill that invaded the place.

Gabriel would come over tomorrow and fix up the banking around the foundation, repair some of the windows, make things snug and tight. In return she'd give him some of the money she had saved, the small amount she was parceling out to the needy. She didn't know why she thought Gabriel was needy. Maybe it was that look in his eyes, so different and yet oddly like Emerson's. And she'd never known a man more needy than Emerson Wyatt MacVey.

She had to stop thinking about him. Had to stop thinking about Gabriel Falconi, for that matter. She wasn't interested in sex—it only led to disaster. She wasn't interested in love, either. Falling in love with Emerson MacVey had been the worst mistake of her life. She had trusted him, and he'd turned out to be a conscienceless snake. It didn't mean she no longer loved him. But she never should have put her town into his ruthless hands. Not to mention her heart.

It was past time for regrets. It was the first Sunday in Advent, Christmas was coming, and despite their depressed economy Angel Falls was going to have the best damned Christmas in memory. Carrie was determined.

GABRIEL STOOD in his tiny room at the Swensens', stooped under the eaves, looking out at the snow-covered town to the factory on the hill. As industrial buildings went, it wasn't a bad-looking building. If only it were someplace like Massachusetts it could have been turned into a trendy apartment building, or an upscale mall.

But the people of Angel Falls had no way to pay for trendy apartments or upscale malls. They could barely afford to live in this demanding climate, much less treat themselves to the luxuries that had once bored him.

And it was his fault. He no longer had any doubts about that— it had been MacVey's corporate greed that had gutted this economy, sending the town on a downhill slide just as the country was pulling itself out of its decline. He could no longer remember the details, or even why he'd done it. That life was becoming hazier and hazier, the man who'd done those deeds seemed only a distant kin to Gabriel Falconi.

But done it he had. And there was no doubt where his second miracle had to come from. He had to somehow make things right, if not for the whole damned town, at least for the Swensen family.

Three years ago it would have been simple. He had money and power to spare. Now he had a gold credit card, a few hundred dollars in cash, and a miracle per person, a power he needed to use wisely.

He glanced over at the book on his dresser. He never read novels, never had the time for them, and he doubted Gertrude/Augusta meant more than a jab at his temporary security. Still, the Swensens were busy with family activities, and he didn't want to intrude. His truck was still broken down, and the wind was howling outside, whipping the snow into a frenzy. He was in no mood to go for a walk.

Unless Carrie Alexander's house was within walking distance, and he knew full well it wasn't. He only had a few weeks here, and he didn't want to waste a moment of it.

But she'd looked frightened of him. He'd recognized that when she'd looked up at him, and he wondered what scared her. His kiss? Or something else?

What had MacVey done to her? For some reason his memory remained blank. He knew he'd fired her—Augusta had gleefully informed him of that. And that she'd been the only one to cry for him when he died.

Had she loved him? He knew he couldn't have slept with her—

Emerson MacVey had been a conscienceless scum but he didn't sleep with his secretaries.

But there was something there. Something in that cockeyed triangle that existed uneasily between them. Between Carrie and Gabriel and his old self. And he wasn't going to get any further with rescuing Carrie until he found out what it was.

He turned away from the snowy landscape, from the brooding hulk of the old brick factory, and picked up the book. The room was chilly with the door closed, so he burrowed down under the quilt Carrie had made. It was soft, warm, and smelled like her perfume. If only she was there with him.

A stupid thought, one Augusta would probably hear from halfway across town and punish him for. This mission was doomed from the start—he might as well enjoy the small amount of time he'd been allotted and then take his punishment like a man.

Opening up the book, he began to read.

CHAPTER NINE

Oh, God, it smelled like cookies. Cinnamon and spice, ginger wafting through the small, decrepit farmhouse when Gabriel let himself in the next morning. Coffee, as well, with the tang of hazelnut to sweeten it. He wasn't sure how he knew it was hazelnut, but there was no doubt in his mind.

Cookies were laid out on sheets of wax paper all over the spotless kitchen. Some with red and green sprinkles, others pressed into ornate shapes. The coffee was on the stove in an old aluminum drip pot, and he could hear the steady splash as it brewed.

The place was bursting with warmth, but then, it was a moderate day outside. He was rapidly growing used to the chill temperatures of Minnesota, so that a sunny high of twenty degrees seemed positively balmy. He shrugged out of the ancient peacoat that seemed to be Gabriel Falconi's defense against the winter and hung it on the wooden peg near the door.

The old house was filled with comfortable sounds, as well as smells. The drip of the coffee, the crackle of the fire, the sound of the shower running. And Carrie's voice, loud and tuneful and surprisingly cheery, singing "God rest ye merry, gentlefolk."

Surely that was wrong? "Merry, gentlemen," wasn't it supposed to be? Lord help him, Carrie Alexander must be a closet feminist, as well as a saint set on self-destruction.

In the past there had been nothing that annoyed MacVey more than feminists. For some reason this morning Gabriel found himself smiling. God rest ye, merry gentlefolk, indeed. It sounded better that way.

Her wood box needed filling. Despite the fact that there was nothing he would have liked better than to sit at her table and drink coffee and eat cookies and wait to see whether she'd emerge from the shower fully dressed or not, the distant memory of Augusta's stern eyes squashed that temptation. It took him three trips to fill the wood box, and he deliberately made enough noise so she wouldn't make the mistake of emerging from the bathroom in a towel, but he still felt a shaft of disappointment when she greeted him at the door wearing a turtleneck tunic that reached from her chin to her knees.

He rose above his baser nature to realize it was a wonderful piece of clothing. Bright red and Christmassy, it was made of a soft cottony yarn, and it molded against her reed-slim dancer's body and moved with her grace.

And then he frowned. She was more than reed slim. She was downright skinny. "You're too thin," he said as he stomped the snow off his feet and kicked the door shut behind him, sounding more gruff than he'd meant to.

Carrie blinked in surprise, and then a slow, luscious smile curved her pale face. "Good morning to you, too," she said cheerfully. "Thanks for filling the wood box. Do you want some coffee?"

"Yes," he said, knowing he sounded grumpy. He moved past her into the living room, dumping the wood with a loud crash before turning to look at her. Her skin was flushed from her shower, and this morning she didn't look the slightest bit wary. She looked firm, decisive, in control. And he found himself wondering if he could make her lose her control.

She'd already moved back into the kitchen, pouring them both mugs of the fragrant coffee, and he told himself he was there to save her, not to sleep with her. He took one of the pressed-back chairs, spun it around and straddled it, accepting the coffee from her with a muttered thanks.

She took the chair farthest from him, a fact that pleased him. Obviously she wasn't as secure as she wanted him to believe. He liked that. "Have a cookie," he said, taking a sip of the coffee. It was good enough to die for.

Carrie shook her head. "I'm not hungry. You have some."

"You're never hungry. You don't eat enough to keep a bird alive."

"Birds eat three times their weight every day."

"You're awfully sassy for a woman who's starving to death."

"I'm not." The light still danced in her eyes, and she seemed to have forgotten she was going to be stern with him. She reached out and took a cookie, popping it into her mouth defiantly.

"Who are the cookies for?"

"What makes you think they're not for me?" she countered.

"Because as far as I can tell, you don't do a damned thing for yourself."

She ate another cookie. "I don't think that's any of your business."

Gabriel shrugged. "I suppose it isn't. I guess I'm just not used to being around saints."

"I'm hardly that." She took a third cookie without realizing it. It was a gingerbread man, and she bit off his head with her sharp white teeth. "As a matter of fact, I've spent too much of my life around people who were only out for their own good. Who squashed anyone or anything that got in their way."

She was talking about MacVey, he knew it. He took a meditative sip of his coffee. "Whoever he was, he obviously didn't appreciate you."

"What are you talking about?" She'd devoured cookie number three, and was on her way into number four, an ornate, pecan-studded horn.

"The man who squashed anyone or anything that got in his way. I take it you were one of the ones he squashed."

He wondered if he'd pushed her too far. He wanted to know what she really thought of Emerson MacVey. Did she still hate him? Did she have reason to? Damn it, if only he could remember!

She put the half-eaten cookie down. "If you're finished with your coffee I can show you what needs doing around here."

"Did you love him?"

He wasn't sure what he expected. Not the faint shadow of sorrow that danced in her blue eyes, not the wry, self-deprecatory smile that curved her mouth. "I did," she said, rising from the table with her dancer's grace. "Hearts are made to be broken, Gabriel. Trust is made to be betrayed. End of discussion." She started toward the door, but Gabriel forestalled her.

"Do you still love him?"

She turned to look up at him. It was still a strange feeling, looking down into her blue eyes. In the past, he hadn't been that much taller than she was.

In the past, he remembered with sudden, shocking clarity, he'd covered her body with his, and the fit had been perfect. She'd wrapped her legs around him, taken him inside her, and for one night and one night alone he'd lost himself and his miserable existence in the sweet pliant warmth of her body.

"He's dead," she said flatly. Her eyes narrowed. "Are you all right? You look as if you'd seen a ghost."

"I just remembered something," he muttered, still reeling from it.

"It mustn't have been anything pleasant."

"I wouldn't say that," he managed to drawl. "So your true love broke your heart, betrayed your trust and then died. It must give you comfort to think of him roasting in the flames of hell for what he did to you.''

"I'm not into revenge, Gabriel,'' she said. "And besides, I don't believe in hell.''

"Do you believe in heaven?''

"Yes.''

"Then what's the good of heaven without hell?''

She smiled then, and her mood seemed to lighten. "When you find out, Gabriel, be sure to let me know.''

It was moments like these, Gabriel thought, watching her step out into the bright winter sunshine, that scared the hell out of him.

She didn't know. She couldn't know. If he tried to tell her she wouldn't believe him. But the eerie appropriateness of her words haunted him as he followed her out into the day.

CARRIE BEGAN BOXING UP the cookies in the various tins she'd been collecting. The sound of a hammer echoed pleasantly beneath the sound of Christmas music on the old stereo, and she smiled to herself as she worked. Gabriel was outside, fixing the banking around the sagging foundation of the old farmhouse, and the steady sound of his work was as soothing as the smell of cinnamon and coffee. He'd looked faintly surprised when she'd shown him around the place, enumerating the things that needed to be done. She wasn't quite sure what he expected.

He might have thought she'd asked him out here for the sake of his beautiful face, but he would have been wrong. He must be used to women coming up with excuses to have him around. There simply weren't that many men who looked like that, with a quiet, nonthreatening manner besides. Not that he was as quiet as he seemed. There was a sharp, mocking intelligence at war with the gentleness in his dark eyes. Whenever she looked at him, really looked, she had the odd notion she was looking into the eyes of two different people.

He was right about one thing, she hadn't manufactured the work she had him do. It was needed, but in other circumstances she would have let it wait.

But he was a stranger in town, stranded, with no work and no money. It was her fault the factory had closed down, her responsibility to help those affected by it. If Precision Industries were still a viable alternative, Gabriel could have worked there through the holiday season.

He wasn't a man who asked for help, a man who wanted to accept help. She could understand that—she felt the same way. There were a great many people in town whose pride got in the way of their need, and Carrie had grown adept at circumventing that pride.

Because there was a major difference between her and the people of Angel Falls. They didn't deserve their misfortune. She did.

She'd berated her ego time and time again. If only she hadn't thought she could save the world. Save the factory, save her beloved Angel Falls, save Emerson MacVey. Instead, her well-meaning actions had brought despair and disaster. And Emerson MacVey had doubtless forgotten her existence months before he died.

Why did she keep thinking about him? Ever since Thanksgiving he'd been haunting her dreams, her waking hours, as well. She'd thought she'd gotten past it all, down to the point where she only thought about him once or twice a week. But suddenly it was all fresh and new, the heat of her attraction to him, the pain of his betrayal, the shock and sorrow of his death. She'd come to terms with it all, knowing her energies needed to be channeled into making a difference, not bemoaning the past.

But he seemed to be hovering just beyond her consciousness, a ghost, a spirit, a longing that she hadn't quite recovered from. She wondered if she ever would.

She wrapped a bright velvet ribbon around the last tin and sighed. They were a small enough offering, but they were something, and she had her deliveries to make that afternoon, once she was certain Gabriel had enough to do. She sank down at the round table, muttering a tired "damn." She'd forgotten to eat yesterday, and sugar cookies for breakfast along with black coffee weren't the most nutritious choice.

She leaned her head back, but the room began to swirl around her. She needed to get up and put wood on the stove, she needed to get up and answer the telephone that had just started ringing. She tried to rise, but the swirling surrounded her once more, and she felt herself start to fall into the blackness. She put out a hand to save herself, but there was no one there, she was alone, in the darkness, and she was falling, falling...

He caught her. Warm strong hands reached for her, pulled her back from that abyss, held her against a hard, muscled body. She could hear his voice, almost from a distance, cursing, she could feel the panicked beat of his heart as he lifted her in his arms. She wanted to say something, to tell him not to make such a fuss, but for some reason the words weren't coming, and she had to close her eyes, to lean her head against his shoulder.

Lord, he had nice shoulders, she thought dizzily. Strong, slightly bony, but so comfortable beneath the faded flannel shirt. She wanted to bury her face against that soft flannel. He smelled of wood smoke and fresh lumber and hazelnut coffee, and she wondered what his mouth would taste like. If she only moved her head a fraction of an inch she would find out.

He set her down on the sofa, and she clung to him for a moment, unwilling to let him go. He was warmth, safety, he was someone she didn't need to take care of. He was someone who would scare away the demons and keep her safe, and she was so tired of fighting.

And then she released him, sinking back against the sofa, her eyes closed. "Sorry," she murmured faintly.

"What happened?"

His voice was rough with concern, and his hands were in her hair, pushing the strands away from her face. She didn't want to open her eyes. If she did, she'd find him staring down at her, and she wasn't sure if she could keep the longing from her own eyes.

"You're right," she said. "I don't eat enough. Too much sugar and caffeine on an empty stomach."

"Damn," he said.

She opened her eyes at that, managed a weak smile. "Don't worry, it's happened before. I'll just make myself a cup of tea and some toast and I'll be fine..."

"You'll stay right there," he said fiercely.

His beautiful face looked enchantingly stern. "Listen, I'm okay," she said, trying to sit up, but Gabriel put one of his large, beautiful hands smack in the middle of her chest and pushed her back down again.

"Stay put," he said, "or I'll sit on you. I'm making you soup, hot milk, toast, and anything else I can find."

His words sent sudden panic through her. "I'm not hungry. Gabriel..."

But he was already rummaging around in the kitchen. She struggled to sit up, but the room whirled around her, and eventually she gave up. She just needed a moment or two to compose herself, and then she'd explain to him...

"You have no food in this house."

He was back too soon, and she wasn't quite up to arguing with him. "Of course I do," she said weakly. "There are at least ten dozen cookies..."

"You have a little bit of sugar and flour left over, and that's that. No milk, no bread, a couple of tea bags, a can of tomato paste, and a can of okra, for heaven's sake. Why in the world would you have a can of okra sitting on your shelves?"

"It was the only thing I couldn't bring myself to eat," she said, unable to resist. "I just haven't had a chance to get to the store recently. I was planning to go out this afternoon after I got you started. I'm going to deliver the cookies and then stop by the store and stock up on my way home."

"You're not driving anywhere."

"I beg your pardon?"

"If you want to go to the store I'll drive you. If you passed out behind the wheel and killed someone I'd never forgive myself." He looked half-surprised at his own words, but nevertheless completely stubborn.

"I'm not going to endanger anyone else," she said quietly.

"When you don't take proper care of yourself you endanger everyone else's peace of mind. Consider that the next time you forget to eat."

She couldn't argue with him. It was an unpalatable truth. Whether she deserved it or not, the people of Angel Falls cared about her. And the odd thing was, she knew they'd love her even when they knew the truth about what had happened to the factory. That it hadn't been some random choice of a power-mad conglomerate. That in her misguided efforts to play God she'd brought about its destruction.

"You can drive me to the store," she said wearily, the fight suddenly leaving her. "But you'll still be getting paid."

"You don't have anything better to do with your money in a town like this?" he countered. "I have to go to the store, too."

She sat up, and the whirling had blessedly stopped, at least for now. "You know, Gabriel, you have the most annoying habit of being right?" she said.

"I do my humble best. You feel up to going now?"

What she wanted to do was crawl under the covers and go to sleep. She was so tired, not even the rest of the pot of coffee could put energy into her. But Gabriel wasn't going to let her hide. Taking him on as another one of her pet projects might prove to be a costly mistake in a life strewn with mistakes.

"Now's as good a time as any," she said brightly, doubting

she'd fooled him even for a moment. Those oddly familiar brown eyes could see her far too clearly.

An hour later she knew she should have been firm. They'd dropped the cookies off at the church, where the Ladies' Fellowship would distribute them, and then headed on to Martinsen's supermarket. Everyone had watched as they traversed the aisles, benign expressions on their faces, and she knew just what they were thinking. And the fact that in another lifetime, she would have wanted it to be true, only made it worse.

To top things off, Gabriel kept throwing things into her grocery cart. A dozen cans of chicken-rice soup, at eighty cents a can. Fruit juice, the expensive kind, imported crackers, yogurt, pasta, garlic, onions...

"What are you doing?" she demanded as he tossed a package of frozen bread sticks into the overflowing basket. "This is too much food for one person."

"Most of it'll keep. And I'm making you dinner tonight."

"Gabriel..."

"Carrie..." he mimicked right back, looking down at her and smiling.

For a moment she couldn't breathe. For a moment all memory of Emerson MacVey and the lifetime of stupid mistakes vanished, as she looked up into the warm brown eyes of Gabriel Falconi and fell in love.

The noise of the store was all around her. Old Mrs. Johannsen was moving past her, heading for the taco chips, Mr. Draper was over by the magazine rack, staring longingly at the computer magazines, and Jeffie Baker was standing near the wine rack looking furtive. Carrie was aware of all of them, but for a moment all she could concentrate on was the man in front of her, so close she could feel his body heat, so close all she had to do was sway against him and his strong arms would come around her and hold her tight and safe.

And then reality intruded. She pulled herself away, turning to watch Jeffie tuck a bottle of wine beneath his bulky down parka.

She didn't think she'd said a word, just made a quiet little sound of distress. No one else noticed what had happened. No one but Gabriel.

He moved with a speed and grace surprising in such a big man. With seeming clumsiness he bumped into Jeffie, knocking him against a small display of wine. The bottle he'd stolen fell with a thump onto the carpeted floor, along with half-a-dozen others.

"God, I'm clumsy," said Gabriel, who had to be the least awkward man Carrie had ever seen. He set the wine bottle back up on the stand, taking the one Jeffie had tried to steal and putting it back where it belonged on the shelf. The small crowd involved in midday shopping quickly returned to their own interests, and the conversation between Jeffie and Gabriel was low pitched enough not to reach her ears.

It looked pleasant enough, if earnest. Jeffie obviously thought Gabriel was God. She only hoped Gabriel had the sense not to humiliate him. It was hard enough to be seventeen, and even harder if you were blessed with such mindlessly intellectual twits as Jeffie had for parents.

She made a furtive trip down the aisles, hoping she'd be able to put a few things back, but Gabriel caught up with her just as she was reshelving the horridly expensive chicken soup, and he took the can out of her hand. "I gave him hell," he said pleasantly.

She was shocked. "You didn't! He's sensitive, Gabriel, you might make things worse...."

"For some reason he takes it from me. Maybe he's just grateful for the attention. He needs someone to knock some sense into him. If my father had caught me doing something like that I wouldn't have sat down for a week."

"But Jeffie's father doesn't even notice."

"I know what that's like, too."

"Make up your mind, Gabriel. Either your father ignored you or he taught you right from wrong. Which is it?"

"I have a vivid imagination. Let's get out of here." He reached over and took two more cans of chicken soup and threw them into the cart.

She didn't have enough money to pay for all the things he'd taken from the shelves. Not and pay him, too, and give Pastor Krieger the money she'd promised for the Christmas fund. People needed that money, to buy food, to buy fuel, far more than she did.

She stared up at him in mute distress, unwilling to tell him the truth. She'd forgotten how astute he was behind those warm brown eyes.

"Why don't you go out to the car and wait for me?" he suggested calmly.

"I have to pay for the groceries."

"No, you don't."

"Yes, I do," she said furiously. "I don't take charity..."

"I know, you give it. Too damned bad, Saint Carrie. I chose this food, I'm paying for it, and I have every intention of eating a good portion of it. If you want to have a screaming row in the middle of the local grocery store I'd be more than happy to give it to you."

"I don't have screaming rows," she said between clenched teeth.

"Maybe you should. It would be good for you."

She stared up at him. The damnable thing about him was he was right. He was bringing up emotions, feelings she thought she'd managed to squash in her effort to atone for her sins. In the week since he'd arrived in Angel Falls she'd experienced lust, love, longing and sheer fury, when all she was used to feeling was quiet regret. It was oddly unnerving.

"I'll write you a check," she said tightly, enjoying the race of blood in her veins, enjoying her temper.

"You do that. When I'm finished my work, you can add it in. After Christmas, when I'm ready to leave."

"I don't have that much work to keep you busy," she protested.

"I take my time. Pay me after Christmas."

She wanted to hit him. She who never had hit anyone in her entire life. She whirled around and stalked toward the door, her dignity around her like a cloak. Mrs. Johannsen's knowing smile only irked her more.

He was out in five minutes, with four overflowing bags of groceries. He was humming under his breath as he stowed them in the back of her car, something familiar yet oddly jaunty. She recognized it with a start of shock. It was an up-tempo version of the Gregorian dirge that passed for Emerson MacVey's taste in Christmas music.

"How did you manage to pay for all that?" she demanded grumpily. "I thought you didn't have much money."

"Yeah, but I have a gold credit card," he said, sliding behind the driver's seat.

"Credit cards have to be paid off sooner or later."

For a moment he looked abashed. Then he started the car. "Don't worry," he drawled. "My credit card's got a rock-solid guarantee."

"Fasten your seat belt."

"You *are* in a grumpy mood, aren't you?" he said cheerfully. "I don't believe in them."

"In my car you wear seat belts," she snapped.

"Yes, ma'am." He seemed almost pleased by her bad temper. "But trust me, it won't matter."

"It can be the difference between life and death."

"Not in my case."

He drove well. Not too fast, his big hands resting on her steering wheel. She tried not to watch him, tried to concentrate on the melting slush on the back roads. Her temper was fading, guilt was setting in. He was only trying to help her, and she was an ungrateful, self-centered bitch to fight him.

"I'm sorry."

"I knew that would happen. Don't be sorry, Carrie. Be mad. I'm high-handed, and you like to be Lady Bountiful. It drives you crazy to have to accept anything in return. Admit it."

"I'm trying to be gracious," she said sharply.

"I like you better when you're honest."

"I don't give a damn what you like."

He turned and smiled at her, that wide, beautiful smile that would have melted the resolve of a saint. "Yes, you do," he murmured, then turned his attention back to the road, humming once more.

"Aren't you driving a little too fast?" she roused herself long enough to ask. The road was wide and blessedly deserted, but her car seemed to be picking up speed as they started down a long winding hill. "This isn't the Indianapolis 500, you know."

"I know." There was a certain tension in his voice, and the hands on the steering wheel were no longer gripping it loosely.

"Then why are you driving so fast?"

He didn't turn to look at her. His face looked grim in the winter light. "Because, Saint Carrie," he said with deceptive calm, "you don't seem to have any brakes."

CHAPTER TEN

He was a hell of a good driver. He realized that later on, but for the moment he'd been too intent on keeping Carrie alive to even think about it. Just as well. Emerson MacVey had been a clumsy, careless driver, treating his Mercedes with a singular lack of respect. If Gabriel had taken the time to consider it they might have ended up wrapped around a tree.

Carrie hadn't said a word as he wrestled with the speeding momentum of the car as it careened toward the bottom of the last hill before her old farmhouse, and he hadn't taken the time to do more than glance at her. Her face was pale, her hands were tightly clasped, but she looked serene, damn it. As if she were waiting for death.

The thought infuriated him enough to make him stomp on the gas just as they slid into a curve. It provided enough momentum to avoid a lethal clump of trees, but then the car went spinning, spinning, across the ice-covered road, finally coming to a shuddering halt. They sat in complete silence for a moment, and then he turned to look at her.

"Are you okay?" His voice was harsh, angry, and he didn't bother to disguise it.

She reached down for her seat belt, and he noticed with fury that her hands weren't even shaking. "Fine. You're a very good driver."

"Don't you even care?" he exploded.

She stared at him in blank surprise. "About what?"

"You could have died. It was a damned close call—we were headed straight for that clump of trees."

"But we didn't," she pointed out with maddening calm.

"But we might have."

She climbed out of the car. "The house is just over the next rise. We might as well start walking."

He tried to follow her, forgetting that he'd put his seat belt on. His own hands were shaking, a fact that infuriated him even further, and then he was following her as she trudged determinedly up the snowy hill.

He didn't say another word as they made their way the quarter mile or so to the house. He didn't worry about her getting too cold in the threadbare coat she was wearing—he was so damned mad it was lucky the entire state of Minnesota didn't melt under the heat of his fury. He followed her into the kitchen, slammed the door behind him, and caught her by the arm as she was starting to pull off her snow-covered coat.

"Do you have a death wish?" he demanded harshly.

She held very still, looking up at him. The snow had melted in her silky blond hair, dampened her long eyelashes, and he couldn't mistake the heated flicker of sexual awareness before she did her best to tamp it down, to give him that maternal, wise look that only increased his fury.

"I'm pragmatic enough to know that when it's my time, there's not much I can do about it. I'm not afraid of death."

"No," he said. "You're afraid of life."

Her face whitened, and she yanked at her arm, trying to free herself. He had no intention of letting her go. "What I'm afraid of is none of your business."

"You're afraid of life, of getting hurt, of making mistakes. You set yourself up as the saint of Angel Falls, ministering to the poor, soothing the weary, healing the sick. Too bad the lake's frozen over or you could show me how you walk on water."

She yanked again, and it only brought her up closer against his body. She was hot, he was hot, and he wondered that the kitchen didn't ignite. "Maybe I have a reason," she said furiously. "Maybe I need to make up to these people for the harm I've done them. Maybe I need to atone..."

"Atone for what? I can't imagine anything you might have done that would be so terrible."

"Then you haven't got a very good imagination."

He stared down at her for a long meditative moment. Her lips were soft, trembling now from anger and emotion, whereas her brush with death had left her unmoved. "I wouldn't say that," he murmured. "When I look at you I can imagine all sorts of things."

For the third time she tried to pull away. She backed up against the basement door, but he was with her, his body pressed up against her, and he wanted to see if he remembered the taste of her mouth, the feel of her body. He wanted to taste the life she was so blasé about losing.

He expected more resistance from her. He put his hand beneath her chin, tilting her face up, and took her mouth with a deep, searing kiss. Her hands were on his shoulders, but instead of pushing him away she was clinging to him. Her lips parted beneath his and she let him kiss her.

He tore his mouth away and stared down at her. "More charity, Carrie?" he said. "How far does your saintliness extend? Passive kisses? Or are you willing to take off your clothes and lie down for the poor itinerant stranger in need of comfort?"

He'd managed to reach behind that calm maternal facade, and her fingers dug into his shoulders as she tried to push him away. "You're disgusting," she said.

"No, I'm not. I'm human. At least for now. And I want you more than I've ever wanted anyone in my life. But I don't want a passive saint sacrificing her virtue. I want someone who wants me in return. I want a woman, not a martyr."

"Damn you," she began furiously.

"That's better," he murmured, and kissed her again.

This time there was no passivity about her. There was fury, passion, everything he'd ever wanted from her. She slid her arms around his neck, slanted her mouth beneath his, and kissed him back.

She was awkward, endearingly, erotically awkward at it, as if she hadn't been kissed enough lately. He remembered that about her. He cupped her face, his long fingers soothing her hair back away from her cheeks, and gentled the kiss, coaxing her, and the soft moan from the back of her throat rewarded him. He could feel her small breasts against his chest. Even through the thick layers of flannel he could feel her nipples harden in undeniable response, and he pulled her more tightly against him, wanting to drown in the physical sensations that were his only for a few short weeks. The heat, the touch, the sounds whirled around in his head, and he knew if he didn't stop there'd be no chance of saving her, or anyone else. Least of all, the very least of all, his own worthless soul.

He didn't pull away from her. He stroked her gently, softening the kiss, moving his mouth to her delicate ear, feeling her shudder in response. He tasted the delicate texture of her skin, breathed in her scent and told himself he had to stop. He held her, his head resting on hers, and waited for her breathing to slow, waited for his own heartbeat to steady, reveling in the fact that he had a heartbeat at all.

When the moment, the fever, seemed to have passed, he pulled away gently and looked down at her. She had a dazed expression in her wonderful blue eyes, and her mouth was soft and damp, and he would have given ten years of his life to kiss her again. But he had no years to give, so he released her, stepping back.

"Sorry," he said. "I shouldn't have done that."

"Why not?" Her voice was so quiet he could hardly hear her words, but he knew them in his soul.

"Because you didn't want it."

She looked up at him, her vision clearing. "Yes, I did." She moved across the room, heading for the telephone. "I'd better call Steve and see what he can do about the car."

She'd ended the subject, which was just as well. If they'd continued it he would have touched her again, and if he had touched her again, he wouldn't have been able to let her go.

The whole thing was damnable, he thought, watching as she spoke into the telephone, running a hand through her sheaf of silvery blond hair. At least this time her hands were shaking. A near brush with death had left her calm and unmoved. A brush with passion, with life, had shaken her to her roots.

"He'll be out as soon as he can," she said, hanging up the phone.

"Why do you need to atone?" he asked abruptly.

"I beg your pardon?"

"You said you had crimes you needed to atone for. Sins committed against this town that you needed to make up for. What were they?"

"None of your business." She put the kettle on the stove, busying herself, refusing to meet his eyes.

"You're right. But I don't pay proper attention to what is and isn't my business, and I fully intend to hound you until you confess your terrible sins. I imagine once you speak them out loud you'll find they aren't nearly so bad as you imagine."

She leaned back against the counter, staring at him. "This is a small town, Gabriel," she said flatly. "The people here relied on two things to survive. The tourist industry, which doesn't account for more than a few dozen families who spend the summer by the lake in makeshift cabins. And the factory. Precision Industries wasn't anything special, the work wasn't state-of-the-art woodcraft, but it provided a living for most of the people in town. With the factory closed down, no one has the money for houses, for food, for medicines, for gasoline. You've heard of infrastructures? Ours collapsed when the factory did."

"And where is your blame in all this? Did you firebomb the mill?"

She shook her head, refusing to meet his eyes. "You've already accused me of thinking I'm a saint. God-like delusions is a little more accurate. I thought I could save the mill, and instead I brought about its ruin."

He didn't want to hear this after all. He knew what was coming, knew with an instinct that transcended common sense, and he wondered if he walked out of the kitchen, climbed into Lars Swensen's beat-up old truck and just kept driving, whether he might live out his remaining three weeks in sybaritic pleasure.

Emerson MacVey would have done just that. But he was finding that he wasn't MacVey any longer. Neither was he Gabriel Falconi. He was some odd, uncomfortable mix of the two.

So he waited. Calmly, implacably, knowing she'd have to tell him. Which she did, her back to him as she stared out into the wintry landscape.

"I used to be a dancer, you know," she said in a dreamy voice. "Not a very good one, unfortunately. How was I to know that the best dancer Angel Falls, Minnesota, had ever seen was no more than adequate in New York City? I couldn't find work, but that wasn't the worst of it. The worst was knowing and accepting the fact that I was mediocre." She glanced over her shoulder at him, and there was a rueful, accepting expression on her face.

"So I took a clerical job in an office. Unfortunately I wasn't very good at that, either. I'd spent so much of my lifetime concentrating on being a dancer that I hadn't applied myself to much else. I managed to get a job working for a private investor in New York. A cold, ruthless bastard, if I do say so. And I made the dire mistake of falling in love with him."

It was like a knife in his heart. It hurt more than the heart attack that had taken his life, it twisted inside him so that he wanted to scream in pain. In reality, he couldn't make a sound.

"Emerson made his money investing in small companies. Time after time he'd buy them and appear to bring them back to financial health, making a tidy profit as he did so. The problem was, I didn't realize how he did it. He cannibalized everything he could, selling off equipment, selling off smaller parts of larger conglomerates. He was utterly ruthless, and I'd fooled myself into thinking he was caring."

"How could you have done that?" Gabriel managed to say,

amazed that his voice sounded no more than casually interested in the story she was telling.

"I thought he was a wounded soul, a good man hidden beneath his unfeeling manner. I thought he needed a good woman's love, I thought he would do the right thing when he was presented with the option."

"And did you? Present him with the option?"

She tried to smile once more, but her expression was bleak. "I told him about Precision Industries. Showed him what an excellent investment opportunity it was, for a man of his organizational skills. Unfortunately, he found it an even better investment opportunity as a tax loss. He sold off the equipment, fired all the workers, and sold the empty factory to the town for one dollar."

"Then the town could sell the place..."

"It's falling into ruin. They've tried. No one's even remotely interested."

"Did you tell him what you thought of him for doing that? Maybe he would have listened if you'd explained to him..."

"I doubt it. You see, he'd already committed the cardinal sin of having sex with me one night, and after that he wasn't ready to even see my face, much less hold a discussion."

"If the two of you made love..."

"We didn't make love. He had sex with me. I made love with him. A subtle difference, I grant you, but enough to matter. He fired me the next day, rather than have to see me."

"Carrie," he said, ready to tell her. Ready to confess his own sins, promise to make things better, to tell her he had cared about her, only he'd been cold and angry and frightened of needing anyone. "Carrie," he said, but the words refused to come.

Augusta had warned him. He could perform miracles, three of them, he could right the wrongs he'd done. But he couldn't tell anyone the truth about why he was here. Even when Carrie needed to hear.

She turned to look at him, and she managed a wry smile. "You're right," she said. "Confession is good for the soul."

"You weren't to blame," he said, wondering how much he'd be allowed to say. "That bastard was."

"Well, he's paid for his sins. He's dead, and has been for almost two years. I have to make up to Angel Falls for the harm I did."

"The harm *he* did."

She shrugged. "Nevertheless. There's nothing that can be done."

"You could sue his estate. He must have left a bundle..."

"No."

He didn't want to ask. He thought he'd heard more than he could bear; for some reason this would be the worst of all. He tried to move toward the door, but his feet were rooted to the floor. "You couldn't force yourself to bring suit..." he suggested in a hoarse voice.

She shook her head. "For this town, I would have done anything. After all, Emerson MacVey was beyond hurting. But his estate was worthless."

"Worthless?" he choked.

"Everything was delicately balanced. With his death, it all collapsed, like a house of cards. There was barely enough for a decent burial."

"How do you know?"

"I used to work for him, remember? One of my co-workers called and told me about it. She was very bitter. She said she'd put up with the arrogant bastard for eight years only to have him keel over and die on her, leaving her with absolutely nothing."

Megan, Gabriel thought, with one of those unexpected flashes of memory. "So it's up to you to rescue the town that he destroyed?"

She shook her head. "I don't think I'm God anymore. It's up to me to make things better, when and where I can. It's that simple."

"Punishing yourself while you do it."

"I'm not punishing myself."

He didn't want to argue with her anymore. She'd told him more things than he was ready to hear. He felt like Scrooge in *A Christmas Carol,* watching the hags argue over his bedclothes after he was dead. He'd died penniless. A worthy end for someone who had only cared about money and power.

"I'll go back and get the food out of the car," he said. "It's getting colder, and we don't want things freezing."

"You don't need to...."

"I do," he said irritably. "You curl up on the sofa with a cup of tea and I'll be back in a few minutes."

She glanced out the window. "It's snowing."

"It's always snowing. Go sit."

SHE WAITED UNTIL she saw him trudge down the driveway through the blowing snow, and then she let out a deep breath, one she hadn't realized she'd been holding. Her eyes were stinging, her heart ached, and she told herself she was coming down with the flu. And she told herself that Gabriel Falconi had far too unsettling an effect on her.

The kettle shrieked, just as she was about to succumb to an absolute orgy of self-pity. She stiffened her shoulders, made herself a cup of orange-spice tea, stirred in more honey than she usually allowed herself and went to curl up on the lumpy sofa in the living room.

He'd done a good job with the wood stove—the heat was still filling the room, but she pulled the quilt around her anyway, for protection as much as warmth. She needed something to hug around her, something to keep her safe.

She was going to send Gabriel Falconi away. Surely Lars could find work for him, or Steve. She couldn't have him in her house. looking at her out of those dark, haunted eyes. She couldn't let him put those elegant, beautiful hands on her, kiss her with that wide, hard mouth. She couldn't let herself be folded in his arms so that she could feel his heart beat, feel his need, a need that matched her own.

She'd loved one man in her life, in a moment of rash stupidity that had ruined not only her own future but that of an entire town. Now she stood on the edge of falling in love again, with a man who would leave in the new year, and for some reason it still felt like the same man. Gabriel Falconi and Emerson MacVey couldn't have been more different. One a glorious Renaissance angel, the other an overbred yuppie. One tall and strong and graceful, the other spare and slender and precise. One the child of immigrants, the other the child of privilege. One who worked with his hands and body, the other who'd never done a day's honest labor in his life.

So different and yet the same. The same lost soul, hidden behind disparate eyes. The same longing calling out to her, a longing that resonated in her heart.

A longing she had every intention of denying. She took a sip of the scalding tea, listening to the wind howl around her tiny house, rattling the windows that needed fresh caulk, knocking against the foundations that still needed banking. She'd have to do it herself.

She heard him come back, stomping into the kitchen, dumping the bags of groceries on her round oak table. She knew she should get up and help him, get up and confront him, but for the time being she stayed where she was, too weary, too comfortable to move.

She must have drifted off. She heard Steve's voice in the kitchen, making disparaging noises about her beloved station wagon. "Second accident in less than a week, Gabriel," he drawled. "You got a death wish or something?"

"Not particularly," he replied. "Her brakes failed. Think you can fix them?"

"Shouldn't be a problem. I'll tow it into town and get right on it. You're not in any hurry for your truck, are you?"

There was a pause, and Carrie found she had enough energy to wonder how he'd respond to that. He wanted to leave, she knew with sudden certainty. He wanted to get out of Angel Falls as much as she wanted him to go. "No hurry," he said finally, his voice resigned.

She should get up and tell Steve her car could wait. After all, Gabriel had bought her enough food to feed the Russian army—she'd have no need to go into town for days.

But she couldn't. She could barely keep her eyes open. She knew when Steve left, knew when Gabriel came back into the room. She wasn't asleep, but she had every intention of pretending to be.

He loaded the wood stove then closed it down again, before coming to stand over her. She didn't want to open her eyes, but suddenly she couldn't resist. She wanted to read the expression on his face.

It was a waste of time. He was more than adept at shielding his emotions, one small thing he had in common with Emerson MacVey. "You need to eat," he said gruffly.

"I will."

"I need to get back to town."

"I know."

He didn't move. He wanted to touch her, she knew it. She wanted him to touch her, as well. But he wasn't going to. "I've got a few things to do," he said. "I don't think I'll be able to come out for a few days."

Despair and relief flooded her. "That would be fine. I'm going to be rather busy myself the next few days. I'm not sure the work can't wait until next spring, if it comes to that."

He knew the nature of the work as well as she did, knew that it couldn't wait. "That might be a good idea," he agreed, moving away from her. "Take care of yourself."

He was saying goodbye. She knew it with a certainty that held no logic, and she felt a tearing of grief inside her. But she couldn't stop him. Couldn't put out her hand to reach him, to make him stay.

And then he was gone. She heard the sound of Lars's old truck as he drove away, and then nothing but silence, broken by the sound of the snow beating against the old windows of her grandmother's house, the dry crackle of the aged wood in the old stove.

She'd promised him she'd eat. She pulled herself off the sofa and wandered into the kitchen, trailing the quilt after her. He'd put all the food away, the first neat man she'd ever met in her lifetime. No, the second. Emerson MacVey had been a neat man, as well. She'd considered it a character flaw.

She didn't have the energy to heat herself some soup, so she made do with a carton of raspberry yogurt, leaning against the refrigerator door as she forced herself to swallow the stuff. Everything was tasting strange nowadays, which was just as well. It meant she had less interest in food and, therefore, could spend what little money she had on more important things.

She was so tired. She used her last bit of energy calling the Swensens' house. Maggie answered, sounded worried, and Carrie remembered belatedly that Lars was in the woods that day, working with Hunsicker's shoddy operation. She wished she could offer words of comfort, but at that moment she needed all her comfort for herself.

"Keep Gabriel from coming out here for a while," she managed to say.

"But why..."

"Trust me, Maggie. It's for the best." She was counting on Maggie's loyalty. Maggie would do anything for her, with many questions asked, of course, but she also accepted a total lack of answers. As she would today.

"Lars has a project he's working on in the evening. Maybe Gabriel will help."

"That would be wonderful," Carrie said wearily.

"Are you all right? You don't sound well."

"Just tired, Maggie. A few days' rest is all I need. I'll see you in church on Sunday."

"Carrie, are you certain...?"

"Wouldn't I tell you if I needed help?" It took all of Carrie's waning energy to sound practical.

"No."

"Keep him busy, Maggie," she said wearily. "I'll be fine."

She didn't convince Maggie, and she didn't convince herself.

She just needed some rest. She wandered back into the living room, sinking down on the sofa. It was too hot in the room, and yet cold, as well, and she huddled deeper into the quilt, looking for something that had already driven away from her, back to the Swensens' house in Angel Falls. Her eyelids felt heavy, her joints ached, her chest burned, and even her teeth hurt. She realized, just before sleep overcame her, that she was sick.

Inconvenient, she thought drowsily. It was a lucky thing she'd already talked with Maggie, gotten rid of Gabriel. She could take care of herself.

It was a simple fever. A case of the flu. It was no wonder she was imagining herself falling in love with the beautiful stranger who'd arrived in their midst. No wonder that she started seeing Emerson MacVey in him, when the two were as different as night and day.

She needed fluids, plenty of rest and quiet. In a few days she'd be her old self, full of energy, compassion, and not a trace of wistful longing for something that would only bring her pain.

In a few days, everything would be just fine.

CHAPTER ELEVEN

So he'd saved her life. Why wasn't that good enough? If she'd been driving when the brakes on her car failed, she probably would have ended up against that tree. So he'd taken care of his first duty, hadn't he? Why did he feel he wasn't through with Carrie Alexander? Maybe because he didn't want to be.

Gabriel maneuvered Lars's truck up the steep, icy driveway, put it into Park and turned it off. It was dark already, and through the brightly lit windows of the old Victorian-style house he could see the family bustling around, all energy and life. A life at which he could only be a spectator.

It was odd. When he'd been alive he hadn't cared about holidays, about family, about friends, even. His parents had divorced and remarried so many times he'd almost lost track of who had actually produced him thirty-two years ago. He'd sat through all the sentimental Christmas movies, listened to all the treacly Christmas songs, and never given a damn.

He did now. He wanted that warmth, that family. He wanted cinnamon rolls dripping with butter, not nouvelle cuisine. He wanted American beer, not French wine. He wanted friends and family, he wanted life. He wanted sex. And he wanted love.

Three people whose lives he'd ruined. Carrie Alexander was number one, and he ought to feel vindicated. He'd saved her life, lectured her on the error of her ways and been summarily banished. If she had any sense she'd pull herself together, head back for a city and shake the dust from this dying town.

Even if she wouldn't, he was no longer to blame. He could forget about her, about her luminous blue eyes and corn-silk hair, her soft mouth and too-thin body that needed pasta and cinnamon buns, as well. Forget how much he wanted to touch her again.

It was now abundantly clear to him just who number two was. He'd ruined the lives of the entire population of Angel Falls, no mean feat for a shallow yuppie. Augusta couldn't be expecting him to fix everyone, but he had little doubt he was living with Lars Swensen for a reason. If he could do something about the Swensens, somehow right the wrong he'd done Lars, then maybe he'd be ready to move on.

He still had no inkling who number three might be, and at that moment he didn't really care. He was tired, still shaken from the near miss in Carrie's rust-bucket of a car, and tense from a frustration that was a great deal more than sexual. He wanted to go up to his room, lock the door and slam his fist against the wall.

But one month didn't allow for wasted time. When he walked into the warmth and light of the old kitchen, baby Carrie looked up at him with a beaming, toothless grin, Lars clapped him on the back, and even Maggie's careworn face warmed at the sight of him.

For a moment he wanted to yell at them. They were fools to trust him—he was the man who'd brought them to this point in the first place. But even if he wanted to tell them, he wouldn't be able to—he'd already discovered that any attempt to tell someone the truth about who and what he was ended in silence.

And he was no longer sure who and what he was. Gabriel Falconi had taken over, Emerson MacVey was fading fast, and like the rest of MacVey's acquaintances, he couldn't mourn him. He was a cold, heartless man, better off dead. And from what little he could see from the time he'd been back on earth, he didn't deserve heaven.

"I need your help, Gabriel," Lars boomed out from his place at the head of the scrubbed table. He had an omnipresent cup of coffee in one big hand, and Gabriel accepted his own from Maggie with automatic thanks. "I'm working on a mahogany railing, and I need it done by Christmas. I don't know how much Carrie has for you, but if you'd feel like giving me a hand..."

"Carrie doesn't need me out there for a few days," he said, wondering if it was a lie. He had the sense, probably wishful thinking on his part, that she needed him very badly. "I'd be glad to help."

"I'll pay you, of course," Lars said carefully. "I'm not sure how much I have right now..."

"Pay me when you get paid," Gabriel replied easily. "I have all that I need right now. A warm place to live, good food, friends..." The moment the word left his mouth it shocked him, but fortunately Lars was too relieved to notice his surprise. He'd never before considered that he had friends.

"We work well together," Lars said. "I wish you could see your way clear to staying past the New Year. I'm doing this railing on spec at the moment, but if we just had a little luck I think we could make a modest go of it.''

"Luck," Maggie said with a snort from her spot at the stove. "A Christmas miracle is more like it.''

Thank you, Augusta, Gabriel said silently. "Miracles have been known to happen," he drawled, drinking his strong coffee and wondering how he'd ever liked tea.

He didn't even think of Carrie for the next few days. At least, not more than once or twice an hour. And all night long, in his dreams, in his waking, in his drifting off to sleep. Instead he concentrated on the long sweep of carved mahogany railing, the hand-carved newel posts that filled most of Lars's workshop. And he concentrated on his Christmas miracle.

In the end he was afraid he'd wasted it.

Alexander Borodin was a millionaire, patron of the arts, industrialist, with an eye for talent. Emerson MacVey had despised him as a sentimental old fool with a weakness for antiquated ways of doing things. Borodin specialized in restoring old mansions with lovingly detailed woodwork—MacVey had preferred chrome and steel.

But Borodin had connections throughout the world—he would see the rare beauty in Lars's work, and he could easily provide enough commissions to keep the Swensen family happily solvent into the millennium and beyond. Last Emerson had heard, he was in the midst of investing in a chain of small, exclusive hotels throughout the world, renovated from some of the small palaces and manor houses that had fallen on hard times. Lars's gift would prove invaluable.

But actually getting in touch with Borodin proved to be no easy matter. Alexander Borodin was not the sort of man one simply called—you had to wade through secretaries and assistants and vice presidents and administrators, and each one had very strong reasons not to let you talk to the man.

One name would have done the trick, opened the lines of communication instantly, but it was a name Gabriel was unable to speak. It was just as well. No one would have believed him anyway.

Three days of trying to reach him, three days of running up long-distance phone bills that would probably rival the national debt, three days of being on hold, and Gabriel had simply closed his eyes, focused on Augusta's stern face, and silently asked.

A moment later Alexander Borodin's accented voice came on

the line. "I gather you've been trying to reach me, young man. What can I do for you?"

After that it was simple enough. No more miracles were required—Gabriel discovered he was fluent enough when he cared to be persuasive, and it didn't take much to persuade Borodin to look at some of Lars's work. Lars had an old camera, Angel Falls came equipped with a one-hour developing service and the U.S. postal service had express mail. The deed was as good as done.

Two down, Gabriel thought, wondering if he should go see Gertrude. He'd been assiduously avoiding her for the past few days, not ready to look at those thick glasses and know the power of a coldhearted eternity lay behind them. He'd have to face her sooner or later. For now, he was content to keep his distance.

Oddly enough, the one person he missed, aside from Carrie, was Jeffie. After their brief run-in at the market, he'd wanted to call him, to talk to him, but he couldn't find a reasonable excuse. And Jeffie, who apparently used to haunt the Swensens' house, was making himself alarmingly scarce.

Probably sulking after being caught trying to shoplift, Gabriel thought, but he didn't quite believe it. For some reason Jeffie seemed to take his strictures with an almost pathetic gratitude. There'd been none of the expected sullen defiance at the store, just a look of such guilt and misery that it almost broke Gabriel's heart.

"Seen Jeffie recently?" he'd managed to ask Nils one day in what he hoped was a suitably offhand voice.

Nils had shrugged. "I saw him in school the other day. He's doing okay, I guess. I asked him if he wanted to come over, work in the shop, but he said no. Said he didn't have anyone to make presents for."

"Poor baby," Maggie had murmured. "Lars, you should go see him."

Lars had set down his paper. "After church on Sunday, Maggie," he agreed. "We'll invite him to dinner, and we won't take no for an answer. It'll give him a chance to talk with Gabe. He seems to think you're some kind of hero," he said with comfortable amusement.

And Gabriel, knowing he should protest, simply nodded, dismissing his unreasoning sense of foreboding.

The days passed with no word from Carrie, and Gabriel worked in the shop beside Lars and told himself his work was done. He'd have no reason to see her again, no reason to talk to her, to touch her. He'd saved her life. Surely things were even now.

And even if Borodin had yet to be in touch, Gabriel had little doubt it would work out. It would take a fool not to see the sheer artistry in Lars's work, and Borodin had never been a fool.

It wasn't until Sunday that Gabriel began to admit to the uneasiness that had been gnawing away at him. An uneasiness that was reflected in Lars's face. Carrie wasn't in church.

"Don't tell me she never misses church," he said, unbelieving as they made their way down the icy church steps. Kirsten had her hand clasped firmly in his, something he was getting dangerously used to.

"Not if she can help it. And certainly not during Advent," Maggie said. "Carrie lives for Christmas. I'm going out to see her once we get home."

"I'll go," Gabriel said, in a voice that brooked no opposition.

Maggie looked at him for a long, considering moment, her face troubled. "I don't think…"

A new voice came from directly behind him. "Let Gabriel go."

Gabriel froze. He'd managed to avoid Gertrude, telling himself he wasn't ready to deal with her. He should have known it wouldn't be up to him.

He turned and looked down at her, at the hunched-over, delicate old-lady figure, the bottle-glass lenses shielding those too-sharp eyes, the kindly expression on her face that masked the look of judge and jury.

"Is she all right?" he demanded sharply.

"I have no idea, young man," Gertrude said sweetly. "I'm just a bit of a matchmaker at heart."

"Go ahead," Lars said, clamping a heavy hand on his shoulder. "Take the truck, and give us a call when you get there. Maggie will save some Sunday dinner for you."

He didn't hesitate any longer. The past few days had been bitter cold, with a wind that blew down from Canada and chilled to the bone. The snow on the roads was packed, sanded, and he drove much too fast toward Carrie's decrepit little farmhouse, all the while telling himself he was ridiculous to be worried, telling himself he should have let Maggie go, should have suggested Maggie at least call, should have got on with the business of finding out who his third soul to save was. He was finished with Carrie, damn it! He'd managed to resist temptation, to do no more than kiss her. He'd saved her life—surely they were quits?

The moment the house came in view all his foreboding tripled. Carrie's car was sitting out front—Steve must have fixed it and brought it back to her, a hell of a lot faster than he was getting around to fixing his truck. But the house looked dark, deserted. And there was no wood smoke coming from the chimney.

He knew for a fact that Carrie had no source of backup heat. All she had was that damnable wood stove in her living room, and on a cold December day if there was no smoke coming from the chimney then there was no heat in the house.

He skidded down the driveway, slammed Lars's truck into Park and jumped out. Her front door was locked, but panic was riding him so hard that he simply kicked it open with his unexpected strength, splintering the wooden frame.

"Carrie!" he shouted. There was no answer. And the homey little kitchen was icy cold.

He slammed the door behind him, but it bounced back open again, letting in a blast of arctic air. He grabbed a chair and shoved it against the door, then raced into the living room.

If he'd had ten years left to live, the sight of her would have taken them off his life. She was lying on the sofa, still and cold, cocooned in a pile of old quilts, with a weak electric heater putting out barely a teaspoonful of heat in the icy room. For a moment he froze, certain she was dead. And then he heard the noisy rasp of her breathing.

He began to curse under his breath, furiously, obscenely, and in Italian. He didn't even take time to be surprised by that fact, as he rushed across the room and knelt by Carrie's unconscious figure. She was burning up with fever, and she stirred under his hand, murmuring something out of dried lips, something he couldn't hear.

The wood box was empty, of course, and obviously she'd been too sick to deal with the fire. His fury vanished into some dark cold place inside him as he sprang into action. It took him ten seconds and one terse sentence to get Lars to find a doctor, and then he concentrated on the wood box. By the time cars started arriving he'd managed to get a roaring fire going, bringing the temperature of the house up to a balmy fifty-five degrees. And Carrie hadn't moved.

He didn't know the man who rushed in with Maggie, but the sight of the black bag did wonders for his barely controlled state of panic. "Doc Browning," Maggie muttered a hurried introduction. "This is Gabriel. Where is she?"

"In the living room. I think it's pneumonia."

Doc Browning, an elderly little urchin of a man with long, tufted eyebrows, looked at him in surprise. "Even without seeing her, I imagine you're probably right," he said. "I warned her." He started into the living room, muttering under his breath. "She needs fluids. Make her some tea."

"The pipes are frozen," Gabriel said dourly. "I'll see what I can do."

There was frozen water in the kettle on the gas stove. He turned on all the burners, hoping to add even a trace of warmth to the frigid house, and then went back to the living room.

He stopped in the doorway. Doc Browning was sitting on the sofa beside Carrie, listening to her breathe. He'd unfastened the shirt she wore, and Gabriel could see her pale skin, the soft curve of her breasts, and he knew he was going to hell for sure, to be lusting after a woman who might very well be dying.

And hell couldn't be that much worse than being around Carrie Alexander and not touching her.

"It's pneumonia, all right," Doc Browning said, pulling her shirt closed again. "She's burning with fever, she's dehydrated, she's too damned thin, and if I had any sense I'd take her to the hospital."

"You can't, Doc," Maggie said. "She doesn't have insurance."

"If she needs the hospital..." Gabriel began.

"We can give it a day," Doc said wearily. "I know Carrie— she hates like hell to be beholden to anyone. She wouldn't take charity, and hospitals don't like to give it. If someone can stay with her, make sure she gets her medicine, fluids, keeps warm, then I can wait a day. These things usually respond to antibiotics quickly."

"I'll stay," Maggie said. "We took care of her last time."

"No," Gabriel said in a calm, sure voice. "I'll stay."

"But she needs a woman to look after her..."

"I don't think she cares much about modesty at this point, Maggie," Doc Browning said. "And Gabriel here is a lot stronger than you are. Besides, someone's got to do something about the water situation. And you're still nursing, and no way am I having that baby come into a sick house."

Maggie was defeated, and she knew it. She took it with good grace. "We'll bring dinner out," she said to Gabriel. "And Lars can come help with the frozen pipes."

Gabriel nodded, staring at Carrie's still figure. Her cheeks were bright red with fever, the rest of her was almost marble white, and it took all his effort to keep his rage and fear under control. She couldn't die, damn it! He refused to let her. And not for any fear for his own eternity. He'd accepted the fact that he deserved hell and would probably end up there.

But Carrie was a different matter. She wouldn't even have to pause at the Waystation. She'd be on an express train straight to heaven, and he'd never see her again.

So he damned well wasn't going to let her go too soon.

Doc Browning was rummaging around in his leather bag. "I'm going to start her with a double dose of penicillin, but after that it's going to be up to you to see that she gets it down. Every six hours, regular as clockwork, and pump those fluids into her. Herb teas, fruit juice, ginger ale. Nothing with caffeine—it'll dry her out even more. You think you're up to it?" He fixed Gabriel with a fierce stare.

"I'm up to it."

Browning nodded, satisfied. "What the hell is this town going to do when I'm out of here?" he demanded of no one in particular.

"You're leaving?" Gabriel asked.

"The whole town's dying. Can't afford to be a doctor for a hundred people—I've got to go where I'm needed. In another month Carrie wouldn't have any choice—you'd have had to drive her to the emergency room." He rose, staring down at her.

"We're just glad you're still here, Doc," Maggie said.

"Hell and damnation!" the old man exploded. "I warned her. She's going to kill herself if she keeps on this way. Never taking care of herself, not eating decent meals, not getting enough sleep. She's run-down, too damned skinny, and this house is as drafty as a gazebo. It's no wonder she's sick."

"I'll take care of the house," Gabriel said. "And I'll take care of her."

Doc just looked at him. And then he smiled, a faint, wintry smile. "I believe you will. Come along, Maggie. We're leaving her in good hands."

Gabriel wasn't so sure. By the time the water in the kettle had melted and begun to boil he'd loaded the wood box with enough firewood to keep the stove going for a couple of days. The temperature had risen to a comfortable level, and he took the electric heater into the bathroom and aimed it at the pipes, giving them a head start, before he made a pot of apple cinnamon tea.

Carrie was burning up when he brought her a cup, laced with honey. She'd kicked off her covers, and she was muttering something underneath her breath, something he couldn't begin to make out. He knelt beside her on the floor, put his arm under her shoulders to raise her, and put the mug to her cracked lips.

She took an instinctive, automatic sip, and he was careful not to let her choke. She drank half the cup slowly and then her eyes fluttered open, fever bright, to stare at him in shocked disbelief.

She tried to say something, but she had no voice beyond a whisper. And then she closed her eyes again, and he set her back on the couch, covering her frail body up once more with the quilt.

If she was going to recuperate here and not in the hospital, they'd need water. He rose, staring down at her, loath to even leave the room. She looked marginally better now, though it was probably only wishful thinking on his part. She wasn't going to die. She was going to sleep, long, healing sleep, while he got the house in working order again. And then he was going to come back into the living room and sit there and watch her. Just watch her. Indulge himself in the sheer, hopeless pleasure of it. Knowing that he only had a couple of weeks left.

THE DREAMS WERE extraordinary. Fever bright, a whirl of colors, dancing around in her head. Once she gave in to them the fear left her, and she drifted like a leaf on the wind through the magic, willingly, the heat and the cold wrapping her in a tight cocoon of forgetfulness.

And then they came, pulling at her, poking at her, forcing things down her throat, and she wanted to tell them all to go away. Until she opened her eyes and saw him through the crystalline haze. And for the first time in years everything felt right again.

She wanted to tell him. She wanted to reach out and touch him, but she was too weak. She couldn't even keep her eyes open, to stare at him in wonder. She felt herself sink back, and she fought it for a moment, terrified he'd leave her once more.

But he wouldn't. She knew that with a certainty. He'd be there, watching over her, taking care of her, for as long as she needed. She didn't have to fight anymore. She was no longer alone.

She could hear him moving around in the kitchen, banging on the pipes. She could feel him all around her. Even behind her closed eyelids she could watch him as he put more wood on the stove, sending blankets of heat through the house. She was cold, chilled, but he seemed to sense that, for he tucked the quilt around her, and brushed the hair away from her face, and she wanted to look at him again, she wanted to tell him she knew him, she wanted to cry.

But there were no tears, no words. She simply slept, secure in the knowledge that he'd come to her when she most needed it. And she never had to be lonely again.

When she woke it was dark. The room was warm, and there was a light on in the kitchen, spreading a pool of illumination into the shadowy living room. There was no sound but the quiet crackle of the wood fire, and she wondered whether she was alone. He'd fed her a second dose of medicine and more tea, and she knew she had to go to the bathroom, but she wasn't sure if she'd manage to crawl. The pipes were frozen, she remembered that. She'd tried to thaw them, but she hadn't the strength—she'd just lain on the couch and coughed.

No, she wasn't alone. She could feel him in the house, nearby. If she turned her head she'd seen him watching over her. Like a guardian angel, protecting her while she fought the monster that squatted on her chest, heavy and smothering. Her mouth moved in a faint smile at the notion, and she heard him move, coming to her side, and she knew he was watching her out of those beautiful dark brown eyes.

She opened her own and smiled up at him, dreaming, fevered, peaceful. "I thought you were dead, Emerson," she whispered. And then she slept again.

GABRIEL DIDN'T MOVE. He was kneeling beside her, one of her hot, dry hands in his large ones, and he was the one who felt chilled.

There had been calm lucidity in her eyes. Despite the fever raging in her frail body, she'd looked into his eyes and seen him, known him, and the thought shattered him in ways he couldn't bear to contemplate. Most of all because he found he didn't want to be Emerson MacVey, ever again.

Why the hell had she loved him? The man he once was had been a shallow, manipulative bastard, capable of destroying a town on a whim, capable of bedding and discarding a vulnerable young woman without even having the guts to do it face-to-face. Emerson MacVey hadn't been mourned when he'd come to his untimely end, and Gabriel Falconi knew why. He'd been merciless, and he deserved no mercy shown toward him.

But Carrie had loved him. Carrie, who seemed to have enough love for all the lost, needy creatures of this earth, Carrie who had enough love for everyone but herself. Carrie had loved him. And that knowledge was his one saving grace.

He sat back on his heels, staring at her in the shadowy darkness.

He'd managed to get the water going—the pipes had burst under the kitchen sink but he could wash the dishes in the bathtub until he replaced them. Lars and Maggie had brought dinner out as promised, staying long enough to worry over Carrie. And now they were alone, he with his guilt and his misplaced desire, she with her fever dreams.

She was shivering, and he knew what that meant. Her fever was spiking again, climbing to dangerous levels, despite all the aspirin he'd poured down her throat. The antibiotic wouldn't start kicking in for at least another few hours, and all he could do was sit there and watch her burn up with fever.

The shivering became shaking. Her skin was scorching, and her eyes opened again, glazed, unseeing, and she began to mutter lost, hopeless words that tore him apart.

He rose, and she clawed at him. "Don't," she whispered in a raw thread of a voice. "Don't leave again." And he didn't know whether she was talking to Gabriel. Or Emerson.

It didn't matter. "I'll be right back," he murmured, stroking her forehead.

It took forever to fill the bathtub with cool water. When he couldn't wait anymore he went back to get her. She was thrashing around, the covers kicked to the floor, and her flannel nightgown was tangled around her long dancer's legs.

He carried her into the bathroom, settling her into the tub, nightgown and all. She jerked in his arms from the shock of the cool water, making a quiet moan of distress, and he felt unexpected tears burn his eyes. He wanted her better. He wanted her to turn suddenly clear, lucid eyes on him and demand to know why she was sitting in a bathtub full of cold water with her nightgown on. He wanted a miracle.

"Augusta, damn it," he muttered. "Or God. I don't care who. Just fix her. Somebody. Make her better. Now."

But this time there was no instant miracle. Carrie's eyes were tightly shut, and she was crying, shaking from cold and fever, and suddenly Gabriel couldn't stand it any longer. He scooped her up, stripped the sopping nightgown from her, wrapped a thick towel around her and carried her back into the living room. He dumped her onto the sofa and threw the quilts over her, staring down at her as she fell back asleep. And then he grabbed his coat and headed out the door.

He'd send Maggie back, he told himself as the chill night air bit into lungs. Or Lars could drive her to the hospital, and Gabriel could use that amazing gold credit card that would never come due. He had to get away from her—he couldn't help her, couldn't save her, and couldn't live with the guilt of watching her as she struggled to breathe.

He yanked at the door to the truck, climbing inside. He had to get away, run away, like the damned coward he was, and had always been. If he'd wondered whether he was Emerson or Gabriel there was no longer any question. Carrie had looked at him through fever-bright eyes and known him. Emerson was the snake who'd abandon a desperately ill woman in the middle of the night. Emerson was the ultimate coward who'd run away from all responsibilities, all caring, all emotion.

He reached for the key, and then his hand dropped, and he put his head on the steering wheel, feeling the shame and guilt wash over him. "Please," he said out loud, not knowing whom he was asking, or even what. "Please," he said again, his voice hoarse and breaking.

This time there was an answer. This was his second miracle, wasted on his own worthless self. Not a miracle for Carrie, to make her instantly better. But the strength for him, to deal with it.

Prayers are always answered, the minister had said, just this morning, and yet it seemed like centuries ago that he'd sat in the little Lutheran church, so consumed with worry about Carrie that he thought he hadn't even been listening. Prayers are answered, but you just might not get the answer you want.

And sometimes you get what you need, Gabriel thought, closing the door silently behind him and staring around Carrie's kitchen. Dumping his jacket onto one of the chairs, he moved silently back into the living room. Carrie lay on the sofa, unmoving, her cheeks still flushed with fever.

And Gabriel sank down on the floor beside the sofa, prepared for a night-long vigil.

CHAPTER TWELVE

Carrie was warm. Cozily, comfortably warm, not burning hot. The pain in her chest had lessened, and as she snuggled down further into the soft mattress she knew an unexpected sense of rightness. She opened her eyes warily, seeing the early-morning light filling her bedroom, and then she turned her head.

Gabriel was asleep beside her. In the dawn she could see the lines of exhaustion on his beautiful face, the scruffy growth of beard. He was wearing jeans and a T-shirt, nothing more, and he lay sprawled out on her double bed, filling it.

She couldn't resist. She lifted her hand, noticing that it was trembling, and touched his mouth with her fingertips.

He murmured something, but he didn't wake up, and Carrie almost leaned forward and touched him with her lips, as well. In time sanity reared its ugly head, and she pulled back, sliding out of the bed silently as Gabriel slept on.

She could barely stand, her legs felt so weak. She glanced down at her body, noting that she was wearing an old T-shirt and nothing else. She hadn't put that T-shirt on her body.

She had hazy memories, of Gabriel putting her in the bathtub, of holding her in his arms as he rocked by the wood stove, of tea and soup and medicine being forced down her throat. At one point Doc Browning had been there, she was sure she'd heard his voice, and the Swensens had come, as well.

But through it all Gabriel had remained, watching over her, taking care of her, a presence, along with her fever dreams. Her fever dreams of Emerson MacVey.

It made no sense that the two of them should be so mixed up in her head. There were never two more dissimilar men. But maybe it all boiled down to one constant. In both cases, she'd made the dire mistake of being stupidly, irrationally attracted to the wrong man.

She had to hold on to the wall as she made her way down the hallway to the bathroom. She looked at her reflection in the mirror and shuddered. She looked like death warmed over. Her face was pinched and pale, her eyes huge in her face, her hair a rat's nest. She needed to use the toilet, she needed to brush her teeth, and she needed to wash her hair.

Her strength held out until halfway through her shower, and then she sagged against the metal side of the stall, too weary to move, trying to summon up enough energy to even turn off the water. She barely heard the door open, and then Gabriel was there, filling the room.

"You're crazy," he said. And then he calmly stepped into the shower with her, turned off the spray and scooped her trembling, wet body up into his arms.

Wrapping her in a towel, he carried her back into the bedroom, setting her down gently on the bed. She was able to gather enough strength to bat his hands away when he began to dry her off with efficient, impersonal care. She didn't want him to be impersonal.

"I can do it," she said crossly.

He smiled. He was wet from the shower, water stains across the dark T-shirt he wore, and his face was weary beneath his good humor. He looked as if he'd been to hell and back. "I wasn't sure that antibiotic was ever going to work."

The towel was huge, enveloping, and he was hardly likely to be tempted by her skinny, unfeminine body, but she wrapped it tightly around her anyway. "How long have I been sick?"

"Years. Centuries," he said. "Actually, I don't know. I found you on Sunday, and today's...God, I think it's Tuesday, but I could be wrong."

"Have you been here all this time? Taking care of me?"

"Yes." He put his hand on her forehead and frowned slightly. "I think your fever's about gone, but maybe I'd better check. Taking a shower was a damned stupid thing to do when you can barely walk. Why did you?"

She was too exhausted to think about what she was saying. "Because I looked horrible," she blurted out.

He stared at her for a brief, astonished moment. And then he threw back his head and laughed.

Carrie scrambled beneath the covers, mortally offended. "It's not funny," she said sulkily.

He leaned forward, kneeling on the bed beside her, his hands cupping her face, his long fingers sliding through her wet hair. "No," he agreed, "it's wonderful. I thought you were too busy being the saint of Angel Falls to waste a precious moment on yourself."

"I'm not a saint."

"No," he said. "And you look wonderful." And he leaned forward and kissed her.

It was a revelation of a kiss. Tender, without being the slightest bit platonic, his mouth touched hers, clinging, warm and damp, and she felt the heat building in her. Something had changed while she'd been sick, something had shifted inside her, and she wanted this man. Wanted him enough to risk taking him.

She lifted her arms, but he'd already stepped away, unaware of her longing. "I'll make you some tea," he said briskly, "and toast, and maybe some applesauce. If you can manage that then maybe we can graduate to eggs."

"I'm not hungry," she said, trying to squash her longing. "And I want coffee."

"Too bad. If you eat enough to satisfy me then maybe I'll let you have a little bit of coffee. Maybe not." He looked down at her, a considering light in his eyes. "You stay put. If you want to get dressed I'll help you, after you have something to eat."

"I can take care of it myself."

"Trust me, Carrie, I've seen you without a stitch on any number of times during the past few days."

"I'm sure you can control your raging passions," she said sharply, "but I want my privacy."

He halted by the door, staring at her. "I wouldn't be sure of any such thing," he said with a crooked smile. "Stay put."

There was something about his smile. Something about the look in his eyes, that made her start wondering whether there might be a future for her after all.

SHE DIDN'T DO as he told her to, but then, Gabriel hadn't expected it. To everyone else she was Lady Bountiful, the saint, the martyr, ready to sacrifice everything for her fellow man. When it came to him she was stubborn, determined and sharp-tongued. He wondered whether it was love.

He hoped not. He'd saved her life twice, above and beyond the call of duty. Surely by now he was quits. He didn't think Augusta would look too kindly on things if Carrie fell in love with him, only to have him vanish in two weeks' time.

He thought about her mouth, tasting of toothpaste and longing. Of her huge eyes, staring up at him with such a troubled expression in their blue depths. He thought of her skinny body that needed food and love and sex, and he thought it just might be worth it.

He'd already been here half his allotted time and it didn't seem as if he'd made any progress at all. Maybe he ought to take what he wanted and prepare to spend eternity in hell. Since he seemed bound there anyway, he might as well have something to remember.

He'd do it, too, if it was only his eternity he had to consider. But Carrie had been through enough. She'd already been used and rejected by Emerson MacVey. If Gabriel entered into an affair with her, knowing it was doomed, then he'd deserve any torment fate could offer him.

It took all his self-control not to go to her when she appeared in the kitchen door, swaying slightly, dressed, triumphant, pale. He wanted to put his arms around her, he wanted to carry her back up to bed, he wanted to make love to her.

He contented himself with glancing her way, then turning back to the stove. "I knew you wouldn't stay put," he said. "I've got the fire cranked up. Go lie down on the sofa and I'll bring you something to eat."

"Are you always this dictatorial?"

He grinned. "Only when I get the chance. Are you always this crabby?"

Her slow, answering smile was a revelation. "Only when I get the chance."

She ate everything he put in front of her, then demanded coffee. Faint color began to reappear in her cheeks, and by the time the Swensens' car pulled up the long, icy driveway she was arguing about who was going to do the dishes.

"It's a miracle," Maggie breathed when she rushed into the room, not taking time to discard her coat. "Yesterday you were at death's door and now you look like the cat that swallowed the canary."

"I told you she'd be all right," Lars said, coming in behind her, his broad face creased with pleasure. "She was in good hands with our Gabriel. A hospital would have been a waste of time and money."

He heard the phrase, "our Gabriel," and the warmth of it sent a shaft of sorrow through him, for the connections he'd never made when he had the chance. He squashed it down—it was too late for recriminations. "You need coffee," he drawled. "I'll get it, while you see if you can put the patient in a more agreeable mood."

Both the Swensens turned to look at Carrie in surprise. "Carrie's always agreeable," Maggie said.

"Of course I am," Carrie said. "Except when a bully like Gabriel tries to boss me around."

Lars looked at Maggie, and the two of them grinned. Gabriel knew what they were thinking, and he wanted to tell them to stop it. There was nothing worth grinning about—he was bad for her, the worst possible man. He could offer her sex and desertion, and she deserved love and commitment.

"Coffee," he said morosely, disappearing into the kitchen.

The day was a stream of visitors. Everyone brought something. Food, flowers, homemade tokens. Gabriel kept himself out of the way, busy with making the drafty old house more secure against the harsh December winds. He caulked windows, fixed the banking on the west side of the house, and was in the midst of stacking firewood when he had an uneasy prickling sensation at the back of his neck. He knew who it was even before he turned.

"You're running out of time, Gabriel," said Gertrude Hansen in Augusta's peremptory tones.

He paused, leaning on the splitting maul, and looked down at her. Emerson had been the same height as Augusta, but here in Minnesota he was taller and she was shorter. He didn't bother pretending to misunderstand. "I have two weeks left."

"And what have you done so far?"

"Saved Carrie's life. Twice. Surely that's enough."

"Could be," the old lady murmured. "It all depends on what kind of state you leave her in. She doesn't need her heart broken again."

"I'm not going to touch her," he snapped.

The old lady just looked at him. "We'll see," she said obscurely, moving past him onto the porch just as Lars and Maggie came out.

"Hi, there, Gertrude," Lars said. "Come to see the invalid? You wouldn't believe how well she's doing. Gabriel's a miracle worker."

Gertrude directed a sour glance back at him. "Is he?" she murmured in the deceptively gentle voice that fooled the Swensens, a far cry from Augusta's autocratic tones. "I would have thought he was the type to save his miracles for himself."

Guilt swamped him, leaving him speechless as Gertrude disappeared inside the house. She was right, damn it. His miracle had been for himself, for his miserable, cowardly self.

"She's an old tartar sometimes," Lars said, putting a hand on Gabriel's shoulder. "Don't pay any attention to her. We've known her all her life, and we're used to her."

It was enough to startle him out of his abstraction. "I thought she was new in town."

"What made you think that?" Maggie asked, perplexed. "She was born here, and as far as I know she's never even left the state in all her eighty-some years."

Gabriel shook his head. Trust Augusta to take care of details. "Just a guess," he said. "How's Carrie doing? Is she getting overtired?"

"Hell, she's fine," Lars boomed, then silenced as Maggie kicked him.

"She's doing quite well," Maggie corrected him, "but I don't think she ought to be left alone. Would you mind staying here a little bit longer?"

It was the last thing he needed, and what he wanted most. The longer he was around her, the harder it was for him to resist her. And resist her was the one thing he had to do. If he hadn't known it already, Gertrude's warning had reminded him.

"She's got enough food to feed the Russian army," he said. "Her fever's normal..."

"She needs you, Gabriel," Maggie said gently.

He wanted to deny it. He wanted to explain to Maggie just how dangerous he was to Carrie Alexander's fragile well-being, but he knew it was a waste of time. "Of course I'll stay," he said, hating the savage relief he felt at having to agree.

"In the excitement, I forgot to tell you," Lars was saying, "someone's coming to look at the railings. He might be interested in commissioning some other work."

"He's got a Russian-sounding name. Something like Boris Gudonov," Maggie said.

"Borodin," Lars corrected her. "His name's Alexander Borodin. He must have money—he's using his own jet to fly into Saint Cloud."

Gabriel closed his eyes for a moment, offering up a silent prayer of thankfulness. "I've heard of him," he said carefully. "If he likes your stuff you've got it made."

"Let's not count our chickens," Maggie said, but she sounded a great deal more cheerful than she had in the past few weeks. She put her hand on Gabriel's arm, and her eyes were suddenly dark with concern. "Do you really not want to stay here, Gabriel? I could come out, or Gertrude, or any number of people would leap at the chance to do something for Carrie, after all she's done for us."

"I'll stay," Gabriel said, putting his hand over Maggie's work-worn one. "I want to."

But he wasn't about to go back into the house as long as Gertrude was there, and she stayed a damnably long time. The sky grew dark early as they neared the shortest day of the year, and he could sense another winter storm in the air, he who'd never paid the slightest bit of attention to the weather. The temperature was dropping, he'd left his jacket inside, and there was a limit to how much wood he could split and stack before his energy gave out. He'd been through two days of hell, two days of panic, spooning medicine and soup and tea down Carrie's throat, moving her from bed to bath and back again, all the while cursing Augusta and the fate that had put her life in his hands. He'd barely slept or eaten since Sunday, and he wanted to sit by the wood stove and look at Carrie. With no one interfering.

"You can go in now." Gertrude strode out the door, her cloth coat buttoned up under her wattled chin, her thick glasses glinting in the waning sunlight. "You behave yourself now. She tires easily."

"I have no intention of tiring her," he said sourly.

Gertrude's smile was no more warming than the weather. "I don't trust you, Gabriel," she said. "You'll have to prove yourself to me." And before he could reply, she was gone, zipping off at an alarmingly fast rate in her sturdy sedan.

He watched her go. "At least she called me Gabriel," he muttered out loud. Right then and there he didn't want to be reminded of who he once was, and would be again in another couple of weeks.

Carrie was fast asleep on the living room sofa. Someone, probably Lars, had loaded the wood stove, and the heat was wonderful after the chill winter air. Gabriel poured himself a cup of coffee, took a brownie from the plate someone had brought that morning, and took a seat by the fire, where he could watch Carrie. He didn't know why fate had given him one more night with her. He only knew it would be his last chance. And he intended to make the most of it. By watching her, simply watching her. So that he'd have something to remember, throughout eternity. Wherever he ended up.

IT WAS AN INTERESTING phenomenon, lusting after a man. Carrie had more than enough time to consider it, advantages, disadvantages and all. In her twenty-seven years she'd never been unduly interested in men. Her sexual experience consisted of a vaguely unsatisfying short-term affair with a fellow student, and the cataclysmic night she'd spent in Emerson MacVey's office.

She'd sworn off sex after that. Sworn off men, relationships, dating, and doing just about anything else a normal, healthy young woman might be interested in doing. Most men, including Steve from the garage, had taken no for an answer. The sexless aura she put forth had been astonishingly convincing.

She wasn't quite sure why it hadn't convinced Gabriel. From his sudden appearance in her life, she'd gone out of her way to be motherly, asexual, a friend and nothing more. But he had a way of seeing through that, of getting under her skin, so that she was aware of him constantly, as she'd been aware of no other man.

She ought to bless the fact that her responses were normal, healthy ones. After all, Gabriel was a devastatingly attractive man, quiet, strong, with a streak of ironic humor that matched her own. He was only going to be around for another few weeks—what could be wrong with indulging her unexpected longings?

She'd gotten support from the most unexpected quarter. Gertrude, maiden schoolteacher and pillar of the community, had taken one look at her and shaken her head.

"It's not the things you do that you regret," she'd murmured, following Carrie's glance out the window toward Gabriel as he stacked firewood with his graceful economy of movement. "It's the things you don't do."

Carrie had turned to look at her, scandalized. "He's leaving in two weeks, Gertrude."

"When did you last do something for yourself? Something just because you wanted to do it, and to hell with the consequences?"

"Are you telling me to have an affair?" Carrie demanded. "Gertrude, you were my seventh-grade social studies teacher!"

"I'm telling you to do what your heart tells you," Gertrude had said placidly. "Nothing more. And nothing less."

But it wasn't her heart talking to her, Carrie thought, staring at Gabriel across the table as she ate more pasta than she'd eaten in the past year. It was something a lot more elemental. She watched his hands, strong, elegant hands that he'd put on her more than once, and she wondered how she could entice him to put them on her again. She looked at his mouth, wide, mobile. That mouth had kissed her when she wasn't sure that she wanted to be kissed.

This time she was sure. But she didn't know how to get him to kiss her.

And damn it, he was keeping his distance, fussing around her like a mother hen, as deliberately asexual as she had been. It was almost as if their roles had been reversed. Suddenly she wanted him to see her as a woman, not a plaster saint. And suddenly, he was coming on like Francis of Assisi.

"You should go to bed," he said when she finished off her third brownie. "You need to rebuild your strength." He began clearing the table, keeping well out of her way, almost as if he suspected she might grab him.

Tempting thought. "I've spent the past week in bed," she countered, rising to help him. "I feel restless."

He turned in the doorway, and she almost ran into him. They were breathlessly, deliciously close, close enough for her to feel the heat from his body, close enough to see the flicker of reaction in his beautiful brown eyes, a reaction he banished so quickly she wondered if it was wishful thinking on her part.

"Are you afraid of me, Gabriel?" she asked suddenly, artlessly.

"Why should I be?"

"You seem to be running away from me," she murmured, beginning to enjoy herself.

"I didn't know there was anything to run from."

She took the plate from his hand and put it on the adjacent counter. "There isn't."

He looked at her. "Don't."

"Don't what?"

"If you've decided to come alive again, hallelujah. But don't come alive with me. I'm not the man for you to experiment on, Carrie. I'll be gone in two weeks, and you need someone who's going to be around for the long haul. You don't need to have your heart broken again."

She flinched, shocked. "What makes you think I've ever had my heart broken?" she demanded.

"Someone hurt you very badly. You don't want to make the same mistakes over and over again. You don't want to pick the same kind of man."

"You're completely different from Emerson," she said stubbornly.

"Am I? Maybe you just don't know me that well."

She put a hand on his arm, but he jerked away as if her touch burned him. "Don't," he said in a tight voice. "For God's sake, just *don't*."

She stared at him, unable to keep the pain and misery from her face. "Sorry," she muttered. "It was stupid of me. I thought you wanted me."

The words were out now, shocking in their very simplicity. He shut his eyes for a moment, as if asking for help. "Of course I want you," he said roughly. "I'd be a fool not to. But you need love and cherishing. You need someone to father your babies and stay with you. All I can offer you is sex."

From somewhere she summoned a wry smile. "I'll take it," she said, moving toward him.

He didn't move, didn't dare move, simply because he wanted to so badly. "Carrie," he said, his voice deep with exasperation. "I'm warning you. For your own sake, leave me alone."

"Chicken," she said softly. And she reached for him.

CHAPTER THIRTEEN

Gabriel had a choice. He'd always had a choice, whether he'd known it or not. She stood in front of him, shy, trembling, filled with a misplaced love and longing. And he wanted her so badly he felt as if he were the one with the fever.

If he touched her, took her, his fate was sealed. There'd be no heaven for the likes of him.

He could move. Push past her and walk out of the house before he could change his mind. Or he could let her down gently, explain that he didn't really want her, that she should pay no attention to that bulge in his jeans.

He could do it, when there was nothing he wanted more than to take her. He could accept an eternity of longing for her, imagining what it might be like. He could punish himself, when it was more than he deserved.

But he couldn't do it to her.

If he walked away from her she'd never reach out again, he knew it with a despairing triumph. She wanted him, wanted him enough to fight for him, and if he turned her down she would never ask again. Leaving her would be just as cruel as taking her.

What was the saying, damned if you do, damned if you don't? He was damned, all right. He might as well enjoy his fate to the fullest.

He reached out and cupped her pale face, his long thumbs brushing against her trembling lips. "You're asking for trouble, Carrie," he said softly.

She smiled up at him, her eyes luminous in the shadows. "I know," she said.

He stared down at her, not saying a word. Maybe, just maybe it would work. She'd told him she'd settle for sex. Maybe if he made love to her it would be enough to make her realize that life was worth living. That if she found pleasure and warmth with him, she could find it with someone else, someone better.

Stupid rationalization, he mocked himself. He was grasping at straws, at some insane justification. Because he'd already gone too far. The moment his hands had touched her, there was no turning back. He was going to carry her up to the big bed beneath the eaves and make love to her, and if he spent eternity in hell for it, it would be worth it.

He put his lips against hers, lightly at first, feeling them tremble. Emerson MacVey had been good at sex—it was one of his cold-hearted talents. Gabriel Falconi had never made love before, and each sensation was overwhelming, exquisite. The way her lips parted beneath the pressure from his mouth, the taste of her on his tongue, the soft, shaky little sigh she emitted when he kissed her ear. The thudding of her heart against his chest when he pulled her against him, pulled her arms up around his neck. The thudding that came from desire, and panic.

One last time his conscience surfaced, and he reached behind his neck and took her cold, trembling hands in his, holding her at arm's length. "Carrie," he said gently. "You don't really want to do this. You told me you weren't into one-night stands and casual sex."

"I lied. I've had dozens of men, Gabriel," she said, almost hiding her desperation. "I know when I want one. You're right about me, I have a saint complex. I need to take care of the world. But I don't need a relationship. I'm a big girl, I know when I have physical needs that need to be met."

Her lies were astounding. And the final straw. Anyone who could kiss with such innocent, untutored longing and lie with such fluency was more than he could resist.

"One night then," he said with a crooked grin. "One night of steamy sex, with no strings attached, is that it?"

"That's it," she said, with a calm expression on her face and desperation in her eyes.

He muttered something under his breath, something Augusta wouldn't approve of. And then, before he could change his mind, he scooped her up in his arms and started up the narrow stairs to the second floor.

He wasn't used to being strong. And she weighed too damned little. He needed to fatten her up, feed her pasta and cheesecake, cannoli and croissants. But most of all he needed to love her. For her sake.

And for his.

THE MOONLIGHT WAS COMING through the frosted windowpanes in her bedroom, and Gabriel didn't bother turning on the light. He set her down on the bed, and Carrie kept her arms around his neck, pulling him down with her, afraid he would change his mind once more.

At least she'd managed to convince him she knew what she wanted, even if she wasn't completely sure herself. For the first time in her life she wanted something just for her. She wanted Gabriel. And she wanted to feel alive again.

He could wipe out the memory of Emerson MacVey. He could make her forget her guilt. One night, that was all she asked out of life. Tomorrow she'd go back to good deeds and sainthood, to denying herself. For now she would take what she needed.

He covered her body with his long, muscular one, settling against her hips, and she could feel his arousal with a mixture of satisfaction and panic. He wouldn't leave her now. Not tonight. There was no turning back.

And then he kissed her, and her fear vanished. His lips were soft, damp, brushing against hers, teasing them apart, and then he used his tongue, tasting her, arousing her, so that the cool Minnesota bedroom began to fade away, and all that existed was the mattress beneath her and the wonder of his mouth.

He rolled to his side, taking her with him, his long legs tangled in hers, and his hands were sliding up underneath her cotton sweater, pulling it up. He broke the kiss long enough to pull it over her head, and she was lying there, skinny and cold, wearing only her plain white bra and baggy sweatpants, and she wondered whether he'd change his mind. He'd be used to gorgeous, voluptuous women, he'd be used to...

He put his mouth on her breast, through the plain white cotton, and she arched off the bed in shocked reaction. He moved swiftly, stripping off the rest of her clothes, and she was shivering, telling herself it was from the chill in the bedroom, knowing it was from something far more elemental.

He stretched out beside her, pulling her body against his fully clothed one, warming her, soothing her with his big hands. "I'm not going to hurt you, Carrie," he murmured in his slow, deep voice. "You can say no at any time."

She believed him. Her fear vanished instantly. "Yes," she said. And she put her mouth against his.

Her night with Emerson had been a blur of sex and wonder. This was different. Every touch, every taste was sharply delineated, etched in her mind. He moved his mouth across her collarbone, nipping, tracing a trail down to her breast, capturing the turgid peak and sucking at it. She made a quiet sound of intense pleasure, threading her hands through his thick, long hair, holding him there as his hands moved between her legs, touching her, with a feather-light touch that was reassuring, and then maddening, and then suddenly there, as she heard her voice choke on his name in the darkness.

He stripped off his clothes swiftly, efficiently, almost before she had a chance to come down, and then he was kneeling between her legs, huge and shadowy in the darkness, and her momentary panic returned as he cupped her hips and pressed against her. She was still trembling, sensitive from what he'd already given her, and she jerked back with a quiet shriek. But he touched her again, soothing her, and then she was ready, she was more than ready, she would die if she didn't have him, and she clutched at him, pulling him toward her, and he sank into her, inch by merciless inch, huge and hard and yet velvet soft.

She shifted on the bed to accommodate him, wrapping her legs around his hips, wondering if this was really going to work, when he finally sank into her fully, resting against her, his head cradled on her shoulder as they absorbed the sensations. She could feel herself rippling around him, and she wondered whether she could take much more. She'd had her pleasure—this was for him. A fair trade, and it was only slightly uncomfortable, and...

"Second thoughts, Carrie?" he whispered in her ear.

She shook her head, a complete lie. She owed him, she'd survive.

He pulled back, just slightly, and surged into her before she had a chance to prepare herself. And it was glorious. She moaned in the back of her throat, and her fingers dug into his shoulders instinctively.

"You weren't sure you were going to like that, were you?" he whispered, his voice low and sexy. "You were going to lie there like a martyr and suffer." He pushed into her again, and there was nothing saintlike about her gasp of pleasure.

He pulled her hands from his shoulders, pushed them down on the mattress and threaded his fingers through hers. "This isn't about pain, or guilt. This is about life." And he put his mouth against her, hot and wet and open, as his body thrust deeply into hers.

She shattered around him, instantly, shockingly, again, but he wasn't through with her yet. He knew how to prolong it, and he did, until she was sobbing, writhing, clutching at him, as he rocked against her over and over again. She was lost in some wild, crazy world of magic and dragons, sweat and desire and fulfillment that threatened to burn her to cinders, and it was endless, wondrous, an eternity that she never wanted to leave, when finally he went rigid in her arms, filling her completely, and she heard his voice, strangled, rasping in her ear. Calling her name across the white-clouded mists of time.

She wanted to hold him in her arms as he slept. She wanted to savor what had happened, relive every moment. But it had been too much, too overwhelming, and her body had its own kind of wisdom. Even as she fought it, it simply shut down, and she was fast asleep before he even lifted his head.

HE DIDN'T WANT to leave her. Didn't want to leave the hot, clinging warmth of her body, the frail yet strong cradle of her arms. He was ready for her again immediately, but he forced himself to pull away from her. She was sound asleep, her face shadowed with exhaustion and tears, and he wondered when she'd cried. If he'd made her cry.

He pulled the covers over them, wrapping her body tightly against his. There was no way he could ignore the fact that he wanted her again, and he had every intention of enjoying that need. It was part of life, a life that was going to be taken from him again far too soon, and he was going to savor everything until that happened.

He reached out and pushed her hair back from her tear-streaked face, and she murmured something in her sleep, nuzzling against his hand with age-old instinct. He could see the shadows beneath her eyes, and he considered calling himself every name in the book for taking advantage of her when she'd been weak and defenseless.

Except that he hadn't. Whatever the consequences, what they'd shared had been glorious, eternal. And if he had to spend that eternity in hell for it, it might just have been worth it.

He didn't sleep. He lay there in the moon-swept darkness, staring at the woman lying in his arms, drinking in the sight of her, shaken and shocked at the feelings burgeoning through the stranger's body he'd inherited, the one that now felt fully like his own.

He was in love with her. Emerson MacVey hadn't known how to love, but Gabriel Falconi did. Gabriel knew how to give his heart, even if it was a mortgaged one. One that had been nothing but a liability. As he lay there in the darkness, he considered the fanciful notion that if Emerson had ever once shared his heart it might not have exploded after thirty-two years. An interesting thought, but of no real importance in the scheme of things. Emerson was dead. It was up to Gabriel to salvage his soul.

He slipped out of bed just as the sun was rising, still achingly hard. She slept on, a faint smile on her face, and he covered her with the quilt, tucking it around her slender body before he left the room silently.

By the time she came downstairs, shy, sleepy, he'd managed to finish up the woodpile, stacking the logs in neat rows, enough for a long, cold winter. The wood stove was kicking out heat, the coffee was warm on the back burner, and he'd made muffins for her. Gabriel Falconi had unforeseen talents, including an aptitude for cooking. He just didn't have a gift for leaving well enough alone.

He fed her, keeping her mouth busy so that she wouldn't say what she wanted to say. He could see it in her eyes, and it terrified him. As long as she didn't say it, he was safe, he had a chance. Once she said it, he was doomed.

The house was banked against the winter, the windows caulked and tight. There was nothing more he could do, nothing that wouldn't be a major remodeling. Not that the place didn't need some solid work, but anything he started now would take months. And he'd be gone in less than two weeks. He had no reason to prolong being there except that he wanted to be with her, needed to be with her.

He fed her pasta and Italian bread for lunch, brownies and ice cream for dessert. He made her cappuccino, improvising with the limited kitchen equipment she'd inherited from her grandparents, watched her as she drank the cinnamony brew and ate every last bit of whipped cream. And when she started to say something, he leaned over and stopped her mouth, tasting the coffee and cinnamon.

When he went out to bring in more firewood she followed him, and just when he was expecting the worst, he ended up with a snowball smack in the middle of his chest. He'd responded appropriately, chasing after her, tossing her in the snow and rolling on top of her, until they were both frozen, breathless, laughing. And he'd kissed her again, and the snow began to melt beneath them, and he knew he wouldn't be able to keep from making love to her one last time.

They made it as far as the living room sofa. He stripped her snow-damp clothes off her as they went, leaving a trail through the kitchen. He kept her so busy she didn't realize that he wasn't letting her touch him, kiss him, caress him. He'd survive this if he could give to her, do for her. If he accepted anything in return he'd be doomed.

She was looking up at him, laughing, when they sank down onto the sofa, and then her laughter stilled as he filled her, thrusting deep, no longer afraid of hurting her. She arched up to meet him, her body tight around him, her arms clinging to him, her face pressed against his shoulder, and it was fierce, hot and fast, a fire-storm of passion that was immediate and eternal, that left them both panting, sated, silent, with only the stillness of the winter afternoon around them, and the crackle of the wood stove breaking the quiet.

He held her, his eyes closed, unwilling, unready to face what he knew would come next, held her, knowing he had to let her go. If Augusta had thought to punish him, she couldn't have come up with a better torment. Even hell would pale compared to the thought of leaving Carrie.

And then he released her, surging to his feet and disappearing into the kitchen. He picked up the trail of clothes he'd pulled off her. He was still wearing his jeans, and he refastened them, rebut-toning his flannel shirt.

She lay curled up on the sofa, a secret, satisfied smile on her face. She looked up at him when he dropped her discarded clothes on top of her, and opened her mouth to tell him she loved him.

He stopped her. "I'll make some coffee," he said. "You stay put."

She smiled lazily. "Are you certain you don't have Scandinavian blood in you? You drink coffee like a Swede."

He had no idea what kind of blood he had in his veins. Whatever kind it was, it was only borrowed. He managed to return her smile, holding himself back from her when he wanted to pull her into his arms. "I used to drink tea."

It was her turn to look startled. "I knew a man who drank tea once," she said in a quiet voice.

Damn, and double damn. "Did you? Only one? I know it's a rare taste nowadays," he said, trying to get the right teasing note in his voice.

But she simply looked at him, confusion darkening her wide blue eyes. "Only one," she said. "Until you." And he knew she wasn't talking about a taste for Earl Grey.

It was already getting dark, the December afternoon closing

down around them. He sat at the kitchen table, a mug of black coffee in his hand, and stared out into the twilight, trying to summon up the strength to leave her. He could hear her rummaging around in the living room, humming beneath her breath, a Christmas carol, and he told himself the dangerous moment over the tea had passed. There was no way she could connect him with the heartless bastard who'd destroyed her life.

She came into the kitchen, coming up behind him, threading her arms around his neck, pressing his head back against her soft breasts, and he could barely stifle a groan. He couldn't stop her this time. He couldn't kiss her into silence, feed her into stillness.

"I love you," she said softly. "You know that, and you've been terrified I was going to tell you. You've been trying to shut me up all day, but it's really nothing to be afraid of." She kissed the side of his face, and his eyes fluttered closed in sudden despair. "It's odd, but it seems like I've always loved you. Even when I was in love with someone else, it seems as if it was you. Ridiculous, isn't it?"

He held himself stiff and still in the cradle of her arms. "I thought you wanted uninvolved sex?" he said in a harsh voice.

"I lied," she said simply, pressing her face against his, following his sightless gaze out into the evening. "I wanted you."

Damned. Damned to hell and back, and he knew it. He'd earned it twice over in this lifetime and the last. He'd taken a woman who was aching and vulnerable, one who was ready to love. He'd taken her, and he was going to abandon her, this time not by his choice but by the cruelties of fate. He'd been given a chance to save her, and he'd only brought her back to the same vulnerable state he'd left her in the last time.

Damn him, he deserved it, he thought bitterly. He deserved the torments of eternity. But she didn't.

He pulled out of her arms carefully, rising from the table and looking at her. He had no choice in leaving her, but he could choose when and how. He could stay with her now, love her for the next two weeks, and abandon her on Christmas Eve without a word of explanation.

Or he could act like a bastard here and now, and make her realize she was well rid of him.

It was no choice at all. The second option would hurt him, start his punishment just a little bit early. It gave her a hope of salvation.

"I'd better be getting back," he said, his voice cool and distant.

"Lars and Maggie will be wondering where I am. You're able to take care of yourself by now, aren't you?"

In the shadowy kitchen he could see the color drain from her face. She took a wary step back from him, searching for something to protect her, and he wanted to put his arms around her, to smooth the pain from her face.

Instead he reached for his coat, hanging on a peg near the door. "If you need anything just give Maggie a call," he said, shrugging into it.

"I'll do that," she said, her voice cool and lifeless.

He managed a jaunty smile. "And keep eating. You don't want to get run-down again. I won't be here next time you get pneumonia."

She flinched, so slightly another man might not have noticed. "No, you won't," she said evenly. "I haven't thanked you..."

"Consider me well rewarded," he said with a deliberate leer.

He might have pushed her too far. Her hands clenched, and he wondered if she was going to hit him. And what he'd do if she did.

She managed a faint smile. "Goodbye, Gabriel," she murmured.

It was worse than the heart attack that had exploded in his chest and ended up killing him. Worse than the paramedics beating on him, worse than the thought of an eternity roasting in the fires of hell.

And it was all he could do for her. "Goodbye, babe," he said, heading out into the frosty night air.

He didn't dare look back. If he saw her crying he wouldn't be able to stand it. Lars's truck started instantly with a low, throaty rumble, and he backed out her driveway, at the last minute glancing in the window. He could see her silhouette standing there, very still, very proud.

She'd make it, he told himself. She was tough, too tough to let a turkey like Emerson MacVey get to her twice in a lifetime. She'd survive.

Thank God, he wouldn't.

NO ONE SEEMED SURPRISED at his reappearance at the Swensen family home. Alexander Borodin had just left, and the place was in an uproar.

"A fortune, Gabriel," Lars boomed out. "The man has offered me a fortune."

"Beware of Greeks bearing gifts," Maggie said, unable to keep the light of hope out of her eyes.

"I thought he was Russian," Gabriel managed to drawl.

"He's an American, by God," Lars said. "Same as you and me."

"A very rich American," Nils piped up. "He's renovating a string of exclusive hotels all over the world, and he's offered Pop the job of redoing the woodwork. There's enough work to last into the year two thousand and beyond."

He'd blown it, Gabriel thought in sudden misery. It had all back-fired. "You'll leave here, then?" he asked in a carefully neutral voice.

"Only to visit the sites. We need to set up a workshop right here in town, do most of the custom work here and then ship it to the hotels. I'd oversee the installation, but I've always liked the thought of a bit of travel. As long as I have Angel Falls to come home to."

"Sounds perfect," Gabriel said, disguising his relief. So he'd managed to do one thing right after all. He wondered how Augusta would stack that up against his seduction of Carrie.

"There's more than enough for you, as well, Gabriel," Maggie said. "Mr. Borodin saw some of your work, and he thinks you're very gifted. Almost as good as my Lars," she said proudly. "He wants you to help."

Gabriel shook his head. "I can't. I told you, I have a job just after Christmas."

"You don't know what kind of money this man is offering," Lars said. "It's unbelievable, it's magnificent, it's..."

"No more than you deserve," Maggie said sharply. "Can't you get out of your next job, Gabriel? Tell them something more important came up. Something with a future."

There was no future for him. He shook his head. "Sorry," he said. "I wish I could. But I'm committed."

"But..." Nils began.

"Leave the man alone," Lars said, looking at him closely, see-ing him more clearly than Gabriel could have wished. "He knows there'll always be a place for him here. He'll always be needed. If he wants to, and he can, he'll be here."

"There are not quite two weeks till Christmas," Gabriel said. "I've finished out at Carrie's—at least I can help you get started."

"First of all, I need to find a place to work. We'll have enough to hire at least a dozen men, and I can think of twelve right now

who need the work. The sooner we get going, the sooner those
men will start bringing in some money,'' Lars said. And then his
eyes narrowed. ''You've finished at Carrie's?''

''Finished,'' he said flatly. ''What about the old mill? Is it still
in working shape?''

''By heavens, you're right. Most of the equipment was sold off,
but some of the really big stuff is still there, and the building's
sound as a dollar.''

''Not much of a recommendation,'' Gabriel said dryly.

''We'll check it out tomorrow. Now why didn't I think of that?''
Lars demanded of the company. ''There are times, Gabriel, when
I think you must be my guardian angel.''

''Not likely,'' he drawled. ''Just someone passing through.''

And outside the old house, the wind began to howl. And it
sounded like the hounds of hell, calling to him.

CHAPTER FOURTEEN

Carrie stood in the darkened kitchen, watching him drive away, a sense of numb disbelief washing over her. She felt nothing but a vast sense of confusion. The pain would come later, she knew it. Once more she'd been a stupid fool, giving her heart to a man who had no interest in it.

For now she could bless the numbness that settled around her. She waited until the headlights disappeared into the gathering night, and then walked slowly back into the living room.

She stared at the sofa, at the rumpled cover and disarranged cushions. She stared at the wood box, filled with a fresh load of firewood, and she wrapped her arms around her body, shivering.

"Damn him," she said out loud, her voice clear and steady and very far from tears. "Damn his soul to hell."

The words shocked her. Suddenly, for some reason, they felt very real. Not a traditional curse without meaning, but a deliberate damning. No one deserved that, even someone who ran at the first sight of love.

"No," she said wearily. "Don't damn him. Just don't let me care."

She glanced around her living room, the rustic wood-paneled walls, the quilted wall-hangings, the snow-crusted windows. She hadn't done a thing to get ready for Christmas, and it was already nearly there. She needed to decorate her house, she needed to clean it, she needed good hard physical activity with no time to think, no time to brood. She needed to wipe the memory of Gabriel Falconi from her mind, from her body. She'd deal with it later, after he was gone.

She was usually far from compulsive about the state of the old farmhouse, but that night and the next day she would have done her Scandinavian grandmother proud. She scrubbed anything that held still, she put out candles and Christmas wreaths and hangings and fragrant boughs of fir, she even dragged in her own sizable Christmas tree, stuck it in a corner and decorated it with tiny white lights and all the quilted decorations she'd made over the year.

On the top of the tree she put the angel she'd made when she heard Emerson MacVey had died. It was a comical sort of angel, with a clownish face, an upturned grin and ineffably sad eyes. While he didn't look the slightest bit like the man she'd once loved, he'd always reminded her of MacVey. For some reason, he reminded her of Gabriel, as well.

She stepped back and surveyed the tree with a critical eye. Perhaps it was just the fact that she'd been fool enough to love two men who had no use for love, or for her. Or maybe there was something else, something she didn't quite understand, that linked the two men. Other than her own foolishness.

She heard the click-clacking of the freezing rain outside the window, slapping against the house. Inside, everything was cozy and warm, Christmassy, with the kitchen radio playing carols, the lights from the tree winking at her. Someone had brought her out a chicken pie among all the other goodies, and it was heating in the oven, sending wonderful smells throughout the house, mixing with the cinnamon potpourri she'd put in a bowl on the stove.

She was still recovering from her bout with pneumonia, she was exhausted from her compulsive housecleaning, and the weather report had gone from winter storm watch to winter storm warning, a full alert for those who understood such things. Carrie knew perfectly well she needed to curl up in front of the stove, eat her chicken pie, read something soothing, and make an early night of it.

She also knew she had no intention of doing so. Something was nagging at her, and all the housecleaning and decorating in the world couldn't drive it from her mind. She ought to give up on Gabriel, count him a lesson well learned, and go back to her solitary life, thanking God she'd been spared anything more painful. She kept trying to squash down her feelings, push herself back into a calm, martyred acceptance, when suddenly they burst forth in a great passionate rush, and along with them came knowledge.

He hadn't run away from her. He'd run away from himself. If he was a cool, heartless womanizer, he would have responded with an easy "I love you, too, babe." Instead, he'd frozen and then run, and she'd curled up like a wounded dog, ready to suffer in silence.

She wasn't ready to suffer any longer. She was going out on this dreadful icy night, and she was going to confront Gabriel Falconi. She was going to fight for him. And damn it, she was going to win.

He didn't move. "Actually, that's a very good question," he said. "I'm not really sure."

"Don't give me that," she said, ripping off her coat with trembling fingers, and whether they trembled from rage or the cold he couldn't guess. Or something else, something even more elemental that was flowing between them, blazing between them, like a forest fire out of control. "You have no right to go to bed with me and then run away when I tell you I love you. No right." She dumped the coat onto Maggie's spotless floor and kept moving toward him.

"You told me you only wanted sex."

"I lied," she said flatly. "And you knew it."

He was backing away from her. Trying to stall, to give her one last chance to save herself. The fury was the best possible thing for her. He needed to feed that life-affirming fury. "Maybe I didn't care."

"Maybe," she said, still coming toward him in the darkened hallway of the Swensens' old house. "Or maybe you cared too much. I believe you when you say you have to leave. That you have no choice in the matter. I don't believe you when you say you don't care about me. You aren't a very good liar."

Emerson MacVey had been a consummate liar. Gabriel reached for that long-lost talent, for anything that would halt Carrie on her determined advance. He needed to convince her he was the worst thing that ever happened to her. Not for his sake—he'd accepted his punishment. For hers.

"Listen," he said, summoning a cool drawl as he ended up against the wall, no place to retreat to. "It's a simple matter of hormones. You were available, I was horny, we had a good time, as long as emotions didn't enter into it. As soon as they did, I figured it was time to leave. You aren't really in love with me. It's always the way with women—they have a good time in bed and then their puritan upbringing convinces them they have to call it love. They aren't allowed to simply enjoy their bodies. That's all it was, Carrie. Great sex. Believe me."

He waited to see her fury fade, her face crumple into pained acceptance. She kept on advancing.

"It doesn't work, Gabriel. Try it again. Tell me it was lust that kept you by my side, spooning tea and soup down my throat, taking care of me."

"Maybe it was guilt."

That halted her, at least momentarily. "Guilt?"

"You're an expert on that, aren't you? You blame yourself for

GABRIEL STRAIGHTENED UP, stretching the kink in his spine, and let out a quiet, miserable groan. He'd spent the day in Lars's workshop, fussing over the details on a newel post, being so finicky that even the perfectionist Lars had teased him. Work wasn't driving her out of his mind. Nothing was.

He didn't want to be around anyone. The buoyant cheerfulness of the Swensen family, now that security was just around the corner, drove him mad. The silence of the house, when they were gone, was even worse.

He should have gone with them that night. The whole lot of them had piled into the pickup and the ancient station wagon and started on a caravan up to the old factory to check out its usefulness. Gabriel hadn't needed to go along with them to know it would suit them just fine. He'd done his part, saved his second victim, and everything was going to fall into place quite neatly, thank you. Besides, he didn't want to visit the scene of the crime. Even looking at the outside of the deserted factory brought a depressing wave of guilt over him.

He wondered how Carrie was doing. He told himself he was only concerned whether she counted as a success or not, and knew he was lying. Maggie had talked to her this morning, and even Gabriel's most careful questioning hadn't been able to elicit anything. Perhaps there was nothing to elicit. Augusta/Gertrude hadn't come to the house, waving thunderbolts and threatening the wrath of God. Perhaps he was ready to concentrate on the third person he had to save.

Not that he had any choice in the matter. The longer he was around Carrie the more he botched things. The deeper he fell, in trouble, in love. He needed to forget his almost unbearable need to see her, he needed to leave bad enough alone.

He needed to find the third person whose life he'd ruined. He'd considered plain out asking Gertrude, but he already knew it would be a waste of time. She expected the worst from him, and she wasn't about to make things easier.

Maybe he ought to get out of town. Steve had finished with his pickup truck, and Gabriel had found he had enough money to pay him. If he got into the truck and started driving away from Angel Falls, maybe his third task would present itself.

He didn't think so. Lars and Carrie were no coincidence, neither was Augusta's presence or the name of the town. Christmas Eve was not much more than a week away. He had that long to find the third person, and then he'd be gone.

He knew where he was going, he'd accepted it. The other place, without question, was the price he had to pay for touching Carrie, for kissing her, for taking what she so sweetly, desperately offered.

And it was worth every moment of eternity.

He was still going to do his damnedest to find number three. Maybe he'd get time off for good behavior. Maybe if he did a good enough job with two of them, Augusta would overlook his failing grade with Carrie. Maybe he'd pass the test without the full extra credit.

Damn it, it wasn't fair! Other people died and didn't have to go through all this crap. Other people lived longer, they weren't cut off in their prime, when they had so much to live for.

And what did Emerson MacVey have to live for? Money. A cold, upscale apartment, a cold, upscale life. In his thirty-two years he'd done more harm than most people did in lives that lasted twice as long. It was just as well his had come to an abrupt end.

Hell, he didn't deserve to go to heaven. He accepted that, but he wasn't ready to give up. He'd find the last person and do his best. The one thing he wouldn't do was bring any more pain to Carrie Alexander. He wasn't going near her again.

The lights in the old kitchen flickered and went out, and Gabriel cursed in the darkness. It took him a few moments to find the matches and candles. In the darkness he could hear the freezing rain rattling against the windows, and he thought of the Swensens, out on such a night.

As if on cue, the phone rang. It took more than five rings for him to find it in the dark. "Gabriel, we're not getting home tonight," Lars boomed over the other end, jovial as ever. "The police have closed the main road, and the ice is murderous. Gertrude's going to put us up for the night."

All Gabriel's suspicions were instantly aroused. "Why Gertrude?" he asked.

"She lives right next to the factory," Lars said patiently. "You'll be all right there, won't you, boy? Don't go out in this stuff. You aren't used to it, and even for someone who knows what they're doing it's damned treacherous."

"I'll stay put. The power's off."

Lars sighed. "It does that. I wish you'd come with us tonight."

"And ended up spending the night at Gertrude's? No thank you. I'll enjoy being alone," he said. "If the lights come on I can get some more work done. Otherwise I'll just go to bed."

"You do that. Stay warm, Gabriel. We'll see you in the m ing."

Gabriel moved to the window, looking out into the dark The white stuff was coating the roads, the cars, the windows, ing a little clicking sound. He stared outside for a momen then his eyes narrowed. Someone was driving down the roa more accurately, someone was sliding down the road, the lights swinging wildly back and forth as they tried to contr vehicle.

They'd be fine, he told himself, trying to squash down his panic. The street was relatively flat. If they just had enough to slide to a stop, to seek shelter, they wouldn't be hurt. A in God's name was stupid enough to go out driving on a ni this?

He watched as the car drifted sideways. Even through t of the wind and the thickness of the storm windows, he h crunch as the front end of the car collided with one of lining the road. He waited for the driver to move, to try the car going. A moment later the headlights turned off, car disappeared into the swirling darkness.

It had parked three houses down, at the Milsoms' plac one obviously coming for the holidays, he told himsel bleakly out into the darkness. Someone who should hav sense to wait for better weather.

But he knew he was fooling himself. Knew, as he sound of her footsteps climbing up the snow-drifted fr knew as he heard her knock on the door, a loud, perempt knew who it was. He just wasn't sure why she'd come.

He considered not answering it, then dismissed it. A he didn't want to see her, he couldn't let her go out int again. She was seven times a fool to have ventured o He wasn't about to let her risk her life again.

He was halfway to the door, the stub of a candle i when it opened. Hardly anyone in Angel Falls locked doors, or even waited very long for a knock to be ans stood there, ice coating her hair, her coat, stood there doorway looking at him.

There was no reproach in her pale, beautiful face. no longing, no heartbreak. There was simple, life-affi

She slammed the door behind her and advanced on the hell do you think you are?" she demanded in a h

everything bad that ever happened in this town. Just because some yuppie jerk closed the mill doesn't mean you're to blame. You were trying your best, but you were playing with fire. MacVey was out of your league from the very beginning, and you should have known it. You did your best, and it backfired. The mill was in trouble long before MacVey got his hands on it—it was just a matter of time.''

Her face was pale. "How do you know his name was MacVey?''

Hell and damnation, he thought. "Maggie said something,'' he improvised swiftly.

"Maggie doesn't know about him.'' Her voice was flat, accusing.

He could feel himself starting to sweat. "Gertrude...''

"Gertrude doesn't know, either. I never told anyone about him. Not by name. Who are you, Gabriel? Why do I feel as if I know you?''

He opened his mouth to tell her, but the words wouldn't come. She deserved no less than the truth, but he couldn't give it to her. "Lars,'' he said abruptly, the inspiration nothing short of a miracle.

"I never told Lars...''

"No, but you told me you were responsible for some coldhearted yuppie buying the factory and then closing it. And Lars knew the name of the man who'd done that. He's negotiating for the use of the building right now.''

"He's not negotiating with MacVey.''

"No,'' Gabriel said. "MacVey's dead. Burning in hell, most likely.''

She stared up at him. "I don't think so,'' she said. "But we're not talking about MacVey. We're talking about you and me.''

"There is no you and me.''

"Guess again,'' she said. "Look at me and tell me that night we spent together was just a one-night stand. A roll in the hay. Tell me you don't feel something for me.''

Damn. She looked brave and strong and alive, the fire of determination burning in her eyes. A woman like Carrie wasn't easily destroyed. A woman like Carrie was ready to fight for what she wanted. He'd warned her, and been damned for it. He could only go to hell once.

"I don't feel *something* for you,'' he said, his voice so flat and uncompromising that the light began to fade from her eyes. "I'm in love with you.''

The expression on her face was worth it. She just looked at him, radiating joy and love, and the sight of her was so beautiful it hurt. He blew out the candle, plunging them into darkness, and pulled her into his arms.

Her mouth was cold, tasting of the winter air. Her body was trembling, and he knew now it had nothing to do with the temperature and everything to do with him. Too late, the words danced in the back of his mind, and he shut them out, scooping her up in his arms.

He made his way through the pitch darkness with unerring instinct. Kissing her slowed him down, and he had to kiss her. They stopped halfway up the flight of stairs, and he let her body slide down against his. She reached up and ripped his flannel shirt open, her greedy hands running up his torso.

"Where are the Swensens?" she whispered, putting her mouth against his chest, tasting him, licking him.

"Gone," he said, his voice strangled as her mouth moved lower, to his stomach, her arms wrapped tight around his waist. She was on her knees on the step beside him, and she put her cheek against the fierce swelling beneath his jeans, and he wondered whether they'd make it to the tiny bedroom beneath the eaves, or whether he was going to take her on the stairs.

They made it as far as the upstairs hallway. He tripped on the frayed carpet, and the two of them fell. She landed on top of him, soft, warm, fragrant, and she found his mouth in the darkness, kissing him, pushing the shirt from his shoulders, sliding her hands down to unfasten his belt buckle.

This time her hands were sure, determined. This time his hands were nervous, clumsy, as he stripped the clothes from her, tossing them away in the darkness, pushing her down onto the worn strip of carpeting, desperate to touch her, to kiss her, to have her.

He wanted to take his time, but she was as fevered as he was. She pulled him up between her legs, and he sank into her sleek, welcoming warmth with a muffled groan.

She arched up to meet him, wrapping her long dancer's legs around him, pulling him in deeper still, and her hands clutched his shoulders, her mouth met his with unerring instincts, and each thrust brought him closer and closer to heaven.

It was darkness, velvet darkness all around them. He cupped her face, kissing her eyelids, her cheekbones, her soft, wonderful mouth. He wanted to be gentle with her, to make it last, but he was hurtling along a dark path toward completion, and she was with him every step of the way, her breathing labored, her body slippery with sweat, her hands clutching him.

He felt her body tighten around him, heard her strangled cry, and then he was lost, thrusting into her, pushing them both over the edge into a star-tossed darkness unlike any he'd ever known.

He could still feel her body rippling, shimmering around him. He kissed her tear-streaked face, her nose, her mouth, and her lips reached up to kiss him back as she clung to him, shaky and breathless.

"You cry too much," he said in a low, tender voice.

"I haven't cried in two years. Not until you walked into my life." He started to pull away, and she clutched at him, suddenly desperate. "Don't," she said. "Don't feel guilty. People need to cry."

He'd never cried in his life. Doubtless another reason why his heart had exploded. "We need a bed," he said, lifting her into his arms, kicking the scattered clothes out of his way as he carried her the absurdly short distance to his bedroom.

The tiny room was very dark—only a fitful light came through the ice-coated window. He put her down onto the narrow iron bed with great care, lying beside her and pulling her into his arms. It was cold up there, and he flipped the heavy quilt over them, wrapping his body around hers.

"What do you think Lars and Maggie will say when they come back and find me here?" she whispered against his chest. "Do you think you'll be horsewhipped?"

"Congratulated is more likely," he said, threading his hands through her silky hair. "He and Maggie have been hardly subtle in their matchmaking efforts."

He could feel her smile in the darkness. "Neither has Gertrude."

Their bodies were entwined too closely for her to miss his start of shock, but luckily she jumped to her own conclusions. "That surprises you, doesn't it? It surprised me. I mean, she was my social studies teacher, for heaven's sake."

"How was she matchmaking?"

"She told me to go to bed with you."

Gabriel closed his eyes. Augusta's motives were beyond his comprehension. Perhaps she'd been stacking the deck against him. More likely giving him the hardest test of all, one he'd failed. One he was damned glad he failed.

"She did, did she?" he murmured. "She's smarter than she

looks. Carrie, I...'' His words were cut off as the sound of the telephone echoed through the house.

Both of them were very still, absurdly guilty. "Don't answer it,'' she whispered, clutching at his shoulders. "It's going to be trouble.''

"I thought you liked trouble.''

"Right now I don't like anything but you.'' The phone stopped ringing, and he began kissing her again, ready for her, knowing she was ready for him.

She was getting very bold, her hand reaching down to capture him, learn him, and he could barely control his groan of pleasure, wanting the world to center down on this narrow bed under the eaves and the woman beside him, the storms of life outside, the warmth of love inside. He kissed her mouth slowly, lingeringly, trailing his lips down her neck to the delineated collarbone, until he captured one nipple, suckling it deeply into his mouth, feeling her instant, fierce response that matched his own, and...

The phone began to ring again. The world, intruding. Carrie was motionless, waiting. It was up to him, he knew it. She would shut out the world, and everyone in it, for him.

And he knew he couldn't do it. He'd spent thirty-two years thinking of nothing but his own needs and desires. Thirty-two selfish, dissatisfied years. He didn't want to bring Carrie to that same lonely spot.

"I have to answer it,'' he said, slowly disentangling himself, half-hoping she'd cling to him.

She let him go. "I know you do,'' she said, and even in the darkness he could see the love shining on her face.

He knocked over the telephone table in the hall as he tried to find it in the dark, and the panicked voice on the other end was that of a strange man.

"Lars, it's Martin Baker. I need your help,'' he said in the anguished voice of a frightened parent. "Something's happened to Jeffie.''

And with a sudden, sinking feeling, Gabriel knew who the third person was. Somehow he'd ruined a seventeen-year-old kid's life. And it was up to him to save him.

CHAPTER FIFTEEN

"What's wrong?" Carrie sat up in bed, the quilt pulled around her, and with the fitful light from the frosted window she could see that he was in the midst of pulling on his clothes.

"I have to go out."

She scrambled from the bed, looking in the darkness for her own clothes. "What's happened?"

He didn't even pause. He seemed like a stranger, distant, determined. More like a saint than she had ever been.

"I have to find Jeffie."

"Who was that on the phone?"

"His father. He was looking for Lars. Apparently Jeffie's parents came home unexpectedly and found he'd been drinking. They had a huge row, and Jeffie took off in the car."

"Oh, God," Carrie said quietly. "I took him practice-driving once. He can barely manage to keep a car on the road in daylight, when the roads are clear and he's sober. He's going to be killed."

"No, he's not," Gabriel said flatly. "I'm going to find him."

"Why you?" She didn't know why she asked the question. Gabriel had seemed like the kind of man who shunned involvement. Risking his own life on icy roads for the sake of a drunken teenager should have seemed unexpected. Oddly enough, it wasn't at all.

"Why not me?" he countered. "His father can't do anything— Jeffie took their only car. Lars has a family depending on him. He shouldn't be risking his life out on a night like this."

"And you should?"

"I don't have that much to lose," he said. "I'll need to take your car."

"Fine," she said. "Where are my clothes?"

"What do you need your clothes for?"

"I'm coming with you, and I think it might be a bit chilly if I went outside naked."

"You're staying here."

"The hell I am. You don't know this area, I do. How do you

expect to find a teenage boy on a night like this without a little
help?''

"Carrie..."

"I'm coming with you. Now where the hell are my clothes?"

They were strewn from one end of the Swensens' house to the
other. She found her jeans at the top of the stairs, her sweater
halfway down the hall, her panties hung over the railing. She never
did find her bra, and she could only hope they'd make it back there,
in daylight, before the Swensens did. While Maggie and Lars might
heartily approve of her being with Gabriel, they might draw the
line at her underclothing decorating their house.

By the time she'd pulled her boots on and headed out into the
ice storm, Gabriel was already at the car, and if she hadn't had the
keys she knew he would have driven off without her. If she hadn't
already discovered he was a better driver than she was she would
have refused to give them to him, but as it was she simply buckled
herself into the passenger seat and waited for him to pull out onto
the ice-covered road.

He drove with maddening slowness, managing far more control
than she'd been able to achieve. "Have you ever driven on ice
before?" she asked, tucking her hands into her pockets to keep
them from clenching.

"I don't remember."

"You have the strangest memory."

"Yes," he said, concentrating on the roads. The headlights
speared through the icy darkness, and she could see his reflection
from the dashboard lights. "Where should we start looking?"

"Your guess is as good as mine. I didn't see him on the road
when I drove here, but I don't know how long he's been gone. For
that matter, I don't know how long I've been with you tonight."

"Not long enough," he said, carefully navigating a turn.

"No," she said, "not long enough."

"I've got an idea," he murmured, and she had to admire his
skill. Each time the car started drifting sideways he corrected it,
keeping his speed careful, even. The sight of the salt truck was a
blessed relief, the sight of the police car trailing it was less reassuring, particularly when the blue lights began to flash at the sight
of Carrie's car.

"You'd better pull over," she said. "Jimmy likes to think he's
Rambo."

The fresh salt on the road gave the cars slightly more purchase, and Gabriel slowed to a halt, grinding down the window of the car as the policeman shone a blinding light at them.

"Seen any sign of Jeffie?"

"How'd you know?" Carrie leaned across Gabriel, breathing in his scent, wishing to God they could have stayed curled up in his narrow little bed.

"His dad called me. We've got a couple of state police looking for him, but we didn't want to get too many people out on a night like this. Make things even worse than they already are. If I were you I'd go back and wait it out."

"All right," Gabriel said dutifully.

"Don't worry, we'll let you know when we find him."

Gabriel nodded, rolling up the window and edging the car forward. Carrie sat back and looked at him, trying to control the surge of disappointment. Disappointment that turned to a measured relief when he turned up toward the school, instead of back to the Swensens.

"I thought you said we were going home to wait it out," she said.

"It doesn't pay to argue with people like Jimmy. If you want I'll drop you off there, but I'm not going in till I find him."

"I'm staying with you. Jeffie needs all the friends he can get. I'd just as soon the police aren't the ones to catch up with him. His father won't have told them he was drinking, and Jeffie's going to have enough to handle without having to deal with the legal ramifications of drunk driving."

"It might be the best thing for him," Gabriel said. "Sooner or later you have to deal with the consequences of your actions."

"Are you talking about Jeffie? Or yourself?"

"I'm talking about everyone. What goes round, comes round," he said.

"Jeffie's already spent most of his life dealing with the consequences of other people's mistakes. His brother's and his parents' included."

There was a sudden, arrested look in his eyes. "Baker," he murmured. "What was his brother's name?"

"Lord, I don't know. Do you mean the name he was born with? Up until the time he dropped out of college and joined a commune, he was Clive Baker."

"Clive," Gabriel said in an odd voice. "Of course."

"What do you mean, of course? Did you know him?"

"No."

"Stupid question. Of course you didn't. Clive spent his life here, until he got accepted at Harvard. If it weren't for a bunch of sadistic preppies..."

"What do you mean?"

She shook with remembered fury. "A group of rich bullies decided to haze Clive, led by some cruel jerk. They teased him so badly he dropped out of school, went off to become one with the universe, and no one's seen him since. The Bakers gave up on both their sons then, I think. And Jeffie's been paying for it."

"And it was all the fault of some college buddies of Clive's?"

"No. But their leader was the catalyst for the disasters that followed."

"Do you think someone should be punished for being a catalyst?" he murmured, moving with a slow, steady speed up the long hill toward the union school. "Do you think they should be judged and found guilty, sentenced...?"

"I don't know," she said. "It's not my place to judge people."

"No," he said in a hollow voice. "Nor mine."

The parking lot outside the sprawling school was dark and deserted, not even the streetlights glowing. The power outage seemed to have hit everywhere, and only in the distance could Carrie see the faint glow of lights. "He's not here," she said, unable to keep the panic and disappointment out of her voice.

"Yes, he is."

"Gabriel, there's no sign of him..."

"He's here," Gabriel said, letting the car slide to a halt. There was no sign of anyone in the vast ice-covered parking lot, but Gabriel unfastened his seat belt and climbed out anyway, leaving the car in neutral.

Without hesitation Carrie followed suit, barely able to stand upright on the glare ice. "Gabriel, he isn't..."

But he was already moving away from her, walking carefully with steady determination across the ice-covered surface. She followed his gaze in the glare of the headlights and saw what she'd missed before. The chain-link fence that surrounded the school property was down.

"Oh, God," she murmured, starting after him, but her feet went out from under her and she went sprawling, hard, on the ice. By the time she scrambled upright again, Gabriel had disappeared beyond the fence, heading down the steep hill.

She fell three times before she reached the fence, and she was half-afraid to look over the side, certain she'd see the Bakers' car a twisted mass of metal and broken flesh. Relief swamped her as she made out the shape of the sedan, still in one piece, resting against a grove of trees. The lights were off, but she could hear the radio playing, Christmas rap music, for God's sake, and she could see Gabriel leaning inside the driver's door.

"Is he all right?" she called, her voice shaking in the night air.

"He's fine," Gabriel called back, his voice rich with relief. "He's got a few cuts and bruises and he feels like hell, but he's fine."

"I'll bring the car closer."

By the time she'd edged the car along the icy surface Gabriel and Jeffie had appeared at the top of the hill. In the glare of the headlights Jeffie's face was pale, and there was a streak of blood across his cheekbone. He didn't look drunk or belligerent, he looked like a scared, lost little boy.

Gabriel bundled him into the back seat, then followed in beside him. "Drive to the hospital, Carrie."

"I thought you said he was all right?" She swallowed her sudden panic at the thought of having to navigate these roads again.

"He's taken some pills. He needs to have his stomach pumped, he needs to be checked out, and he needs to talk with someone. A professional. Can you manage it?"

"Yes," she said, because she had to.

"And turn on the radio, would you? Jeffie and I need to talk?"

It was maddening, it was terrifying, it was one of the hardest things she had ever had to do. She turned on the radio, finding something middle-of-the-road and innocuous, and began the endless slide to the hospital.

She wondered what they were saying back there in such low, serious voices. Was Gabriel giving him hell? Was Jeffie whining, or coming up with excuses?

Damn it, she wanted to be the one to lecture him, to take care of him, to make everything better. Letting someone else handle it was impossible, and good for her. She needed Gabriel around for more than the pleasure of his company. She needed him to prove that she wasn't indispensable. Someone else could be responsible for the state of the world. Responsible for one lost little boy she hadn't been able to help.

He took Jeffie into the emergency room while Carrie called his parents. When Gabriel finally emerged, he was alone, looking weary, sorrowful, like a man who'd looked into the face of hell and seen his own reflection.

"Is he all right?" she asked, rushing up to him, wanting to put her arms around him, afraid he wouldn't let her.

He pulled her tight against him, burying his face in her neck, and she clung to him, love flowing through her. "He'll be fine," he murmured. And then he lifted his head, looking past her.

The Bakers were coming toward them. Martin Baker looked more disturbed than she'd ever seen him, and Carolyn, usually the best-dressed woman in Angel Falls, wore one earring, ripped stockings, and her coat was buttoned awry. Her eyes were puffy with tears, and Martin's were suspiciously bright.

"Where is he?" Martin demanded. "Where's my boy?"

It's about time, Carrie wanted to snap at him, but she bit back the words. "He's in with a counselor," Gabriel answered for her. "He'll be released in a short while."

"I can't thank you enough," Carolyn began, her usually arch voice shaky with emotion. "When I think what might have happened..."

Gabriel just looked at her, and there was no judgment, no censure, only sorrow and understanding. "Life is too precious to throw away," he said. "Love is too precious to waste. Even for a moment." And putting his arms around Carrie's shoulder, he led her out of the hospital into the chill midnight air.

CARRIE DIDN'T SAY A WORD when they left the hospital, and for that Gabriel could be profoundly grateful. The past few hours had been the most harrowing of any lifetime. He could accept responsibility for a woman's broken heart and shattered life. He could accept responsibility for the economic collapse of an entire town. But the fate of one teenage boy was more than he could bear.

She simply fastened the seat belt around her, waiting for him to make the first move. When he tugged at her she went silently, willingly, resting her head on his lap as he made the long, slow drive back to the Swensens.

This time there was no tossing of clothes as they made their way upstairs. This time, when they made love, they did it in the narrow bed, sweetly, slowly, letting the pleasure stretch and grow, taking their time, savoring each other. And when they finished he looked down at her, cradling her head in his arms, and kissed her eyelids. "Carrie, I..."

"No," she whispered. "Don't say it. We have a little more than a week. Let's not talk about it. Let's just live it. No promises, no regrets."

And instead of telling her all the things he wanted to and couldn't, he told her with his lips and his body, arousing her all over again, until the night slid into daylight, and together they slept.

IT WAS A WEEK OF HEAVEN, and a week of hell. A week of love-making, cookie-making, a week spent feeding Carrie, body and soul. And a week spent feeding himself.

Two out of three ain't bad, he told himself, knowing Augusta wouldn't agree. Lars had already begun setting up shop in the old mill, Jeffie was going to AA meetings and family counseling and beginning to lose that sullen, haunted look. Only Carrie was going to suffer, and there was nothing he could do about it.

She steadfastly refused to talk about it. She knew he was leaving, knew nothing would change that. And yet she took each day, each hour, each minute with a delight that moved him, as well.

"Welcome, stranger," Lars greeted him when he walked into the kitchen. "It's Christmas Eve, my boy. You'll be coming to church with us, won't you?"

"Of course, he will," Maggie piped up, looking downright cheerful as she nursed the baby. "Carrie wouldn't let him miss it. And don't tease the man about making himself scarce. He's had better things to do."

"Am I complaining?" Lars said plaintively, his blue eyes twinkling. "He's been at the mill every day, and I can't imagine what I'd do without him. It's a rare gift you have, my boy."

He heard the words with numb despair. "It's Christmas Eve," he agreed. "And I have another job to go to."

The silence in the kitchen was palpable. "I thought you'd changed your mind about that," Maggie said softly.

Gabriel shook his head. "I'm afraid I'm committed. I just wanted to settle up my rent, and say goodbye."

"Don't be ridiculous!" Lars said gruffly. "It's me who owes you money, after all that hard work you've put in at the mill..."

Gabriel shook his head. "We agreed that would wait until you got your advance from Borodin. You can send it to me."

"But..."

"We agreed," Gabriel said sternly, counting out some money and dropping it onto the table. "And I'm a man of my word." He managed a faint grin. "Look at it this way, you'll still have time to get that train set Nils is longing for."

He was still good at manipulating people, he thought absently.

That much of Emerson MacVey remained. The Swensens wouldn't accept the money for themselves, but they would for their children.

"My things are already in the car," he said. "I just wanted to say goodbye."

Lars looked shocked. "You can't be leaving already! No one expects you to be on a job site on Christmas Eve."

Gabriel's smile was wry. "You don't know my future boss. I'll miss you."

"You'll come back?"

He wondered whether he ought to lie. If he ended up where he expected, there'd be no way he'd ever see any of the Swensens again. They were good people—there'd be no question where they'd end up come Judgment Day. No sending the likes of them back for extra credit.

"If I can," he temporized.

"Have you already said goodbye to Carrie?" Maggie asked softly.

"I'm on my way there."

"She knows you're going?"

"She's always known I had to go," Gabriel said. "I never lied to her." At least, not in this lifetime.

Lars rose and shook his hand, and the Christmas cheer in his ruddy face had vanished. "We'll miss you, boy. Come back when you can."

"Is Gabriel leaving?" Nils wandered into the room, munching on a sugar cookie.

"Remember, he said he could only stay till Christmas," Maggie said.

"Oh, yeah," said Harald. "By the way, Gertrude told me to tell you she wants to see you. This afternoon. Four-thirty sharp."

He must have arrived in Minnesota around four-thirty, on Thanksgiving. It was such a short while ago, and yet it was a lifetime. He'd crammed more into those weeks than he had into his previous thirty-two years of living.

But he had no intention of going quietly to his doom, or trying to plead his case. Augusta had made up her mind long before he'd come back, she'd even conspired to make it harder for him. He wasn't going to make it easier for her. When she was ready to take him back she could damned well come and find him.

The roads were in decent shape—it hadn't snowed for several days, and the road crew had managed to clear up the mess from the ice storm. It was supposed to snow that night, a white Christmas, Carrie had said, managing to smile. He wouldn't be there to see it.

She was waiting for him. She'd dressed in something lively and red, and she was wearing jingle-bell earrings that rang when she turned her head. She was relentlessly, infuriatingly cheerful, handing him a mug of hazelnut coffee, chattering about the Christmas Eve service.

"I suppose you have to leave before then," she chattered onward, bustling around the kitchen.

"I suppose," he said, sitting and watching her, storing up the sight of her for the eternity to come.

"By the way, Gertrude called. She said to tell you she wants you to stop by on your way out of town."

"I got the message," he said lazily. "Are you going to keep running away from me or are you going to perch for a moment?"

She turned, startled, and gave him a wary smile. "I'll perch," she said, coming over and sitting on his lap, her arms around his neck. She was smiling very, very brightly, and he wanted to kiss that phony smile off her face. But somehow he knew she needed it. She needed the energy, the smile, the careless bravery. The only thing he could do was give it to her.

"I'm glad you're taking this so well," he said.

He heard the faint shudder of swallowed tears. "Of course I am," she said cheerfully. "I've always known you've had to leave. It's not as if you ever lied to me about it. I'll miss you, of course. But I expect that sooner or later you'll be back..."

"No."

The smile on her face faded for a moment. "No?"

"Damn it, Carrie, I told you...!"

"All right," she said firmly. "You won't be back. So I'll marry Steve, have half-a-dozen children who'll all be bald by the time they're twenty, and I'll think of you every Christmas Eve with a tear or two when I've had too much brandied eggnog. I'll be perfectly fine."

He rose, setting her on her feet, his hands lingering on her narrow waist. "I've already hurt you enough."

"Never," she said flatly. "Name one thing you've done."

He knew that he couldn't. Instead, he kissed her, long and deep and hard, kissed the lying smile off her face, kissed the brave eyelids that blinked back tears.

And then the bravery and tears vanished, and she began to sob deep shuddering tears that she cursed as she wept. "Pay no attention to me,'' she sobbed against his shoulder as he held her with tender hands. ''I always cry at Christmastime. And I'll miss you— I'm allowed to say that, aren't I?''

''Of course,'' he murmured into her hair.

''Couldn't you lie to me?'' She tilted her face up, and she looked very vulnerable, very sweet. ''Tell me you'll try to get back to me? Even if you don't really want to, a little lie won't hurt you.''

He looked at her, and the pain in his heart was worse than anything he'd ever endured. Massive cardiac arrest was a piece of cake compared to a simple, permanent break. ''Damn it, Carrie...'' he said.

''All right then, don't lie,'' she said. ''Don't say anything at all.'' And her mouth stopped his protest.

He left her sleeping. She was curled up on the living room sofa, the bright red dress flowing around her, the salty path of her tears drying on her pale cheeks. It was four-thirty, but already pitch-black outside, and he knew there was no escape. He knelt down beside her, stroking her hair, touching her so lightly he knew she wouldn't awake. And then he rose, carrying the sight and the scent and the feel of her with him, into eternity.

He recognized the ancient Dodge Dart that squatted at the end of Carrie's driveway like a malevolent blue bug. His truck was still parked there, and he wondered what would happen if he got in, started it and tried to ram Gertrude. It was an idle thought, enough to summon a wry amusement from him, and he strolled down the long, winding driveway toward the waiting car.

''Get in,'' Gertrude said, rolling down the window.

He got in. He didn't bother with the seat belt—it wouldn't make much of a difference where he was going. ''I must say, I wouldn't have thought it would be a GM product that would carry me across the river Styx.''

''I'm glad you can still find something amusing about your situation, Mr. MacVey.'' There was no longer any sign of Gertrude in the old car. Augusta drove with her customary arrogance, and the slippery roads had no choice but to obey her.

He glanced out the window and realized they weren't driving on the roads. He leaned back against the seat with a weary sigh. ''You've got your wish, Augusta. I did my best, and I failed.''

''Indeed, Mr. MacVey.''

''Don't call me that,'' he said mildly enough, determined not to let her get to him.

''Why not? It's your name. And there is no river Styx, and I am hardly Charon, the evil boatman. You're going back for the trial. I have my own opinion as to where you belong, and the answer might surprise you. But it's not my decision alone.''

He glanced at her. She was glowing in the darkness, and he realized with a sense of shock that he was glowing, as well. "You mean there's hope for me?''

"Oh, there's always been hope for you,'' she said. "Mind your manners, and we'll see what happens.''

CARRIE HEARD HIM LEAVE. She knew he didn't want her to say goodbye, so she'd pretended to be asleep, holding herself relaxed and still as his hand brushed her face, his lips brushed her eyelids.

She listened to his footsteps in the kitchen as he headed for the door, and she stuffed her fist into her mouth to keep from calling out to him. A moment later the rumble of a car, and he drove away, out of her life, forever.

She closed her eyes, absorbing the pain. She would survive. She always did, no matter what kind of mess she got herself into, no matter what kind of blows life dealt her. She wasn't sure if this current situation was her own fault, and she didn't really care. No matter how long she ached for him, hurt for him, waited for him, the days spent with him were worth it.

She was so tired. She'd been running on nervous energy, unwilling to rest while her time with him was so limited. That time was over now. She could close her eyes and let sleep come. Sweet, drugging sleep, where she could find Gabriel again in her dreams.

HE WAS WEARING his Italian wool suit once more, and his silk tie was too tight around his neck. He was glad the Waystation didn't come equipped with mirrors. He didn't want to look at his reflection and see Emerson MacVey's blandly handsome face. He'd had no choice but to leave Gabriel behind, a fallen angel. But that didn't mean he had to like it.

He sat alone in one of the waiting rooms, wrapped in that vast cocoon of nothingness. The smells were gone, he realized, the smells of Christmas. No cinnamon and hazelnut, no fir trees and gingerbread and hot chocolate. He was back in the void, and for a brief, savage moment he thought even hell would be preferable.

And then he wasn't alone. Augusta was there, tall, disdainful, staring down at him out of her cool blue eyes. "The decision has been made,'' she said.

He found he didn't want to hope. Heaven or hell made no difference to him at that point. Any place without Carrie was eternal torment.

"It's been determined that you tried very hard. To be sure, you wasted your miracles. One was for your own self, one was for a phone call, and you could have found Jeffie without divine intervention. Nevertheless, in two of the three cases you have done very well, indeed, and we're pleased with you."

He barely glanced at her. "What's the punch line?"

"You've broken Carrie Alexander's heart."

He stared down at his fingers as they idly drummed the arm of the chair. Short fingers, well manicured. Soft hands. "So? That's nothing new, is it? Apparently I'd already done so."

"I'm sorry, but she's in more trouble this time. Before she was simply suffering from an infatuation. This time she's not going to recover. Broken lives and broken bones mend. Broken hearts do not. She'll never marry, and she'll think of you every day of her life."

"Don't!" he said furiously, lunging to his feet. "She's too strong for that. She won't waste her life for a worthless bastard like me."

Augusta smiled. "She knows how to love, Mr. Falconi."

"Of course she does. It's not fair that she…" His voice trailed off as he realized he was looking down at Augusta. Augusta, who had stood eye to eye with Emerson MacVey. "What did you call me?"

"Why, your name, Mr. Falconi," she said. "You haven't earned your place in heaven, I'm afraid, so we have no choice but to send you to the other place. But you've been under a misapprehension. There is no such place as hell. The other place is life."

"Life?" He knew that deep voice. It was Gabriel's. It was his. He looked down at his hands. Large, graceful, scarred with the nicks and scratches that came from working with wood.

"Angel Falls, Minnesota. You're going back to Carrie, Mr. Falconi. You're being given a second chance. See that you get it right this time."

The blue light exploded in his eyes, and he was falling, falling, the pain sharp and cold and clear, and he wanted to scream, but when he tried, nothing came, and he reached out, and his hand came in contact with something solid. He took a deep, shuddering breath, deep into his lungs, and looked around him.

He was standing on Carrie's porch. The moon had risen, and a light snow was falling. He glanced up at the sky, and for one brief, mad moment he thought he could hear sleigh bells.

The house was still and quiet when he let himself inside. Carrie lay sleeping on the sofa, a quilt tossed over her, and as he glanced at the old grandfather clock he noticed in shock that it was one minute to midnight. He thought he'd been gone a matter of minutes. Or a matter of years.

The hand moved, the clock began to chime, a low, stately chime, and Carrie opened her eyes. She looked at him in wondering disbelief.

"You get me instead of coal in your stocking," he said, his voice hoarse.

"For how long?"

He thought back to the past few hours. It was distant, fading, like an old forties movie that he could hardly remember. It didn't matter. All that mattered was the future.

"Eternity," he said, reaching for her.

She came into his arms with her dancer's grace, and he lifted her high, holding her tightly. She was everything that had ever mattered to him, his heart and soul, his very life, and for a moment he just held her, absorbing her heat. And then he reached for the quilt, wrapped it around her, and he carried her through the house, out onto the icy porch, just as the clock finished striking midnight. In the distance they could hear the church bells ringing in Christmas, and he smiled at her.

"Merry Christmas, love," she said to him, her heart in her eyes.

And looking down at her, he knew he'd found his own heaven.

HARLEQUIN®
Makes any time special.™

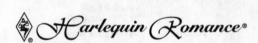

HEART OF THE WEST

Every Man Has His Price!

Lost Springs Ranch was famous for turning young mavericks into good men. So word that the ranch was in financial trouble sent a herd of loyal bachelors stampeding back to Wyoming to put themselves on the auction block!

HARLEQUIN®
Makes any time special ™

EXTRA! EXTRA!

The book all your favorite authors are raving about is finally here!

The 1999 Harlequin and Silhouette coupon book.

Each page is alive with savings that can't be beat!

Getting this incredible coupon book is as easy as 1, 2, 3.

1. During the months of November and December 1999 buy any 2 Harlequin or Silhouette books.

2. Send us your name, address and 2 proofs of purchase (cash receipt) to the address below.

3. Harlequin will send you a coupon book worth $10.00 off future purchases of Harlequin or Silhouette books in 2000.

Send us 3 cash register receipts as proofs of purchase and we will send you 2 coupon books worth a total saving of $20.00 (limit of 2 coupon books per customer).

Saving money has never been this easy.

Please allow 4-6 weeks for delivery. Offer expires December 31, 1999.

I accept your offer! Please send me (a) coupon booklet(s):

Name: _____

Address: _____ City: _____

State/Prov.: _____ Zip/Postal Code: _____

Send your name and address, along with your cash register receipts as proofs of purchase, to:

In the U.S.: Harlequin Books, P.O. Box 9057, Buffalo, N.Y. 14269

In Canada: Harlequin Books, P.O. Box 622, Fort Erie, Ontario L2A 5X3

Order your books and accept this coupon offer through our web site
http://www.romance.net
Valid in U.S. and Canada only.   PHQ4994R_T6

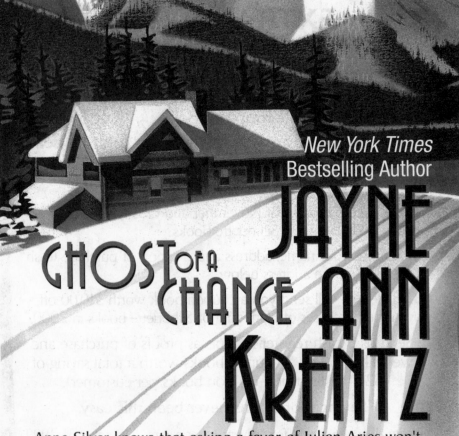

New York Times
Bestselling Author

JAYNE ANN KRENTZ

GHOST OF A CHANCE

Anne Silver knows that asking a favor of Julian Aries won't be easy. They'd almost been lovers once—until they parted on no uncertain terms. Now she needs his expertise as an investigator to uncover false claims of psychics.

Julian listens to her plan, and promptly accepts the challenge. But as they investigate the world of mystics together, Anne finds herself haunted by a passion from the past, and a love that never died.

"A master of the genre…nobody does it better."
—*Romantic Times*

On sale mid-December 1999 wherever paperbacks are sold.

MIRA